NICHOLAS RAVEN

AND THE

WIZARDS' WEB

VOLUME 2

~ CHAPTERS 40 - 85 ~

THOMAS J. PRESTOPNIK

Visit Thomas J. Prestopnik's website at **www.TomPresto.com**.

Cover Artist: Kelly McGrogan
Cover Layout: Ryan McGrogan
Maps: Thomas J. Prestopnik

Nicholas Raven and the Wizards' Web - Volume 2
ISBN-13: 978-1511432429
ISBN-10: 151143242X

Library of Congress Control Number: 2015905654
CreateSpace Independent Publishing Platform
North Charleston, SC

Printed in the United States of America

For every reader in search
of an exciting adventure.
I hope you find one
inside these pages.

CONTENTS

PART SIX
SEARCH AND RESCUE

PART SIX
(Continued)

PART SEVEN
A CLASH OF ARMIES

PART SEVEN
(Continued)

PART EIGHT
LOOSE THREADS

MAPS

Map One
The Lands of Laparia

Map Two
The Kingdom of Arrondale

Map Three
The County of Litchfield

Map Four
The Village of Kanesbury

Each map follows twice.
First as a two-page spread, and then on a single page.

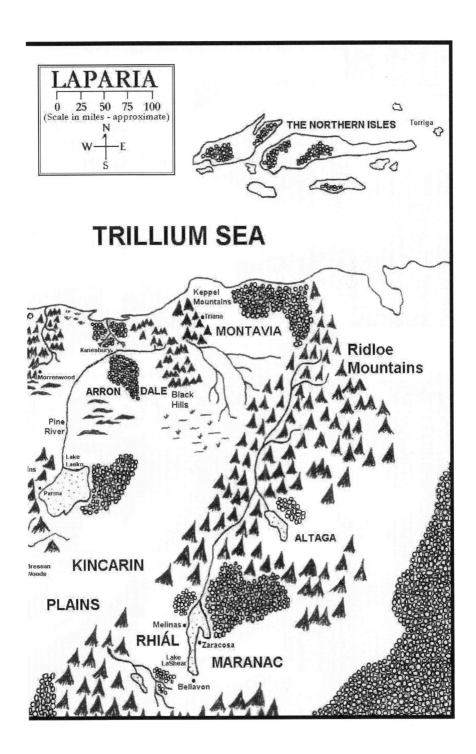

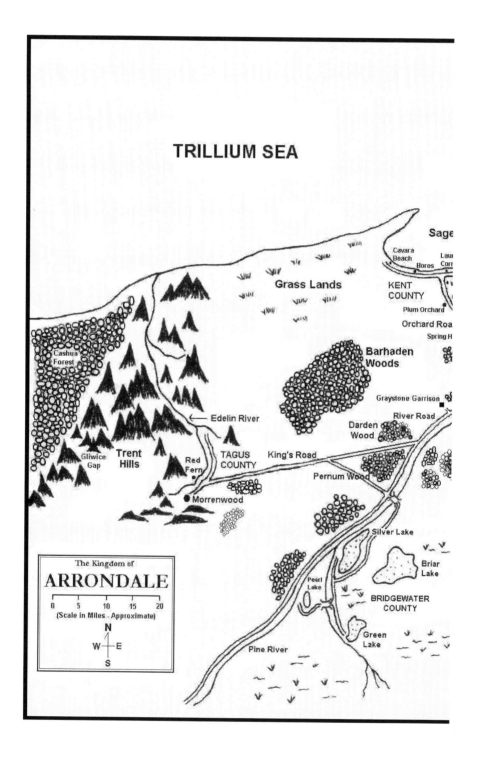

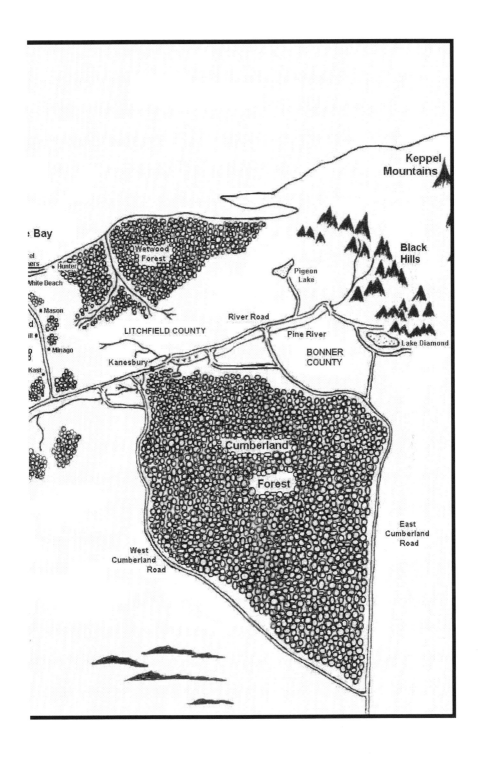

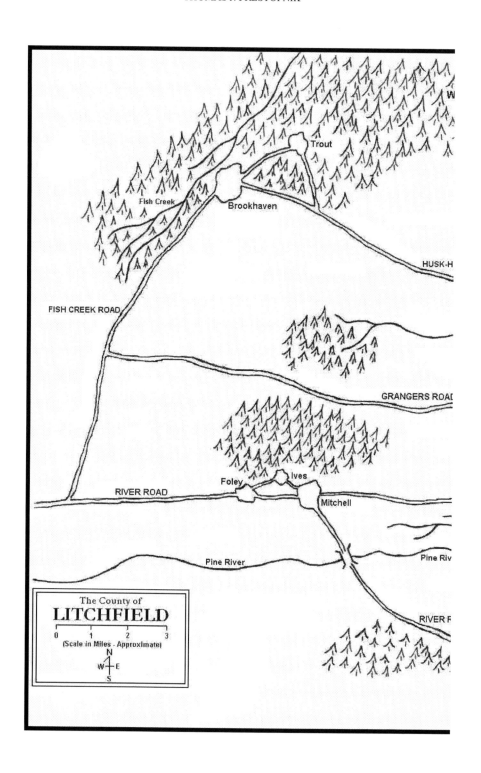

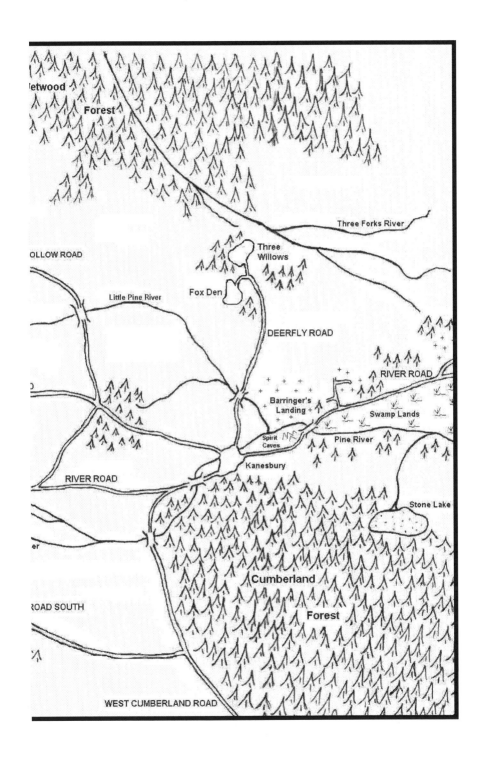

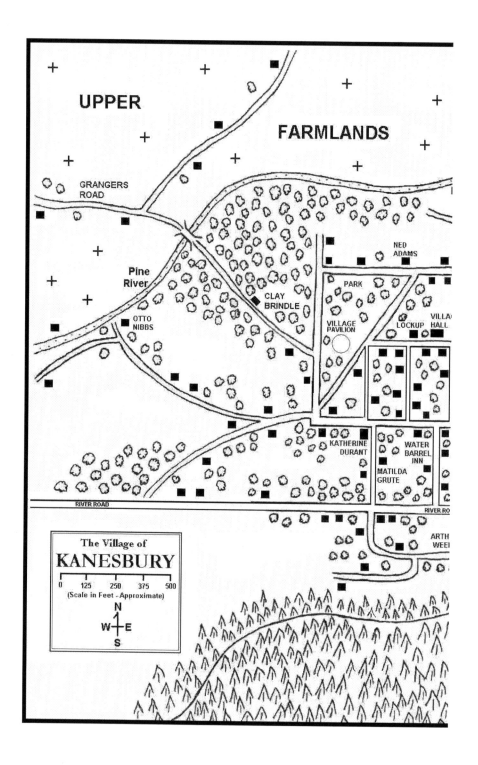

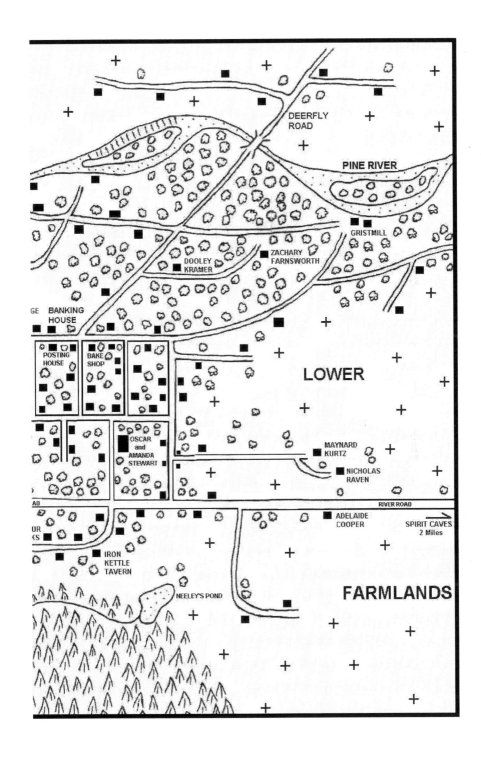

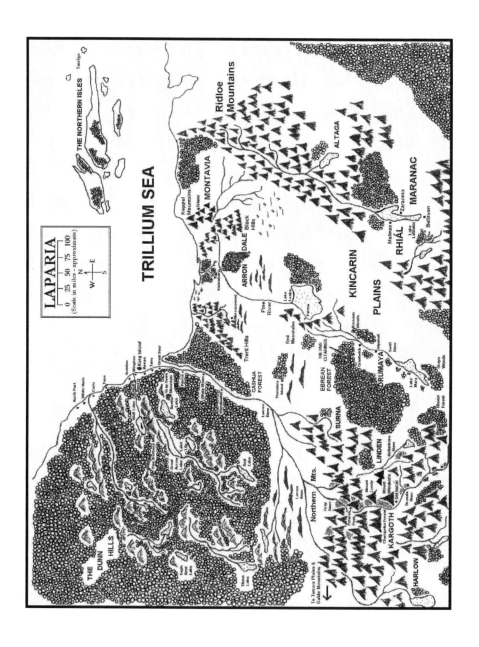

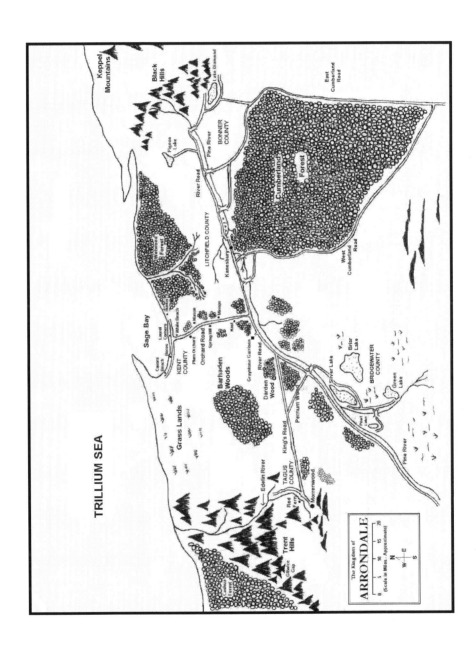

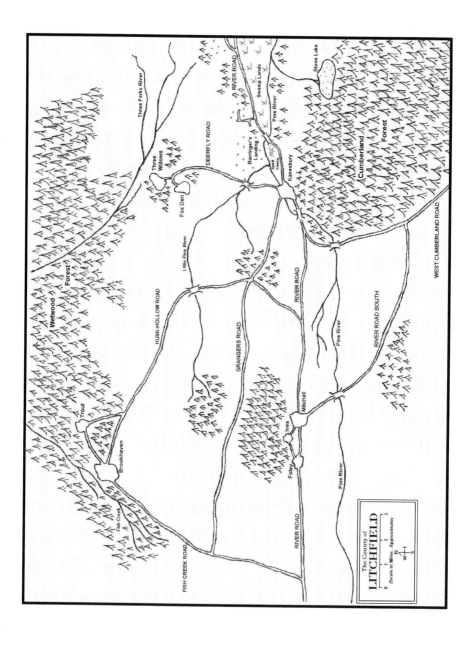

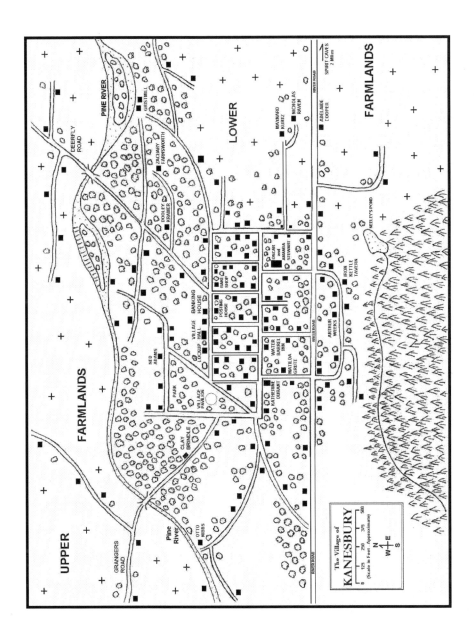

NICHOLAS RAVEN

AND THE

WIZARDS' WEB

VOLUME 2

~ CHAPTERS 40 - 85 ~

PART FIVE
BATTLE ON THE HOME FRONT

CHAPTER 40

The Gathering

A patchwork of gray clouds plastered the sky shortly after midnight. It was the next to last day of Mid Autumn. The glow of the veiled Bear Moon, still a few days from full as it dipped in the west, added an eerie sheen to the chilled Kanesbury landscape. In the dim light, Dooley Kramer tried to find the correct key to unlock the main storage building of Ned Adams' gristmill. The rattling key ring echoed loudly in the dead silence.

"Why didn't you select the right key before you left your house?" Zachary Farnsworth muttered. He stood with his back against the building, emitting a weary sigh.

"Be thankful that I *have* the keys," Dooley replied. "How about a bit more light?"

"No! Not until we're inside. Someone might spot us."

"There isn't a soul awake in the entire village," he whispered. "Besides, who'd see us here by the river?"

"I want no mistakes with this meeting," Farnsworth softly spoke, his ghostly breath rising. "We've given Caldurian enough reasons to question our usefulness. Let's not add another to the list by announcing our presence here."

"I suppose." Dooley exhaled sharply as he fumbled with the keys. "I'll be glad when this night is over. First it was facing

Adelaide and him at the swamps earlier, and now this. When will it all end so I can get my due?"

"Soon," Farnsworth said, eyeing him in the shadows.

"I hope so," he replied distractedly. "I can't wait–ah, here we go! Door opened."

"About time. Get inside. The others should be here soon."

They entered in darkness. Only after making their way to a windowless area did they dare light any oil lamps. The storage room was partially filled with flour sacks intended for the local market. Dooley had already delivered the final out-of-town shipments for the year. He sat on a small crate and folded his arms, nervously awaiting the start of the meeting as Farnsworth paced about. Dooley had purposely avoided most of their meetings with the wizard, but today it couldn't be helped. Matters were moving on several fronts and information needed to be shared. And though he was only a small cog in a great machine, he would have to make his own report to earn his promised compensation. A part of him wished he had simply given Farnsworth the key to the Spirit Box years ago and severed all ties with the man–or had never stolen the dreadful object in the first place–but he realized it was too late to turn back now.

"So we don't mention the swamp?" Dooley asked after a prolonged silence.

Farnsworth, who had been thinking in a corner of the room, turned and bolted toward him. "No! A thousand times *no!* Do we even need to discuss that anymore? Caldurian is never to know anything about it. He doesn't like loose ends, and our two guests there are just that. When the wizard departs Kanesbury, we'll find a permanent solution." He shook his head, wishing he had left Dooley on the swamp island as well. "Speak as little as you must tonight. Who knows if we'll be given any last assignments before Caldurian leaves us to enjoy the village. But we're close now. Let's not panic."

"All right," he replied, cloaking himself with a thin veneer of confidence. "I can get through this." His heart beat rapidly and his breathing felt constricted.

Shortly after, when he heard the shuffle of feet outside, he knew he had no choice in the matter. The meeting was about to begin. Dooley Kramer envisioned a long and tortuous night ahead.

Everyone arrived within the half hour. Dooley guided them inside the storage room as Farnsworth greeted each visitor in the dull light. Caldurian took a seat on a chair Dooley had brought in from Ned's office. Also present were Madeline and Mune who each sat on a low pile of flour sacks. A fourth arrival stood silently in the corner shadows, his arms folded, carefully observing the goings-on. Farnsworth stood at attention between Dooley and Mune, directly across from the wizard.

"Not the most luxurious accommodations, but they will suffice for our purposes," Caldurian said, straightening the folds of his black cloak.

"They are secure and out of the way," Farnsworth replied, not certain if the wizard's dark eyes were showing disappointment.

"This will do fine," he continued. "It's good to have all of us here at one time. It's rare that our schedules allow it. We'll discuss Vellan's business before my own as that is the main reason for this gathering. Mune, you may as well start the proceedings. Bring us up to date on what's happened."

"Certainly," he said, uncomfortably eyeing Farnsworth and Dooley. "*Everything?*"

The wizard nodded. "Yes, Mune. There can be no secrets among us now. We're too far into this to limit information."

"Very well," he said, caressing his goatee. "I had met with Madeline at the Plum Orchard Inn over a month ago. She told me about the war council, the information compliments of her old friend in the Citadel kitchen, Dell Hawks. I sent the specifics to you through Gavin." Suddenly there was the fluttering of wings above in the darkness. Mune looked up in the shadowy rafters, spotting a pair of black eyes reflecting the light of the oil lamps. "Oh, there you are. I thought you were going to be a no-show."

"Not on your life, Mr. Mune," the crow sharply replied.

Mune addressed the wizard. "Did you make use of that bit of intelligence?"

"Yes," he said, glancing at Dooley. "We were able to get a pair of ears and eyes into the war council, but we'll discuss that later. Continue."

"All right," Mune replied. "But there is another piece of news that I didn't send along with Gavin, only because Madeline and I were unsure of the outcome."

"Oh?" Caldurian remarked. "Now you have me intrigued."

"But you'll be pleased with the result," Madeline chimed in, her willowy body warmly wrapped in a cloak lined with fox fur. Strands of flaming red hair peeked out beneath her black kerchief.

"Indeed you will," Mune continued. "By happenstance, Dell Hawks spotted the King's granddaughter, Princess Megan, in that area. He followed her to the Plum Orchard Inn the day before my arrival. Dell informed Madeline of this and attempted to kidnap the princess, though failed." He noted the incredulous look on Caldurian's face. "Trust me, I'm sober. It was the princess. We arranged for her kidnapping a few days later in Boros before taking her to our meeting spot above the grasslands with Commander Uta. I'll provide the particulars later, but Princess Megan is now in the capable yet reluctant hands of one Captain Tarosius Lok of the Northern Isles."

"The princess was taken to the Isles?" Caldurian asked, both delighted and stunned by the unexpected bit of information.

Mune smirked. "No, even better. Since the Islanders are sending troops and supplies to Vellan up the Lorren River, they've confiscated a small island near the mouth of the Lorren from which they direct their operation."

"Karg Island. Yes, I know of it," the wizard replied.

"That is where we left the princess," Madeline explained. "She's being held prisoner under Lok's supervision, if or until you should need her."

Caldurian raised an eyebrow and smiled. "She'll yet be a useful bargaining piece, even twenty years later. You've redeemed us from our dreadful error in the past."

"I thought that, too," she replied, pleased with his reaction.

Dooley, meanwhile, watched with bubbling curiosity as he listened to their story. This was the second time he had heard about Princess Megan's kidnapping. The first time, however, was from the princess herself when she recounted the story while he was hidden among the rafters in the war council chamber two weeks ago. While there, he also learned that a girl named Ivy had traded places with Princess Megan and had been accidentally kidnapped instead. Apparently Madeline and Mune never learned of this deception. He felt suddenly empowered knowing that he possessed vital information of which they were not aware. When he returned from

Morrenwood, Dooley told Farnsworth that he had heard Nicholas Raven and the princess speak after the war council and planned to tell Caldurian tonight. He looked forward to deflating Mune, Madeline and the wizard's sense of superiority by informing them that they had kidnapped the wrong girl. He glanced at Farnsworth, silently acknowledging what was about to unfold.

"There was nearly a slip-up," Mune continued, sensing the wizard's concern, "but I only mention it because all turned out well in the end. The princess was briefly rescued from her tent by two men before we got her back and took her aboard Uta's ship. I don't know who they were since Princess Megan refused to tell us."

"But she is safely on Karg Island?" Caldurian asked.

"Most definitely," Madeline assured him. "Mune and I sailed there ourselves with Commander Uta and dropped her off. On the return trip, Uta and Captain Burlu, along with a hundred of their finest soldiers, were dropped above the Trent Hills and are making their way south toward Morrenwood. They'll hide out there until you need them."

"You have done your jobs admirably," the wizard replied.

"All in a month's work," Mune said with a satisfied smile. "The ship later dropped Madeline and me above the Wetwood Forest and then continued sailing east where I suppose it joined up with your little invasion party in Montavia. Can't wait to hear all about that adventure."

"In good time," the wizard said. He turned to Dooley who sat quietly hunched upon his crate. "But now it is time for our spy to speak. We were fortunate to be able to have him slip into the war council."

"Exactly how?" Mune wondered aloud, unable to imagine someone infiltrating King Justin's secret council. After the wizard explained that Dooley had replaced Nicholas Raven at the gristmill and made deliveries to the Blue Citadel, Mune settled back on his seat of flour sacks, expecting an intriguing tale.

"Well…" Dooley softly said, nervously clearing his throat, "I did manage to sneak into the council before it convened, thanks in part to some unknowing assistance from Len Harold. He's a member of our village council who attended the meeting," he added, glancing at Madeline and Mune, though receiving only stony expressions in return. "Anyway, as I relayed to Caldurian through Gavin, I didn't learn many specifics at the council. King Justin and the others had agreed to send forces to the war in Rhiál and to counter the recent invasion in Montavia, but the details were to be hashed out at a later, private meeting," he lied, happy to be partially hidden in the shadows. For an instant he feared that Caldurian might be able to read his mind and discover that he had fallen asleep in the rafters.

Mune grunted with contempt. "So after all that planning and infiltrating, we learn that King Justin's grand plans are to counterattack? Brilliant work on your part, Mr. Kramer. I could have told you exactly that while sitting beside a fire with my feet up and enjoying some ale. Do you know when he plans to launch his offensive? From which direction? How many men? Armaments?"

"Maybe you found out what color banners they'll be waving when they make their charge," Madeline dryly added.

"Let him finish," Caldurian said, raising a hand to signal them to retreat from their verbal attacks.

Dooley, his face warm with disdain, took a deep breath and exhaled before answering, knowing they were looking down upon him, waiting for him to slip up. "As I said, those technical issues were to be discussed at a later meeting that I wasn't able to worm my way into. However, I did learn some interesting news immediately after the war council concluded. After nearly everyone had left, King Justin remained behind with a handful of people. Soon afterward, four individuals arrived with the most unexpected news." He remembered his surprise upon hearing Nicholas' voice in the King's chamber and his shock that he was apparently good friends with Princess Megan. But Dooley planned to withhold that information for a little while longer, savoring the announcement.

"Tell them what you discovered," the wizard said.

Dooley glanced at Farnsworth for encouragement before going on. "To make a long story short, the key to the Spirit Box was rediscovered and brought to the Citadel."

"Do you mean the enemy has it now?" Madeline asked. "How did that happen? How is it possible? I learned from Mune that after the Enâri were released from the Spirit Caves, a disloyal servant to Vellan ran away to search for the key."

"And he found it," Caldurian said, explaining how Jagga had stolen the key and killed Arthur Weeks in the process.

"It was melted down into a lump of metal afterward," Dooley continued, "and fashioned into a medallion that was presented to King Justin after the council had concluded. They discussed how the medallion was to be secretly delivered by two people to the wizard Frist to be reforged into the key." He couldn't conceal a grin as he sat up straight on his crate. "Luckily, I overheard a few particulars about that mission and sent them on to Caldurian while he was in Montavia." Dooley looked at the wizard with wild expectations. "Can I assume that my information proved useful?"

Caldurian nodded, offering a hint of a smile. "Tell you what, why don't I let him explain everything," the wizard replied, indicating the man standing silently in the corner shadows. "He'll let you know precisely how useful your information was."

"Wonderful!" Dooley said, feeling at ease for the first time.

"Yes, the message you had delivered helped me immensely," the man said, stepping out of the darkness. Standing in the dim light, tall and of stern expression, was Maynard Kurtz, his silvery-black hair rolling over his shoulders. "Your information assisted me greatly in tracking down the wrong two people!"

Dooley's smiled suddenly sagged. "Wrong two–*what*?"

"You heard me," Maynard said, glaring at him. "I followed the two who had left the Citadel at dawn, traveling south. I searched their campsite on the edge of the Ebrean Forest one night and didn't find the medallion. I then tracked them through the woods to a small cabin, but they denied they possessed the medallion. After I slew one of them, the younger boy admitted that two other people were delivering the medallion to the wizard Frist, though he claimed not to know the wizard's whereabouts. Before I left, I searched both bodies and the cabin, but found no medallion."

Dooley swallowed hard. "*Both bodies*? You killed the other one, too?"

Maynard smiled grimly, his eyes cold and distant. "I pushed the second one out a window. He was breathing when I left, so he may have survived. I cared not. All I sought was the medallion, but it was not there. Your information was false."

"That's impossible!" Dooley said.

Maynard advanced a step. "There was no medallion!"

"Perhaps they hid it. You might've overlooked it."

"You doubt me?" he sputtered, ready to erupt. He suddenly raised his arms high in the air like vulture's wings and his body swiftly transformed into the wizard Arileez, the shock of his dark, lifeless eyes, his skeletal face and his deathly white hair pummeling Dooley into temporary silence. The other onlookers were aghast at the preternatural display. "I ask you again, Dooley Kramer. Do you still doubt my word?"

"No!" he replied, shielding his eyes with a raised hand, the word barely able to escape his lips.

Caldurian stood up. "All right, Arileez. You've made your point. We don't need raised voices this night. We are here to discuss, not to argue."

Arileez locked gazes with him, glowering at the assault upon his trustworthiness from one of the wizard's underlings. A moment later, after his breathing settled and the muscles in his face relaxed, he reverted to his former manifestation and was once again Maynard Kurtz. He stepped back into the shadows.

Caldurian sighed, taking his seat. "When Arileez returned from the cabin and reported to me, he mentioned that the two boys, both blond, had called each other William and Brendan. I can only assume that they were the sibling princes of Montavia, sent purposely as decoys or accidentally caught up in matters of which they had no knowledge. But none of that makes any difference now. So have you anything else to say, Dooley?"

He looked up, and though the sudden appearance of Arileez had rattled him, he knew he was not to blame for his failing to recover the medallion. Yet he did feel responsible for something else. Though Arileez had murdered Brendan, Dooley felt responsible for the boy's death as his information had led Arileez directly to him. He gazed into a dark corner of the room, his shoulders slumped and his throat tightened, tuning out the words of the others for a moment as a wave of guilt swept over him. "I do not doubt Arileez' account," he finally said, "but while eavesdropping on the council, I had clearly heard that the two people with the key would be leaving at dawn on the fourteenth day of Mid Autumn, a little over three days after I departed the Citadel. I told Gavin that very thing, instructing him to remain behind and follow the pair when they left before sending word back to you."

"He did speak those very words to me," the crow gruffly muttered from above.

"I did my part!" Dooley snapped. "In fact, more than I was supposed to. If it wasn't for me, none of us would even know of the key's whereabouts."

"But we still don't have it," the impostor Maynard complained. "So what good did you accomplish?"

"Let me think for a moment," Caldurian said, attempting to calm the stir of ill feelings. "If what everybody said is true, then we were just outsmarted. No sense in arguing about it further."

"Still, all is not lost," Farnsworth said, hoping to put a positive spin on dreadful news. "If the medallion was taken away to be remade into the key, it's only logical that it will be brought back to the Citadel. At least we still know where the key will end up."

"Yes, right alongside the Spirit Box," Mune said defeatedly, "waiting for King Justin to use it and destroy the Enâri with a turn of his wrist. How convenient for him."

"Now now, Mune," Caldurian said. "Have a little faith. We aren't defeated yet. Part of the reason I have Commander Uta and his troops wending their way down to Morrenwood is to retrieve the Spirit Box. No reason they can't swipe the key as well if it's returned. You and Madeline will go there to take possession of the items once the deed is done. However, I'd like to be guaranteed possession of at least one of them. Let me think for another minute," he said, holding up his hand for silence as he pondered things. "Gavin, since you followed the decoys south, let's assume that the real mission to find the wizard Frist went in a different direction." He mentally wandered for another moment or two. "I had met Frist a few times on the road before our perilous encounter in Kanesbury twenty years ago when he cast the Enâri into a deep sleep. He often mentioned his fondness for the Dunn Hills region in the west and spent much time there wandering along the lakes and climbing the mountains."

"Do you think that's where his guide was instructed to take him?" Madeline asked.

"Perhaps. If the key went east, it would be going deeper into Arrondale. North would take it to the Trillium Sea. I don't think Frist would have journeyed in either of those directions," he said. "I can almost guarantee they are heading west to the Dunn Hills."

"But that's a vast region," Mune said. "How would we ever locate them now?"

"Our chances are slim to none," Caldurian reasoned, "so we won't be tracking them. But since men from the Northern Isles are traveling up the Lorren River to Kargoth, it would be but a little imposition for some of them to scout about the area on the off chance of finding the travelers. It is worth a try. Gavin!"

"Yes, Caldurian," the crow said, flapping its wings and settling down upon a sack of flour.

"If the two were supposed to set out from Morrenwood on the fourteenth day of Mid Autumn as Dooley said, that would be about a week and a half ago," he calculated. "By giving or taking a day regarding their actual departure in light of the decoys, our travelers are probably just reaching the Lorren River now, more or less, preparing to enter the Dunn Hills. The nearest villages on the river west of Morrenwood are Woodwater, White Stone and Pierce, so I'll guess they would enter the Hills after visiting one of them for supplies." Caldurian glanced at Gavin. "After this meeting, fly to the mouth of the Lorren and contact whatever ship is anchored there from the Isles. If they can spare a dozen men to watch the three villages and the surrounding main roads and possibly fan out into the Dunn Hills from each location, we may get fortunate and stumble upon the medallion–or the key–depending on which form it is in at the time. It may be a futile effort, but I'll regret not taking the chance. I can't send Arileez again as we are ready to proceed with plans both here in Kanesbury and in Morrenwood."

"Speaking of plans," Mune jumped in, "are we finally going to get the remaining details about your grand design to take the Blue Citadel? Since Madeline and I have taken great pains to set your ideas in motion–"

"–you think it's about time that I let you in on the secret?" Caldurian added, a mischievous gleam in his eyes. "Rest assured, Mune, before this gathering departs, you will know all that I know– or nearly everything. There are many threads in this tapestry. But before I delve into the details, let us allow Dooley to finish."

"Yes, continue," Madeline said. "I'd like to know more about how that medallion came to King Justin's doorstep. I can't imagine that that traitorous Enâr willingly brought it there himself. Did someone steal it from him?"

"No," Dooley said, pushing his melancholy aside. "Apparently Jagga–that is the Enâr's name–befriended a somewhat eccentric woman on the road named Carmella and–"

"*Carmella?*" Madeline blurted out the name in shock. "A woman roughly my age? A wildly dressed, pretender-of-a-wizard?"

"As a matter of fact, yes," he replied. "She said that Jagga had met her on the road and gave her the medallion as a gift. Apparently Carmella provided him food and the lofty position–at least in her eyes–as her personal driver."

Madeline fumed. "That insufferable poser! A wizard she is definitely not. My cousin is a fake. A fraud!"

"That's right. She's your cousin," Dooley said. "I remember now, Madeline, that your name–and even yours, Mune–were both mentioned at the council."

Mune furrowed his brow. "My name. Why would Carmella mention that? I've never met the woman."

"To be accurate, Carmella didn't actually speak your name. Someone else did. You see, besides Jagga, three other people had accompanied her to the Blue Citadel," he explained. "They were the ones who provided some enlightening facts about you and Madeline and your brilliant escapade above the grasslands."

"And what's that supposed to mean?" Mune fired back.

"Yes, tell us," Caldurian calmly added, though fearing the worst. He sensed that Dooley was far too eager to reveal the forthcoming details.

"Happily," he said as he stood up, feeling the control of the meeting flow his way. "I would have mentioned this sooner when you talked about kidnapping Princess Megan and shipping her off to Karg Island, but I didn't want to interrupt until I had heard everything."

"*Meaning?*" asked Madeline with impatience.

"Meaning," Dooley continued, "that Princess Megan herself was one of the three people who accompanied Carmella to the Citadel. She and two other gentlemen, the very same men who attempted to rescue the woman you actually did kidnap."

Mune shook his head, at a loss for words. The incredulous look upon his face, coupled with Madeline's stony expression, brought a silent joy to Dooley's heart. Now *they* were failures in

Caldurian's eyes and Dooley was only too happy to dish out subtle insults as eagerly as they had a short while ago.

"No, no, no! Are you purposely trying to undermine our efforts?" Mune asked. "What kind of ridiculous story are you attempting to pass off as truth? Madeline and I arranged for the kidnapping of Princess Megan. We spoke to her ourselves and delivered her to Karg Island. We even saw the silver medallion she wore around her neck indicating her royal lineage."

"He speaks the truth," Madeline insisted. "I lifted it off the girl's neck to examine while we held her prisoner in a root cellar near Cavara Beach." She looked at Caldurian, her swift glance pleading for him to believe her story, yet a vague uneasiness gnawed at the pit of her stomach. Was it remotely possible that they had made a mistake? The wizard indicated for Dooley to continue.

"Though it pains me to contradict you both, the woman I heard speaking claimed to be Princess Megan of Arrondale," he said with subdued glee. "And since King Justin lovingly greeted her as his granddaughter, what greater proof do you need?"

"If this is true," Caldurian said, "then who is the other girl?"

"According to the story I heard, the kidnapped individual goes by the name of Ivy. It seems Princess Megan reluctantly agreed to some sort of switch while in Boros, a change of identities," Dooley told them. "And it seems to have worked."

Upon hearing the name Ivy, both Madeline and Mune were visibly shaken. Their skin grew pale, their expressions morose. Both recalled that the girl whom they assumed was Princess Megan had insisted her name was Ivy. When they mentioned this to Caldurian, the frustration and simmering anger upon the wizard's face indicated that he believed Dooley's story.

"What better way to convince you that she was the Princess than by denying it," Caldurian commented. "No doubt the real Princess Megan lent her the royal medallion to aid her performance."

"And we were taken in by the deception," Mune said contritely, hoping such an admission would temper the wizard's ire.

"Though Megan's abduction wasn't part of your assignment, the loss is still a disappointment," Caldurian said with surprising calm. "Captain Lok is wasting his time guarding a girl who is not a princess. We'll have to get word to him."

Mune grunted. "I'd rather you took your time doing that, Caldurian. I found Lok to be a most obnoxious and arrogant sort. He wasn't too pleased having the girl in his care, and the longer he has to continue doing so, the happier I'll be."

"In that case, Mune, send word to him when it suits you."

"With pleasure."

"Well, I'm glad that all worked out," Dooley said, his words steeped with sarcasm, wishing that Caldurian had shown a bit more anger toward his two closest allies. But the thought quickly dissipated when the wizard posed his next question.

"By the way, Dooley, who were the two men who tried to rescue Ivy above the grasslands and accompanied the princess to Morrenwood?" Caldurian asked. "What can you tell us about them?"

"*What?*" he asked uncomfortably, never expecting he'd have to answer such a question, assuming Caldurian only wanted information about Princess Megan.

"What were the names of the two men with Princess Megan?"

"Uh, they were just a couple of locals she met on the road," he said, returning to his seat on the crate. "Farmhands, I guess. So tell us what happened in Montavia?" he added rather quickly.

Far too quickly for Caldurian's liking. "I'll do so in a moment, Dooley. But first I'd like the names of those two men. You must have heard them when you were hidden in the rafters."

Dooley cleared his throat. "I'm trying to recall..." He cast a subtle glance at Farnsworth for assistance, but none was forthcoming. The last thing he wanted to tell the wizard was that Nicholas Raven, the man he and Farnsworth were supposed to run out of Kanesbury, now had the fate of the Enâri race in his very hands.

"Dooley!" Caldurian snapped as he glared at the man. "Their names please."

Dooley Kramer squirmed in his seat. "Well, one of them was Leo Marsh, I believe. An apple grower from Minago. As for the other one, his name may have been..." Dooley wiped beads of sweat from his brow.

"*Yes?*"

"I think it might have been–*Nicholas Raven?*"

The wizard remained stone still as he absorbed the information, though no one could fathom if he was on the verge of an explosive fit or a boisterous laugh. He finally glanced at Dooley with the most composed demeanor, posing a simple question.

"*Our* Nicholas Raven?"

Dooley nodded. "Yes, sir. And I was reluctant to say so, knowing that you'd probably get upset since he was the person you had ordered Farnsworth and me to get rid of from the start. But in our defense," he quickly added, "we did get rid of him, clear out of Kanesbury. That he later met up with Princess Megan and is now delivering the medallion to the wizard Frist are just two unfortunate developments."

"He is the one King Justin chose for the mission?" Caldurian incredulously added.

Dooley nodded timidly. "He and Leo Marsh, yes."

Caldurian paced around the storage room, sputtering as he tried to keep his anger in check. "Intellectually, I know this isn't your fault, Mr. Kramer. Nor yours, Mr. Farnsworth. After all, I hired you to get Nicholas Raven out of the way, out of his abode. And you did just that in your own unique way, framing Nicholas to get his job. Perhaps it might have been best if I simply asked you to kill him as you did with the real Maynard Kurtz." He spun around and glared at Dooley. "You did get rid of him properly, didn't you? Arileez informed me that you and Farnsworth carted away Kurtz' body after Arileez put him under a sleeping spell before assuming his place in Kanesbury society."

"We did," Dooley said, nodding several times.

"Yes," Farnsworth added, sensing the need to jump in and save Dooley. "Maynard Kurtz is now lying at the bottom of a swamp. You needn't worry about him anymore. He won't show his face in this village ever again–at least not the real Maynard Kurtz."

Farnsworth crossed his arms and offered a reassuring nod, thankful that neither wizard could read his mind. If they discovered that Maynard was still alive and sleeping in a tiny shed on an island in the swamps–and only a short distance from Adelaide Cooper, of all things–he feared that both he and Dooley would find themselves permanently under water before the night was over. Though admitting to himself that he and Dooley were dishonest schemers of the first order, Farnsworth realized that neither had the stomach for killing by his own hand. But certain that their loose ends in the swamp were going to catch up with them eventually, he knew he'd have to arrange for a permanent solution after Caldurian and Arileez left the village for good–and it couldn't be too soon for his liking.

Caldurian combed a hand through his tangles of iron gray hair, feeling exhausted. "I suppose this is just another setback we'll have to accept. But how is it that every time we have dealings with the princess from Morrenwood, that slippery key to the Spirit Box or even a local bumpkin from Kanesbury, they always seem to come back and prick us like a nest of kalaberry thorns? It doesn't seem possible!" He flung his arms in the air in frustration. "Is there anything else I should know?" he asked, retuning to his seat.

Dooley, first glancing at Farnsworth for his silent permission, raised his hand before asking his next question. He figured Caldurian couldn't get any more upset, so now would be the perfect time. "Sir, I was just wondering why you hired us to get Nicholas Raven out of his home in the first place. You never did tell us."

Caldurian buried his face in his hands and sighed before looking up at Dooley. "I think that by now it would be obvious, but as I'm learning more and more each moment about whom I dealing with, perhaps not." The wizard leaned back in his chair, vowing to keep his temper in check. "My friend, Arileez, is doing a favor for me in Kanesbury, namely, taking the place of Maynard Kurtz, if you haven't already noticed. Later he'll go to Morrenwood and attend to Vellan's assignment."

"I noticed," Dooley whispered.

"That's a start. In the meantime, I meet regularly with him to discuss my plans for the village," the wizard continued, "and it would be very difficult to do that in secret with Nicholas Raven living in the adjacent cottage, thus my need to get rid of him. That's not too complicated a reason, is it, Dooley?"

"No, sir."

"Good. And if you and Farnsworth needed to know that earlier, I would have told you. And now if you're done questioning, I'll tell you about my time in Montavia before going on to other matters," he said, briefly recounting how he, along with the Enâri creatures and forces from the Northern Isles, stormed the city of Triana and usurped the seat of power from King Rowan. "I left Commander Jarrin in charge during my absence while Gwyn dutifully keeps an eye on the Enâri troops. When exactly King Justin plans his assault will be a surprise to us all, though I hope our Island allies send reinforcements soon. Most seem to be going up the Lorren River to Vellan himself. I fear our leader is spreading our resources too thin. Still, we must do what we can for Vellan with what we have. But now on to my agenda regarding Kanesbury." Caldurian detected a slight grimace on Mune's face. "Don't fret, Mune. It will only take about a week to accomplish what I have in mind for this trifling village. And best of all, you and Madeline need not involve yourselves. I'll have men from the Northern Isles to assist me. You may leave for the Trent Hills as soon as we conclude here. Arileez will follow in due course."

Mune instantly perked up. "In that case, I'm quite interested."

"So am I," Farnsworth added. Now that his direct interests were being discussed, he grew suddenly wary of Caldurian's tone. "Men from the Northern Isles? What exactly do you have in mind for Kanesbury? You promised to leave it in one piece after you left."

"And it will be," the wizard said. "For the most part anyway. I'm more concerned with Otto Nibbs and making sure he gets his due. After the misery and public humiliation I suffered at his hands twenty years ago, he'll be lucky if the citizens of Kanesbury don't hang him in the public square when I get through." Caldurian chuckled as he pondered the revenge he had been cultivating for two decades. "Mayor Otto Nibbs will be the talk of the town the day after tomorrow after he makes his secret appearances."

"Where is he?" Dooley asked. "No one has seen Otto since he went to meet with the Enâri at Barringer's Landing near the end of last month."

"Otto Nibbs is still there, sound asleep and safely hidden in an abandoned barn," Caldurian said. "Isn't that right, Arileez?"

"Yes," he said softly from the shadows, still in the guise of Maynard Kurtz.

"You see, when Otto received his late night visit from one of the Enâri creatures, it was really Arileez in disguise," the wizard explained. "All of the real Enâri were with me, ready to invade Montavia. Arileez later met Otto at Barringer's Landing and cast a sleeping spell upon him. Your mayor will contentedly doze there until I need him in a few more days."

"Then how will Otto make an appearance in the village the day after tomorrow if he's asleep?" Dooley asked.

Caldurian sighed. "Arileez will play the part for him. If he can assume the shape of Maynard Kurtz or one of the Enâri, he can certainly transform into Otto Nibbs as necessary."

Dooley squirmed in the shadows. "Yes, of course. That makes sense."

Caldurian smiled as he observed his attentive audience, eager to reveal the details of Vellan's greatest plan. "But Arileez' most masterful performance is yet to come, and soon, when he finally performs the role of King Justin himself. Now that will be an act worth seeing!" the wizard said with pride. "And Arrondale will never be the same."

CHAPTER 41

Words of Warning

Two nights later, Ned Adams trudged wearily down a creaky staircase in the dark of night. He wondered if he had dreamed that knock on the front door. Certainly his wife hadn't heard it as she continued sleeping soundly. He carried a burning candle which cast dancing shadows upon the wall. He suddenly stopped. There it was again–definitely a knock. But who would stop by at this hour? More frantic knocks rattled the front door.

"I'm coming," he muttered, rubbing his bleary eyes. He wanted so much to return to bed, wishing this were a dream.

Before opening the door, Ned nosed up to the nearest window pane for a glance at his nighttime visitor. He saw nothing in the pitch blackness. He cautiously unlocked the door and opened it a crack, planting a foot in front. He held up the candle as he peered outside, straining to see the face of his caller. A cool draft rushed in and extinguished the flame, but not before Ned recognized the man who had rudely awakened him. His jaw dropped.

"Ned, I need to speak to you. It's urgent!"

Ned opened the door and invited the man inside. "I– I can't believe it's you. Why are you here?" he asked, shocked out of his lethargy. "And where have you been for the last month?"

"I'll explain everything, Ned. But we have to hurry. There's not much time!"

Less than an hour later, a similar knock was heard upon the back kitchen door of Oscar and Amanda Stewart's home. A gentle yellow glow spilled out through the windows and onto the lawn after one of the kitchen oil lamps had been lit. A suspicious face peered through the window from within, investigating the disturbance. Morris, one of the Stewarts' oldest servants, noted a dark figure standing outside among the birch trees and pines, all silhouettes against the inky, predawn sky. His eyes widened in shock when he distinguished the stranger's facial features in the soft light. He hurriedly opened the door and invited the unexpected guest inside.

"Please, come in! Come in!" he said, dressed in a black night robe. He offered the visitor a chair. "I can't believe you're back, and here of all places. I must get Mr. Stewart at once."

"Yes, please do, Morris. I need to speak with Oscar. It's of the utmost importance."

"Certainly," he said with a bemused expression, exiting the kitchen. "I'll wake him immediately."

A few minutes later, Oscar Stewart stepped into the room, a dark, red robe over his sleeping clothes, his hair uncombed and his mouth agape. He stared at the man seated in the kitchen, knowing that his wife would scold him if he didn't wake her up to witness this strange visitation.

"It really is you, just as Morris had said," Oscar whispered, though still in disbelief. "Where have you been? I–" He shook his head, not knowing what to think or say. "Let me have Morris put on some tea while I get Amanda, then we can talk. My head is swimming right now," he said. "I can hardly believe you're back, Otto."

"Though not for long," Otto Nibbs replied with a grave sigh. "I escaped from the Enâri after they kidnapped me at Barringer's Landing, but I can't stay. Wake your wife, Oscar, and I'll explain everything. But hurry. I have other people to visit before dawn."

By midmorning, word spread swiftly that Mayor Otto Nibbs had made a number of mysterious appearances to several people in Kanesbury, including all five members of the village council and Maynard Kurtz. And though speculation about Otto's brief return was rampant, the explanations for his second disappearance afterward were equally wild and widespread. As the day wore on, Maynard, in his role as acting mayor, sent word to the members of the council that an emergency meeting would be held at the village hall, in private, to sort out the details of Otto's predawn visits.

As crisp, purple twilight wrapped itself around the buildings and trees of Kanesbury, Maynard sat down with the five council members that included Ned Adams, Oscar Stewart and Len Harold. And though they had desired a confidential meeting until matters were settled, a curious crowd soon gathered near the outer steps of the village hall, hoping to be let in on the discussion.

"Thanks for attending on such short notice," Maynard said to the council. "I thought it best that we address Otto's strange reappearances and warnings to us before rumors get out of hand."

"Not just to us," Len Harold said. "I've heard from a handful of people who said Otto stopped by in the middle of the night to talk to them, too. When I was at the banking house earlier, both Horace Ulm and Zachary Farnsworth said they each had been visited." The other council members likewise admitted to hearing similar stories.

"That explains the crowd gathered outside," Maynard said. "Constable Brindle assigned one of his deputies to keep them at bay until we're finished, but I suppose it might be better to let them inside as Otto's visits are no longer secret."

"I suppose you're right," replied Oscar. "But since I was chosen as head of this council since your appointment as mayor, I think we should agree to a plan of action before we include the others. Otto warned all of us that trouble was coming to Kanesbury, and though he was vague on specifics, I could tell he was deadly serious. I saw fear in his eyes."

"As did I," Maynard said. "That alone convinced me."

As the other members nodded in agreement, the wizard Arileez, in Maynard Kurtz' form, thought how easily he had these people trapped in Caldurian's web of deceit as he sat before them. They willingly followed him because of a few carefully chosen words or a reassuring smile. It was almost too easy playing the part of their mayor, but enjoyable nonetheless after enduring years of island imprisonment. Arileez was happy to repay Caldurian with this performance after he had rescued him from Torriga with Vellan's magical potion. But his future impersonation of King Justin would be an even greater challenge as soon as this stint in Kanesbury was completed. Arileez looked forward to assuming the reins of power in the Blue Citadel.

"What should we do when trouble comes our way?" Len Harold asked.

"*If,*" Maynard cautioned him. "Despite our concerns, let's not turn Otto's dire warnings into reality just yet."

"But he said the Enâri threatened to launch attacks against our village in order to find the Spirit Box," Len continued with a slight quiver in his voice, "despite the fact that Otto insisted the box was now in Morrenwood."

"And Otto told me that others in league with the Enâri and that horrible wizard Caldurian would be doing their bidding," Ned Adams said. "Men from the Northern Isles!"

"That's not the worst of it," Oscar said as he looked at his friends around the table. The rows of empty benches stared back with chilling silence. "Otto fled Kanesbury this morning before the sun rose, fearing for his life should the attacks occur. And he warned us to do the same. What are people going to think about that? Mayor Otto Nibbs, of all people, abandoning his village!"

"Otto suggested that I flee as well," Maynard said. "I was shocked and disheartened to hear those words coming from him." He paused a moment, indicating for the others to listen to the voices in the street rising in volume above the sputtering oil lamps on the white walls. "But I think word has already spread through the village about everything Otto said. What will result I believe, for good or for ill, will be determined here tonight. Therefore, gentlemen, we have no choice but to invite everyone inside and deal with this mess honestly. The rain has fallen, as they say, and there is no putting it back into the clouds."

A few moments later, Len Harold walked slowly to the front of the building and opened the main doors just enough to recognize Tyler Harkin, one of Constable Brindle's deputies, standing guard near the entrance. The air was abuzz with uneasy conversation. A second afterward, Constable Brindle himself looked inside, curiously eyeing Len's pale countenance.

"How are things going?"

"Fine, constable. Just fine," he softly said. "You couldn't keep away either."

"Well, the crowd has grown a bit," Clay replied, wiping his forehead with a handkerchief. "Finished? Should I send them home?"

Len shook his head. "No. Send them in here. The council has decided to open up the discussion. Seems everyone is in the know, more or less, so we might as well make it official, right?"

"Good idea," the constable replied. "You take your seat, Len, and we'll open up the doors nice and slow so everyone doesn't stampede inside like crazed cattle."

Len nodded. "Thanks, Clay," he said before rushing back to prepare the others for the onslaught. He suspected it was going to be a long and trying night.

People entered the village hall up the center aisle in an orderly rush, trying to get seats on the benches closest to the front or on the sides closest to the table. Katherine Durant stood near the interior doorway in the small entrance hall, gazing into the main chamber as people filed inside. She painfully recalled the visit that she and her mother had received from Otto Nibbs early that morning. Both were so happy to see him again yet brokenhearted after he had abruptly left. Katherine's mother, Sophia, was especially melancholy after her brother's brief call, unable to comprehend the man's behavior. She had commented that Otto behaved so unlike the caring brother she had known all her life.

"Katherine, are you coming inside with the rest of us?" a voice asked.

She spun around, startled from her somber musings. "I suppose in a moment," she said automatically, staring at the vaguely familiar face before her. A tall, young man with short black hair and a pleasant smile stared back with genuine concern. Katherine's eyes widened with surprise. "Lewis! I hardly recognized you for a moment. I haven't seen you since…"

"Since our last encounter here over a month ago," he replied. "On the night Maynard was appointed as acting mayor in your uncle's place."

"I remember," she said. "But where have you been lately? I haven't run into you when I've visited Amanda Stewart with my mother. She's over there now having tea. Mother didn't want to face these crowds tonight."

"I'm not surprised as the topic of conversation is all about her brother," Lewis said with understanding. "Anyway, I've been felling trees and splitting wood in the Cumberland with some of Oscar's other laborers, then hauling it back for the winter orders. It's hard work, but it pays more. Better than scrubbing pots in the kitchen." Lewis grinned, recalling his old job of washing dishes and hauling up ice from the cellar, though it had all been made tolerable whenever he had met Katherine there.

"Outdoor work agrees with you," she said, noting that Lewis appeared less the lanky and awkward individual she once fretted about because he might possibly ask her to the pavilion dance. "You're apparently eating more because of your new job and..." She smiled. "I'm not used to seeing you with short hair. It suits you."

Lewis blushed. "It was getting in my eyes while chopping wood," he said, before lowering his voice. "Besides, Mrs. Stewart politely suggested that I pay more attention to my appearance now that she and her husband were employing me in areas with more responsibility." He chuckled. "I think she wanted to say in areas more visible to the public, but left that for me to figure out."

Katherine laughed as well, knowing how strictly Amanda Stewart ran her home and addressed her employees. "Still, she means only the best for you, Lewis."

"I know."

Katherine took a deep breath and sighed as the last of the crowd entered the main room. "I suppose we should go in before the meeting begins," she said with little enthusiasm, wondering if she should have stayed with her mother for tea as it would have been less taxing on her nerves.

"I'd be happy to sit next to you," Lewis said, noting her uneasiness. "With your permission, of course."

"I'd like that," she replied, feeling less anxious. "But I think we're going to be relegated to the back row. Everywhere else is filled."

"Then we'll be the first ones to leave when it's over," Lewis said, holding open the door and escorting Katherine to their seats.

The meeting lasted over an hour, though most of the discussion and arguments voiced at the end of the night were simply rehashing issues raised at the beginning. In the end, everything regarding Otto's kidnapping and unexpected reappearance boiled down to three questions. *When were the attacks upon the village to be launched? What could be done to stop them? And why would Otto Nibbs abandon his beloved village to save himself?* The last question was the cruelest of all and tore at the hearts of everyone gathered.

"I can't believe that Otto would slink out of town and leave Kanesbury to whatever horror awaits us!" someone said in a fit of ire.

"We must defend the village!" another cried out, though sadly acknowledging that several of the younger and stronger men had already joined up with the King's Guard earlier in the year.

"Still, we have enough good men to do what needs to be done!" Horace Ulm shouted out as he rose to his feet. "I'll gladly pick up a sword to defend our homes."

"You don't even own a sword," one of his neighbors muttered from across the room to a burst of laughter.

"Then I'll grab a pitchfork!" he retorted, slightly miffed. "And I'm sure Zachary Farnsworth and my other employees at the banking house will stand by my side."

"Of course we will!" Farnsworth replied, sitting in back of the room.

"But how can we defend ourselves against men from the Northern Isles? They live to fight. I heard someone say that Otto told someone else that they would invade our very homes!" said a woman near the main table. "And what if the Enâri return?"

"Maybe we should seek help from the other villages," someone suggested. "We could send word to Mitchell or Three Willows for starters!" A chorus of agreement rose.

"Now settle down, everybody!" Maynard said, standing up. He pounded the flat of his hand upon the table several times to get their attention. "First, let's not panic. No one has attacked our village yet, and just because Otto Nibbs told many of us that it would come to pass, doesn't mean that it will. Don't invite trouble where none is."

"But what if Kanesbury *is* invaded? What then?" a lone voice inquired.

"Then we'll deal with it," he replied, modulating his voice to a more soothing tone. "I'm not suggesting that we don't take these threats seriously, but let's prepare in a rational, orderly fashion. We are citizens of Kanesbury. We take pride in our village and in ourselves, and I intend to utilize our resources and ingenuity first and foremost before raising the alarm all over the county like a flock of frightened geese."

"Sounds good when you say it like that," Dooley Kramer said. He stood up to address the crowd, sitting a couple benches in front of Katherine and Lewis. "But can you assure us that we'll be safe from whatever is out there? Apparently Otto Nibbs couldn't, which is probably why he left the village under cover of darkness, saving himself and giving us just enough warning to appease his conscience."

Maynard held up a hand for silence when Dooley's comment received applause from some and contradictory remarks from others who felt that he was being too harsh on Otto. But as Maynard closely observed the crowd's behavior as it settled down, he noticed that everyone had a few things in common–they were all confused, all upset and all on edge to one degree or another, traits that would work to his advantage to advance Caldurian's plan. Dooley's question and comment elicited the response he had hoped to hear. Maynard was pleased that Dooley had spoken the words just as he was instructed.

"Let's not direct any anger at Otto as he is not here to defend himself," Maynard pleaded. "Yet after saying that, I can understand why some of you are upset with him. After all, there are many questions that I would still like to ask him, but Otto would only visit with me for a few minutes. Now I understand why–Otto wanted to warn as many people as he could before he left for whatever reason he deemed necessary."

"He didn't visit me!" someone shouted from off to one side.

"Me neither!" another cried.

And that was followed by still another chorus of voices who bitterly complained that they received no warning of any kind from their former mayor.

"Apparently some in Kanesbury are more worthy of being saved by the great Otto Nibbs than the rest of us! Well it's good to know who your friends are," a woman complained from the back.

Several moments passed before Maynard was able to quell the latest squabble. He appeared both frustrated and saddened as he stood before his fellow villagers, telling them that they had to cooperate and give others the benefit of the doubt or they would all regret it should danger actually arrive at their doorsteps. But in his thoughts, the wizard Arileez was delighted with the tenor of the meeting, confident that the unease and suspicion percolating inside these walls would easily seep into every household in Kanesbury. The next two incidents planned for later in the evening would unsettle the local population even more and pave the way for Caldurian's arrival.

"Now that was a gathering to remember," Lewis said as he escorted Katherine out of the village hall into the cool streets a few steps ahead of the talkative crowd. The Bear Moon, approaching full, rose high in the east under clear, crisp skies.

"I suppose I should have said something to defend my uncle," Katherine remarked with regret as she and Lewis took refuge beneath a maple tree, its bare branches webbed in moonlight. "But I…"

"What is it?" Lewis asked, noting her mixed emotions. He knew that attending the meeting couldn't have been easy for her since she probably expected that negative comments about her uncle would be inevitable.

"Lewis, though I love Uncle Otto dearly, a part of me was saddened that he left after giving so many people such dire warnings." She looked into Lewis' eyes and suspected how much he truly cared for her. At the moment, she was happy that he did. "And why did he not warn others, some of whom were good friends?"

"For that matter, why didn't he just ring the village bell, wake up everybody this morning and say what he had to say?" Lewis suggested with a touch of humor.

"Maybe he should have done that," she replied with a forced smile before reverting to her previous consternation. "Still, Otto's behavior was so unlike–*Otto*! My mother said as much this morning after he left us, after we had a chance to absorb what happened. I thought so too, though maybe our heads were still swimming with sleep at the time and affected our judgment." Katherine shrugged helplessly. "Right now I don't know what to think, Lewis. I need to walk and clear my head."

"Then I shall walk you home," he suggested, feeling brave enough to state his wish rather than ask it.

"I accept," she said. "However, you may walk with me to the Stewarts' house instead so I can pick up my mother. She and Amanda should be thoroughly talked out by now." Katherine scanned the thinning crowd in the street as people hurried back to their homes. "I'll fill them in on what happened tonight since I don't see the council members leaving yet. I'm sure Amanda is eagerly awaiting Oscar's report."

"Very well," Lewis said, offering his arm to her. "I'll escort you to the Stewart residence," he added with feigned formality, hoping to elicit a laugh from Katherine. She delightfully obliged.

But they hadn't walked two blocks under the icy stars when their moment of good cheer suddenly turned sour. A brief ruckus near the Water Barrel Inn was audible on the street parallel to them. Several people were shouting and the sound of galloping horses could be heard fading in the west. Katherine and Lewis insisted to one another that they had heard the sound of breaking glass.

"This way!" Lewis said, hurrying south down a narrow lane before taking a right at the next corner. Katherine grabbed his hand as they dashed west through the shadows toward the Water Barrel Inn where a large crowd had gathered beneath bony trees and splashes of moonlight.

"...and took off down the road and out the village!" someone was saying as they drew closer. About twenty people were gathered near the inn with others approaching in several directions.

"What happened?" Lewis asked, noticing that two of the inn's window panes had been smashed.

"Three men on horses rode by and threw rocks through the windows!" Bob Hawkins exclaimed. "I nearly got hit by one!"

"You did not!" said a man standing next to him.

"Well I saw one of the stones break the glass," Bob insisted. "Close enough to being hit, if you ask me!"

"Did anyone give chase?" Katherine asked. "Or contact Constable Brindle?"

"Gill Meddy went to get the constable," Bob said. "As for chasing those hooligans, well, it happened so fast that they were out of sight before we even stepped outside to see what was going on."

"Why would anyone do such a thing?" someone wondered aloud with disgust.

Several people asked similar questions while others examined the damage to the windows, pointing at the broken glass as the glow of yellow light poured onto the street. A few in the crowd who had just returned from the village hall commented that this could be the beginning of the trouble that Otto had warned them about.

"Maybe it was soldiers from the Isles. Did anyone get a good look at them?" an elderly man asked.

"Or maybe they were ghosts!" a slightly inebriated man said with a boisterous laugh, still clutching his mug of ale. "Though probably just a bunch of pranksters."

"This was hardly a prank!" Bob Hawkins replied with disgust. "I expect to enjoy good food and spirits when I'm settled down at the Water Barrel, not rocks sailing over my head!"

Soon Constable Brindle arrived with Gill Meddy at his side. He was immediately bombarded with detailed descriptions of the event. People demanded a thorough investigation as well as armed patrols throughout the village. As the constable calmly addressed their concerns, Lewis took Katherine aside and suggested that they continue on to Amanda's house as they would learn nothing more right now.

"We'll inform everyone there about what happened," he said. "Then I'll walk you and your mother back home."

"You needn't do that, Lewis. We can walk a few blocks in the moonlight," she replied, though she was touched by his offer.

"I insist," he said. "It'll make me feel better after all that's happened today."

Katherine agreed with a smile as they proceeded down the road. "Do you think those men could have been from the Northern Isles?" she added after a few moments of uneasy silence.

"Anything is possible. But regardless where they're from, their intentions were still the same. Somebody is meaning to stir up trouble as Otto warned, but I'm not sure why."

"I wish you were wrong, Lewis, yet I have a feeling that you aren't," she said. "But this was plenty of excitement for tonight. Kanesbury has experienced enough problems over the last few weeks to last us until springtime."

She couldn't help thinking about Nicholas Raven, Adelaide Cooper and the death of Arthur Weeks. Coupled with the release of the Enâri creatures from the Spirit Caves and the strange appearances of her uncle, Katherine wondered if those incidents were all somehow related. And though she couldn't figure it out, she was grateful that Lewis was by her side.

Many hours later, Kanesbury lay silent as the Bear Moon dipped in the west behind a drifting bank of clouds. The previous day's turmoil had been temporarily forgotten in the deep, collective sleep that embraced the villagers in the hours before dawn. A waning crescent Fox Moon climbed in the east, its softer, subtler light reflecting off the waters of the Pine River near Ned Adams' gristmill. A light breeze stirred among the pine trees, swaying their evergreen tips in hypnotic union.

Moments later, the flickering light mirrored upon the river grew brighter and more savage. An acrid stench quickly filled the air. Dark plumes of smoke rose high into the sky, barely visible against the ebony background. Crackling flames leaped up like snake tongues as the gristmill was swiftly engulfed in a devilish blaze that burned for many minutes in blatant anonymity. Not until after a single, sleepless voice began to cry in alarm while going door to door, did the residents of Kanesbury finally awaken to the horrible conflagration consuming one of the village's most important businesses. Men and women rushed to the river with buckets to form water lines in a battle against the wall of orange and yellow flames, though most already knew their efforts would be in vain to save the building. Now it was just a matter of preventing the fire from spreading to the trees.

As the bucket brigade frantically kept to its task, the warnings from Otto Nibbs were foremost on people's minds. The trouble had finally begun, just as he predicted, but what else was to follow? Everyone laboring along the river wondered, searching for answers in the dragon-like flames, the delicate touch of moonlight and the cold, gray breath of approaching dawn.

CHAPTER 42

The Arrival

The charred remains of the gristmill produced an ethereal haze above the treetops late the following morning. Cold rays of sunlight stabbed the smoldering mass that lay like the carcass of a huge, mythical beast struck down by a torrent of fiery arrows. A gawking crowd had thinned since sunrise, though onlookers continually wandered by to examine the spectacular damage. Ned Adams stood alone beneath an oak tree, his coat unbuttoned, his arms folded, contemplating the ruin and the task of rebuilding. His wife was talking with several ladies nearby, but he had spoken to enough people already and wanted a few moments alone. But when he noticed Dooley Kramer lingering near the river's edge, he signaled for him to approach. Dooley raced over at once.

"I was hoping we could talk, Mr. Adams, but I didn't want to bother you," Dooley said, his face as pale as the wet ash.

"It's never a bother when I hear from one of my employees," he replied. "I suspect we'll be having several conversations, Dooley. I'd like your opinion about rebuilding this place, after all. I want to make it better!"

"That's a good attitude, sir." Dooley nodded as a thin breeze brushed through his dirty blond hair. He felt that Ned was taking this financial setback rather well, even better than himself. He felt sick to his stomach upon witnessing the destruction of his livelihood. He knew that Caldurian had some distasteful events planned for Kanesbury as part of his revenge, but he never expected anything like this. Had he been warned, he would have vigorously objected. Now he feared what else the wizard had in mind. How were he and Farnsworth supposed to collect their due if there was nothing left of the village after Caldurian departed?

"Rest assured, Dooley, that I plan to look after you and the other employees until this place is up and running again," Ned promised. "Some of the local farmers have offered to hire a few of you part-time after we get this mess cleaned up, but I can certainly use you all to help rebuild come springtime."

"Count me in!"

"I will. We'll meet later so we can start getting our accounts in order." Ned shook his head, nearly overwhelmed. "All our books have been destroyed along with everything else. It'll be like starting a brand new business." He managed a smile. "I'll bet you didn't expect to be this busy over the winter, did you?"

"No," Dooley honestly said, wondering if his association with Farnsworth and Caldurian was worth such headaches. He promised Ned to be at his disposal when needed and then hurried to the banking house after their conversation, wanting desperately to speak to Zachary Farnsworth.

"How many times have I told you not to bother me here?"

Zachary Farnsworth smoothed out the wrinkles on his red vest as he stood up behind his office desk at the banking house he managed for Horace Ulm. He opened the door and glanced into the main room. One man working behind the front counter attended to a customer while two other employees sat at their tables dutifully scribbling into the account books. A stream of bright, dusty sunlight shot through one of the tiny windows. Farnsworth quietly closed the door and returned to his desk.

"I'm sorry, but I needed to talk to you before tonight," Dooley said, seated in a wooden chair. "The place where I worked just burned to the ground, in case you haven't noticed!"

"How could I not?" Farnsworth bitterly quipped. "Your clothes reek of smoke. And keep the voice down."

"Fine," he whispered irritably. "But did you know about the fire beforehand? Did you know that that was part of Caldurian's plan?"

"Of course not! I'd have said something otherwise. Do you think the wizard gives me every detail about what he intends to do?"

"We should have asked for more information before we agreed to his terms."

Farnsworth leaned forward, steadying his voice. "Look, Dooley, let's not be naïve and think that Kanesbury is going to be unscathed before this is all over. But Caldurian promised us control of the village when he's through, and that's what matters. So if we have to endure a few bumps along the way, we do. The gristmill fire was out of line, but just be thankful the wizard is on our side," he emphasized with a jab of his finger in the air. "He could have plotted his revenge on Otto Nibbs without our help, and who knows what condition this village would have been in afterward in that case."

Dooley grimaced. That was not the answer he wanted to hear, but he knew that Farnsworth was correct. What could either of them do against Caldurian or Arileez? They both had the power and were directing the theatrics, so all he and Farnsworth could do was watch and wait for their time to arrive. He shuddered, unable to determine which of the two wizards frightened him the most.

"If you learn anything new, let me know," Dooley said. "Chances are that I'll be busy working with Ned Adams on his customers' accounts."

"You do that," Farnsworth replied. "It'll keep you out of trouble. In the meantime, stay away from here. You're lucky that Horace isn't around today. The last thing we need is that chatterbox poking his nose into our business. Now get out of my office, Dooley, and don't come back!"

The gristmill fire was the main topic of conversation that day, with opinions as strong as the bittersweet scent of smoke lingering above the rooftops. The wanton destruction of Ned's property tore at the heart of every citizen. Constable Brindle and his men thoroughly investigated the matter, but after Otto's cryptic warnings and the previous night's damage to the Water Barrel Inn, most people were certain that the fire had been no accident. Many fretfully speculated about what might happen next as talk once again veered to enlisting help from other villages. And though Maynard Kurtz had deemed such a step unnecessary, many began to have second thoughts.

Constable Brindle, in the meantime, organized a series of nighttime patrols on both foot and horseback to sweep the village from sunset until sunrise beginning that very night. Volunteers eagerly signed up for three-hour shifts, determined to protect their homes and loved ones. An announcement was also made that the doors to the village hall would remain unlocked so that if some nefarious activity was discovered, anyone could access the belfry to sound the alarm.

Yet amid all the turmoil, feelings of resentment and mistrust toward Otto Nibbs grew quietly in the hearts and minds of most citizens. Despite his last-minute warning of impending trouble, Otto had forfeited any respect or admiration he might have earned because of it by fleeing the village. The man who was once the epitome of friendliness and integrity was now perceived as a selfish coward. And though few expressed those words on the open street, that sentiment thrived behind closed doors and around dinner tables. It was only a matter of time, most felt, before the name Otto Nibbs would be uttered on the streets loudly and with fiery contempt.

Katherine stepped out the front door of Amanda Stewart's house later that evening, bathed in the soft light from a pair of oil lamps on either side of the stone pathway. The second night of Old Autumn was cool and clear, touched by the silvery glow of the nearly full rising Bear Moon. She was bundled in a cloak and wore a pair of thin gloves while walking up the leafy street on her way to the village hall to locate Oscar and Maynard who were nearly late for dinner.

She and her mother, along with the acting mayor, had been invited by the Stewarts for a meal that evening. Katherine had hoped to run into Lewis at the house, but learned with disappointment that he had left shortly before she and her mother had arrived.

As she strolled past the Water Barrel Inn, she noted that the two broken windows had been replaced and that the eating, drinking and merrymaking continued on within as if nothing had happened. She turned a corner and continued north up the next street, fondly recalling that the Water Barrel was one of Nicholas Raven's favorite haunts. It seemed a lifetime since he had walked out the door of the ice cellar and fled into the darkness, yet it had been just over a month and a half ago. She worried about him and hoped that he was safe, wondering if he would ever step foot in Kanesbury again.

Soon the village hall loomed in view, its windows comfortably awash in yellow light amid the encroaching darkness. As Katherine neared the front steps, she noticed Ned Adams approaching.

"How are you this evening, Ned?" she asked as he neared. She suspected that the fire had fully engaged his time and thoughts during the day.

"Oh, hello, Katherine," he replied absentmindedly, his focus still elsewhere. "I, uh– What did you say?"

She smiled. "I wanted to know how you were doing," she repeated, gently touching his shoulder. "I imagine not too well after what happened."

"Maybe not at first," he said, "but surprisingly my wife and I are managing all right, at least for today. Many people have been so kind, including your mother. She sent over a pot of beef and barley soup and a loaf of bread. We're more than grateful."

"I'm glad to hear that," she replied. After they conversed for several minutes, she inquired if he had seen Oscar and Maynard.

"They're still meeting inside, I suspect. That's where I'm heading now," he explained. "I told them I'd probably be late." He took Katherine's arm and escorted her up the few steps to the front doors of the village hall. "They're discussing measures to protect the village, including the patrols Clay Brindle has suggested. I guess after the fire, people are taking Otto's warning more seriously despite him sneaking off like a scared jackrabbit." Ned was about to open the door and then paused, shaking his head. "I'm sorry, Katherine, but I didn't mean to disparage your uncle like that. It's just that..."

"I'm not offended, Ned. It's understandable after all you've endured." She wrapped the folds of her garment tightly about her shoulders. "I suspect many are thinking the same thing. Uncle Otto has fallen out of the good graces of most after the way he behaved. Even I can't understand it. Otto acted so unlike himself when my mother and I spoke to him the other morning. He seemed..."

"Yes?"

"Not himself, I guess." She sighed. "He possessed a faraway look that I've never seen before, as if he were a shadow of his former self. My mother thought so, too. I imagine being kidnapped by the Enâri would unnerve anybody, yet Uncle Otto seemed a completely different person. Does that make any sense, Ned?"

"I felt the same way when I spoke to Otto, too."

"You don't have to humor me," she replied. "I'm probably sounding like a foolish girl who let her imagination fly. It must have been the shock of seeing my uncle after so long and in such an unexpected manner that caused me to experience those feelings."

"But you said your mother had reacted similarly."

"That's true."

"So believe me when I say that Otto appeared different to me as well, though I also tried to explain it away to the strangeness of the situation and the early morning hour. But he isn't the only one. Why, I was even thinking that–"

Katherine looked up as Ned stopped in mid-sentence, detecting a hint of uncertainty in his voice. "What were you going to say, Ned? I'd like to know."

He grinned with embarrassment. "I'm going to sound like I'm the one with a lively imagination, but I was going to say that, well..." Ned uncomfortably cleared his throat as he fingered his coat collar. "Ever since Maynard was appointed as acting mayor, he seems to be a bit different, too. More distant perhaps? Still friendly and all, but just not quite the Maynard I know, if you understand me."

"I do!" Katherine said. "Though I never mentioned it to anyone, I attributed his cool demeanor at times to the fact that Nicholas had run away and Adelaide Cooper was missing. Maynard was very fond of them both."

"Having two such dear people torn out of his life must have been a shock. How would we behave if it had happened to either one of us? Yet you and Nicholas were good friends and you appear to still be as gracious as ever."

"Thank you. Nicholas and I were well acquainted, though not for nearly as long as he and Adelaide had been with Maynard. It saddens me that Maynard is roaming around the farmstead all alone these past several weeks."

"His extra duties as mayor will do him good," Ned remarked. "Take his mind off of being alone."

"I suppose so."

"But I still find it odd," he continued, "that Adelaide's disappearance, the robbery at my mill and Arthur Weeks' murder all occurred at the same time those Enâri creatures escaped from the Spirit Caves. Then Otto later meets with the Enâri at Barringer's Landing, was apparently kidnapped and escaped, and now flees his own village? It doesn't make sense. I believe Caldurian is mixed up in this, though I can't prove it. Kanesbury is sinking into trouble all over again like twenty years ago. It sickens me!"

Ned appeared visibly shaken, combing a hand through his thinning hair. If anything upset him even more than the destruction of his business, it was the devastation that was about to be unleashed upon his beloved village according to Otto Nibbs. That Otto was nowhere to be found only multiplied his anxiety.

"Many feel as you do, Ned. You've lived in Kanesbury your whole life and built up a successful business. An attack on either one is like an attack on your family. You should be angry."

"I am, though I must keep my senses or I'll be of no use to anyone." He sighed regretfully. "I suppose, Katherine, that I lost my senses on the night Nicholas ran away. Being accused of robbery and murder would be enough to make anyone do something rash. I should have believed him when he expressed his innocence despite what the evidence looked like. I'm guessing that Nicholas might also have been caught up unawares in whatever trouble is brewing here. He had no reason to rob me or kill Arthur Weeks." He scratched behind his neck. "But Dooley claimed that Nicholas attacked him and then killed Arthur, so maybe Nicholas *did* rob me. Oh, but I just can't seem to figure it out! And now my head's starting to ache." He placed a hand on the door, preparing to step inside. "Well, we've chatted enough. Let's go in and find out what the council is up to."

"Wait," Katherine said, carefully contemplating her next words. "Ned, there's something you need to know. I probably should have told you or somebody else a long time ago, but I made a promise and..." She looked uneasily into his eyes. "Since there is more at stake now than my own safety, I must speak up."

"What are you talking about? You look positively distressed."

She signaled for Ned to follow her down the steps toward a nearby maple tree, desiring more privacy. "As I said, I made a promise to someone not to reveal the information I'm about to tell you," she told him, glancing around at the nearly empty street to make sure no one was in earshot. "He insisted that I do so for my own safety, but now the safety of everyone in Kanesbury is at issue."

"What are you saying? And who did you make a promise to?"

She hesitated before answering. "It was to Nicholas. I promised not to say anything when we talked on the first night of the Harvest Festival. He was hiding in the ice cellar at Oscar and Amanda's house during the party after he was accused by Arthur Weeks of being a thief."

Ned's eyes widened in amazement. "I was at that party, though I left early because I was so upset about the robbery and learning that Nicholas had been fingered as the culprit."

"He insisted that he didn't commit the crime," Katherine said. "I gave him some food and let him sleep awhile in the cellar. He had planned to go back to Maynard's farmhouse after things calmed down, but they only got worse."

"Arthur Weeks was stabbed to death." Ned sadly recalled the horrific details of that night. "Dooley claimed that Nicholas had hit him before killing Arthur."

"But Nicholas had been asleep in the ice cellar. I woke him later and told him the horrible news."

Ned placed his hands upon his hips, his face tightening as he contemplated a dozen questions at once. He paced a few steps, replaying the events of that night in his mind.

"If what you say is true, then Dooley lied to everyone. And Arthur also lied by claiming that Nicholas had returned to the gristmill after hours when Arthur was cleaning up the place."

"I'm telling you the truth, Ned."

"But why would Arthur lie? Did he and Dooley steal the flour sacks–and my money–and place them in Nicholas' shanty?" Ned raised his hands, at a loss. "For what purpose?"

"I don't know. But Dooley does have Nicholas' job now."

Ned felt his limbs grow cold. "Would Dooley arrange all that just to get Nicholas' job? I find it hard to believe." He looked up at

Katherine with fear in his eyes. "Worse yet, do you think that Dooley was the one who killed Arthur?"

"I don't know," she said. "I suppose it's possible, but I find it difficult to believe that even he would do something like that."

"Agreed," he replied. "There must be more to this conspiracy. But if you can vouch for Nicholas' whereabouts at the time of the murder, then at the very least, Dooley Kramer is a liar. Whether he is a murderer is yet to be determined."

"That's why Nicholas made me promise not to reveal this information to anyone, not even to Constable Brindle. It would simply have been my word against Dooley's regarding Nicholas' innocence," she said. "Nicholas feared that I might get hurt, or worse, if I implicated Dooley. Since there was already one dead body, he didn't want to chance a second one. I urged Nicholas to flee, hoping that Clay Brindle would uncover the truth on his own."

Ned placed an arm around her shoulder as if Katherine was his own daughter. "You did the right thing under the circumstances. But the question is–what do we do now?"

"Perhaps it's best if we say nothing for now and simply keep our guard up. Dooley is working at your side, so what better way to keep an eye on him if he is involved in the recent goings-on?"

"I suppose you're right," he said. "If we accuse him now of lying or murder without proof, he'll become cautious and possibly dangerous if he is up to something."

"Then we'll go about our business as if nothing has changed, keeping a close watch all the while."

"Agreed, Katherine," Ned replied. "And a very close watch at that. Who knows what trouble may yet be lurking in the shadows?"

As the Bear Moon continued its steady ascent in the eastern sky, a sheet of high, gauzy clouds drifted in from the west, blanketing the village and scattering bluish moonlight through a fine veil of crystalline ice. The streets lay quiet as most people were sitting down to an evening meal. Shops had closed for business. Heads of cattle in pastures were being paraded into barns to pass the frosty night in straw beds. Elsewhere around the village, the first few patrols had been released into the streets by Constable Brindle to begin their watches, some on horseback and others on foot, and all with a seriousness of purpose and a renewed affection for Kanesbury.

"We were lucky to draw the early shift," said a man named Arnie. He and his patrol partner wandered south along the western edge of the park. The road was mostly lined with trees and shadows that quivered in the light of their fluttering torches. Only a few houses had been built at either end of the long lane. "This isn't too bad of a job to handle, Lucas."

"Well don't get too used to it," he replied. "Constable Brindle said he's going to rotate the patrols to be fair, so we're going to get stuck with some rotten hours one of these days." He spat on the side of the road. "Don't know why I let him talk me into this."

"Because you know it's the right thing to do," Arnie said, a hood draped over his head and a pair of wool gloves warming his fingers. "We're protecting our village, and after what happened to Ned's gristmill and the Water Barrel Inn the other night, she needs all the protecting she can get."

Lucas grunted. "I don't expect she needs much protecting during the dinner hour. I rushed through a bowl of potato soup to be here on time. My wife promised me a proper meal when I get back home. I should have brought some food along. I'll be starving after walking for three hours!"

"Oh, don't be dim, Lucas. There's nothing preventing us from stopping at the Water Barrel for a break now and then. It's in our section of the village we're supposed to patrol, after all."

"I suppose we could do that," he replied, cheering up.

"Of course we can! This isn't our real job. We're our own bosses now," Arnie said, slapping Lucas on the back. "Think of it that way, my friend."

"I guess I will," he said with a smile, his prospects suddenly looking up. Then a frown appeared on his face and his mood darkened. "Hey, where are we supposed to go for a bite or a quick pint when we're stuck out here in the cold gloom a few hours before dawn? The Water Barrel won't be open to us then."

"Why do you have to dampen every good thought like a passing rain cloud?" Arnie replied with amused disgust. "When we're out here in the bleak hours, we'll bring along a pot of stew, a loaf of bread and eat on the pavilion steps, okay?"

"I was just wondering, is all. Don't fault me for that."

Arnie burst out laughing. "You and your stomach. Maybe you should ask your wife to wake up in the middle of our late patrols and run down here with a picnic lunch!"

"Oh, quit it, Arnie, will you? I can take it out here in the cold if you can. I was just–" Lucas stopped in mid sentence when he thought he detected the sound of grunting horses through a thicket of trees along Grangers Road nearby. The long country highway began at a point several yards ahead and to their right, continuing out of the village to the northwest for miles through Litchfield County. "I bet that's the Bessel brothers. They're supposed to be roaming about on this side of the village, too." Lucas glanced at Arnie with a wicked grin. "Let's give them a scare!"

"All right," he muttered, knowing he wouldn't be able to talk Lucas out of it. "Just have at it and get it out of your system."

"Follow me," Lucas whispered, lowering his torch and stepping off the road to his right. He led Arnie across a patch of dried weeds and freshly fallen leaves nestled beneath a scattering of trees. Grangers Road appeared just ahead of them and they could see the outline of several horses farther up the road to their right. "Get ready," he softly said, glancing back at Arnie with a smirk. "I guarantee that one of them screams out loud."

Arnie nodded, urging him on. "Just do it already."

"Okay," he replied, preparing to dash out of the trees. "*Now!*"

At that instant, Lucas darted out of hiding and onto Grangers Road, heading straight toward the shadowy men on horses as he waved his torch like a madman. Arnie obediently followed, but with less enthusiasm. Though both expected a boisterous reaction from the Bessel brothers, neither were prepared for what awaited them–a dozen men on horseback sitting tall and stern, and the metallic swish of twelve drawn swords reflecting traces of moonlight and the flickering torches. Lucas and Arnie stopped dead in their tracks, shocked and confused.

"You're not the Bessel brothers," Lucas muttered, his mouth agape when facing the sharp tip of a sword blade inches from his nose. He glanced at Arnie, his face clouded with dread, realizing their hours of patrolling had just come to an abrupt end.

"No, we're not," the man closest to him gruffly replied.

"Who are you?" Arnie asked defiantly, his heart racing.

"Oh, you'll find out soon," one of the other men answered.

"Quiet!" the first man scolded, apparently the leader of the group. He glared at Lucas and Arnie, demanding to know their names and why they were wandering in this section of the village. A moment of uneasy silence followed. "Answer me!"

"We were just... Just out walking," Lucas uttered, taking a half step backward from the gleaming sword.

The man raised a doubtful eyebrow. "We expect a better answer than that."

"*Oh?*"

"How about you?" the man said, addressing Arnie. "Why are you here? Why did you try to sneak up on us?"

Arnie looked up, not having the slightest idea what to say, when he was suddenly inspired to act in a quite unusual manner. From the tips of the twelve swords to the strangers' foreboding presence, Arnie knew that the full brunt of the trouble that Otto Nibbs had warned everyone about had finally arrived in Kanesbury. If he didn't act immediately to sound a warning, he would never get a second chance. And if he didn't utilize this brief spurt of courage surging through him now, it would surely go to waste. He breathed steadily as a peculiar sense of calm settled upon him.

"I'll tell you why we're here," Arnie said, lowering his torch as he fixed his gaze challengingly upon the man. "But on second thought..."

Suddenly, he flung his torch somersaulting into the trees near the point where he and Lucas had exited. The men on horseback instinctively turned their heads to follow the path of the burning light. At the same instant, Arnie fled, sprinting down Grangers Road until he reached the lane that he and Lucas had been patrolling earlier. He dashed through the adjacent park past the pavilion, his lungs burning as he sucked in the cold night air, determined to reach the village hall and sound the warning bell. He hoped Lucas would forgive him for running off, but he knew he had no other choice. Trouble had arrived and he wondered if Kanesbury would survive the night.

"Shall I give chase?" one of the men on horseback asked, returning his sword to its sheath. He wore a long brown sea coat and black boots as did all the men who had accompanied him from the Northern Isles.

"Not important," his leader replied. "They'll know of our arrival shortly, with or without his warning. And as the village is surrounded, where will anyone go?" The man glanced at Lucas who was still wide-eyed and petrified. "Lead us to the center of town. We're anxious to see what kind of place Kanesbury is since we'll be making this our home for a time."

They had nearly finished eating dinner when Amanda Stewart, in mid-sentence, silently indicated for Morris to prepare a kettle of tea to accompany the dessert cake. He politely nodded and exited the room as she concluded her point without missing a beat, eliciting laughter from her husband and her three invited dinner guests, Katherine Durant, her mother, Sophia, and Maynard Kurtz. Oscar refilled their glasses with plum wine as Maynard finished off the last morsel of roast pork on his plate, running it through a splash of bacon-mushroom gravy with his fork.

"You've outdone yourself tonight, Amanda," Maynard said, raising his drink in her honor. The flickering candles upon the harvest colored table linen reflected off his glass.

"The cook has done an outstanding job," she agreed. "Luckily Katherine dragged you and Oscar back here in time before all this food went to waste."

"They were hard at work," Katherine admitted, "so I suppose we must forgive their tardiness."

"That depends if they accomplished anything at their meeting," Sophia joked, taking a sip of wine. Her appearance, though similar to her daughter's, had been delicately aged by time. Sophia's long, brown hair was fastened in back with a set of elegantly painted hair sticks and her eyes were a shade lighter and less intense than Katherine's.

"Now that we've finished eating, we can change the subject to more robust matters, namely, the discussion at the village hall," Amanda said, casting a curious gaze upon Maynard. "What plans have you and Constable Brindle concocted to protect our village? Poor Ned Adams. His entire livelihood disappeared in smoke overnight and is now nothing but a pile of gray ash."

"A great shame," Maynard agreed. "But as Oscar can confirm, we've made substantial progress."

"He's right, dear," Oscar said, peering over his wine glass as he smiled at his wife, her silvery hair highlighted by the glow of the candles. "For one thing, we started the village patrols this evening. Clay Brindle has some of his men and plenty of volunteers out there right now keeping watch over our streets."

"A sensible first step," she said as Morris returned and began clearing away the dishes. "I understand that five of my employees have signed up. Do keep them safe, Maynard."

"Amanda, they're the ones keeping us safe," Oscar said. "At the first sign of trouble, they'll ring the bell in the village hall as a warning. Fear not, my dear."

"Some very fine men are watching out for all of us," Katherine agreed, with thoughts of Lewis on her mind.

"Pardon me for interrupting," Morris said as he continued to gather the empty plates, "but when I was in the kitchen moments ago, I heard the bell ringing through one of the open windows. The staff and I were wondering what was going on."

"A practice run perhaps?" Sophia asked.

"Not that I'm aware of," Maynard replied with a shrug.

"Quiet for a moment," Amanda requested with a raised hand, tilting her head slightly to better hear as the room succumbed to silence. "I do hear the bell pealing."

"Odd that it's sounding now," Oscar muttered. "What's Brindle up to? Ringing lessons in the belfry?"

"Perhaps somebody encountered a stray squirrel and got excited," Maynard lightly added as he reached for his wine glass. Suddenly there was a piercing scream from a distant street that everybody heard through the closed windows and above the laughter.

"What was that?" Katherine said, gripped with uneasiness as she sat arrow-straight in her chair, her heart aflutter. "That sounded awfully unpleasant."

"Let me investigate," Morris said, hurrying out of the dining room with an armful of clattering dishes.

"You don't suppose there's trouble already," Sophia said, fearing that her brother Otto's predictions had come true. Her face appeared strained, her complexion pale. "I had begged him to stay and help us prepare, but he simply refused. I can't understand why."

Katherine gently placed a hand upon her mother's arm. "Perhaps it's nothing. Let's wait to hear from Morris." But it was not to be. As soon as those words had left Katherine's lips, the sounds of shouting in the streets grew suddenly and ominously louder, punctuated by the thunder of horse hoofs and the banging of fists upon doors. She looked at the others, for a horrifying instant stunned by the chaotic sounds in their streets.

"What's going on in our village?" Oscar sputtered as he jumped up from his seat and headed out the room.

"Let's find out," Maynard replied, following him.

Amanda glanced at Katherine and Sophia who both appeared as distraught as she was, yet all were deeply intrigued by the mysterious goings-on. The trio of ladies hastened out of the room as the clamor outdoors continued to grow, yet no one expected or was prepared for what happened next.

An instant later, the front door burst open. Six soldiers from the Northern Isles stormed inside, riding on the wave of cold air and autumn leaves that blasted through the hallway. The men rushed in with swords drawn and boots pounding upon the stone tiles, stopping in unison when one of the servants approached after having dashed out of the kitchen. The worker froze in mid-step, imagining the thrust of cold steel through her body. Oscar and Maynard were only a few paces behind, their faces painted with shock.

"What's going on?" Oscar hollered, dumbfounded at the sight. "Who are you? Why have you entered my home?"

"We're looking for a man named Oscar Stewart. He is supposed to be a member of the village council," the soldier in front said, his face grim and unshaven. "Is that man you? Do you serve in that capacity?"

"It is and I do," Oscar said defiantly, gently taking his stunned servant by the arm and pulling her away from the soldier and sending her back to the kitchen.

"But you haven't answered *his* question!" Maynard jumped in with a show of equal disdain. "Why are you in this house? Under whose authority–"

"Enough!" the man said, taking a step forward, his sword at the ready. "I ask the questions. And for starters, what is your name?"

Maynard stood tall, equal in height to the man. "I'm Maynard Kurtz, the acting mayor of Kanesbury. Your invasion of this home is an invasion of my village."

The soldier smirked. "Well, *acting* mayor, a few things are going to change around your village starting now." He glanced at his companions. "Apparently, men, we struck it rich here, finding Oscar Stewart and the mayor in one place. Now my team will get the credit for finding two of you when we take you in."

"Take them where?" an angry voice demanded from in back of the crowded hallway. Amanda weaved her way through several servants to stand by her husband's side, locking her arm around his. "You aren't taking my husband anywhere. Get out of my house!"

The soldier in charge sighed, sheathing his sword. "I don't wish for bloodshed, but at my direction, that unpleasant reality will be unleashed in this house if my orders are not followed. Your husband and the mayor will accompany us to the village hall immediately or suffer the consequences. I have other men surrounding this house and throughout the village, so there's no hope of escape. Therefore, the question to your husband is this–will he follow us peacefully, or must we resort to other methods?" He noted the palpable fear in Amanda Stewart's eyes. "His choice."

Before Amanda could say a word, she felt the warm hand of her husband upon her own and already knew his answer. She held him tightly, unable to accept his response but knowing there was no other way.

"We'll both go with you," Oscar said, his words laced with defeat. He received a reassuring nod from Maynard. "But I want your word that no harm will come to my wife or anyone else in this house."

"We have no interest in hurting anyone," the soldier replied. "They can go back to whatever matters they were engaged in. My soldiers will depart immediately."

Oscar accepted the man's word and assured his wife that he and Maynard would be fine. "Perhaps I'll be home for breakfast," he gently told her before kissing her goodbye. She reluctantly released her hand from his.

After being allowed to don their coats, Oscar and Maynard were silently led out of the house and into the black night, surrounded by the soldiers. Amanda Stewart watched in bewildered horror with Katherine and Sophia attentively at her side, all temporarily at a loss for words and wondering if they would ever see the two men again.

CHAPTER 43

Breakfast with the Enemy

Oscar Stewart and Maynard Kurtz were led through the main doors of the village hall under the watchful eyes of their captors. Most of the streets had been deserted on their way over as soldiers from the Northern Isles had ordered everyone to remain inside their homes. Kanesbury was under siege and Oscar had never felt so helpless in his life. As a businessman and community leader, he was used to developing great plans and having his orders followed, but that way of life had been shattered in an instant. Though the shock of the situation nearly overwhelmed him, he kept telling himself not to panic and to observe the people and goings-on around him. That was of utmost importance if he were to survive this ordeal, yet a part of him wondered if he would even live through the night.

When they were escorted into the meeting chamber, Oscar and Maynard were relieved to see the other four council members and Constable Brindle talking among themselves while seated on benches near the main table. About twenty soldiers stood guard, some near each entrance while others paced along the sides.

"Go with your friends," the soldier in charge ordered before stepping away to consult with his colleagues. Oscar and Maynard quickly joined their companions.

"It's good to see you two," Len Harold said with a weary smile, shaking their hands. "We wondered if you had been taken elsewhere or maybe escaped."

"No chance of that," Maynard replied. "Kanesbury is crawling with these brutes. How are the five of you holding up?"

"My day keeps getting better and better," Ned Adams grimly joked. "First the fire and now this. Can't wait to see what tomorrow brings."

"What *will* it bring?" Oscar wondered aloud. "Have they told you anything?"

"Nothing," Constable Brindle said, glancing cautiously at the display of force scattered about the room.

"I'd rather not engage any of these soldiers in conversation just now," one of the other council members said. "They don't appear to be the amiable type."

"That they aren't," the constable agreed. "And though they haven't hurt anyone yet from what I've heard, I can see in their eyes that they wouldn't hesitate to strike down a man if provoked." Clay glanced at Maynard, his eyes welling with regret. "I'm sorry, but there were too many of them for my deputies and volunteers to handle. A few hundred maybe from the reports I received before they took me prisoner. I can't say for sure."

"We were all overwhelmed, Clay. No need to apologize," he said. "I should have listened and sent for help as soon as Otto gave his warning. But who would have expected this?" He indicated the slew of armed soldiers and noted the stunned disbelief still evident on the faces of his companions.

"So what do we do now?" Len asked.

Maynard took a deep breath. "I'll tell you one thing–we just don't stand here like cattle chewing their cuds." He removed his coat and folded it over a bench, then spotted one of the soldiers who he thought might be in charge. "I'm still mayor, after all, despite the threat of a sword. I intend to find out what's happening to my village. Excuse me, gentlemen." He confidently strode over to one corner of the room where several soldiers were engaged in conversation.

"Maynard, wait!" Ned warned, fearing for his safety.

But Maynard ignored his words and walked over to the soldiers. They saw him approaching at once, however, and ordered him to stop with the show of swords.

"Back with your friends!" one of the men barked.

"We want to know what's going on," he pleaded. "As mayor of Kanesbury, it is my duty to inquire."

The soldier marched forward, grabbed Maynard by the arm and dragged him back to his friends. "Right now you are mayor in name only. Your power means nothing," he said with contempt.

"Why are you holding us?" Oscar demanded.

"You'll find out tomorrow when the new leader of Kanesbury makes his arrival." The soldier noted the surprise on their faces with amusement. "He'll answer your questions then. In the meantime, this is your home for the night. We'll provide food and blankets later if you don't annoy us any further."

He abruptly left to finish his conversation. Maynard and the others sat down on the benches, forming a tight circle as they continued their discussion, speculating about who was behind this cruel invasion of their lives and how their families were holding up in the process. Most felt as if the morning sun would never arrive.

Oscar opened his eyes, wondering where he had passed the night in such an uncomfortable bed. His back ached and his cheeks and the tip of his nose felt cool to the touch. The walls and ceiling were painted with the cold, gray of morning. As he sat up, a wool blanket slipped off him, revealing his coat snugly buttoned all the way up to the neck. Now he remembered, having chosen to sleep on the floor rather than the benches as they were too narrow and uncomfortable. The oil lamps attached to the walls had been turned low during the night. He grinned when he saw his friends dozing on the floor as well, but they were abruptly awakened moments later by the thunderous tolling of the bell above the building.

"What in blazes was that?" Clay Brindle shouted, sitting up like a corpse brought suddenly back to life. He gazed about the room, wide-eyed and confused.

"It's to signal the change of the guard around the village," a soldier explained as he added wood to the fireplace.

"Well a fine way to greet a new day," the constable muttered as he stretched the knots out of his neck and shoulders. "I hoped it might have been a call to breakfast. You do plan to provide us that, don't you?"

"Eventually," said a voice from behind him. Another soldier approached, appearing to be in charge. "But first we'll allow you time to gather your wits and wash up. We want you looking your best when we leave."

"Where are we going?" Maynard asked, sitting on one of the benches and appearing very tired. He rubbed a hand over his face and yawned.

"To breakfast, of course," the soldier replied. "And to meet your new leader."

"That'll be the day," Ned Adams said with icy bitterness.

"Easy," Oscar cautioned him, not wanting to cause trouble and risk harm to anyone. "The sun has barely risen yet. Let's save that emotion until after we find out who we're dealing with."

"A wise suggestion," the soldier replied.

A stream of air disgustedly escaped between Ned's pursed lips. "I already suspect who we're dealing with, Oscar. But I'll behave until we learn what kind of a fix we're in."

"Where are we going?" Maynard asked again.

"Not far," the soldier replied. "Somewhere with a table large enough to accommodate all of you, unless you'd prefer to eat here."

"I didn't even want to sleep here," Len Harold joked.

"Then it's settled. We leave in an hour," the soldier said, walking away to attend to other business as Maynard and his six puzzled companions continued to discuss matters among themselves.

They departed the village hall on foot precisely one hour later, heading west for almost two blocks until they reached the park. A small contingent of soldiers led the way while several more followed from behind through the cold, deserted streets. Patches of dirty white clouds drifted overhead upon a chilly breeze. The seven prisoners followed the angled street southwest along the park until they turned onto another road curving northwest all the way to the Pine River. Few houses were built on this particular street, though everyone knew who owned the last home near the water's edge.

"Are we going where I think we're going?" Ned whispered to Clay Brindle who walked beside him.

"I think so," he curiously replied. "Of all places, considering everything that's happened. And I thought these last few days couldn't get any stranger."

Most everyone thought the same thing as they neared Otto Nibbs' house, a large, one-story building built of gray stones of various hues with oak beams and a clay tile roof. It stood quietly nestled on the banks of the river among a healthy thicket of maple and pine trees. Delicate trails of bluish smoke rose from the chimney in a series of graceful swirls, slowly dissipating in the milky skies. If he hadn't known otherwise, Ned would have guessed that Otto had started a welcoming fire and placed a pot of tea on, waiting to receive his friends for breakfast on a fine autumn morning. But he was more than sure who really awaited them on this troubling day.

Two soldiers stood guard near the front door and several others patrolled the grounds. As Maynard Kurtz, Constable Brindle and the five council members walked up a stone pathway to the entrance, the door suddenly flew open. A tall man in a long, black cloak stepped out of the shadows. Ned smirked as soon as he noted the man's unkempt tangles of iron gray hair, a pointed beard and a pair of dark, menacing eyes, his worst fears unsurprisingly confirmed.

"Did you set fire to my gristmill yourself, Caldurian, or did you hire one of your thugs?" he sputtered.

"And good morning to you, too, Mr. Adams," the wizard replied, unfazed by the comment. "I'm pleased that you remember me after twenty years."

"We all do," Maynard said dryly. "Tell us, why are we here? And more importantly, why are *you* here? I don't recall extending you an invitation to visit our village. The last time any of us saw the great wizard Caldurian, he and his friend, Madeline, were being escorted out of our village by a company of King Justin's finest soldiers–and neither of you looked too happy about it."

"You were both marched to the southern border of Arrondale like common criminals and told never to return," Oscar gleefully recounted. "Did you forget that part?"

"Apparently I have trouble following directions," Caldurian said with good humor. "Now if you're through flinging such obvious taunts, you're all invited to join me for breakfast where we can have a real conversation."

"About what?" Ned asked.

"About the new order of things," he replied. "I'm sure you'll find the details most intriguing."

The eight sat down to their meal in a large kitchen warmed by a crackling fire. A table was already set for breakfast. In the center was a mouthwatering display of food–a crock of steaming scrambled eggs with wild mushrooms and herbs, a platter of fried beef strips, loaves of freshly baked bread alongside bowls of butter and honey, and on either end, bunches of purple grapes and glistening red apples. Caldurian served them tea from a large kettle hanging on the hearth before he sat down, signaling for everyone to dig in before the food got cold. A few of the soldiers stood guard in the adjacent rooms, allowing the wizard privacy with his guests.

"Let it not be said that I wasn't civil to my captives," the wizard remarked as he buttered a slice of bread to have with his tea.

"The raid upon my house last night was anything but civil," Oscar replied as he gulped down a forkful of eggs and beef. "So don't think that this elaborate meal is going to excuse it."

"I apologize if my colleagues from the Isles were less than courteous, but I had instructed them to lay down the law–*my* law," he explained. "However, if you promise to give me your cooperation and help keep the peace, there is no reason why my stay in Kanesbury need be unpleasant for anybody." He noted a frosty glare from Ned Adams. "Unpleasant from this point forward anyway."

"Cooperation with what?" Constable Brindle asked. "Why don't you just come out and say what you have to say? No need to pretend to act all friendly and such by providing us breakfast," he added as he stabbed a second slice of beef with his fork and plopped it on his plate. "We're still your prisoners, after all."

"I agree," Maynard said. "And though I appreciate the pleasantries, they'll do nothing to excuse your presence in my village. You're an invader, Caldurian. A criminal. So we expect you to be blunt. What exactly do you want?"

The wizard leaned back in his chair, enjoying a quiet laugh. "I admire your desire to get right to the point, Mayor Kurtz, so I will do just that. Simply put, I am taking over your village as well as the odd piece of property here and there to accommodate my needs. And if I don't have the cooperation of each citizen in Kanesbury, there will be dire consequences, perhaps even deadly ones." He sipped his tea, punctuating his point with a raised eyebrow. "Blunt enough for you?"

Ned slapped his fork on his plate and pushed it aside. "What's your game, Caldurian? You couldn't destroy Kanesbury twenty years ago, so you've come back to finish the job? We know your creatures have been released from the Spirit Caves, so why bother us now?"

"I have my reasons," he said, getting up from his chair to wander about the room. Faint splashes of sunshine flowed in through a small eastern window while a view of the Pine River was visible through a larger window in the west wall. "But I will tell you that my demands must be followed–or else."

Maynard sighed as he tossed a cloth napkin on the table and glanced at Caldurian. "All right, wizard. I'll play along with your little game. Tell us what you want. We can't wait to hear," he said sarcastically, eliciting a few grins from the others. "And you apparently can't wait to tell us either."

"As a matter of fact, I can't," he said, standing at the head of the table while addressing his prisoners, enjoying the fact that they were helpless to do anything but listen. "First, though I have already taken control of Kanesbury, I want all of you to give me your approval at a public announcement in the village hall so that the citizens can witness this transfer of power."

"Ridiculous!" Maynard shouted. "I won't do it. Nobody would believe it."

"I don't care if they believe it, sir. I only want them to experience the spectacle," the wizard said. "Besides, if the public doesn't support me–and that means first supporting you–why, the alternative methods to force their cooperation might be a tad, shall I say, *unsavory*?"

Maynard looked at Oscar and Constable Brindle, noting the expressions of helpless resignation upon their faces that matched those of the other council members. He realized that the men were angry and disgusted at what the wizard was saying, yet helpless to do anything about it while the village was held hostage. He nodded sympathetically to his friends, displaying an equal amount of subdued rage and revulsion. But inside, Arileez was delighted that Caldurian was handling the situation with such seasoned aplomb.

"Tell us what else you want!" Maynard said, his tone icy.

"As my second demand, I want you to serve as my intermediary," the wizard continued. "Whether I get the pretended or actual support of your people, with it will inevitably come a slew of demands and complaints that I have no desire to deal with firsthand. I require someone people will trust to weed out those few matters that I truly need to address, and that person is you, Maynard. Subjects that don't require my attention will be left to you and your associates to handle through my captains."

"Does that mean he's still our mayor?" Len Harold asked.

"Call him what you will," the wizard replied, "but just know that he answers to me at the end of the day. I'm running this village."

Constable Brindle leaned back doubtfully, folding his arms. "Pardon my skepticism, but just how do you intend to enforce all of this? How can you take over a village in the kingdom of Arrondale without anybody outside discovering it? Or without any of us inside fighting back or escaping?"

"Excellent questions," Caldurian said, pointing at the constable with mock pride as if he were a student. "But I have considered those points from all angles and am quite satisfied with my plan. Taking your last point first, escape is nearly impossible."

"How so?" Oscar curiously asked.

The wizard retook his seat, helping himself to more bread and tea as if he were talking among old friends. "Already I have posted a large contingent of soldiers at each of the four main entrances to the village, all armed but dressed in civilian garb. They'll be there all day and night gathered around large bonfires to get people's attention. Groups are stationed at both ends of River Road, and another group each to Grangers and Deerfly Roads as well. As winter is fast approaching and the harvesting is done, travel between the villages has already slowed to a trickle. But since redlin fever has swept through the village, no one from the outside will have any desire to visit Kanesbury for a time and poke their noses in my business."

"Redlin fever? What are you talking about?" one of the other councilmen asked. "There's no such epidemic here nor has there been for over thirty years."

"Well there is now," Caldurian replied. "At least there'll be rumor of one, and that will be just as effective as the actual fever.

Anyone approaching the village along either end of River Road will be informed that redlin fever has spread through Kanesbury, and if they choose, will be quickly escorted through the village and on their merry way. The few houses on the main road will be vacated. Strips of red cloth will be nailed to those porch posts as a warning of the fever as is custom during such an epidemic."

"You've thought this through," Ned remarked with grudging respect.

"I've had twenty years," the wizard said. "And anyone trying to enter the village from either Grangers Road or Deerfly Road will be turned back and told to make their way around the village by other roads. Those two roads lead into the heart of Kanesbury and pose too much of a risk to my operation even with an escort."

"You may have the roads covered," Maynard countered, "but some of us could easily escape through the Cumberland Forest on our southern border or across the Pine River to the north. And there's plenty of farmland at either end to flee through. Surely you can't seal us inside this village completely."

"Oh, I think I can." He offered a grim smile. "I'm afraid escape won't be possible, and this is where I'll especially need your voice to convince the citizens to obey my orders. I have countless soldiers hidden in the eaves of the Cumberland and among the trees along the river. They're also patrolling every open section encircling the village, hiding among the weeds and rocks or inside barns and sheds. Anywhere and everywhere. And these men are some of the finest archers from the Northern Isles. I've ordered them to fire upon anyone trying to escape–*anyone*. No warnings. No questions asked. Just an arrow sailing noiselessly through the air–and then a dead body falling. And the corpse will be left on the ground where it falls to rot or become food for the night scavengers," the wizard coldly promised. "So if some family members frantically report a missing relative after you instruct them about my guidelines, well, they'll get no sympathy from me."

"They will not accept it!" Oscar fumed, slamming his hand upon the table. "You cannot treat people like this."

"But they have no choice," Caldurian responded as if his point exuded only pure logic and was incapable of being misunderstood. "My armed men outnumber your unarmed villagers and outmatch them in strength and ability. We are the superior force.

It's as simple as that. And while you may be bothered by questions of morality and inconvenience, I am not. I've defeated your village and that is the plain truth. Your righteous words will neither repel a sword nor change my mind. So unless you can raise a force strong enough to overthrow me, then I'm here to stay as long as I choose. And that is why I make the rules," he said, savoring another sip of tea.

The village officials sat speechless, their mouths agape and shoulders slumped. In their minds they knew that Caldurian spoke the truth and had them beat, yet their hearts couldn't accept such a fate, not even for a second. But the pummeling of their spirits continued when the wizard outlined more of his instructions. This included the seizure of certain, larger properties for the use of housing and feeding his troops, the confiscation of all food contained in root cellars and storage sheds for redistribution among the population, and the assignment of citizens to various jobs for the proper running of the village. Resistance to these orders, he emphasized, would result in summary imprisonment.

"And you will make a sincere effort to convince your people that these things must be done," Caldurian instructed the mayor.

"And if he refuses?" Ned asked.

The wizard threw a sharp glance at Ned, his eyes smoldering with ire. "You should not want to have that discussion, Mr. Adams. It will not be pleasant."

"Well I think that—"

"Please wait," Maynard said, raising a hand as he sadly nodded. "The wizard is right, I'm sorry to say. At the moment we have no choice but to do as he wishes, as detestable as that prospect may be. The safety and lives of everyone in Kanesbury are at stake, and as long as I'm mayor, I won't risk bringing them death and destruction just to make us feel better at this table." He glared at the wizard, pointing his finger at the man. "But don't think for a moment that I won't do everything in my power to oppose you and finally run you and your brutes out of town."

"I'd be disappointed if you *didn't* try," Caldurian replied with an amused smile. "My time here would be awfully dull otherwise, so good luck with that."

A meeting was scheduled for noontime that same day inside the village hall with one resident of each household required to attend. A sea of scared and angry faces stared back at the wizard enrobed in his black cloak and towering silently in front of the meeting table with a seemingly uncomfortable Maynard Kurtz at his side. The five members of the village council sat on the bench off to one side while armed guards were scattered around the room. After Maynard explained the situation and highlighted Caldurian's demands, it took some time to calm the expected outrage and settle raw nerves. At one point, the troops unsheathed their swords for effect, the sunlight reflecting off the deadly steel. But even that display couldn't quell the crowd completely.

"You will not tell us how to live!" someone shouted out.

"And you will learn to listen and obey!" Caldurian shot back.

"Who's going to make us?" another person defiantly replied.

With his patience wearing thin, the wizard stepped forward while uttering a few inaudible words and extended both arms like the wings of a vulture, causing all the windows along both sides of the chamber to suddenly burst outward into tiny shards of glass. People screamed and ducked for safety as gusts of cold air rushed into the room, dispelling any remaining thoughts of rebellion or feelings of bravado that lingered only moments ago.

As Caldurian lowered his arms, Maynard took a step away from him, appearing frail and frightened despite his equal stature to the wizard. The room fell silent as the villagers stared transfixed at the man who now controlled their fates. The wizard nodded at one of the armed guards to return his sword to its sheath. The others simultaneously followed his lead. After what seemed a long stretch of uncomfortable silence, the wizard spoke again.

"That will be the last demonstration I give to prove that I am in charge of your lives," he said in a low, steady tone. "From here on, I will let the deadly tip of a cold sword or a swift arrow make my point. And trust me, there will be no second warnings. So now that the interruptions are concluded, Mayor Kurtz can continue to speak. And when he talks of reassigning some of you to new jobs, one of the first will be to replace all of these windows. It's suddenly gotten rather chilly in here, hasn't it?"

The sun had nearly set when Katherine Durant found herself working in familiar surroundings–laboring in the kitchen of Oscar and Amanda Stewart's home. Their property had been one of many that Caldurian seized, though still having a modicum of influence, Oscar was able to request many of the people he would like to see working in his home after it was turned into a dining facility for the wizard's troops. Katherine told him that she was more than happy to help.

"I heard that some of my friends had to assist in clearing out root cellars and transporting the food to nearby barns where it would be stored and distributed as needed." Katherine attempted a smile as she set down a stack of dirty plates on a counter. "I guess serving meals and scrubbing dishes isn't so bad after all," she whispered to Oscar as she stepped out of the room to clear more of the makeshift tables hastily built out of wooden planks that had been set up in several rooms around the house.

"The front and back lawns have been trampled to death!" Amanda complained at the same instant to her husband as she entered the kitchen after a brief inspection of the premises, her complexion painted in scarlet hues. "I have half a mind to grab a fire poker and teach some of these Islanders a thing or two!"

"Now, my dear, that would be most unwise," Oscar said, gently taking his wife by the arm and leading her into the pantry near the ice boxes. He noted the confusion and melancholy in her eyes and felt his own spirit entwined in the same poisonous bonds. "We must remain strong, Amanda, or else we'll never get out of this mess."

"I know," she said, on the verge of tears, "but I don't like it. I don't want this. This isn't the way life is supposed to be!"

"That's why we have to fight," Oscar said. "And we will." He glanced back into the kitchen, and seeing that no one was close enough to hear, he leaned toward his wife and whispered into her ear. "There are already plans in motion to set up a resistance. Some of us are meeting later in secret–Maynard, Ned and a few others." Oscar smiled tenderly. "We'll teach that wizard a lesson yet."

Amanda blinked away a few tears, grateful for those words of hope. "I know you will," she softly replied, hugging him before quickly composing herself. "Now I suppose I should act like the supervisor I'm supposed to be."

"And I'll leave to make sure the next shipment of food is delivered for tomorrow's breakfast," Oscar said, leading her back to the kitchen. "I suppose Morris will never want to crack another egg when this is all over!"

Katherine sighed with weariness as she cleaned up another table in a side room, now empty of soldiers as the evening mealtime was winding down. The steady drone of voices and occasional laughter drifted in from the main room where several other girls were attending to the last diners of the night. Several soldiers congregated outside, smoking pipes and sharing stories before continuing on to their assigned duties or sleeping stations in other houses or barns. Katherine was glad to work here and return to her home at the end of the day which was sure to be warm and wafting with the scent of freshly baked bread since her mother had been designated as one of the bread suppliers for the village. She also wondered how Lewis was faring, splitting and hauling wood to supply the ovens and fireplaces around the village. Though he was one of a handful of employees who regularly performed that work for Oscar, a small host of men had now been recruited to fell trees on the edge of the Cumberland to keep Caldurian's operation going. Katherine hoped to see him next time he made a delivery here.

"Look where you're going, woman!" someone shouted from the next room. "I'll ask to have you reassigned to barn work if you don't watch yourself!"

Katherine hurried around the corner to see what was going on. A chorus of scornful laughter erupted from three soldiers who sauntered past a young girl and left the room upon a cloud of arrogance. A few soldiers sitting at another table left shortly afterward, having also finished their meals. A tall, young man with dark hair glanced at Katherine and the other girl as he left, his unshaven face expressionless.

"I'm truly sorry," the young girl meekly responded to no one in particular, stooping over to pick up the pieces of a broken plate she had dropped. Katherine bent down to help clean up the mess.

"Are you all right, Lana? I've seen dogs eat their meals with better manners than some of these men," she said in a playful tone, hoping to cheer her up.

The girl nodded. "I'll be fine. I was just a little nervous and tired. It's been such a long day."

"For all of us," Katherine agreed, gathering up the last of the broken bits. She helped Lana carry the remaining dirty dishes into the kitchen and told her to sit down at a table in the corner of the room bustling with washers and cooks against a background of crackling flames, steaming pots and cluttered counters. "Have you eaten?"

Lana shook her head. "It's been so busy. The other girls took their turns first."

"That's no reason to go hungry yourself." Katherine hurriedly prepared the girl a plate of food and a cup of hot tea and set it down before her. "Now eat and let the rest of us finish clearing the tables. The mad rush is over as most everybody has left."

"At least until tomorrow," Lana replied with a thin laugh. "Then we get to do it all over again!"

"That's the spirit," Katherine said encouragingly, noting that the supply of firewood near the main oven was getting low. "I'll fetch another armful of wood outside. I could use a bit of fresh air right now." She slipped out the back door into the shadowy darkness splashed with lunar light from the nearly full Bear Moon ascending in the east. A gentle glow from the kitchen fire and oil lamps radiated through the steamed window panes.

Katherine wandered past the shrubbery, inhaling the cool, sweet air of a dying autumn night. The voices of several soldiers in the near distance stirred up angry revulsion in her heart, causing her to wonder how such a fate had befallen the village. The events of the past few days seemed so unreal, as if she were trapped in an unending nightmare. But here she was, a captive in her own village, forced to work in the kitchen of some dear friends whose house had been invaded by strangers. She didn't know whether to laugh or cry, but realized she must fight back if this cruel injustice were to end. But she had no idea where to begin.

"Maybe next time your clumsy friend will learn how to handle a plate if she doesn't want to be made fun of in the dining hall!" spouted a soldier in the darkness.

Katherine glanced to her left as she wandered along the house, seeing a tall figure striding toward her, for a moment confused as her thoughts had been interrupted. "What?" she softly asked. "Were you speaking to me?"

"Sure I was," he said, walking up to Katherine and now speaking in a voice just loud enough for his fellow soldiers in the distance to hear. "Where'd she learn to serve meals anyway?" A ripple of laughter emanated from his friends standing under some trees near the north side of the property.

Katherine turned in disgust and hurried in the opposite direction as the man quickly followed. "Go amuse yourself somewhere else! I have better things to do than listen to you," she sharply replied. "Cleaning out a horse stable comes to mind."

"Well have fun doing that," he taunted as they walked around the southeast corner of the house. The man spoke in lower tones now, confident he was out of earshot of his friends.

"Why are you following me?" Katherine asked, stopping and planting her feet in the dried grass. In the moon glow and the light from the windows, she could see that the man was only a few years older than her, his dark hair slightly unkempt, his face unshaven. And though she expressed nothing but contempt for him, when she stared into his eyes, she sensed a kindness that belied his provocative attitude.

"I truly don't mean to bother you," he whispered, glancing around to make sure nobody was watching them. "I only wish to apologize for how those men treated your friend inside. I watched them leave and saw you helping the girl."

"And I'm supposed to think what?" Katherine replied, unnerved by his presence though not prepared to show it. "It's a funny thing to apologize for something while causing all this tumult at the same time."

"I agree," the man continued, "but I'm sorry nonetheless. I just wanted you to know that not all of us agree with what's happening."

"Then why are you here?" she bluntly countered.

The man shook his head sadly, staring at the ground for a moment before looking at Katherine, obviously troubled. "I don't have time to explain since I have to return to the others, but you must realize that life in the Northern Isles is nothing like in Arrondale. We're forced to serve for a time in our military, and since the aim of our leaders is expanding our influence off the Isles and acquiring more land, well, we end up involved in missions like the invasion of Montavia and in alliances with Vellan himself."

Katherine appeared skeptical. "But this is Kanesbury? Surely we are not of any strategic value."

The soldier grinned. "No, you aren't. But Caldurian has his own personal agenda from rumors I've heard, and our commanders have compelled us to do his bidding." The young man leaned in and whispered. "There are some of us who think about running away now that we're off the Island, but it's a dangerous risk. Several who unsuccessfully tried in Montavia have been imprisoned. A few even killed. But maybe one day I'll make a run for it if the timing is right."

"Then I wish you luck," Katherine replied, feeling a bit sorry for the man.

"My name is Paraquin, by the way. And again, I'm sorry for the trouble."

Katherine was about to give him her name, but hesitated, still not fully trusting the man. "Though I sense that your words are heartfelt, I still have a difficult time forgiving you."

"I'm not asking for your forgiveness, nor do I believe I deserve it," he replied. "Still, I wanted you to know. So if there's ever anything I can do…"

"You can march your army out of here. That would surely convince me of your sincerity." She grew suddenly downcast. "Or return some of my friends to me. I'm convinced Caldurian is somehow connected to their fates."

"What are you talking about?" Paraquin asked.

Katherine shook her head apologetically. "I suppose you're not to blame for that," she said, briefly telling him about Nicholas' abrupt departure and Adelaide Cooper's disappearance. "It's just that their troubles occurred as the Enâri creatures reawakened and escaped from the Spirit Caves east of our village. I can't help feel that Caldurian is somehow responsible, though I can't prove it. And while I believe Nicholas is safe, I can't imagine where Adelaide might be or if she's even still alive." Katherine wiped away a tear. "You'd better go back to your friends before they grow suspicious. I still have much work to do before I can go home."

"Very well," Paraquin said. "I hope this ends soon. I really mean that."

NICHOLAS RAVEN AND THE WIZARDS' WEB - VOLUME 2

"So do I," she softly replied, watching him disappear around the corner of the house as the rising Bear Moon illuminated the treetops with its cold, harsh stare. Katherine let a few more moments pass before she casually walked back to the kitchen door to face a second night in captivity.

CHAPTER 44

Dark Discussions

They sat in cold darkness, unwilling to risk lighting even one candle for fear of being discovered. The empty root cellar smelled of the potatoes, carrots, radishes and other food stores that had been hauled away the previous day to one of the local barns. Oscar earlier suggested that there wouldn't be a better place to hold the first meeting of the resistance than in one of the cleaned out cellars since the enemy would have no reason to return. Maynard agreed that it was an inspired idea. So on the third night of the invasion, ten people secretly gathered to discuss retaking their village.

They had approached the root cellar behind Freddy Dobbin's house one at a time and at five minute intervals so as not to be noticed, scurrying through trees and shadows when the way was clear from roving patrols and suspicious eyes. When the last man finally arrived, the meeting was called to order despite that fact that no one could see each other's faces.

"Thanks for showing up tonight," Maynard whispered, his voice deadened by the wall of rock surrounding them as if they were entombed inside a crypt. "You all took quite a risk for our beloved village, but it'll be worth it in the end. And thanks to Freddy for allowing us to use his place."

"It's my honor," Freddy responded in the inky blackness. "And thank you to Oscar for recruiting me. After they raided my place, my wife and I vowed to do whatever we could to rid Caldurian and his mob from Kanesbury. But not to worry. I didn't say a word to her about this meeting."

"Very good, Freddy. I knew you'd be an excellent choice for this initial group," Oscar replied, "though I suspect we'll need to enlist more people than just the ten of us to make this work."

Also in the root cellar were Ned Adams and Len Harold, along with Len's son, Owen. When Oscar first confided with Maynard about choosing people, they mutually decided that it would be safest not to involve all the members of the village council or Constable Brindle in case their plot was discovered. Oscar also invited Lewis Ames and three other villagers to round out the group.

"What's our first move?" Lewis asked, proud to be involved with the resistance. Secretly, he hoped that Katherine Durant would some day be impressed with him for joining the fight to save Kanesbury when his contribution could be made public.

"First we think," Oscar said, "followed by some careful planning. When we're ready to act, Lewis, we'll count on the younger and more eager members, such as you, Owen and some of the others to implement most of the grunt work. Stealth, sharp eyes and quick legs will be needed if we're to make a go of this."

"You can depend on us," Owen said, his father smiling proudly in the darkness.

"That's the attitude!" Ned replied. "Just leave it to those of us who are less nimble of foot to develop the ideas. Together, we'll show those Islanders a thing or two."

"That we will," Len agreed. "But don't make us all sound like we're confined to a porch chair or walking with a cane. I'm just as willing as my son to fight or ride or–climb rooftops!–if need be to save this village."

"Climb rooftops?" Oscar asked curiously. "What did you have in mind?"

Len, flush with embarrassment, was glad that nobody could see him. "Well, nothing yet, Oscar. Guess I'm just excited to get this movement underway. I'll shut up and listen now."

"All right," he replied, happy that his group wasn't lacking for enthusiasm. "But now we need to hear some solid ideas. Maynard, would you care to begin? Any suggestions on how we can start our little rebellion?"

"That's the crux of the matter," he replied, sitting on a cold, stone step. "Can we actually fight our way out of this, or must we somehow escape and seek assistance? From what Caldurian has told us and what we've seen with our own eyes, I certainly favor the latter. Even if we were fully armed, this community is no match for the forces surrounding us, and I say that with the utmost respect for everyone in Kanesbury."

"We aren't a match," Owen said, recalling with pride the soldiers he had observed training in Morrenwood when he accompanied his father to the war council. "And as much as I would love to wield a sword or pick up a bow and arrow–"

"Assuming we had any!" Lewis joked.

"–I must agree with Mayor Kurtz that we are outmatched militarily. We have to send word to Morrenwood for help as well as alert the nearby communities about what's happened here. Maybe they can offer assistance in the meantime."

"Makes sense to me," Lewis replied. "But how do we do that?"

"Exactly," agreed another voice in the darkness. "We're surrounded. There's not a safe opening through tree or river or field."

"And forget the roads," added Freddy. "We'd need a cattle stampede to break through."

"Perhaps one of us could grow wings and fly out," someone else joked, eliciting a round of quiet laughter.

"All interesting suggestions, but not quite practical," Maynard said appreciatively. "We need something a bit less dramatic and a little more–"

Suddenly the village bell tolled mournfully in the distance. The change of the evening guard had begun.

"There they go," Ned whispered. Everyone listened for a few moments in silence, though all they could hear was an occasional voice in the distance or the muffled clip clop of a passing horse. "To think that we would find ourselves in such a situation, hiding out in our own village," he added with an air of disgust.

"Then let's think harder and figure out how to fight back," Lewis said. "Every day without a plan is another day living under that wizard's boot, and I don't like it."

"You have a lot of company there," Len Harold said. "So whenever you're willing to start that cattle stampede..."

Another round of soft laughter filled the root cellar until Oscar called for everyone's attention. "Despite our amusement, Freddy's idea might not be so far off the trail of commonsense."

"Surely you don't plan to run a herd of cattle down River Road and bust out of here, do you?" Ned asked with a note of skepticism.

"Not cattle," he said. "Horses!"

"I'm intrigued," Freddy said. "Explain."

"I think my plan–inspired by Freddy, of course–is just outlandish enough, but not too much so, to actually work," Oscar said, his growing enthusiasm apparent as he put the pieces together. "I always check in on Lewis and my other workers a few times a day as they harvest wood on the northeast edge of the Cumberland Forest below Neeley's Pond. But near the pond itself is where the Islanders have corralled all the horses within the village not in use. They're under guard but the security detail is light. Maybe three or four men at most from what I've seen passing by."

"What do you suggest?" Owen asked with growing interest.

"I think that one of these nights we send a group to release all the horses at once and drive them out of the village along River Road, storming right through the Islanders barricading the west entrance," he explained. "They'll have no choice but to move aside or be trampled to death. At the same time, a handful of the younger and better riders among us will be atop a few of the horses in the middle of the herd, dressed in dark clothes, lying low and breaking out to freedom. They can ride to the nearby villages for assistance and send word to Morrenwood." A moment of silence followed as everyone pondered Oscar's plan.

"Intriguing," Maynard finally said.

"I'll say," Freddy added, his imagination fired up as he ran the scene through his mind. "And I had only been joking when I first talked about the cattle."

"But the stampede is only half the strategy," Oscar continued. "In the meantime, we'll have two or three other men hidden around the village, say in an old shack here or an abandoned house there."

"For what purpose?"

"For our diversion," he said, offering a smile no one could see. "Those men will start fires to the buildings first, and amid the ensuing commotion, the horses can be released." Oscar then snapped his fingers. "And we can use the village bell to coordinate our moves! As it tolls for the changing of the evening guard, that will be the signal for the fires to be set. When the men hiding out near the horses deem the commotion is sufficient, they can release them from the stables and ride to victory!"

Ned cleared his throat, catching everyone's attention. "Just one minor question, Oscar. How are we to get by the Islanders guarding the horses?"

"Well, uh, that's a detail I still have to work out. But we'll think it through," he assured him. "We'll think it through."

"All right," Ned replied. "I'm willing to give it a try since our options are few."

"As am I, but think it through we must," Maynard said. "Still, it's a viable plan if we work out the knots. Given a few more days of preparation, we just may have the answer to regaining our freedom from that miserable scourge of a wizard."

"I think so," Oscar said, pleased that everyone was taking his idea seriously. "Now not a word of this to anyone," he cautioned. "Only those in on the plan should know of it. We can't risk a single detail reaching unfriendly ears by an inadvertent slip of the tongue."

"That would be the death of our movement, and perhaps us as well," Maynard replied, his words chilling and grave, though contradictory to the snake-like smile forming upon his face that no one could see in the inky darkness of the root cellar.

The following day dawned cool and misty, though the air warmed slightly as the morning progressed. A blanket of tattered clouds, thinning like a scrap of old fabric, allowed the glare of the muted sun to pass through. Nearly all the leafy trees had been rendered bare, awaiting a cold, deep sleep through the approaching winter. Lines of blue-gray chimney smoke rose above the rooftops, blending with the pungent-sweet scent of decaying leaves that wafted through unsettled streets and eerily silent woodland. The Pine River flowed south on its journey to Lake Lasko near the Red Mountains, carrying a scattering of yellow and orange leaves upon its watery back for the long, quiet ride.

The citizens of Kanesbury lumbered through the village, grudgingly going about their assigned tasks while steering clear of River Road. Many people avoided eye contact whenever a soldier from the Northern Isles happened by, most fearing that any hint of defiance might bring harm not only to themselves but to their loved ones. Occasionally, however, and with little or no provocation, certain individuals were arrested from time to time and thrown into the village lockup, usually for half a day before being released. Other prisoners would quickly take their places and receive the same brief incarceration.

"The Islanders are keeping us off balance," one man said to his wife when they saw two people being marched into the lockup. "It's part of their plan."

"And what plan is that?" asked his wife.

The man scratched his head and shrugged as they walked on. "I'm not quite sure, dear. I'm not quite sure."

Nobody saw Caldurian since the raucous meeting in the village hall two days ago, assuming that the wizard chose to remain holed up in Otto Nibbs' house to implement his devious plans. Many admitted to being glad that Caldurian was living it up in the former mayor's home, satisfied that Otto had received at least some penalty for his cowardly absence. Though Otto had saved himself and condemned the rest of the village to tyranny, a modicum of justice had been seemingly served.

Katherine Durant and her mother were more than aware of such talk, though they rarely brought it up in conversation as it was too painful to address. Sophia still couldn't grasp the fact that her brother had abandoned his beloved village and condemned it to such misery. His actions were so unbelievable coming from the kind and generous man she had known all her life. Katherine felt the same way about her uncle as she sat down with her mother later that night to a quiet meal at home, happy to be away from the unending tension at the Stewart household.

"It's nice simply to sit here and wallow in silence," Katherine said, seated across from her mother at a small table near a blazing fireplace. The thick window drapes were closed, blocking out the night. A pair of candles flickered between them and the scent of freshly baked bread filled the air.

"I can't disagree," Sophia replied, appearing tired as she leaned back in her chair and sighed. "If I never see another loaf of bread, it'll be too soon."

"Maybe we should switch jobs," Katherine said facetiously.

"I'd probably get thrown in the lockup for insulting a soldier or purposely spilling a bowl of stew in his lap," she replied with a chuckle. "No, I'm better off here where I won't let my temper get the best of me."

"I suppose you're right," her daughter said, standing up and clearing the table. "I'll put on tea while you sit here and relax. You deserve it, Mother."

"Tonight, Katherine, I won't put up an argument. I—"

A knock sounded at the back kitchen door. Both women looked at one another, cautiously puzzled.

"Who could that be at this hour?" Katherine said with a trace of apprehension as she hurried to the kitchen. "You stay in here, Mother, while I find out."

Katherine stepped into the room where another low fire crackled in a stone oven. The wooden door was bolted shut. She peered out a small window above the counter, hoping to get a glimpse of the late-night visitor in the faint glow of the Bear Moon rising in the east. She saw the silhouette of a tall man patiently waiting at the doorstep, unable to discern his features until he stepped out of the shadows and into a splash of moonlight. Katherine pulled back, slightly startled yet equally intrigued. She slid back the metal bolt before cautiously opening the door a tiny bit. She glanced outside as the man stepped forward.

"Why are you here?" she whispered suspiciously, now seeing Paraquin's features fully revealed in the light from the kitchen.

"Forgive me for disturbing you at this late hour," the soldier replied, "but I need to speak if you have a moment. It's very important, or at least I think it might be."

"About what?" Katherine asked, hesitant to meet with him either inside or out. "I think you should leave."

Paraquin raised his eyes in a silent plea for her trust. "I haven't much time. But I have some information." He looked about through the trees to the nearby road to assure himself that no one was around. "It's about one of your missing friends."

Katherine's heart beat wildly upon hearing his words. She opened the door wider. "Nicholas? Adelaide?"

He nodded. "Yes. The woman."

Katherine thought for a moment and then signaled for him to step inside. "All right. I'll give you a moment. Hurry. It's miserably cold out."

"I'd rather not," he said. "I only have a short while before I go on guard duty. I'd prefer to talk in the shadows. It's best if we're not seen together in a private dwelling. People would be suspicious."

"I understand. Let me grab my cloak." Katherine closed the door and returned to the dining area where her mother anxiously waited near the fireplace.

"Who was that?" Sophia asked, fearing the worst.

"Everything's fine, Mother. There's nothing to worry about," she replied as she removed her cloak from a hook near the front doorway. "I need to step out for a moment. I'll be right back."

"But who stopped by?"

"Just a–*friend*. I'll explain later, Mother. Please trust me," she said, hastening out of the room as the cloak was wrapped around her shoulders in a colorful swirl.

Moments later, Katherine joined Paraquin in the shadows among some fragrant pine trees. She stared at the soldier for a moment, still distrustful of him but not afraid.

"Again, forgive the late intrusion, but for obvious reasons I can't stop by in the middle of the day and chat with you on the front porch," he said with a boyish grin.

"I suppose not," Katherine agreed, quickly put at ease by his relaxed tone. "But tell me what you know, including how you found out where I live."

"Forgive me a second time, but I observed you from a distance walking to your house late this morning," he explained. "I was on patrol and saw you leaving the Stewart household."

"I went home to visit my mother on one of my long breaks, if you must know. Were you spying on me?"

"No, Katherine. It was just by chance that I saw you. And luckily so, because I had information I wanted to give you in private."

"*Katherine*? I recall purposely not giving you my name the other night."

"And I don't blame you. But that mystery was easier to solve as I had heard it uttered a few times by some of the other serving girls when I had my meals at the Stewart place," he said, appearing impatient. "I *am* pressed for time."

"Very well," she said with a slightly apologetic tone to her voice. "As you're taking a chance coming here, I suppose I should listen. So what is this information about Adelaide? Though I can't imagine how you would know anything about her."

Paraquin blew into his hands to warm them. "I heard something late last night while on guard duty. I'm stationed with a few other soldiers at the east entrance to your village on River Road. Each night I've been there has been painfully dull as not a soul has showed up requesting to enter the village."

"That's not surprising so late in the day at this time of year."

"True. But what surprised us last night was seeing two people trying to leave the village in a horse-drawn wagon," he told her.

"Leave the village?" Katherine furrowed her brow. "Why would anybody leave in such an obvious manner since Caldurian has Kanesbury surrounded? They might've been killed."

"Exactly. So when the men approached after midnight, we immediately advanced with swords drawn, prepared to haul them off to the lockup," he continued. "The man driving the cart, however, held out a folded note and handed it to one of my fellow soldiers, asking us not to delay him. He had a smug expression on his face."

"Who?" Katherine asked, greatly intrigued. "And what was written on the note?"

Though already speaking softly, Paraquin lowered his voice further. "The note was apparently written by Caldurian, giving the two men permission to leave the village at will and without question. We were skeptical and prepared to arrest them. But the tone of the driver's voice and the hardened look in his eyes made us think twice when he warned us that we'd be in terrible trouble with the wizard if we harassed them. Anyway, one of the soldiers ran off to find our captain to confirm the authenticity of the letter."

"What did he discover?" Katherine asked, unable to believe what she was hearing.

"The letter was authentic," Paraquin said. "It seems someone had forgotten to inform all of the guard shifts about this one exception to the wizard's rule about not leaving the village."

Katherine hugged herself in the gnawing chill as the scent of pine needles danced about. "But why would Caldurian allow any of the locals to leave? That doesn't–" A grim realization suddenly hit her and her heart sank. She slowly looked up at Paraquin. "Unless one of my fellow villagers is conspiring with him."

"I'm afraid so, Katherine. *Two* villagers in this case."

"But who? Why?"

"I don't know why since the men wouldn't tell us their business as they waited for the letter to be authenticated. But I did learn the names of the men since they were both mentioned in the letter," he replied. Even in the shadows, Paraquin noted the eagerness for an answer in Katherine's wide eyes, yet he sensed that she was filled with dread as well, waiting to learn the identities of the two traitors in her dear village.

"Tell me their names," she said coldly, almost reluctantly.

Paraquin nodded. "Their names were Zachary Farnsworth and Dooley Kramer. Do you know them?"

"Yes," she whispered, turning aside as she tried to make sense of the startling information.

"Who are they?"

"Apparently men of no honor," she replied with a disgusted sigh, leaning against the tree trunk and folding her arms. In the bits of filtered moonlight, her careworn expression was obvious to Paraquin who patiently waited for more information. "Zachary Farnsworth manages the local banking house for Horace Ulm. I don't know Mr. Farnsworth personally, though I've heard from others who do that he'd like nothing better than to own the banking house himself someday. Horace, however, seems to be in no hurry to retire. Some have characterized Mr. Farnsworth as quietly ambitious and maybe a little aloof, but he earns a fine living and does his job well."

"Ambition isn't a crime," he remarked.

"But unbridled ambition can lead one down a wrong path, as apparently it has with him," she said. "Dooley, on the other hand, is quite the opposite of his neighbor."

"They're neighbors?"

"Who've apparently conspired against Kanesbury," she said. "Dooley frequents the Iron Kettle Tavern regularly and worked at the gristmill before it burned down. Now he has Nicholas' job." Katherine smiled grimly. "I suspected that Dooley and Arthur Weeks had a hand in Nicholas' downfall, but could never figure out why. And I still don't know why, but if Dooley is mixed up with the wizard, his actions and recent events are beginning to make more sense." She noted the lost look on Paraquin's face. "Oh, sorry," she said, her thoughts returning to the moment. "I was thinking out loud. But what does any of this have to do with Adelaide Cooper?"

"While we were waiting for confirmation of Caldurian's letter, those of us on guard ordered Farnsworth to pull his cart off the road until the matter was settled," Paraquin went on. "He wasn't too eager to comply, but as we were armed and he wasn't, he had no choice. I could hear him now and then in a quiet but heated conversation with his associate. Neither was happy with the turn of events."

"I can imagine. But what about Adelaide?"

He looked around before answering. "It may be nothing or everything, but during snippets of conversation I overheard, I caught the name *Adelaide* being bandied about."

Katherine's heart fluttered. "What did they say about her?"

"I heard no specifics as the two men were trying to be discreet as they talked," he said. "But as voices travel, I heard a few words, thinking nothing of them at the time until the name *Adelaide* reached my ears. Like I said, it may be nothing–"

"–or everything." Katherine's thoughts and emotions were in a whirl. "I see no reason why Zachary and Dooley would be discussing Adelaide Cooper unless they knew something about her."

"Or were involved in her disappearance," he suggested.

"Perhaps. Adelaide lived across the road from Nicholas. If Dooley, and now Mr. Farnsworth, were involved in Nicholas' fate, maybe they had something to do with Adelaide's disappearance, too." She nervously placed her hands to her face, not knowing what to believe. "I can't think straight. There's so much to ponder and just as much that I'd rather *not* ponder, if you understand."

"I do," he said. "It must be awful to have people in your village plotting against you. But what are you going to do about it?"

"Good question," she replied, her breath rising among the pine branches.

And though she was ecstatically grateful for Paraquin's assistance, another question haunted her later that night through hours of fitful sleep. Was there anything she *could* do about it, especially now that the village was under siege? She hated to face the harsh truth, namely, that the answer at the moment was probably *no*. And now that there were traitors among the population, Katherine wondered if she could trust another soul with this new information.

Later that same evening, Caldurian poured himself a glass of wine, sipping it leisurely as he sat in front of the fireplace in Otto Nibbs' parlor. He silently delighted in the former mayor's change of fortune as he savored the beverage. He extended his legs upon the hearth, the fire warming him and driving months of weary road travel from his tired limbs. At last he was finally enjoying some sweet revenge against Otto for the defeat and public humiliation he had caused him twenty years ago. But there would be more vengeance to come–and soon. The wizard smiled, imagining Otto fast asleep near Barringer's Landing under Arileez' spell, perhaps dreaming pleasantly now, but totally unprepared for what was to hit him next.

Moments later he heard tapping upon a window, startled from his musings. When he noted the distinctive rap a second time, he stood and glanced out the window into the moonlit night. There upon the ledge was a large crow, its dark, piercing eyes gazing at the wizard as if expecting to be let in. Caldurian sighed, more out of amusement than irritation, and quickly unfastened the latch and let the bird flutter inside where it landed in the middle of the room.

"Your mode of arrival is unconventional tonight," the wizard said, relocking the window. He closed the drapes and shut a door to the next room, assuring their privacy. "Though none of my guards are inside, I don't want to take a chance that someone might see you."

Suddenly the crow changed shape into its natural form of Arileez, his tall figure casting a menacing shadow upon the wall. "Understood," he replied, taking a seat near the fire, his lifeless eyes beneath his hood given a hint of animation as they reflected the snapping flames.

Caldurian sat opposite him, always fascinated whenever he witnessed one of Arileez' incredible transformations. He recalled the first time he had seen him turn into a bird after gaining his trust while a prisoner on the island of Torriga. But only after Arileez had consumed Vellan's potion to counteract the confining spell was the Umarikaya finally able to fully appreciate his own transformational abilities. And all it took was a few sips of a magic liquid that Vellan had created. Caldurian unobtrusively placed a hand upon one of his deep, cloak pockets, feeling a small, glass vial within filled with the remaining amount of the potion that had given Arileez his freedom– plus a little extra something as well.

Caldurian almost felt sorry for the ruse he and Vellan were playing upon Arileez, using him for their own purposes at the same time they were deceiving him. But Vellan convinced Caldurian that it had to be done if they were to maintain their dominance throughout Laparia. Though Arileez was now an ally, he might one day become a threat with his strange and far-reaching powers. Those abilities had to be extinguished, though slowly and imperceptibly. The additional spell added to the potion and now running through Arileez' veins would do just that.

In a few weeks, Vellan planned to achieve victory over Arrondale by replacing King Justin with the impostor Arileez in guise of the monarch. Soon after, Arileez would suddenly find his own powers reduced to that of a mere mortal–to nothing. By then, Vellan's grip over Arrondale and all of Laparia would be complete. Arileez would no longer be needed, being reduced to a shadow of his former self. What a powerful potion it was, Caldurian mused as he gazed upon the other wizard. What a devious plot he and Vellan had gleefully devised. He was glad he had kept a portion of the liquid for his own future needs.

"I had expected a visit from Mayor Kurtz. He was to brief me on the daily affairs of my village," Caldurian said with a slight smirk. "What happened?"

"I grow weary of playing that part," Arileez replied, "and treated myself to a flight under the glow of the Bear Moon. I am here nonetheless."

"I can't say that I blame you, possessing such a magnificent power," he replied. "But I assure you that our work here will be done in a few days. Then it will be on to bigger and more exciting prospects in Morrenwood."

"I look forward to it, Caldurian. I'm feeling as restricted here as I did on Torriga."

"Those terrible days are over. Now tell me, how are plans coming along for the grand escape from Kanesbury?" the wizard asked. "Did the resistance have another meeting in an empty root cellar tonight?"

Arileez nodded. "We did, with several more eager recruits attending. Now we have enough people to go forward with Oscar Stewart's plan, but we need a few more days to prepare."

"That shouldn't be a problem. Excellent work," Caldurian said, pleased with the swift progress. "But I still want to do a little something tomorrow to divert any suspicion from Mayor Kurtz and perhaps bolster his standing in the community at the same time. Just to be on the safe side before the big day."

"What did you have in mind for me?" Arileez asked.

"Nothing too fancy, but perhaps the mayor needs to stand up to me in public to rally his supporters," Caldurian said, taking a sip of wine. "*Hmmm*, but I think it's time I stepped up the random arrests in the village, don't you?"

CHAPTER 45

Bell, Fire and Horses

Caldurian ordered his soldiers to step up random arrests the following day, which they did with a fury. Some people were dragged away from the breakfast table while others were taken from their jobs in the middle of the morning, all unceremoniously marched to the village lockup where they were interned for several hours. None were given any reason for the arrest, though their names were printed on a continually updated list posted outside the lockup. To add insult to injury, whenever people were released, they were told not to repeat their offenses even though they were unaware of what crime they had committed in the first place.

"This tears at me!" Constable Brindle muttered as he examined the list of the latest accused, his face reddening with disgust. "I don't even know where they're putting all these people. We have only two cells in the lockup."

What irked him most was that he had been forbidden to step inside the lockup and was assigned to help repair the broken windows in the village hall next door. He had stopped to examine the list during one of his work breaks, commiserating with fellow citizens.

"Clay, this has gone too far!" a man angrily whispered as they stepped away from the list so others could look. Several armed soldiers walked past, amused at the fuss by those craning their necks

NICHOLAS RAVEN AND THE WIZARDS' WEB - VOLUME 2

to view the arrest record. "My son-in-law was hauled away near dawn before he had even finished his eggs. Right in front of his wife and kids, too! He's been released since, but it isn't right, I tell you. It isn't right."

"You think I don't know that, Albert?"

"Someone's going to get hurt, or worse," said a woman who emerged from the crowd after scrutinizing the list. "Sooner or later people are going to fight back despite not being armed, and you know where that's going to lead? Bloodshed! Broken bones! You must put a stop to this," she pleaded, her ashen complexion and fearful eyes mirroring many who wandered the frosty streets.

"You have to talk to Maynard," Albert added, turning up his collar and shoving his calloused hands into his coat pocket as he stormed away. "And soon!"

The woman agreed, nodding to the constable as she departed. Clay silently indicated that he would do his best. By lunchtime he made good on his promise, tracking down the mayor at a candle shop where Maynard had just finished receiving an earful of similar complaints from the owner.

"Maynard, we need to talk," Clay said, the scent of melting wax thick in the air inside the store. "These arrests have got to stop!"

"Clay, I was just on my way to the village hall to see you," he said as they exited the building. "I've had complaints all morning and plan to take my case to Caldurian. If he wants me to serve as his go-between, then he'd better be prepared to listen to me. I just wanted to get your take on the situation first."

"Everything you've heard from the others goes double for me." Clay was happy to see Maynard riled up at the outrageous treatment of his fellow citizens. "I say we march to Otto's house right now and give that wizard a piece of our minds. Are you with me?"

"I'm with you," he said, "but I think it's time we made him come to us. I'll inform one of the captains at the lockup that we demand a meeting with Caldurian at once. In the meantime, round up whoever you can and get them there for the confrontation. There's strength in numbers, my friend."

"Good!" replied Clay, a giddy smile plastered upon his apple red face until a look of fear slowly settled upon his features. "But what if they unleash their swords? What if Caldurian doesn't show? This dispute could be over before it starts."

"My guess is that Caldurian's people don't want trouble if they can help it," he said. "As much as they threaten us with violence, they'd probably rather settle things peacefully. Much less work for them, see?" Maynard patted Clay on the back before he headed to the lockup. "Trust me on this. I have a feeling Caldurian will show up. He's enjoying himself too much to risk a rebellion in the streets."

To the surprise of many, Caldurian appeared in front of the lockup less than an hour later. Maynard stood at his side looking pale yet confident. A small crowd of onlookers were bursting with pride that Maynard had even gotten this far with the wizard, successfully drawing him out of his lair. It was a minor victory to savor, though they hoped for better things.

"Apparently too many of you seem to be without a work assignment," Caldurian said, his voice calm but cool beneath the gray overcast. "That can be easily remedied."

"We're here to talk about another matter," Maynard insisted while wagging a finger. Murmurs of agreement rippled through the gathering. "You must order your men to stop these ridiculous arrests. You're disrupting lives and causing hardships that won't be tolerated much longer."

"And what do you plan to do about it?" uttered a soldier standing near the front entrance, a sneering grin upon his face.

"I asked for no comment from you!" Caldurian snapped, upon which he ordered the soldier indoors. He glanced at Maynard, folding his arms as if he were addressing a friend in casual conversation. "I understand that some of my men have been perhaps a little too eager in their duties?"

"That's an understatement," Maynard replied, detailing the rash of recent arrests. "The people won't take it any longer!"

"Yeah!" a voice boisterously shouted from within the crowd.

Caldurian nearly smiled at the response. "Well, Mr. Mayor, I do admire your blunt appraisal of the situation and your courage to bring it to my attention. And in my defense, I wasn't aware that such harsh tactics had been employed by my Island associates," he said. "Though I'm sure people have been arrested from time to time for serious infractions against my rule, I never ordered nor condoned these mass detentions of which you speak."

Most believed no such thing, stunned that Caldurian bothered to make such a confession. A few people, however, felt the tiniest bit of admiration for the wizard's apparent sense of fairness, unaware that they were nodding with approval as he spoke.

"Is there anything you can do?" Maynard asked, softening his agitated tone. "Most everyone in the village has cooperated with your decrees so far."

"For which I'm most grateful," he replied, extending an appreciative hand to the crowd while contemplating his next step.

The people collectively held their breath, as did Maynard, all awaiting Caldurian's pronouncement. A moment later, the wizard snapped his fingers and indicated for one of the captains in charge to approach. The man hurried forward.

"What can I do for you, sir?" he asked.

"I've considered the situation and have concluded that some of the men under your command have taken liberties with their authority, making arrests when there was no reason to," he said to the delight and amazement of those gathered. "I, too, will shoulder some of the blame for not paying attention while attending to other duties in my quarters. However, that is in the past. From this moment forward, your men will cease these random and unnecessary arrests and release all those whom you are now holding." Cheers erupted from the onlookers as many whispered to one another that a ray of hope had at last returned to their village. Maynard especially grew more admired and respected in people's eyes for having confronted the wizard on their behalf. "After all, though I demand discipline," Caldurian continued, "I neither seek chaos nor wish to mete out undeserved punishment. I have a village to run, and these disruptions only hinder our achievements, not help them."

Additional nods of agreement punctuated the wizard's flowery words as they drifted through the chilly air. A few people went so far as to politely applaud Caldurian's statement. When he concluded a short time later, he instructed the captain to consult with Maynard to oversee the immediate release of the prisoners.

"And, captain," the wizard pointedly added as he began to walk away, "tear down that arrest list at once and burn it. Our village has no need for such a divisive instrument."

As Caldurian headed back to Otto Nibbs' house accompanied by several soldiers, he was delighted to hear a wave of cheers and applause wash over the landscape upon the announcement of his last order. Though Maynard had been surely elevated in stature because of his feigned confrontation with the wizard, Caldurian took immense satisfaction that several people in town would more than likely sing his own praises, too, an achievement that humored and astounded him at the same time. It had been all too easy.

Katherine was helping to clean up in the Stewart kitchen later that evening after the last group of soldiers had been served dinner. Amanda sat at a small table in the adjacent pantry which served as a makeshift desk, busily planning the meals for the following day. The clatter of plates, pots and pans competed with the swishing of hot, soapy water and the crackling flames in the ovens and fireplace. Katherine had just stored a stack of clean plates in one of the cabinets when Lewis entered though the back door. She greeted him with a delighted smile when their eyes met.

"This is a pleasant surprise," she said. "I thought you'd be home asleep right now, considering all the work you've been doing."

"I feel as if I felled half the Cumberland Forest in the last few weeks," he replied with a grin, his face reddened from the cold as he rubbed his hands in the warm air. "But it feels good to enjoy the results of my labor," he added, indicating the roaring fire.

"Do you need to see Oscar?"

"No. I just saw him a while ago when–" Lewis suddenly caught himself, not wanting to reveal that he had returned from another meeting of the resistance. "No, I don't need to see him. I stopped by to see if I could get a bite to eat–and to see you."

Katherine blushed. "I think both can be arranged. And you shall have a place of honor right here in the kitchen, Lewis," she said, leading him to a table in one corner and insisting that he sit down and rest. Moments later, she served him a plate of steaming food and a mug of hot cider before joining him with a cup of tea and a biscuit. "I'm long past due for a break myself. It's been a hectic evening."

"I hope you're not overworking, Katherine. And your mother shouldn't be either," he said with concern.

"You're the one to talk, Lewis. When was the last time you had a proper day off?" She patted him on the arm. "Even before the village was overrun, you and the others had been working nonstop on the winter's wood supply."

"Oscar pays us well," he said, stabbing a cube of roasted potato with his fork. "And he has given us some days off before the wizard arrived, though I admit that this week has been a busy one. When I go home, I'll be asleep before my boots are off."

Katherine sipped her tea, silently fuming. "I'd like to give that Caldurian a piece of my mind. Oh, what a troublemaker that man is!"

"He'll get what's coming to him," Lewis softly said. "We must be patient."

Katherine looked around to make sure no one was in earshot as Lewis ate his meal with gusto. She drew her chair closer to his and leaned in. "I hear there are plans in the works to fight back." Lewis looked up, the weariness driven from his eyes, his face awash with surprise. "Is this true?"

"What are you talking about?" he asked with a shrug, taking a sip of cider. He uncomfortably stared at his plate while he ate. "I haven't heard anything."

Katherine smiled. "You're not a very good liar, Lewis. But don't worry. I won't say anything."

He shrugged again. "I still don't know what you mean, Katherine. Would you like another biscuit?"

"Thank you, but no." Katherine wrapped her hands around the tea cup for warmth. "Let's just say that I accidentally overheard a few words between Oscar and Amanda when I stepped into the pantry the other day to get something from the ice boxes."

"Accidentally?"

"Yes, Lewis. It was perfectly innocent. Anyway, from the few words I gathered and by the looks on their faces when they saw me, I concluded that something was being planned to challenge Caldurian's authority." She glanced around the room again before continuing. "You needn't give me details, Lewis, but merely a nod to verify."

Lewis sat hunched over his plate, avoiding eye contact. "I really can't comment," he whispered, pushing the food around with his fork. "Perhaps you misinterpreted what you overheard."

"I don't think so," she assured him. She sipped her tea and sighed. "But what bothers me most," she continued, "is not that you won't tell me what's going on, but that Amanda was included and I wasn't."

Lewis looked at her, slowing shaking his head. "Amanda's not involved, so you needn't be–" He quickly caught himself, though it was too late as he blushed with embarrassment.

"Thanks for the confirmation, Lewis," she lightly replied. "But as I said, don't worry. Your secret is safe."

"But apparently not safe with Oscar."

Katherine giggled. "Though I love the Stewarts dearly, I don't think Oscar would be able to keep a secret from Amanda no matter how hard he tried. But you needn't worry about her telling anyone either."

Lewis nodded while finishing his meal. "I suppose. And it's not that I don't trust you, Katherine. It's just that..."

"I understand." She stood up, telling him that she had to get back to work. "You finish and I'll bring you a slice of pumpkin bread and tea to top off that meal," she kindly said, affectionately running a hand across his shoulders as she stepped away. Lewis turned his head to watch her leave, a tired yet contented smile upon his face.

Fifteen minutes later, Lewis finished his pumpkin bread and left the table, searching for Katherine to say goodnight. He made a quick check of the dining areas, nearly empty of soldiers, but found no sign of her. None of the other workers had seen her in the last few minutes either.

"Perhaps she went down to the ice cellar or stepped outside for more firewood," one of the girls suggested.

"Thanks. I'll check," Lewis said, returning to the kitchen and exiting the back door into the inky night.

A gentle glow from the nearly risen Bear Moon radiated along the eastern horizon. The voices of several soldiers smoking beneath the trees on the border of the property resonated sharply in the cold night. Lewis walked about the back of the house looking for Katherine, but found no sign of her. He figured she must be hard at work again inside and decided to go home. He peeked around the southeast corner of the house for a last check and suddenly stopped, his heart beating rapidly.

There, standing several yards ahead with their backs to him were Katherine Durant and one of the soldiers from the Northern Isles, deeply engaged in quiet conversation. A moment later the soldier departed to the west, opposite of Lewis' position in an apparent hurry. Katherine watched the man disappear into the shadows before turning around to walk back to the kitchen. As she neared the corner of the house, she noticed Lewis in the darkness, the glow of the horizon behind him.

"*Lewis?*" The tone of her voice indicated that she was both surprised to see him and uncomfortable that he had seen her. "What are you doing here?"

"I wanted to thank you for dinner," he stated flatly, his mind reeling with speculation about what she and the solider had been talking about. Had it been merely a chance, innocent meeting, or something else entirely? Lewis thought the familiarity the two had seemed to share while speaking might indicate the latter.

"You're welcome for dinner," Katherine replied with equal unease, wrapping the folds of her cloak about her. "Stop by anytime."

"Yes, well..." He fidgeted uncomfortably. "I couldn't leave without saying goodbye either." He attempted a casual smile. "So, um–goodbye, I guess." He dug the toe of his boot into the grass, searching for a coherent thought. "Better get going," he clumsily added, beginning to walk away with a wave of his hand. But Lewis had only taken a few steps when he summoned up his nerve and spun around, facing Katherine who hadn't yet moved. "Katherine, was that soldier bothering you? Because if he was..."

"No. Nothing like that, Lewis. He was a perfect gentleman."

"Oh?" He slumped his shoulders, almost wishing that she had answered otherwise. "Because when I saw the two of you together– you and an enemy solider–I just thought that..." He swallowed, feeling as if their recent time together had been an illusion and that he was once again washing dishes and filling the ice boxes in Amanda Stewart's kitchen while admiring Katherine Durant from a distance.

"We were just talking, Lewis. He wanted to update me about–" She caught herself, not prepared to tell him about the information that Paraquin had provided her. Tonight, the soldier informed her that Zachary Farnsworth and Dooley Kramer made no additional excursions outside the village since their last one two nights ago. He promised Katherine that he'd keep a vigilant watch.

"Update you about what?"

Katherine stared at the ground. "I'd rather not say right now, Lewis. I need to find out more information first." She looked up. "But as soon as I do…"

"I see." Lewis stuck his hands in his coat pockets. "And not that you have to tell me, since it's none of my business, but can I ask why you were talking to that soldier at all? Why would the enemy even have information for you? It doesn't make sense."

"It would if I told you everything, but right now I cannot. I'd rather not," she replied. "It's safer for everyone this way."

"Okay," he said with a defeated sigh, his white breath dissipating in the night air. "I wouldn't speak of our resistance plans earlier, so I guess I shouldn't expect you to tell me about whatever it is that you're doing."

"Thank you," she kindly said, though Katherine could still see that he was riddled with doubt and unease.

Lewis, slightly agitated and unable to contain the words boiling inside him, looked into her eyes which reflected the slowly rising moon to ask the one question that was really on his mind. "Are you seeing him, Katherine? That soldier, I mean. Do you–"

"Of course not, Lewis! Is that what you're thinking?"

He tried to smile. "It had crossed my mind."

"Well rid yourself of that thought this instant! I have no feelings for that man, other than being grateful for some chance information he provided a couple nights ago." Katherine grimaced. "Besides, I would never associate with the enemy in that way. What would people think?"

"I'm glad to hear it," he replied, rocking back and forth on the soles of his boots. "And you're right, of course. People might think all sorts of things if they ever saw you with one of the Islanders."

"Just like you did?" She smiled, more flattered than angered by his reaction. "But I forgive you, Lewis, not that it's necessary. I know you have nothing but the best intentions for me."

"Exactly, so…" He stopped rocking, at a loss for words as he stared at the ground for a moment before gazing at Katherine. "What do you think people might say in passing if they saw you in the company of someone like me from time to time?"

Katherine smiled again. "I'm not sure that I would care what others thought," she said playfully. "Though I suspect that some folks might think I was quite lucky to be with you."

"They would?"

"I certainly would."

"*Hmmm*, interesting to know," he said, concealing a grin as he nodded thoughtfully, feeling so close to Katherine at this moment and sensing that she felt the same way about him. "Please correct me if I'm wrong, but I'm supposing that you might not care either if I did–*this*?" Lewis leaned forward and kissed her in the moonlit shadows, their arms tenderly wrapping around one another as both momentarily forgot the troubles in the uneasy streets of Kanesbury.

"You supposed correctly," Katherine whispered, her face flushed and beaming in the moonlight. She and Lewis held hands as they looked at one another in the cold night that suddenly felt as warm and inviting as a summer afternoon. "And I'm so glad you stopped to say goodbye, Lewis."

"Me too. But now I don't want to leave," he replied, touching his lips to the back of her hand. "Maybe we can…"

"Most definitely," she replied, confirming their unspoken plans. "I know it'll be another busy day tomorrow, but stop by for dinner again. We can sit and talk and…"

"I can't wait," he said, unable to contain a string of smiles as he stood there helplessly lost in the intoxicating moment.

Several minutes later, both reluctantly departed. Katherine returned to the kitchen to help clean up and prepare for another grueling day tomorrow. Yet all the while, she felt as if she hadn't a care in the world, thinking only of Lewis and their time together as she cleared the last dinner table and wiped down the counters. Lewis, meanwhile, walked home through the shadowy streets, equally elated and eager for dawn's arrival. He couldn't wait to see Katherine again, to talk to her and hold her hand. All thoughts of the resistance movement and its impending plans had been temporarily driven from his mind like a whirling leaf carried away upon a capricious breeze.

"Gentlemen, any final questions?" Oscar Stewart spoke in a low voice while cloaked in the suffocating blackness inside Freddy Dobbin's root cellar the following night. He had just reviewed their plans for the escape from Kanesbury in excruciating detail one last time, double checking to make sure that each person knew his part. "This is our last meeting, so there won't be time to make changes if we overlooked something."

"Don't worry. We haven't overlooked anything," Ned Adams insisted. "They all know what to do, Oscar."

"I just want to be sure."

"And you've done a fine job, deserving of a round of applause," Maynard interjected. "But that honor might reveal us to the enemy, so our quiet thanks is all you'll get tonight," he added with a touch of humor. "But Ned is right—don't worry. This caper will go swimmingly. I'm sure of it. Now I suggest we depart one by one as usual and go home. I'm getting hungry."

"Me too," Ned replied. "So if nobody minds, I'll leave first." He found his way to the door and felt for the handle. "Best of luck to you all. We'll listen for the village bell tomorrow night at the changing of the guard," he whispered before cautiously opening the door. After assuring himself that it was safe to leave, he stepped outside and closed the door. He hurried up a few stone stairs before dashing across Freddy's yard into the safety of some nearby trees before heading home.

"Are you sure you want to go through with this?" Len Harold whispered to his son in one corner of the room. Though he was proud that Owen had volunteered to ride one of the horses during the escape and send word to Morrenwood, his father was having second thoughts. What if he was captured—or worse?

"I'll be fine, Father. I'm a good rider, just like the others," he replied. "I'll lie low and it'll be dark. But how about you? Having doubts?"

Len chuckled. "I have the easy part," he said. "Pour some oil, wait for the bell to toll, start a fire and then run away. What's difficult about that?"

"It may not be difficult, but everything depends on you and the other two fire starters," Lewis commented, unable to help overhearing their conversation. "We don't make a move with the horses until we see the distant glow of flames and hear the commotion. So make sure you keep out of the Water Barrel Inn tomorrow night so you're not late for your appointment," he joked.

Oscar grunted. "The Water Barrel is not worth going to now that Caldurian has turned it into another place to feed his troops. A fine establishment gone to waste!"

"Just one more reason we must succeed tomorrow," Maynard said. "Let's put that wizard and those Islanders in their place once and for all. Now whose turn is it to leave?"

The eighth day of Old Autumn was greeted by a fine flurry of snow that dusted the pine trees and rooftops of Kanesbury during the still hours before sunrise. Somersaulting trails of blue and gray chimney smoke reached for a fleet of clouds passing overhead. The awakening village lay peaceful and picturesque, nestled up against the Cumberland Forest like a napping dog upon a warm hearth. Yet the apparent serenity belied another day of captivity. By midmorning, the pristine ground had been riddled with the muddy footprints from the Island soldiers on patrol. Grim-faced villagers trudged about to complete their assignments, wondering if the last five and a half days had been but a strange dream from which they would soon awake, or at least hoping so.

Oscar returned home early that evening to enjoy a meal with his wife in the pantry. The couple hadn't seen much of each other lately since his duties coordinating firewood shipments had kept him away from home most of the day. But tonight, a short while before the bell was to toll for the changing of the guard, Oscar managed to finish up work early to spend time with Amanda. Though he hadn't revealed the plans to his wife, she could sense by his anxious behavior that something was afoot, perhaps for that very night. Katherine, too, noted Oscar's edgy demeanor when she served the Stewarts their meal, though decided to mind her business and not inquire about his plans or Lewis' whereabouts.

At that same moment, Lewis, Owen and eight other men had positioned themselves on the edge of the woods around Neeley's Pond where all the horses in the village had been corralled. Only three soldiers were on guard tonight, casually patrolling the area since rarely did anybody pass by after sunset as it was far from the village proper. While all ten men were silently positioning themselves to overpower the guards and release the horses in a grand stampede to the west entrance of the village, only Owen and two other individuals would actually ride upon the horses to freedom, crouched down on the animals in the center of the galloping storm. All hoped that speed and darkness would keep them concealed from the eyes and arrows of the enemy.

Meanwhile in three northern parts of the village, Len Harold and two other men arrived at their separate destinations–abandoned houses or shacks that were beyond repair. Placed inside each structure was a small container of lamp oil, a bit of tinder, kindling and a pair of fire stones, all the necessary ingredients to start a fast blaze. These items had been secretly placed there over the last two days by members of the resistance. When Len arrived at his location, a dilapidated one-story cottage in the woody, northwest section of town, he immediately started a tiny bonfire. He warmed his hands over the flames while waiting for the village bell to toll before he would spread the oil and ignite the diversionary blaze. He envisioned the men in the two other locations doing exactly as he was right now, waiting with nervous anticipation for the guard bell to ring.

Something then caught his attention. A snapping twig? Some rustling leaves? Perhaps the crackling fire was playing tricks on his ears. He stood and went to the next room where cracks in the wall allowed inside a constant breeze from the outdoors. He peered through one of the splits, seeing only shadows and darkness, yet tormented by a vague uneasiness. Was somebody nearby? Had someone followed him?

He heard it again, a shuffle of footsteps through the dry grass and weeds. But Len could see nothing through the narrow crack in the wall as it was too dark outside. Perhaps it was a deer feeding or a loose dog from a nearby home, he speculated. Suddenly, all was silent again. Len exhaled, his face tight with worry. He returned to his fire to await the tolling bell, unaware of the swords being unsheathed by approaching soldiers among the thick shadows surrounding the cottage.

The workers in the Stewart household began to clean up after another day of serving meals. Katherine prepared an extra strong brew of tea to serve Oscar and Amanda who sat at the corner kitchen table after having dined in private. Amanda invited Katherine to join them after she poured their drinks from a steaming kettle.

"You look tired," she said, indicating for Katherine to sit and have some tea. "Perhaps you should stay home tomorrow. You can help Sophia bake bread."

"Mother has enough help for that," she said. "I would only be in the way. Besides, she has a system."

"Then arrive a few hours late," Amanda suggested. "You're here more than you should be."

Katherine blushed, suspecting that neither Oscar nor Amanda knew of her strong feelings for Lewis. She felt embarrassed to tell them why she had worked extra hours in their house lately, hoping to see Lewis more often since he was one of Oscar's employees. But in light of recent events, that ploy hadn't worked well as Lewis was rarely around the house anymore. But with the Stewarts now at her side, she decided to tell them of their budding relationship. There was no reason to hide it as they were each responsible adults of seventeen, despite Amanda Stewart frowning upon distracting relationships between her employees.

But Katherine barely got the first word out of her mouth when Oscar suddenly sat up straight in his chair as if he had been stabbed in the back. Katherine and Amanda looked at him with concern. In the distance, above the din of clattering dishes and kitchen conversations, the mournful tolling of the village bell could be heard. The changing of the evening guard had commenced.

"What's the matter, Oscar?" his wife asked, placing her hands upon his. Amanda thought she detected a slight trembling when she touched his cool skin. "You're nearly as pale as this morning's dusting of snow."

"Overworked, I guess. I need some fresh air." Oscar stood, making his way to the front door with Amanda and Katherine trailing behind. He grabbed his coat from a hallway peg and slipped it on. The remaining soldiers who had been recently dining had since left.

He inhaled the cool air when he stepped out the door, holding his breath for a moment to calm himself. The two oil lamps on either side of the front stone path cast a warm glow upon the fallen leaves that had been raked aside. The dark, tree-lined street stood deathly still. Moments later, Amanda and Katherine were at his side, each wrapped in a warm, flowing cloak. Oscar's wife slipped her arm inside his, holding him close.

"What's bothering you, Oscar?" she asked in worried tones. "I've never seen you so rattled."

"I just had to step out. I'm..." Oscar looked up the street to the north, gazing past the distant houses and treetops, desperately seeking a sign. He expected to see the glow of firelight any moment now. But as the seconds drifted by, and then another minute or two, he began to worry. He walked across the lawn, still facing north, yet the horizon lay dark and the sky was blanketed with clouds.

"What are you looking for?" Katherine whispered. She was unable to observe Oscar's expression in the dense shadows, yet could sense the tension that gripped him.

Oscar turned to his wife and Katherine, rubbing a hand nervously across his face. "I suppose I can tell you now since the men are in motion," he softly said, looking around to make sure no one was in earshot. "Tonight is the night we've been planning for these last few days."

Amanda let out a small gasp. "You mean–?"

Oscar nodded. "Our little resistance movement is about to have its first test. The tolling of the village bell was the signal to begin." He scanned the northern horizon again, still as black as coal. "But we seem to be a little behind schedule."

"What's supposed to happen?" Amanda asked. "What are you looking for?"

Oscar was about to fill them in on the specifics of his inspired plan when the sound of distant voices at the south end of the road caught their attention. As they turned and walked back to the front of the house, Oscar could see two Island soldiers riding upon horses as they slowly made their way up the street, having just turned up the corner off River Road. Behind the two riders walked a group of ten local men surrounded by a small company of armed soldiers, their swords unsheathed and reflecting the light from the flickering torches that several held aloft. As the group passed by the house, Oscar noted that the ten villagers all had their hands tied in front of them, their heads bowed despondently. He was shocked into silence as he watched them advance.

"Where are you taking these men?" he finally called out to one of the riders. "What have they done?"

"Go inside," a voice gruffly commanded. "There's nothing of concern here."

"But what have they done?" Katherine demanded to know. "You simply cannot–" Suddenly her heart froze when one of the prisoners turned his head to her as he walked by. Lewis gazed upon her, troubled and frightened, yet tried to smile to comfort her. Katherine was stunned, nearly losing her balance before Oscar caught her by the arm.

"These criminals, along with three more apprehended elsewhere, will be dealt with by the wizard himself," the soldier continued. "Do not interfere. I'm sure they will be accorded a fair trial before their sentences are announced." A wave of laughter rippled through the Island troops as they disappeared up the road and turned left at the next corner, swallowed up in the shadows.

"That was Lewis!" Katherine exclaimed, looking to Oscar for an answer. "Why was he there? What was he doing?"

"Tell us," Amanda pleaded, her voice quivering. "What did you plan for tonight? And what do we do now?"

Oscar swallowed hard as fear gripped him, his mouth slightly agape in the glow of the lamplight. But all he could do was shake his head, dumbfounded by the sight of Lewis Ames and the others being marched away as prisoners. Had someone made a terrible mistake? Or had they all been betrayed? In either case, Oscar could only blame himself at the moment.

"This cannot be," he mournfully whispered as the world around him dissolved into a dizzying blur. "What have I done?"

CHAPTER 46

A Wizard's Revenge

News spread rapidly throughout the night about the arrest of thirteen villagers who had challenged Caldurian's authority. Though the wizard had labeled the men as conspirators, the citizens of Kanesbury looked upon them as heroes. And while the men were endlessly praised, most people harbored no illusions regarding their fate, fearing that callous retribution would be meted out at once.

Nobody was allowed to visit the prisoners after they were hauled off to the lockup. Maynard had made a public spectacle the next morning in front of the building, asking to see the thirteen. But a few soldiers only blocked his entrance until he received further orders from Caldurian who was contemplating the matter in his quarters. Maynard then marched to Otto's house with a group of villagers in tow, demanding to speak to the wizard, but all were refused a meeting. Armed soldiers dispersed the crowd, explaining that Caldurian would make a public announcement later that morning.

An hour before noon, one of the captains rode up on horseback to the village hall with a message from the wizard. He dismounted and walked to the top step where a crowd eagerly gathered, all bundled up beneath a swirl of gray clouds and intermittent snowflakes. The stern-faced soldier held up one hand to settle everyone before unfolding a sheet of parchment to read.

"The wizard Caldurian hereby orders that the thirteen conspirators captured last night will be paraded in front of the gathered populace at noon today inside the village hall to receive their just sentences. All work assignments will be suspended so the citizens of Kanesbury may attend this most grave occasion. Threats posed by these lawbreakers have interfered with the orderly running of our village. Such disruptive behavior cannot be tolerated." The soldier looked up at the crowd, lowering the piece of parchment. "That is all." He turned and walked away.

"So now we wait," a woman whispered anxiously to another at her side. "It will be a long hour to endure."

"Especially for the prisoners," her friend replied helplessly as the crowd dispersed. "It doesn't look good for them."

"No," the woman replied with a sigh. "I suspect not."

Kanesbury was at a standstill an hour later as everyone converged upon the village hall, filling the benches to capacity. Many stood among the soldiers along the side walls and in back while others were forced to remain outside for lack of room. The table and chairs usually in front for the village council meetings had been removed, lending a cold emptiness to the interior. The room, however, was sufficiently warmed by the body heat and endless chatter of the crowd as people speculated about what would happen. Someone sarcastically suggested that Caldurian might shatter all the repaired windows once again, though another didn't put such an action past him. But all voices fell silent by the unexpected ringing of the village bell. It solemnly tolled three times, after which the interior doors of the building were opened.

Slowly, the thirteen prisoners were escorted up the center aisle by armed soldiers to the empty space in front. People turned around to watch the grim procession, noting the prisoners' pale faces and weary eyes. Their hands were tied in front as if common criminals. Katherine, sitting in one of the middle aisles next to her mother, trembled when she saw Lewis pass by in a frightened daze. She clasped her mother's hand for support as her heart ached and her eyes welled with tears. The prisoners were instructed to stand in a slight semicircle and face their fellow citizens as they awaited Caldurian's arrival. Finally, after moments of excruciating silence, the wizard appeared through a side door and strode confidently to the front of the crowd.

"I will get right to the point," he said in a low, commanding voice, his thin face and iron gray hair punctuated by a pair of dark eyes filled with indignation. "The thirteen men standing here have defied my authority. All have been thoroughly questioned. Yet to a man, not even one will reveal the instigator behind their devious plot. So before this day is done, they will pay the consequences for their hideous actions."

"Let them go!" someone shouted. "They've done nothing wrong."

Caldurian stood tall and intimidating, wrapped in a black cloak that mirrored the gloom of the outdoors. He extended an arm with the swiftness of a drawn sword, pointing at the prisoners. "They have challenged my authority, regardless of the failure of their mission! That by itself is a grievous crime, and so punishment must be doled out to restore order. This will be accompanied by food rations throughout the village and additional arrests for the slightest infractions." Groans of disapproval rose from the crowd. "All to discourage similar misbehavior in the future. I don't want to do this, but I have no choice."

"You *do* have a choice!" Maynard said, standing up by one of the side benches. "You're pushing us too far, Caldurian, and others may revolt if you continue."

"I'm doing what needs to be done to run this village!" he boomed, silencing the crowd. "However," he quickly followed, his voice softening and more pleasant, "I would be more than amenable to releasing all of the thirteen prisoners and lifting the new arrest and food rationing orders on one condition."

"What?" Ned Adams asked skeptically, sitting near Maynard.

"Simply this," the wizard replied. "I want to know the identity of the person–or persons–who instigated this rebellion. Whoever had the impudence to think he could challenge me should step forward right now to save these misguided individuals. Or if anyone happens to know the identity of such a ringleader, you may disclose that name to me now or to one of my captains later and anonymously if you prefer." Caldurian scanned the worried faces of the crowd. "Is there anyone with integrity enough to step forward and admit complicity in this affair right now? Or others brave enough to turn in a fellow citizen? *Anyone?*"

The wizard waited for several moments, allowing those gathered to search their thoughts and shoot furtive glances at one another. Yet no one acceded to Caldurian's wishes. The room remained as still as a moonless, winter night. Katherine stared at Oscar Stewart who sat across the room with Amanda, wondering if he would dare speak up. But Oscar held his tongue, as did Maynard, Ned and a few other men who Katherine assumed had been involved in the resistance. She couldn't imagine how this day would end.

After another minute of uncomfortable silence, the wizard's voice broke the unbearable tension. "It appears that no one wishes to take responsibility for the rebellion. And apparently no one wants to turn in those who were behind it either–at least not in public. Therefore, I will take the extra step and demonstrate one final act of mercy–but only one–and give you until sunset tonight to come forward with the information I seek. But if by then no one claims responsibility or identifies those behind these acts, then I'll have no choice but to pronounce my sentence."

"Do as you must," Len Harold definitely stated, standing behind Caldurian with his hands bound. "We take full responsibility for our actions and implicate no one else."

A snake-like smile spread across the wizard's face. "As you wish," he said, grabbing Len by one arm and pulling him forward. He randomly chose a second man from the group, bringing Lewis Ames forward as well so that he stood side by side with Len. "If information is not presented to me by sunset, then these two gentlemen will pay for the crimes of this group with their very lives, forfeited at the point of a sword. The remaining eleven will be marched north and either conscripted into the army from the Northern Isles or imprisoned across the sea." Caldurian awaited a response from the crowd but was greeted with horrified silence. "So I guess I have made myself perfectly clear. Until this evening then."

Without hesitation, Caldurian walked off and disappeared through a side door, the folds of his cloak trailing behind like a billowing wisp of black cloud. Soldiers escorted the prisoners down the center aisle and out the village hall, with Len Harold and Lewis Ames pushed in front of the group, their faces pale and their thoughts whirling. As the thirteen men walked past in silence,

Katherine wanted to rush over to Lewis and comfort him, wondering amid warm tears if anyone could save Lewis and the others from either certain death or expulsion from their beloved homes.

Less than an hour later, Maynard stood in the ice cellar of the Stewart household with Oscar and Ned discussing what was to be done. Oscar paced nervously, his frosty breath rising in the harsh glow of candlelight.

"This is my fault," he whispered, finally sitting down on a block of ice covered with straw. "It was a foolish plan I proposed! Why did you people listen to me?"

"Your idea was sound," Maynard assured him. "But apparently someone found out. The enemy was tipped off."

"By who?" Ned asked. "Someone from our group?"

Maynard nodded sadly. "Either that or one of Caldurian's soldiers overheard something in passing. After all, we conspirators grew to a large number near the end. But regardless of the reason, we only have until sunset to save the lives of Len and Lewis. And we certainly can't condemn the others to conscription or imprisonment in the Northern Isles. That might be worse than death itself, so I–"

"Agreed!" Oscar nervously interrupted, only half listening to what Maynard had said. "Therefore, I shall turn myself in and accept the consequences. It's the only way."

"Oscar, you're speaking nonsense!" Ned told him. "Besides, you have a wife and businesses and employees to care for. There has to be another way. We must make some sort of deal with the wizard to spare everyone."

Maynard sighed dejectedly, shaking his head and drawing the alarmed attention of the others. "Oscar is right. There is no other way–and no time either. We must do something soon even if it means sacrificing one of us in exchange for the others." He looked up at the faces of his two companions, both pale with worry and fright. "But it won't be you, Oscar, who shall make that sacrifice. It will be me."

"What? You can't do that, Maynard."

"I have to."

"Certainly not!" Ned added. "You're our mayor, after all, and our go-between with Caldurian. These past few days would have been much worse without you talking at least a bit of sense into that crazed wizard."

"Perhaps, but I still must do this," he insisted. "Unlike you two, I have no family, so if something happens to me…"

Ned flung up his arms in desperation. "There has to be some other way, Maynard! Go to the wizard and talk to him. Convince him to change his mind."

Maynard looked helpless. "He won't do that, and you know it, Ned."

Oscar nodded. "That I agree with. The expression on Caldurian's face as he stood in front of the prisoners chilled me to the bone. He will not compromise regardless of any arguments we present." He glanced at his friends, his eyes glistening in the candlelight. "We have no choice. It's up to us to save them."

After another futile attempt to change his mind, Ned finally agreed that Maynard should give himself up at sunset and hope for the best, though both he and Oscar privately thought that a ghastly outcome was inevitable. When Oscar later informed Amanda and Katherine of their decision while they worked in the kitchen, both women were horrified, fearing the worst.

"With the little time we have, what else could we do?" Oscar explained as his wife and Katherine stood on the verge of tears. "Given that Maynard has cultivated a bit of trust with the wizard, maybe Caldurian will judge him less severely."

Amanda scoffed. "Given that Maynard broke that trust, Caldurian might respond all the more harshly. I fear Maynard Kurtz is walking to his doom."

Katherine agreed despite the knowledge that Lewis' life would be spared. "It is a noble sacrifice, but a foolish one."

Oscar shrugged. "You may be right, Katherine, but Maynard won't budge in his decision. As he is both the mayor *and* stubborn, he'll definitely have his way. At sunset, we will witness the full extent of his loyalty to our village."

"I fear it will cost him and the village dearly," Amanda replied, holding her husband close to dispel the emptiness that overwhelmed her spirit. She dreaded the hours to follow.

The village bell tolled as the sun sank in the southwest, its reddish-orange rays filtering through a bank of tattered clouds.

People hurried to the village hall, having grown accustomed to the throng of armed soldiers scattered in the streets as if they were as natural a part of the surroundings as the trees, stone walls and chimney tops. Inside, the drone of competing conversations hung heavily in the air. Hearts were filled with dread and despair. Few grasped what was happening or knew how to oppose it, so most simply waited, expecting the worst and hoping to survive it.

The thirteen prisoners were again marched inside and lined up, their hands bound in front. Caldurian appeared shortly afterward, his expression cold and stony. Additional armed soldiers were stationed about the hall in anticipation of trouble from the villagers should the wizard's harsh sentence against Len Harold and Lewis Ames be carried out.

Katherine sat between her mother and Amanda Stewart, watching the proceedings nervously. Oscar, Ned and the two other council members sat on a side bench next to Maynard Kurtz in a show of unity. Zachary Farnsworth and Dooley Kramer occupied seats in separate parts of the hall, each engrossed in the grim proceedings. The last rays of the setting sun stabbed through the western windows, setting the glass aflame in lustrous shades of orange and crimson, but only for a moment. Soon the window panes were leached of their color, dissolving into muddy shades of gray and black as the sun dipped below the horizon.

Caldurian gazed at the crowd and the prisoners before indicating to one of his soldiers to bring Len and Lewis forward. The soldier brusquely grabbed each man by an arm and positioned them helplessly in front, the focus of the room's horrified attention.

"I needn't rehash my demands from earlier since everybody knows why we're here," the wizard said, pointing to the two men. "Certainly these two are aware of the significance of what's about to unfold. So before I ask my question one last time, I hope everyone has had a good think these past few hours. Much depends on your response—or lack thereof." No one spoke as they waited uneasily for Caldurian's question, though all knew what he would say. It was what would happen afterward that caused many hearts in the room to beat rapidly or gazes to sink to the floor. "Who in this village is responsible for planning the failed escape attempt last night? Speak now, or all blame will be assigned to these thirteen men, two of whom will pay for the outrage with their lives this very night."

The hall was deathly still as the villagers looked on, several heads craning this way and that to see if someone might step up to claim responsibility. A few whispered words were hastily uttered as Caldurian watched, his dark eyes scanning the rows of benches for any hint of compliance. But just as he was about to speak, Maynard Kurtz slowly rose to his feet to both the relief and dismay of his fellow citizens. Yet despite his willingness to turn himself in, the mayor didn't have a chance to address his audience. Everyone's attention was suddenly directed toward the back of the room.

The astonished voices of those standing outdoors and huddled within the entryway grew louder, reverberating throughout the hall. A commotion was brewing near the main doors, causing everyone to stand up and turn around. Soon gasps of shock and surprise were audible from one end of the building to the other as people observed a slightly stocky man slowly walking up the center aisle, his eyes wide in confusion and his mouth agape. The familiar figure was dressed in rumpled clothing, his thin, stringy hair tied up in back with a black band. He looked around as if in a state of drunken wonderment, halting when he caught sight of his sister and his niece.

Sophia Durant raised a trembling hand to her lips, thinking for a moment that she was seeing an illusion. But when the man returned an equally astounded gaze, Sophia knew that her brother had finally returned home.

"*Otto*! Where have you been?" she asked excitedly, clasping Katherine's hand for support.

"I– I'm not really sure," he whispered. He looked around in bewilderment. "What's happening here? And who are these armed men?" Sophia and Katherine, as well as several people within earshot, appeared astonished by the question.

"Don't you know?" Katherine asked, recalling the string of pre-dawn visits her uncle had made to certain residents of the village eight days ago, warning them of the trouble to come. "You had told us that something bad was about to happen to the village."

"I did?"

"You did!" someone shouted. "And then you went slinking off like a scared cat before the worst arrived!"

"Yeah! A lot of help you were, Otto!" another voice burst out. "Go back to where you came from!"

"Huh?" Otto asked, in a mild stupor as he gazed around during the competing outbursts. *"This* is where I come from." He glanced at Katherine, a trace of fear in his eyes. "What's going on?" "It's difficult to explain," she said. "You see, Uncle Otto–"

"You're a traitor is what's going on!" interrupted a farmer near the front of the hall, receiving a chorus of support from some sitting next to him. "Warning so many of your friends about what was going to happen before running away. How come you didn't visit me, Otto?" The man grew red from a simmering rage.

"Or me!" exclaimed the farmer's closest neighbor. "Nor any of my relatives in Kanesbury. Guess our families just weren't good enough!" He stuck out his chin with contempt, glaring at Otto. "Ashamed to ever call you my mayor again," he muttered with disgust as more voices rose up.

"Millard, what kind of talk is that?" Otto asked, standing in the aisle with his arms outstretched. "I don't know what's happened. I truly don't. Tell me what's going on. Tell me what I've done."

"You betrayed us, Otto!" Bob Hawkins shouted as he jumped to his feet, his chest puffed up and his eyes filled with disdain. "It's just like the man said–you're a traitor!"

"Now wait one minute!" Maynard shouted, pushing through a forest of bodies that had slowly gathered around Otto, but he was quickly blocked out. "Let's give the man a chance to–"

"He had his chance when he decided to warn only some of us villagers and not the rest!" a teary-eyed woman cried out while shaking her clenched fist in the air. "My husband was arrested twice because of Otto's selfishness. And now he has the audacity to stand there and pretend he doesn't know what's happened? The nerve!"

More people shouted in derision as they tightened the ring around their former mayor like a circle of vultures, leaving Otto Nibbs flummoxed and scratching his head. But the ghastly expressions upon the faces of his friends and colleagues, along with their harsh words, were all too real, sending a sickening chill through him. When he noted that Sophia and Katherine simply stared back with horrified looks, it confirmed in his mind that Kanesbury had been thrown into unimaginable turmoil during his mysterious absence, however long that had been. And apparently he was to blame, though for what specifically, Otto could only guess.

Finally, another man stood up on his seat and shouted at Caldurian who remained standing calmly in front, ignored for the moment by the boisterous, bubbling crowd. "If you really want to know who was behind last night's trouble, you're looking at him!" The man pointed down at Otto as if he were some mighty judge pronouncing a stinging verdict. "Otto arranged everything! He organized the escape, hoping to make up for abandoning us to the invasion," the man bellowed out, his voice hoarse with anger. "It was all Otto's plan, failure though it was. Every single bit of it!"

"It sure was!" another man hollered, likewise getting to his feet and glaring at Otto as several people cheered him on. "Arrest him, Caldurian, if you're looking for the true culprit! Arrest Otto and let the others go!"

"*Caldurian?*" Otto whispered that bitter name from the past in stunned revulsion, not yet having noticed the wizard through the throng of people. He was still enveloped in a haze of bewilderment after having awakened from a long and fitful sleeping spell only moments ago, sprawled out on a pile of leaves off the road just down the street. Otto spun around to look for the wizard as some in the crowd stepped aside, allowing their mayor to locate his nemesis who had terrorized the village twenty years ago. When Otto locked gazes with Caldurian, the cold shock of recognition snapped his senses awake, though he was now rendered even more confused than when he had first walked into the hall. "*You?*" Otto's eyes widened with dread, though the contempt in his voice was as hard as stone. "What are you doing here, wizard? What is happening?"

Caldurian chuckled. "Quite a change of circumstances from twenty years ago, don't you think?" But all Otto could do was shake his head in disbelief. "And as for what I'm doing here, Mr. Nibbs, well, I'm running your village as it *should* be run," he replied with delight.

"Nonsense! You're a troublemaker of the worst kind, Caldurian, and no one in this room will disagree," he shot back.

"Perhaps not," he replied with mild amusement. "But at least I'm not a traitor, deserting my people in the dead of night to save myself as apparently you have."

As murmurs of agreement swept through the room, Otto sensed that the crowd would favor the wizard over himself should it come to a contest. He wondered if everyone was under the influence of some vile, magical spell.

"I'm not a traitor!" Otto shouted. "I would never desert Kanesbury."

"Then why did you warn some of us about the trouble to come just before fleeing the village?" asked a woman standing directly behind him, her eyes filled with contempt. "What kind of a leader does that to his people?"

"I agree," the wizard said, nodding sympathetically at the woman. "Only a heartless, conniving and ruthless man could do such a thing. It's shameful in every way."

"I fled nowhere!" Otto insisted. "After I traveled to Barringer's Landing to negotiate with the Enâri creatures, I—" He shook his head. "I just don't remember what happened. I arrived there and searched among the fields, but found no one. The place was deserted. I hiked toward one of the abandoned barns and..." Otto looked up, helplessly pleading for anyone to believe in him.

"And *what*?" Bob Hawkins asked.

Otto sighed. "And nothing. I remember nothing from that point on until I woke up only moments ago down the street from here," he explained. "I was lying on a pile of leaves, feeling as if I had been sleeping for ages."

"No doubt passed out drunk!" someone joked, receiving a round of boisterous laughter from the others. "So that's where you've been all this time? Living off gin and ale in the wild?"

"Is this true, Otto?" Caldurian asked with feigned shock.

"No!" he shouted. "I don't know where I was, but as soon as I woke up, I heard many of you gathered outside the village hall. So I walked this way, wondering what had happened to me while wondering at the same time what was happening here." Otto looked at several people for an answer, his voice faltering. "And by the way, if I might ask, why do some of you want me arrested?"

"Better you than them!" Millard said, pointing at the thirteen prisoners standing in utter bewilderment near Caldurian. "Because of your disloyalty to the village, they're now paying the price."

"All too true!" someone replied with vigorous disgust. "All too true! You should be up there instead, Otto, for what you've done. They're being punished for trying to save this village when all the trouble can be traced back to you for abandoning us to chaos."

"I say arrest Otto Nibbs and let the others go!" a voice shouted, echoing previous sentiments. Others quickly joined in until a raucous chant erupted, filling the village hall to its rafters with an explosion of pent up rage and frustration.

"Arrest Otto Nibbs! Arrest Otto Nibbs!" most of the villagers shouted at once, many stomping their feet in the process.

"Make him pay for what he did!" a lone voice hollered among the uproar.

Otto looked on in stunned disbelief, wondering if he had gone insane. The shouts of *Arrest Otto Nibbs*! rang painfully in his ears. Sophia and Katherine tried to catch a glimpse of their forlorn relative, eyeing him with pity through the human barrier surrounding the man, wondering if there was anything they could do to save him. But the crowd was unrelenting in its condemnation of the former mayor as their shouts for his incarceration grew only louder and louder.

"Arrest Otto Nibbs! Arrest Otto Nibbs!"

Caldurian looked upon the spectacle with a stony expression, but inside, his spirit was swimming in a sea of euphoria as he savored the scorn and contempt heaped upon Otto by his own people. After a long and cruel wait, he was at last witnessing the scene he had played in his mind for twenty years, finally dining upon a visual meal whose aroma had enticed him for far too long. He had at last achieved a small victory and looked forward to many more.

Through the crowd and turmoil and swirl of emotions, Caldurian and Otto locked stares for a few brief but weighty moments, each realizing that their roles had been reversed from two decades ago. Otto detected the hint of smug satisfaction oozing from the wizard's vague smile, knowing for the moment that he was defeated, but not understanding how. Caldurian simply studied the face of his victim with contentment, silently savoring Otto's utter demise.

After he had had his fill of victory, Caldurian signaled to several of his captains to quell the crowd and to arrest Otto, instructing the soldiers to escort the man to the front of the room with the other prisoners. A burst of ecstatic applause reverberated throughout the hall as Otto Nibbs was walked up the remainder of the aisle with a guard on either side clutching his arms. The prisoner was ordered to stand near the wizard and face the crowd before accepting his sentence.

"I must admit that even I was surprised by this turn of events," Caldurian said, quieting the celebration. Not a single whisper disturbed the heavy silence. "And though ordinarily I would take some time to consider my next pronouncement, it appears beyond a doubt that the people here tonight have made their wishes known in the starkest terms." Neither Otto nor Caldurian could ignore the sea of nodding heads before them. "So who am I to disregard such an overwhelming desire of these fine citizens to exact a bit of justice on one who so rightly deserves it?"

The people of Kanesbury collectively held their breaths, anticipating the wizard's verdict. The heat and pressure inside the village hall climbed rapidly in those few moments as the fate of the thirteen prisoners hung in the balance. The life of Otto Nibbs at the moment seemed an awfully small price to pay for their release, and most had no qualms about turning him over to Caldurian. Otto deserved a merciless fate considering the cruelty Kanesbury had been forced to suffer because of his cowardice and selfishness. Few were willing to shed a tear for him.

"Therefore," the wizard continued with much loftiness in his tone and gestures, "in accordance with the wishes of those gathered here, I am charging Otto Nibbs with the crimes of conspiring against the authority of this village and for attempting to raise chaos in the streets and against its people, and thus formally arrest him now. He will be sentenced after a public trial conducted by the very people he has offended. In the meantime, he'll be incarcerated in the village lockup. A fitting fate for such a detestable criminal," he emphasized with a sharp nod. "And in light of this new development, I hereby rescind all charges against the thirteen other prisoners and order that they immediately be set free. Guards, release them!"

The spectators erupted in cheers of jubilation and relief, jumping to their feet and applauding as their spirits soared and their worries melted away. Caldurian soaked it all in. One by one, the prisoners' hands were untied and the thirteen men were free to leave, immediately greeted by the hugs and tears of their family members. Otto, at the same time, was unceremoniously hustled out of the hall through the side door at the wizard's command and taken to the village lockup. Caldurian planned to question him later that night.

But for now he would quietly return to his quarters by the river–Otto's quarters–and enjoy a fine meal and a glass of wine to celebrate. This battle was finally over, the wizard mused as he slipped out the building, leaving the others to their celebration.

Katherine, at the same time, had asked her mother to stay close to Amanda Stewart and find their way out of the hall while she waded through the crowd, hoping to reach her uncle before he was led away. She was too late, just glimpsing the back of Otto's head as he was rushed out the side door.

"I need to see my Uncle Otto!" she pleaded with one of the soldiers amid the uproar, barely able to get the man's attention. "Can you take me to him? I beg you!"

"Not tonight, miss," he said flatly. "The wizard will want to question him first."

"But I must talk to–"

"Stop by tomorrow. Make your case to one of the guards on duty," he brusquely replied, brushing her aside as he walked away to help disperse the crowd.

Katherine sighed, feeling helpless amid the bustling mass of people. As she turned to make her way back, she caught sight of Lewis in the embrace of his parents and younger brother and sister, her heart warming for that bit of good news. Lewis noticed her as well and their gazes connected, acutely aware of each other's conflicting emotions. Unable to make her way over, Katherine signaled to him that she would attempt to see him later. Lewis nodded likewise, silently promising to stop by when he could. Their wordless conversation across the crowd was cut short a few seconds later when Katherine was nudged away by a line of soldiers hurriedly passing by, leaving her feeling as alone and abandoned as Otto Nibbs.

CHAPTER 47

A Shift in Power

Katherine spotted her mother and Amanda Stewart outdoors after the raucous meeting in the village hall had concluded. People poured out the front doors into the cold evening air and the warm glow of torchlight and oil lamps. The crescent Fox Moon shimmered behind a veil of clouds in the west. Katherine promised her mother that they would visit the lockup first thing in the morning and demand to see Otto.

"I'll go with you," Amanda insisted, indignant at the way Otto had been treated during the wizard's shameful spectacle. "We shall take Oscar and Maynard with us if necessary. Most may have turned against your brother and uncle, but we certainly won't!"

"Thank you," Sophia replied, deeply touched as she wiped away a tear. "I can't believe this is happening."

"Me either," Katherine said. "But don't worry, Mother. We won't abandon Uncle Otto," she promised, hugging her tightly. "There must be a logical explanation why he fled the village before all this trouble erupted. There *must* be."

Soon after, Katherine bid goodbye to the women, deciding to wait awhile and speak with Lewis before returning home. She stood in the lonely, crowded street, imagining Otto languishing behind a locked door and feeling very much a prisoner herself.

"Sorry to hear the bad news about your uncle," said a voice in the shadows. Katherine spun around, surprised to see Dooley Kramer walking toward her, his hands shoved in his coat pockets to keep them warm. His mop of dirty blond hair sprouted out from beneath the floppy brim of a brown hat. "I suspect it's just as difficult for you and your mother to bear this terrible hardship as it is for Otto."

"It certainly is," Katherine replied, appearing appreciative of Dooley's remark while at the same time detesting him. All she could think about was the information Paraquin had provided her regarding Dooley and Zachary Farnsworth's ability to leave the village in the dead of night. She wondered what kind of deal they had struck with Caldurian and who in the process had been harmed.

"If there's anything I can do, please don't hesitate to ask," he added with a pleasant smile, hoping to win her respect and perhaps a modicum of affection as well. "At times like these, the village needs to pull together to help one another, don't you think?"

Katherine nodded, her face softening as she put on an air of graciousness. Though she desired to lash out at Dooley for consorting with the enemy, she wondered if she could use this moment to her advantage. Would it be wise to confront him now about his hand in Nicholas Raven's troubles? She knew that that might cause an emotional stir on his part, and the subsequent reaction on Dooley's face might confirm his guilt. She also wondered if she should casually drop Adelaide's name into the conversation in an attempt to worm some details about his possible involvement in her disappearance.

But Katherine decided not to tread those dangerous waters just yet, fearing that accusing him without proof might push Dooley away at a time when she desperately needed information. Keeping him and Farnsworth ignorant that she was on to them might serve her best for now. The wisest course of action would be to play the spy, hoping to catch them off guard. Perhaps Paraquin would discover more information in the meantime.

"Thank you for sharing your concern, Dooley. I appreciate it, especially on an awful night like this," she said. "Caldurian turned this village upside down, hasn't he?"

"He's a villain of the first order," Dooley remarked. "Why, he's got me on one of the leaf burning details on the east end of town, though I suppose it's better than chopping wood or emptying root cellars."

"It seems neither of us has a glamorous job. I'm serving meals to the Island soldiers–and what appetites they have!" she joked, putting Dooley at ease. "What task has your neighbor, Mr. Farnsworth, been forced to do? Cleaning out horse stalls?"

Dooley laughed. "As a matter of fact, he still works at his current job in the banking house. Apparently the wizard realizes that some businesses in the village have to continue running properly amid the chaos."

"How fortunate for him," she replied. "I hear that Mr. Farnsworth is a fine worker, so that's a benefit for all of Kanesbury. Horace Ulm must be proud to have hired such a dedicated and outstanding citizen."

"Outstanding indeed," Dooley said, clearing his throat in the dry air, for a moment unable to look Katherine in the eyes. "Well, I suppose I must be going before the Islanders shoo us all home. Just wanted to offer my good wishes, Miss Katherine."

"Thank you again, Dooley."

"Uh, might I walk you to your house?" he added somewhat eagerly, nearly stumbling on his words. He hoped that Katherine didn't notice. "It is dark out, after all, and you are alone."

She smiled graciously. "I appreciate the offer, Dooley, but there's someone I need to talk to before I leave," she replied, glancing over at Lewis who was still surrounded by family and friends near the entrance of the village hall. "But thank you anyway."

Dooley nodded. "Very well. But do be careful and watch yourself," he added as he strolled away with a wave of his hand.

"Oh, I will," she replied, eyeing Dooley until he disappeared into the murky shadows down the street. "And I shall be watching you as well," she whispered.

Zachary Farnsworth poured himself a mug of ale and then ladled out a bowl of pork stew from a simmering pot over his kitchen fire when he heard a strange noise in the house later that night. He ignored it at first while sitting down at a table, prepared to enjoy a quiet evening after enduring Caldurian's theatrics at the village hall. He shoveled down a few spoonfuls of stew which he enjoyed with some bread and cheese, and then sipped his drink and sighed wearily. Though he continued to do his job at the banking house, the presence of the wizard and his soldiers was wearing on him despite the fact that he had been secretly allowed to keep his food stores. His root cellar had remained untouched. He wondered when Caldurian would leave so he could have the village to himself as agreed.

He then heard the sound again as if something was frantically scraping against a piece of wood. Perhaps there was a squirrel on the roof or a mouse in the wood pile. But Farnsworth was too tired to care, preparing to retire early with the hope that tomorrow would bring better news. Now that Caldurian had had his revenge by destroying Otto Nibbs, what more could he want?

Farnsworth slammed his hand on the table when the scraping sound persisted, annoying him to no end. He grabbed a lit candle and wandered through the shadowy rooms to track it down, ending up in the front hallway. He unlocked the door and cautiously opened it, greeted only by silence and the chilly blackness. He opened the door wider, peering into the night, his dark eyes and perplexed frown aglow in candlelight. Suddenly a low, dark shape brushed past his leg and slipped into the house, startling him so that he yelled out in fright. He slammed the door shut and spun around, gazing into the shadowy hallway, the candlelight reflecting eerily in the wall mirror.

"Where are you?" he uttered harshly.

As he wildly moved the candle through the air, he caught the gleam of a pair of eyes low to the floor, golden-yellow in color and staring back with a paralyzing intensity. Farnsworth flinched, quickly stepping back, but slowly approached again when seeing that the creature remained perfectly still. When shining more light closer to the animal, its rusty red fur, pricked up ears and narrow snout became visible, causing him to grin.

"Looking for a meal, little fox?" he asked.

The fox remained perfectly still, studying Farnsworth for a moment before growing larger and distorting its shape. Farnsworth stepped back, frightened for a moment before realizing what was happening. Soon Maynard Kurtz stood before him, his long silvery-black hair framing a mischievous grin.

"I'm not particularly hungry at the moment, but thanks all the same," Maynard replied, stretching his arms as he again accustomed himself to the shape he had been living in for most of these past several weeks. "Forgive my entrance, but I didn't want to be spotted walking to your house as either the mayor or in my natural state for obvious reasons. And any chance to exercise my transformational abilities, I happily take."

"Guess I can't blame you," Farnsworth said, smiling clumsily. As intimidated and uncomfortable as he felt when dealing with Caldurian, those moments couldn't begin to compare to the apprehension he experienced when alone with Arileez regardless of his physical manifestation. This wizard had spooked him from the very first night they had met. "How can I help you? You were the last person I expected to see tonight."

"I'm here only to deliver a message from Caldurian, and then I shall be off," he said, bathed in the glow of candlelight.

"Would you like to sit down?" Farnsworth politely offered, though hoping that Arileez would refuse.

"Not necessary. This will only take a moment," he continued. "Caldurian wanted me to tell you that he and his troops will be leaving Kanesbury–in secret–two nights from tonight. He wanted you to know that he hadn't forgotten your agreement."

"I never suspected that he would," Farnsworth said, hoping his demeanor appeared casual and unconcerned. But he celebrated inside, already tasting the power he soon hoped to wield.

"After Caldurian and his forces return to Montavia in the dead of night, the village will be both delighted and shocked the following morning to find them gone and their lives back to normal," he said.

"I can imagine."

"Then as everyone goes about the business of setting things right, I shall appoint you as the newest member of the village council, Mr. Farnsworth."

"Village council? But there are already five members on it."

"True. And though Caldurian and I were going to develop a ploy to assure an opening for you, Ned Adams has already taken care of that problem for us," he explained. "Ned talked to me in private yesterday, saying that he would remain on the council only until Caldurian was either defeated or run out of the village. After that, he needed to devote his free time to rebuilding his gristmill."

"Well, lucky for me then," Farnsworth replied sarcastically, sitting on a bench against the wall. He set the candle on a shelf. Maynard noted his disappointment. "Not pleased with a mere seat on the village council?" he inquired. "That's a step up in society for a man like you."

Farnsworth looked at his visitor with mild contempt, sighing disgustedly. For the moment he didn't care how mighty a wizard this man was. He simply wanted his due.

"A seat on the council is nice, but after all the groundwork I did to assist Caldurian in taking over the village, I had expected something more."

Maynard chuckled. "Caldurian is right. You are impatient. And easily provoked, too. And we both know what you're after, but do not worry, Mr. Farnsworth. You shall be justly compensated."

"How?"

"It's simple," he said. "A few days after you're appointed to the council and the village has had a chance to recover, I'll announce plans to travel to Morrenwood, saying that I must consult with King Justin about Caldurian's reappearance. In my absence, I'll highly recommend that you be appointed acting mayor." Farnsworth looked up, visibly cheered by this bit of good news. "Being the respected citizen and banking manager that you are, the rest of the council should readily agree after my show of support. Besides, with all the commotion that the other council members have been through this past week, I should think they would want a break from the rigors of politics and would have no interest in being mayor themselves."

Farnsworth stood, eager to take the reins of power at once. "Well that's more like it!" he said, giddy with delight. At last, all his careful years of plotting and planning were about to pay off, and all because he had happened to notice Dooley Kramer fingering that silly little key on his doorstep five years ago.

"Who you appoint to take your place on the council afterward is up to you. My work here will be done."

"Are you joining Caldurian in Montavia?" asked Farnsworth.

Maynard shook his head. "Have you forgotten what Caldurian told you during our meeting at the gristmill? I shall be going to Morrenwood, just like I said. Not to meet with King Justin, however, but to replace him. And after walking around in this body and in this trifling village for far too long, it is a challenge I look forward to." Maynard rolled his eyes. "In all honesty, Mr. Farnsworth, both Caldurian and I wish never to step foot in your village again. I'm not sure what you see in this place, but you're welcome to it, sir."

Farnsworth grinned, tasting victory at last. "You can have the rest of the kingdom to do with as you like, Arileez. Even all of Laparia, for all I care. Just allow me this little slice of it right here. That's all I ask and all I ever wanted."

"And you've succeeded," he said with a nod of respect, preparing to leave. "But just remember–grabbing power is one thing. Hanging on to it is the real test."

"I'll remember," Farnsworth replied, half listening to those words while envisioning the exhilarating days ahead as the candlelight flickered wildly in the darkened hallway. He couldn't wait to assume his new place in Kanesbury society.

END OF PART FIVE

PART SIX
SEARCH AND RESCUE

CHAPTER 48

The Road West

Nicholas and Leo sauntered across a small stone bridge on horseback beneath a starry, moonless sky. They had said goodbye to Nedry an hour ago and left the Blue Citadel, traveling west along the Edelin River. It was now past midnight on the fourteenth day of Mid Autumn. The crisp air swirled with the sweet scent of decaying leaves as the gentle rush of river water below wound its way through the Trent Hills. The young men, bundled in long, hooded wool coats, tasted adventure in the air, yet also felt pangs of sadness when leaving behind the people they cared for so much.

Leo couldn't help seeing Princess Megan's cheerful smile in the murky shadows or hear echoes of her voice in the thin breeze, imagining that she was sleeplessly wandering the corridors of the Citadel, counting down the days until his return. Nicholas, though, could only wonder where Ivy was, believing she was a prisoner in the Northern Isles. As difficult as the journey ahead would be, he knew it couldn't compare to the hardship and despair that she must now be enduring. If only he and Leo had been more prepared for their fight above the grasslands. If only Ivy had not agreed to change places with Megan in the village of Boros. *If only…*

He sighed, knowing he was uselessly torturing himself. He silently vowed to find Ivy and bring her home. He didn't quite know how to do that or where to begin his search, but Nicholas Raven promised himself that it was the one task in this world he must complete–or die trying.

"Thinking about the medallion?" Leo asked as they cleared the bridge and followed a dirt road on the opposite side of the river. "Or is it Ivy again?"

"Ivy," he whispered. The medallion hanging from his neck by a leather cord seemed an afterthought.

Locating the wizard Frist in the Dunn Hills to reforge the piece of metal into a key hardly seemed important at the moment. Nicholas guessed that Leo sensed his lapse into melancholy, knowing he shouldn't indulge such emotions too often if their mission was to succeed. The lives and freedom of many people depended on them. He would have to be strong until the task was completed. Maybe afterward he might find a way to rescue the woman with whom he had fallen helplessly in love. He placed a hand in his coat pocket, fingering the scarf he had purchased for Ivy in Boros and recalling how happy he was when he found it lying on the shoreline along the Trillium Sea. He never had a chance to return it to her above the grasslands, hoping one day to hand it back amid smiles of delight.

They traveled for another hour under cover of darkness before turning off the road into a thicket of pine trees to spend the night. "Beginning tomorrow, we can travel in daylight," Nicholas said. "I think we're far enough away from the Citadel to elude any possible spies, though I don't see how anybody could know about our mission."

"I don't either," Leo replied. "Only ten of us were in the chamber when we swore our oath. With luck, this will be an uneventful mission to Wolf Lake and back. Scenic, but uneventful."

"After all we've been through, uneventful sounds fine," he said, guiding his horse toward some fragrant pines towering against a starry backdrop. "But right now a night of uninterrupted sleep sounds even better."

Leo agreed. After building a small fire, they each wrapped themselves in a fur-lined blanket that Nedry had provided and promptly fell asleep on the cold ground to the sound of creaking branches and the restless grunting of their steeds.

NICHOLAS RAVEN AND THE WIZARDS' WEB - VOLUME 2

The southern portion of the Trent Hills divided into two branches separated by an open region that was grassy and fertile in some places and rocky and barren in others. Tiny villages and farmsteads dotted the landscape where conditions were favorable for hunting and cultivating crops. The capital city of Morrenwood was located on the southeastern and less formidable branch of the Trent Hills along the Edelin River. After crossing the waterway on the first night of their journey, it took Nicholas and Leo only a few hours the next day to emerge through the low, green mountains late in the cold morning. Open terrain greeted them beneath a lemon yellow sun as the southwestern branch of the Trent Hills loomed like faint shadows in the distance. There, the Gliwice Gap would lead them directly to the Cashua Forest and beyond. Nicholas reined his horse to a halt and pulled out a map Tolapari had provided. Leo stopped beside him.

"Lost already?" he joked.

"Just comparing this map to what I see before me. I want to gage how competent the King's mapmakers are." He gazed at the black, green and blue lines on the map and pointed directly west. "Straight ahead to the western branch of the Trent and to Gliwice Gap. About a day and a half, I'd estimate. Less than another day after that to get through the hills."

"Sounds about right," Leo said, remembering their time with the wizard to plan their secret route. "Bear southwest after we leave the Gap to the forest beyond. That's where we'll sell or abandon our horses and go on foot. In the meantime, enjoy the ride."

"No one promised us an easy journey," Nicholas said as he stored away the map and continued on, the warm sunlight touching his face and easing his worries. For a moment he felt at peace from all the troubles that had plagued him recently. "After slogging along the dreary grasslands, this path should be a treat."

"I hope so," Leo said, happy to see Nicholas in a cheerful mood as their horses contentedly wandered across the brittle grass turning brown with autumn's frosty touch. "And I hope the wizard is still alive, otherwise this journey will be for nothing. Tolapari hadn't seen Frist since he guided him to Wolf Lake years ago."

"He'll be there," he confidently replied. "Tolapari also said he could feel magic within the medallion even though the spell had been altered and weakened. I'll take that as proof that Frist still lives.

Regardless, our road to the Dunn Hills will take us close to where the Islanders are moving upriver. Who knows, but maybe we'll stumble on some information that would lead us to Ivy. If she's been taken to the Northern Isles..."

Leo glanced skeptically at Nicholas, sympathizing with his friend's personal pain but knowing that he was spouting unrealistic words. "I don't want to wring all hope out of you, but if you think you're simply going to chat with some Islander rafting up the Lorren who'll happen to know something about Ivy, you're in for a huge disappointment."

Nicholas grunted. "I'm not naïve, Leo, but I was just thinking that maybe..."

"Maybe what?"

He shrugged, not ready to reveal his intentions to Leo just yet. It was too early in their journey to tell him. They needed to find the wizard and reforge the key before other plans could be discussed.

"Nothing," Nicholas casually replied. "It's not important. Let's ride a few more miles and then we'll take a break."

"Suit yourself," he said. "But whenever you want to tell me what's on your mind, I'm here to listen."

"Thanks," he replied, dreading that future conversation.

Should their task be successful, Nicholas was confident that Leo could take the key to Morrenwood on his own so the Spirit Box could be unlocked. He hoped his friend would understand his need to depart midway through their journey. After their planning sessions with Tolapari, who had instructed them about the geography of the Dunn Hills, Nicholas felt confident that he could make it to the shores of the Trillium Sea from Wolf Lake on his own. From there he could travel south along the shoreline to the mouth of the Lorren River where ships from the Isles were arriving and sending men and supplies to Vellan's stronghold in Kargoth. Would it be possible to stow away on one of those vessels and sail to the Isles to find Ivy?

Nicholas admitted that the idea sounded preposterous and so was hesitant to tell Leo, but what other alternative was there? He felt responsible for Ivy's kidnapping and vowed to find her. And though they had only known each other a short while, his affection for the young woman had grown in their brief time together and during their abrupt separation. He convinced himself that he had to attempt a rescue no matter how improbable the odds were for success.

He cast a furtive glance at Leo as they continued silently under the midmorning sun. He promised himself to tell him of his plan only after they completed their mission. Such a revelation might be a distraction otherwise. Nicholas nodded, confident he was making the correct decision. Besides, that would give Leo less time to talk him out of such a foolhardy notion.

They passed through two villages during their travels that day, eating sparse meals on the side of the road and enjoying the sunshine while their horses grazed and drank from nearby streams. They made camp for the night on the edge of a field after the sun had set and the purple-red glow of twilight cloaked the landscape. The Fox Moon, just past first quarter, sailed through a sea of icy stars. After dining on strips of fried beef, apples and biscuits, Leo turned in for the night, lying on folded blankets next to a crackling fire while bundled in his hooded coat with another blanket draped over him.

"Have the innkeeper wake me at sunrise," he mumbled.

"Consider it done," Nicholas replied, sitting comfortably near the flames in quiet contemplation. "I'm going to tend to the fire. I'm not sleepy."

"All right," Leo said through the blanket before dozing off.

Nicholas added twigs to the fire, studying the flames while thinking about Ivy. He wondered about life in Kanesbury and how his friends were faring after his departure thirty-two days ago. He had learned from King Justin that Maynard Kurtz was now acting mayor and that Otto Nibbs was missing. What shocked him even more was that the five hundred Enâri cast asleep in the Spirits Caves had awakened and escaped. He fingered the medallion hidden beneath his shirt, astounded that the fate of those creatures and others like them was tied to such a nondescript piece of metal.

He felt a surge of power course through him, realizing the enormity of his task. Yet he also experienced a paralyzing awe knowing that he controlled the lives of so many. Though the Enâri deserved defeat for the destruction they had caused to so many over the years, Nicholas' thoughts turned to Jagga who had remained behind at the Citadel under Carmella's guardianship. As an individual, that one Enâr seemed friendly enough, almost comical, and he wondered if others in the group had likewise turned away from Vellan in thought or in deed. Still, Jagga had been part of the force that created havoc in Kanesbury twenty years ago and had probably murdered Arthur Weeks, so his momentary bout of compassion for the creature quickly diminished. Perhaps it was fitting that one of the Enâri should serve as the conduit for their own demise.

Nicholas let go of the medallion, believing that events would play out as they should despite what he thought. But for good or ill, he knew there was no turning back now. He accepted that this is where he was meant to be. Maybe all the chaos at home and in his personal life had happened for a reason, preparing him and flinging him out in the wilderness for just this task.

He sighed and glanced up at the stars before grinning, realizing the lofty pedestal he had just climbed upon in his mind. Maybe he had blindly stumbled into this affair instead and was simply doing the best he could. In either case, he would move forward with determination and a bit of humility, hoping that all would work out in the end. Perhaps when this chaos was behind him, he could one day walk hand in hand with Ivy along the lazy back roads or by the quiet winding river of his village and enjoy a few moments of simple, silent peace. Right now, that's all he truly wanted.

Around noon the following day, after traversing miles of dirt roads, soft grassy fields and desolate patches of hard, stony ground, Nicholas and Leo paused near the entrance of Gliwice Gap in the southwestern arm of the Trent Hills. The skies had turned cloudy and the air was damp, but the two travelers' spirits were lifted as they had arrived this far without any problems other than a lack of sleep and some aching muscles.

"So far, so good," Leo said. "Tolapari's instructions were right on target."

"Now another day of traveling through these hills until we see the woods of the Cashua," Nicholas replied. "Yet as pleasant as this stage of the journey has been, I'll be glad to slip into the trees for more privacy. The farther we go, the more uneasy I become."

"I understand. That thing around your neck must be a weight on your mind."

Nicholas nodded. "Though I keep it hidden, I sometimes imagine that people we've passed on the road somehow suspect that

NICHOLAS RAVEN AND THE WIZARDS' WEB - VOLUME 2

I'm carrying something of value, something dangerous." He appeared slightly embarrassed by his confession. "Perhaps that sounded silly, but it is how I feel. I'll be glad when Frist reshapes it into a proper key for us."

Leo chuckled. "So instead of a medallion around your neck, you'll have a key. And we'll have to retrace our journey back to Morrenwood with an even more perilous object in our possession. But that's what we agreed to do."

"Yes," Nicholas replied as he imagined a ship sailing toward the Northern Isles upon restless waves. Pangs of guilt swept over him, nearly causing him to reveal his plan to abandon Leo and search for Ivy after their mission. But he held his tongue. "That is the task we agreed to, Leo. And it will be done–one way or another."

"I'm sure of it," he replied, looking askance at Nicholas when hearing the faraway tone in his friend's voice. He knew something was on his mind, but didn't pursue it. Leo snapped the reins of his horse and led the way into Gliwice Gap, signaling with a smile and an easy sense of confidence for Nicholas to follow.

Gliwice Gap stretched on for about five miles, the slightly undulating landscape winding here and there and varying in width at spots for up to a mile or more. They crossed several streams flowing down from both the northern and southern hills, the clear, crisp water reflecting the ashen skies like a finely polished mirror. Acres of lush pine and nearly leafless trees dotted the landscape. Occasional farmhouses were visible in the distance as they neared the western border of Arrondale. Neither Nicholas nor Leo had ever stepped foot outside the kingdom and both looked forward to the sights and adventure that awaited them.

Several hours passed uneventfully as the majority of their path took them through deserted woodland or fallow pastures awaiting a distant spring. Both were happy to see cattle grazing near a haystack at one point, though they encountered no one to talk to on the few roads they traveled upon. They took their time passing through Gliwice Gap since they had no plans to enter the Cashua Forest until the following morning. They only wanted to arrive at the edge of the woods before dark to allow themselves some rest before the more difficult part of the journey commenced.

Near mid-afternoon with about a mile to go before leaving the Gap, they observed in awe the distant green swath of the Cashua

Forest looming on the western horizon. They stopped to eat an early dinner which they washed down with cold stream water. Nicholas gazed in the distance, more eager than ever to reach the edge of the woods before sundown.

"I see a farmhouse beyond that next field," he said, pointing. "We can try to sell our horses there. I hope you're ready for some serious walking."

"Suddenly this adventure is going to require a bit more effort," Leo joked. "Too late to turn back?"

Nicholas laughed. "Such talk won't stand you in good stead with Princess Megan."

"Or her grandfather," he replied. "King Justin seems amiable and formidable at the same time. But I think he took a liking to me, at least from what Megan said." As Leo sat in the grass leaning back on his hands, he couldn't help but chuckle in the cool serenity of the late afternoon.

"What's so funny?" Nicholas asked, munching on a biscuit.

"Just realizing where I am," he replied. "Not long ago I was selling apples for my father up and down Orchard Road and cleaning out horse stalls with Henry. Now I've been to the Blue Citadel, met the King of Arrondale and am smitten with his granddaughter, a princess." He looked at Nicholas, his face scrunched up in disbelief. "How did that happen?"

Nicholas laughed. "I'm still wondering why I was framed for robbery, accused of murder and run out of town. And you expect me to figure out *your* life? We should give up worrying about the *whys* and just see where it leads us."

"Maybe that's all we can do," he agreed. He stood up and brushed the grass off his pants. "In the meantime, let's sell these horses and get to the woods. Daylight is fading fast, and with these thickening clouds, we'll get no help from the Fox Moon."

They continued on, arriving at the farmhouse and successfully making a deal with its owner to buy the pair of horses, claiming they were going to explore the Cashua Forest before seeking out their fortune and a new life along the narrow stretch of land surrounding the eastern edge of the Dunn Hills. While examining the horses near the main house, the farmer introduced himself as Larry Kerns and wondered why the two men were leaving so late in the year.

"We like to take risks," Leo said, putting on an air of bravado as he leaned against one of the horses with his arms folded. "We wanted a little adventure on the way to our new lives, whatever they turn out to be. Things back home on the farm were getting dull. I mean, how many crates of apples can a man pick every year before going completely mad? And don't get me started on raking out the horse stalls day after day, right, Nick?"

"Something like that," he replied, biting the inside of his cheek to keep from laughing at Leo's slightly dramatic burst. But whether the farmer believed Leo's story or not, he didn't indicate one way or another.

"Well good luck to you both wherever you end up," Mr. Kerns said as they concluded their deal. "I hear that many young and adventurous souls have built lives for themselves in the villages scattered up and down the Crescent. But it must be a hard, lonely existence, lodged in that narrow strip between the sea and the forest with no one to protect them except themselves."

"We'll put in a good word for Arrondale," Nicholas said. "Perhaps one day they'll petition to join our kingdom."

"Don't know about that. Most there are fiercely independent from what I've been told," Mr. Kerns replied. "Still, I hear stories from people passing this way from the west that men from the Northern Isles have been sailing into the area. I'm not sure why, but maybe they've got their eyes on expanding onto the mainland. The protection of King Justin might not be such a bad thing for them."

"We've heard similar rumors," Leo said.

"It's more than rumor," the farmer insisted before raising his head and sniffing the air as a smile appeared on his face. "I smell bacon from my wife's kitchen!"

To the delight of Nicholas and Leo, they were invited to sit down to a meal of bacon stew and freshly baked apple bread with Mr. Kerns and his wife who allowed them to sleep in their barn that night. And though it would delay an early start the next day as they would still have to travel the remaining distance to the Cashua Forest, the two men felt that a fine meal and a good night's rest were worth it. By early evening, each was sound asleep on a warm pile of straw, blissfully unaware of the handful of horses and cows sharing their quarters that night.

The sun peeked over the eastern horizon the following morning, casting its cold, pale light through a veil of torn clouds and swirling mist. After trudging to the barn and waking Nicholas and Leo, Mr. Kerns invited them to the house for an early breakfast. While seated at the table, the farmer insisted that they ride their former horses the rest of the way to the forest to save them some traveling time.

"I'll ride with you and take my purchases back with me," he said, envying their journey. "Besides, I deserve an occasional break from the farm and intend to take one."

Nicholas smiled gratefully as he savored a cup of hot tea while relishing the sound of crackling wood ablaze in the fireplace. "We appreciate the offer, Mr. Kerns, and gladly accept, though you and your wife have been far too generous already."

"Happy to do it," he said, cutting into a fried pork chop that Mrs. Kerns had just set upon his plate.

"I'll fix you up some breakfast leftovers along with bread, apples and cheese to take with you," she added. "Who knows how long it'll be until you're with people again? Can't have you starving to death in the middle of the forest."

Shortly after, as the mist evaporated and the morning shadows lazily stretched across the sleepy autumn landscape, the trio departed the farmhouse. Mrs. Kerns waved goodbye near the front door, telling her husband she expected him back before lunchtime as he still had chores to do. He promised her so as the trio disappeared down the road.

The journey to the border of the Cashua took less than two hours, though longer than Nicholas and Leo had hoped since Mr. Kerns was far more interested in telling them stories and pointing out and discussing particular parts of the landscape. But as the man and his wife had been so kind to them, they happily showed an interest in his enthusiastic offerings. They traveled slightly southwest after leaving the Gliwice Gap as Tolapari had instructed until they reached the edge of the woods. There they dismounted and returned the horses to Mr. Kerns, thanking him several times over for his help as they donned their heavily laden backpacks for the journey ahead.

"You'll have several days of hiking before you," the farmer said, "though the falling leaves will allow you more daylight on your way. Still, watch yourselves. I suspect some of the terrain will be treacherous."

"But it'll be many days and miles less compared to going around the forest," Nicholas said. "Or at least I hope so, assuming we don't get lost."

"Thanks again," Leo said as he and Nicholas shook hands with Mr. Kerns and watched him depart with the horses Nedry had given them three nights ago. The two travelers turned around and faced the Cashua Forest, its leaves shedding and brilliant color fading as autumn raced past its midpoint. The vast collection of maple, beech, elm and pine trees solemnly welcomed them with a bittersweet scent of fallen foliage, pungent soil and stony silence, punctuated occasionally by the caw of a distant crow or the sound of a blue jay winging over the grand and thinning canopy.

Nicholas glanced at Leo, noting the same tinge of uncertainty in his eyes that he himself was feeling. "Well, no sense thinking about it any longer. Let's go," he said. "It's about time we earned those extravagant wages the King is paying us for this mission."

"Remind me how much," Leo quietly remarked as the two men stepped into the woods, the crunch of dry leaves underfoot sounding like harsh whispers.

CHAPTER 49

Cashua Forest

Clouds thickened as morning progressed, dampening Nicholas and Leo's spirits as they hiked across the leafy forest floor. Yet the sweet scents of damp wood, mossy undergrowth and rich soil slowly provided a homelike sense of comfort. The terrain proved easy at first as the ground was fairly level and the trees wide apart. But after two hours of hiking and a few stops for brief breaks, the woods gradually encroached upon them like troubling thoughts. When glancing over their shoulders, they noted that the visible edges of the forest had long disappeared.

"Tolapari mentioned a dry river bed and ravine a couple miles in," Leo said. "Shouldn't we have come upon that by now?"

"I would think so," Nicholas agreed, stopping to scan the area ahead. "Assuming we entered the woods at the right spot. Maybe we should veer a little more to our left. As the ground seems to gradually slope down that way, ancient streams would have fed into a river in that direction."

"Makes sense. Take your best guess and lead on."

"As long as I don't get blamed if we end up even more lost," Nicholas said. "Perhaps we should have gone around the forest."

"I don't know," he replied. "Tolapari showed us the maps. Going around would have added almost a hundred miles to our journey. And though it might've been easier on horseback, he wasn't sure how safe it would be if secrecy is our goal. We can't be sure that Island soldiers rafting up the Lorren River haven't made temporary settlements between the water and the western edge of the Cashua. If we encountered any, would they ignore us, question us–or worse?"

"Best not to chance it then."

"If we get through this forest, all we'll need to do is cross the river to the village of Woodwater. That'll be a treat compared to this," Leo added, indicating the vastness of the woodland with a sweep of his arm.

"It's not so bad," Nicholas said, slapping him on the shoulder as he hiked onward. "We've only started, after all. When we find the river bed, our situation will look better. Give it another day or two and you'll see."

"I'm just planning my schedule to dinnertime," he joked. "The next day or two seems about as far away to me as next month."

Two days later, they felt as if they had been traveling for a month, with no sign of a dry river bed or ravine in sight. Their spirits, not yet on the edge of despair, had deflated somewhat on this third day of wandering in the Cashua. Their limbs ached and their feet were sore, causing them to stop now and then to tend to annoying blisters or sheer exhaustion. At one point, Nicholas signaled for a halt as they passed through some brambly undergrowth near a small stream to soak a particularly sore foot in the water despite its icy coolness. After quickly drying off, he replaced his heavy sock and boot and plopped down on the ground against a tree trunk.

"I need a nap, Leo. Even more so than food."

Leo nodded, his eyes and expression tinged with fatigue. "Me too." He sat down nearby, unable to keep his eyelids open. "So why don't we do just that? We'll kill ourselves if we keep up this pace."

"Being lost makes you step things up a bit, doesn't it?"

Leo closed his eyes. "Did Tolapari specifically mention when he last hiked through these woods? Maybe that river bed has been overgrown for years."

"Or we missed it completely–which doesn't say much for our sense of direction."

"At least we can build a fire," Leo replied lethargically, unable to suppress a yawn. His head slowly dropped to his chest. "I'm taking you up on that nap idea. Wake me–*whenever...*"

"Sure..." Nicholas mumbled, too exhausted to argue or care. He also succumbed to his need for rest and promptly fell asleep against the tree as if it were a comfortable chair.

Neither man moved for several hours, finally opening their eyes as the sun dipped in the southwest and dusky twilight advanced like stealthy soldiers through the tall trees. The air was cold and damp, and the woods silent. They quickly got to their feet when they realized how long they had slept, their muscles aching and chilled. Neither particularly cared that they were behind whatever schedule they had once prepared within the walls of the Blue Citadel since both realized how sleep-deprived this adventure had rendered them. Reality in the wild was turning out to be quite different from the map work and conversations back in Morrenwood. The two travelers, now revived, moved forward in silence, planning to hike as far as the fading light would allow them. They hoped their fourth day tomorrow would prove more productive.

They awoke the next morning after spending the night bundled up beneath a thicket of pine trees whose invigorating scent nourished them almost as much as their breakfast. Despite the long nap they had taken before settling down the previous evening, neither had awakened once during the passing night.

"We have no excuse to be tired today," Nicholas said as he cleaned off a metal skillet and repacked it in his bundle. "And the longer we travel, the lighter our loads get."

"Not too light, I hope. Our food has to last until we're out of the woods," Leo said, "or we'll be eating utensils and spare clothes."

"If we keep heading west, we'll be okay. I've given up on finding any dry river bed or ravine that might've made our hike easier. We'll have a word with Tolapari next time we see him. But I suppose even a wizard can make a mistake from time to time."

Leo grunted with laughter. "I guess so! Just look at Vellan. He's one continuous mistake if you ask me–though I don't think I'd say that to his face if I ever met the man. He'd probably turn me into a worm or freeze my blood."

"Or make you scrub all the floors in his stronghold."

"That actually would be worse," he deadpanned. "I can't imagine us having a mug of ale with him as we did with Tolapari. They're two very different wizards, I'm sure."

"And if we help to destroy his Enâri pets," Nicholas added, "he'd be the last person either of us would want to see. So maybe being stuck here in these woods for a while isn't so bad. Imagine visiting Kargoth?"

"Only in my worst dream." Leo donned his heavy pack for what seemed the hundredth time in the last few days. "Ready for another lovely stroll through the woods?"

"I'm ready, but I'm not so sure about my feet," he said while fixing his pack. "But lead on. They'll catch up eventually."

"That's the attitude," Leo cheerfully said, feeling much better with a full stomach and a rested body.

They trudged onward as clouds drifted overhead, hoping for a glimpse of the sun at least once today before darkness descended. By late morning they had gotten their wish as a small patch of blue slowly opened up above them, growing wider as the clouds began to break on a freshening breeze. Soon the sun was out in her full glory, crossing the southern sky while lighting their way and their spirits. And though the temperature had cooled somewhat at the same time, both were happy for the tradeoff.

The rest of that day and midway into the next was blessed with clean, mischievous gusts brushing across the treetops and swirling the fallen leaves like confetti. The incessant creaking of the swaying branches proved intimidating at first, but after a few hours the two hikers grew accustomed to the sound. Near sunset, the weather calmed and feathery clouds tinted red and orange drifted overhead among the first budding stars. After dinner, they fell asleep close to the fading fire and awoke the next morning to a pile of cold, gray ash, marking the start of their sixth day inside the Cashua.

"After we return from Wolf Lake, we might consider going around the woods on our way back," Leo suggested later that afternoon as they marched through the seemingly never-ending forest. His pace was brisk as he led the way up a slight incline and through a patch of dried fern. They maneuvered around several stunted trees overshadowed by the larger canopy of maple and pine towering above them. "By then we'll know what kind of opposition we face from the Isles. If the way is safe, it'll be quicker."

"You may be right," Nicholas said coolly as he marched a few steps behind his friend, wondering if maybe he should now tell Leo about his plan to separate after their mission so he could search for Ivy. Perhaps a little forewarning might be the wisest approach. Leo would be on his own for most of the return journey. It wouldn't be fair to spring the news on him at the last moment.

Nicholas now regretted not having more people in their group. Though he and Leo planned to hire a guide in the village of Woodwater to lead them to Wolf Lake, that guide would only return to Woodwater when the mission was done. After that, Leo would be alone with the key to the Spirit Box. Nicholas considered the fate of their mission if Leo was injured or lost. His departure might put the lives of many at risk. He wondered if he had a right to ask Leo to shoulder this task alone to suit his own purposes. He decided to tell Leo of his plan, knowing he owed his friend that much.

He looked up, seeing Leo's backpack swiftly moving several yards ahead. "Leo, I need to—"

"Nicholas!" He stopped and spun around, up to his waist in fern and grinning as if he had just stumbled upon hidden treasure. "You won't believe what I found."

"What?" he asked curiously as he ran toward his friend. "You look as if you—" His jaw dropped as he gazed past the sea of fern.

Several yards ahead, beyond the muted shades of greens and browns, the ground suddenly opened up. A narrow fissure ran roughly east to west for many yards and was only visible at this higher elevation. They looked at one another with renewed hope, realizing that Tolapari had been partially correct.

"The ravine at last," Nicholas whispered as he inched up to the edge and looked down at a drop of forty feet. It was about twenty-five feet to the opposite side. The bottom was littered with stones, weeds and rotting branches.

"We apparently entered the woods at the wrong spot and missed earlier sections of this completely, or Tolapari's memory of where he encountered the ravine was a little off," Leo said. "In either case we found it, so our way out of here should be easier."

"*Should* be," Nicholas remarked. "I hope we haven't walked in circles and are just picking up this trail now when we should have days ago."

"Too late to worry about that. Shall we climb down?" he asked. "It doesn't look too steep and there are plenty of crevices in the rock face."

"Let's follow it on top for a bit first," Nicholas replied. "Maybe we'll find an easier spot to climb down. Anyway, we'll have a better view from up here."

They continued along the edge of the ravine for a short time, happy at last to have a proper path to follow. Within the half hour, the terrain gradually sloped downward, the ground grew barer and the steepest sides of the ravine lessened in height. They climbed down what remained of the rocky edge so as to give themselves something of a challenge before the ravine itself disappeared.

Leo went over first, getting a steady foothold on the rock face before lowering himself. There were plenty of fissures and small outcrops in the dark rock to grab onto, as well as a few slender trees that had taken root. Nicholas followed, pleased with the ease at which he and Leo descended to the dry river bed below. In a few minutes they were on the bottom looking up.

"Let's follow this path before the light fades in a few hours," Nicholas said between sips from his water skin.

They moved forward along the weedy, bumpy terrain, observing the cliffs on either side of the narrow passageway. Parts were bare rock while other sections were coated with damp moss, fern or tree saplings that had sprouted from some of the soil-filled crevices. And though the path was no easier to traverse than any other part of the woods, at least it provided a visual feast from the monotony that the weary travelers had endured for six days.

After stopping for a short break an hour later, they moved on for one more hike before nightfall, eventually making camp near a large outcropping of rock that provided a bit of shelter. And while the dry river bed was still visible, this portion of the ravine walls had gradually disappeared into the landscape so that the travelers saw level ground beyond on either side. Soon they built a small fire, ate a meager meal and were off to sleep as the crescent Bear Moon drifted overhead toward the west. Both were eager to get an early start hiking the following morning.

They made swift progress through the Cashua Forest the next day, or at least they thought so now that there was a semblance of a path to follow. But by early afternoon the skies darkened and a steady rain fell, deflating their spirits and lessening their pace. With a muddy ground coated with slippery leaves, their progress slowed to a near standstill. Bone-chilling dampness permeated every layer of clothing. After a few more hours battling the elements, Leo pointed out a thicket of tall pines which would serve as shelter. Nicholas needed no convincing and followed him underneath one of the tallest and fullest trees where it was nearly dry and heavy with the scent of pine. The large, lower branches were splayed out like protective arms, thick with needles and providing adequate roofing.

"No chance of starting a fire tonight," Leo muttered tiredly as he removed his pack and sat against a tree trunk. "Besides, I'm too tired to start one anyway."

"I just want to sleep," Nicholas replied, equally exhausted as he reclined against the opposite side of the trunk. He was too cold and weary even to fish out something to eat from his backpack, grabbing instead only the driest blanket he could find to wrap around himself. He sneezed a few times and felt a chill run through him before the steady patter of raindrops lulled him into a deep but restless sleep.

When he opened his eyes later the next day, the rain was steadily falling and the daylight gray and miserable, but a current of warm air and the scent of smoke permeated the area. He was lying on the ground, still wrapped in a blanket and using the corner of his pack as a pillow. He slowly sat up, felling chilled and achy, yet managed a brief smile when seeing the small fire blazing a few feet away. He noticed Leo standing near the edge of the tree, gazing into the drenched woodland.

"How'd you manage that?" he asked, indicating the fire with a tilt of his head when Leo turned around.

"The rain let up a few hours ago while you were dead to the world. I went out and gathered what dry sticks I could find buried beneath the leaves," he said amid the rising sweet smoke. "I filled our water bottles in a nearby stream, too. So drink up. We can refill them when we leave."

"What time is it?"

162

"Probably past noon."

"At least one of us has been productive today," Nicholas said, lying back down, his body plagued by a bone-deep lethargy. "I don't think I can hike today, Leo. I feel awful."

"You *look* awful," he replied, noting his friend's pale color. "You're not going to put in any miles today. I'll make us something to eat, then you can go back to sleep."

"I won't argue."

"This heavy rain is going to stick around for a while," he added. "We wouldn't have made much progress anyway and we both could use a day off."

They remained beneath the pines for the rest of that day until shortly past noon the next, sleeping away most of the hours and regaining their strength and stamina. When Nicholas opened his eyes again, his head felt cool and light. The air smelled sweet, and despite the lingering gray clouds, the rain had ceased and the sky lightened. He sat up with little difficulty and breathed freely, relieved that whatever sickness had briefly infected him had left. Leo was sound asleep nearby next to a low fire and Nicholas allowed him to rest until he awoke on his own about an hour later. After a meal of ham, potatoes and bread, the refreshed travelers abandoned their shelter beneath the pines and continued on, certain that the western edge of the Cashua Forest couldn't be much farther away.

After putting several more miles behind them that day and early into the next, the traces of dry river bed disappeared due to years of wild undergrowth, soil erosion and the ravages of time. Just like at the start of their journey, they would have to trust to luck and what hiking skills they had developed to traverse the final miles of their road. When they stopped for lunch beside a stream, Nicholas again considered telling Leo of his idea to search for Ivy. He quietly laughed to himself. If he couldn't make it out of the Cashua, how would he ever find his way out of the Dunn Hills? He wondered if his ambitions for a search and rescue mission were out of proportion to his strength and abilities, deciding to keep his plan secret for a little while longer.

"I will never complain about the monotony of the apple run if I ever make deliveries for my father again," Leo said while munching on one of their last apples as he sat against a slender elm.

Patches of blue sky were visible through a parade of grayish-white clouds that sailed overheard. "After slogging through this forest, driving up and down Orchard Road with a cart full of apple crates will feel like an easy dream."

"Even with Princess Megan at your side giving you an earful?" Nicholas joked.

"Especially with that," he replied with a smile. "I wonder what she's doing right now. I do miss her so. I'm glad my father came across the two of you on the road. My life would be as dull as river rocks right now if he hadn't."

"A little dullness might not be such a bad thing–at least for a day or two," Nicholas said as he refilled his water skin in the stream. "I've never worked so hard in my life as I have these past few weeks." He secured his pack before hoisting it upon his back, indicating that it was time to go. Leo nodded and reluctantly stood up, convincing his mind and legs that they needed to navigate several more miles of hard ground and forest before he could rest again.

But one by one, the monotonous hours drifted by as they had done since entering the Cashua Forest nine days ago. The hikers made steady progress, yet with every passing mile, they began to wonder if their food supplies would hold out before they reached civilization. Other than a few squirrels or an occasional deer, they had encountered little wildlife. If it came to hunting for a meal, the pickings would be scarce.

About an hour before sunset, the hikers collectively slumped their shoulders when a steep bank dotted with trees loomed in the distance. As it stretched north and south as far as they could see in the deepening gloom, there was no way to go around it without going off course. Neither man wanted to attempt the climb so late in the day as they were tired and hungry, yet putting off the climb until morning would waste an hour of daylight.

Nicholas looked discouragingly up the hill as he ground one foot into the soil, his arms akimbo. He glanced at Leo, seeing the same weary attitude reflected back.

"I'm beyond tired, but I'd rather do this now than tomorrow," he said. "You?"

Leo smirked, feeling as if fate were keeping them from their real task. "I'd hate to make camp here and let the light go to waste. It'd feel like we we're going backward."

Nicholas fished out a biscuit from his pack and split it between them. After they drank some water, the two men began the slow and steady ascent up the hill, slippery with loose soil and leaves. They grabbed onto small trees along the way to keep steady and pull themselves forward, stopping several times to catch their breaths. It proved a grueling climb so late in the day when dinner and a full night's sleep beckoned to them.

They made it halfway up the hill as the last rays of sunlight cut across the trees from the southwest. The clouds had thinned even more during the day so that now large patches of deep blue sky were visible. A handful of the brightest stars were just noticeable in the dying light. Leo finally signaled for them to rest briefly and drink some water. But just as they were prepared to continue on, a distant sound caught their attention. They glanced at each other, momentarily questioning their senses.

Leo raised an eyebrow. "Was *that*...?"

Nicholas held up a hand, his ears searching out the twilight sounds playing on the night breezes. Several long moments later they heard it again, the very same sound.

"We're not hearing things, Leo," he said with a smile.

Suddenly the two men continued their climb with renewed vigor, digging their boots into the stubborn soil, grabbing thin tree trunks and branches to help pull them up, all the while ignoring previous aches and pains and heavy shoulder packs as a new energy spurred them up the hill in the last remnants of golden sunlight. When they finally reached the top, they stood upright again and the pressure on their backs and knees disappeared. They encountered another stretch of trees before them, yet their hearts beat with unbearable joy because they could see wide swaths of countryside splashed in shades of purple twilight just beyond.

They raced through the woods until they finally emerged into the open air of a cool autumn evening, having at last escaped the confines of the Cashua. The vast dome of the sky was dotted with icy stars, and the glow of the Bear Moon, just past first quarter, rose high in the east amid a trace of gauzy clouds. They stood on the edge of a wide field in the local farming district with patches of dry grass beneath their well-worn boots, though at the moment it felt like soft feathers after the punishing terrain inside the forest. About a half mile to the southwest, Leo pointed out the subtle yellow glow of a farmhouse silhouetted against the horizon. A moment later, the two men heard the noise that had caught their attention earlier, grinning at one another in the fading light.

"*Cows*," Nicholas said, delighted with the discovery. "And they never sounded so sweet."

CHAPTER 50

Some Friendly Assistance

Nicholas and Leo made camp along the edge of the woods. Having escaped the suffocating confines of the Cashua Forest, they were too exhausted to explore the open region that greeted them like a long, lost friend. After starting a small fire and enjoying a leisurely dinner from their thinning food supplies, the two men drifted off to sleep under a veil of stars, neither one waking even once during the long, cold night.

Not until midmorning the following day did they finally stir, but the travelers felt only partially refreshed after their ordeal, each yearning for more rest. Nicholas gazed out upon a vista of browning fields and scattered trees, knowing he and Leo would have to continue hiking west to find the Lorren River.

"It shouldn't be too far to the water," he told Leo after glancing at his map. "A few miles at most. The village of Woodwater is on the opposite side."

"So what are we waiting for?" he replied, eager to move on.

Less than two hours later, after trudging across vast, windswept fields, crossing an occasional stream or following wheel-rutted dirt roads, they finally saw the Lorren River looming ahead. It cut through the land as it snaked down from the distant Northern Mountains and emptied into the Trillium Sea. But when they reached its eastern bank, their hearts sank as they stared across the water at another vast stretch of grass and scrubland.

"We obviously missed the mark," Nicholas said, wondering if they had exited the woods either too far to the north or the south. "No sign of any village here. So which direction do we take?"

Leo shrugged, shading his eyes as he scanned the area. "I don't see signs of civilization anywhere. Not even a trail of chimney smoke to give us a clue."

"My instincts tell me we should head south. Agreed?" he asked, getting a nod of approval from Leo. After walking along the banks of the Lorren for less than an hour, their choice was confirmed. A farmer, hauling a cartload of fresh hay, happily stopped to give them directions.

"Woodwater's a good seven or eight miles more to the south," he stated, indicating the way with a thumb pointed across his shoulder. "But you'll have to cross the river to get there."

They thanked him for his assistance, realizing they had emerged from the Cashua Forest too far north. Both hungrily plodded ahead through grassy fields and patches of woodland. But as twilight approached, a scattering of lights appeared one by one across the Lorren River less than a mile to the south, giving them hope that the punishing trek had been worth the struggle. The village of Woodwater was at last in sight.

"Finally!" Nicholas said, a sense of relief washing over him.

He and Leo had hurried to cover the remaining distance to a point on the Lorren River opposite the village. The glow of the waxing gibbous Bear Moon rising in the east behind a veil of clouds cast a cool, silvery light upon the dark waters of the river. The two shadowy figures stood on the edge of the Lorren and gazed across, their white breaths rising in the cold autumn night. Tomorrow they would find a way to the other side, but for now they basked in the pride of having traveled so far in their quest.

Nicholas recalled looking at a map of this area in one of King Justin's chambers, tracing the length of the Lorren River with his finger and wondering if he and Leo had the will and stamina to reach the waterway. But now that he actually stood upon its grassy banks, he felt there was nothing he couldn't do if he put his mind to the task–including finding and rescuing Ivy. A sense of renewed hope seized him. He could hardly wait until morning to continue.

Leo nudged him with an elbow. "What's that?" he said, pointing downriver to the north.

Nicholas turned and focused on the spot about a quarter mile away on the water. A faint glow of what appeared to be three torch lights floating down the river grabbed his attention. He and Leo gazed at them curiously, amused and mesmerized by the weird sight of floating points of light in the middle of the Lorren. Moments later, Nicholas detected the vague outline of three large log rafts, each one with several men upon it methodically poling upriver. He suddenly understood what he was seeing and flopped onto the grass bank, pulling Leo down with him.

"What are you–?"

"*Shhh!*" he whispered, lying on his stomach and pointing across the water. "Those are troops from the Northern Isles," he softly said.

Leo focused as the men and rafts drifted closer into view, his mouth agape. "You're right," he whispered back, estimating about a dozen men on each of the three, long rafts. A single torch had been affixed to the front of each vessel, and as they passed through a shaft of moonlight, Leo noted that the rafts were also laden with several wooden crates, barrels and other supplies covered with canvas tarps.

"They're heading upriver into the Northern Mountains to Kargoth," Nicholas said, imagining the long and lonely journey ahead for those men. "It makes our trek in the Cashua seem like a stroll through the countryside."

"And there's nobody here to stop them. The Islanders have free rein to do what they want."

Nicholas sighed. "So it seems."

As there was no established kingdom or standing army in this thinly populated strip of Laparia, troops from the Northern Isles expected no resistance to their plan to supply Kargoth with men, weapons and goods. Nicholas wondered if the Islanders would have designs on this region afterward. Now that they had arrived, what was stopping them from establishing a permanent colony? They had invaded Montavia in the east and would soon engage a large portion of King Justin's troops in battle there. But what forces would stop them here in the west? Now more than ever, the urgency of his and

Leo's mission became clear. The key had to be reforged and the Enâri destroyed to give Arrondale and the other free realms a fighting chance against the forces of Vellan.

Several minutes later after the three rafts had poled upriver and out of sight, Nicholas and Leo stood and brushed themselves off, fully realizing the danger they faced. They moved on in gloomy silence to find a place to pass the night.

Billowing clouds of gray and black filled the sky late the following morning, threatening to unleash a harsh rainfall at any moment. Nicholas and Leo had slept long past daybreak beneath a clump of pine trees on a field's edge close to the river. They needed to find better shelter soon or risk getting soaked. A farmhouse lay about a half mile up a dirt road and the two men decided to seek refuge there. Afterward, they would contact the owner about securing passage across the river to Woodwater and hopefully obtain information about the Island troops in the process.

Raindrops pelted the ground minutes later as they raced across a narrow stretch of field to a large, whitewashed barn. They rushed inside, greeted by the smell of damp hay and dirty stalls. Several cows and a few horses grazed contentedly outdoors in an adjacent field, unfazed by the weather. A stone house, guarded by a few bare maple trees, stood several yards away down a dirt pathway, its chimney releasing curls of bluish smoke into the raucous skies.

"Let's schedule our next mission in summertime," Nicholas joked as he pulled out his water skin and took several refreshing gulps. "I'd prefer more accommodating weather."

"I'll mention your suggestion to Nedry," Leo said, setting down his backpack to enjoy a much needed stretch. He peered outdoors at the pounding rain, knowing they might be stuck here for some time. The steady patter upon the roof sounded both melancholy and hypnotic.

"When it lets up, we'll knock at the house and see about getting across the Lorren," Nicholas said, removing his pack as well. "Maybe the owner can recommend an experienced guide in Woodwater."

"One we can afford." Leo plopped down on the ground and reclined against his pack. "We need to buy more food supplies, too. I think we're down to biscuit crumbs and moldy cheese."

"You're the apple salesman. I'll leave the negotiating to you."

"I won't disappoint you," Leo replied, closing his eyes. "Now if you'll excuse me, I'd like to take a short nap as long as we're trapped here."

"Rest away," Nicholas replied, strolling about the barn to examine the interior. He recalled life back on Maynard Kurtz's farm and all the hours he had spent there working the fields, tending to the animals and mending broken fences. It seemed like a lifetime ago.

He wondered how Maynard was carrying on, hoping his adoptive father would forgive him for running away should he ever return. But now that Maynard was acting mayor according to King Justin, perhaps the man had no time to worry about such things. He wasn't the only person in the world with problems, after all. But before Nicholas could ponder the matter further, he detected a fleeting shadow behind him and spun around, standing face to face with a man holding up the pointed end of a pitchfork aimed directly at his chest.

"Mind telling me exactly where you two came from?" the man asked, his voice steady and confident. He was about twice Nicholas' age, unshaven, and his head of hair in desperate need of combing.

Nicholas took a step back as Leo snapped opened his eyes. Both looked fearfully at the man who presumably owned the property. Leo swallowed and sat up on the floor, scuttling backward on his hands and feet to a safe distance before standing up.

"We apologize for trespassing," Nicholas said, "but we needed a place to get out of the rain. We don't mean any harm and will leave right now if you want."

The man suspiciously glanced at their backpacks. "You from around these parts?" They simultaneously shook their heads. "Then where are you from? And more importantly, where are you going?"

"We're from Arrondale," Leo said calmly. "My friend, Nicholas Raven, is from the village of Kanesbury. I'm from a small place called Minago. My name is Leo Marsh."

"We just spent nine days hiking through the Cashua Forest and are on our way into the Dunn Hills," Nicholas added. "But first we need to cross the river to Woodwater and find ourselves a guide and buy some supplies."

The man lowered the pitchfork slightly, inclined to believe the two young men by the tone of their voices, but his fears and suspicions were still not allayed. "What's so important in the Dunn Hills that you traipsed all the way here from Arrondale?"

Nicholas and Leo looked at one another, not prepared to reveal the details of their mission. Yet both knew they had to tell the man something if they were to leave unscathed.

"The reason for our trip is personal, though we may be able to give you some details later," Nicholas said. "But you must believe us that we don't want to cause you any trouble. All we're looking for is a way across the river and a guide for our journey."

"That's all you need?" the man asked.

"Well, a bath, a shave and a few days of rest wouldn't hurt either," Leo uncomfortably joked as he combed a hand through his hair, hoping to appear less threatening.

As the man continued to study them intently, Nicholas thought he detected a flicker of growing trust in his wide, brown eyes. "What's your name, if I may ask?"

"You may ask, though I'm not prepared to answer just yet." The man turned to Leo. "Name the King of Morrenwood."

"*Huh?*"

"Tell me the name of the King of Morrenwood. You say you're from Arrondale, so you should know. It's a simple request."

"King Justin," he said matter-of-factly.

"And his son?" he added, pointing at Nicholas. "Quick!"

"Prince Gregory," Nicholas replied with a straight face, slightly amused that this man was testing their honesty but not wanting to show it.

The man nodded and lowered the pitch fork. "Prince Gregory. Correct. Most people claiming to be from Arrondale might have known King Justin's name, but few, I suppose, would have recalled his son's name so quickly. So I'm guessing you're not with those troublemaking men from the Northern Isles."

"They're the last people we want to see," Nicholas said, explaining how he and Leo saw three rafts floating up the river the previous night. "We're fully aware of their incursion into this area and their mission to supply Kargoth. You can trust Leo and me when we say that the allies of Vellan are no friends of ours."

"That's good to hear," the man said, rubbing his curious face. "Will Fish. That's my name. And I've decided to trust you up to a point. For now anyway. But tell me, how do you know so much about what the Islanders are up to? Why exactly are you here?"

Nicholas and Leo hesitated, at a loss for words. They knew they had to be careful about revealing explicit details of their mission, yet needed this man's help to continue on their journey. Leo indicated for Nicholas to play along.

"Mr. Fish, at the risk of jeopardizing our safety, I'm going to tell you that Nicholas and I are here at King Justin's bidding." Both Will Fish and Nicholas nearly gasped at his statement. "We're on a secret mission, and should you wish to assist us, your help will be greatly appreciated."

The farmer leaned on the handle of his pitchfork, intrigued as he eyed the two men with renewed wonder. "I don't know if I totally believe you, gentlemen, but you definitely have my attention. Let's discuss this further over a bowl of hot corn chowder my wife is fixing for lunch. This rain is chilling me to the bone."

Within the next hour, Nicholas and Leo were each polishing off a second helping of corn chowder with buttered bread and fresh milk at the Fishes' kitchen table. Will and his wife, Beth Ann, along with their two teenage sons and a younger daughter, were excited to have unexpected company during this dreary time of year. All quickly warmed up to their guests and treated them as if they were long-lost relatives. Beth Ann served tea and honey biscuits after the meal while one of her sons added more wood to the fireplace. Outside, murky skies deluged the landscape with rain and raw breezes, glazing the window panes with rippling sheets of gray water. Inside, however, Nicholas and Leo savored the joyful and talkative mayhem that surrounded them, thankful for a welcomed respite from the grueling rigors of the road.

But as the afternoon wore on and the rain showed no sign of letting up, Beth Ann suggested that they spend the night in the barn, refusing to take no for an answer. It took little cajoling on her part for them to accept since both admitted that a few days of rest would be more beneficial to the speed and success of their journey than simply plowing onward while sore and exhausted. Mrs. Fish playfully ordered her husband and their two guests off to another part of the house, knowing they had much to discuss in private.

"The children and I will clean up the kitchen while you all talk about the goings-on up and down the river," she said with a motherly sort of smile as she refilled Nicholas and Leo's mugs with tea. She handed her husband his pipe and a small pouch of tobacco before shooing them out of the room. "Holler if you need anything."

"Thanks, Mrs. Fish," Nicholas said, his voice trailing off through the doorway.

Several minutes later the three men sat in wooden chairs beneath a cloud of pipe smoke in front of a small fireplace. Leo carefully detailed a less-than-truthful version of their mission, but only with the best of intentions. The safety of the Fishes and the ability to complete their task in secrecy was foremost on his mind. He explained to Will Fish that he and Nicholas were gathering information on the extent to which soldiers from the Northern Isles had overrun the area along the Lorren River and whether they intended to stay, mentioning nothing of the medallion.

"Other teams are exploring different areas in the region," he said, spreading out one of their maps before him for effect. "We'll report back to King Justin in the weeks ahead. Nicholas and I were ordered to hike into a nearby section of the Dunn Hills to see if there is any infiltration of Islanders there, too."

"So you're both royal spies?" Mr. Fish excitedly asked as he puffed on his pipe, filling the air with sweet smoke.

"Something like that," Nicholas said with a nod before slyly throwing an uneasy glance Leo's way. "For security reasons, we were reluctant to reveal our true intentions when we first met you."

"Of course. I understand completely," Will replied before giving them a rundown of recent Islander activity in the area. "It's a good hundred miles or so north to the Trillium Sea, so I can only imagine what the men from the Isles are doing down there when their ships come in. But out here, we see rafts filled with men and supplies poling upriver regularly. Thankfully, no one has come ashore in our area, but I've heard rumors how they've made camp miles north and south of here, occasionally plundering farms and households just for sport. You can see why I was quick with my pitchfork."

"Point well taken," Leo joked.

"Now that we understand each other," Will continued, "I know just the person to help you find your way into the Dunn Hills."

"*You?*" Nicholas asked.

"Good gracious, no!" he replied, nearly choking on his smoke. "I'm a farmer at heart, happy to remain here on my land. I was referring to my brother, Lane, who lives a few minutes down the road. He's always rowing a boat over to Woodwater, selling his homemade grape and apple wines, maple syrup, honey and whatnot, depending on the season."

Leo perked up. "He grows apples? Which variety? How many trees?"

Nicholas held up a hand. "Easy does it, Leo. No time for that discussion."

"Oh, sorry…"

"Anyway," Will continued, "if anyone is sure to find you a proper guide, it'll be Lane. He knows everybody in Woodwater. If my brother doesn't show up later today or by tomorrow, we'll visit him ourselves."

"That'd be terrific," Nicholas said gratefully. "We can't wait to meet him."

But as the rain continued falling relentlessly, there was no sign of Lane Fish or anyone else upon the road all afternoon or evening. Nicholas and Leo contentedly resigned themselves to the fact that they could spend a relaxing and uneventful evening in the company of newfound friends, renewing their stamina and spirits at the same time.

"I've boiled extra water and set it in the washroom in back," Mrs. Fish later informed them with an easy familiarity as if they had been lodging in her home for weeks. "You can each take turns cleaning up and shaving those scruffy faces before dinner. And if you have clean sets of clothes left in your packs, put them on. I'll wash all the others and hang them by the fire to dry so you'll be ready to travel properly. And no arguments from either of you!" she quickly added as Nicholas and Leo were on the verge of protesting her tireless assistance.

They did as instructed, and after enjoying a warm meal later that evening, Nicholas and Leo insisted that they would clean up the kitchen before retiring for the night. When the task was complete, they offered Will and Beth Ann their profound thanks before shuffling off to the barn. The rain had let up somewhat by then and they each passed a restful night on piles of warm hay beneath clean blankets until the milky gray light of dawn touched the eastern horizon.

The morning blossomed cool, dry and breezy. Clouds sailed overhead, allowing the sun to peek through and evaporate the remnants of yesterday's downpour. Nicholas and Leo sat down with the Fish family at midmorning for tea and bread when there was a knock at the door. Lane Fish popped his smiling head inside, happily greeting his niece and nephews who christened his arrival with shouts of joy. Lane, who was a few years older than his brother though similar in appearance, joined everyone at the table. Will filled him in on Nicholas and Leo's plan to explore the Dunn Hills, leaving out any mention of King Justin and the Northern Isles.

"If you'd like to take Mr. Raven and Mr. Marsh over to Woodwater and help them secure a proper guide, that would be most helpful," Will said to his brother.

"I'm taking a shipment over the day after tomorrow," Lane informed them. "You're welcome to come along. I know just the man for the job, too. His name is Hobin. More likely than not, we'll find him at the Mossy Rock."

"The Mossy Rock?" Leo asked curiously.

"A small eating establishment I like to frequent whenever I cross the river," he said. "Norma Delving serves a fine lamb stew there which, by the way, goes down nicely with some of my wines I'll be delivering. Norma owns and runs the Mossy Rock."

"Leo and I insist on buying you lunch in exchange for your help," Nicholas said. "It's the least we can do."

Lane thanked them for their offer and made arrangements to meet at midmorning in two days at his farm down the road. But for the rest of the current day and the next, Nicholas and Leo helped Will and his sons around the farm as repayment for the family's kindness. Will was grateful as there was fencing to be mended, stalls to be cleaned and other tasks piling up that had been delayed by the rain.

"I hire several locals to help during the busy growing season," Mr. Fish said, "but let them go by this time of year as I have my boys to rely on now that they're grown. But your assistance is appreciated. If you two ever wander back this way, stop by again."

"We promise to," Leo said, feeling as if he were back home in Minago. "Right, Nicholas?"

Nicholas looked up, fumbling his initial words as he sought a suitable reply. "Sure," he finally said, his voice slightly wavering. "If I ever pass this way, I'll be sure to knock on the front door instead of sneaking off to your barn."

Nicholas glanced at Leo, hoping his friend didn't detect his unease as he offered a strained smile. Time after time he had planned to tell him of his intention to separate after they completed their mission, yet he always found an excuse to back out. Now that he and Leo were getting closer to the Dunn Hills, time was running out. If he was serious about finding his way to the Trillium Sea to search for Ivy, he knew he had to level with his friend–and soon. It was the only honorable thing to do.

"I packed enough food to last a day or so until you can buy more provisions in Woodwater," Mrs. Fish said two days later on a cold morning blessed with sapphire blue skies and abundant sunshine. She gave Nicholas and Leo each a motherly hug. "As Will said, come back any time you're in the area. We'd love to see you again."

"As would we," Nicholas replied. He and Leo thanked the couple profusely for all their kindness.

Beth Ann wiped away a small teardrop. "Now you'd better be off. Lane is waiting and he likes to keep to a schedule." She looked at her oldest son, Tim, who planned to accompany them to his uncle's farm. "And promise me no dallying after you take Uncle Lane's horse back to his barn. Your father has plenty of work for you to do here."

"I promise, Mother," Tim replied with an exasperated sigh.

Will shook hands with Nicholas and Leo while the other children waved goodbye as the travelers walked down the road to Lane's farmhouse with their brother. After a short hike along a dirt road rutted with wheel tracks, the trio spotted Lane directing a small horse-drawn cart down his front weedy pathway. Several wooden crates, some containing crocks of honey and others filled with pears, were piled on back next to a few small casks of various wines. Tim waved to his uncle, a grin upon his freckled face.

"Hop on," Lane said, indicating for Nicholas and Leo to climb up on the front seat after they stowed their packs in back. Tim clambered onto the back of the cart. "My boat is tied up on the river. You can help me load the goods."

After a short ride to the river's edge, Nicholas and Leo helped Lane haul his items to a rowboat tied up at a tiny wooden dock that Lane had built several years ago. When they finished, Tim eagerly climbed up on the front of the cart and grabbed the reins to take the horse back to his uncle's farm. Lane handed him two copper half-pieces for his help.

"Spend it wisely," he told his nephew before the boy drove off and left the others on the river's grassy edge. Lane turned to his passengers and guided them onto the boat. "Let's move. I've got sales to make and you have a journey to take. With luck, Hobin will be available to guide you. He's spent years exploring and mapping the lakes and mountains in the Dunn Hills. He'd rather do that than most anything."

"He sounds like just the man we need," Leo said as Lane untied the boat and pushed off with one of the wooden paddles.

Moments later they were gliding across the Lorren River on the second day of Old Autumn as bright sunlight danced upon the water. Lane sat in the center, expertly dipping his paddle into the water from side to side while Nicholas and Leo enjoyed the view at either end. In the near distance lay the tiny village of Woodwater nestled on the edge of the Dunn Hills. The vast spread of tall trees and distant rolling mountains exploded in brilliant and welcoming shades of green, brown, yellow, red and gold while ominously veiled in mystery and doubt at the same time. As they neared the western bank, Nicholas and Leo already felt lost. They knew their jaunt through the Cashua Forest would seem easy compared to the anticipated hike through the Dunn Hills. The two friends exchanged tired glances before having taken their first steps.

Another horse and cart was waiting on the other side of the river when Lane paddled his boat to a low, stony spot on shore. He tied up the vessel to a nearby pine tree and breathed in the fresh morning air, happy in his element.

"Where'd that come from?" Nicholas asked, pointing to the horse secured beneath a second tree.

"I made a trip across earlier this morning. Hired out the horse and cart for the day from a local farmer like I always do," Lane replied. "He dropped it off a short time ago as I instructed. Untie her, Nicholas, and bring the cart close to the boat so we can load up. It's only a few minutes into town along that road," he said, pointing west. "I need to make two deliveries on the way. We can stop at the Mossy Boulder for lunch. If Hobin isn't around, I'll take you to his house."

About an hour later inside the village of Woodwater, Lane's cart rattled up a dirt road that was thickly lined with pine trees. An area opened up near a curve in the road. On the left side stood the Mossy Boulder, a low pinewood building with small windows on either side of the front entrance. Several maple trees nearly stripped of their leaves stood guard in back of the slouching diner. Nearby, a huge mud puddle lay on the ground like a small lake. Sweet wood smoke issued out of three chimneys spaced evenly on the roof. Off to the right of the building and along the left side of the road sat a huge boulder, the bottom quarter buried in the ground. Leo thought it looked as if some giant, fantastical creature had slammed the enormous rock into the soil and left it there. Serving as the inspiration for the eatery's name were patches of dry, brown moss clinging to sections of the boulder like worn out pieces of old carpeting.

"I hope the cooking is better than the view," Leo softly commented.

"Oh, the Mossy Boulder is not much to look at, I'll admit," Lane replied with a chuckle, "but you'll be more than happy with Norma's menu. She's a fine cook."

"Let's put her to the test," Nicholas said, leading the way to the door after tying up the horse.

Upon stepping inside, they were greeted by murmuring voices and the clatter of plates amid the sun splashed and candlelit interior. Flames crackled in a large, brick fireplace, its billowing heat warming the several rooms and grateful patrons on a chilly autumn day. A dozen or so people sat at several tables near the fire enjoying their noontime lunch. Two other men, looking tired and unshaven, silently sat at a table against a far wall picking at the remains of a roasted pheasant on a platter between them. Lane spotted an empty table near one of the windows. After placing their orders with a server, he, Nicholas and Leo soon enjoyed cold ale, buttered bread, a wedge of cheese and three large bowls of lamb stew.

"You're right," Leo said, tearing a piece of bread and dipping it into his bowl. "This is delicious!"

"I said Norma is a great cook," Lane replied as he attacked his meal with gusto. "You won't ever go wrong stopping here."

"That's the nicest thing anybody's said to me all day," a woman replied as she approached the table, a dull, white apron tied around her waist. She smiled at the trio, appearing weary and cheerful at the same time. "Did you bring my wine and pears, Lane?"

"And some honey, too, if you're getting low," he said before introducing Norma Delving to his two companions.

"I can use more," she said, glancing at Nicholas and Leo. "Lane is my best customer from across the river. Has he finally took my advice and hired help? He tries to run that farm all by himself."

"And I nearly do," he replied with a playful grin.

"Lane is helping us," Nicholas said.

"We're looking for Hobin," Lane said between sips of ale. "These two want to hire him as a guide. Plan to scout around the Dunn Hills for a while."

"He was in this morning for breakfast and told me he had a busy day ahead," Norma explained. "I don't expect to see him here until tomorrow, if that."

"No matter. I'll drop these boys off near his road before I make my next delivery," he said. "Did Hobin mention what he was planning to do today? Will he be around?"

Norma laughed out loud, drawing the attention of several customers. "You know Hobin. He could be off on a whim for days at a time or holed up in his house poring over his maps for just as long." She removed one of the empty plates from the table. "If you'd like, my son can run over there now and let Hobin know he can expect some visitors later in case he plans to disappear into the woods."

"Assuming he hasn't done so already," Lane said.

"We appreciate the offer, but that won't be necessary," Leo told her. "We'll take our chances that Hobin will be there. We've been lucky so far in our travels."

"They've come all the way from Arrondale," Lane informed her. "Now they want to explore our section of the world."

"Well you won't find a more beautiful spot in all of Laparia," Norma said with a smile. "Now can I get you gentlemen another helping of stew?"

"Please," Nicholas said as he sopped up the last of the gravy in his bowl with a piece of bread. "And some more of that fine ale will hit the spot, too."

Over the next half hour, Nicholas, Leo and Lane enjoyed their food, drink and several laughs before realizing that it was time to move on to more important matters. Leo paid for their meal, and then after he and Nicholas helped Lane deliver the food supplies to Norma's kitchen, they exited the Mossy Boulder and rattled down the dirt road in the rented horse cart.

As they drove past the huge boulder alongside the road, they took little notice of two men standing near the rock, one smoking a pipe while engaged in quiet conversation with the other. They were the same men who had been inside the restaurant earlier dining on the roasted pheasant, discreetly listening to the conversation that Nicholas, Leo and Lane were having with Norma Delving. What caught their attention most was learning that Nicholas and Leo had traveled all the way from Arrondale and were planning to head into the Dunn Hills.

"Think those two are who the wizard is looking for?" one of the men asked.

The other man took a long draw on his pipe and exhaled a stream of smoke into the chilly air. "How many pairs of travelers from Arrondale do you think pass this way every day? Of course it must be them! And what a stroke of luck," he said with a grin. "As we're the team that found them, imagine what kind of reward we'll get. And here I was ready to give up after only three days on the lookout."

"But we have to make sure they really are the right ones. We have to track them."

"Leave the particulars to me," the second man replied, puffing on his pipe. "We can follow them easily enough in this tiny place." He softly laughed, rubbing his whiskered face. "I guess this job beats poling one of those blasted rafts up the Lorren River for days on end, don't you think?"

CHAPTER 51

The Guide

"Hobin lives over there," Lane said. He reined his horse to a halt along a dirt road on the outskirts of Woodwater. He pointed down a long, narrow pathway of drying mud and grass that wound through a small field and into a dark stretch of woods.

"Exactly *where*?" Leo asked with a shrug, seeing no dwelling of any kind.

Lane grinned knowingly. "He built a small cabin among those pines just inside the tree line. Hobin likes his privacy and isn't particularly fond of intruders."

"That'll help our cause," Nicholas replied with a sarcastic edge to his voice. "Are you certain he's our best choice for a guide?"

"Once you tell him that I recommended his services, he'll take to you like a frog to pond water." Lane again pointed toward the towering pines, indicating a trail of wood smoke rising among the treetops against the cobalt blue sky. "Look, he's home."

"Maybe you can come with us and make some introductions," Leo suggested.

"No, no," he replied. "We'd get to talking and drinking ale and I'd lose half my daylight. Today's for work, not socializing. I'll catch up with Hobin someday at the Mossy Boulder over a plate of Norma's finest. In the meantime, I need to push on while you two hire a guide. The days are getting shorter, my friends, so wherever you're going, you'd better get going now. Soon the snow will fly and you'll wish you were back in Arrondale."

"I'm sort of wishing that now," Nicholas said, only half jokingly. "But you're right. We've delayed long enough. It's time to move on."

Nicholas and Leo grabbed their packs from the cart and slung them on their shoulders, anticipating the cumbersome weight of the many long miles ahead. They thanked Lane for his help and guidance, asking him to extend their appreciation to Will and Beth Ann one final time and promising to visit again if ever possible. Lane gently snapped the reins and proceeded down the road to finish his deliveries, waving over his shoulder as he disappeared into the sun-splashed hues of the woody countryside.

Nicholas took a deep breath as he soaked in the surroundings. "Here we go again," he said, contemplating where in Laparia he might be standing another week or month from now, uncertain if they would be any closer to their goal.

"Let's get this over with," Leo said. He started down the path, his words tinged with weariness as he imagined the grueling footsteps to Wolf Lake. "Why couldn't the wizard Frist have retired at a comfortable inn that serves fine food and drink? Now that's a journey I would have volunteered for without thinking twice."

"Next time," Nicholas replied as he followed his friend down the path still spongy and wet in spots from the rain a few days ago.

They quickly hiked over three quarters of the distance to Hobin's residence, eager to meet the man and strike a deal. The towering pines loomed like giants just ahead, the air thick with their sweet, clean scent. Leo suddenly stopped, thinking he had heard a rustle in the shadows beneath the trees.

"Not more cows, I'm sure," Nicholas said.

Before Leo could respond, two large dogs bounded out of the trees and bolted up the path. The snarling, hairy animals, one brown and one black, barked incessantly as they targeted Nicholas and Leo before stopping in the middle of the trail, blocking their way forward. The two canines bared their sharp teeth and gazed at the unexpected arrivals, studying them amid a series of distrustful growls and intermittent barks. Nicholas and Leo took a cautious step backward, feeling more terrified than when Will Fish had confronted them with his pitchfork.

NICHOLAS RAVEN AND THE WIZARDS' WEB - VOLUME 2

"I'll assume these two beasts belong to Hobin," Leo said, swallowing hard as he kept his eyes fixed on the huge animals. "Charming pets."

"Let's hope they already ate lunch," Nicholas added, frozen in place. "So what'll we do now, Leo? Go forward? Or turn around, run like horses and hire somebody else?"

"If you boys don't go forward, you'll never get to where you're going," a sturdy voice called out from the trees. "But before you take that next step, the three of us need to have a little talk."

Slowly, a tall man stepped out of the pine shadows and ambled confidently along the path toward them, scrutinizing the pair with an eagle-like gaze. He wore a brown coat that fell below his waist, its hood flopped back, and the material well-worn and stained from its many journeys through the woods. His dark boots had seen similar wear and tear over the miles. A large knife was secured inside a sheath attached to his side. After he observed the strangers for a moment, he leaned back, folded his arms and slowly massaged his chin as if in deep thought. Nicholas and Leo silently looked on with a mix of unease and curiosity, wondering who would speak first. The man made the decision for them.

"I guess you can't be all bad," he said, his voice firm yet cheerfully pleasant. "After all, my dogs decided not to take a bite out of either one of you."

"For which we're much appreciative," Nicholas replied, studying the man with interest. He was over twice his age with a head of light brown hair that was beginning to thin and gray, growing almost to his shoulders. His wide, whiskered countenance was punctuated with a set of aqua-colored eyes radiating joyous enthusiasm and a seriousness of purpose at the same time. "Are you Hobin?"

"I am," he casually replied. "But how do you know my name? I don't recall seeing either of you in the village before."

"We crossed the river with Lane Fish earlier today," Leo explained, wanting to get to the heart of the matter so that Hobin would call off his dogs. "He recommended that we seek you out since we're interested in hiring a guide to take us into the Dunn Hills."

"To Wolf Lake," Nicholas clarified. "We'll pay whatever fee you think is fair."

"That's definitely an offer in my favor," he replied.

"I'm Nicholas Raven and this is my friend, Leo Marsh," he said, still slightly uncomfortable. "Can we discuss terms?"

"Only if we discuss them over a drink," Hobin said, snapping his fingers twice and pointing toward the pine trees behind him. Suddenly the two dogs stopped growling and ran off into the woods, leaving the three men alone. Nicholas and Leo were visibly relieved at the canines' departure. Hobin chuckled. "Frank and Gus wouldn't have harmed you–at least not without my say-so. We watch out for each other around here. Where's Lane?"

"We just had lunch with him at the Mossy Boulder," Leo said.

"I'm sure he recommended the lamb stew. Norma makes a fine kettle."

"She certainly did. Lane dropped us off here before leaving to make his deliveries," Leo continued, quickly filling in Hobin on how he and Nicholas had met him and his brother. "Lane insisted that you were the perfect choice for a guide."

"Kind of him to say–and accurate." With a wave of his hand, Hobin indicated for them to follow him to his home. "I had planned to slip away into the hills and go to Lake Lily for a few days starting tomorrow, but as I haven't been to Wolf Lake in quite some time, I could easily convince myself to hike there instead." He glanced at the two men as they neared the soaring pines. "Why do you want to go there anyway? There are some strange tales out of that region."

Nicholas and Leo glanced at each other, again confronted with the task of how much of their business they could or should reveal to their prospective guide. Hobin, however, instantly picked up on their hesitation and let them off the hook for the moment.

"But I suppose that can wait until we're settled inside. Some food and drink by the fire is our first order of business, gentlemen. You can tell me as much as you're inclined to," he said, putting them temporarily at ease. "Based on that, I'll make my decision as to whether I'll be your guide or not. Sound fair?"

"More than fair," Nicholas said as they passed under the low hanging branches of some pine trees. They were suddenly consumed in shadows and filtered sunlight.

Moments later they approached a large, rectangular one-story cabin constructed of pine logs. It stood in the middle of a small clearing, its stone chimney issuing curls of blue smoke into the early afternoon sky. The waters of a nearby creek washed hypnotically over a series of smooth, mossy rocks. Several stacks of split firewood had been piled against one side of the cabin in anticipation of a brutal winter ahead. Behind the cabin were the fallow remains of a modest field that had grown corn, potatoes, beans, carrots, pumpkin and squash during the summer. A line of five apple trees stood farther away in the open light, long since plucked of their ripened fruit. Nicholas noted that Hobin's appearance and demeanor were perfectly reflected in the roughhewn surroundings and the staggering sense of isolation that oozed up from the soil between the trunks of the creaking pines. For one who felt so much at home among the trees and in the outdoors, Nicholas knew beyond a doubt that Hobin would be the perfect guide.

Hobin sliced up a loaf of pumpkin bread. He, Nicholas and Leo enjoyed the tasty treat with generous servings of ale. The trio sat at a table next to a fire in the central room of the cabin. Four smaller rooms were accessible from the main area, two on either side. Frank and Gus lay near the hearth, each gnawing on a beef bone.

"If Wolf Lake is your destination, I suggest we head north to Beetle Lake first," Hobin said after downing a mouthful of ale. "Gray Hawk Mountain is just east of that lake. We can climb and get a view of the Five Brothers and of Wolf Lake just beyond them."

"Five Brothers? Who are they?" Leo asked.

"They're mountains," Hobin said. "A string of five beautiful mountains just south of Wolf Lake."

"One moment," Nicholas said. He went to his backpack and fished out a map of the Dunn Hills. He spread it out on the table before them. "This might help."

Hobin stood up and leaned over the map, nodding and muttering as he scanned the lines and representations of the hills and lakes he loved so much. "A fine map," he said, looking up. "At least for someone who only wants to study the Dunn Hills from the comfort of a chair miles away from the real thing." He went to a shelf and rifled through some rolled up pieces of sturdy parchment until he found the one he desired. He returned to the table and spread out another map over the one Nicholas had displayed. "If you really want to know where you're going, this is the proper map for the job."

Nicholas and Leo's jaws dropped when they saw the detailed drawings upon the map. It depicted a section of the Dunn Hills encompassing the area around Lake Lily, Beetle Lake and Wolf Lake. The black, brown, blue and green ink sketching was breathtaking to behold in both its beauty and meticulous detail. Hobin noted the appreciative amazement upon their faces and was silently pleased.

"Where did you get this map?" Leo asked.

"I drew it," Hobin replied matter-of-factly. "Kind of a hobby. Very accurate, too. I've explored the Dunn Hills for over the last twenty years and have mapped all of it to one extent or another. I need to refine some of my drawings to make them as precise as this one, but that takes time."

"Still, if your other maps are only half as good as this one, that's quite an accomplishment," Nicholas said, tracing a finger along the small river leading from the eastern end of Wolf Lake to the Trillium Sea. Visions of Ivy swept through his mind. "They should have such accurate maps in the Blue Citadel," he added, not thinking about what he was saying. "The royal cartographers could learn a thing or two from you."

Hobin looked askance at his guests. "You've been frequenting the halls of the Citadel? There must be quite a story behind that."

Nicholas looked up, horrified at his verbal slip. Leo glanced at Hobin, feeling guilty for not explaining the true purpose of their journey, yet knowing that they would now be forced to tell their host part or all of the truth if he was ever going to trust them and agree to be their guide. But Hobin said nothing, seemingly unfazed by the comment as he leaned back in his chair, allowing the uneasy silence to work its will.

"There is a story," Nicholas said before downing the last bit of ale in his cup. "And quite a complicated one, too. I suppose Leo and I owe you an explanation about the purpose of our journey before you decide to be our guide. As our task is a well-guarded secret, I don't envision any danger to us–other than what we might face in the wild. But you should be made aware of some aspects of our mission despite the oath we took."

"First you mention the Blue Citadel, and then a secret task and an oath?" Hobin rubbed his hands together. "Now you have me really intrigued."

"We'll bring you up to date on how we arrived at your doorstep," Leo said, "and then you can make your decision."

"Fair enough." Hobin peered inside his nearly empty cup and glanced up at his guests. "Uh, will this be a long and rambling tale?"

Nicholas nodded. "It can be, depending on how many details you'd like."

"Perfect! Let me tap the ale cask one more time so I can enjoy your story properly," he said, grabbing an empty wooden pitcher from the table and hurrying off to another room to refill it. Soon he returned, and after topping off everyone's cup with a frothy head of foam and throwing more wood on the fire, he settled back in his chair and stretched his legs, eagerly awaiting their account. "If your grand quest is leading you into the Dunn Hills, a place I hold dear to my heart, then I'd like to know how you arrived here and what you plan on doing." He took a gulp of ale and signaled for them to proceed.

And neither one of his guests disappointed Hobin. They took turns recounting their adventures in the villages of Kanesbury, Minago and Boros, to the sprawling grasslands along the Trillium Sea, and within the corridors of the Blue Citadel itself. He was touched by Leo's budding relationship with a princess and seemed genuinely moved when Nicholas explained how Ivy had been ripped from his life just as the possibility of true love had begun to blossom. The story of the Enâri especially intrigued him as well as their encounter with Carmella, Jagga and the soldiers from the Northern Isles. Guessing that Hobin had seen the lighted rafts being poled upriver at night and probably viewed them as invaders, Nicholas hoped that he would be sympathetic to their cause. When a half hour or so of storytelling had passed, with a few questions from Hobin tossed in, Nicholas was delighted to be proven correct.

"If anything irks me more than good ale gone bad or unwanted and annoying visitors–present company excepted–it's the sight of those blasted Islanders slipping into our territory with death and destruction on their minds." Hobin pounded a fist on the table. "I've seen them at night when I wander down by the river, floating by as if they own the place. There have even been rumors from up and down the river of how they've come ashore in spots and cause trouble just for sport. Mostly I hear that they're traveling to Kargoth as quick as they can like you said. Apparently Vellan needs more help than his own soldiers can provide." He glanced at Nicholas, his face crinkled with doubt. "So they really exist–those Enâri creatures you spoke of?"

"They do. The stories of their attack on my village twenty years ago are legion," he replied. "Now they're causing trouble in Montavia as well as in the trio of mountain nations near Kargoth."

"And if a journey to Wolf Lake will help put an end to them, it's well worth the effort," Leo added. "Nicholas and I don't plan to give up, but we could sure use your experience at this point. Will you help us?"

Hobin extended a hand and snapped his fingers once. Immediately, Frank and Gus looked up and whimpered from their comfortable positions on the hearth, a beef bone still clamped in each of their mouths. "No, not you two," Hobin said to the dogs, indicating for them to go back to their treats. He addressed Nicholas, rubbing his fingers together. "Let me see it please, if that doesn't violate your oath any further."

Nicholas realized that he was referring to the medallion, hesitant to respond to his request. Yet their host had been nothing but gracious so far and had been highly recommended by Lane Fish, so the caution in Nicholas' mind was soon overcome by the trust in his heart. He carefully lifted the leather cord over his head, revealing the medallion from its hiding place beneath his shirt. He handed the cold piece of metal to Hobin who examined it in the glow of the firelight.

"Doesn't look like much to me," he muttered, squinting as he brought it close to his eyes. "And as I know nothing about magic, I can't feel any of the power you say is swirling inside this thing."

"Tolapari assured us that the spell had been altered somewhat, or even diminished, when the key was subjected to the heat of the forge," Nicholas explained. "But it's still a potent object nonetheless."

"And this wizard Frist is supposed to fix it up nice for you?" Hobin asked, glancing at the unremarkable object in his hand.

"Assuming that Frist is still alive," Leo added uneasily. "But we have to try in spite of the odds. If we're successful, the gains would be unimaginable."

"I suppose so." Hobin handed the medallion back to Nicholas who hid it beneath his shirt again, feeling protective of the mysterious object. "And I suppose I'll take up the offer to serve as your guide, too. Whether this wizard is alive or not, it'll still be a fine jaunt to Wolf Lake. I haven't been there in a while and am due for a trip back. And as you two seem like decent folk, I wouldn't want you to get lost. The Dunn Hills can be treacherous to the uninitiated despite the many miles of trails I've marked. Even I could get disoriented in the gloom or if bad weather should spring up on the sly."

"In the short time we've gotten to know you, Nicholas and I have complete confidence in your abilities," Leo said. "What could go wrong?"

"Oh, lots of things," Hobin warned. "One of my basic rules is never to be complacent when wandering through the wild. It could kill you in a snap–or worse."

Nicholas looked at him in bafflement. "What's worse than death?"

Hobin appeared surprised. "Why, you could get seriously injured and forever lost, which wouldn't be a more attractive alternative. So you were smart to seek me out. And after hearing your story, I know we face an additional challenge."

"What?" Leo asked.

"That Frist character you spoke of. I told you earlier that I had heard strange stories from around the Wolf Lake region," he said, lightly drumming his fingers on the tabletop. "This explains all those rumors then. There's a wizard about."

"I don't think we have to worry about any danger from Frist," Nicholas said. "He helped save my village twenty years ago. He's one of the good ones. He never let his power get the best of him."

"I hope you're right, Nicholas. Because if only half of what I've been told about the wizard Vellan in the Northern Mountains is true, then I'd step gingerly around the whole pack of those magic men, if you understand."

"We do," Leo said. "But I think we'll be fine."

"And we really appreciate your help, Hobin, and will definitely let King Justin know of your contribution to our cause," Nicholas added before inquiring about how much he would charge them for his guide services on behalf of the King of Arrondale.

"We can discuss the particulars after another round of ale and a second bite to eat. I'm hungry again after all this talking," he said. "But you can lessen a portion of my fee by contributing to the costs of our provisions. I have more than enough in my home for the first leg of our journey to Beetle Lake, but we'll need to resupply once we arrive. There are a few villages along the water."

"A deal," Nicholas replied, sealing their agreement by raising his cup.

"And it wouldn't hurt either if you'd mention my mapmaking skills to your King," he modestly mentioned. "If he'd like copies of my works to update his libraries, why, I'm sure his aides and I could negotiate a fair price. Perhaps he'd even want to hire me from time to time to survey parts of his kingdom. Who's to say?" he said with a shrug before downing the rest of his ale. "But again, we can discuss the particulars later. Now I'm simply hungry."

The trio indulged themselves with more ale and a second meal, talking until the sun set and the deepening dusk of twilight silently wrapped itself around the trees and the cabin. As darkness fully settled in, Nicholas and Leo helped Hobin finish some outside chores that needed attending to before their departure the following morning. Later, the trio prepared their packs, filling them with enough food and other supplies to get them to Beetle Lake.

"I'd like to leave shortly after sunrise," Hobin said. "We'll drive to a farm a couple miles down the main road. I have an arrangement with the owner to leave Frank and Gus there whenever I go on some of my longer adventures. My dogs only accompany me on the shorter ones. We'll enter the Dunn Hills from there and be on our way."

"How long until we get to Wolf Lake?" Leo asked, wearily recalling their time in the Cashua Forest.

"The stretch of woods to Beetle Lake will be the toughest, most monotonous part of our journey," he bluntly explained. "Expect a handful of days on your feet, depending on how ambitious we are and how the weather cooperates. But once we arrive there, the scenery will pick up your spirits. The lakes and tree-covered mountains are a sight to behold. We'll still have about a third of the journey left to complete once we arrive at Beetle Lake, but it'll be a much more pleasant endeavor from there on."

"Well, if Leo and I survived nine days roaming aimlessly inside the Cashua, then I suppose we can survive this, too." Nicholas smirked at his friend. "Just think of all the stories you'll get to tell Megan when you return."

"Oh, I'm sure she'll want to hear about every tree I walked past. And just when I stopped having dreams about being lost in the woods," he joked. "But if that's the path before us, I intend to start out with a good night's sleep. Imagining the road ahead–not to mention drinking one too many cups of ale–has brought me to the brink of exhaustion. So if you'll point me to my spot on the floor, Hobin, I think I'll turn in."

"Good advice for us all," he replied, indicating that Frank and Gus would be more than happy to forfeit their sleeping space near the hearth for one night.

As the nearly full Bear Moon rose high in the east in a bitter autumn sky, the three travelers succumbed to deep and dreamless sleep to prepare for the tiring journey ahead. Wood smoke continued to issue from the chimney throughout the night, climbing high above the tips of the pine trees that surrounded the cabin like silent sentries as a field of icy-white stars watched from above.

Another pair of eyes also watched the cabin from deep inside the woods, securely hidden among trees and rocks and dried fern. The individual was one of the two men who had observed Nicholas and Leo leave the Mossy Boulder with Lane Fish earlier that day. The other man was lying on the ground nearby, fast asleep as they took turns spying on Hobin's cabin. Both men were now wearing the long, brown coats typical of a soldier from the Northern Isles, an article of clothing they had temporarily abandoned while spying among the population of Woodwater for the past few days.

The soldier wrapped his arms around himself for warmth, his hood over his head, wondering if rafting up the Lorren River would have been so bad compared to this monotonous duty. But if the two men who had arrived here earlier in the day possessed the unmade key to the Spirit Box, then securing that prize for the wizard Caldurian would do much for his career. The two soldiers had earlier decided to steal the medallion whenever the first opportunity presented itself, whether the object had been remade into a key by then or not. All they had to do now was wait for the men inside the cabin to begin their journey and then follow them. After that, it was simply a matter of biding their time and striking at the right moment. The man exhaled a puff of ghostly white breath into the frosty, moonlit night, continuing his lonely watch.

CHAPTER 52

Trees and Footsteps

Nicholas and Leo awoke to cold darkness and throbbing temples, wanting only another hour's rest when they heard Hobin stirring in an adjacent room. When he strolled into the main section of the cabin, his booming voice roused them fully awake. Nicholas knew that he and Leo could no longer delay the inevitable. It was time to move on and seek out the wizard Frist.

"Two fewer rounds of ale last night would have been a wise decision," he groggily muttered as he stood and stretched by the glowing embers in the fireplace. Nicholas leaned on the mantel, burying his head in his arms. "I could sleep right here."

"A few gulps of cold stream water will revive you," Hobin said, seeming in cheerful spirits. "That particular brew does have a delayed kick if you're not used to it."

Leo nodded as he raked his fingers through his hair and plodded silently out the front door. Hobin chuckled and started to make breakfast.

Less than two hours later, after enjoying a filling meal and a pot of hot tea, the trio departed the cabin. They headed up the long path to the main road in a rickety, horse-drawn cart, with Frank and Gus lying lazily in back among the heavy packs. The sky was painted a rich shade of blue and blazed with sunshine, yet the air contained a biting chill. Soon they arrived at a farm where Hobin dropped off his beloved canines with the owner, promising to be back in a couple of weeks. After donning their backpacks, the trio continued down the road on foot for a few minutes until Hobin pointed out a small stream emanating from within the trees to their left.

"We'll enter the Dunn Hills along that watercourse and follow it for a mile or so," he said, leading the way into the thick woods. "Now the fun begins!" he added with childlike excitement.

They entered the trees unceremoniously, accompanied by the pleasant gurgle of creek water to their right and a flurry of private thoughts swirling in their minds. Whether it was the abundant sunshine or because they had an experienced guide with them, Nicholas and Leo both commented that the woodland atmosphere seemed more hospitable and less encroaching here than when they had entered the Cashua Forest fifteen days ago. But after several hours into the grueling hike with a few rest stops, both men again endured an unrelenting test of their patience and endurance, yearning for the sight of the open air or a spread of clear, blue water.

"I warned you that this first stretch to Beetle Lake would be the toughest. There's nothing but trees upon trees until we arrive," Hobin said, contentedly hiking across the leaf-littered floor with a piece of a long maple branch in hand to use as a walking stick.

"And you kept your promise to a fault," Leo joked. "But I don't expect to get lost this time, so we have that going for us."

"Still, it is beautiful here," Nicholas said, observing the slanted rays of sunlight stabbing through the rich green pines and the nearly leafless maple, elm and birch trees. "I suppose the more you wander through the woods, the more you appreciate them."

"How true," Hobin replied. "And just wait until the lakes and hills unfold before your eyes. You'll never want to leave."

"I wouldn't go that far," Nicholas said. "But what possessed you to devote so much of your life to exploring this region?"

Hobin, leading the group, stopped and turned to his companions. "Because it's my passion," he said as if the answer should have been obvious. "As you said, I appreciate the woods. I fell in love with them many years ago," he explained before continuing at his typically brisk pace.

"When did you first start exploring?" Leo asked, sensing that Hobin was willing to open up a bit and wanting to learn more about their guide.

"I was about your age. Maybe a little younger. My cousin and I decided to explore the hills for a few days out of sheer boredom from working on my uncle's farm." Hobin spaced his words between the rhythmic pattern of his deep breaths and steady footsteps. "Well, my cousin grew weary of all the hiking required for such an endeavor and became annoyed with my persistent requests to explore the Dunn region even further. He preferred a more leisurely existence in the open air. I, however, was captivated with this place when I climbed my first mountain and saw Lake Lily in the distance gleaming with the most brilliant shade of blue under the dazzling sunshine. I returned countless times over the years and met several wonderful people living in the villages along Lake Lily's northwestern shore and along Great Arrow Lake just beyond."

"Why would folks want to live among these hills?" Leo asked, wondering what possessed one to carve out a life in such confining surroundings.

"While the scattered populations aren't very large, some of the heartier souls in Laparia have chosen to make their homes in this region or were born here," Hobin said. "When we arrive near the lakes, you'll see that some of the land has been cleared and tilled and life goes on pretty much like in other parts of the world. Day to day living here can be tougher though, being cut off from much of the world and enduring extremely harsh winters from time to time. Still, some people thrive in it."

"Including you?" Nicholas asked.

Hobin laughed. "To a point. After all, I always return to my life in Woodwater, though I did live on Lake Lily for nearly a year in my younger days." He grew silent, the dull pounding of his walking stick upon the hard soil audible in the cool autumn air. "I had almost stayed there too, but..."

Leo gently prodded him. "But what?"

"Oh, I don't want to bore you two with ancient history," he said, pointing up a slight incline as he quickly changed the subject. "If my memory proves correct, there should be a small clearing just a few minutes away. We can stop there to rest and have lunch. My feet are feeling the miles, I'm not ashamed to say."

"Mine too," Nicholas added as the tree trunks, branches and fallen leaves passed by in a blur of faded colors. He tried to calculate how many miles he had walked since fleeing Kanesbury forty-nine days ago. He wondered what Katherine was doing at this moment, unaware that she and her friends and neighbors were seated inside the village hall listening in horrified amazement as the wizard Caldurian claimed control over Kanesbury, shattering all the windows inside the hall with a single blast of magic to demonstrate his seriousness.

He also wondered how King Justin's preparations for the counterattacks in Montavia and Rhiál were progressing as he and Prince Gregory gathered and supplied two separate armies for the long marches ahead. What Nicholas didn't know was that Prince William and a man named Eucádus were also readying additional forces with King Cedric of Drumaya. They were two days from departing over the Kincarin Plains to launch the first strike against Vellan's ruthless puppet, King Drogin.

And amid that wild whirl of speculation, both joyful and heartbreaking images of Ivy were never far from Nicholas' thoughts. She was the one constant he carried with him in his heart and mind as he slogged on. Though he imagined one day rescuing her, he fearfully wondered if those dreams would forever remain unrealized. Did he truly possess the ability, resources and sheer luck to find her? And was she really still alive? For a moment, he speculated whether he was simply holding on to an improbable vision in order to avoid facing a grim reality–that Ivy would never again be found. His face tightened as he tried to dismiss such horrid musings.

"What are you thinking about?" Leo's voice finally broke down the mental barrier between Nicholas and the rest of the world.

He looked up. "*Huh?*"

Leo shook his head in amusement, walking beside his friend as Hobin swiftly led the way through the woods. "I've been trying to get your attention for the last minute. Your expression looked as hard as stone. I thought you might be walking in your sleep."

"Had a few things on my mind. Did you want something?"

"Only wondering what was bothering you as you appeared troubled," Leo said with concern. "Thinking about Ivy?"

"When don't I?"

"Who can blame you?" he replied, wishing there was something he could do or say to make a difference. "Anything else you want to talk about? We have all the time in the world."

"No, I'm fine," Nicholas said appreciatively. "Not really in the talking mood."

"Okay," Leo replied.

"But perhaps you're in the eating mood?" Hobin said as he suddenly stopped and pointed ahead. "We're at the clearing. If you gentlemen are prepared to take a breather, this is the place to do it. I'll get a fire going as there's plenty of dry kindling around. A hot lunch will do you good as you acclimate to what will be your new home for the next several days."

"If the Cashua Forest hasn't already done that, nothing will!" Leo said with a laugh, recalling that tortuous journey with a mix of pride and dread. "But I won't turn my nose up at a hot lunch. So if you're willing to cook the first one, I'll dig out the tin plates."

They enjoyed a leisurely meal and an extended rest, delighted to see a swath of blue sky and sunshine above them for a short while. They continued on as the maze of trees and undergrowth silently enveloped them again. Hours later, as twilight turned to nightfall, the trio made camp among a clump of pine trees beside a tiny stream. Nicholas built a fire, recalling that cold, dark morning in Aunt Castella's house where he set some kindling ablaze at the kitchen hearth with Ivy kneeling at his side. It seemed so long ago. After Leo and Hobin prepared dinner, the tired travelers sat in front of the crackling fire, enjoying some quiet conversation with their meal.

An hour later, as the flickering tips of the red and orange flames licked the cold air, a fleet of clouds moved in. The stars were blotted out and the glow of the Bear Moon, a day shy of full, climbed in the east. The trees stood still amid the thick and oppressive silence. The glowing embers at the base of the fire dimmed and brightened like dozens of watchful eyes. Soon after, Nicholas, Leo and Hobin each found a spot near the flames, and wrapped snugly in their coats and blankets, they fell promptly to sleep.

Nicholas opened his eyes to blinding darkness, not sure what time of the night it was, or for a moment, even where he was until he recognized the glow of the dying fire and the stark silhouettes of towering trees. Had a disturbance in the forest awakened him? A snapped twig perhaps? Or was it merely a noise from a dream? He sat up and clutched a blanket around his shoulders. Leo was fast asleep nearby. When he scanned the ground by the fire, his heart skipped a beat. Hobin was missing. His blankets had been left in a pile. Nicholas got to his feet and looked around, turning in a slow, steady circle.

He noticed a flash of light deep in the trees behind him, gone for one moment and then reappearing the next. It bobbed slightly up and down as if magically floating. Slowly the light grew nearer and burned steadier, mesmerizing Nicholas who had it locked in his gaze. Soon the outline of a body was visible in the glow of the flame and then the features of a familiar face. Nicholas exhaled, relieved that Hobin had returned.

"What's going on?" he whispered. "Where have you been?"

"Sorry I woke you," he softly replied, bending down and placing the flaming torch into the fire. "I was scouting the area. I thought I heard movement through the woods. Woke me out of a sound sleep." He indicated for Nicholas to lean in closer. "I thought I heard voices."

"Did you find anything?"

Hobin shook his head. "No. But maybe tomorrow I'll see something in the full light of day. I'm not convinced we're alone."

A chill ran through Nicholas upon hearing those words. Leo stirred, raising his head while still on the verge of a deep sleep.

"Did you load the apple cart yet?" he muttered, his heavy eyelids barely raised.

"All taken care of," Nicholas said. "Go back to sleep, Leo. I'll wake you when it's time for deliveries."

"Okay," he was barely able to reply, his head dropping back into the crook of his arm as sleep again consumed him. "I just..."

Nicholas looked askance at Hobin. "Apples on the brain. But back to those noises. Are you certain someone is out there?"

"Or some*thing.* Deer perhaps? But as I heard voices, I'm more inclined to guess a some*one.*"

"That's comforting news. Should we be worried?"

Hobin shrugged. "Depends on who they are. Maybe they're other travelers just like us, though I've rarely encountered anyone

wandering in these unpopulated regions during my years of travel."
He lowered his voice further. "Are you sure no one else knows of
your mission?"

Nicholas crinkled his face, certain that that was impossible.
"How? There were only ten of us in King Justin's chamber when we
took our oath. The doors were closed and guarded from the outside.
Who else could have known?"

"Maybe we're fretting over nothing," he replied. "But as a
precaution, I'm going to sit up for an hour or two. I'm far from
sleepy now, and as dawn is still hours away, I can get enough rest
when I close my eyes again later."

"All right," Nicholas said. "But promise to wake me before
you go back to sleep so I can watch for a while, too. I mean, as long
as we're being cautious…"

But their vigil in the darkness proved either unnecessary or
very effective as there were no further disturbances during the night.
When Leo awoke refreshed the following gray morning and
commented that Hobin and Nicholas both looked less than ready to
march, Nicholas explained what had happened the previous night.

"Then I *had* spoken to you," Leo said, trying to recall his
words. "I thought I dreamed that you and Hobin were talking to each
other by the fire. What'd I talk about?"

"Apples, of course," Nicholas replied with a laugh.

Later, Hobin scouted about the area as soon as there was
sufficient light. And though he found no individuals to go with the
voices, he did find suspicious signs that maybe others had been
about, including disturbances in the leafy ground covering and
freshly crushed undergrowth in spots, all in areas that his group had
not traversed. Yet he detected no trail he could follow at any length
nor had the time to search for one.

"If others are tracking us, they're clever enough to remain
hidden. But we can't spare the daylight to seek them out. We must
move on," Hobin insisted.

They continued their trek after a hasty breakfast, at the
moment fearing a change in the weather more than anything else.
The graying skies had been accompanied by a dampening air that
chilled them to the bone as they started out on their second day of
hiking. Their ghostly breaths rose and leisurely lingered in the cold

and clammy atmosphere. The gray, monotonous hours blended into one another, forming a colorless blot of time that epitomized their expedition for the remainder of that day and all the next, wringing any traces of enthusiasm out of their spirits and conversation.

It wasn't until the following day that the air began to dry and the clouds started to break, allowing glorious patches of blue sky and splashes of sunshine to entertain them from above. Though the air still harbored late autumn's cold bite, the vexing dampness and persistent melancholy had dissipated to the delight of all.

They made camp before twilight as the reddish glow of the sun gently soaked through the trees in the southwest. The sky above was crisp and clean. There had been no further disturbances to their sleep since that first incident three nights ago which gave them hope that maybe they were reading more into the episode than was really there. The trio enjoyed hot stew with biscuits and apples as they sat near the fire, pleased to have concluded their fourth day of traveling.

"We're making excellent time," Hobin remarked before taking a gulp from his water skin and wiping his lips upon a coat sleeve. "At the rate we're going, we should see the shores of Beetle Lake tomorrow and the woody slopes of Gray Hawk Mountain standing beside it. It'll be a welcome change of scenery from this endless parade of trees."

"I look forward to it," Leo said. "And I'm eager to climb Gray Hawk, too."

"That's one of the smaller mountains in the Dunn Hills region, but it still affords a wonderful view as there aren't many trees near its stony top," Hobin explained. "We've been gradually climbing in elevation over the last day. When we reach the actual mountain tomorrow, it'll be a quick three hour hike or so to the summit. It's one of the more pleasant climbs I've made. A few of the higher peaks might take me all day to reach the top, but all the views are spectacular."

"A quick three hours?" Nicholas asked skeptically. "Isn't that an unneeded delay?"

"But the fun will be worth it!" Hobin's laughter shattered the gathering stillness of twilight. "Besides, when are you ever going to be in these parts again? You should add at least one climb to your list of accomplishments. When we make the final hike to Wolf Lake, we'll pass between the last two easternmost peaks of the Five

Brothers but won't have the time to scale either of them. They're much higher and more challenging."

"Since you're the guide, I'll leave the particulars to you, Hobin. After all, Leo and I want our money's worth," Nicholas quipped.

"I'll try not to disappoint," he said. "Now I think I'll turn in early tonight and catch up on some sleep. Tend to the fire as long as you want. We'll leave after sunup."

With that, Hobin grabbed a rolled up pelt from his pack and tossed it on the ground just inside the glow of the fire. He lay down upon it, covering himself with a heavy blanket. Soon he was fast asleep, snoring occasionally in the deepening night.

"I'm not very tired," Nicholas said. He got up from a large, flat stone he had been sitting upon and added a few sticks to the fire. "If you want to turn in, go ahead, Leo. I'll sit here and think for a bit while I stoke the flames."

"Not yet," Leo commented matter-of-factly, noting the tension and unease in Nicholas' face in the steady glow. He sat against a nearby tree and stretched his legs, warming his boots by the fire. When Nicholas returned to his seat, Leo could tell that his friend had much on his mind yet sensed his unwillingness to talk about it.

"Want anything else to eat?" Nicholas asked. "The stew is gone, but there's still a biscuit sitting out."

"Save it for tomorrow. One of us will appreciate it after climbing up Gray Hawk."

"I suppose," he said, staring at the snapping flames while trying to find order in their erratic nature.

Leo glanced at him, noting the faraway look in his eyes. He had an idea of what his friend was thinking about now and over the past few days, deciding to broach the subject as Nicholas seemed unwilling to do so himself. He folded his arms and rested his head against the tree, staring off into the darkness beyond the dancing tips of the bonfire.

"Do you think I should go around the Cashua Forest on the way back? After all, going through it alone might mean the death of me," Leo softly said. "Or perhaps I could convince Hobin to guide me through the woods. We'll have enough money left to pay him. I can find my way back to Morrenwood easily enough once I'm on the other side." He massaged his chin, feigning deep thought. "Then again, Hobin might want to travel with me all the way to the Blue Citadel. There he'd have a chance to show King Justin some of his maps and maybe earn a temporary job in the royal library. There are probably several parts of the kingdom that need to be mapped out as meticulously as Hobin has done with the Dunn Hills." He turned to his friend. "What do you think?"

Nicholas shifted his gaze from the flames and stared at Leo, half listening to what he had been saying. "What are you talking about? Why would you be going through the Cashua alone, Leo? And did you say something about hiring Hobin to return with us?"

Leo smiled in the darkness. "You heard what I said, Nicholas. I just want your honest opinion. Think I can make it back to Morrenwood on my own, or should I ask Hobin to tag along? For a fee, of course."

Nicholas felt his blood run warm as if caught in a lie, surprised to hear such talk from Leo. "Why are you asking ridiculous questions? Do you think I'm going to fall off a cliff before this mission is over, or maybe drown in Beetle Lake when we get there?" His words sounded strained. "Why wouldn't I accompany you back to Morrenwood?"

Leo looked at him with heartfelt support. "Because you'll be making your way to the Trillium Sea to search for Ivy. That's why."

Nicholas tried to look surprised, grateful that it was dark enough so he could at least pretend to appear so. He felt somewhat foolish to actually hear one of his deepest thoughts spoken out loud, wondering if Leo assumed it was a ridiculous and impractical notion as well. Nicholas kept silent for a moment, uncomfortably searching for the right words to explain himself.

"I suppose I should ask you where you came up with that silly idea," he finally said, continuing to stare at the fire. "But who am I kidding? That's all I've been thinking about these past few weeks on the road."

"What *road*?" Leo joked. "Anyway, I could tell that you've had something on your mind for a while, walking around all moody and preoccupied. And the few times you tried to broach the subject, you only skirted about the edges before changing the topic which made me even more suspicious."

"Not very subtle, was I."

"Not really," Leo said. "When I saw you trace your finger over the map on Hobin's table–along the river that leads from Wolf Lake to the Trillium Sea–well, it doesn't take a wizard's mind to put it all together."

"I suppose not." Nicholas turned to him, relieved to finally open up. "Whenever I tried to mention this to you, I always found an excuse to back out. I felt that if I left this mission halfway through, it would be abandoning both my duty and my friend–not to mention breaking my oath."

Leo smirked. "You wouldn't really be breaking your oath, Nicholas, since we only swore to keep the mission a secret unless it proved successful. We didn't swear to see it through to the end under any and all circumstances. And since we gave Hobin the details, I don't think we have to worry about not breaking that particular oath anymore."

"It was out of necessity," Nicholas reminded him. "He wouldn't have agreed to be our guide otherwise."

"I know."

Nicholas grew silent again, composing his thoughts before speaking. "So just how foolhardy do you think I would be to try to find her? Ivy's been gone a long time. She was forced on that boat forty days ago this very night," he softly said, his voice nearly choking as the sound of lapping sea waves echoed in his memory. "I can still see her face as she struggled with those men in the boat. I was so close to her, though I don't know how I would have saved her with only a dagger in hand. But I'm glad I tried." He stared into Leo's eyes, his determination evident. "And I need to try again."

Leo nodded. "I know. But where would you go? How would you find her?"

Nicholas shrugged helplessly as he tossed a few twigs into the fire. "I've no idea. First I'd have to find a way to the Northern Isles. And then after that? There'd be a lot of improvising, I guess."

"That's not much of a plan."

"I know, but it's all I have." He tried to lighten the mood. "Since there are ships sailing from the Isles to the mouth of the Lorren River filled with troops and supplies, they eventually must sail back to get more. Maybe I can sign on for a job as a deckhand or a cook's helper," he said. "I figure that would be easier than stowing away. Don't know how I'd accomplish that though."

"Well, it's a plan," Leo replied, unconvinced about its viability. "And let's say you make it to the Northern Isles. What then? How would you even find out who has Ivy or where they took her? And what makes you think you'd have the freedom to wander around the Isles after signing on with a vessel? I hear life is awfully strict over there. You're told how to live and where you can go. You're not really in charge of your own existence. That's one of the last places in the world I'd want to visit."

"But that's where Ivy is, so what other choice do I have?"

"I suppose none–if it's what you really intend to do."

"It is," Nicholas said. "And as crazy as my idea sounds, I have to try at least once. For her sake anyway. I owe her that much."

Leo nodded, knowing that Nicholas' decision was already cast in stone. "Then I won't try and stop you by reason or by force."

"Not that you could either way," Nicholas said, grinning. "Anyway, it'll put my mind at ease if Hobin agrees to guide you back through the Cashua Forest. A person with his skills should know how to tackle any outdoors obstacle, including one he hasn't encountered before."

"He *will* and he *does*," Hobin called out groggily from beneath the blanket covering his face. "Now if you gentlemen wouldn't mind finishing your conversation jackrabbit-fast, we can discuss the particulars in the morning. I'd like a full night's sleep."

"Sorry, Hobin," Leo said. "We'll turn in shortly."

"Good!" he muttered before drifting off once again.

Nicholas lowered his voice to just above a whisper, a hint of amusement upon his face. "That was easy enough, recruiting you an expert guide for back home. The key will be in safe hands."

"But who will guide you, Nicholas, to where you're going?"

"I guess I'm on my own again," he said, accepting his fate with an air of nonchalance. "And since the first leg of my journey will simply be following a river to the Trillium Sea, how could I possibly foul that up?"

"It's what'll happen afterward that worries me," Leo said, anxiously resigning himself to his friend's decision. "But like Hobin said, we'll discuss the particulars in the morning. Perhaps we'll dream up a better plan for you to find your way to the Isles."

"That's the attitude!" Nicholas said, standing up to dig out the sleeping gear from his pack. "Maybe in the light of day my idea won't sound so farfetched."

"Maybe," Leo replied, unable to suppress a good-natured snicker. "But I doubt it."

CHAPTER 53

On Gray Hawk Mountain

They awoke the next day to a cold, colorless morning. After a quick breakfast, they loaded their gear upon tired shoulders and moved on, all anxiously awaiting the view of Beetle Lake they assumed was only a few hours away. Nicholas decided not to bring up the subject of searching for Ivy until they had a few more miles under their belts and more food in their stomachs. The matter could wait until after the sun burned off the thin layer of clouds and the misty tendrils of fog nuzzling the tree trunks like slinking cats.

They made swift and steady progress. Their heavy footfalls snapped twigs and rustled dry and decomposing leaves that had fallen over the past few weeks. Eventually the sky cleared and warm streaks of sunlight shot through the collage of trees, lending a tint of cheerful color to the monotonous backdrop of greens and browns that dominated the landscape.

When they were about to stop for a midmorning break where the woods had thinned out, Nicholas was delighted to see a rise of trees looming in the distance to the northeast. Hobin verified that that was Gray Hawk Mountain. When they stopped to rest, he showed them on the map how far they had traveled over the last five days.

"We'll approach the eastern tip of Beetle Lake first before climbing the mountain," Hobin said. "There are a few small settlements along that end of the water where we can purchase provisions and be on our way."

"No time for a hot meal?" Leo asked longingly. "Or even a mug of ale? To sit on a real chair for a while would be a treat."

"Sorry," Hobin said. "I want to start hiking up Gray Hawk as soon as possible while the daylight lasts."

Leo sighed. "I didn't expect so, but I thought I'd ask."

"Oh, lounging on these cold, hard rocks is equal to any comfortable chair by a fireside," Nicholas said with mock seriousness. "And who needs ale when you can drink the purest, lung-freezing stream water a person could desire?"

"Not to mention the root-stuffed, dirt mattresses we've been using day after day. Some of the finest this side of the Trent Hills, I hear," Leo added facetiously.

Hobin smiled at their antics as he readied his pack for the next leg of the hike, assuming that his two charges were rather enjoying the adventure in spite of its hardships. As he carefully folded up his map and placed it in a side pouch of his backpack, a few small items spilled out onto the ground, including a small, flat stone about the size of a tiny plum with a bluish color and faint traces of a silvery hue which sparkled in direct sunlight. After Hobin replaced all the other items in his pack, he picked up the stone and slipped it in his front coat pocket and gently patted it.

"Do you like to collect stones?" Nicholas asked upon observing the small act. "That one looked rather colorful."

"*Hmmm?*" He looked up, distracted from a distant thought.

"The stone," Nicholas said, pointing at Hobin's coat pocket. "You collect them?"

"No. Just this one." He fished out the stone and tossed it to Nicholas to examine. "Sometimes I carry it with me. Other times it's in my pack. But I always have it whenever I'm traveling through the Dunn Hills. It brings me good luck."

"We'll take all the luck we can get," Leo said.

"It's beautiful," Nicholas remarked as the smooth stone faintly glimmered in the afternoon sunshine. He handed it back to Hobin, noting a faraway look in his eyes. "Where'd you find it?"

"On the shore of Lake Lily," he wistfully replied as he placed it back in his pocket. "We found it lying next to another stone nearly identical to it."

"*We?*" Nicholas asked, his curiosity piqued.

Hobin nodded. "It was over twenty years ago when I lived along the lake for several months one year–from Mid Spring to Old Autumn. It was a glorious time. I was around your age. We had the finest stretch of weather on the lake which is quite unusual in these parts. But weather eventually changes, right?" He patted his coat pocket again. "The stone is a reminder of better times. That's all."

"Where's the matching stone?" Leo casually asked as he readied his own pack.

"Someone else has it," Hobin said, hoisting his pack upon his shoulders. A slight smile spread across his face when he looked up and noted that Nicholas and Leo were eagerly awaiting a reply. He let a stream of air escape out the corner of his mouth. "Her name was Emma," he said, before turning around and leading the way to Gray Hawk Mountain. "And no, I'm not going to tell you all about her. We have a journey to finish," he called to them without looking back. "So put those boots to work, men, and get a move on!"

Nicholas and Leo glanced at one another as they gathered their things, grinning at Hobin's good-natured marching orders.

"*Hmmm.* Emma from Lake Lily," Leo curiously commented as he eased his pack onto his shoulders. "I'll bet he's told Frank and Gus stories about her."

Nicholas chuckled as he walked past him. "Maybe. But you heard the man. Get a move on."

Shortly after noontime the trees began to thin out. The sweet fragrance of wood smoke lingered upon a breeze stirring beneath the cobalt blue sky. And like the parting of heavy drapes in front of a sunny window, the trees in this section of the Dunn Hills opened up around the trio of exhausted hikers, revealing the glittering blue waters on the eastern tip of Beetle Lake. The rooftops of several small houses and shops in the nearest village were visible a half mile away as a haze of blue-gray smoke issued from their stone chimneys. About that same distance farther east of the lake stood Gray Hawk Mountain, covered with leafless trees and towering pines as it watched over its watery companion. Nicholas stopped and let his backpack fall from his shoulders, closing his eyes and deeply inhaling the fresh lake air. He was astounded that he had made it this far, suddenly feeling the many miles that had piled up underfoot.

"This was definitely worth the sore feet and pulled muscles," Leo said, also taking in the view with awestruck wonder. The sun drifted across the sky behind them, reflecting upon the water's wavy surface in a glittering dance.

"Didn't I tell you?" Hobin replied, enjoying the vista himself which he hadn't experienced in many years. "But just wait until you see the view from atop Gray Hawk. You won't want to leave."

"Then what are we waiting for?" Nicholas said.

They headed into the nearby village of Pomeroy to buy provisions for the rest of their journey, happy to see some new faces after five days in the wild. Hobin ran into a few people he hadn't seen in years and quickly caught up on the latest in the area which hadn't changed all that much since his last visit. And despite his earlier refusal, Hobin carved out half an hour in their schedule for a bowl of beef stew and a cup of ale at a local eatery on the lakeshore.

An hour later the trio was back in the woods, scaling the western slope of Gray Hawk Mountain as if their brief excursion into Pomeroy had been an illusion. The blur of miles over the past five days had again taken root in their minds, and coupled with the heavier packs now loaded with new supplies, the journey to Wolf Lake seemed as if it would never end. As the climb to the summit eventually passed the three-hour mark that Hobin had earlier estimated, slowly turning into four, both Nicholas and Leo wondered if this detour was such a good idea after all.

"Perhaps we should have just hiked on and avoided this climb altogether," Nicholas said, the growing frustration evident in his voice. "I am so getting tired of seeing a tree in front of my face every second of the day, one after another after another."

Leo silently agreed, too tired to utter a complaint.

"You didn't think I steered you wrong when you admitted how beautiful Beetle Lake was when you first saw it," Hobin said as he continued to lead the way to the top.

"I didn't," Nicholas muttered, his head down low. He clambered up a steep incline littered with small rocks embedded among a thicket of scraggly trees which he grabbed onto for support. Leo followed closely behind.

"Then you'll be twice as happy when I show you this."

"Show me what?"

Nicholas looked up, pausing in his last few steps before he reached the top of the slope. His face was sweaty and streaked with dirt. He could barely catch a breath. Leo's condition appeared much the same. Hobin stood above them both, grinning knowingly.

"Show you *this!*" he shouted, sporting a lively grin while extending an arm through the air. "We're here."

"We are?" Leo uttered, his eyes open wide with gratitude.

Hobin urged them forward until Nicholas and Leo completed the last few grueling steps and clambered to the top. At last they were able to stand up straight and feel a cold breeze upon their faces, feeling for a moment as if they had already completed their journey. The top of Gray Hawk was composed primarily of stone and hard patches of moss and lichen. A few stunted trees and some straggly shrubs managed to sprout up here and there on the summit.

Nicholas inhaled the cool, crisp air as if drinking the finest ale he had ever tasted. He set his pack down and walked toward the center of the rocky summit, and then slowly turned around to take in the glorious panoramic view of the surrounding mountains, trees and lakes, basking in silent awe. To the west lay the blue expanse of Beetle Lake, sitting like a brilliant gemstone among a cushion of green velvet. The Five Brothers stood proudly in a line to the northwest, the tip of each mountaintop sun-splashed and wind-burned as they kept their silent watch. The vague outlines of more distant mountains were visible here and there among a sea of trees that made up the majority of Nicholas' view. But as he turned, scanning from the northeast to the east, he noted a stretch of pale and hazy blue beyond the greens and browns of the woodland, knowing that the Trillium Sea lay in that direction. As he remembered walking along its cold and lonely shoreline while attempting to rescue Ivy, a tinge of melancholy infused his heart while he imagined the massive body of water separating him from one so dear.

"I take back every unspoken curse that passed through my mind on our way up here," Leo said, standing with his arms akimbo and gazing across the sun-soaked horizon. "The view is amazing, don't you think, Nicholas?"

He turned to Leo when hearing his voice upon the edge of his drifting thoughts. "Yes, it is."

"There are the Five Brothers." Hobin delightfully pointed out the range of mountaintops as if he had created them himself. "We'll make our way between the farthest two mountains on the right which will lead us directly to Wolf Lake. You can see parts of that body of water between the peaks." He removed another map from his pack and carefully spread it open upon the ground so the constant gusts of wind wouldn't rip it from his hands and carry it away. This particular map depicted the exact same view they were now observing.

"Your lines are incredibly accurate now that I can compare them to the real thing," Leo said as he looked over his shoulder. "How long does it take you to draw a map?"

"Hours upon hours," Hobin replied, "which then add up to days upon days. But I enjoy doing it. I always make detailed sketches atop each mountain I climb to aid me in my work, but there's no time for that today. I just wanted to show you some of the results of my years of travel through the Dunn Hills."

"You should be proud," Nicholas said. "If you show your work to King Justin, I have no doubt that he would have his royal scribes create copies for the Citadel library and perhaps hire you to create maps of Arrondale."

"I would seriously consider that," he replied, putting the map away. "After I guide Leo back to your capital, I'll be happy to speak to the King if he'll grant me an audience."

"King Justin met with the likes of Nicholas and me, so I'm sure he'd be delighted to talk about mapmaking with you," Leo said. "He's quite an amiable fellow for a king–not that I've met any others, mind you. I think you two would get along just fine."

"Then I look forward to it. Now we must be off this mountain before darkness settles in," he said.

"Or bad weather approaches," Nicholas added, pointing out a section in the far western sky. A distant bank of ashen clouds was slowly drifting their way, its forward edges brushed with sunlight. "Rain tonight?"

"Or maybe snow," Hobin commented. "The weather can be very fickle in these parts. But we'll get what we get in spite of our wishes or complaints. Let's go."

They hiked down Gray Hawk Mountain, happy with a quicker descent after the grueling climb up. Even though they planned to travel to the northwest to reach two of the Five Brothers, they stayed on the western slope for a time as it was the easier course. Hobin told Nicholas and Leo that their next climb would seem much less difficult now that they had the first one under their belts.

"Next climb?" Leo asked. "First let me recover from this."

"It won't be during this journey, though I wish I had time to take you up one of the Five Brothers," Hobin replied. "That would be a sight worth seeing. But if ever I'm in Arrondale surveying for the King, I could always use a few reliable assistants. Something to think about, especially if the pay is good."

"I might take you up on your offer," Nicholas said. "It'd be fun to take a break from working as a bookkeeper in Ned Adams' gristmill–that is, if I ever get my old job back."

"You will," Leo assured him. "Once Ned and the others learn what Carmella told us about the murder, they'll realize you're innocent. And it might be fun helping Hobin map parts of Arrondale. A break from selling apples would be nice. It's about time my brother picked up some of the slack and learned the business."

"Kind of like he is now?" Nicholas asked with a smirk.

"I hope so," he replied.

"You two can mull it over," Hobin said as he eased his way down a stony slope covered by a blanket of decaying leaves that crunched underfoot.

"Do you think your father would mind you taking time off from the family business?" Nicholas asked Leo.

"I don't see why not. It'd only be temporary. I still want to cultivate my own orchards. What worries me is how Megan would react!"

"Good point," Hobin replied. "Until you settle any matter with the woman in your life, then it's simply not settled."

"And would that advice come from your past relationship with Emma?" Leo playfully inquired. "You can tell us."

"From that and commonsense."

"I'm sorry things didn't work out between the two of you," Nicholas said.

"Things were working out between us just fine," Hobin remarked, his eyes fixed on the ground ahead as it slowly leveled out.

"Oh? I just assumed that something happened between the two of you. Something that hadn't been settled, as you put it."

"That probably would have been best, Nicholas, parting on a point of contention. But fate had another surprise in store for us." He slowed down as he approached a quartet of tall pines among a swath of maple trees. A gurgling stream flowed behind them over a series of mossy rocks.

"What happened?" Nicholas asked, assuming that Hobin had stopped to tell them his life's story. He and Leo gazed at him in eager anticipation of a narrative both heartfelt and tumultuous.

Hobin shook his head as he ground the tip of his boot into the soil. "As I told you boys, I have no intention of telling you anything more about Emma and me. So don't take this as a personal insult because it's not, but–it's just not any of your business."

"Got it," Leo said. "So then why are we stopping here?"

"Because it's time to change course. I just want to get my bearings first."

Nicholas nodded. "Right. That makes sense. Verify directions. No talk of Emma."

"Now you're catching on," Hobin said, slapping him on the shoulder. He pointed beyond the pines to the northwest. "Now our path takes us that way. We're more than halfway down Gray Hawk, and as the terrain has leveled out, we can make our turn toward the Five Brothers. We'll head for the narrow valley between the last two mountains on the east end of the chain." He looked up at the dimming patch of blue among the treetops. "No clouds yet, but the light is fading. Let's travel for another hour if we can, then we'll camp for the night. With luck, we'll be passing between the mountains in about a day and a half."

"If exhaustion doesn't kill us first," Leo muttered. "I'm starting to feel like I'm in the Cashua Forest again. And let me tell you, I didn't like it much the first time."

"But you didn't have an expert guide like me with you then. That would have made all the difference."

They made camp in the deepening twilight, and after a brief meal around a crackling fire, they were soon fast asleep. The trio awoke the next day to dreary, leaden skies. The air felt colder and sharper. Occasionally light snow flurries would dance upon the air between the creaking trees. Their sixth day of hiking through the woods passed uneventfully, and by nightfall, once again exhausted and bleary-eyed, they made camp and built a fire before enjoying a meal of venison, potatoes and hot tea. It tasted like a feast.

"By this time tomorrow, or nearly so, we will have passed between two of the Brothers depending on our pace," Hobin said.

"And once we're through?" Leo asked.

"Then it's less than a day's journey to Wolf Lake where you can consult with your wizard friend, assuming he's still living there." Hobin looked up, his face reflecting the wavering flames. "But you'd better be prepared for the possibility that he's not. Be ready for bitter disappointment. You were given no guarantees."

"We're not even sure that Frist is alive," Nicholas said. "Tolapari hadn't seen him in years. This could all be for nothing."

"Then definitely don't get your hopes up," Hobin uttered as he finished his meal. "You'll only fall that much harder afterward."

They turned in soon after darkness. The clouds that had plagued them throughout the day continued to sail slowly overhead, obscuring the stars and the black, moonless sky. The orange-red glow from the fire cast dancing shadows upon the tree trunks and branches, sputtering and popping throughout the chilly night until it slowly consumed its fuel and reduced itself to glowing, hot coals. An owl called in the night as a small herd of deer weaved quietly through the distant trees.

Hobin opened his eyes to blackness, startled awake. The cold, clammy air felt oppressive as he wavered between consciousness and the remnants of a pleasant dream on the shores of Lake Lily. Then he heard it, the softest of sounds, as if the sole of a boot were carefully pressing down upon a patch of frosted and decaying leaves. He raised his head, detecting the movement of murky silhouettes near where they had stored their packs. He opened his eyes wider, trying to separate reality from imagination. As his vision slowly adjusted to the darkness, he noted the faint glow of the Bear Moon, not yet at third quarter, buried behind thick clouds high above. It provided just enough light to help him realize that the shifting shadows were the outlines of two people and not remnants of lingering sleep. He sat up, realizing they were about to be robbed–or worse.

He threw off his blanket and sprang to his feet, emitting a bloodcurdling call that instantly awoke Nicholas and Leo. The mysterious intruders spun around and unsheathed metal daggers in the darkness. Hobin did likewise as Nicholas and Leo sat up, each ripped from a deep sleep while still swimming in a fog of confusion.

"Intruders!" Hobin cried in the darkness. "Two of them!"

Suddenly an explosion of yellow, red and orange sparks shot in the air as Hobin jammed a few sticks into the pile of glowing embers left from last night's fire. The flash of pyrotechnics illuminated the area for an instant, allowing Nicholas, Leo and Hobin a glimpse of the enemy and the cold glint of their knives. As the woods succumbed to darkness again, one of the two men rushed at Hobin while the other headed toward Nicholas. Leo, on the opposite side of the fire, leaped over the embers to assist his friends.

The voices of Hobin and his assailant were distinguishable in the darkness as they struggled in hand-to-hand combat, their boots searching for a foothold against the slippery leaves on the hard ground. In that same moment, Nicholas saw the second man barreling toward him before the light had dimmed. He grabbed a large stick of firewood and raised it low above the ground, swinging it blindly at the man as he approached. A painful scream arose as the attacker stumbled forward. Nicholas had found his mark, cracking the piece of wood directly below the stranger's knees. But as the man cried in pain, he lunged at Leo who had hurried forward at that same moment, yanking him backward by the arm and tackling him to the ground, the full weight of his body upon him. Leo cried out in agony and then went silent. His assailant scrambled to his feet and dashed through the woods, his legs searing with pain and his mind in chaos.

Then something that sounded like a dry, choking gasp was audible in the darkness just beyond the glow of the fire that had come alive once again. Just as quickly, an eerie silence again enveloped the area. Nicholas looked around, still holding the piece of wood, his heart pounding, his breathing erratic. The muscles in his arms throbbed with the painful vibrations from the damage he had done to the man who had fled.

"Leo?" he called, fearing the worst. "*Hobin?*" Nicholas grabbed one of the now-burning sticks Hobin had shoved into the embers and held it aloft as a torch, dispelling the gloom. "Are you two all right?"

A moment later a shaken voice quietly replied.

"I'm fine," Hobin answered as he slowly stepped out of the shadows and approached the fire. He also grabbed a flaming stick and held it up, highlighting the horror in his eyes and the blood and dirt upon his face. "Are you hurt?"

"No," Nicholas said, catching his breath. He looked around, sweeping the torch through the air. "Leo, where are you? Are you okay? Answer me."

Hobin moved to one side to help search in the darkness. "Leo?"

"I think he's over there," Nicholas said, pointing past the fire. "The man who tried to attack me went after Leo just after I hit him." He hurried forward. "He should be—"

Nicholas froze when seeing a body sprawled upon the ground next to a large rock. He and Hobin rushed toward it, dispersing the shadows with their light. When he leaned forward, Nicholas could see that it was Leo, lying face down with his left arm extended underneath his chest at an awkward angle. Nicholas could hardly catch a breath when he saw his friend lying there. His blood ran cold with anguish and fear.

"Let's carefully turn him," Hobin whispered, taking charge. He set his torch against the rock and gently rolled Leo over so that he was now upon his back. His face was pale and bruised on one side when he had fallen.

Nicholas stared at him in shock, looking at Hobin for an answer. A moment later, Leo's chest rose as he took a shallow breath, slowly followed by another. His eyes darted beneath his closed lids. Nicholas couldn't help but smile. His friend was alive.

CHAPTER 54

To the Shores of Wolf Lake

Leo opened his eyes several minutes later. Nicholas and Hobin stared back at him as they knelt close by in the glow of the torches. For a few moments he couldn't remember where he was or what had happened, at first thinking they were waking him up in Hobin's cabin to begin their journey. Slowly, the bewildering string of events flooded his memory and Leo closed his eyes again.

"My head hurts," he softly muttered. He moved his left arm and winced in pain. "And my shoulder *really* hurts." Leo opened his eyes and took several labored breaths, a veil of disappointment upon his pale face. "Maybe you two should leave me here and go on when it's light. I'll recover–eventually."

"We've discussed that," Nicholas said lightly. "With luck, some deer or a bear might wander by and take care of you until we get back."

"Or have me for a meal."

He nodded. "Yeah, or that. Can you hold on until then?"

"I'll try."

"It's a good sign you can make jokes. Maybe your injury isn't too serious," Hobin said. "Can you raise your arm and bend it?"

Leo did so, very slowly, experiencing a sharp pain as he extended the limb. He lowered his arm to rest it, feeling exhausted after the minor movement. A deep, dull and persistent ache washed over his left shoulder while he remained still.

"Was that man trying to yank my arm out of its socket?" he muttered, attempting a bit more humor though the severe pain in his voice was evident.

"Since you can move your arm, I'm hoping you didn't break any bones," Hobin said. "But something was damaged in the attack."

"Who were those men?" Leo asked. "What did they want? And what happened to the one who attacked you?"

"They were from the Northern Isles, probably the ones who were following us a few days ago. I had assumed then that they were simply other hikers who we had crossed paths with, but now I realize they had been tracking us. And they were good at it, too. I saw no signs of them since that first time."

"They had to have been after the medallion," Nicholas said, fingering the leather cord around his neck. "Though I don't know how they could have found out about it."

"That has to be the answer," Leo said, closing his eyes again for a few moments before glancing at Hobin. "But how do you know they're from the Northern Isles? Did you get a good look at the one who attacked you?"

"You could say that," he replied, glancing knowingly at Nicholas. "But we can discuss that later. Right now, you should get some sleep, Leo. It's still many hours until sunrise. You need the rest after what you've been through."

"I agree," Nicholas said. He grabbed the blanket Leo had been lying upon earlier and brought it over. Leo eased his body onto it, wincing whenever his left shoulder moved. Nicholas gave him some water and covered him with another blanket to keep warm.

"What, no bedtime story?" he asked. But before Nicholas could reply, Leo had already closed his eyes and drifted off to sleep.

"That's the best medicine for him right now," Hobin said, grabbing his torch and walking to the fire. He added several more sticks and ignited the blaze to a crackling roar. "I doubt our other friend will return, especially after you whacked him in the knees, but we should keep guard until morning. I'll take the first watch."

"Okay," Nicholas said, joining him by the flames. He lowered his voice even though he was certain that Leo wouldn't wake up. "So tell me, Hobin–how are you so sure those men were from the Northern Isles?"

"I'll show you," he said, grabbing the torch and leading Nicholas to where he and his attacker had fought. Moments later, Nicholas noted the outline of a body lying upon the ground. A nauseating chill ran through him.

"Is he...?"

Hobin nodded. "I stabbed him before he could stab me." He rubbed a hand over his face, visibly upset at what had transpired. "I never killed a man before. I never had a reason to in all my life." He held the torch close to the dead body, its eyes still open. The unshaven man was dressed in a long brown coat and black boots traditional to soldiers from the Northern Isles. A dagger lying on the ground next to the body had markings indigenous to the Isles similar to those on a ring on one of the man's fingers.

Nicholas stared at the dead stranger for several moments, both numb and horrified by the sight. A more terrifying thought struck him and he slowly turned his head and eyed Hobin. "Do you think there are more of them?"

"I hope not, Nicholas. And since we didn't encounter any signs of others tracking us along the way, I'll take it as an indication that these were the only two." He tried to sound confident. "Still, let's act as if there may be more lurking about. That means the three of us can't sleep at the same time. One should always be on watch."

Nicholas agreed. "And what about him?" he added, pointing to the body.

"We'll bury it tomorrow. He won't be going anywhere," Hobin stated, a mix of coldness and pity laced among his words. He indicated for Nicholas to follow him back to the fire where he would begin his silent watch for the next couple of hours, needing time alone to think about what he had just been forced to do to save himself and his two charges. Hobin knew it would be a chilly and empty night ahead, wishing more than anything that he were walking in the warm light of day.

Dawn broke several hours later under ash gray clouds that moved in slowly from the west. When Nicholas opened his eyes, he found himself sitting against a tree and wrapped in a blanket near the dying remains of the fire. His back and neck felt sore. He decided a few more minutes of sleep would do him some good when he suddenly realized that he had drifted off while on watch. Hobin had awakened him two hours ago before going back to sleep himself.

He jumped up and looked around, his heart pounding. He saw Leo still dozing where they had left him during the night. Hobin was also sound asleep nearby, his head buried in a blanket. He breathed a sigh of relief. Everyone was safe despite him nodding off and letting the fire die out. He added kindling to the glowing embers to reignite the flames and soon had a roaring fire going. Half an hour later, Hobin stirred and sat up.

"How'd your watch go, Nicholas?"

"Just fine," he replied. "No problems."

"Good. Our other visitor must still be licking his wounds."

"Apparently so. I saw no sign of him last night," Nicholas said as he fished through his belongings, his back to Hobin. He decided not to tell him that he had slept through the majority of his watch. He prepared breakfast for both of them instead, feeling that that should more than adequately make up for his mistake.

They let Leo sleep, knowing it would help in his recuperation. After their meal, Hobin fashioned a digging implement out of a large stick using his knife and dug a shallow grave so he and Nicholas could bury the body of the Island soldier. By midmorning they had completed the task, marking the grave with that same stick. Hobin also stuck the man's knife into the ground next to the marker to indicate who was buried there.

"If his friend returns, he's sure to spot this," he said. He stood and brushed the dirt off his clothes. "But I have a feeling we've seen the last of him."

"Let's hope so. But now what do we do? We certainly can't carry Leo if he's unable to walk very far."

"We'll get to Wolf Lake and find your wizard. Don't worry about that," Hobin replied in a reassuring voice. "We'll let Leo sleep for as long as he needs to and then try to hike a few miles. I think we're entitled to an easy day after the distance we've put in already. We could all use the rest."

Leo finally stirred shortly after noontime and had something to eat and drink. He felt rested but his left shoulder still throbbed with a dull and persistent ache. If he moved his arm or shoulder suddenly, a sharp pain shot through him. Nicholas and Hobin carried as much of his gear as they could to lighten his pack, but after hiking only a mile, the trio felt as if they were slogging through a muddy swamp and stopped to rest.

"We'll never get there at this rate," Leo said apologetically. "Maybe I should wait here until you return."

"We're not leaving you," Nicholas said.

"He's right," Hobin agreed. "I won't abandon one of my charges–especially when you're paying me for my guidance." He rubbed his whiskered face, deep in thought before digging out one of Leo's spare shirts from his pack. "I've got an idea."

Moments later, Hobin gently tied the shirt around Leo's arm, neck and shoulder, fashioning a sling of sorts to keep his left arm from jostling too much during the hike. Leo walked a few steps to test it out, happy to report that it greatly helped him.

"It still aches like mad, but the sharp pains have diminished now that I can keep my arm still."

"Maybe I can help with that, too," Hobin said as he rummaged though his pack again. "I almost forgot about some of the supplies I'd purchased from a local apothecary last time I visited Red Lake. He sold me yoratelli leaves which are supposed to ease pain in the muscles and joints when steeped in hot water." He pulled out a folded piece of cloth from the bottom of his pack containing about three dozen, small green leaves with pointed tips. "Now's as good a time as any to try them out, don't you think?"

Leo grinned. "Who am I to argue with an apothecary from Red Lake? My specialty is apples."

While Nicholas started a fire and heated some water, Hobin crushed two of the leaves into a cup. After they filled it with the steaming liquid, a soothing and minty aroma filled the air and reminded them of happier times. Leo took the cup with his good hand, sniffed the concoction and took a sip, grimacing.

"It's not awful," he said, "but this yoratelli definitely smells better than it tastes. Still, I'll give it a try." He slowly drank the medicine, happy to finish the last few drops.

"Hope it helps," Hobin said as Nicholas doused the fire with water from a nearby stream. "When you're ready, we'll move on."

"Let's go now," Leo said. "I've held us up long enough. I'll let you know if you got your money's worth from that apothecary."

Less than an hour later, Leo reported that the pain in his shoulder had greatly subsided, allowing him to increase his hiking speed. Nicholas and Hobin also noted that the tension in his face had disappeared. Leo looked like his old, cheerful self again, confirming to them that he wasn't just pretending to feel better.

"Worth every one of those eight copper half pieces," Hobin remarked with a cheery laugh.

Nonetheless, they stopped for extra breaks along the way, allowing Leo to rest as often as possible. And they made camp for the night earlier than usual, about an hour before sundown, which enabled them to enjoy a more leisurely meal and gather additional wood for a larger fire. During this time, Hobin and Nicholas told Leo about the fate of the second attacker. But what they didn't tell him was that they planned to keep a secret watch for one more night just as a precaution. After Leo finally went to sleep, Hobin took the first three-hour shift and allowed Nicholas to get some rest, promising to wake him for his turn. They planned to alternate in three-hour increments until sunrise. Nicholas agreed and quickly dozed off, awaiting his turn on guard.

There were no surprise visitors during the night. Nicholas was glad to see the first glimmer of daylight in the southeast when he completed his second round on watch. Neither he nor Hobin planned to reveal to Leo that they had lost valuable sleep to keep their vigil, knowing that he would have raised a fuss for not being included. But he was none the wiser during breakfast, again feeling an agonizing pain in his shoulder.

"I'll fix up another brew of the yoratelli leaves," Hobin said. "That'll keep you going all day. By the time we make camp tonight, we should be passing between the peaks of the last two Brothers. We'll arrive at Wolf Lake tomorrow."

"I hope so," Leo said, his words labored and weary.

And though he assured the others that the pain in his shoulder wasn't severe, Nicholas and Hobin believed otherwise, observing his glassy-eyed stare and tense facial muscles. But an hour later, after drinking a second cup of the yoratelli brew, Leo perked up and his pain lessened substantially. They continued hiking for the rest of the day as if he had never been injured at all. An hour before sundown, as on the previous night, they made camp, having nearly passed

NICHOLAS RAVEN AND THE WIZARDS' WEB - VOLUME 2

through the region between the two easternmost peaks of the Five Brothers. By then the clouds had thinned, allowing the nearly first quarter Fox Moon to lend a subtle glow from above as twilight deepened. After a quick meal, the trio retired to their warm, fur lined blankets and varied dreams. As they had passed the previous night without incident, Hobin and Nicholas agreed that a second night on watch was unnecessary.

The following morning dawned cold, gray and breezy, marking the ninth day since they had left Woodwater. After breakfast they moved on. Leo refused another dose of Hobin's brew, despite his obvious pain. He wanted to see how far he could hike without it. But by midmorning he relented as the soreness in his shoulder grew unbearable. By noontime they had entered an area beyond the northern slopes of the Five Brothers, having at last cleared the passage between the two easternmost peaks. In this spot the trees had thinned and allowed a view of the surroundings. When Nicholas turned and gazed south from where they had traveled, he could see the forested slopes of the two peaks, gazing up at both in awe. Each was several hundred feet higher than Gray Hawk Mountain.

"Now that I can see the peaks up close, I really do want to climb them," he said to Hobin, admiring their beauty. "Unfortunately we won't have the time."

"Or a fully able member of the party," Leo joked. "Maybe some day we can return–by an easier route, of course."

"It's a difficult climb, but worth the effort," Hobin said as he eased the pack off his tired shoulders. "And as long as we've stopped, we might as well have lunch here. You won't find a better view until you get closer to the lake in a few hours."

They ate a cold meal and rested for a few minutes before resuming their trek. And under four hours later, just as Hobin had predicted, the choppy, bluish-gray waters of Wolf Lake slowly came into view through the distant trees. They hurried to the shoreline situated on the edge of the woods as a light snow flurry descended from a billowy fleet of dirty, gray clouds.

"There aren't any villages on this end of the lake," Hobin said, throwing a hood over his head. Nicholas and Leo were similarly attired. "There are a few on the western edge, but we won't be going near them. Our path will take us to a small island on the water several miles west and about a half mile off the shoreline. You can just make it out from where we're standing." He pointed at the island. Nicholas and Leo craned their necks to catch a glimpse of the wizard Frist's dwelling through the finely blowing snow.

"Tolapari mentioned he had guided Frist there to make his final home," Nicholas said, barely able to see the dark dot upon the water. He shoved his gloved hands into his coat pockets for extra warmth. "He also said that Frist used to roam about the Dunn Hills and climb these very mountains just like you, Hobin. Do you think there's a bit of wizard's blood in your veins?" he lightly added.

"I don't have the patience or composure of a wizard. We both just happen to appreciate the beauty of this area, that's all."

Nicholas chuckled. "Patience, maybe. But composure? That doesn't describe either Vellan or Caldurian. From what I've learned, they're two of the most out-of-control wizards I've ever heard described. You'd be a better wizard than either of those two by far."

"I thank you for that compliment, Nicholas, but being a wizard is not one of my goals in life," Hobin replied. "I have enough to do without dabbling in magic."

"Still, I think you'd be a great one, don't you, Leo?"

"*Hmmm?*" he replied, looking up while leaning against a tree. He hadn't been paying close attention to their conversation, and both men could see right away that he was in pain again.

"The medicine is wearing off," Hobin said. "I'll crush three leaves next time."

Leo shook his head, his face strained. "I don't want any more. I just want to get to the island. When we arrive, maybe I can sleep for a day or two." He glanced helplessly at Nicholas. "I don't know how I'm going to get back home in this condition."

"We'll figure something out," Nicholas replied, detecting a tinge of fear in his friend's eyes, certain that Megan and his family were foremost on Leo's mind. "First let's have something to eat before we leave. There's still time to get to the island before nightfall, right, Hobin?"

"Just barely," he said, "providing we don't stop for any more breaks. But you're almost at the end–and to think you made it all this way from Morrenwood."

"From Kanesbury and Minago," Nicholas corrected him. "And a few side trips included. I can't believe the miles we've traveled. These were some of the most grueling."

"If you plan to reach the Trillium Sea, there are plenty more punishing miles ahead, Nicholas. Let's eat and move on so we can first end this journey," Hobin said, rummaging through his backpack. "As there's no time to build a fire, what'll it be, gentlemen? Cold strips of venison or cold strips of beef? Your choice."

After a hasty meal, they continued through the bare trees with the lapping waters of Wolf Lake to their right. A veil of fine snow flurries swirled through the air and dusted the decaying leaves upon the forest floor. They had hiked for less than an hour as the light began to fade, their pace slowing due to Leo's sluggish steps. But eventually the island increased in size. They drew closer until they were at a point on the shoreline directly opposite the wizard's home located a quarter mile from the water's edge. Suddenly Nicholas voiced exactly what Leo and Hobin were both thinking.

"How are we supposed to get over there?" He scratched the back of his neck, a slight grin upon his face. "To tell you the truth, I never really thought about it until now."

"Doesn't say much for our planning," Leo said, rubbing his sore shoulder with his right hand. His left arm was still in its sling.

"We'll construct a small raft," Hobin decided as if it were only a minor inconvenience. "I'll start first thing in the morning. I have a small axe in my pack and there are plenty of trees."

"What about rope to lash it together?" Nicholas asked.

"No need. A few deep notches here and there will do the trick. It'll be nothing fancy, mind you, but it'll float us over to that island." He wandered deeper in the woods with Nicholas, examining some of the smaller trees and pointing out which ones they might use, eagerly anticipating how to attack the project.

"We've come all this way and now we're stuck on the water's edge," Nicholas complained with an exasperated sigh. "Maybe I should just swim over there, Hobin."

"Uh, I don't think that will be necessary," Leo called out, gazing suspiciously across the water as Nicholas and Hobin turned around and wandered back to shore.

"Why not?" he asked as they emerged through the trees.

Leo pointed across the surface of the lake, now dusted with twilight as the snow began to subside. "Look."

Nicholas and Hobin shifted their gazes to the spot that Leo had indicated. After their eyes adjusted to the dimming light, their mouths were instantly agape. Slowly, and no doubt magically, a small, wooden canoe was floating across the water from the island toward their location on shore with no one inside the craft to propel it forward. It moved in a straight, steady line, unaffected by the mild wind and the choppy waves. The three men glanced at one another, each dumbfounded yet delighted at the same time.

"I guess Frist is alive and home after all," Nicholas softly said. "And apparently he wants us to pay him a visit."

CHAPTER 55

The Wizard Frist

Hobin stepped into the water's edge and pulled the empty canoe onto shore, contemplating the vast powers of the wizard who had sent it across the lake. Inside were two wooden paddles and room enough for three passengers. He grunted in amusement.

"Exactly what we need," he muttered. "And perfectly timed."

"What was that?" Nicholas asked as he gathered two of the packs to load them into the canoe.

"Just wondering how this wizard knew we were coming." Hobin scratched his head. "Maybe he has a network of spies who've been tracking us."

"Spies or no spies, we have a boat," Leo said. He grabbed his pack with his good arm and walked it slowly to the canoe. "Saves us from building one so we can finish this mission that much sooner."

"Doesn't sound like your heart is in this adventure anymore," Nicholas said. He took Leo's pack and set it in the boat. "You can sit in the middle. Hobin and I will paddle."

After helping Leo into the canoe, Nicholas and Hobin slowly pushed it back into the water, climbed in and started paddling toward the island. Nicholas sat in front, gazing at the mass of land before them shrouded in purple twilight. Intermittent snow flurries swirled upon a light breeze.

The island appeared oval in shape, stretching a quarter mile in length and half that distance in width. The surface, higher in some parts than others, was covered with a variety of trees, thickets of dense brush and a range of low rock cliffs along portions of the island. They glided across the lake's surface accompanied by the gentle whoosh of water against the paddles. It reminded Nicholas of his time along the Trillium Sea while searching for Ivy. But before he could indulge himself in those memories again, the island drew swiftly nearer as if magically pulling them toward it. Minutes later the bottom of the canoe scraped against the sandy shoreline and they came to an abrupt halt.

"Here we are," Nicholas said, his words swallowed in the deepening darkness. He looked at his companions with uncertainty. "Shall we make our visit now or wait for sunup?"

Leo grimaced in pain. "I'm willing to search now."

Hobin cleared his throat before Nicholas could respond. "Not necessary," he whispered, pointing to the edge of the trees to his left. "Somebody has already found *us*."

Nicholas and Leo turned their heads, startled to see a man with a flickering torch standing on the edge of the tree line. The erratic light cast shadows all about him. Though they were not close enough to see his face in detail, the stranger appeared far too young to be the wizard.

"We're getting prompt service for being uninvited guests," Nicholas remarked as he stepped out of the canoe and helped Leo onto shore. He and Hobin removed the packs and set them away from the water's edge before pulling the canoe farther inland.

"He's waiting for us," Leo whispered, glancing at the man who stood unmoving the entire time. "Let's introduce ourselves."

They walked up to the figure, curious about him yet not fearful. He appeared to be in his mid twenties, tall with long, black hair and wearing plain clothes and a heavy coat similar to the people they had briefly met in the village of Pomeroy on Beetle Lake. He smiled and bowed his head as the trio approached.

"I'm guessing you sent that canoe to us," Nicholas said in a friendly tone to break the tension. "We appreciate it."

"You can thank Frist for that bit of convenience," he politely replied. "He's been expecting you for about two days now."

"How?" Hobin asked. "Were his spies patrolling the woods?"

"Frist has no spies. I am his sole assistant from time to time." He stepped forward to shake hands with his guests, noting with concern Leo's injured left arm in its sling. "My name is Rustin. And I suppose I should rephrase my last comment. Frist has been expecting *someone* for about two days now, someone carrying something he had never expected to see again."

Nicholas suspected that Rustin was referring to the medallion. He decided not to make mention of the object until he met the wizard in person.

"Frist is very perceptive," he replied. "We hope to meet him."

"That's why he sent you the canoe and asked me to take you to him," Rustin said. "He'll answer the many questions I'm sure you all have. Are you ready?"

"As we'll ever be," Leo said, eager to continue. "Is it far?"

"Only a few minutes to his abode," Rustin said. "Though this island has plenty of room for one man, it's still not very large."

"Please lead on," Nicholas said, feeling their fortune changing for the better.

"Before you do," Hobin interjected, "I'll respectfully wait here and make camp until you return. After all, whatever happens beyond this point is really Nicholas and Leo's business, not mine. I was only hired as their guide."

"Are you sure?" Nicholas asked.

"I appreciate you confiding in me, but you and Leo were appointed by King Justin to see this matter through. I'll let you two handle the negotiations. I'll build a fire here and set up camp. With your permission, of course," he added, eyeing Rustin.

"As you wish." Rustin bent down and grabbed a large stick and set it aflame with his torch. He handed it to Hobin. "You'll need some light. Night is fast approaching."

"Then you three had better be off before it gets here," Hobin replied, shooing them away before the trio disappeared into the darkening woods.

They followed Rustin along a well-worn path through the trees. Darkness quickly settled in as a cold breeze weaved its way through the creaking maples and pines. The light snow had stopped, but billowing, coal gray clouds portended a severe winter ahead.

"Are you from these parts?" Nicholas asked, curious about how Rustin had come to know the wizard.

"I was born in a village about a two hour walk west along the lake," he said, telling them of his life in the Dunn Hills and how Frist had taken him on as an apprentice three years ago. "But he is a much older wizard and says that I should seek out a younger teacher if I really want to learn the craft. Though he has taught me many things, I think I aid him better as a servant than as an apprentice," he admitted, explaining how he brought in supplies for Frist from time to time, apprised him of goings-on in the area and told the wizard stories to keep him entertained. "It's not the grandest apprenticeship, I'm sure, but to be privy to his vast knowledge of the wizarding world has been a great honor indeed."

"Why doesn't Frist live inside one of the villages if he likes this area so much?" Leo asked. "Why does he isolate himself?"

Rustin shrugged, unable to fully answer the question. "Though he makes an occasional appearance in the surrounding communities, living a secluded life is the way of the wizards–at least of the original race that wandered from the Valley of the Wizards in the Gable Mountains far in the west. Those who are fit enough in their later lives–reaching ages far older than we ever will–tend to seek out a place they had grown fond of during their travels to spend their final years. I don't particularly understand it, but it is their way. You might ask Frist more about it if you desire."

Leo shook his head, appearing doubtful. "Now that I hear you discuss it, I think not. Sounds like it's none of my business. We should be thankful that he's willing to take the time to meet us." He grimaced, grabbing his sore shoulder.

"Are you in more pain?" Nicholas asked.

"That last dose of yoratelli is wearing off," he said, stopping for a moment. He took a deep breath and exhaled, appearing pale in the flickering torch flame.

"Perhaps you'll allow Frist to take a look at your arm," Rustin said. "He has cured many minor injuries and others not so minor. Ah, we are nearly there," he said as they turned right along another dirt trail. "He lives past the large boulder at the end of this path. Here you can rest and have some food. I prepared extra soup and fish earlier as we were expecting company."

"We're grateful for your hospitality. It's been quite a journey from Morrenwood," Nicholas replied, though in the back of his mind he knew that his days on the road were only just beginning if he intended to go through with his plan to search for Ivy. But for now he would try to enjoy this brief respite, knowing that Leo needed a sustained and recuperative rest before he could return to the Citadel with the key.

As they neared the end of the path, a large boulder half buried in the ground loomed ahead to their right. Here the trees had been cleared, opening up enough space for a small house and a bit of land for cultivating several gardens. Off to the left was a modest, one-story building constructed of clay bricks and wood. Bluish-gray smoke rose in mischievous swirls through a round chimney. A faint yellow glow was visible around the edges of thick, wooden shutters covering several circular windows. A door constructed of hewn oak, not quite square at the angles, closed out the night.

"We are here," Rustin said, leading his visitors to the house. He gently knocked on the front door and called out to the wizard. "Frist, it is Rustin. I've returned with guests. May we enter?"

"Of course, of course!" a voice replied from within. "You needn't knock every time you step out to run an errand, gather wood or fetch strangers." Suddenly the door swung open and the old, frail wizard stood outlined against the interior glow, bundled in woolen garb and holding a steaming cup of tea. Despite his thinning gray hair and unshaven face, his quiet, blue eyes emitted a youthful spark from time to time. He eyed Nicholas and Leo for a moment, and after greeting them and asking their names, the wizard introduced himself with a pleasant smile. "Rustin can be too polite sometimes. I tell my apprentice that a good wizard requires a bit of nettles and bad cider about him–attitude wise, of course–as well as patience, foresight and, well, all the rest." He beckoned the trio to step into the welcoming warmth of his home. "Sit by the fire. I'll pour you tea."

"Thank you," Nicholas replied, stepping into the room and suddenly noticing that the wizard was staring at him with a puzzled intensity which made him feel both guilty and uncomfortable. "Is something the matter?"

The wizard stroked his chin. "You look awfully familiar, Nicholas. Have we met before?"

"I doubt that very much, sir. I had only just been born the last time you were in my village of Kanesbury about twenty years ago."

"Ah, you know of my visit."

"Stories of the Enâri were rampant when I was growing up. Your name was spoken of fondly and often," Nicholas replied.

"Yes, well we can discuss that later," Frist said, continuing to usher his guests inside while still trying to jog his memory regarding Nicholas' familiar appearance.

When the door closed behind them, almost immediately Nicholas and Leo felt the weariness of their travels dissipate as if there was some magical quality to the air inside that was slowly healing them. But even if it was only their imaginations playing tricks, they welcomed the restorative effects. Soon they were drinking tea with the wizard while Rustin prepared a meal at a nearby table. But before Nicholas could explain the purpose of their visit or ask the wizard how he knew they were on their way to his home, Frist attended to other matters.

"What happened to your arm, Leo? How did you injure it?"

"It's my shoulder actually," he replied, again feeling the pain despite his initial euphoria upon entering the house. He recounted how he was attacked almost three days ago, at which point Nicholas jumped into the conversation, wanting to tell Frist about the medallion and why the Islanders had sought him out in the wild.

"I suspect I already know," Frist said, interrupting him. "Your attackers were after that key I created twenty years ago, or at least after something *like* that key."

"Yes," Nicholas said. "But how did you know?"

Frist smiled. "Because I can still sense the magic inside it. I have for about two days now which is how I knew someone was looking for me. Its presence grew stronger with your every step closer to this island." The wizard tilted his head slightly as a look of vague confusion settled upon his countenance. "But something is not quite right about my key, am I correct? I'm certain it's my magic spell that I detect, but has the object itself been altered? Has it succumbed to a counter spell?"

Nicholas removed the medallion from around his neck and held it up for the wizard to see. "The key fell victim to the hot fires of a forge and several hammer blows thanks to one of the Enâri creatures who had stolen it," he said, handing the piece of metal to the wizard who was eager to examine it. "That's what's left of your key, sir. Leo and I brought it here from Morrenwood at the behest of King Justin, hoping you could refashion it back into a copy of the original. The wizard Tolapari gave us your location in secret and helped prepare us for this journey."

Frist smiled upon hearing the name of his former student and raised his eyes while clutching the medallion. "And how is my old friend and loyal guide? He accompanied me to this place many years ago, pleased that I had chosen him for that honor."

"He's quite well," Nicholas said. "There's a good part of nettles and bad cider about him, as you would say."

"He tolerates nonsense from no one," the wizard said. "That's why we got along so well and why I agreed to advance his training." Frist grew silent while examining the medallion, recalling the effort he had put forth to create it that nearly consumed him both physically and mentally. "And the Spirit Box? What has become of that?"

"It's safe, too," Leo said. "The box is under guard in the Blue Citadel. The King is prepared to open it upon our return, or I should say has ordered it be opened upon our return. King Justin and his army will be on their way to Rhiál by then, or possibly already there, when the key is returned. And Prince Gregory will lead a second army to Montavia. Troops from the Northern Isles, along with the five hundred Enâri you had cast under a sleeping spell, have recently occupied that kingdom. King Rowan's two grandsons escaped to the Citadel and told us of the invasion."

"So my sleeping spell wore off," Frist commented with an air of disappointment.

"No, it didn't," Nicholas said, recalling details that King Justin had learned from Len Harold during a private conversation before the war council. "Apparently one of my fellow villagers from Kanesbury had been duped into entering the Spirit Caves and unknowingly helped awaken the Enâri." He told the story of George Bane, a glass sphere and an eerie blue fog that somehow brought the Enâri back to consciousness.

"It seems I have missed much in the outside world," the wizard said, "so perhaps you should tell me everything that's happened while we have our supper. I especially want to know more about how my simple, yet elegant key became this metallic monstrosity." He held up the medallion by the leather cord. "I'm sure it's a fascinating tale."

"I'll be happy to recount all that's happened," Nicholas said. "But first, is there anything you can do to ease Leo's pain?" He glanced at his friend sitting in a wooden chair closest to the fireplace. And though Leo made an effort to participate in the conversation as if nothing were the matter, Nicholas could detect the severe discomfort he was trying to hide.

"I can do better than that," Frist replied. "I'm still a capable wizard from the Gable Mountains despite my advancing years."

"We should handle matters with the key first," Leo said, his arm resting again in the makeshift sling after he had removed his coat. "My shoulder can wait. I don't want to waste valuable time."

"If you plan to return to Morrenwood with the key intact, then you must be intact as well." He looked reassuringly at Leo. "Trust me. You will feel no pain. I have administered to worse injuries than this." He handed the medallion back to Nicholas and then stood beside Leo, gently pressing his fingertips upon his left shoulder. "In earlier days I would often receive a basket of fresh eggs for my labors. Once I was presented a slab of bacon. Mostly fish around these parts now, though I haven't been about in some time."

"We have a little money to pay you," Nicholas said.

The wizard chuckled. "I am not angling for compensation but merely making conversation. What you two are doing for King Justin is more than payment enough. Many people will be in your debt." He stepped away from Leo and thought for a moment before slowly walking into an adjoining room. "I believe I have a solution," he said, his voice rising above the sudden clatter of glass vials and clay jars. "Rustin, fill a cup with hot water please."

Leo glanced at Nicholas with horrified amusement. "I hope I'm not getting another dose of yoratelli."

"Definitely not," Frist announced as he returned to the room and took the cup of hot water that Rustin had prepared, adding a few drops of an amber-colored liquid from a tiny vial. "Though yoratelli would help ease your pain temporarily, I have something better." Frist handed him the steaming cup. "Drink this for starters."

"For *starters*?" Leo raised his eyes skeptically. "What is it? And what follows?"

"This is the first half of your cure," Frist replied. "Trust me, it will not harm you and will taste much better than even the freshest yoratelli leaves."

"I guess that's a plus," he muttered before taking a cautious first sip. He was pleasantly surprised though how palatable the drink was and took several more swallows. "Not bad. It's chasing the damp chill right out of my body."

"Much like Hobin's ale?" Nicholas joked.

"But hopefully without the same effects the day after."

"This is better than ale," the wizard said, taking the empty cup from Leo after he had finished his drink. "Now I can complete your cure if you're ready."

"Ready as ever," he replied, appearing more relaxed and less concerned about the wizard's plan for his shoulder. "How long will this take?"

"Not long for me," Frist replied, standing at his side. He placed one hand upon Leo's injured shoulder and another just above his elbow. He closed his eyes and began to whisper words that neither Leo nor Nicholas could comprehend. As Frist continued to speak, his voice grew lower and softer and his facial muscles tightened. Slowly his eyes closed, and though his lips continued to move, the wizard's voice was silent as he cast his healing spell.

Soon Leo's eyelids grew heavy as a deep and recuperative sleep overwhelmed him. A moment later his eyelids dropped as his head leaned comfortably against the back of the chair. He took a deep breath and exhaled, a slight smile of relief upon his face. Frist opened his eyes and removed his hands from Leo's arm and shoulder. His spell was now fully administered.

Nicholas glanced at the wizard, unsure whether he should break the solemn silence, but did so with a whisper. "How is he?"

"He's sleeping," Frist replied matter-of-factly.

"For how long?"

"For a few hours. It will do him a world of good."

"Will his shoulder be all right?"

"The spell is healing it as we speak, so there is no need to worry. Leo will be fine," he promised. "In the meantime, let us eat the supper that Rustin has graciously made and talk more about that key of mine–or what remains of it."

While Leo soundly slept, Nicholas, Rustin and the wizard ate at the table and discussed the goings-on in Arrondale and elsewhere. Nicholas told them about the war between Rhiál and Maranac and of the invasion of Montavia, as well as his and Leo's journey with Princess Megan and their failed rescue of Ivy above the grasslands. Frist was touched when Nicholas spoke of reluctantly abandoning Leo and Hobin to resume his search for Ivy, planning to leave the reforged key in their trust.

"I'm confident they'll deliver the key to Morrenwood," he said. "But I must move on to the greater cause in my heart."

As Nicholas continued to discuss his adventures, Frist was especially interested in hearing how Jagga had murdered Arthur Weeks and stole the key to the Spirit Box. He found it darkly comical that the Enâr had gone to so much trouble to melt down the key and dispose of it, only to have the object end up in the hands of the very wizard who created it.

"I had put some of my very life force into that key," Frist said. "And though I recovered from the strenuous effort over time, I felt that I was never whole again. It was an exhausting endeavor, almost debilitating to me."

Nicholas looked at the elderly wizard, nearly on the verge of hopelessness, wondering if Frist was about to tell him that his and Leo's journey had been for nothing. "Is it impossible to repair it?"

"No, I'm not saying that at all," he replied, taking a spoonful of soup. "You and Leo did not travel here in vain. I shall be able to remake the key, though it will be a monumental effort. The spell still resides within the medallion, though somewhat misshapen by the forging process. It will require several hours to reform the key and fix the spell, but it shall be done—and it shall be done tonight. Rustin will have to get a fire started outdoors."

"We have a small forge built into the base of a rock face just beyond the second garden," Rustin said. "Anyone could easily melt the medallion there, but only Frist has the power to remake his creation."

"And I willingly accept the challenge," he said.

"Yet I respectfully suggest that perhaps..." Rustin's voice faded when he glanced at his two companions with an obvious sense of worry. "It might be best if—"

The wizard interrupted Rustin with a soft chuckle. "What my apprentice is trying to say is that creating such an elaborate spell–or in this case, repairing it–might be too laborious a task for an old wizard like me," he explained to Nicholas.

"You have experienced extreme fatigue and dizziness teaching me some lesser spells over the last months," Rustin said. "That's why I have not pushed you for many lessons in recent weeks and have returned to my village for longer stays than I used to."

"Still, I'm a teacher at heart and wish to do what I love best."

Rustin nodded appreciatively. "Then I will accede to your wishes if your mind is truly decided."

"It is," the wizard said.

Nicholas noted the determination in the old man's eyes, yet he also wondered if the task might be too much for him. But as Frist continued to talk about the necessity of opening the Spirit Box, he knew the wizard would never be talked out of making the attempt. After supper, Frist instructed his apprentice to prepare a fire in the forge so he could begin the elaborate process later that evening. Rustin bowed obediently as he got up from the table, grabbed his coat and then stepped outdoors, heading for the rock face.

Nicholas and Frist in the meantime, continued to discuss the troublesome events plaguing Laparia, each speculating whether the small part they were playing would have any effect on the spreading wars. When the wizard refilled their cups with more tea, Nicholas took it as a sign that he was in the mood for more conversation and seized the opportunity to pose several questions about Vellan. He was rewarded with the story of Vellan's towering ambition and his expulsion from the Valley of the Wizards at the age of twenty-eight.

"That was fifty years ago, yet the memory is still etched clearly in my mind," Frist said, recounting those dark days. "For all of his skill, intelligence and potential to do good, Vellan's one weakness was his love of himself and of his grand ideas to the point where he could see nothing else. His behavior was obsessive and childish." The wizard sighed wearily. "Vellan was perpetually consumed with creating a world where everyone should bow to his will and greatness, and as the years passed, his warped vision–if he can even remember what it originally was–has led to war, poverty and economic chaos in all lands marked by his evil touch." Frist leaned back in his chair. "It's ironic that the hands of a potential healer have caused so much misery and destruction. Besides using our magic for practical applications and entertainment from time to time, some of the best wizards have developed and perfected spells and potions to combat the ailments that have inflicted men and women for years. Healing is a noble calling for any wizard, but one which Vellan has willfully and selfishly cast to the winds."

"Luckily for Leo that you hadn't," Nicholas said, glancing at his friend who was still sound asleep in the chair. "You performed a compassionate act."

"Any wizard who is truly good at heart would have done the same," Frist softly said as he stared at his patient, observing Leo's breathing pattern, facial hue and expression. He went silent for a long moment, contemplating a jumble of images from the past until his eyes widened in sudden recognition. Frist turned his head and stared at Nicholas, a slow smile forming upon his face. "*Now* I know where I've seen you before! I tried to save your life after the Enâri attack."

Nicholas was taken aback. "Excuse me?"

Frist quickly shook his head. "My thoughts are getting ahead of my words. Not *your* life, of course, but a man I assume was your father—someone named Jack Raven." The wizard suddenly appeared melancholy as he recalled that terrible time. "Yet I had failed back then in my task. I had failed."

Nicholas looked askance at the wizard. "I don't understand. Failed at what? And how do you know my father's name?"

"When I first saw your face at the doorway, Nicholas, I was certain we had met before. But given your age, and considering how long I've lived here, that would be impossible. But now that distant memories have been jogged, I realize that it was your father whom I had met in Kanesbury twenty years ago while combating the Enâri." Frist stared at Nicholas. "You look remarkably like Jack Raven when he was about your age."

"So I've been told by others who knew him well," Nicholas said, both troubled and perplexed by the wizard's words. "But how could you have met my father? And how could you have tried to save him from an Enâri attack? He died in a terrible storm one night shortly before I was born. He was thrown from a horse."

The wizard returned a skeptical gaze. "Was there another Jack Raven living in Kanesbury? A relative with the same name?"

"No," Nicholas said. "He was the only one. He died from the injuries sustained during a fall."

"But if I'm not mistaken, his wife's name was…" The wizard thought for a moment, again reaching back in time for a faded memory. "Alice, I believe."

Nicholas slowly nodded, his mouth agape. "Alice was my mother. She died when I was five. But how…?"

"Then it is your father who I'm thinking of and tried to cure," Frist replied, observing Nicholas' stunned expression. Then the realization suddenly hit him, but it was too late. The wizard knew there was no taking back the words he had already spoken. "Dear me, but I can see now that you were never told the truth about your father's death," he continued, sorry that he had ever broached the subject. "I had just assumed…"

Nicholas sat silently for a moment, not fully comprehending what he had just heard. When he was almost five years old, he vaguely remembered his mother once explaining to him why he didn't have a father. He had asked her for a reason when seeing other children walking or playing with their own fathers. He recalled the pained look upon his mother's face, remembering her explaining something about a terrible storm and a wild horse. Only after her death, when Nicholas was raised for several years on his uncle's farm, did he hear the full story of Jack Raven's accidental demise which he accepted as truth. Years later, when Maynard and Tessa Kurtz eventually adopted him, they also related the same story if ever the subject of his father's death surfaced. The account had become a melancholy piece of personal history that Nicholas carried with him. But with a few words, Frist had turned this sad fact upside down.

"Tell me of the Enâri attack you spoke of," Nicholas said after giving a brief account to the wizard of what he had been told as a child. "What do you know?"

"First let me apologize for my carelessness. I–"

"No need to," he calmly jumped in. "I just want to know the truth. You certainly couldn't have known that my father's fate would be hidden from me years later."

The wizard offered a heartfelt smile. "I'm sure your family members were only trying to conceal a terrible truth from a young boy, not wanting you to grow up bitter or resentful if you knew what really happened."

Nicholas nodded. "I now know that and have no ill feelings toward the people I love because of it. How could I after all they've done for me? Still, I need to know what happened to my father."

The wizard told Nicholas how he had traveled in haste to Kanesbury with King Justin and his troops twenty years ago after Otto Nibbs sent word that his village was under an Enâri attack. They arrived to discover that Caldurian and his associates had taken refuge near Kanesbury after the attempted kidnapping of Princess Megan in the Citadel. In anger and desperation, Caldurian had unleashed the Enâri upon the village after Mayor Nibbs refused to act as a go-between with his cousin, the King, to help encourage an alliance between Arrondale and Kargoth.

"After several days of terror, the uprising was quashed upon the arrival of King Justin's forces," Frist explained. "The Enâri fled to the caves outside the village and were trapped within by the royal guard. Caldurian and Madeline were arrested and his eagle, Xavier, captured. As you know from local stories, I cast a sleeping spell over the creatures to avoid further bloodshed, creating a contained spirit to destroy them should they ever awake and escape in the future. But as I was attempting to challenge a creation of Vellan's, my spirit needed years of incubation to gain the strength and potency to be effective. I suspected that such a magical weapon would never be needed in the future." Frist took a sip of tea. "Seems I was wrong."

"But fortunately you created the Spirit Box. And I have every confidence that you can repair the key that opens it," Nicholas said. "But right now I just want to know what happened to my father."

"Of course," he replied with understanding. "You see, Nicholas, just before King Justin and I had arrived, your father and several other men had been involved in a skirmish with a large group of the Enâri. Your father was severely wounded while trying to lead your mother to safety. He was one of the injured people I tended to while the King's soldiers were safeguarding the village. Your mother was at his side through the entire ordeal as I remember, at the time with child. It must have been only days from your birth." The wizard looked at Nicholas with sincere regret. "I tried everything I knew, but his wounds were just too grave. As powerful as I am, Nicholas, I cannot hold back death when it wants its way. Wizard though I am, and as long-lived as our race is, we are mortal in the end."

"I understand."

"I wish there had been more I could have done for your father, and especially for your mother and her unborn son. But alas, Vellan's evil sting had reached both your family and your village during those several days." A faint, hopeful smile appeared on the wizard's countenance as he looked into Nicholas' eyes. "Yet judging by the persistence you have shown and the hardships you've endured to bring this medallion to me, I can only conclude that Jack Raven must have been a decent soul to have fathered such a fine son. He would have been very proud of you."

Nicholas grew misty-eyed as the wizard spoke, remembering the many stories his mother had told him about his father. He found it difficult to put into words what his heart knew to be true about the man he was acquainted with only through the kind words and gentle recollections of others.

"Maybe," Nicholas finally said. "But I'm even more proud to walk in Jack Raven's footsteps, along with those of my mother and Maynard and so many others who have prepared me for this journey. I'm only now beginning to realize it."

"That knowledge will help sustain you in place of actual memories of your father," the wizard said. "Perhaps one day you can share it with your own son or daughter and honor him through the generations."

"I plan to," he replied with a wistful smile.

The wizard downed the rest of his tea and set the cup on the table. "And now the time for talk is over," he said, slowly standing up. "Rustin should have the forge glowing white-hot by now. After all, I have taught him some superb spells regarding the ignition and manipulation of fire. He has quite the aptitude."

"Do you need assistance?" Nicholas asked. "I possess zero magical skills, but…"

"Thank you," Frist replied with an appreciative smile. "But neither you nor Rustin can help me at this point. What I must do, I must do alone. I thought my task was done twenty years ago, but fate has determined otherwise. It is best that no one interrupts me until it is finished." He noted the look of disappointment on Nicholas' face. "But please walk with me to the forge. It's not very far. Just past the second garden. After your long journey, you at least deserve to see where this deed will be done. I'm sure Rustin is patiently awaiting my arrival. You can keep him company in the garden while I fulfill my assignment. But check in on Leo from time to time. I'm not sure when he'll awake. The spell works at varying speeds depending on the individual, and as he is young and appears quite healthy, I suspect it will take fewer hours instead of more in his case."

"I'll keep an eye on him," Nicholas promised as he helped the wizard slip on his cloak before putting on his own coat. He opened the door into the chilly night and took Frist by the arm, leading the aged wizard along a snow-dusted path through a thicket of trees to the second garden.

CHAPTER 56

Metal and Fire

Nicholas guided Frist to the second garden. Rustin awaited them with a torch in hand near a white birch tree, leafless and bony amid the flittering shadows. They walked several more yards to a tall rock face, the line of dark stone scarred with cracks, fissures and ornamented in spots with saplings and scraggly pines growing out of its side. Thickening black clouds hovered above. A warm, yellow glow emanated from a small opening to a tiny cave at the base of the rock. The entrance was only high enough so that a tall man had to stoop before going inside.

"The forge is ready," Rustin said in uneasy tones.

"Thank you." The wizard eyed the cave and then turned to his companions. "Now I must do what needs to be done to help save Laparia. By dawn we'll know how good of a wizard I am," he added with a wink. He turned to Nicholas. "May I have the medallion?"

"Of course." He carefully removed the metal disk from around his neck and handed it to the wizard. "Good luck to you."

"Frist needs no luck," Rustin said with a confident smile. "He is one of the greats."

Frist gently patted him on the arm. "You have been a good apprentice. I know you will go far beyond what I have already taught you." He looked at both men and nodded. "Now I must finish what I started. You may wait in the garden or go back to the house where it is warm. This I must do alone."

Nicholas and Rustin watched as the wizard neared the rock face, stooped slightly and entered the gentle glow of the cave, the hem of his cloak sweeping across the ground and disappearing behind him. Nicholas looked at Rustin with a questioning gaze yet sensed that the apprentice knew little about what to expect.

"Should we go?" he whispered.

Rustin nodded, leading the way back to the second garden, now fallow and littered with the dried remains of a once thriving crop. There they lingered for over an hour, sitting on rocks and talking softly to one another about the wizard. Rustin told Nicholas all that he knew about him including Frist's early days in the Valley of the Wizards.

"I spoke to him for the first time when I was ten," Rustin said. "He was passing through my village as he had on previous occasions while journeying around the lake to explore. Frist was stopped by a woman with her daughter of four in her arms who had a terrible and persistent cough. He examined the child on the spot and cast a brief spell over her. But an additional part of her treatment required some kaníya berry seeds which he didn't have in his pack. I was nearby and knew where a patch of those berry bushes grew and volunteered to run into the woods and bring him what he needed." Rustin grinned as he recalled that fond memory. "Frist had barely finished uttering his consent and instructions before I had dashed off to fulfill the errand."

"And the sick child?"

"She was as good as new two days later, running and playing with the other children. Her mother was beyond grateful," Rustin said. "I was beyond astounded that the wizard could do such good and that I had had a small part in it. I then wanted to learn more about wizardry as I was usually bored in my studies at school. Anyway, after I saw Frist on several more occasions in the village over the years, he employed me from time to time to gather certain leaves, berries and barks that he couldn't obtain near his island. He'd have me dry them and properly store them in wrapped cloth or clay jars as required and then purchase or trade for them on his next visit to our village. My family was delighted with the extra income and sensed that I had an aptitude for something greater than working on a farm, fishing on the lake or apprenticing in another business. And though I did finally go to work with one of the local apothecaries, I felt there was more in the world I wanted to do."

"Like apprenticing with the wizard?" Nicholas asked.

Rustin nodded. "About four years ago I saw Frist again and suggested that very idea to him. He was reluctant to take me on as his student, preferring to spend his elder years exploring the region and dabbling in wizardry only when the occasion required. I approached him several other times over the next few months until he finally relented somewhat, telling me that he would consider my request. In the meantime, he instructed me to create a complicated potion that required difficult-to-gather ingredients, including one found only on the summit of the middle mountain of the Five Brothers. I even had to recite incantations over the concoction for hours at a time in the middle of the night under particular phases of the moons. But I did everything Frist asked of me and kept a complete record on parchment. I even saved extra samples of every item I had gathered for the potion. Finally, two months later, he returned to evaluate my results."

"What did he say?" Nicholas eagerly asked.

Rustin smirked. "After I handed Frist the clay jar with my completed potion and showed him all my records and samples, he seemed mildly impressed, merely raising an eyebrow in response. We then walked to the edge of the lake in silence. There Frist opened the jar, and without so much as looking inside, he tipped it upside down and dumped the contents into the water. I was stunned, thinking I had failed the old man."

Nicholas appeared as astonished as Rustin had described himself those years ago, finding it difficult to believe that the wizard had treated him so harshly. "Why would he do such a thing after all the work you had put in? Did you make a mistake?"

"Not quite," he replied with a chuckle. "After Frist handed back the empty container he simply uttered four words that I will never forget—*I will teach you.*"

Nicholas shrugged. "I don't understand. What was the point of you making the potion?"

"That was my thought at the time," he said. "As it turns out, what I created was—nothing. A pretend brew. Frist had tested me to find out if I was willing to follow difficult directions without question and to see if I really desired the life I claimed to want. He told me that anyone who had so meticulously followed the ridiculous and convoluted instructions he provided was worthy of at least one opportunity to be called his student."

Nicholas laughed softly in the night shadows. "So all those hours you spent chanting in the moonlight over a container of who-knows-what…?"

"Made-up spells, of course. I'm just glad I was away from the village where nobody could see or hear me. But I've come a long way since."

"Frist certainly has a flair for the dramatic," Nicholas said.

Suddenly the faint glow at the entrance of the cave grew intensely brighter as the voice of the wizard drifted through the air like a swift brush of wind, his words strange, whispered and harsh. A heavy silence enveloped the area moments later and the fiery illumination near the cave returned to its previous, subtle glow.

"He certainly does," Rustin agreed.

Nicholas walked back to the house an hour later to check on Leo. Rustin, though, had refused to leave the garden, insisting on keeping a nighttime vigil until the wizard emerged from his cave. Nicholas promised to return shortly with some food and a hot drink.

The fire was burning low when he stepped inside the house. Leo was still fast asleep in his chair just as they had left him. Nicholas placed more wood in the fireplace to revive the flames and then prepared a small plate of bread and cheese and a cup of hot tea for Rustin. Soon Leo began to stir, awakened by the sound of the snapping flames. He sat up in his chair, stretching his right arm.

"Could you ask Ron or Mabel if the kitchen is still open?" he lazily asked. "I could go for more of that roast pork right now. And some ale, too."

Nicholas smirked as he poured hot water for the tea. "I hate to disappoint you, Leo, but we're not at the Plum Orchard Inn. We're in the wizard's house on Wolf Lake. How's your shoulder?"

"*Huh?*" He looked down, noticing the sling around his left arm. Slowly the fog lifted from his mind. "Now I remember. I thought I had drifted off in the common room. How long have I been out?" He looked around the empty room. "Where is everybody?"

"First things first," Nicholas said, walking over to him. "How do you feel?"

"Quite well," he said. He moved his injured shoulder and carefully raised his left arm, smiling with relief that there was no pain or restriction of motion. "I guess the wizard did it." Leo hastily removed the sling and walked about, turning his shoulder in several directions. "This is amazing. Where is he so I can thank him?"

Nicholas told him where Frist was and their buoyant mood dissipated. Though their intention was for the wizard to remake the key and reconstitute the spell within it, now that he was actually performing the deed, Nicholas grew afraid that the task might be more than the elderly man could handle. He filled Leo in on the details while preparing him a late supper, and as he began to eat, Nicholas brought out the plate of food to Rustin and learned that the wizard had not yet stepped foot outside the cave. When he returned to the house, Leo was pouring himself a second cup of tea. Nicholas joined him at the table and appeared moody and quiet.

"Frist was going to do this task regardless of the consequences," Leo said as he continued to eat, famished after enduring the wizard's spell. "Don't blame yourself for his decision."

"That's not what I'm brooding about," he replied. "I'm thinking about something Frist had told me earlier." He looked up at Leo with mixed emotions. "Something about my father."

Leo appeared perplexed. "Your father? What do you mean?"

Nicholas explained the disturbing news the wizard had revealed about Jack Raven's death, wondering if he would have been better off not knowing. "I can see why Maynard and Tessa never told me the truth when I was older. What would I have done with that information all those years later? It might have just made me angry and vengeful while growing up."

"Possibly," he said with concern. "Yet I think I'd rather have the truth than not. But as you can't change the past, don't let it beat you up or you'll never move forward."

Nicholas looked up, his face hardened. "Part of me wants to run to Morrenwood with that key as fast as I can and open the Spirit Box. Vellan's Enâri army deserves what's coming to it, as do Vellan and Caldurian." He sipped his tea, his mind spinning with vengeful notions. Then, whether because thoughts of Ivy tugged at his heart or he was enveloped in the magical atmosphere on the wizard's island, he suddenly grew calm. The tension in his face disappeared and he sounded like his old self again. "But I know I have another job to do first, Leo, and carrying around newfound hatred because of what I learned will only hinder me. And you're right–I can't change the past, but I'm not going to let it change *me* either."

"Wise choice," he said between bites of food. "Besides, we've nearly accomplished what we came here to do. No reason for you to go all Vellan-crazy now. That wizard will get his one of these days for all the trouble he's caused. Trust me."

Nicholas was happy to hear himself laugh, knowing he was still on the right track in both his quest and his attitude. But how it would all end was still as dark and roily as the clouds hovering above the wizard's rooftop.

The island stood silent in the darkness several hours later as dawn crept closer to the eastern horizon. Suddenly Rustin burst through the front door of the house, awakening Nicholas and Leo who had fallen asleep in their chairs near the fireplace. They each looked up, neither knowing what to expect.

"What?" Nicholas asked, fully awake yet less than refreshed after his brief slumber.

"Frist wants to see you," he said with a sense of urgency.

Nicholas and Leo followed him past the second garden to the cave as the bitter air nipped at their faces. They stooped low and stepped through the entrance, the warmth inside washing over them. The barren, rocky interior glowed from the red-hot embers within the crudely built forge. A small stool and anvil stood off to one side. Nicholas saw the wizard sitting upon the ground in the shadows, his back slumped against the wall. Though he appeared essentially the same man physically, he seemed to have aged in both spirit and presence. Nicholas and Leo went to him as Rustin stood nearby. Frist looked up with a faint smile, indicating for Nicholas to approach closer. He knelt down on one knee next to him, noting that the once lively glow in the wizard's eyes now seemed to be slowly fading.

"I have finished," he softly said. With an effort, Frist held up a metal key of minimal design with a slight oval loop on one end. Through it was strung the leather cord that had been tied around the medallion. Frist handed it to Nicholas who accepted it with a bit of reluctance. "Since you brought it all the way to me, I shall hand it over to you first. Though I suspect another will take possession of it shortly," he added, glancing at Leo.

"Thank you," Nicholas said, examining the key with amazement before he placed it over his neck. "But how are you feeling? That is what's most important."

The wizard smiled again, noting the concern of his three visitors. "I feel like I've done all I was supposed to do in this world," he said. "And perhaps a little more. Now I think I'm due for a long sleep. A long and permanent sleep." Rustin was about to speak when Frist held up a hand to quiet him. "I have earned it, my friend. You have been a loyal apprentice, but it is time for both of us to move on. I told you a few days ago when I first sensed the medallion's presence that this might happen, that this might be my fate."

Rustin nodded, on the verge of tears. "You did," he said, his voice unsteady.

Frist beckoned him forward, and as Rustin knelt beside him, the wizard took his hand and placed a gold coin inside the palm. "Never spend this in the marketplace. Keep it with you until the day you find another wizard to help you continue your studies. Give it to him and he will instantly know that you are a loyal and serious wizard-in-training, worthy to be his student. You will go far, my friend. Of that I am sure. In the meantime, remain on this island for as long as you wish. Take what possessions of mine you require for your chosen life and give away anything else of value as you see fit."

"I will," Rustin said as a tear rolled down his cheek. "Thank you." He kissed the wizard's hand and stepped back with a heavy heart.

He called forth Nicholas once more who knelt beside him with a puzzled look. "I have one more item for you." Frist removed a round, silver object with obscure markings etched upon it that was attached to a thin, sturdy chain of the same material and handed it to Nicholas. "I fashioned this amulet and Rustin's gold coin before I remade the key, knowing they wouldn't tax my remaining strength as much as my final feat."

"What is it?" Nicholas asked, examining the wizard's gift with wonder.

"A guide and a protector as you journey alone," he replied. "May it lead you to those whom you wish to find and preserve life where death and destruction are lurking."

"I don't know what to say," Nicholas whispered, clutching the amulet in his hand.

Frist smiled. "I couldn't save your father twenty years ago, but maybe through this gift I can save you from afar if need arises."

Nicholas bowed his head with gratitude and stood up. "Thank you, Frist. I'll remember you in my travels."

"And my thanks to all of you," the wizard replied as he fondly looked upon the trio. "It has been quite a memorable day."

"It has," Rustin said, gazing upon the old man with bittersweet emotion, wishing they had more time to talk and discuss the ways of the world.

"But now is the moment," he added, gazing upon them one last time.

Frist then took a final breath and his body went still. And though his eyes remained open and their color yet sharp, the wizard's face and hands seemed to pale slightly. The air inside the cave grew cold despite the hot embers glowing in the forge. Slowly, a faint white mist rose from Frist's body like a warm spring rain evaporating beneath a rising sun. As the mist intensified, the wizard's body gradually faded away until only his garments and boots remained upon the ground in a shapeless pile.

Nicholas, Leo and Rustin looked at one another in disbelief, feeling as hollow and empty as the cave. Outside, a quickening breeze stirred through the bare tree branches and creaking pine boughs, creating a soft white flurry from the newly fallen snow that danced wildly upon the night air for a brief and wondrous moment. Then everything was quiet once again, solemnly awaiting the dawn.

CHAPTER 57

Unfinished Business

Nicholas, Leo and Rustin returned to the house with heavy hearts as the first light of morning touched the eastern sky. Rustin carried Frist's boots and folded clothing with him to burn later in a private ceremony. In the meantime, he insisted that Nicholas and Leo help themselves to some of the food stores remaining in the pantry.

"It will come in handy on your journeys ahead," he said. "And since Frist had cast a preservation spell upon all of his edibles, the food will last a long time before showing signs of spoilage. And, Nicholas, take the boat, too," he added. "I have another. It will save you much time on your way to the sea."

"What will you do now?" Leo asked.

"I'll stay here for a few days as my heart is filled with sorrow," he replied, sitting by the fire. "I'll later distribute what food and goods remain to the nearby villages as Frist requested. When that is done, I don't think I shall ever return to this island."

"I can understand," Nicholas said, sharing in his grief though he had only known Frist for a short time. "I hope one day you apprentice with another wizard, though I'm guessing you're ready to go out in the world on your own and follow in Frist's footsteps. I think he would be honored."

"The honor will be mine," he replied with a smile.

"I understand that, too," Nicholas said.

Within the hour, after partaking of a brief breakfast and filling two small sacks with some food for their travels, Nicholas and Leo thanked Rustin and said farewell before returning to the shore alone. There they found Hobin sitting by a fire under the milky gray clouds of midmorning, munching on a biscuit and drinking tea. Both were delighted to see their guide again, recounting all that had happened during the night.

"I'm glad the wizard was able to patch you up, Leo, though it's a shame he's no longer in our world," Hobin said. "With several more Frists and a lot fewer Vellans, this world would be a much better place."

After throwing water on the fire and packing up the boat with the supplies, they were again on their way across the lake. Leo took one of the paddles this time to try out his new shoulder, happy to report that it felt pain-free and stronger than ever.

They paddled east along the lakeshore for a few miles in the direction they had come from until the island was once again a small dot upon the water behind them. There they decided to make camp and rest for most of the day as none of them had gotten much sleep the previous night.

"It won't make sense to continue on while our eyelids are drooping," Hobin said as he searched for kindling to start a fire. "In the meantime, we'll have a chance to discuss our return trips." He glanced at Nicholas. "You have to decide now if you truly mean to search for Ivy. There's no turning back from here."

"I know that," he said. "And I have no intention of changing my mind—or listening to others trying to change it for me despite their best intentions," he added with an appreciative smile. Nicholas removed the key from around his neck and handed it to Leo who stared at it with mild trepidation. "Take it, Leo. You might as well start carrying it. I still have the amulet. Make sure this key gets to Morrenwood as quickly as possible."

"I will," he said, taking the object from Nicholas and placing it around his neck. He held the key between his fingers and stared at it, logically aware of the power it could unleash. Yet his heart and spirit couldn't fully comprehend that the fate of the Enâri race was in his very hands. He hid the key beneath his shirt, anticipating a long and grueling journey back to the Blue Citadel.

They awoke at daybreak though the sun was still obscured behind a slowly moving band of clouds. All were well rested and eager to move on after a night of uninterrupted sleep. After a brief breakfast, everyone collected their gear near the edge of Wolf Lake, prepared to face the inevitable and go their separate ways. Nicholas shook hands with Hobin and thanked him for his fine service.

"Happy to have been a part of this grand adventure," Hobin replied. "And since you only have to follow the river now, you won't need a guide. Still, watch out for yourself. And if you're ever in Woodwater, look me up. We'll share another mug of ale."

"That's a promise," Nicholas replied before glancing at Leo, saddened at leaving him to complete the mission without his help. He would miss Leo's friendship after all they had been through together on the long and weary road for nearly two months. "I'll bet you never expected any of this when you agreed to drive Megan and me to Boros in your apple cart," he said with a chuckle. "Kidnappings, bruised limbs and endless treks through the woods."

"No, I did not," Leo said with amusement. "Still, I got to meet a princess and plan to see her again soon, so I guess I came out ahead on the deal." He shook hands with Nicholas and hugged him goodbye. "Now it's time for you to find Ivy and bring her back."

"I plan to," he said, nearly choking on his words as he looked upon his companions framed against the cold and melancholy waters of the lake. He picked up his pack, set it on the boat and slid it into the water, knowing that if he didn't leave now he might never have the heart to do so. After settling in and picking up one of the paddles, he looked up at Leo and Hobin as a thin breeze skimmed the lake's surface. "I'll get word to you both no matter what happens," he promised before pushing off and paddling eastward along the shoreline. "Count on it."

"You'd better," Leo said, offering a wave goodbye.

He and Hobin shouldered their packs and turned southeast, planning to return through the same passage between the last two mountains in the Five Brothers chain. Moments later, the shoreline along Wolf Lake stood vacant and silent in the dreary morning chill as if nobody had been there in ages.

Nicholas glided along the lake at a leisurely pace, entranced by the rhythm of his paddling while the mosaic of windblown waves upon the water and constant thoughts of Ivy played in his mind. He moved parallel to the shoreline for nearly an hour until he saw the eastern tip of the lake coming into focus. He stopped for a moment and removed the hood from his head, observing how far he had traveled and how much longer he had to go until Wolf Lake funneled into the river that would lead him to the Trillium Sea. Though not the longest lake in the Dunn Hills, Wolf Lake was still a large body of water and Nicholas felt it so while bobbing upon the surface.

After a short rest he continued. A half hour later he was nearing the entrance to the river. Here the lake narrowed and the water flowed faster. Soon he found himself paddling along Wolf River, and for the first time he truly felt the absence of his friends. Since that night he encountered Princess Megan in the Darden Wood along King's Road, Nicholas Raven was once again all alone in the wilderness. Alone and searching.

He traveled downriver until twilight, disembarking twice and carrying the canoe along the shoreline when he encountered stretches of rocky falls impossible to maneuver through. Though it temporarily delayed him, he was grateful that the canoe proved very light to carry in addition to his pack. No doubt there was a bit of Frist's magic in its construction, the same magic dangling from the amulet around his neck. The notion brought comfort to Nicholas with every step.

At nightfall he made camp and built a fire, and while the air held the chill of late autumn, the weather seemed more tolerable as the terrain had been gradually decreasing in elevation the farther he moved away from the Five Brothers and Wolf Lake. Nicholas hoped to be out of the woods by the end of the next day at the earliest if both the weather and topography cooperated. He couldn't wait to see the vastness of the Trillium Sea again, and with luck, one or more ships from the Northern Isles anchored offshore. That very thought lulled him to sleep near the crackling flames of his fire later that night.

He opened his eyes the following morning, wrapped tightly beneath his fur coverings. His nose and cheeks felt damp and the scent of soil and decaying leaves permeated the air. The fire had long since gone out and faint mist hugged the ground. When

Nicholas sat up and stretched his aching limbs, he noticed a thicker layer of fog upon the river. The clouds lounging above the treetops appeared thinner than of late and he hoped the sun might break through as the day progressed. When fully awake, he ate a filling breakfast of cold beef, biscuits and water, not even attempting to build another fire. About an hour after he had awakened, he pushed his boat into the misty river and paddled silently onward.

The river was not very wide, yet the swirling white mist made him feel as if he were paddling while lost upon a vast ocean despite the view of many trees. But as the morning grew brighter and the clouds began to break, the mist dissipated and the Wolf River was once again a grayish-blue strip of water meandering through the leaf-strewn forest. Occasionally a ray of sunshine would find its way through, lifting Nicholas' spirits. He wondered how far Leo and Hobin had traveled, wishing he could be there when the Spirit Box was opened. He guessed that his father would be proud of him for playing a part in restoring the key and bringing about the downfall of the Enâri, and possibly, Vellan himself. But only time would tell.

He paddled to shore early in the afternoon as another series of rapids presented themselves a short distance ahead. Since the sun was burning off the remaining cloud cover and brightening the interior, Nicholas decided to have lunch and enjoy the warmth. After eating and taking a short nap, he again donned his pack and lugged the canoe over a quarter mile along the water's edge before the river was once again calm enough to navigate. He paddled for the next several hours, taking one short break to eat and one longer break after portaging his canoe an additional half mile beyond more rapids. After slogging through dense, tangled undergrowth, he was back on the water, exhausted yet pleased with his progress.

As the sun sank in the southwest behind a wispy collage of purple and orange tinted clouds, Nicholas decided to paddle ashore and call it a day, feeling as weary as after some of his worst days of hiking through the Cashua Forest. He was disappointed that he hadn't reached the eastern border of the Dunn Hills yet, though knew that it couldn't be too far away. More than anything, he yearned to view the Trillium Sea again and walk along its coast.

He made for the southern bank of the river and went ashore before twilight. Streaks of sunlight stabbed through nearby tree branches. A handful of bright stars were visible through breaks in the clouds. He gathered kindling and built a fire, looking forward to a hot meal and a full night's rest. It was his second day traveling alone, and though he missed talking and joking with his companions, he realized he wasn't especially bothered by the loneliness and the quiet. The distant cry of a sparrow, a meandering breeze rustling through the trees and the snapping flames dispelled any sense of isolation. He sat against a tree and ate a biscuit while waiting for some water to boil, enjoying his time alone.

He then heard a crunch of leaves nearby, now convinced that he was not alone. His heart pounded. Nicholas jumped up and grabbed a burning stick to use as a torch in the swiftly fading daylight. He patted the handle of a dagger attached to his side, giving him a modicum of security and comfort as he took a few cautious steps through the woods. Soon he noticed several dark shadows drifting past each other only yards ahead. He held aloft the torch.

"Who's there?" he asked, his voice steady though his nerves were on edge.

When receiving no response, he advanced, slowly waving the torch back and forth to throw off additional light. Then he saw it–a pair of eyes glowing in the murky twilight. There was a second pair close by staring curiously back at him. By the time Nicholas noted a third arrival, his own eyes had adapted to the gloom. He finally recognized the identity of the trio before him. He exhaled, not realizing how tightly he had been holding his breath. He chuckled to himself as he lowered the torch.

"Following me, huh?" he said, admiring three large deer that were searching for food. "I'd like to share, but I don't know when I'll stumble upon another inn to refill my pack." The deer continued to stare at him. Nicholas couldn't help but smile. "I suppose I could spare a few apples I got from the wizard's pantry," he added, stooping over his pack and rummaging through it. "Mind you, there is a preservation spell involved, so I don't know if it'll affect you differently than people." He glanced up at the deer. "So don't blame me if you start learning to talk or sing or–climb trees." He chuckled as he searched for the apples in the growing darkness until he grasped a piece of the fruit. "Ah, found them," he said, grabbing three apples before slowly walking toward the animals.

He avoided getting too close, fearing they would run away, and simply tossed the apples one at a time toward the hungry deer.

After a moment's hesitation, the deer stepped forward and sniffed out the round pieces of fruit before taking greedy yet appreciative bites. Nicholas could see the enjoyment on their faces in the glow of the torch and from the nearby fire, delightfully amused at the crunching and chewing noises they made with every mouthful.

"Now you're making me hungrier than ever," he said, still waiting to have his dinner as he watched the deer eat. "Better enjoy it because that's all you're getting," he added, turning around to go back to the fire and check on his small pot of boiling water.

He suddenly froze, his heart revving up the instant he saw a man standing in front of the flames, a silent silhouette whose shadow fluttered upon the ground with sinister intent. Nicholas held the torch aloft but was unable to recognize the stranger's face.

"Who are you?" he asked, stunned that anyone else was in the vicinity.

"Forgotten already?" the tall man asked, dressed in a long dark coat that nearly matched the night. "I'd been hiking this way for a few days when I spotted you on the river late yesterday. I've kept a close watch ever since. I suspected who you were from the start but wanted to make sure." The man raised a hand, revealing a dagger that reflected the garish red glow of the firelight. "Now I'm sure."

"That doesn't answer my question," Nicholas said, attempting to remain calm by controlling his breathing and keeping a fixed stare upon the individual. "Who are you? Where'd you come from?"

"I come from across the sea," he stated. "And as to who I am? Well, I'm the man who's going to kill you, just like you and your companions killed my friend. I wandered back two days later and found where you buried him. But before your corpse is cold, I'm going to take that medallion, or key, or whatever it is at the moment, and then find my way back to my ship." The man gently rubbed the area below one of his knees. "The left one hurts more than the right, though both were banged up thanks to you. I could barely walk that first day after I fled your campsite."

"Serves you right," Nicholas countered, "considering how you injured my friend." He realized he was dealing with one of the two Island soldiers who had attacked his traveling party days ago, never having expected to see him again. "But you'll be happy to know that he's as good as new, unlike yourself."

"Too bad," he muttered, waving the tip of his knife at Nicholas. "Now hand over the key. I'm only going to ask you once."

"I don't have it," he said with a shrug.

"Then give me the medallion," he replied with growing impatience. "The wizard Caldurian sent word to my superiors that you would have either one or the other."

Nicholas grunted with contempt. "It figures that troublemaker would have his nose stuck in our business," he said, wondering how Caldurian had learned about the mission. To buy some time, he slowly drew out the amulet that Frist had given him, pretending it was the medallion that the solider sought. "Are you looking for this?" He held up the piece of engraved silver still secured around his neck by the leather cord.

"Never found your wizard to repair it?" the soldier asked. "Too bad. Now hand it over."

Nicholas smirked. "Well, since we couldn't make it into a key again, I don't think you really have any need for it. I'll keep it for a memento." He let the amulet drop to his chest. In the brief moment that the soldier's eyes remained transfixed on the falling piece of silver, Nicholas flung the burning torch at him and then ran deep into the woods away from the river.

The man vaulted to one side as the somersaulting flames sailed by and then spun around and ran after Nicholas, temporarily losing him in the darkness. The three deer scattered, their rustling of leaves and undergrowth further throwing the Island soldier off Nicholas' track.

"You come back here!" he cried, pausing to get his bearings. He caught a glimpse of Nicholas' fleeing shape and was off again in wild pursuit.

Nicholas, in the meantime, unsheathed his knife and took refuge behind a large tree, his back against it as he rested to catch his breath. He could hear his heart beating loudly, wondering what he should do as the shuffle of footsteps grew closer and closer through a trail of dried leaves and brittle twigs. He tried to guess what Hobin would have advised him in such a situation, and for the first time since their departure, Nicholas truly missed his friends. But he would never betray them and so purposely led his pursuer to believe that he still possessed the medallion. He clutched the amulet, hoping it would protect him as the wizard Frist had promised. He placed it down his shirt again to keep it safe, knowing he had only seconds to act or make another run. He suspected that the soldier knew approximately where he was hiding and peeked around the tree for a better look.

He inched over to one side, hugging his body close to the tree as the pungent scent of bark perfumed the air. He peered into a thick swath of shadows, but when he shifted his gaze slightly, he could see the distant flames of the campfire. He wondered if the soldier had run in a different direction than what he had first suspected. Or was the Islander perhaps using his expert tracking skills and circling about, ready to pounce upon him from behind? Nicholas gripped the dagger handle and shot a glance over his shoulder, wondering if his luck had finally run out. He felt foolish to believe he could make it on his own through such wilderness to rescue Ivy. An overwhelming sense of dread and defeat crept around the edges of his thoughts, causing him to wonder if he would survive this ordeal.

But just as those anxious feelings took root in his mind, Nicholas saw a shadow pass in front of the distant flames and was startled back into the moment. The figure appeared shorter in stature for being so close, but Nicholas would not let it scare him off, preparing to leap out and attack head on since he knew he couldn't hide among the trees forever and win this fight.

He raised his knife and took a cautious step out from behind the tree, gazing in the direction where he had seen the moving shadow. Now he saw nothing. He was about to step back to his hiding spot when he heard the tiny snap of a twig behind him. He spun around just as the black form of the Island soldier rose above him like a wave. The man grabbed Nicholas by the shoulders and heaved him onto the ground on his back. Nicholas landed upon a tree root, wincing in pain as the knife fell out of his hand. The soldier rushed forward and pressed his boot on Nicholas' ankle while holding the dagger in front of him so that it faintly reflected the snapping flames of the distant fire.

"I told you I would have that medallion," the man said. "And your life. Now remove it from around your neck and hand it to me. While you're at it, tell me where your other two friends are."

"Not a chance," Nicholas said as he slowly removed the amulet while looking up at his captor. He was preparing to fling it into the trees, hoping to buy a few seconds to escape, but as he collected the chain and small circle of silver into his palm, the soldier was already mindful of his intention.

"Don't even think it!" he said, waving the knife above him.

"*Fine*," Nicholas replied.

He reluctantly raised his arm to deposit the amulet into the man's outstretched hand. But as he opened his fingers and let the metal chain pour onto the soldier's palm, Nicholas grabbed the man's wrist and yanked him forward, throwing him off balance just long enough so that he could scramble to his feet. But he didn't get far. Nicholas had taken only a few steps when the soldier was upon him from behind, grabbing and turning him before pinning him against a tree. The Islander pressed his left arm to his chest. Nicholas saw the whites of the man's eyes and the point of his dagger only inches from his face. His hot breath rolled across his cheeks. Nicholas didn't have time to catch his breath and speak, knowing that it was all over as the man pulled back the knife, preparing to thrust the cold piece of metal into Nicholas' body as he offered a vindictive grin.

But in the next instant, the man's spine went rigid and he stood up straight, gazing at Nicholas as if in a trance. Slowly, the vindictive grin melted off his face. His right arm dropped to his side and the metal dagger fell from his fingers. The soldier's body slumped and toppled to the ground in a heavy mass. Nicholas looked down in shock, unable to believe what he was seeing. He wondered if his eyes were playing tricks on him. Or was that truly an arrow sticking out of the dead man's back?

CHAPTER 58

A New Recruit

Nicholas looked up from the dead body sprawled upon the ground. He peered into the darkness, half expecting a second arrow to fly through the air and kill him. But all he saw was a small figure stooping over the fire, and moments later, it walked toward him carrying two burning sticks.

"Are you all right?" A woman spoke, her voice containing a stony quality that veiled a more genial nature just below the surface. She handed Nicholas one of the makeshift torches and smiled. "You seemed to need help, so I finally decided to step in."

"Thanks," Nicholas said, his mind still reeling. "Uh, *finally* decided?"

The woman nodded. "I'd been tracking you both for over an hour through the woods and along the river while I was hunting." She bent down and looked at the dead man's face, fingering his coat sleeve with much interest. "I don't know how long he had been tracking you."

"Since late yesterday." He curiously watched the woman as she studied the body. "That's what he told me before he tried to kill me."

"*Hmmm*," she replied, but Nicholas wasn't sure if she was responding to his comment or was thinking about something else as she examined the dead man's coat. She stood and handed Nicholas the amulet she removed from the soldier's lifeless hand. "Yours?"

"Yes," he said, grateful to have the wizard's gift back. He draped it around his neck and concealed it under his shirt.

"Are you hungry?"

"Haven't really thought about it, being almost killed."

The woman chuckled softly. "You're welcome to follow me home and get something to eat," she said. "And while you're doing so, I'd like to know why a man from the Northern Isles was trying to put an end to your young life." She looked around. "I didn't see anyone else while I was tracking this one. I think we're safe."

"There were only two of them. They attacked us a few days ago," Nicholas said.

"Us?"

"I was with some friends who have since taken a different road," he explained. "The other Islander is dead, too."

"There must be an interesting story behind that. I'd like to hear it," she said. "Will you come with me?"

Nicholas, still in shock, nodded. He felt he could trust the woman to an extent as she had just saved his life, and hoped he might glean some information from her about the incursion of the Islanders into the area. She apparently was knowledgeable about them, and anything he could learn might help him in his search for Ivy. "Thanks. A meal would be great." He studied the woman's face in the glow of the torch flames, noting a gritty exterior than still radiated a youthful beauty that belied her fifty years of life. "My name is Nicholas."

"I'm Hannah." She stuck her torch into the ground and then leaned over the dead body. "Could you give me a hand?"

Nicholas looked at her askance. "A hand? With what?"

"I need to remove this coat before the body goes cold," she said. "A shame that my arrow tore a hole through the back, such nice material and all."

Nicholas looked slightly aghast. "You want his coat? Are you serious?"

She grunted with laughter. "Not for me. And yes, I realize this seems ghoulish."

"Just a bit," he said. He gazed back with morbid curiosity, rethinking whether he should accompany Hannah to her house.

"But I do need the coat," she insisted. "And the man's dagger and sheath. We can leave the boots."

"May I ask why?"

"You may ask, but I can't tell you. Not just yet anyway."

Nicholas sighed, not knowing what to think. But since Hannah appeared quite rational to him at the moment, he simply shook his head and bent down to assist her. "Considering that you saved my life, I'll give you the benefit of the doubt about why you're doing this. But if you don't need the coat, who does?"

"My brother," she replied as she attempted to pull one sleeve off the dead man's arm, tugging at it with a clenched jaw. "Not that Arch plans to wear it himself, but he might be able to use it for a project he's working on. As I said, maybe I'll tell you about it later. In the meantime, help me turn him over. He's quite heavy."

"Sure..."

"And let's be careful so we don't rip the coat any worse on the arrow." Hannah paused for a moment when an idea struck her. "This might help." She grabbed the arrow with both hands near its base and snapped off most of the shaft. She casually tossed it aside. "There. Now it should be easier."

Nicholas recoiled with disgust. "Should we even do this? Won't we be cursed or something?"

"Don't get squeamish on me now, Nicholas. This man just tried to kill you. But there's a good reason for what I'm doing. Still, if it'll make you feel better, we'll come back and bury the body in the morning. It'll be very cold tonight. He should be fine until sunup, assuming no animals come sniffing around for a meal." She smiled, freeing one of the sleeves from the man's arm. "There! Now let's work on the other one."

A short time later, Hannah led the way through the woods to her cabin, carrying a torch along with her bow and quiver of arrows. Nicholas followed, again shouldering his pack as well as carrying the heavy coat and cold dagger worn only moments ago by a dead man.

They traveled less than two miles when Hannah pointed out her home, a small one-story cabin built of pine logs. The seams between the logs were filled with a mixture of mud, clay and straw. A small, adjacent clearing contained the remains of a vegetable garden. A nearby stream cascaded over several rocks before emptying into the Wolf River.

Hannah invited Nicholas inside. While he attended to the cold fireplace, she prepared them something to eat. Soon they dined at a table by the warm flames on strips of venison and gravy, steaming squash soup and bread. Nicholas devoured first and second helpings to Hannah's delight, telling her how delicious the food tasted.

"Nearly losing one's life gives you an appetite," he joked.

"I'm just happy for any compliment about my cooking," she replied. "As you probably guessed, I don't get many visitors here."

"Where's your brother live?" He noted a hint of worry in Hannah's blue eyes and in the subtle lines on a face framed by long, straight locks of dirty blond hair. "Will he join us tonight?"

"No, but I'm going to visit him soon," she replied. "He and his wife live in the village of Illingboc on the seacoast. I'm leaving the day after tomorrow for an extended stay as I do a few times each year." Hannah looked up at her guest with a sense of eagerness. "Perhaps you'd like to go with me? You can tell them the story about how we found the Island soldier's coat. I'm sure Arch will be interested in hearing the details."

"I'm sure that you'd like some more information, too, before we go to your brother's house." Nicholas sensed there was a more serious and troubled side to his dinner host, concerned that she was not being completely forthright about some matter or other, but he didn't want to press her.

"I think I'm entitled to a little, saving your life and all," she pleasantly said before taking a sip of hot tea. "How does a young man all the way from– By the way, you never did tell me where your home is."

"Kanesbury," he said, feeling that she deserved to know a little bit about him. "It's a small village in the middle of Arrondale."

"Never heard of it. But how does a young man from there nearly end up dying so close to my doorstep? Why was that soldier after you?" Hannah set her cup on the table as the fire crackled in the dimly lit room. "And I'm also curious to know about that thing around your neck. Is it valuable enough to kill for?"

Nicholas leaned back in his chair, troubled that he again had to explain his business. But since Leo and Hobin were miles away and their fate was out of his hands, he didn't have to be so secretive and evasive anymore, a trait he did not treasure.

"I'm searching for a dear friend," he finally admitted, happy to tell his story even if it was with a woman whose motives weren't quite apparent. "My friend was kidnapped over five weeks ago by men from the Northern Isles. Her name is Ivy." A trace of melancholy quickly enveloped him. "That's why I was heading down Wolf River to the sea. I need to get on a ship to the Isles if any are still in the vicinity. I assume Ivy was taken there. But how I plan to locate her if I make it to the Isles is a whole other story." He anxiously drummed his fingers on the side of the chair, his heart and mind sensing the apparent futility of his plan.

Hannah leaned forward, resting her chin upon her folded hands. "That's quite the beginning of a story, Nicholas. Ivy must mean a great deal to you."

"She does, though we've only known each other a short time." His coat was draped over the back of his chair. He reached inside a pocket and removed the gauzy scarf. The subtle autumn colors were illuminated in the glow of the fire. "This is a gift I gave Ivy after we first met. More than anything, I want to give this back to her as soon as possible."

"It's very pretty," Hannah said, admiring the material before he tucked it safely away. "Is the man who attacked you one of the men who kidnapped Ivy?"

"No. Those were other troublemakers from the same place. It seems those Islanders are up to no good all over Laparia." He picked at the remaining food on his plate while Hannah waited patiently for more of his story. "The man who tried to kill me had attacked me and two of my friends several days ago. He and another were after something we had. Our guide killed one of them. The other escaped and found me by chance just now."

"Was he after that?" she said, indicating the amulet.

"No," he replied, deciding that he could trust Hannah enough to tell her about his journey to see the wizard Frist, at least a condensed version, without risking any harm to Leo or Hobin. He hoped by doing so that she would open up to him and eventually help him find a way to the Northern Isles.

Hannah listened in fascination as Nicholas explained about the Enâri race and their connection to Kanesbury, and of a stolen magic key that was destroyed and turned into a medallion and then back again into a key. "Will the entire Enâri race be destroyed if the Spirit Box is opened?" she asked.

"That's the plan. We'll see in the days ahead if it's so."

"Well, if the wizard's new key works as well as that amulet he gave you, there should be no problem," she said with a smile. "That fine piece of silver jewelry saved your life, did it not?"

"*You* saved me," Nicholas replied with an appreciative smile.

Hannah shrugged. "Amulet. Arrow. You're still breathing and walking, right?"

"I guess so," he said, pouring himself another cup of tea. "And now that I thoroughly discussed my comings and goings over the last several weeks, I'd sure like to hear more about you."

"Such as?"

"Such as why you're living here in the middle of nowhere."

Hannah grinned. "It's not in the middle of nowhere, Nicholas. We're quite close to the edge of the woods. It's only a few miles to the eastern border of the Dunn Hills, and then just a few more miles to the seacoast. I'm not as isolated as you think."

"But why do you live here? Why not in Illingboc where you have family?" Nicholas hoped he wasn't prying too much.

"Because I like it here. But as I said, I do visit the coast several times a year to see family and friends and to buy and barter for supplies that I can't grow, make or find for myself. I fell in love with the woods years ago and value my independence. I work with my hands and survive by my wits. It's as simple as that," she admitted. "Maybe when I get a little older I'll move back to the coast when living alone is more of a challenge. But right now I'm happy where I am."

"Sounds like someone else I know," he said, recalling when he met Hobin. He glanced at Hannah with a more serious eye. "Still, there's one thing I hope you can tell me about. Why did you...?"

Hannah leaned back in her chair. "Why did I *what*, Nicholas?"

He looked uncomfortably at the tabletop before eyeing his host. "Why did you take that dead man's coat?"

Hannah stood and added wood to the fire from a pile of dried and split logs. "That's a long story which perhaps my brother could better explain." She noted an expression of restrained surprise upon his face. "Now I realize you did me the courtesy of detailing your recent adventures and are probably expecting the same in return, but I have my reasons." After stoking the blaze, she joined Nicholas at the table again. "And it's not that I don't trust you with the information, but matters relating to that coat and such are best left for Arch to make clear. Still, I think my brother will be more than happy to bring you into the discussion after he hears your story."

"All right. I'm patient. I can wait until we arrive in Illingboc."

Hannah sensed his disappointment and decided to relent a bit despite her better judgment. "Nicholas, maybe I shouldn't tell you this, but perhaps there is–" She paused abruptly, reconsidering her words. "Well, maybe I shouldn't get your hopes up."

He leaned forward. "Perhaps there is *what*? If you can tell me anything, I'd like to hear it."

"I know. And I don't wish to divulge secrets, but seeing as how you want to go to the Northern Isles and find Ivy, perhaps there is a way to get you on one of those ships near the coastline." She noted Nicholas' skepticism. "I'm being quite serious."

As much as he wanted to believe her, Nicholas couldn't imagine how a woman he met by chance living all alone in the woods could have any means to get him aboard a ship from the Isles. It seemed awfully convenient that she could provide him the one thing he so desperately needed–a way to Ivy. He grew suspicious of her all over again, particularly because of the stolen coat off of the dead man. He wondered if Hannah was merely a woman out of touch with reality and was simply leading him on for her own entertainment and companionship. Or did she have some other motive, attempting to secure his trust and lure him onward? He began to wonder if she really had a brother living in Illingboc, knowing only time would tell.

"Thanks for the offer," he said. "Maybe we can discuss boarding one of the ships after we get to your brother's house."

"Sure," she replied with a friendly smile, certain that he didn't believe her. "We'll leave the day after tomorrow if you don't mind staying here until then. First we have to bury the dead Islander and then I have to pack supplies for the trip and tend to a few other matters before I leave. I plan to be gone for a few weeks."

"I'll give you a hand," Nicholas said. "Tell me what to do."

"Thanks. I have extra blankets so you can sleep by the fire," she replied, pointing to his empty bowl. "So now that we've sized each other up, more or less, would you like more soup? There's still plenty in the kettle."

The following morning while Hannah attended to her chores, Nicholas buried the dead man near the spot where he was killed. When he finished the somber task, he paddled his canoe to the cabin and brought it ashore. After lunch, he split and piled firewood and burned the last of the dried remains from the vegetable garden while Hannah packed and tidied up the cabin before their departure. After a late supper, the two retired for the night and awakened at dawn, prepared to depart by midmorning.

"If you don't mind, I'll throw some of my things in your canoe," Hannah said, carrying a small sack in one arm and lugging a second over her shoulder as they tramped along a leafy dirt path to the river. Nicholas followed, similarly burdened. "I'm usually weighed down on my trips to and from Illingboc. I should get a second canoe or build a small raft to load with my supplies and drag behind me. Maybe the Islanders will sell me one of theirs," she joked.

"You're familiar with their excursions up the Lorren River to Kargoth?" Nicholas asked.

"Of course," she said. "I've seen their tall ships and heard stories about how they build rafts along our coastline away from populated villages with utter impunity. The few communities scattered along the Crescent have no standing army like Arrondale nor the proper number of men to form one capable of challenging a threat from the Isles."

"So I've heard," Nicholas said as they arrived at the river and loaded the boats. He was amazed at Hannah's knowledge of the situation.

"But maybe one day the villages might unite into a nation of sorts as the population grows," she replied. "Right now, however, places such as Illingboc, Reese, Great Bear–and even the village of Woodwater where your guide lives–are simply small communities where people enjoy being left alone to pursue their lives without interference from the outside world."

"Until now," Nicholas said.

"Until now," she softly echoed. "But maybe that can change," she added without explanation before heading off to the cabin to gather more supplies, including the coat from the dead man. Nicholas wondered if that remark portended anything more than wishful thinking. But he was too mentally fatigued to pursue the matter and would wait until he was introduced to Hannah's brother before asking more questions.

They departed a few hours later beneath overhanging treetops, ragged gray clouds and intermittent sunshine. The air was cool as they paddled their canoes side by side down the Wolf River, hoping to reach Illingboc by nightfall. The water, scattered with a handful of autumn leaves, mirrored the somber fleet of clouds and the occasional sparks of sunlight as their journey peacefully progressed.

"Though I value my privacy, it's lovely to make this trip to Illingboc with somebody," Hannah remarked. "Yet after a few weeks with Arch and his wife, and of course all the socializing through the winter with several friends, I usually find myself content to return home alone. I guess it all balances out in the end." She expertly dipped her paddle into the water, alternating from side to side.

"You should get a dog or two to fill up those lonely hours," Nicholas suggested, recalling Frank and Gus with amusement.

"Maybe one day. But usually I'm just too busy to get lonely. There is always another task on my list. Living here is a glorious treasure, but it's an awful lot of work, too. So I do enjoy a few weeks of leisure now and then at Arch's place, though I suspect this visit might not be as restful as the others."

"Why?" Nicholas asked, noting a faraway look in her eyes.

"*Hmmm?*" she finally replied, as if momentarily forgetting that he was beside her in the next boat. "What'd you say?"

"Nothing important. Are we near the end of the trees yet?"

"It shouldn't be too long. We can go ashore and have lunch."

"Good. I've seen nothing but forest for days on end," he said. "I need a change of scenery. I can't wait to look out across the Trillium Sea again. There were times I thought I'd never get back."

Nicholas remembered unsuccessfully asking King Justin for assistance in searching for Ivy, finding it difficult then to think that he would ever again stand upon the coastline. But now he was nearly there, his long journey almost complete. Yet the search for Ivy was only beginning. He felt proud of himself nonetheless as he contemplated all the miles and hardships he had endured to get this far. And though Ivy might still be miles and weeks away from being rescued, Nicholas felt closer to her now than he had in a long time. He wondered if she felt that same connection to him, praying that Ivy hadn't given up hope that he would somehow find her.

They emerged from the woods within the hour. The world suddenly opened up before them as they floated past the last of the trees along the water's tranquil surface. The late-afternoon sunlight, tempered by a veil of gauzy clouds, gently illuminated stretches of low, rolling hills, lonely scrublands and an occasional farm field on either side of the river, all tinted in muted shades of greens and browns of a dying autumn. The colder, open air caused them to bundle up tightly in their coats and hoods as a light but biting breeze played across the landscape. Nicholas didn't mind though, knowing he had only a few more miles to paddle until he could bask in the humbling sight of the Trillium Sea, wishing that Ivy could share the moment with him.

Hannah suggested they stop for another break as the sun dipped behind them in the southwest, but soon after they were back on the river. At last the clouds began to thin and disperse, opening up large patches of deep blue sky that dispelled some of the visual monotony. About an hour later, the surrounding lands grew flat and the scent of salty seawater lingered in the air. At the first hint of encroaching twilight, Nicholas finally caught a glimpse of the Trillium Sea spread out in the distance like a giant swath of dark, blue velvet. He stopped paddling and let the current of the Wolf River carry him onward for a few moments as he soaked up the wondrous sight, its distant waters absorbing the last, weak rays of the setting sun.

"I can't believe I made it, Hannah," he whispered, his gaze locked on the far horizon before he turned to his companion. "And I have you to thank."

"You have many people to thank from what you told me," she said. "But I'm happy to be on the list. Now let's pick up the pace and get to Illingboc before the darkness completely swallows us. It's less than two miles from here on the southern bank. Arch's wife, Natalie, will feed us well when we get there. You can count on it."

They moved on with renewed vigor and soon saw the spread of lights in the village on the south side of the river to their right. As they paddled closer to shore, the river slowly opened up into the sea itself. The community of Illingboc was situated on the corner of land where the coastline intersected with the southern bank of the river, though some additional homes and businesses were sprouting up on the northern side of Wolf River in recent years as the population slowly grew.

Hannah guided Nicholas to a tiny wooden dock along the last section of the river where they tied up their canoes and stepped ashore, stretching their aching limbs and inhaling the fresh sea air. The grassy area was vacant and silent. Nicholas removed his hood and closed his eyes for a moment, letting the breeze wash across his face and cleanse his weary mind.

"We can walk to Arch's place from here," Hannah said. "It's only a few minutes away. We'll return with a horse and cart for our things afterward. They'll be safe."

"Lead on," he replied. "I'm looking forward to that meal you promised from your sister-in-law, as well as a good night's sleep."

"All in due time," she said as she stepped off the dock and walked along a trampled path through the grass. "I know Arch will want to talk with you first about your travels–over some fine wine or ale, of course. So it won't be too taxing an evening."

"That I can handle," he replied, picturing himself in front of a roaring fire and sipping his drink as if he were back relaxing at the Water Barrel Inn.

Soon they arrived at an elegant stone house in the middle of town, several of its windows glowing with soft light in the deepening darkness. The Fox Moon, now a few days from full, rose high in the east and gently scattered its light across the seawater. A handful of tall, sinewy trees stood guard around the property, gently bending in the night breeze. Though a much smaller house, it reminded Nicholas of Oscar and Amanda's home in Kanesbury and of better times.

"Your brother seems to have done well for himself," Nicholas remarked as they approached the red painted front door illuminated by an oil lamp suspended from an overhanging iron fixture.

"He's an astute businessman with his fingers in several endeavors," Hannah replied, "unlike his sister who is content to live life in the woods. Still, I do enjoy the fruits of his labor when I visit which he happily shares, yet Arch has spent time at my place in the woods for a couple of days now and then. He says it's primarily to check on my wellbeing, though he does appear more rested and content after he leaves than when he arrives. I think the breaks from his day-to-day work are good for him. Maybe one day he'll build a second home in the wild simply as a refuge from life in Illingboc."

Hannah knocked on the front door and was promptly greeted by her surprised and delighted sister-in-law, Natalie. The woman was a few years younger than Hannah and attired in a light blue dress and a white shawl with decorative embroidery. She greeted Hannah with a hug and embraced Nicholas with equal affection after he was introduced.

"Only three days ago I was telling Arch that I think we were long overdue for a visit from you, Hannah. I instructed Eva to freshen up your room just in case–I had her wash the drapes and the feather comforter–and well, here you are! Eva has the night off this evening which is why I'm answering the door. But I don't mind. Arch spoils me too much with the house help. So anyway, if you'll just give me a few minutes, I'll dig something out of the pantry for both of you to eat and drink. How's chicken sound? Nicholas, do you like chicken? Now come along!" she said with an enthusiastic wave of her hand, having taken only a few steps down the hallway since she opened the door. "Arch is in the sitting room poring over one of his ledgers, a habit I can't seem to break him of even after work hours. But he is a dear! My, we'll be able to have a lovely conversation tonight in front of the fire. Oh, I'm so glad you're here!"

As they followed the woman into the next room, Hannah glanced at Nicholas with an amused glint in her eyes, silently letting him know that he had just met the love of her brother's life. Nicholas grinned back, wondering if they would have a chance to participate in any conversation with Natalie at the helm. Still, the woman was charming in her way and he was grateful for her hospitality given so freely to a stranger such as himself.

When they entered the sitting room, Arch was working behind a corner desk leafing through the yellowed pages of a ledger illuminated by the bright light of an oil lamp. He looked up and smiled when seeing his sister and stood to greet her with a hug. Arch Boland was a tall man with thick, dark hair and a trimmed mustache beneath a set of rich brown eyes. Nicholas thought they conveyed a hint of weariness and concern despite his cheerful demeanor and firm handshake he offered after he was introduced by Hannah.

"Any friend of my sister is welcomed in my house," he said.

"I'll always be in her debt after what she did for me," Nicholas replied. As they sat around the fire, he was soon providing details to Arch and his wife about how Hannah had saved his life two nights ago in the forest. Arch and Natalie listened attentively and with much concern when they learned that two soldiers from the Northern Isles had penetrated so far into the Dunn Hills.

"I wonder if there are others," Arch said. "For more than a year they have been heading up the Lorren River on rafts they construct with wood harvested from the forests only miles away from our villages. Yet we were not aware of any incursions into other parts of our homeland until now. We just assumed that their goal was to supply Kargoth with goods and soldiers."

"As far as I know, the two soldiers who were after me and my friends were looking for us specifically," Nicholas said. "Maybe they were the only ones sent into the Dunn Hills." He informed Arch and his wife about the invasion of Montavia. "I'd guess that the manpower of the Northern Isles is limited like in any other place. Maybe a war in Montavia along with their tribute of men and supplies to Vellan is all they can handle right now."

"Perhaps my Arch is needlessly worrying about problems that are merely the handiwork of his imagination," Natalie suggested with a pleasant smile.

"If only it were so, Natalie," he replied. "Yet I and others worry that when the Islanders are through fulfilling their agreement with Vellan, they may have their eyes focused on our lands. They're not blind to our resources, and goodness knows they can plainly see that we pose no military threat." He sighed discouragingly as he stroked his chin. "It's only a matter of time, I fear, before the battle reaches our shores."

Natalie served dinner, and shortly after eating, Nicholas and Hannah returned to the dock with a horse and cart to retrieve their belongings. Later, everyone gathered around the fire for more drinks and conversation. Arch and his wife were enthralled by Nicholas' adventures on the road. They were deeply touched that he planned to make his way to the Northern Isles and search for Ivy despite their warnings of danger. Nicholas wondered if he was telling these people too much about his personal life, but the heat of the fire and the delicious wine provided him some much needed relaxation. He willingly offered details about his life as he was more than grateful to accept help where he could find it.

"Your King must have been proud of you, Nicholas, when you agreed to venture into the wild and seek out that wizard," Arch said. "The world needs more individuals like you who'll temporarily put aside the conveniences of life to protect the people and lands that they love."

"I was only doing what I thought was right," he replied. "Before I fled my village I had planned to join up with the King's Guard, yet I ended up at the Blue Citadel in his service anyway."

"Maybe it was fate," Hannah suggested.

"Maybe," he replied with a shrug. "Many strange things have happened to me, so I'm open to any explanation."

"Maybe it was fate that also brought you to my home in the woods," she added, glancing at Nicholas before looking askance at her brother. "I have something for you, Arch, out on the wagon. I'll just be a moment."

"Hannah, dear, you needn't bring us a gift every time you visit," Natalie said to her sister-in-law as she exited the room.

"This is much more than a gift," she replied, her voice drifting back with a tone of mystery just before she stepped out of the house.

"Perhaps she brought us back a deer carcass," Arch joked while his wife refilled everyone's cup with wine.

Moments later Hannah reentered the room with a large brown coat draped over one arm. Arch and Natalie looked up, not quite sure what she held. Nicholas, however, grew immediately uncomfortable, knowing the origins of that item of clothing, yet was curious to learn why Hannah was so preoccupied with the dead soldier's coat.

"What have you there?" Arch asked, eyeing the heavy material. "Did you wrap something in that?"

"No," Hannah said. "This is the item I was talking about. Maybe you'll recognize it when I hold it up to the firelight."

Hannah stepped close to the fireplace, and after grabbing the garment by its shoulders, she raised it in front of her so everyone could plainly see that it was a coat traditionally worn by the soldiers from the Northern Isles. Arch recognized it immediately and seemed surprised that his sister possessed such an item.

"You confiscated it from the dead man?" he asked.

"And his dagger, too. I thought you might be able to use them," she replied before indicating Nicholas with a turn of her head. "And perhaps him?"

Arch Boland understood his sister's intent. "Have you brought me a recruit for the cause?" he asked, wanting to make sure they were thinking along the same lines.

"If he's willing," Hannah replied. "He did say he means to go to the Northern Isles. Perhaps you can make use of him somehow."

Nicholas slowly turned his head and stared at Hannah, his mouth slightly agape. "Is this why you brought me here? To be a recruit?" Hannah smiled guiltily as she folded the coat over her arm again. "For what exactly?"

She sat down in her chair, resting the coat upon her lap and pressing out the wrinkles with a few swipes of her hand over the coarse material. "Now don't be angry with me, Nicholas, because I only had the best of intentions for both you and my brother. And didn't I promise you a way on board one of the ships from the Isles?"

"You did," he replied, "though I had my doubts. Now I'm not so sure. After hearing your brother speak and seeing his reaction to the coat, well, I don't know what to think." He glanced at Arch, his eyes filled with questions and concerns. "What were you referring to when you asked Hannah if I was here as a recruit?"

Arch looked silently at his sister while weighing his words.

"I didn't tell him specifics–not that I know many myself," Hannah told her brother somewhat defensively. "I'm aware of how much you value the secrecy of your operation, yet I was convinced that Nicholas might be an asset to your cause."

"So am I," Arch said. "After hearing his story, there is no doubt which side Nicholas is on. But he does not live here. He has no stake in our fight."

Nicholas folded his arms, a thin stream of air escaping from the side of his mouth. After all the wine he had drunk, he was not shy about expressing his thoughts in the home of a stranger. "Not to be rude, but could you please tell me what you're all talking about?"

"You'd better tell him, dear, now that you and Hannah have spoken words you can't take back," Natalie instructed her husband. "In the meantime, I'll clean up in the kitchen. Military matters are beyond my area of expertise." She affectionately kissed her husband on top of the head and smiled before strolling out of the room.

Nicholas' curiosity was piqued. "Military matters?"

"So to speak," Arch said, clearing his throat and leaning back in his chair. "I'll get right to the point, Nicholas. Though the villages up and down the Crescent have no formal army, each locality defends its own as best it can. And there's a loose cooperation among the villages when need arises. But after ships from the Northern Isles started to arrive intermittently beginning last year, we knew that we couldn't prevent them from doing as they pleased. Our villages were easily outnumbered and out-armed by their forces. Any notion of ridding them from the area died quickly at the sight of their ship flags waving in the breezes–along with our sense of isolation, security and freedom from the outside world."

"I'm guessing that you've mounted some kind of resistance," Nicholas said, eager to hear more.

"We did. Several people from each village had the same idea that something had to be done to push back such a blatant incursion," he explained, his voice steady and low. "Word spread from village to village up and down the coast. Meetings were held to plot a strategy. The gatherings were secret so as not to generate wild rumors and possibly reveal our intentions to the enemy."

"What were your intentions?"

"To defeat the men of the Northern Isles and drive them out, of course," Arch said. "Well, that was our wish anyway, though most of us recognized from the start that that was an unrealistic aim. Eventually we settled upon ways to disrupt their steady line of rafts going up the Lorren River. We had to try something, though our successes were few and far between."

"Still, it was very brave of you to try," Hannah said.

Arch shrugged. "I don't know if *brave* is the right word. In the end, we had more meetings with each other than actual clashes with the Islanders. Limited manpower and fear of reprisals had dampened our original enthusiasm. Nothing much happened last year involving our group as the men from the Isles built their rafts with wood from our forests. They stayed away from any population centers, occupying points along the many miles of empty space between villages." Arch leaned forward with a gleam in his eyes. "However, we have had some successes in recent months and are on the verge of making a name for ourselves despite the possible repercussions."

"How do you plan to do that?" Nicholas asked, recalling the many conversations he and Leo had with Tolapari as they planned for their journey to Wolf Lake. Arch reminded him of the wizard in some ways as he enthusiastically commented on the political intrigue and economic implications of the current situation.

"I'd love to share that information with you, Nicholas, but I may have said more than I should have at the moment." Arch noted a look of disappointment on his face. "Yet that doesn't mean you won't be privy to our plans, but just not tonight."

"Oh, tell the boy what plot you're cooking up and don't make such a big production out of it," Hannah said as she downed another gulp of wine.

Arch grinned at his sister. "And I won't tell you either, Hannah, for the same reason. I'm not at liberty to disclose all the details yet. This isn't just any operation, after all. Others are involved, too. I have taken an oath of secrecy."

"That I understand," Nicholas replied. "But when can you tell me? As much as I appreciate your hospitality and enjoy these surroundings, I can't remain in Illingboc indefinitely. I must get aboard a ship to the Isles."

Arch wrinkled his brow, seemingly at odds with his unspoken plans and Nicholas' desire to find Ivy. He paused for a long moment before coming to a decision.

"I'm meeting with someone tomorrow to discuss our next step," he said. "If you want, you can sit in on our talk, Nicholas. Maybe you might wish to join us after all the trouble those two

Islanders caused you and your friends. And then again, maybe you won't," he added, both his tone and expression inscrutable.

"If it'll help get me any closer to Ivy, I'll be happy to, Arch."

"I can't promise you that," he hastily replied, raising a hand in mild protest. "Let's be clear on that point. You may not like hearing what we have to discuss."

"Now you have me intrigued," he replied as the fire slowly died down and the corner of the room darkened.

"Me, too," Hannah said before addressing Nicholas. "And I'm sorry about getting your hopes up when I suggested that I could get you aboard one of the ships. I guess I was assuming certain things about my brother's plan to deal with the Island threat."

"I guess we'll both be surprised," he said as he downed the last of his wine. "In the meantime, Arch, I'll take you and your wife up on that offer of a bed and a good night's sleep," he added with a yawn. "My accommodations lately have been floorboards, barn floors and hard soil since I left the Citadel. I haven't slept in a real bed since I was a guest in Morrenwood." Nicholas scratched his head as he stretched, already on the verge of a deep slumber. "I hope I haven't forgotten how."

CHAPTER 59

A Seaside Chat

Nicholas slept late the following morning. When he opened his eyes and felt his head sunk deep in a soft pillow and his body collapsed upon a feather mattress, he smiled, unable to remember when he last enjoyed an uninterrupted night of restful slumber. He heard voices in the rooms below and inhaled the tantalizing scent of bacon and eggs that finally nudged him out of bed. After he washed and dressed, he joined Hannah, Arch and Natalie for a leisurely breakfast in the dining room. Brilliant sunshine peeked through gauzy white curtains and reflected off the burnished wood floor.

"Natalie insisted that we postpone breakfast until midmorning to give you a chance to rest," Arch said as he munched on an herb biscuit with hot cinnamon tea.

"Thanks, but you didn't have to change your schedule to accommodate me," Nicholas replied. "I'm used to waking up in the early morning, though I did enjoy the extra sleep."

"So did I," Hannah admitted, "which is why I suggested a late breakfast to Natalie before I retired last night."

"And as Eva is back this morning cooking in the kitchen, I had no objections," Natalie said with a chuckle.

"I'm glad everyone is in fine spirits," Arch said, indicating for Nicholas to dig into his meal. "Natalie, if you and Hannah would like to stroll through town, I'll drive down the coast a few miles with

Nicholas. We'll only be gone a short while." He looked at his guest. "There's something I need to show you."

"Sure," he replied as he helped himself to more bacon off a fine white platter. "Where are we going, Arch?"

A cool breeze pushed billowy, white clouds eastward across the sun-splashed sea later that morning when Nicholas and Arch left Illingboc. A pair of chestnut-brown horses pulled them in an open cart along a hard, dirt road parallel to the coastline, the water a short distance to their left and acres of low grass and scattered farmland to their right. The village of Reese, the next community in their direction, lay twenty miles ahead. But Arch only needed to travel three miles down the coast to show Nicholas what he wanted.

"Until last year when the first ships from the Northern Isles arrived, the villages scattered up and down the Crescent pretty much ignored the outside world," Arch explained as they moved down the coastline. Distant waves lapped against the sandy shore. "And I don't say that in a smug way. It's just that most folks living around here enjoy life without worrying about the predicaments plaguing other parts of Laparia. We have enough of our own troubles, especially with the rough winters and occasional bad growing seasons. But we've endured for generations, and as our population and small industry slowly develop, life will get steadily easier. But right now—"

"—you weren't expecting the Islanders," Nicholas said.

"Exactly." Arch focused his steely, brown eyes on the road ahead as the wind tousled his hair. "That forced the leaders and businessmen in our communities to rethink how we operate and endure as a group. Forced us to consider how to defend ourselves from threats other than the usual, minor types that crop up from time to time." He offered a faraway smile as they moved steadily down the road. "I suppose we were a bit naïve to think that the outside world would never find us, or to at least imagine we would be ready when it finally did. But here we are."

"Still, you've recognized that something needs to be done," Nicholas said. "That's a start."

"A few of us have, but many up and down the coast hope the Islanders will simply disappear from our shores after they finish their dealings with Kargoth. Many don't want to consider the possible alternative–a very unpleasant one."

"That the Islanders will stay?"

Arch nodded, explaining how some members of the respective communities had gathered to discuss their common problem and what to do about it. "As I said yesterday, we didn't accomplish much last year. We discussed raising some type of combined army among the villages even though we didn't yet have the population base to face a real military threat. But it was a minor first step."

"You'd be surprised how a few good leaders can shape a group of untrained men into proper soldiers," Nicholas said. "While in Morrenwood, I trained for a few days with some of King Justin's finest in preparation for my journey to Wolf Lake and learned quite a bit. I admit there's much more that I don't know and probably never will, but strong, dedicated men like you can accomplish great things."

"I'm not a military leader, Nicholas, nor pretend to be."

"But you bring other types of leadership to assist those who *can* run a proper military, Arch. That includes raising finances, recruiting the right people for the job and having the passion to see it through," he said encouragingly. He told Arch all he had learned about the results of the war council. "When good men and women get together to fight a just cause, much can be accomplished with few resources. I've seen it up close."

"Your words comfort me, Nicholas. Yet having sufficient men, swords and ships on your side is a good thing, too!" he added with a laugh. "Your King Justin should seriously consider developing a naval fleet to patrol his shoreline after this latest incursion from the Isles. You said yesterday that the Islanders are in Montavia, too. They are coming at us from two points on this shoreline–and it is a long shoreline."

"The King may think along those lines one day," Nicholas speculated. "But right now he has his hands full with part of his army heading to Montavia and the other part to the war between Rhiál and Maranac." He recalled that King Justin's troops were to have left for battle much sooner than those going to Montavia. "They may be engaged with Drogin's men as we speak," he said, his complexion paling with the somber realization. "Or it may all be over by now, one way or the other. I've been on the road for so long that I'm forgetting other people's lives are moving as swiftly as mine." He gazed at the water, feeling as separated from his friends as he was from Ivy. "I wish I knew what was happening to them."

"Your friends are probably thinking the same about you," Arch kindly replied. "But for now you must each tend to your separate tasks." He gently pulled at the reins to slow the horses. "This is far enough." He guided the wagon off the road into a small field with a few straggly trees sprouting up here and there. A small stream nearby wound its way to the Trillium Sea now about thirty yards away.

Arch unhitched his team to let them graze and drink while he and Nicholas wandered to the seashore as the gentle waves lapped upon its sandy surface. Nicholas inhaled the salty air and couldn't help but recall Ivy's face with every breath. He glanced at Arch and shrugged, silently questioning why he had brought him all this way when they could have gazed across the water in Illingboc. Arch immediately understood.

"I could have brought you to the shoreline at home, Nicholas, but then you wouldn't have been able to see that," he said, pointing across the water.

Nicholas placed a hand above his eyes to shield them from the glare of the sun which peeked out among the parade of swiftly moving clouds. "What am I looking at?" he asked. "I don't see anything except–" Suddenly he noticed a vague patch of color a few miles out upon the sea that nearly blended in with the water and the constant barrage of shadows passing over its surface. "What is that?"

"That's Karg Island," Arch said. "A long and wide piece of land with a few trees and rocks, but not much else. And if you look closely to the right you'll–"

"Is that a ship?" Nicholas vaguely detected an object bobbing upon the surface near the island.

"Precisely. It sailed here from the Northern Isles. According to my sources, it's the last ship to visit us before winter sets in."

"Your sources?" Nicholas asked. "Who are they? And how would they know anything about the comings and goings of ships from the Isles?"

"Because," Arch said as he ground the tip of his boot into the wet sand, "my sources are *from* the Isles."

Nicholas looked at him, for a moment slightly confused until the man's words fully registered in his mind. His face went blank and he took a step backward. "You're in contact with men from the Northern Isles? You're in league with them?"

"Yes," Arch replied matter-of-factly. "In contact with them, but not in league with them, at least not in the way you're thinking. The people I'm talking with are on our side."

"And how sure are you about that?"

"Quite sure. You see, a good number of the soldiers on those ships don't support their nation's alliance with Vellan nor have any desire to go to war," he explained. "Yet the young men of the Isles are forced to serve a number of years in military service or face imprisonment–or worse. Most have no choice, or think they don't."

"I've heard similar stories at the Citadel," he replied. "Several of King Justin's men and other soldiers from Montavia training with them kept Leo and me entertained for hours with tales from abroad." Nicholas gazed out across the water again, eyeing the ship with interest. "If that's the last ship of the year from the Isles, when did it arrive? And more importantly, when is it returning?"

Arch understood the point of Nicholas' question, sensing his desire to board that ship and sail back to the Isles to find Ivy. Yet he knew that the young man would not be very happy once he learned the fate his associates had in store for that vessel.

"The *Bretic* arrived about a week or so ago. That's the name of the ship," Arch said. "It will leave within a matter of days."

"So all the soldiers that sailed over on that ship are now moving up the Lorren River to Kargoth?"

"Probably, or soon will be." Arch signaled for Nicholas to walk with him along the shore. "They may be constructing the last rafts now to take them there. You see, I've been told–and have secretly observed the operation in part–that after a ship arrives here from the Isles, it anchors off Karg Island. Its captain meets with the administrator overseeing the process. The ship then sails south along the coast to an area between the villages of Great Bear and Pierce."

"What's there?" Nicholas asked.

"Nothing but empty space," he replied. "There are miles of forest and shoreline between those two villages except for an occasional farmstead. No interference from the public. It's the perfect location for the Island soldiers to make their camps, harvest our lumber and construct their rafts unimpeded. When the rafts are loaded with men, armaments and other supplies, they pole along the shoreline until the sea funnels them into the Lorren River which they follow to Kargoth. The ship, in the meantime, returns briefly to Karg Island before going back to the Northern Isles. Another vessel usually shows up a week or so later to repeat the process."

"I don't understand," Nicholas said. "If the *Bretic* already unloaded its men and supplies, why is it still anchored off the island and not going home? You said it would leave in a matter of days."

"I was told that the administrator on Karg Island will shortly sail back to the Isles on the *Bretic* once he finishes his work for the year," Arch explained, quietly laughing to himself.

"What's so funny?"

"I'm recalling a few stories I've been told about the man in charge," he said. "Apparently he is a reluctant administrator at best, having been assigned to his dismal post as a punishment. He's not a happy or stable individual from what I've heard."

"Serves him right," Nicholas said. "If he can ruin so many other people's lives, it's only fair that he endures some boredom and inconvenience in the process, though it's far less misery than he probably deserves."

"I couldn't agree more," Arch replied somewhat distractedly, his pace slowing as he pointed ahead in the distance. "There's somebody I want you to meet, Nicholas."

"Who's that?" he asked, looking up with a mix of curiosity and subdued suspicion. He noticed a figure on horseback about a half mile away on the road, growing larger as it slowly approached.

"A friend from the Isles," Arch said. "This is the meeting I mentioned yesterday. My contact's name is Arteen. He'll be happy to answer any of your questions."

"Good, because I have several."

A few minutes later, a tall man on a horse veered off the road and sauntered over. He wore a light brown coat with a hood cast over his head, dressed much like anyone else from the local villages. He greeted Arch with a nod as he removed his hood, allowing the light breeze to blow through his mop of dirty-blond hair. Though he was only a handful of years older than Nicholas, there was an air of maturity which hung about him that exceeded his age and was evident in the sharp focus of his light green eyes.

"You brought company," Arteen said after climbing off his horse and shaking hands with Arch.

"This is Nicholas Raven. He's friends with me and my sister."

"Then that makes him a friend of mine, too." Arteen offered his hand to Nicholas.

Nicholas almost hesitated before shaking it, deciding at the last instant to give Arteen the benefit of the doubt as to his loyalties.

"Pleased to meet you," Nicholas said pleasantly enough, though in the back of his mind questions and suspicions still lingered. "Arch told me you're from the Northern Isles and don't agree with what your leaders are doing in these parts."

Arteen smiled amiably. "You get right to the point, Nicholas. I like that sense of directness in an individual. And I suppose if you were being completely direct, you might add that you don't trust me, at least not fully yet."

"Your observation is an astute one," he replied with a hint of good humor. "I'll hold off judgment until you have your say, but at least you don't look or act like the Islanders I've met in my travels recently, so that's a point in your favor."

"Thanks," he replied, glancing at Arch. "So you've taken him into your confidence?"

"I trust Nicholas though I've only met him a short while ago," he said. "And given his recent history with your people, he may wish to help us. My sister vouches for him, too."

"Then that's good enough for me." Arteen took his horse by the reins and walked up the beach with Nicholas and Arch in the direction they had come from. "So tell me, Nicholas, what do you wish to know about me? Or should I just reveal the latest information I have and take it from there?"

"That'll be fine for starters. I can throw in an odd question as it suits my curiosity," he said.

"Fair enough."

"Good," Arch calmly remarked. "Now that the preliminaries are settled, perhaps Arteen can start talking so we can start listening. What news do you bring?"

"Simply this," he replied. "My friends and I have set a time for our raid on the *Bretic*. Three nights from tonight. The last of the rafts will have departed up the Lorren by then, and along with them those soldiers who are still loyal to the Isles and its cause."

"You're planning to take the ship?" Nicholas jumped in, his heart leaping in his chest as hopes for rescuing Ivy grew more realistic by the moment. He could already feel the spray of cold seawater upon his face and hear the snapping of flags suspended from the mast lines as he sailed across the Trillium to the Northern Isles. His farfetched dream was at last becoming a possibility.

"Of course we're taking the ship," Arteen said as if that should have been obvious. "And the few buildings and written records on Karg Island as well. That has been our aim from the start." He gently rubbed a hand through his horse's mane as they walked, his face tightening. "Then we plan to destroy them all in a blaze of fire. Maybe that'll send a message to the Isles that their intentions are corrupt and their support is wearing thin."

Nicholas stopped dead in his tracks, the pit of his stomach in knots. "Wait. You're going to do–*what*?" he asked, hoping he had misinterpreted what Arteen had said.

He and Arch turned and faced Nicholas who looked pale and on the verge of despair. Arteen appeared puzzled by his reaction. Arch had expected it and offered a weak smile.

"I told you yesterday, Nicholas, that you may not like what I have to say regarding our plans," Arch explained. "Or in this case, what Arteen had to say. His men have been planning this operation for quite some time. It's what they think is best for their cause and for our cause as well. And I agree with them."

"Wouldn't keeping the ship be better?" Nicholas desperately asked before telling Arteen about Ivy and his plan to rescue her from the Isles.

"Where would we take the ship?" Arteen asked. "Back home, after which we'd all be arrested or killed?" He shook his head, dismissing Nicholas' plan outright. "We need to take this action. It's a small start, I know, but maybe more will grow from it. When word reaches the Isles about our attack, maybe others will have the courage to act against our corrupt leaders as well. They've been destroying our nation for years, using its people and resources for their own gain to the point where some citizens are fleeing the Isles in secret to start new lives in Laparia and beyond. Others continue to fight to change things from within. That includes the captain of the

Bretic. He is on our side and will assist us when we return to the ship in three nights."

"Nicholas, you can't expect Arteen's men to put their plans on hold for you," Arch said. "Despite the nobility of your cause, they must strike while they have the chance. Perhaps someday you'll be reunited with Ivy when another opportunity presents itself."

Nicholas scowled. "Do you really believe that, Arch? This is my only chance!"

"I want what's best for the most people," he continued, truly concerned for Nicholas yet knowing his demand for using the ship was unrealistic. "Maybe there's another way you can help save lives, both here and abroad. Your journey to my village and this region need not be in vain, Nicholas. There is still much for you to do."

Nicholas tried to hold his growing anger in check. "What are you talking about?"

Arch looked him in the eyes, hoping the young man would still accept him as a friend after his slight deception. "To be honest, when Hannah first brought you to my home, I never planned to involve you in these activities even after hearing about your encounter with the Islanders. Arteen and his men have enough people in place to achieve their aims. But as you told me about your growing friendship with King Justin and his granddaughter, and how he had placed so much trust in you in such a short time, well, I knew that that relationship might be useful to our cause here."

"What? Are you simply using me for your own gain?"

"No! No! Not for my gain, Nicholas, but for all those families who live along the Crescent," Arch hastily assured him. "Maybe I should have been honest about my intentions from the start, but I wanted you first to see up close exactly what we're facing here. Getting you involved with this operation would do just that, or so I had hoped. As much as our villages value independence, an alliance with Arrondale might be a good thing as we develop into a unified nation in the years ahead. But now that the Islanders have stepped foot onto our shores, an alliance is an idea whose time has come."

"Then send representatives to Morrenwood yourself. Why involve me?"

"Some have suggested that very thing, Nicholas, though most expect King Justin has more important matters than worrying about us here on the edge of nowhere," he replied. "And after what you told me about Arrondale involving itself on two battlefronts, I can guarantee that our scattered villages of Illingboc, North Port, Tana and all the rest would be the least of King Justin's worries. But if you went back to the Blue Citadel and told him of our plight, he might take it seriously. And since you have successfully completed your mission at Wolf Lake, he would trust your judgment even more so if you put in a good word for us."

Nicholas shoved his hands in his coat pockets and looked out onto the sea as Arch waited for a reply. Arteen kept a few paces back, standing next to his horse in silence.

"I thought I had doubts about Arteen," he said as he gazed across the water. He turned to Arch, grimfaced. "Now I'm not so sure about *you*."

"Surely you can trust me, Nicholas. After all, I've given you food and a place to stay. And Hannah saved your life."

"Oh, her I trust completely."

Arch grinned. "I suppose I deserved that."

Arteen stepped forward. "In Arch's defense, he and many others like him in the various villages have provided those of us willing to fight against the Isles much assistance and safety. We've been given food, clothing and places to stay while we've secretly prepared our offensive over the weeks. We've been allowed to blend in at much risk to those living here. It was never our intention to involve the locals in this fight, but they have willingly assisted."

"How did you two meet?" Nicholas asked.

"That happened months after the Islanders first arrived last year," Arch explained. "After some of us in the villages formed our first alliance, we would spy on the Islanders and learned of their plans to construct rafts to supply Vellan. One evening, a small group of us had been spied upon by three Islanders who followed us back home. Arteen was part of that trio. Anyway, to make a long story short, we learned of their efforts to thwart the leadership in the Northern Isles and eventually volunteered to help them in their cause."

Arteen smiled. "Fortunately for Arch and his companions, they were discovered by me and my friends. I dread to think what might have happened to them had some of my other colleagues caught them spying. Their little resistance movement would have been over before it started."

"It's true," Arch said. "Arteen and his followers have concealed knowledge of our involvement for our own protection. If the administrator on Karg Island ever suspected that we fed and housed them, or assisted them in their previous raid, he might have sent troops to the villages long ago and dealt with us in a not-so-pleasant way."

"Previous raid?" Nicholas glanced curiously at Arteen for an explanation. "What have you done prior to the planned takeover of the *Bretic*?"

"Several weeks ago a group of us set fire to some half finished rafts and cut timber that had been left ashore awaiting the arrival of the next ship. It put them behind schedule for many days," he said. "But since then, soldiers stay behind and guard their base until fresh troops arrive. Word got back to us through our network of spies that the administrator was on the verge of hysterics when learning that a rebellion had formed among his own people."

"So now you want to outdo yourselves with this next action."

"I think burning down the *Bretic* would accomplish that, Nicholas." Arteen's gaze was sober and unflinching.

"You won't reconsider?" Nicholas inquired, though merely for the sake of asking. He already knew that Arteen was fully committed to his course of action. He saw the same stubborn determination in Arch's eyes as well. "And I'm just supposed to accept it? To return to Morrenwood and intercede with King Justin on your behalf?"

"It's only a suggestion," Arch said. "But I implore you as a friend–though you might not think of me as such right now–to seriously consider what I've said. And sometime before next spring when more ships are likely to arrive, we'll send a small delegation to Morrenwood to seek an audience with King Justin. Hopefully he will anticipate our arrival if he hears from you ahead of time, but that is ultimately in your hands."

Nicholas smirked at what he believed was Arch's naïve belief in his influence with the King. "Even if King Justin heeded my plea for your cause, the outcome of the wars in Montavia and Rhiál will supersede everything. If our side fails to win those battles, there may soon be more ships than you can count sailing from the

Isles and landing upon the shores of the Trillium up and down the entire coastline. Your situation here won't even be an afterthought to Arrondale if that happens."

"Yet victory may find its way to both the war in the south and in Montavia," Arch replied. "If that happens, Vellan will need all the reinforcements he can get from the Isles to protect himself in Kargoth. Our homes along the Crescent may be in the center of this conflict one day no matter which way the wars turn."

"No one knows what will happen," Arteen said. "All we can do is prepare wisely."

Nicholas squinted against the dull glare, appearing perplexed. "If uncertainty is the case, then why do you assume that destroying the *Bretic* is the wisest course? Maybe you should save the ship to help fight the war if it spreads this way. That would send an equally powerful message to the Isles." Nicholas clung to a last bit of hope that Arteen might see matters his way. He appealed to Arch's desire to bolster relations with Arrondale. "Giving the ship to King Justin could be a show of good faith for this alliance you wish to create. That would surely get his attention to your cause."

"Perhaps," Arch said, "but it is not my call, Nicholas. It's ultimately up to Arteen and his men as to which path we'll follow."

"Please reconsider," Nicholas softly pleaded. "I must get to the Isles before it's too late–though it may already be," he added, nearly choking on his words. "Can't you talk to the captain of the *Bretic* one more time? Surely he must have second thoughts about burning down his own ship."

Arteen shook his head. "Sorry, Nicholas, but it was Captain Kellig's idea to destroy the *Bretic*, though it will pain him to do so. He has tried to change the way things operate from within, subtly of course, though with little success. But suspicions have grown as to his loyalty, so he's decided to take this drastic action before he is found out."

Nicholas sighed in defeat as he watched the waves lap upon the shore. They reminded him of that awful night when Ivy was taken away upon a boat as her cries for help drowned in the night breezes. He looked askance at Arteen. "Is there a chance I could talk to Captain Kellig? Perhaps I could change his mind."

"I sincerely doubt that, Nicholas," he replied. "Captain Kellig is steadfast and determined. He's committed to this decision and means to send a fiery message to the Isles. Doing that, as well as putting Administrator Tarosius Lok in his place once and for all, is worth ending his career. He has told me so on several occasions–and all of them while sober," he added with a laugh.

Nicholas' ears pricked up upon hearing the name Tarosius Lok. He stared at the sand beneath his feet, letting Arteen's words swim around in his mind as a chill ran up his back. He slowly looked up at him, doing all he could to remain calm.

"Did you just say the name *Tarosius Lok?*"

Arteen nodded. "Yes. He's the administrator on Karg Island. *Captain* Tarosius Lok, to be exact," he said with a scornful smirk. "But his current position is a demotion if you asked him."

Nicholas was nonplussed. "So let me understand–Captain Lok is on Karg Island right now?" He pointed at the island across the water to emphasize his point. "That very island?"

"Yes," Arteen said with a shrug, wondering why Nicholas was emphasizing such a minor fact. "He's been the administrator here for the last five weeks or so. The previous one had been in ill health for some time and was finally replaced."

"Five weeks?"

"More or less."

"Why is that important to you?" Arch asked, noting Nicholas' sudden pale complexion and dazed demeanor. "Are you feeling ill?"

"No," he whispered, sorting through a few details in his mind before a faint smile appeared on his face. "Ivy was kidnapped above the grasslands fifty-one days ago. It was the twenty-second day of New Autumn and I'll never forget it. That's a little over five and a half weeks ago."

Arteen raised an eyebrow. "And that means...?"

Nicholas took a step closer to the men, speaking softly to them as if revealing a huge secret while trying to contain his excitement at the same time. Arch noticed that his hands were trembling.

"When I rescued Ivy from her tent that night, we talked for a few moments in the tall grass," he said. "Ivy mentioned that she was going to be sailing away under the watchful eye of a man named Tarosius Lok, but she didn't know to where. He had been ordered to keep her under guard since they all believed she was Princess

Megan. I just assumed they would sail back to the Northern Isles. But I never learned anything more because we had to move quickly to escape. After reuniting with Leo, the Island soldiers were soon after us. We were attacked in the tall grass and..." Nicholas took a deep breath, recalling the painful memories. "Ivy was taken away and I lost consciousness trying to save her. When I awoke hours later, the ship was gone. I could only imagine with horror that Ivy was sailing across the sea to the Northern Isles, alone, frightened and wondering if she would ever see her home again."

Arch looked on in disbelief. "You mean Ivy might be on Karg Island right now?"

"That's what I'm hoping," Nicholas said, unable to conceal a smile. "As Arteen said, Captain Lok arrived here shortly after that ship had departed from the grasslands. There wouldn't have been time to return to the Isles first. And if Lok was supposed to keep Ivy under guard for safekeeping, what better place than here close to the mainland where she could be retrieved quickly if needed."

"That's an incredible story," Arteen said. "And though I didn't see Lok's ship arrive as I was deep in the forest on one of our missions, I did get word later about what had happened. It was Commander Uta's ship, the *Hara Nor*, that brought Lok to Karg Island," he clarified. "It had only anchored here for one day before departing, leaving behind a very miserable Tarosius Lok and presumably your friend, Ivy." He chuckled. "I later learned that a Captain Burlu was originally supposed to take over as administrator and that Lok was scheduled to participate on some important mission with Commander Uta himself. But for whatever reason, Lok was sent here and Burlu was awarded the assignment in his stead. No doubt Captain Lok was the victim of his own arrogance and ill-spoken words. His reputation for such is well known among the naval ranks."

"I don't really care what the reason was," Nicholas replied. "I just need to get on Karg Island." He locked gazes with Arteen. "Burn that ship to the water if you'd like, just take me with you first. I'll swim to Karg Island from there."

"I've no objection, though we'll have to find you some appropriate attire as we'll all be dressed in our uniforms and overcoats," Arteen said, glancing at Arch.

"Oh, that shouldn't be a problem," Arch replied as he casually folded his arms and smiled at Nicholas who burst out with a grin. "Thanks to my sister, I know of a suitable Island coat that'll fit Nicholas perfectly."

CHAPTER 60

The *Bretic* and the *Hara Nor*

The following day, Arch Boland met with eight contacts from the Northern Isles who secretly resided in Illingboc and Braiden, the adjacent village north along the coast. Nicholas traveled with him to a few houses and farmsteads as Arch informed his people about the plan to take the *Bretic* in two nights. He listened closely and asked questions as he would be accompanying them on the raid.

"Arteen and his men will be waiting here with three large rafts to take you across," Arch told each individual, indicating on a map where to meet. "Captain Kellig and members of his crew will be ready with rope ladders to bring you on board the ship. But you must be swift. Though there is only a small crew left on the *Bretic* for the return trip to the Isles, less than half are loyal to the captain. The others still offer their allegiance to Administrator Lok. They must be subdued at once."

Twilight deepened into night when Nicholas and Arch returned home after contacting all the men in the two villages. Arteen had assigned others to inform the remaining men living in the villages farther down shore. Nicholas noted a contented expression upon Arch's face in the light of the nearly full Fox Moon, yet detected that the man wasn't completely satisfied with their progress.

"What's the matter, Arch? You seem less than enthused now that we're ready to move forward with the plan." Nicholas tasted the cool night air and felt the rumble of the horses as they galloped onward. "Worried that it won't work?"

"Quite the opposite," he replied with a short sigh. "I have full confidence that it will. It's just that a part of me wishes I was going along. Coordinating behind the scenes is one thing, but sometimes I'd like to dirty my hands a bit, if you understand."

"I do," he said with an empathetic smile.

Arch laughed. "But who am I kidding? The task ahead is for younger men. Besides, Natalie would never allow me to participate in such a dangerous mission. I know it would break her heart with worry if I did. We'll wait beside our fireplace for word to get back to us about your blazing success."

"Let's hope so–and much more," Nicholas replied, gazing out across the sea and thinking of Ivy. He felt as if the next two days would drag on forever as they rattled down the road to Illingboc, seemingly frozen in time as the inky landscape drifted past.

Two nights later the sky was a patchwork of charcoal gray clouds and bright, white stars. Nicholas rode on horseback with the eight other men from the Isles whom he and Arch had contacted earlier. The group silently headed to the meeting place located a half mile from where he and Arch had met Arteen along the seashore. There they would rendezvous with Arteen and thirteen more men arriving from the other direction. Together, twenty of them would row over to the *Bretic* and take the ship with help from Captain Kellig and other crewmen loyal to him.

Nicholas had thought it sounded like a good plan two days ago when Arteen went over the details. But now as he rode along the seashore, its dark waters illuminated by the rising full Fox Moon peeking out from behind the clouds from time to time, he wondered if he should get his hopes up as many things could go wrong. Still, Nicholas knew that if he could make it to the ship, get his bearings and keep his wits, he would be within reach of finding Ivy. He would do anything to achieve that including jumping off the *Bretic* and swimming to Karg Island.

As they galloped along the narrow dirt road, grassy in some spots and rutted in most, Nicholas glanced at the men riding in front of him, wondering what was drifting through their heads. Though they were all identically dressed in the long, brown overcoats and armed with swords and daggers, he suspected their thoughts were far afield from his own. But he didn't bother to make small talk or ask questions during their ride, noting that all appeared preoccupied with the task ahead, seeming to prefer the cold, dark quiet that guided them onward like the pull of an invisible hand.

Less than an hour later, the group approached the meeting place. As they grew near, Nicholas thought he observed a flash of light farther up shore, and then all was black again. Soon they arrived at a spot where Arteen and thirteen other Islanders waited beside a large stream that emptied into the sea. On its nearest bank lay three log rafts with room enough for eight people on each.

"My men built these rafts over the last few weeks in the nearby woods," Arteen told Nicholas when he greeted him. "They aren't as large or heavy as the ones constructed to sail up the Lorren River to Kargoth, but they'll get us to the *Bretic* just the same."

"When do we launch?" he asked, eager to proceed.

"Right now," another man answered who was a few years older than Arteen. He had a head of shortly cropped brown hair and had not shaved in several days. He gazed suspiciously at Nicholas. "I'm Ragus. Arteen said you'd be joining us tonight." He turned to Arteen with a knowing grin. "You're right. He is in a hurry. But for what purpose?"

"His business is his own," Arteen replied, glancing at Nicholas to indicate that any information about Ivy would be kept secret. "And since his friends in Illingboc have assisted us, the least we can do is allow him passage with us to the ship."

"But why does he need to go there?" Ragus persisted.

"I need to get to Karg Island," Nicholas jumped in before Arteen responded. "I have my reasons but I assure you that they will not interfere with your plans."

"So you say," Ragus muttered before turning away to speak with some of the other Islanders, occasionally looking distrustfully over his shoulder at Nicholas.

"Don't worry about Ragus," said another man who was not much older than Nicholas. His easy smile seemed to match his carefree nature. "My name is Brin Mota. And the one thing to know about Ragus is that he's wary of most anyone he first meets. So don't be offended."

"I'm not," Nicholas replied. "I guess nobody can be too sure about anyone you first meet in these times."

"Brin is correct about Ragus," Arteen confirmed. "Ragus is a very good soldier, both true and loyal, but his brusque and suspicious exterior is just his way. You may start to get used to it before the night is over."

"I already am."

Arteen addressed the crowd. "If everyone is ready, we'll board the rafts and make for the sea. Soon we'll find out if our plotting and planning has been worth the effort."

They divided into three groups and pushed the rafts into the stream, splashing through the dark waters before climbing on board. Three of the men stayed behind to tend to the horses. After grabbing some wooden paddles, the men on the rafts propelled their way down the last portion of the stream and were soon adrift upon the sea. Nicholas sailed on the same raft with Arteen, Brin and Ragus, excited to finally be in open waters. He spotted Karg Island and the *Bretic* in the distance, both gently soaked in filtered moonlight. Several lights flickered on both the island and the ship. Nicholas wondered if anyone on either place could see them approaching as they occasionally drifted through a shaft of lunar light. His nerves were on edge as every paddle stroke brought him closer to Ivy. All he could imagine was seeing her surprised and beautiful smile when he returned the scarf he had given to her in Boros. It seemed a lifetime ago. A soft voice brought him back to the present.

"Steady," Arteen whispered. "We'll make for the port side."

Nicholas looked up as he raised his paddle, amazed at how close to the ship they had moved. The starboard side of the vessel loomed steadily ahead like a sprawling, black cliff, the bow facing eastward toward the Northern Isles as if anticipating its journey home. The tall masts and myriad rope lines bereft of sails looked like a gigantic spider web in the intermittent lunar light. After a few more strokes, the rafts glided past the bow and then veered left to the more shadowy port side that would better conceal them. Soon after, Arteen ordered everyone to lift their paddles out of the water, allowing the raft to drift closer to the ship on its own momentum.

"How do they know when to expect us?" Nicholas whispered.

"One of my men had signaled them from shore with a flash of torchlight just as you were arriving,"Arteen replied. "In response, a second light was displayed in one of the windows in the captain's cabin near the stern. That was a signal to us that all was safe on board and that our plan could proceed. Captain Kellig's men will be dropping the rope ladders upon our arrival."

"And then?" he asked.

"When the ship is secure, we'll consult with the captain about advancing upon Karg Island. Lok has only a small contingent of men with him there, so it shouldn't be a difficult operation," he explained. "We'll use our rafts and some of the rowboats on the *Bretic* to make our way over. Hopefully you'll find who you're looking for there."

Nicholas smiled in the gloom. "I can't thank you enough."

"You can intercede with King Justin next time you speak to him, as Arch requested. That will be thanks enough. It may provide more help for this region of Laparia than anything I or my men could ever do to repay our debt."

"I promise to do my best," Nicholas replied when another voice in the darkness interrupted their conversation.

"*Shhh*," Ragus said, tapping Arteen on the shoulder from behind. "We're here."

Arteen nodded and silently directed his raft to edge up alongside the ship near its center. The two other vessels flanked his raft at a short distance, one on either side. Moments later, three rope ladders dropped from the deck above, unraveling on cue, their bottom rungs dangling along the side of the ship, one near each of the small crafts. One man on each vessel secured his raft with a length of rope to each of the ladders. Arteen gave a signal and the men began to silently clamber up the side of the ship like dark lines of ants scaling the trunk of an enormous tree.

When it was his turn, Nicholas grabbed the ladder and hoisted himself up on the bottom rung and started to climb, looking down at the oily, black water as the Fox Moon shimmered through a nebulous layer of clouds. The vessel appeared much higher and intimidating while hanging from its side than when looking up at it from below. He climbed steadily, feeling the sway of the ladder in the breeze and the minor rocking of the ship, realizing how small he was compared to some things in the world yet amazed that a group of men were able to construct such an enormous vessel. When he finally maneuvered himself over the top rail, he experienced the same sense of satisfaction he had when reaching the summit of Gray Hawk Mountain, though the resulting views were hardly comparable.

On deck, two men at each ladder wordlessly greeted him and the other Islanders, raising fingers to their lips to signal for absolute silence. They were similarly dressed in long, brown overcoats with the hoods drawn over their heads. One man carried an oil lamp which provided the only light other than an occasional appearance of the Fox Moon and the distant glow from the captain's cabin. A few lighted windows were visible on Karg Island about a quarter mile away west. Arteen climbed over the rail last of all and leaned close to the man who was holding the oil lamp.

"Where is Captain Kellig?" he whispered.

"Inside his cabin," the young man replied, pointing to the stern. "He awaits your presence. My name is Peltus. The rest of you should split into two groups and follow my men. They'll lead you to others in the crew not loyal to our cause. Most are in their sleeping quarters below deck. A few are still on duty. We must move fast."

Arteen nodded and informed his crew of the plan, dividing them into two groups. "Nicholas, stay close by me. We shall meet with the captain together."

"All right, though you could probably make better use of me elsewhere," he said.

"Keeping you safe is my first priority." But before Nicholas could protest, Arteen raised a hand. "I do so not for your sake, but for the one whom you seek."

"Well, in that case…"

Arteen dispersed his troops, with nine following two of the men and the remaining nine following the others to separate parts of the ship. Meanwhile, Nicholas and Arteen hurried off to meet with Captain Kellig and discuss their next move, following Peltus along the port side while bathed in the glow of the oil lamp. As they walked toward the back of the ship, the wind picked up, snapping several flags attached to the lines above. The Fox Moon again revealed herself from behind an inky cloud drifting eastward.

When they reached the cabin, Nicholas peered through a small window to one side and saw a man sitting on a wooden stool while hunched over a desk. He held a quill pen, apparently writing in a ledger. An ink bottle, some bound books and several leaves of loose parchment were scattered across the desktop amid the sickly glow of an oil lamp. The walls were painted bright white and sparsely adorned with nautical-themed decorations–a replica helmsman's wheel, a silver boatswain's whistle and a bundle of clean rope neatly looped, tied and hanging from a large hook.

Peltus glanced at Nicholas and Arteen, indicating for them to follow him to the entrance. He grabbed the door handle, and after looking about the deck as if to make sure they hadn't been followed, he nodded to his companions and opened the door. He hurried inside as Nicholas and Arteen followed, closing the door behind them.

"We're here, captain," he said in a calm voice as he placed the oil lamp on a nearby table.

Nicholas and Arteen stared at the man seated at the desk, his head hung low as he continued to scribble in the ledger. He calmly placed the quill pen in the ink bottle and closed the book before looking up, a tight, thin smile drawn across his face.

"Welcome to my ship, gentlemen," he said, his words and demeanor as cold as the vacant stare emitted from a pair of dark eyes set beneath a head of thinning hair. A small scar ran along his left cheek close to the earlobe. "I've been awaiting your arrival."

Nicholas thought the captain's manner was off-putting at first glance, looking askance at Arteen. But when he saw Arteen's mouth agape, he felt tightness in the pit of his stomach and knew that something was wrong. He heard a single word uttered and his worst fears were confirmed.

"Lok!" Arteen uttered the man's name with contempt. "Where is Captain Kellig?" he demanded, reaching for his sword.

In that instant, Peltus stepped back and drew his own sword, pointing the sharp tip just below Arteen's chin. "I don't think you want to do that," he remarked.

"I agree," Captain Lok said as he got up off his stool. "The floor in here was just scrubbed the other day. It would be a shame to stain it with your blood. Or his," he added, indicating Nicholas.

Arteen lowered his sword and handed it to Peltus. Just then, several armed soldiers entered the cabin from an adjacent room. A half dozen others could be seen through the windows standing guard outside. They disarmed Arteen and Nicholas and ordered them to one corner of the room. Moments later another man was pushed toward them who had been concealed behind the soldiers. The tall, unshaven individual was Captain Kellig, appearing pale and disheartened.

Arteen looked shocked at seeing him in such a state. "What happened, sir?"

"We were betrayed," he muttered, rubbing a hand across his face as he shook his head in disbelief.

Arteen was speechless for a moment, wondering who could have turned against them. "Who did this? I'll avenge him myself."

"One of your own," Lok said with much delight. "Did you really think you could get away with such a bold maneuver? Your dishonor to the Isles disgusts me."

"Not as much as you disgust me," Nicholas said, glaring at Tarosius Lok.

Nicholas was overwhelmed with a desire to lunge at the man as he speculated upon the harm and mental anguish he inflicted upon Ivy. He imagined himself rushing at Lok and choking the life out of him, but not before forcing the man to reveal exactly where Ivy was being held on Karg Island. But he kept his composure, gritting his teeth until he could size up the situation.

Captain Lok stepped close to Nicholas, breathing down upon the unfamiliar face. "What ship did you sail on to get here?" he asked, thumping a finger against his chest. "And how did you manage to involve yourself in this criminal's vicious plot against me?" He tilted his head at Arteen.

"He came over on the *Durósk* a few weeks ago," Arteen jumped in, knowing that Nicholas needed help to conceal his identity.

"Can he not speak for himself?" Lok snarled before glaring at Nicholas. "Talk to me like that one more time and your blood will be staining this floor before the night is over–though that may yet happen regardless."

There was a knock at the door and one of the soldiers who had helped lower the rope ladders excitedly entered. "The other traitors have been subdued and disarmed, Captain Lok."

"Excellent!" he replied, smiling. "Any injuries? Deaths?"

"None, sir. They were taken completely by surprise as you predicted," he said. "Your orders, sir?"

"Assemble them all on deck so I can address the sorry lot." Lok smirked at Arteen and Nicholas. "Some revolt you put together. I had hoped for a bit more of a challenge." He turned to the soldier. "We'll be out shortly. You are dismissed."

"Yes, Captain Lok," he replied, exiting in a breathless rush.

"What do you plan?" Arteen asked. "Sail us back to the Isles so you can parade us around in public and pretend to be a hero?"

"Oh, I can imagine much better punishments to mete out to you and your traitorous friends. You can think about it while we go on deck," he said. He signaled some of his soldiers and they promptly marched Nicholas, Arteen and Captain Kellig out of the cabin into the cool, night air.

Moments later they neared an open area on the starboard side where the rest of Arteen's men had been assembled. Those few in the crew who had remained loyal to Captain Kellig were still imprisoned below. As the clouds began to disperse on a freshening breeze, the brush of moonlight across the prisoners' faces accentuated their defeated expressions. Nicholas noted fear in some of their eyes and wondered what trouble loomed ahead as the mournful creaking of the vessel reverberated in the night.

"I can only imagine that several of you now regret following the bizarre whims of your failed leaders." Lok stared at both Arteen and Captain Kellig when he said this, eliciting a few chuckles from his supporters. "Those who think they can take up arms against the Isles will soon learn the folly of their ways."

"We aren't the only Islanders opposed to this madness," Arteen said. "Some will follow in our steps no matter what you do to us. Others sent off to war will simply desert into the forests and hillsides of Laparia the first chance they get." He glared at Captain Lok. "Some of them might even join the opposition before it's all over. The rebellion against the Island leadership is more far-reaching than you know."

Lok appeared unfazed by Arteen's words, though they gnawed at him deep inside. But he wouldn't give him the satisfaction of knowing so and simply smiled.

"Idle words won't help you here." Lok looked around at the sea of faces and focused on one of Arteen's men and signaled him to approach. "So tell me, Mr. Mota. Is there anything more I need to know about this failed endeavor? Or shall I proceed to announce sentences on these traitors?"

A palpable sense of shock arose from Arteen and his followers when Brin Mota stepped forward, the apparent and unsuspected traitor to their cause. Brin looked uncomfortably at Arteen before averting his eyes to address Lok.

"Captain, the only item not mentioned in my last report is something I learned about just a short time ago," Brin said, shooting a cool glance at Nicholas. "There is one among Arteen's men who is not from the Isles, sir. One of the mainlanders has participated in this botched raid."

Lok's curiosity was sparked. "I was aware from your reports that Arteen and his followers were getting assistance from the nearby villages. However, I didn't expect any of the locals to join in the attack. Who is this man?"

Brin pointed at Nicholas, enjoying his moment of power. "Him, sir. His name is Nicholas Raven. He traveled from his home in Arrondale. While on our way here, I overheard him in conversation with Arteen. Mr. Raven is apparently on speaking terms with King Justin. To what extent, I do not know. But if he has the King's ear, then there is more about him than his appearance would indicate."

Before Lok answered, Arteen snickered loudly. "Not only do you turn on your friends, Brin, but you're an eavesdropper as well."

"I'll do whatever it takes to perform my duty," he proudly replied.

"And we'll do whatever it takes to make you pay for your disloyalty," Ragus sputtered with disgust. "That's a promise!"

"Enough!" Lok said. He stepped toward Nicholas, eyeing him suspiciously. "I had a feeling the moment I saw you that you weren't one of us. A spy for the King perhaps?"

"Maybe," Nicholas replied tauntingly, refusing to say anything more in case he should accidentally reveal his true purpose.

"Well if spy you are, you're not a very good one!"

"The man claimed that he needed to get to Karg Island," Brin added. "Being a part of this raid was not his true purpose."

Lok appeared taken aback. One of his aides close by glanced at him with concern.

"Could he have come looking for her?" he asked. "Maybe he *is* a spy."

"Silence!" Lok muttered.

Nicholas' heart fluttered upon hearing the soldier speak those words to Lok, certain that the man could only be referring to Ivy. But he forced himself to appear uninterested in their verbal exchange.

"But if he is a spy, maybe there are others like him," the aide nervously continued. "Maybe they're already among us."

"I said silence!" Lok shouted. "Certain conversations are not meant for all ears. Do you understand?"

"Yes," he whispered, nodding in apology.

Lok studied Nicholas' face again and seemed to relax. "Just as I sensed in the cabin that you were not one of us, I'm now beginning to suspect that you have come here alone. So whether or not you are a spy for King Justin is irrelevant as you are now my prisoner. What you have come here for is of little concern to me. In the end you'll be treated just like all the other traitors in this group and suffer the consequences."

"And what might those be?" Captain Kellig asked. "Don't keep us in suspense."

"You won't find the situation so amusing when you stand before the high judges during your tribunal," Lok dryly replied. "Nor will *you*," he added with a caustic look at Arteen. "You and Captain Kellig, along with the handful of your allies on this ship who are imprisoned below deck, will face charges of treason during the inquiry. And after my testimony, I have little doubt that a death sentence awaits all of you. I'd administer it myself right now, but you know how the political and naval higher-ups will want to make a show out of it for their benefit. I can't deny them their fun, can I?"

Lok's followers laughed, but Arteen and Captain Kellig stood there with stony expressions, each afraid to consider the fate of their remaining followers standing before them. Arteen finally posed the question when the commotion died down.

"What of my men on deck?" he asked. "They're citizens of the Isles, too. They deserve to make their case and be judged fairly."

"They've already been judged by me," Lok said. "They have forfeited any judicial consideration due other men since they have been apprehended in the midst of traitorous acts. There is no doubt of their guilt, or of yours. But I'm allowing you, Captain Kellig and the men below to return to the Isles to appease my superiors. They would surely hound me if I handed down a sweeping verdict here myself–though I have that right as we are out to sea. But the rest of your sorry crew will face my immediate judgment. Their sentences will be carried out forthwith."

Captain Kellig looked on with disbelief. "You can't be serious, Lok! We are not out to sea as you claim. And even if we were, only someone with the rank of vice-commander or higher can exercise such authority. You are out of your bounds, sir!"

"But I am in charge, am I not?" Lok's tone was bitter and spiteful. "Commander Uta banished me to this desolate island to run it as I see fit. So in a sense I am carrying the proper authority. Let Uta and Burlu seek glory elsewhere. I have the power here and I shall wield it!" Murmurs of agreement reverberated among his men, bolstering Lok's belief in his argument. "And in my judgment, all twenty men involved in this conspiracy against me, my ship and my island are found guilty of treason in the first order." He poked his finger in the cold air to emphasize his words. "Therefore, Captain Kellig and Arteen will be imprisoned below with the others until they are returned to the Isles to face a public sentence. But the remaining eighteen traitors shall be executed forthwith and thrown overboard as they are not worthy to stand on the deck of the *Bretic*, the very ship they plotted to destroy. And when their bodies wash ashore, let the birds and the elements do with them as they wish, though in my eyes it is a sentence still too lenient for their crimes."

A heavy silence pervaded the ship as the remaining clouds broke up and dispersed, revealing a field of stars above. All of Lok's men as well as those he accused of treason stood in utter disbelief, each wondering if he had heard the captain's words correctly. Their stunned faces were awash in a sharp breeze off the sea and the steady glow of the Fox Moon. Captain Lok, who had expected a rousing chorus of support from his troops, looked upon their silence with mild irritation.

"Is there a problem?" he asked, eyeing some of his closest aides who returned only tentative glances. Finally, one of them found the nerve to speak.

"Captain Lok, I'm wondering if..." The man froze in mid-sentence, intimidated by Lok's vulture-like scrutiny.

"Yes? Say what's on your mind."

After a moment's hesitation, the soldier nervously cleared his throat. "I'm wondering if you might reconsider your decision, sir. I think you may have misspoken–unintentionally, of course!"

Lok glowered at the man, and while everyone expected him to erupt in rage, the captain simply shook his head and sighed. "Misspoken? No, I don't think so. I meant what I said. My order will be carried out. Is that understood?" The man nodded nervously. "Good! Then if there aren't any other questions, we'll proceed."

"Not if I have anything to say about it," Arteen said. "Do you think you can get away with such an irrational scheme?"

"You can state your argument when we return to the Isles," Lok said. "But unless you want to join your fellow conspirators and share in their fate now, I suggest you keep quiet."

"We'll do no such thing!" Captain Kellig jumped in. "Even your own men are horrified that you'd suggest such a grotesque idea, Lok. It is out of the bounds of decency. It is even out of the bounds of Island law." He growled with disgust. "Propose all the lunatic ideas you want, but I suspect that even your most loyal soldier will not follow your orders down such a dark and treacherous path."

"They will follow me, or they will join the traitors!"

"*You* are the traitor, to reason and sanity."

"Enough! I am in charge, Mr. Kellig, and I hereby strip you of your rank. Now not another word from anyone." Lok unsheathed his sword and raised it with one arm for all to see. "Let the blood of these renegades stain this sword tonight and seep into the waters of the Trillium. I will accept full responsibility for their fate." He handed the weapon to his nearest soldier, directing him to walk one of the prisoners to the railing and strike the first deadly blow. "You can start with that one," Lok ordered, pointing at Nicholas.

"*What?*" Nicholas looked back wide-eyed, his mouth agape. Before he could utter another word, Arteen spoke up in his defense.

"You cannot kill him, Lok, without risking the wrath of the mainlanders. They have assisted us greatly, though in secret. But should they find out that you murdered one of their own in cold blood, one who is dear to the family of our greatest supporter, they would rise up against you without a single thought for their safety."

"Well, Arteen, that is where you're wrong," he replied. "When the villagers find eighteen dead bodies washed up on shore, fear will spread like wildfire along the Crescent. Their horror will be my greatest weapon. It will crush their budding rebellion before it grows stronger roots. The Isles won't want to waste time, resources and troops to keep them in line if they ever revolted. So just think how pleased the leadership will be when learning that I already have the locals in line. I might earn a promotion when it's over."

"I doubt that," Arteen said, glancing at Brin who stood ill at ease nearby. He addressed the young soldier. "Having second thoughts now about throwing in your lot with the likes of him?"

"Address my men no further, Arteen. You're trying to confuse them with your twisted words," Lok said, moderating his strident tone. "Despite my harsh sentence, my troops know that I'm right. And I will stand by my decision since that is a sign of a truly great leader, is it not?"

As Lok scanned an eye over his troops, hoping for an inkling of support, he was disappointed and incensed that most of his men had cast their gazes out across the water, taking it as a sign of silent dishonor. If he lost their support now, he knew his authority would be compromised beyond repair. Even though he had quelled the uprising and defeated the traitors, he would still be on the losing end as far as his soldiers were concerned, their grudging respect and fear forever lost.

"What insubordination is this?" he angrily lashed out, grabbing his sword back from the soldier and driving the sharp tip into the deck. "I demand your attention! My orders will be followed!"

"Captain Lok," whispered one of his aides. "Commander Uta's—"

"I don't want to hear another word about Commander Uta or anyone else on the Isles who might object to my instructions. Do you understand? They are not here to—"

"But, sir," the aide persisted, pointing to the southeast. "Commander Uta's ship is approaching. The *Hara Nor* is here."

Lok was dumbstruck, turning around and gazing out across the water where everyone else was looking. "Impossible," he whispered to himself. He glanced hard at his aide. "This cannot be. Commander Uta is about to lead a vital mission far from here. That cannot possibly be his ship."

"But it is, Captain," another aide replied. "His flag is visible on one of the mast lines. The Fox Moon illuminates it from behind."

The man pointed out the stark yet glorious sight to Captain Lok who continued to look on with utter incredulity. As the *Hara Nor* swiftly glided over the dark waters of the Trillium, ablaze in moonlight, Lok's plans for a magnificent night of personal triumph dissolved into bitterness as old wounds quickly surfaced. His shoulders slumped at the sight of the *Hara Nor* as his breath involuntarily escaped from his aching lungs.

"Why is he here?" he muttered, walking to the railing and clutching it, his fingernails digging into the wood. "This is *my* ship. This is *my* night. Hasn't Uta ruined my life enough already?"

"What shall we do with the prisoners, captain?"

The voice of his aide echoed in Lok's ears as he stared hypnotically over the railing. The *Hara Nor* was fast approaching.

"I need a moment to think," Lok wearily replied, his eyes fixed on the ship. Slowly he loosened his grip on the railing. A hint of a smile spread across his face while the gears in his mind rapidly turned. "Perhaps I can still make this work," he said, turning to his aide. "But we'll have to move fast!"

CHAPTER 61

A Change of Command

The *Hara Nor* lowered her sails and dropped anchor when she was parallel to the *Bretic's* starboard side. The vessel was the grander of the two ships, much larger, more stately and one of the finest in the fleet. Commander Uta was proud to call it his own, flying his military standard just below the official flag of the Isles. But Uta was not on board the *Hara Nor* at the moment. A small rowboat was lowered from the deck and minutes later a handful of men climbed aboard the *Bretic*. Captain Lok greeted them, slightly miffed by their presence. Brin and a few other soldiers were at his side. Though Lok knew that Commander Uta was working his way down the Trent Hills for a future raid on the Citadel, he half expected him to be here with his ship. Instead, a tall man with a finely trimmed beard upon a thin face extended a hand in greeting. Lok tentatively accepted it.

"Welcome aboard the *Bretic*, Vice-Commander Ovek. This is an unexpected pleasure," Lok said with a perfunctory dryness. "It is rare that Commander Uta's ship sails without him on board."

"He trusts me with it," Ovek replied before introducing his aides. Lok did the same. "I had almost hoped that Captain Kellig would be greeting me tonight as this is his ship, but I guess what I heard is true."

THOMAS J. PRESTOPNIK

Lok raised a suspicious eyebrow at the comment, wondering what the vice-commander was referring to. "What you *heard*?"

"Now don't be modest, Captain Lok. That is so unlike you," he said with a grin. "I want to congratulate you on apprehending the band of traitors intent on taking and destroying this ship." Lok stared back at Ovek, his mouth agape. "I'm assuming this is the case as I see no signs of fighting or bloodshed. And as Captain Kellig is nowhere in sight, I must be correct in my assumption, am I not?"

"You are indeed, sir," Lok grudgingly responded, his voice nearly a whisper. But his thoughts swirled with suspicion, wondering how Ovek received word of his triumph and how he showed up precisely at this moment. Most of all, he warily suspected that nothing good would come of it. "But how do you know of this treason and my response to it? Events unfolded only moments ago. The prisoners had just been taken below deck as you arrived." Lok wrinkled his brow. "I do not understand."

"I was informed in advance of your plan to let the traitors converge on this ship so that you could capture them in the act," he said approvingly. "It was quite a risk but one that apparently paid off handsomely."

"Who told you?" Lok asked, keeping a boiling anger in check.

Vice-Commander Ovek threw a glance at Lok's men which sent a chill through the captain. Brin stepped forward, eyeing Captain Lok without fear or intimidation.

"I have been keeping Vice-Commander Ovek apprised of this situation for the past several weeks," he calmly stated.

"Explain yourself!" Lok said.

Brin complied. "Ever since I heard rumors of Arteen's organization months ago when I arrived on these shores, I decided to find out all I could, hoping one day to crush it. It pained me to learn that there were Islanders fleeing their military companies to start new lives on the mainland. It incensed me even more to find out that some of them were hiding in the area to wage war against us. That is why I ran away from my post one night after we had finished working on our rafts for the day," he explained. "I wandered through the woods and about the shoreline for over a week before being spotted by a small group of Islanders who had also fled. They were part of Arteen's group plotting against us. When I told them of my

312

disgust for the Isles' military endeavors and my plans to start a new life on the mainland, they brought me to Arteen and integrated me into their group. It was exactly where I wanted to be. Soon I gained their trust and their secrets."

"And then you came to me," Lok said, still wondering how Ovek was given the same information.

"Yes, but only after weeks of going off alone on spying missions or acting as a messenger among our contacts in the nearby villages," Brin said. "I first had to play the part of a traitor to fully convince Arteen and the others that I was one of them. Finally, I was sent off to the village of Illingboc to pass on information to a few of our soldiers hiding out there and to some of the locals supporting us. As I was on my own for a few days, I stole a small boat from shore one night and paddled to Karg Island and presented my case to you."

"I remember that night," Lok replied. "I encouraged you to continue your pretense and to keep me informed so we could eventually crush the rebellion."

"And so I did, visiting you in person on a few more occasions when it was feasible, or sending messages to you from time to time via trusted soldiers on other visiting ships." A snake-like smile spread across Brin's face. "When I finally learned about the planned raid on the last ship to arrive here before winter, I knew it was our best chance to expose the traitors and destroy the network Arteen had developed. I quickly got that information to you."

"But how did Vice-Commander Ovek learn of all this?"

"Simple," Ovek said. "Mr. Mota also sent word to me through a few of his contacts on the ships returning to the Isles. He is a smart and ambitious soldier. I, in turn, let Commander Uta know what was going on the last time I saw him before he and Burlu departed on their mission. I got word back to Brin to keep me informed, telling him I would be in the area on the *Hara Nor* when the last ship arrived. I hid my vessel in a deserted cove several miles down the coast. Brin contacted me before dawn yesterday about tonight's proceedings, and well, here I am."

"But why?" Lok sputtered, unable to contain his seething anger. "I had the situation under control. I knew how to deal with the traitors and put an end to the insurgency once and for all. Why did you have to show up?" He glared at Brin. "And why did you have to contact the Vice-Commander? Why would you deceive me?"

"Lok, watch your tone," Ovek said, his growing disdain for the man evident. "Brin is no fool. He contacted me with vital information like any soldier would who was trying to make a name for himself. You of all people should understand that, given the path that your career has taken over the years."

"Yes. And it landed me on that stinking patch of dirt!" he fumed, pointing a bony finger at Karg Island. "Commander Uta purposely did this to me. And now he wants to take credit for my capture of the traitors for his own political ambitions."

"And if you're smart," Ovek warned, "you'll play along and perhaps redeem yourself in Uta's eyes. If he should rise in leadership, he just might reward you for your role in this incident, much like he punished you by sending you here. Your choice."

Lok shook his head and sighed, realizing how close he was to being insubordinate with the Vice-Commander. But despite Ovek's promise of possible rewards from a grateful Uta, Captain Lok couldn't find it within himself to cooperate. He had had enough of others taking credit for his successes and stomping on his dreams. It had to stop now.

"At least allow me to handle the prisoners as I see fit, Vice-Commander. I believe I have earned that much," he calmly petitioned. "If Commander Uta wants to share in the credit afterward, then I welcome him. But I think I deserve to be captain at the helm of this ship when it returns to the Isles. That would only be appropriate, don't you think?"

Captain Lok was moderately encouraged when Ovek seemed to seriously consider his request. His mood soured when Brin raised his voice in protest.

"Vice-Commander, I believe it is my duty to inform you just how Captain Lok planned to handle his prisoners," Brin said, briefly looking askance at Lok. "He was about to execute eighteen of them right here on deck and toss their bodies overboard as a warning to the villages on the mainland."

"That was just one of many possibilities I was considering!" Lok snapped.

"If you had not arrived when you did," Brin continued, "I fear there may have been a bloodbath."

"Is this true?" a stunned Ovek asked, his tone harsh.

Lok slowly fumed, glaring at Brin. "But it is nothing less than the traitors deserve. They will probably get as much at a tribunal."

"Nevertheless, that is for the judges to decide, not a ship's captain!" Ovek replied, his disgust growing. "What an astoundingly stupid act you were about to commit. As of this moment, your role in this affair is terminated, Captain Lok. You'll have nothing more to do with the prisoners and will accompany me home on the *Hara Nor* at daybreak."

"Vice-Commander, I must protest this–"

"Duly noted!" Ovek continued with a brusque wave of his hand. "I hereby put the *Bretic* in the hands of my trusted aide, Langlin." He glanced at a tall, weather-beaten man standing next to him. "Mr. Langlin, you will follow the *Hara Nor* on the return trip home with the prisoners." Ovek looked at Brin. "And you I promote to the position of captain's assistant. You can serve in this role beside Mr. Langlin on the voyage back."

"Thank you, sir," Brin replied, keeping a stern countenance. "Your trust in me is not misplaced."

"I believe that," Ovek said. "And with that attitude, I don't think it'll be too long before you make full captain."

"How lucky for him," Lok snidely remarked. "Perhaps we should celebrate."

"Perhaps we should have a private talk," Ovek said.

"You can say anything you wish about me in front of these men," he replied, beyond caring about his reputation. He had little respect left for any of the individuals gathered about.

"The talk is not about you, Lok, but about the princess," Ovek clarified. "For your ears only."

"Oh. We can speak alone in my cabin. Or shall I say *his* cabin," he added, glancing at Langlin.

"One moment, sir," Brin called out to the Vice-Commander. "I would be remiss not to let you know that one of the prisoners below is not from the Isles but is from Arrondale. His name is Nicholas Raven and he has apparently been in communication with King Justin."

"Is this true, Lok?"

"Yes, Vice-Commander."

"And, sir," Brin continued, "this individual's sole purpose for coming aboard the ship was to get to Karg Island. I suspect that he may have been trying to rescue the girl. No doubt one of King Justin's spies."

"This has turned into quite an interesting visit," Ovek said. "Bring Nicholas Raven to the cabin at once. I wish to speak with him." He headed toward the stern, indicating for Lok to follow as if he were merely an afterthought. Lok did so, muttering to himself.

When they entered the captain's cabin, Lok grudgingly offered the Vice-Commander a chair while he sat on the stool at his desk. "Forgive the mess, but I had brought over some of my ledgers, papers and other effects from the island. It seems that I shall have to move them again, this time to your ship."

Ovek grunted. "Enough of your whining, Lok. Tell me about the girl. Is she all right?"

"Of course," he replied. "I went out of my way to keep her safe as Commander Uta had instructed when he dropped me on the wretched island. I even ordered some of my men to construct the princess her own quarters. They are not the luxury she is accustomed to, but they are her own. And as she has been under guard at all times, escape was never an issue. Still, she was a headache I wish I didn't have to deal with. I had enough problems getting men and supplies up the Lorren River."

"That's good," Ovek said, nodding as if another thought was distracting him.

Lok folded his arms and gazed impatiently at the man, his chin resting in one hand while waiting for Ovek to make his point. "So what is it that you needed to tell me in secret?" he finally asked, wishing the meeting were already over.

Vice-Commander Ovek smiled uncomfortably. "It's about Princess Megan. You might find this amusing, Lok, but she's not..."

"Yes?"

"Apparently she's not really the princess," he said with a bit of a chuckle. "We seem to have the wrong woman."

"What?" Lok slowly rubbed his hand over his mouth while he stared at Ovek, wondering if the man was serious or simply making a strange joke. He was in no mood for humor of any kind. "Not a princess? What are you talking about?"

Ovek explained how he received word nearly ten days ago from Caldurian's messenger crow that Princess Megan was back safely in Morrenwood, witnessed by one of the wizard's spies. "It seems a simple hoax was perpetrated for Princess Megan's protection. A switch was made and the kidnappers procured the wrong individual. So the woman you've been watching for these past several weeks is–"

"–a nobody?"

"We suspect so, but we'll take her back to the Isles just to be sure. She may still be a spy of sorts. Commander Uta and I thought it best to keep this matter quiet so as not to cause you any embarrassment."

Captain Lok stared incredulously at Ovek. "Cause *me* any embarrassment? Your concern is misplaced, Vice-Commander. I'm more than happy to let others know that we've wasted so much of our time and resources caring for one of Uta's mistakes."

Ovek stood and pointed a finger at Lok. "You will keep this matter private, Captain Lok, on Uta's direct order. Any records of her stay on Karg Island will be turned over to me. Understood?"

Lok studied Ovek's reddening face with mirth, unable to conceal a smirk. "So I'm supposed to happily relinquish control of the *Bretic* as well as taking credit for capturing the traitors. And on top of that, you want me to keep quiet about Uta's blunder? I suppose holding a princess prisoner who turns out not to be royalty might be a tad embarrassing for a man with political ambitions." Lok enjoyed seeing the sour grimace on Ovek's face. "Let me guess–did Uta spread word among his circle of supporters that he was holding Princess Megan to use against Arrondale when needed? I'll bet he had grand plans to use her to make himself a national hero."

"That is enough, Lok."

"By your tone, I'll take that as a *yes*." He then looked wide-eyed at Ovek as a delicious notion popped into his head. "Uta didn't happen to send word to Kargoth about his prized princess, did he?"

"I said that's enough!"

"Perhaps to Vellan himself?" Lok chuckled. "Now how would Commander Uta look if word got out about an embarrassing slip-up such as that? Misleading Vellan, deliberately or otherwise, surely can't be good for one's career."

"Lok, you are treading in waters where you should not!" Ovek warned.

"I will not be a scapegoat for Commander Uta or for you!" he blasted back. "Your reputation is linked to this royal mess as much as Uta's, and if the truth seeps out, you'll both look like the incompetent fools you've turned out to be. Don't think I don't realize what's going on."

"Think as you please, but you'll keep this quiet if you know what's good for you. And that isn't just my suggestion," Ovek said. "This comes from Uta himself. But if you want to put your career in jeopardy–or even your life–then go ahead. Talk up a storm."

"My career has already been jeopardized by Uta while I was doing my job. Any additional threats from you, Ovek, will not–"

A hurried knock at the door cut Lok off in mid-sentence. Brin had arrived with Nicholas. Vice-Commander Ovek beckoned them to enter at once. He eyed Nicholas with suspicion, mildly disgusted that he was wearing the coat of a Northern Isles soldier.

"Arteen was very thorough, stealing an extra coat for you."

"He was," Nicholas coolly replied, having no intention of telling him how Hannah had actually attained the item. "But I assume you didn't bring me here to talk about clothing. What do you want?"

Before answering, Ovek glanced at Brin. "Thank you, but that will be all for now. We wish to speak with this man alone. Go wait outside with the others until you are needed."

"As you wish, Vice-Commander," Brin said with a slight hesitation, having assumed that he would be part of this meeting. "If I can be of further assistance–"

"Yes, of course," Ovek hastily replied, his impatience evident. He remained silent until Brin had left the cabin and then turned to Nicholas with a stony expression. "I have questions, Mr. Raven, and I want swift and honest answers. If I don't get them, the woman on Karg Island will face punishment for your obstinacy. Am I clear?"

"Perfectly," he grudgingly replied, unable to bear the thought of Ivy suffering for his bravado.

"Good. We agree." Ovek began to pace the room. "I've learned from some well-placed sources that the young lady on the island is not Princess Megan, so there is no use in pretending otherwise." He studied Nicholas' face and detected a tinge of fear and surprise in the young man's eyes. "Who is she and what is her name? And remember our agreement," he cautioned.

Nicholas looked up at the ceiling and along the dark timbers evenly spaced about the walls as they caught the garish glow of the oil lamp. He wondered how he ended up in this room, so close to his goal yet seemingly a thousand miles away. "Her name is Ivy," he softly said, a sense of defeat slowly encroaching about him. "She's also from Arrondale and works as a housekeeper in the village of Boros, if you must know."

"Boros? Never heard of it."

"Perhaps you ought to look at a map now and then."

Ovek grunted. "And perhaps you should be a better judge of character, getting involved with the likes of Captain Kellig and Arteen. But back to the woman. I'm guessing you have affections for her judging by that heartsick expression on your face and your willingness to answer my questions so quickly. So here are a few more." He posed them in rapid-fire fashion. "How did you meet Ivy? How did you meet the real princess? And what is their connection that caused one woman to pose as the other?"

Nicholas carefully considered how he should answer. Would the truth work to his advantage and save Ivy, or simply land them in more trouble? But when looking at Ovek and Lok and sensing deception and corruption in both men, he realized that his fate was probably determined no matter what he said. He decided to tell them the truth, up to a point, and hope for the best.

"Several weeks ago I met Princess Megan traveling alone on the road. After escorting her to Boros to visit her great aunt, I subsequently met Ivy, the aunt's housekeeper." Captain Lok and Vice-Commander Ovek stared at Nicholas in utter disbelief. "Well, that's the story in brief. I suppose you'll want a few more details."

"A few, yes," Lok replied dryly.

Nicholas elaborated on meeting the two women and Leo. He left out any mention of their encounter with Carmella and Jagga, his knowledge of the war council and his journey to find the wizard Frist, simply presenting his story as the travels of four friends.

"In the end, Ivy wanted to help keep Princess Megan safely hidden in Boros until the people after her were gone. That's why she suggested switching identities," he continued. "But Ivy was kidnapped in the end and…" Nicholas sighed, shaking his head. "Megan had given Ivy her silver medallion beforehand which only convinced her kidnappers even more that Ivy was the princess." He gazed at his captors, silently pleading with them to release Ivy. "Though I fell in with Arteen and his men, my only reason was to gain access to the island, rescue Ivy and then leave. I have no desire to get involved with the politics of your cause. To tell you the truth, I don't really care who's on whose side," he said, hoping they believed him. "All I ever wanted was to save Ivy so we could run off and start a life together away from this strife. Neither of us is a threat to your operation, and if you let us go, we'll never bother you again."

"A touching story," Ovek replied with a hint of sarcasm. "And I do believe you," he added, receiving a grateful look from Nicholas and a scowl from Lok. "However, I am a thorough man and will have others hear your story, and Ivy's, before a decision about your fates is decided. That is the wise and prudent thing to do."

"The girl has not revealed much to me," Lok informed him. "Yet my men and I did not press her much since we assumed that Commander Uta would not approve."

"That was when you thought she was a princess," Ovek said. "Now we know she is not and can perhaps be a bit more vigorous in our questioning if it is so warranted."

"What do you mean to do?" Nicholas asked, his fear for Ivy's safety spiking at Ovek's ominous words.

"You shall both be taken to the Northern Isles where a complete investigation can be conducted. The two of you might still be found out to be spies in the end, two very clever spies," Ovek suggested. "But my agents will determine that, one way or another."

"We're not spies!" Nicholas insisted. "Just let us go. Please."

Ovek shook his head. "Sorry, but this meeting is over. You'll be sent below with the other prisoners and my men will bring Ivy aboard the *Hara Nor*."

"Not necessary," Lok jumped in. "My men can handle that duty. In fact, I would like a word with the girl myself before I transfer her to your ship." His tone sounded too eager as Nicholas looked on with subdued horror.

"Thank you, Captain Lok, but your assistance is no longer required," the vice-commander replied. "You will be escorted to the

Hara Nor as well where a room will be provided for your comfort and privacy."

"Excuse me?"

"You heard me, Lok. Your business here is done."

"But I must finish my work on Karg Island before I return home. There is much yet to do," he insisted, growing red in the face, knowing that Ovek was wringing the last bit of authority out of him.

"My men will crate up your personal belongings and all the official records and such on Karg Island and bring them aboard the ship for you. You needn't worry," he replied with a thin smile.

"You're shutting me out!" Lok cried, jumping up from his stool so fast that he hit the front of his desk and nearly knocked over the oil lamp, catching it just in time. He angrily pointed a finger at Ovek. "I still know what I know–remember that. You and Uta cannot silence me nor hide your ineptitude regarding this situation. I'll let important people know what really happened here. Word will spread–possibly to Vellan himself if I can arrange it."

"Well, you can try, Lok."

"Don't think that this is over, Vice-Commander."

"This conversation is over!" he snapped, pushing past Nicholas and opening the door. Ovek called outside to Brin and another of his aides and they came rushing to him. "Take Mr. Raven back with the other prisoners," he instructed Brin. "On second thought, find a place below deck where he can be isolated. I want no one talking to him without my permission. Is that understood?"

"Yes, sir," Brin replied, eager to have a role in whatever was happening regarding Nicholas and his attempt to get to Karg Island. Brin assumed he had some connection to Princess Megan and wished he were privy to more details. He grabbed Nicholas by the arm and they exited the room, closing the door behind them.

Ovek then instructed his aide to escort Captain Lok to the *Hara Nor* immediately. He made Lok hand over his sword which he grudgingly did. "Find him private quarters somewhere and post a guard outside his door." Ovek glanced at Lok. "For your protection, of course."

"Of course," Lok replied bitterly as his world crumbled about him. He took several deep breaths, his face hot with anger and betrayal, and silently vowed not to let his adversaries get away with this humiliation. He doubted he would survive a voyage back to the

Isles, suspecting that Ovek or his cronies might try to kill him midway through the trip. How convenient it would be for Ovek and Uta if he were accidentally lost at sea. He knew he had little time to act and snapped his fingers.

"Vice-Commander, I know you are forbidding me to go back to Karg Island for my records and such," he said. "But may I at least retrieve a few personal effects from my desk, sir?"

Ovek rolled his eyes with impatience. "Fine," he said, standing at the door with one hand on the knob while clutching Lok's sheathed sword in the other. "Make it fast."

Lok walked around the desk, opened one of the drawers and rifled through a stack of parchment in the sickly glow of the oil lamp. Ovek glanced at his aide, silently indicating for him to keep an extra sharp eye on their prisoner. The aide stood at attention, placing a hand gently upon the hilt of his sword. Lok caught their brief exchange out of the corners of his eyes and looked up with a disappointed smile.

"*Seriously?* You already took my weapon, Vice-Commander. What do you think I'm going to attack you with?" he remarked with an amused grunt, holding up a handful of parchment. "These musty accounts of the number of fish barrels going to Kargoth?" Lok disgustedly tossed the leaflets into the air and glared at Ovek as they rained down on the floor in front of the desk.

"Was that necessary?" he snapped back with equal disdain.

"Yes. As is this!" Lok suddenly grabbed the oil lamp and hurled it at the floor among the fallen parchment. It smashed in an explosion of glass shards and oil droplets, followed by a demonic whoosh of red and orange flames.

"What are you doing?" Ovek shouted in disbelief as a wave of fire instantly engulfed the desk and the spread of parchment between them. He lunged back against the door as the flames leaped in his direction.

"Sir!" the Vice-Commander's aide shouted as he stood off to the side. "You're coat is on fire!"

The young man raced to his superior as Ovek looked down and saw the hem of his coat had ignited where some of the oil had splashed upon it. He dropped Lok's sword and struggled to remove the coat as the flames grew. His aide helped him rip it off and then opened the door to escape the searing heat. He pulled Vice-

Commander Ovek out onto the deck as a cold sea breeze blew inside and stirred up the flames into an even greater frenzy. Billows of smoke followed them out of the cabin. Ovek angrily whipped his coat upon the deck until the flame was extinguished. When he looked up, his face contorted and dotted with sweat, he realized that Lok could not follow them out through the growing inferno. A paralyzing fear took hold when he also realized that the fire was out of control. He glanced at his aide, knowing that the *Bretic* was already lost.

Lok, during those same moments, grabbed the bundle of rope hanging on the wall and hurried to the back windows. He knew he had only a short time to escape before the smoke, heat and flames overpowered him. He unfastened a metal latch and swung open a panel of windows inward, allowing a strong, westerly breeze inside which temporarily cleared the smoke around him and slammed the main door shut. He longingly viewed Karg Island through the darkness. He swiftly unraveled the rope, tied one end to a support post and dropped the other end out the window. It fell like a dead snake as it plopped into the water. He raced over and peered through the portside window and spotted the three rafts that Arteen and his men had used to board the ship. He knew he would have to swim a short distance to reach the nearest one, but it couldn't be helped.

With little time left, Lok returned to the back windows and climbed out, preparing to make his way down the rope as the snapping flames spread in his direction. As he positioned one foot on a ledge just outside the opening, a serpentine smile spread across his face as he wondered how Vice-Commander Ovek would be able to explain the loss of a ship to his superiors.

"Looks like Arteen is going to get his wish after all," he muttered in amusement, expertly lowering himself down the rope as the flicking snake tongues of fire advanced, tasting the cold sea air.

CHAPTER 62

On Karg Island

Nicholas walked beside Brin across the creaking deck of the *Bretic* after they had exited the captain's cabin. The ship's masts and rigging caught the moonlight like a giant spider web. Flags above them and on the nearby *Hara Nor* flapped in the breeze.

Nicholas wondered if he should run for it and jump overboard before Brin locked him below deck. But even if he did escape, he knew it wouldn't be long before Ovek's soldiers stormed Karg Island, the only place where he could go and wanted to be. But before he reached a decision, Brin grabbed him by the arm and pulled him into a deserted section of the ship swimming in shadows.

"Hey, what are you–!"

"Quiet!" Brin ordered, pushing his prisoner against a towering wooden post strung above with ropes and pulleys. "Listen to me or I'll throw you in confinement right now. I guarantee you'll never see that lovely princess again. Understand?"

Nicholas agreed with a quick nod. "What do you want?" He looked calmly into his captor's eyes, hoping to form some sort of bond or play upon the sympathies of a young man not much older than himself. He also decided to keep pretending that it really was Princess Megan on Karg Island, realizing it was no use giving up one of his few advantages.

"I need to know everything Vice-Commander Ovek and that fool-of-a-captain Lok discussed with you inside the cabin," Brin whispered. "It was all about Princess Megan, right? And since I'm now assistant captain of this ship, I should be privy to that information."

Nicholas smirked. "Why should I tell you after you betrayed Arteen and his friends?"

"Arteen betrayed the Northern Isles!" he angrily replied. He quickly calmed down and looked around to make sure no one was in earshot. "Besides, I'm armed and you're not. So tell me what the three of you talked about before I really lose my temper."

Nicholas studied the man's contorted expression and frowned more out of disgust than fear. "You're just like all the others–Lok, Ovek, the wizard Caldurian. Even Vellan himself. It's all about opportunity and power to you people. And whoever gets hurt along the way is an afterthought, if that."

Brin glared at Nicholas, knowing he had little time left to get what he was after. "You're in no position to lecture me," he said, pulling out a dagger and turning the blade in front of Nicholas' face as it reflected the cold light of the Fox Moon. "Don't make me resort to more distasteful methods."

"If you kill me, you'll never get any information."

"Who said anything about killing you?" Brin's icy words complemented his vacant stare as he moved the blade tip closer to Nicholas' face. "Do I make myself clear?"

"I think so," he said, certain that Brin wasn't bluffing and wondering what he could say to protect Ivy.

"Good. Now for the last time, tell me what the three of you discussed or you'll wish you had never stepped foot on this ship."

Nicholas nodded as a veil of defeat spread across his face. "I'll tell you, though I'm not sure if it'll help."

"I'll be the judge of that. Speak!"

"All right. Ovek was telling us that–" Nicholas suddenly stopped talking, gazing curiously into the air as if some ominous presence had caught his attention.

"Ovek was telling you *what*?" he asked impatiently.

Nicholas sniffed the air, detecting an acrid smell of smoke coming from the stern. Slowly his eyes widened as he saw a devilish display of red and orange flames raging behind the windows of the captain's cabin.

"It's on fire," he calmly stated.

"*On fire?* That doesn't make sense. Did Ovek say–?"

Suddenly Brin understood as he locked gazes with Nicholas and saw the reflection of flames in his prisoner's eyes. An instant later there was an explosion of glass as several of the windows in the cabin blew outward from the intense heat and pressure of the roaring fire. Brin spun around to witness the scene for himself as the flames leaped out of their confinement, reaching far into the night sky, refreshed and strengthened by a blast of cold sea air.

"What's happening to my ship?" he muttered as he raked a hand through his hair, shocked at the sight. He took an unsteady step forward, mesmerized by the flames.

"We have to move away!" Nicholas urged. But now that the knife blade was pulled away from his face, he thought he might have a chance to escape. But Arteen and the others were being held below deck. He knew he couldn't leave without freeing them first.

"*Fire!*" Brin shouted, moving closer to the stern until the conflagration was in full view, a wave of wild flames that quickly spread. "There's a fire in the–!"

But his cries were drowned out as similarly panicked shouts of fire and a multitude of calls for abandoning ship echoed from bow to stern. Vice-Commander Ovek's voice boomed from elsewhere on deck, sounding above them all as the flames rapidly engulfed more of the ship, whipped into a fury by the steady sea breezes.

"Lower the boats and make for the *Hara Nor!*" Ovek's order was dispatched with steady forcefulness that defied the erratic nature of the growing inferno. "Release the prisoners from below deck!"

"This can't be happening!" Brin muttered, his eyes transfixed on the advancing flames as he fumed with boiling anger reminiscent of Captain Lok. Brin drove the point of his dagger into a wooden rail in frustration and then turned around to confront Nicholas, snarling like a chained dog.

In that instant, Nicholas slammed his fist into Brin's jaw, knocking the man down onto a pile of coiled rope as he writhed in pain. Nicholas grabbed the dagger stuck in the wood and fled toward the bow of the ship, his heart racing and his hand burning with excruciating pain. He ran to a section of railing on the starboard side as wisps of pungent smoke began to engulf much of the ship. He ducked for a moment behind a large rain barrel as a soldier raced by, fearing he may have been spotted. But the man apparently didn't see him or didn't care as he disappeared amid the clamor.

Nicholas' eyes stung and he started to cough, now hearing a growing cacophony of terrified voices and discordant shouts from all over the ship. And though some men were frantically lowering a few row boats closer to the bow of the ship, Nicholas saw other men jumping wildly over the rail to escape the flames. He thought he recognized a couple of men from Arteen's group and knew that the prisoners had been released, but there was no order among any of the troops. He couldn't distinguish guard from prisoner and assumed that chaos had taken over with every man looking out for himself. He decided to do the same, knowing he had to get off the *Bretic* before it was too late. The flames steadily crept forward along the deck with tendrils of dark smoke swirling in the breeze. The Fox Moon silently watched the mayhem below.

Nicholas started to cough again. His stinging eyes watered until he was nearly blinded by the tears. He wiped his face and scrambled out of his hiding spot behind the rain barrel, knowing he must escape now or face certain death. He decided to jump off the deck like so many others, knowing he dare not get on one of the rowboats. He raced to a section of the railing away from where the boats were being lowered and looked over into the moonlit water, wondering if he could swim the nearly quarter mile to Karg Island without freezing to death. But he had no choice. After shoving the dagger under his belt, he placed one foot on the base of the railing and hoisted himself up, gulping a lungful of air. But as he positioned his body to make the jump, a hand suddenly grabbed him by the shoulder in the swirling smoke and pulled him back onto the deck.

"Not so fast," a voice whispered.

Nicholas spun around and reached for his dagger, ready to defend himself against Brin who he assumed had followed him through the smoke. He broke out in a smile, seeing Ragus' whiskered face grinning back at him. "Ragus! How did you–"

"No time for talk," the man calmly replied, signaling for Nicholas to follow him to the port side of the ship where fewer people had congregated. Most had been fleeing on the starboard side in view of the *Hara Nor*. "Arteen told us to keep an eye out for you," he said as they made for the railing. "Looks like I'll get the prize."

"What are we going to do?" Nicholas asked as a gust of smoke rushed at them like the hot breath from a deadly dragon. He and Ragus instinctively turned away and covered their eyes until it passed and then made for the railing.

"We're going to escape," Ragus said, running his hands along the rail until he found what he was looking for. "The smart way."

"*Huh?*" Nicholas peered over the side and saw the middle raft he had helped paddle over from the mainland. Ragus had located the rope ladder leading down to it.

"Let's go before we're spotted or others get the same idea," he said, climbing over the railing and moving quickly and steadily down the swaying ladder.

Nicholas followed, breathing a blast of cold air rushing past his face. He looked up as he descended the ladder, amazed at how fast the flames were consuming the *Bretic*. He knew it would only be a matter of minutes before the ship was totally destroyed as red and orange fire leaped up from the tip of one of the lower masts. After they both touched down on the raft, Ragus borrowed Nicholas' dagger and cut them loose. He grabbed a paddle and gave one to Nicholas, indicating for him to start rowing toward the island.

"Shouldn't we wait for any of the others?" Nicholas asked, feeling guilty for abandoning them to the fiery tempest.

"They'll find a way off," Ragus assured him. "There are two more rafts. Anyway, Arteen wanted one of us to get you to Karg Island as soon as possible to find your friend. Maybe that lunatic Captain Lok or the one in charge on the other ship will send some men there as well. We have to get ashore first."

"That may not be possible," he replied, glancing toward the stern as they pushed away from the side of the ship. He swallowed hard as he looked at Ragus. "One of the other rafts is missing."

"What?" Ragus craned his neck forward and was surprised to find that one raft had been cut loose. "I wonder who beat us here."

"*He* did," Nicholas said, pointing as they cleared the ship's stern and made for the island. "Look."

Ragus stared ahead and discerned a shadowy figure on the missing raft paddling steadily toward Karg Island in the moonlight. The vessel was nearly ashore. "Who's that?"

"Lok," he uttered with a heartbreaking sigh. "I'm guessing he started the fire, too." Nicholas paddled as fast as he could, looking at Ragus in fear. "We have to stop him before–"

"I know," he whispered, keeping pace with Nicholas' stroke. "I know."

As they drew nearer to shore, Nicholas' arm, back and shoulder muscles burned as furiously as the *Bretic*, yet he continued to paddle with Ragus, his eyes fixed forward and his breathing deep and steady. The inevitable then happened and Nicholas shuddered– Lok's raft had touched shore. In the glow of moonlight, he watched as Lok disembarked, his first few steps unsteady as if he were drunk or half asleep. The man wrapped his arms tightly around himself, rapidly rubbing his upper arms and the sides of his chest before tiredly trudging up the shore and into the thin stretch of woods. A handful of distant lights emanated from within the trees where a few wooden buildings and been constructed for the administration of the ships arriving from the Isles.

"Faster!" Nicholas whispered to himself, though he and Ragus were already propelling the raft as quickly as they could.

A few minutes later the tips of their paddles touched the sandy bottom near the shoreline. Nicholas jumped off the raft as it glided onto shore, his boots splashing through the water as he raced to dry land. Ragus quickly followed, worried that Nicholas was too emotionally caught up in the situation to think clearly about his next step. The young man simply raced into the woods and bolted toward the nearest lights.

"Slow down!" Ragus muttered, nearly out of breath.

But Nicholas didn't hear him or refused to listen, his mind only on Ivy and her safety. He called out her name several times to warn her of Lok's approach.

"Ivy!" he desperately cried, starting to feel winded and barely able to focus on the path ahead. "Ivy!"

The thicket of trees flew past them like a blur of shadows as their feet pounded the hard, dirt path. Suddenly a large clearing opened up and three low buildings popped into view, the few windows in each glowing with yellow light. But Captain Lok was nowhere in view. Nicholas and Ragus rushed into the closest and largest of the three structures, bursting through a wooden door. The building was empty as they searched. The main room was a large office area with a desk and several shelves cluttered with ledgers, loose parchment leaves, maps and other items. Smaller tables in various states of disarray were scattered about. A large, cold fireplace yawned in one corner and a few oil lamps brightly burned by the windows and on the main desk. The other rooms consisted of Lok's living quarters where Ragus helped himself to a long dagger he found hanging from one of the walls.

"Let's search the other buildings!" Nicholas frantically cried as they both bounded outside. He directed Ragus toward one while he investigated the other.

But these also proved to be dead ends. One structure was living quarters for up to a dozen soldiers and the other a storehouse for foodstuff and survival supplies, both deserted. When they met outdoors again, both appeared anxious and worried.

"She's got to be here," Ragus said, hoping to bestow a bit of encouragement upon Nicholas who was at his wit's end.

"But where?" Nicholas turned around in a slow circle, surveying the terrain until a chilling notion struck him. "You don't suppose she was already on board the *Bretic*, do you? Maybe Lok had brought her over and wasn't telling Ovek."

"I don't know," he replied, not wanting to consider such a horrendous notion as the *Bretic* burned on the water behind them.

"Or maybe he–" Nicholas stopped suddenly, pointing to a spot farther into the woods just ahead. "Look! I see another light."

Ragus peered into the trees and soon made out a faint point of light partially masked by the glow of the Fox Moon. "Another building?" he whispered. But Nicholas didn't wait for any words of confirmation. He shot off like an arrow directly toward it. "Nicholas, wait!" Ragus cried, racing after him.

Seconds later they entered another small clearing where a tiny, one-room structure had been built in an obviously hasty manner as indicated by the roughly hewn logs and corners that were slightly off plumb. A faint light was visible from two small windows. A trail of wood smoke drifted out of a narrow chimney. Nicholas paused when seeing no one in the vicinity and looked hopelessly at Ragus.

"She must be here," he said as if seeking reassurance from him before approaching the building. But Nicholas hadn't taken a handful of steps when the front door suddenly opened. Captain Lok stepped out into the moonlight, his clothes dripping wet from his brief swim in the sea and an arrogant smile plastered upon his face.

"You're too late," he told them with satisfaction, eyeing Nicholas in particular. "Your long journey has been for nothing. And I'll bet you thought you were so clever."

"Is she in there?" Ragus asked, seeing that Nicholas was unable to speak, his face riddled with ire and anguish.

Lok smiled again and unsheathed his dagger. "Like I said, you're too late."

But Nicholas felt no fear and removed Brin's knife from his belt, his fingers tightly gripping the handle. Lok flinched ever so slightly, but whether from the cold or out of fear, Nicholas couldn't tell. All that was on his mind was killing Lok. Ragus realized this and knew he had to do something in the next moment before he had two dead men on his hands.

"It ends now," Nicholas said, his voice choked and hoarse as he raised the knife, preparing to lunge in Lok's direction.

But Lok sprang first and ran toward Nicholas, wildly brandishing his dagger. Anticipating such a move, Ragus pulled Nicholas aside and spoke close to his ear.

"I'll take care of Lok," he said, reaching for his dagger. "Go inside to Ivy. That is where you should be." He pushed Nicholas out of the way as Lok barreled toward them.

With the sound of metal knives clashing and tears streaming down his face, Nicholas veered away from the fight and ran to the small cabin, dreading what he might find inside. He knew that Ragus was right. He should be with Ivy now whatever her fate. He could always return later to hunt down Lok and make him pay for his crimes.

When Nicholas opened the door, dim shadows greeted him. A low fire, barely alive, flickered in the hearth. Several candles on a table, sputtering and dripping wax along their sides, added extra light to the deathly quiet. He looked about, his heart pounding as echoes of the fight outdoors lingered in the background. Then he saw it and his heart went cold. A body lay on the floor behind a table near the doorway to an adjacent room. He ran to it, dreading what he would find. As he approached, something about the figure appeared strange as it lay on its side, the face hidden.

After he pushed aside a chair and knelt by the body, Nicholas saw that it was too large to be Ivy. He exhaled deeply as relief washed over him. The body moved and he heard a slight groan. He carefully turned it over and was face to face with an Island soldier. Nicholas was startled and jumped back, thinking it was a trap until he realized that the man was drifting in and out of consciousness. His hands and feet were bound with rope. A long stick of oak wood rested on the floor close by. Nicholas thought for a moment, wondering if this was Ivy's handiwork. Had she already escaped? Was he too late? Or had something else transpired?

He shook the body and lightly tapped the man's cheek. "Where's the girl? Tell me!" But the man wouldn't open his eyes. Nicholas didn't expect him to for some time, leaving him to wonder where on this island–or elsewhere–Ivy might have gone.

The voices of Ragus and Lok shook him back to reality as they drew nearer to the cabin. Nicholas could still hear fighting as the sharp ringing of metal blades pierced the air. He knew Ragus needed help and ran out of the cabin wielding his dagger, his emotions boiling with rage. But as he stepped into the moonlight, his heart sank. He saw Ragus being shoved face first against a tree, his knife flying out of his hand, his breath forced from his lungs. The left sleeve of Ragus' coat was stained with blood. Lok pressed an arm against the back of his neck and clutched a dagger in his right hand, ready to drive the cold piece of metal into the man's back.

"Wait!" Nicholas cried, causing Lok to momentarily hold back his deadly strike as Ragus struggled in pain against the tree.

Lok glared at Nicholas, his eyes filled with disdain. "You're next!" he promised, his face contorted with rage.

Nicholas returned an icy stare, knowing he wouldn't have time to reach his friend before Lok could kill him. "You said earlier that I was too late. But you're the one who was too late regarding Ivy," he taunted, hoping to buy some time as he inched another step closer. "Ivy wasn't inside, Lok. She escaped before you could get to her. So congratulations. You lost both the girl and the *Bretic*–and all in one day."

"I'll show you!" he cried out, brandishing his dagger behind Ragus.

NICHOLAS RAVEN AND THE WIZARDS' WEB - VOLUME 2

But as they were talking, Nicholas noted that Ragus had slowly raised his right boot between Lok's legs, anticipating a defensive move on his part. In order to buy a few more precious seconds, Nicholas called out to Lok in a more conciliatory tone. "Maybe we can reach an agreement," he suggested. To Lok's utter surprise, Nicholas casually tossed his knife aside where it landed in the dirt with a dull thud. "Let Ragus go and take me as your prisoner instead. He's done nothing to you."

"He's a traitor!" Lok sputtered. "I want no prisoners. If I have my way, you'll both be dead soon. So don't try to–"

Suddenly Ragus made his move. He kicked his boot forcefully sideways into Lok's right shin and threw his captor off balance. As Lok staggered sideways, Ragus slammed an elbow into the man's sternum, dropping Lok backward into the dirt as he gasped painfully for air. But he quickly got to his feet and lunged back with a vengeance, though this time Ragus was ready, having spun around as Lok barreled toward him. He grabbed Lok's right wrist with both hands, preventing him from maneuvering his dagger. Lok fought back, pushing his left palm against Ragus' face. But despite his injury, Ragus summoned up his remaining strength and pulled down hard on Lok's right arm like a lever, plunging the blade squarely into the man's gut and backing away against the tree. Lok froze for a moment as he stared down at the knife handle protruding from his body, unable to take a full breath amid his paralyzing pain. He took an awkward step backward and looked up at Ragus, lightheaded, his lips forming a thin line as a trickle of blood streamed out of the corner of his mouth. Lok then collapsed to the ground like a heavy rock and lay sprawled out upon his back, unmoving, his vacant eyes staring lifelessly at the cold stars above.

Nicholas hurried over and knelt by Ragus' side as the man slowly slid down against the tree truck until he was sitting on the ground and clutching his left arm. He looked at Nicholas and smiled.

"I guess I won," he said, nearly out of breath.

"I guess so," Nicholas said with a nervous smile, staring at Ragus' bloody sleeve. "I need to get you help right away."

"I'll be all right, Nicholas. It's not a deep wound and looks worse than it really is," he said. "I'll tend to it shortly. I'm just worried about how the others made out." He struggled to turn his head and looked through the trees toward the ships. The *Bretic* was fully engulfed in flames. Distant shouts filled the air, some sounding closer than others.

"Do you think Ovek's men will come here?"

"No doubt, so maybe we ought to think about hiding," Ragus recommended, noting the sadness on Nicholas' face. "What'd you find inside?"

Nicholas told him, briefly smiling when he informed him that Ivy had already escaped or that someone had helped her to do so. "But when? And where could she have gone to?" he helplessly asked, staring at the ground in utter bewilderment before looking up at his friend. "What am I going to do now? How shall I find her?"

"Well, I'd first suggest that–" But Ragus cut short his reply as his eyes opened wide with wonder, now fully awake and staring straight ahead over Nicholas' shoulder toward the edge of the nearby woods. Nicholas looked curiously at him, puzzled by his sudden change in demeanor.

"What's the matter, Ragus? Are you hurt worse than you're letting on?"

He shook his head, unable to conceal a delighted smile. "No, not hurt, my friend. And as for finding Ivy, I don't think you'll have to do anything, Nicholas, except turn around."

He shrugged with bewilderment. "What are you talking about?"

Ragus chuckled. "*Turn around*," he repeated with a drunken smile. "Behind you."

Nicholas glanced over his shoulder, casting his gaze among the trees awash in moonlight when he noticed a young woman standing there wearing a dark blue cloak. She had light brown hair down to her shoulders and a sweet yet astonished smile upon her face. Nicholas beamed with disbelief as he slowly got to his feet, astounded at the sight of Ivy who stood only a few steps away.

"Is it really you?" he softly asked as he gazed at her in stunned silence.

Ivy nodded, on the verge of tears. Nicholas ran to her and they hugged, holding each other tightly while weeping and laughing with unimaginable joy. He looked at Ivy, gently touching her face with trembling hands and losing himself in her soft eyes and moonlit tears.

"How did you ever find me?" she asked, hugging Nicholas again before he could answer. They kissed among the trees and shadows, and for a short time were unaware of their surroundings and the distant turmoil upon the sea. Nicholas stepped back and reached into his coat pocket.

"I have something for you," he said with childlike excitement.

"What?" she asked.

Nicholas removed the scarf he had given her on a sunny day in Boros that seemed so long ago. "I found this above the grasslands. I never had a chance to return it after I freed you from the tent."

Ivy smiled in wonderment and disbelief. "I released it to the wind with a prayer, hoping against hope that it would lead you back to me." She took the scarf and caressed it softly against her cheek. "I can't believe you found it, Nicholas."

"And I can't believe that I finally found *you*," he replied, neither ever wanting to leave the other's side as they embraced in a cool breeze rolling off the tumultuous sea.

CHAPTER 63

Friends and Foes

Nicholas and Ivy held each other tightly, never wanting to let go. For a time they were in a world of their own, feeling each other's heart beating as they exchanged tender whispered words, wondering if this moment was merely a dream. Ragus' words scattered inaudibly past them in the moonlight as if they were statues.

"I *said* I think we should be going now," he repeated, clearing his throat for emphasis as he sat against the tree.

Nicholas looked back at him sheepishly. "Oh, sorry, Ragus. I forgot you were still here," he joked. He took Ivy's hand and walked to his injured friend. "Ivy, this is Ragus. He's from the Northern Isles but isn't like the others you've met."

"So I've noticed," she said, glancing warily at Lok's dead body nearby as if her captor might reawaken. "It's nice to meet you, Ragus. Thank you for helping to rescue me."

"I was just along for laughs," he replied as he slowly stood. Nicholas stepped forward to give him a hand. "This was all Nicholas' idea–finding his way to Karg Island to save you."

She looked at Nicholas and smiled gratefully, falling more in love with him. "To be rescued once is one thing. But *twice*? Now that makes a woman feel special."

Nicholas smiled playfully. "That first attempt along the grasslands wasn't my finest effort, I'll admit," he said. "But I'll pretend otherwise if you will."

"Agreed," she said, noticing Ragus' injured arm. "There's a basin of water inside my cabin. We should wash and bandage that arm. There must be some medicinal balm in the storehouse."

"First we should move deeper into the woods," Ragus replied. "Sounds like others have landed on shore. They'll be here soon."

"Who?" Ivy asked with apprehension.

"Some of Ovek's men," Nicholas answered as he took her hand again and hurried into the woods with Ragus close behind.

The trio rushed past Ivy's cabin and went deeper into the trees, halting near a large boulder to listen for signs of troops from the *Hara Nor*. A short time later the voices grew louder. Nicholas guessed that the men had arrived at the three buildings. It wouldn't be long before they spotted Ivy's cabin and revived the unconscious soldier inside and conducted a thorough search of the island.

"We should get as far away as possible," Nicholas whispered. "Perhaps there's a small boat along shore we can take back to the mainland."

They started to move farther into the island just as a group of men approached the last building. Time was fast running out. But Nicholas and Ivy hadn't taken another step when Ragus tapped their shoulders and indicated for them to stop. He listened closely to the scattered conversations and began to smile.

"We can turn around," he said. "That's Arteen speaking. It sounds like he's giving the orders." Nicholas listened closely and confirmed Ragus' observation. Their friends had made it safely to Karg Island.

A short time later, Ragus was reunited with his fellow soldiers. Also among them were Captain Kellig and a handful of officers loyal to him. Arteen explained how they had escaped to the island on the remaining raft and a few row boats lowered from the *Bretic*. Some of the men had jumped to escape the flames and swam to one of the boats, but all had steered clear of the *Hara Nor*. In the ensuing commotion, Vice-Commander Ovek and his men were too busy saving their own lives to worry about the escaped prisoners and chose to let them go.

"I think Ovek will have enough problems explaining to his superiors about the destruction of the *Bretic* and the disappearance of Captain Lok," Arteen said, having already directed a few of his men to remove Lok's body and bury it.

"But that doesn't mean he won't return to these parts," Captain Kellig warned. "More ships may sail back here in the spring to feed Kargoth's appetite. And it's still possible that Ovek might order another ship here sooner to pursue *us*."

The men agreed, but for the moment their victory was enough to keep them in high spirits throughout the night. Fires were built in the four buildings and spare uniforms were found to clothe those who had jumped or fallen into the Trillium Sea, but not before Ivy was asked how she had overwhelmed the soldier tied up in her cabin.

"Don't be too harsh with him," she pleaded. "He was the youngest of Lok's men and his heart wasn't really in this mission. I had befriended him when he was on guard duty near my cabin or escorting me when I was allowed to walk around parts of the island. I found my best opportunity to escape when Lok and his men rowed over to the *Bretic* to stop your attack. The young soldier stayed behind to watch me."

"He apparently didn't to a good job," Ragus said.

"I invited him inside for some stew I was cooking. When I had my chance, well–let's just say that a certain piece of oak wood came in handy," she said with an apologetic grin. "I had hoped to escape if I could find a boat. Later, I saw the ship on fire and wondered what was happening. When I heard someone approach, I hid in the woods, though if I had known it was Lok all by himself, I may have confronted him," she added in all seriousness. "Soon after, I heard Nicholas call my name and was nearly in shock, almost not believing it was you."

"I was never going to stop looking for you, Ivy," he said. "I was prepared to go to the Isles themselves."

"That's true," Arteen confirmed, delighted that she was safe. "But now you don't have to worry about a thing. We'll get you back to the mainland in the morning."

"Thank you," she replied. "But again, promise me you won't be too harsh with the man I clobbered with that stick. My guess is that he'll be more than happy to join your cause after observing Lok's authority up close."

"Captain Kellig and I will talk with him before we make a decision," Arteen said. "But for now, we have some hungry and wet men to take care of, and Ragus' arm needs tending to. Let's inspect Lok's quarters and storehouse and see how well he's been living here. It's high time he paid us back for all the trouble he caused."

Arteen divided up his men to search each building while he and Captain Kellig planned their next move. Nicholas and Ivy, in the meantime, patched up Ragus' wound which wasn't as deep as they had feared, and then later enjoyed some of Ivy's stew and hot tea near a roaring fire. As they sat in front of the warm hearth, Nicholas glanced at Ivy and smiled, silently recalling their time in Aunt Castella's kitchen when they built a fire before dawn had peeked through the windows. Ivy smiled back and Nicholas couldn't help but believe that she was remembering that same moment with equal fondness. He couldn't wait to create more of them with her in the days and years ahead.

Nicholas and Ivy prepared to leave the island late the next morning, standing on the shoreline where the three rafts and a few rowboats from the *Bretic* were lying upon the sand like beached animals. They held hands and gazed silently out upon the sea where the blackened remains of the *Bretic* smoldered under an overcast sky. The vessel had collapsed upon itself and a few of its blackened timbers protruded through the water's surface.

"Certain people on the Isles will not be happy to learn of that ship's fate," Arteen said as he walked up to the couple from behind. "There will be questions and a formal inquiry, something I'm sure Vice-Commander Ovek will not particularly enjoy."

"But I suppose you will," Nicholas replied.

Arteen smiled. "I'll have to be content only imagining how it will unfold. Still, she was a good ship. Captain Kellig doesn't yet have the heart to stand here and look upon his once great vessel."

"I can't blame him," Ivy softly said.

Arteen handed a piece of folded parchment to Nicholas that had been sealed with blue wax. "Please deliver this message to Arch Boland when you return to Illingboc. It explains what transpired here. The villages along the Crescent can rest easy now that the

Islanders are no longer in the vicinity–a least in the short term. We'll have to wait to see what springtime produces and how the battles in the south and east play out."

"Will you visit Arch soon?" Nicholas asked.

"Definitely. But first Captain Kellig and the rest of us have much to decide over the next few days. Shall we stay here and make a future stand, if that is even necessary? Or do we move on to new lives on the mainland or deeper into Laparia?" He shrugged. "But we'll figure out the right course while we inventory what's left on the island and go through Captain Lok's journals and letters. In the meantime, I wish you good fortune when you both return to your homes in Arrondale."

"Neither of us can wait for that day," Ivy said as she placed an arm around Nicholas and affectionately leaned her head upon his shoulder. "It's been a grueling journey for both of us."

"Well, it wasn't exactly a picnic for us either," a voice interjected good-naturedly from beneath the nearby trees. Ragus emerged from the shadows with two other men, his left arm bandaged up and a smile upon his face. "And you were right, miss, about that soldier in the cabin. After Arteen and the captain talked to him during the night, he's fitting in just fine with the rest of us, telling stories about Captain Lok and his lofty plans. I think the boy will make a fine addition to our group."

"Unlike Brin," Nicholas said. "After my encounters with both him and Lok, I'm guessing they must be related. It's almost spooky how similar their personalities were as well as their lust for power."

"I imagine Brin and Vice-Commander Ovek are coordinating their stories to present to the tribunal that will investigate this matter," Arteen said. "Good riddance to them both. But we may have a minor problem with Brin's cousin, Cale."

"Who's he?" Nicholas asked.

"Cale was one of the three men who stayed back to watch the horses. He and Brin were very close. It wouldn't surprise me if they were in league together. My men here will bring him back for questioning if he's still around. But if he saw the fire last night and was on Brin's side, I'm guessing he may have fled, believing that we were victorious."

On that wary note, everyone said their final goodbyes. Nicholas and Ivy stepped into a rowboat with the two men who had accompanied Ragus. Arteen instructed them to give Nicholas and Ivy a pair of horses to ride back to Illingboc and wherever the road might take them afterward. Minutes later, the boat was gliding across the slightly choppy waters of the Trillium. Arteen and Ragus watched it grow smaller against the horizon before turning around and heading back into the woods.

At that moment, nearly a third of the way around the island's shoreline, Brin Mota hid among a thicket of pines and intently watched the boat as it proceeded to the mainland, having a good idea that two of its passengers would be going to Arch Boland's house in Illingboc. He had been there himself on occasion, having delivered messages to Arch when he had infiltrated Arteen's group. He knew that Nicholas was friends with the man.

Brin smiled to himself despite being cold and hungry, though he couldn't risk building a fire. He would hike to the far end of the island first before doing so. Later after dark, he planned to steal a boat and make his way to shore and then to Arch Boland's house where he would track down Nicholas Raven and Princess Megan, doing what Captain Lok and Vice-Commander Ovek were too incompetent to do. Brin had great plans, believing he was far more capable of accomplishing them on his own after witnessing the disastrous events of last night. He decided to seek out someone who could truly make use of a princess and a King's spy in the political war against Arrondale, someone who would reward him handsomely because of his efforts.

Brin stepped back deeper into the woods as Nicholas and Ivy's boat faded in the gray morning. He would sleep until dark before making his next move, anticipating nothing but great opportunities awaiting him in Kargoth.

After Nicholas and Ivy arrived on the mainland with their escorts, they soon located two of the three soldiers who had remained behind to guard the horses. As Arteen had anticipated, Brin's cousin had fled in secret during the night after stealing a pair of horses. Any doubt of his involvement with Brin and Captain Lok was quickly laid to rest. The two soldiers had witnessed the towering flames on the *Bretic* from shore last evening and planned to paddle back to Karg Island to see the destroyed remains for themselves.

In the meantime, Nicholas and Ivy accepted two of the horses. After thanking the men for their help, they were soon traveling along the road to Illingboc. The couple took their time during the short journey, happy to be alone as they exchanged heartfelt words and tender glances.

"I don't want this time to end," Nicholas said as the horses sauntered along a narrow stretch of road dotted with tufts of grass and shallow ruts. He reached over and held Ivy's hand, her fingers warm to the touch despite the brisk air and a faint whisper of snow flurries drifting in careless flight. "I enjoy spending time together and talking with you." He bent his head for a moment, his words caught with emotion. "I thought I might never see you again, Ivy."

"I felt like that at times," she replied, gently squeezing his hand. "Sometimes I resigned myself to the possibility that I would never again visit my home or talk to anyone dear to me. But somehow I would find the strength to carry on for just one more day. And you, Nicholas, were one of the people foremost in my thoughts. You had come after me once and I always tried to believe that you would do it again. When I heard you call my name on the island..." Ivy was caught somewhere between tears and a smile.

"You don't have to say anything," he gently told her, caressing her hand. "Being next to you is all that matters right now. We can talk things through another time when you're ready. I'll always be here when you need me." Nicholas flashed a playful grin. "And even those times when you don't."

"You had better be," she replied, her spirits quickly restored. "It'll be a long time before I tire of having you around. I hope you can get used to that."

"I already am," he said, a contented smile upon his face. He gently held the reins and looked out at the long road ahead.

They arrived in Illingboc shortly after noontime. Arch was splitting wood on the side of the house as a trail of blue smoke rose from the chimney, weaving its way through a dusting of snowflakes. He smiled with delight when he looked up, happy to see a woman at Nicholas' side whom he guessed was Ivy. He congratulated Nicholas on the success of the mission, not appearing particularly surprised at the outcome.

"I saw a sharp glow of yellow light far out on the water last night, and now here you are with the lovely Ivy," he remarked. "I just assumed that Arteen's plan worked splendidly." He noted a slight smirk on Nicholas' face. "Did it not?"

"Let's just say that it took an unexpected turn," he replied as they walked the horses to a large stall in back of the house. "We'll explain shortly." He handed Arch the note from Arteen. "This will help, too."

"I look forward to our conversation, as will Natalie and Hannah." Arch invited them inside so he could hear the details. "And you're just in time for lunch."

Nicholas and Ivy each took turns explaining their side of the story which made for an extended meal. But nobody minded as the winds across the sea had picked up. The clouds continued to roll in thicker and darker until a light but steady snowfall descended upon Illingboc. Everyone later moved into the sitting room around the fireplace as Eva served hot tea and dessert cakes.

"I feel as if I'm in the Blue Citadel after hearing Nicholas talk about it," Ivy said while sipping her tea. "My accommodations of late had been rather plain, to put it mildly. And as for the company..."

"That's how I feel when I visit my brother's house," Hannah said. "I enjoy where I live immensely, but Arch and Natalie do tend to spoil me when I stay here."

"We're happy to," Natalie replied before addressing Nicholas and Ivy. "And I shall enjoy having two more guests in the house. How long can you both stay?"

Nicholas glanced at Ivy, neither having thought about anything but returning home as soon as possible. But after all that Ivy had been through, Nicholas realized it would be a good idea for her to spend a few days in Illingboc to recover. They would have a long road ahead of them with some stops in between.

"I suppose we can't refuse a few days of rest," Nicholas said gratefully. "But only a few. Winter is on our doorstep. We should leave while traveling is still bearable."

"Don't let that bit of snow outside intimidate you," Arch said, glancing out a window from his chair. "A good, hard winter is still weeks away in these parts."

"But the gloom and early nights can be one long and dreary stretch until spring," Natalie added, her words accompanied by a weary sigh.

"Which is why she and her friends will plan so many parties over the coming months," he remarked with a laugh. Arch brought out a bottle of wine from a cabinet, filled some glasses and passed them around.

"Oh, you enjoy attending them as much as we enjoy arranging them," Natalie responded, playfully scolding him. "Now, Nicholas and Ivy, you must at least stay for the initial celebration. It's only eight days away on winter's first evening. Nearly everyone in town attends in the village common. There's food and dancing—"

"—and fine libations, too," Hannah interjected as she raised her wine glass. "The local brewers outdo themselves every year."

"Then it's settled," Nicholas said with a nod of support from Ivy. "We look forward to it."

On a cold but comfortable evening eight days later, the residents of Illingboc gathered in the village common to celebrate the first day of New Winter. The sun dipped behind a patchwork of clouds along the southwest horizon, their edges tinted in striking shades of purple and orange. As part of the celebration, colorful cloth streamers dangled from rope lines, and a series of flickering torches were attached to metal posts encircling the perimeter of the common, flooding the area with warm, inviting light. Bonfires crackled in the background while glowing oil lamps hung from tree branches and adorned tabletops in the sitting section. Food and drink tables laden with steaming platters and bowls of the finest fare were set up in open tents nearby. Various brews of ale, wine and winter punches freely flowed alongside a steady line of dinner plates.

A second area with a spectacular view of the sea had been reserved for dancing later on, though crowds mingled there now as people began arriving. Music drifted through the air as a group of locals played passionately on fiddles, flutes and drums, enveloping the common with sweet sounds and foot-tapping melodies.

Nicholas and Ivy arrived with Arch, Natalie and Hannah. They walked under the stars and a waxing gibbous Bear Moon shrouded behind a veil of gauzy clouds. For a few moments, Nicholas felt as if he were attending a Harvest Festival, recalling his missed opportunity to dance with Katherine at the village pavilion. He smiled when he glanced at Ivy, eager to dance with her and noting how beautiful she looked in the new dress and cloak that Natalie had bought for her. Ivy caught his boyish grin and smiled back.

"What is it?" she curiously asked while holding his hand.

"Nothing," he replied. "Just thinking how life seems to work out once in a while." He lightly squeezed her hand. "For now I just want to enjoy the music and festivities with you at my side."

"As do I," she replied, happy to see Nicholas shedding the troubles that had plagued him for too long, or at least temporarily doing so. She realized they had both been through difficult times and hoped that tonight they could forget about all the trials and heartache they had endured and simply enjoy life for a few hours.

Shortly after sunset the main celebration commenced, with food, drink and laughter flowing as freely as the music. While finishing up a bite to eat at one of the tables, Natalie asked Nicholas and Ivy to reconsider their decision to leave Illingboc.

"Hannah plans to stay a couple more weeks, so why don't you? We'd love to have the company," she said, imploring them with her sweet voice and wide, hopeful eyes. "We could hire messengers to inform your families and friends that you're safe."

"What do you say, Nicholas?" Hannah asked.

"As tempting as your offer sounds, Ivy and I will stick to our plan," he replied. "We'll leave the day after tomorrow. It's a long road to Morrenwood and then to Laurel Corners where Ivy's parents live. We must also stop in Boros to see Castella, of course."

"And then to Kanesbury," Ivy added. "You can't forget that, Nicholas. You'll have a fine time straightening matters out there."

Nicholas sipped some ale. "I've gathered new information since I left which I'm sure will intrigue Constable Brindle. It'll be an interesting visit to say the least."

"I wish I could be there to watch it unfold," Arch said, "but I understand how anxious you must be to get back. And I'll happily provide the horses and wagon to get you there. Natalie will also have

Eva fix up a basket of food and other supplies to last you for several days on the road."

"Thank you very much," Nicholas replied, deeply touched by their generosity and genuinely sad that he couldn't stay longer. "I wish I could be around when Arteen and his friends on the island contact you again. Wish them well for me whatever they decide."

"I will. But enough of this melancholy talk," he said as the music again picked up its tempo. "You and Ivy should enjoy some dancing while the night is early." Arch looked at his wife who was sipping her wine. "And I think you and I should heed that same advice, dear."

"Consider it heeded!" she said, taking her husband's hand and strolling away with him to the dance area.

"Will you join us, Hannah?" Nicholas asked.

"I'll watch from here, thank you," she replied. "With another cup of ale, of course. You two go and have a good time."

Nicholas and Ivy waved goodbye and hurried to the adjacent area where Arch, Natalie and several other couples were engaged in a lively dance native to the villages along the Crescent. The young couple wasted no time in picking up the basic steps, laughing and smiling as they weaved their way among the others bathed in the glow of firelight beneath the frosted stars. Nicholas couldn't keep his gaze off Ivy's joyous smile as they danced, savoring each word of conversation and note of laughter as they spent the next several numbers close to each other as if they had been acquainted for years. Neither of them thought such a moment would have been possible during the previous weeks when life had come crashing down upon them. But now the moment was perfect and they thought only of each other.

Hidden among a small crowd beneath a nearby tree, a man watched as Nicholas and Ivy danced, noting the smiles of pure contentment upon their faces and believing they were far too pleased with themselves. Brin Mota massaged his jaw which still ached after Nicholas had punched him on the *Bretic*. He sported a short beard and wore a rumpled coat and a brown hat he had stolen from a farmstead outside the village. He had been keeping tabs on Nicholas from a discreet distance over the last few days as well as the young woman with him who Brin still believed to be Princess Megan.

Once a day since he had boated over from Karg Island, Brin would spy out Arch Boland's house, usually from afar, though on occasion briefly walking past it to make sure that Nicholas was still living there. He had plans for them and would set it all in motion as soon as the couple left the area, knowing they wouldn't stay in Illingboc indefinitely. He would wait them out and make a name for himself with people who really mattered. Brin Mota was a patient man and hoped that Cale, his cousin, was just as patient while waiting for him with the men on the last raft somewhere along the banks of the Lorren River.

After he had secretly escaped from Karg Island, Brin met with his cousin at an appointed spot and was given one of the two horses Cale had stolen. But instead of joining Brin on the road, Cale was given instructions to ride south as fast as he could and stop the last raft going up the Lorren River. Brin ordered his cousin to notify the crew to wait along the western bank until he returned with some very special passengers and to assure them that it would be financially worth their while to do so.

In the meantime, Brin strolled back to the food tables for a second meal, having had to scrape by lately doing odd jobs for people or stealing whenever he had the chance. But he didn't care. His hardships now would only make his final victory in Kargoth that much sweeter in the end.

The party wound down before midnight. People gradually drifted home, pleased with the success of the first and largest party of the winter season. While Nicholas and Ivy were saying goodbye to a few people they had met that evening, Natalie hurried over and indicated for them to follow her to one of the food tents.

"I mentioned to some of my friends that you two were traveling to Arrondale the day after tomorrow," she said. "And since there are so many leftovers, a couple of the ladies have kindly put together a food basket for you to take along. It should last for days in the cold outdoors. You'll appreciate it when you're on the road and villages are few and far between."

"That's very kind," Ivy said, "and we gladly accept."

"Wonderful!" Natalie ushered them underneath a tent where her friends had filled up a willow basket with various items and covered it with a piece of plaid material. Natalie signaled for Arch, who was standing nearby with Hannah, to help carry it home.

"This will last us quite a while," Nicholas said as he and Arch each grabbed one of the basket handles. But before they could lift it up off the table, a young woman named Miriam hurried over.

"Wait! I have one more thing for you," she said, placing an item wrapped in a small, clean towel on top of the basket. "It's a loaf of currant bread you can share at the breakfast table tomorrow. We had several left over."

"Much appreciated," Arch replied.

"Yes, thanks," Nicholas added, glancing up at the lady with light blond hair and a heavy shawl draped over her shoulders. "That's very kind of..." His voice slowly trailed off as something about her attire suddenly caught his eye.

Miriam, who was not much older than Ivy, wondered if Nicholas recognized her from somewhere. She grew uncomfortable with his persistent gaze. "Is something the matter, sir?" she finally asked to break the tension.

"Pardon me for staring," he said, "but I can't help noticing that pendant around your neck. Where did you get it?"

Miriam held up a small, flat stone with a tiny hole bored into it at one end through which a leather string had been looped and tied in a knot to form a simple necklace. The stone was slightly blue in color with flashes of silver visible in the glow of the firelight.

"This old thing?" she said. "My aunt gave it to me a few years ago."

"You seem fascinated by it, Nicholas," Ivy said, delightfully curious. "Any reason why?"

"There is," he replied before addressing Miriam. "Does your aunt happen to be named Emma, by any chance?"

A look of surprise registered on the young girl's face. "Yes. Emma Covey. But how did you know?" The others were equally intrigued.

"Because I recently saw another stone nearly identical to yours," Nicholas explained. "It was in the possession of a man named Hobin whom I hired for a guide through the Dunn Hills."

"I remember you telling me about him," Ivy said. "But you had mentioned nothing about this mysterious stone. Is it significant?"

"Yes," he replied, noting that Miriam was nodding while everyone eagerly awaited her explanation.

"When I turned seventeen, my Aunt Emma gave this to me as a gift, telling me that she was the same age when the stone was first given to her." Miriam gently rubbed the blue object between her fingers, recounting her aunt's story about how she had fallen in love with a man named Hobin along the shores of Lake Lily where she lived many years ago. "When they spotted the matching stones along the lakeshore, they each kept one to remember the other by. It was very romantic." Ivy, Natalie and Hannah sighed and listened intently. "And though Hobin returned to his home later in autumn, both he and Emma had expected to reunite at the lake the following summer."

"But they didn't," Nicholas said, remembering what little information Hobin had told him and Leo during their hike to Wolf Lake. "Hobin didn't tell us why they never saw each other again, but I could tell he still had feelings for Emma after all these years. Maybe he explores the Dunn Hills to relive past memories. He probably never expected to find Emma there again, but maybe it helped him get by day after day."

"My aunt said that her father moved the family away from Lake Lily at the first sign of spring the following year," Miriam continued. "Her mother had been seriously ill that winter, which was an especially harsh one, and food and work were difficult to come by. Aunt Emma wrote a letter for Hobin telling him where they were going and left it with a neighbor, but she never saw him again and always wondered if he ever received the note. And even if he had seen it, Aunt Emma and her family moved several more times over that year and the next, eventually leaving the Dunn Hills and settling down along the Crescent near the sea."

"What a touching story," Natalie said, her eyes glistening in the cool night air.

Miriam removed the stone from around her neck and handed it to Nicholas. "You must visit my aunt and return this to her," she kindly insisted. "Tell her about Hobin. Even though she married once, I could sense that Aunt Emma had always loved him as she recounted her story to me."

Nicholas appeared uncomfortable with Miriam's request which Ivy quickly picked up on. "Where does she live now?" she inquired. "And where is her husband?"

"Aunt Emma lives in a small farming community midway between Illingboc and Reese, the next village to the south. You'll pass right by it on your way home," Miriam said. "But she lives alone now. Her husband, my Uncle Udell, drowned several years ago in a fishing accident when they lived closer to the sea. That's why Aunt Emma moved away. Now she has two sad memories to endure."

"We'd love to meet her, wouldn't we, Nicholas?" Ivy said. "It'll be a brief visit."

Nicholas smiled awkwardly and relented. "Sure. I'll be happy to return the stone to your aunt and tell her all about Hobin."

"Thank you so much!" Miriam replied, giving him a hug. "It will do her heart a world of good. Maybe they can meet again after all these years."

"Perhaps," he said, making no promises. "But it'll be up to the two of them to decide." He looked at Ivy, feeling slightly put upon but happy to do this special favor for her nonetheless. "Are we ready now?"

Ivy grinned. "Now don't look so inconvenienced, Nicholas. After all, you should know better than anyone about searching for somebody you love. Don't you want to help Emma and Hobin?"

"I'd prefer Hobin's permission first, knowing how he is, but if you do then I do," he replied smiling, noting a slight nod from Arch which indicated that he had provided Ivy with the correct answer.

"So I guess you really do love me," she said, kissing Nicholas on the cheek and wrapping her arms around him.

"I guess I do," he softly replied, holding her tightly.

A short time later, he and Arch lugged the food-laden willow basket home as Ivy, Natalie and Hannah followed, all of them happily chatting about what a wonderful night they had enjoyed as the Bear Moon slowly sank in the west. In the meantime, Brin watched them depart while cloaked in the shade of some nearby evergreens, especially noting the large food basket the two men were carrying through the streets. He was suddenly inspired with an idea that would make the next step in his scheme far simpler than he had originally planned. He smiled as he slipped through the trees and disappeared into the night, having a few more details to attend to before dawn.

Nicholas and Ivy departed at midmorning two days later after an early breakfast and a series of heartfelt goodbyes to Arch, Natalie and Hannah. Both promised to visit in the future when their personal lives, and hopefully, the state of Laparia, were back to normal. Ivy waved farewell to their hosts one last time as Nicholas gently snapped the reins of the covered cart Arch had provided them, drawn by two brown horses through the cloudy third day of New Winter.

Several minutes after they had cleared the outskirts of the village, another man on a horse departed Illingboc as well, sauntering down the road in no apparent hurry, keeping a discreet distance between himself and the two travelers ahead. Brin was bundled up in a coat and wore a thick pair of gloves, the rim of his hat down over his forehead. He knew he would have to bide his time until he found the perfect moment to make his move, yet confident that he was close to achieving his goal.

Nicholas slowed down his team when he and Ivy neared Emma's farmhouse just off the main road before noontime. The sod brick building with a thatched roof stood close to a sprawling, bare oak tree standing as a silhouette against the charcoal gray sky. Several houses of similar construction dotted the landscape. Nicholas had followed Miriam's directions and was now midway between Illingboc and Reese. The Trillium Sea lay less than a mile away, forming the dark, turquoise line of the horizon.

With Ivy at his side, he prepared to knock on the windowless front door a short time later. "I hope she doesn't mind unexpected guests," he said.

"She'll be glad you stopped by. Trust me," she assured him, indicating for Nicholas to knock. "Do you have the pendant?"

Nicholas held back the knock and then patted one of his front coat pockets. "Safe and secure. Though I still think you should have worn it until we arrived here. It looked so beautiful when I asked you to try it on at the house."

"Thank you, but I wouldn't have felt right doing so," Ivy said. "Besides, I'm wearing Princess Megan's silver medallion, though I keep it hidden. You'll just have to find me something of my own."

"I have the amulet Frist created," he reminded her. "You could wear that for a while. It will keep you safe."

"You told me Frist said that it would keep *you* safe, so you'd better not take it off until we get home."

Nicholas shrugged. "I suppose if the magic in it is genuine, it should aid whoever wears it," he replied somewhat distractedly as a realization just hit him. "The wizard also hoped that it would lead me to people I wished to find," he said, glancing at Ivy with affection. "So I suppose it must work. I found you, after all, and I didn't have to sail all the way to the Northern Isles to do so."

"Lucky for both of us," she replied. "And you also found Miriam who led you to this place on Hobin's behalf. So you can't tell me that some wizardry isn't at work here."

"Let's agree that Frist is somehow lending us a hand these last few days. Either that or the two of us have been very lucky." He winked at Ivy before knocking on the door. "Now can we begin our visit?"

Ivy nodded. As Nicholas was about to knock, the door suddenly swung open. Standing before them was a woman about twice Nicholas' age with shoulder-length blond hair and deep, green eyes that appeared sad and vibrant at the same time. She wore a heavy woolen sweater and a long skirt, and draped over her shoulders was a light gray shawl to ward off winter's biting chill.

"Good morning," she pleasantly greeted them, assuming that Nicholas and Ivy were lost. "I thought I had heard voices outside. May I help you?"

"Actually, we're here to help you," Nicholas replied before introducing himself and Ivy. "Are you Emma Covey? And do you have a niece named Miriam?"

"Yes to both questions," she said curiously. "But why are you here to help me?"

"We met your lovely niece at a village celebration in Illingboc a few days ago," Ivy explained, looking askance at Nicholas. "Maybe you better show it to her first."

"Show me what?"

"Good idea," Nicholas said, reaching into his coat pocket and producing the bluish-silver stone pendant. "Miriam gave this to us to give back to you," he continued, uncertain how Emma would react.

Emma was suspiciously surprised to see the treasured piece of jewelry dangling from Nicholas' fingers. "I gave that to Miriam for her seventeenth birthday. She told me she loved it very much."

"And she still does," Ivy assured her.

"Miriam's all right, isn't she?" Emma asked, suddenly anticipating the worst. "It's been several weeks since I've seen her."

"She's quite well," Nicholas said, fearing that he was needlessly making her upset.

"That's the first bit of good news out of this conversation," she quipped, taking the pendant from Nicholas and gazing at it for several moments, her thoughts transported to another time and place. She looked up at Nicholas. "So tell me–why did Miriam want me to have this back?"

Nicholas looked apprehensively at Ivy for a moment before answering. "She thought you might want it back once you learned that, um…"

Emma raised her eyebrows, slightly impatient yet wholly intrigued. "Once I learned that…?"

Nicholas smiled uncomfortably. "Once you learned that I had located the other stone identical to this one which you found near Lake Lily. I recently met the man who currently possesses it." Emma's eyes widened in amazement. "His name is Hobin."

"*Hobin*?" she whispered. Emma took a deep breath as she leaned against the door frame, appearing somewhat disoriented. She held up her hand when Nicholas and Ivy reached out to her. "I'm all right. Just a little bit surprised." She smiled. "Well, perhaps a lot surprised. Overwhelmed." Emma stared at her guests, temporarily at a loss for words as the architecture of her current world began to crack at the seams. "I would love to hear more of your story. Do you have time for a cup of tea?"

While they joined Emma inside and informed her about Hobin's current life, Brin saw his chance to act. He had been following Nicholas and Ivy from a safe distance, keeping them always in his sight but out of hearing range. Occasionally he would direct his horse over a small side road or through a nearby field and observe his prey from a different angle, correctly anticipating where they were heading while at the same time lessening his chances of being spotted. Now he was prepared to strike.

He tied up his horse in a thicket of trees along a narrow stream a good distance from Emma's residence and well away from the next closest farmhouse. Brin ran alongside the waterway and then veered right and scrambled toward Nicholas' cart nearby, hoping no one would spot him from one of the few windows facing his direction. As he approached the cart, he kept it positioned between himself and the house, pausing for a moment to rest and listen. When nobody exited the house, Brin assumed that he had not been seen and methodically went to work.

He climbed into the back of the covered cart and spotted the basket of leftover food from the party. But what interested him more were the two filled water skins lying next to it. He smiled while reaching into his coat pocket and removed a small glass vial containing a pale green liquid which he opened and set aside. Brin grabbed one of the water skins, removed its oak stopper and carefully poured half the contents of the vial into it, gently swirling the water a few times to thoroughly mix it. Before he replaced the stopper, he sniffed the water and could detect no odor. The local apothecary he had purchased the concoction from said it would have a slightly sweet taste when diluted in water. Brin poured the remaining liquid into the second water skin, knowing that the apothecary would have never sold him the potion if he had known what he was really planning to do with it.

With the task completed, Brin placed the pair of water skins back where he found them and shoved the empty vial into his coat pocket before climbing out of the cart. The two horses merely grunted at his presence, paying scant attention to him as they munched on some dry grass. Brin peered around the corner of the cart at Emma's house, and when seeing no one out front and hearing no voices, he dashed back to the wood thicket for safety. He untied his horse and fed it a small apple from his saddlebag which the animal greedily gobbled up.

"Now we wait," Brin softly said as he stroked the horse's mane while gazing at the house. "I don't know why they stopped here, but I sure hope they don't plan to make a day of it. Cousin Cale and the others are waiting for me along the river–or at least they had better be." Brin eyed the steed while adjusting his hat. "So how about another apple? And this time I'll join you."

Nicholas and Ivy hugged Emma goodbye when they left her house less than an hour later as if she were an aunt or an old family friend. She had talked long and animatedly about her relationship with Hobin when he had visited her village on Lake Lily where they fell in love. As she held the blue-silvery stone in her hands, she admitted that she had never fallen out of love with him through all the intervening years. Nicholas promised to leave word with the farmer in Woodwater who was caring for Hobin's dogs in his absence.

"Hobin will probably still be in Morrenwood with Leo," Nicholas told her. "Ivy and I are sure to see him there. We'll let him know where to find you. I promise."

Emma held that promise warmly in her heart as she watched the cart disappear down the road before stepping back inside. She never saw nor heard Brin saunter past on his horse several minutes afterward, heading in the same direction.

Almost two hours later, Nicholas pulled the cart off the road near a towering oak alongside a small pond to stop for lunch and allow the horses to rest. The Trillium Sea was a distant blue-green patch of water at this spot as the main road had veered slightly away from the shoreline for the last mile or so and passed through more fertile farmland. As the weather had stayed cool through the morning, Nicholas decided to build a small fire while Ivy rounded up some food for their meal.

"If there was an inn along the way, I would spoil you there with a fine meal," Nicholas said as he gathered up an armful of twigs. "Right now it's just miles of nothing."

"That's fine with me," Ivy said, carrying some of the food and the water skins to the oak tree where he was starting the fire. "Now we have a chance to talk and get to know each other better."

Nicholas looked up. "I feel as if I've known you all my life, Ivy, if that makes any sense."

She smiled. "I feel the same way, too." She set the items down and helped Nicholas arrange the kindling, each of them gazing at one another from time to time with the same curious excitement of a first encounter as well as the comfortable familiarity of having

355

been together for years. Neither one of them could have been happier.

Brin directed his horse south around a long, sweeping curve in the road running parallel to a stretch of pine trees on his right. He had passed only one other person about an hour ago since he had left the area near Emma's house. The road was lonely and desolate. When it finally straightened out, he noticed a trail of blue-gray wood smoke rising in the distance close to a tall oak tree. A cart with two horses stood patiently nearby. Brin stopped his horse and waited in the middle of the dirt road, gazing ahead for a few minutes for any sign of activity. But as there was none, he snapped the reins and ambled forward.

He approached the stationary cart from behind and to his left. Brin smelled the sweet smoke and heard the crackling flames. He moved slowly alongside the cart and the two horses in front until the oak tree and small fire were fully revealed in his line of sight. He pulled on the reins and his horse stopped a short distance from the tree. Brin looked down and saw the familiar face of the man who had hit him on the deck of the *Bretic*. Nicholas was sitting on the ground with his back to the tree. His eyes were closed as he soundly slept. Ivy sat next to him, also fast asleep, her head resting upon Nicholas' shoulder while his head gently touched hers. Some partially eaten food and two water skins lay nearby.

"Hello," Brin called out, his word quickly dying in the cold emptiness. "*Hello?*"

There was no response. He quickly dismounted and scanned the terrain to make sure no one was in the vicinity. He wanted no witnesses when he carried each of the bodies and placed them in back of the cart. Brin moved fast, eager to find his cousin and, hopefully, a raft and crew waiting for him on the river. If he could reach them by morning, he would consider himself lucky as he didn't think the sleeping elixir would last much time beyond that according to what the apothecary had told him.

As Brin knelt down on one knee next to Ivy to lift her over his shoulder, he noticed a gold chain around her neck. He pulled it out from beneath her blouse and studied the silver medallion attached to it. On the front was depicted an immense stone structure guarded by pine trees with mountains and a winding river in the background. The other side showed a horse galloping through a field of tall grass under two rising full moons with a sword engraved on either side of the image. From his studies on the Northern Isles, he instantly recognized the image of the Blue Citadel.

"I'm delighted to finally meet you, Princess Megan," he whispered while slipping the medallion back underneath her clothing. "Oh, and no need to introduce your friend. I've already met King Justin's personal spy–and I presume the love of your life by the way I saw you two dancing." He chuckled softly while looking upon the sleeping couple. "So, ready to begin our journey? Vellan will be pleased to meet you both when I take you to Kargoth. Very pleased indeed," he said, anticipating with drunken giddiness the rewards that Vellan would bestow upon him once he presented the wizard with such valuable prizes.

END OF PART SIX

PART SEVEN
A CLASH OF ARMIES

CHAPTER 64

A Brief Parley

Eucádus stood unmoving upon the morning field. He stared down King Drogin's forces poised atop a low ridge across the browning grass less than a mile away. Upon Lake LaShear to his left, a fleet of ships from Zaracosa were gathered on the water like silent vultures eyeing their prey. Though the armies of King Basil, King Cedric and those from the tiny nations in the Northern Mountains had planned a surprise attack on Drogin, they now found themselves beaten to the punch on their very doorstep.

Eucádus wondered if Drogin's spies had intercepted their plans for the secret attack. Or had they been given faulty information from the Hamilod Resistance about Drogin's final push up the coast and across the lake? In either case, war had found them, though not fully unprepared. As the lingering tendrils of ghostly white fog evaporated in the growing light and on a freshening breeze, the young but weary soldier from Harlow anticipated a day of bloodshed and sadness. As the horrified whispers of the men around him mingled with the crackling bonfires, Eucádus' heart broke and his throat tightened. He wondered how many of these brave soldiers under his leadership would survive to see the sun rising tomorrow morning over the glorious blue waters of the lake.

A soldier from Drogin's army was dispatched on horseback to request a parley within the hour with King Basil of Rhiál or his representatives. The man, a native of the Northern Isles, returned to his leaders with the message that such a meeting would be accommodated. Soon afterward, Eucádus, King Cedric, Captain Silas and a handful of other captains gathered in a large tent upon the field in view of King Basil's estate to debate their next move.

"No doubt Drogin will want to discuss terms of our surrender," muttered Ranen, defiantly pacing upon the cold, hard ground. His long black hair, tied in back with a piece of scarlet material, highlighted the tension in his facial muscles. "Well, he will get no such response from me!"

"Nor from any of us," Eucádus replied, silently noting that Ranen was exhibiting the same steely determination now that he always did when solving even lesser matters as leader of the Oak Clearing. Yet that was why Eucádus could trust him as a friend and fellow soldier.

"We will confront Drogin, not surrender," Captain Silas assured everyone, "whatever our fates afterward. And if I may be so bold as to speak for King Basil, I know he would echo those same sentiments. We have not gathered the best of our countrymen and those from abroad to simply lie down at the first sight of the enemy. We will indulge their words and then send them on their merry way before we draw swords."

"Those indeed are my sentiments–and nicely phrased."

A voice spoke from behind them, low and weak, yet still with the force of authority. When the men turned their heads, they saw that King Basil had stepped through the tent flap with one of his aides beside him holding onto his arm to keep him steady. The King wore a heavy brown cloak with silver embroidery. His unruly gray hair of late had been combed so that he appeared like the monarch of old.

"Sir, what are you doing here?" Captain Silas asked with fearful surprise. "You should be resting at the estate. I had planned to send constant dispatches to you regarding the battle."

"I know, I know," he replied dismissively with a wave of his hand. "And I could have watched the battle unfold from my bedroom window as well, but that wouldn't have been as entertaining either," he added with a playful wink.

"Have a seat, my friend," King Cedric kindly encouraged him. "Your advice will be for naught if your weakened state prevents you from thinking properly."

"Please," Eucádus urged, offering him a small wooden bench to sit upon near a large table where a crude topographic map of the local terrain had been spread out.

King Basil graciously accepted and was soon immersed in the military discussion with his peers as if the upcoming parley had already occurred and had been soundly rejected. Captain Silas and Eucádus presented their plan of attack to the others, explaining that there would be a two-prong assault–one south on the field and one east along the docks and shoreline of Lake LaShear.

"I'll direct the campaign along the water and Eucádus will confront Drogin's men to the south," Captain Silas said as he traced his finger over the corresponding locations on the map.

"Captain Tiber and I will go with you, Eucádus," King Cedric added. "Our forces have been together since they combined in Drumaya and endured the long road across the Kincarin Plains. There is no reason why we should not join now in battle."

Eucádus nodded. "I will be honored to ride with you into the storm, King Cedric."

In the end, Jeremias, leader of the Fox Clearing, would also charge onto the battlefield with Eucádus. Ramsey vowed to accompany them as well. Ranen volunteered to make a stand along the docks with Captain Silas who would also be joined by Uland and Torr, leaders of the Pumpkin and Haystack Clearings. They, along with other captains and the thousands of men gathered on the south and west fields along the King's estate, pledged their lives to preserving a free and prosperous Rhiál. They were still outnumbered by several thousand troops. The enemy from Kargoth and the Northern Isles was fiercely committed to seizing Rhiál for both Vellan and Drogin's designs.

The discussions were abruptly concluded when someone outside the tent uttered three simple words in a bleak and ominous tone. "Here they come."

Eucádus looked up, a hint of a smile upon his face. "Time to greet our guests. Let's not keep them waiting."

"The sharpened point of my sword is eager to greet them," Captain Tiber replied, his eyebrows arched above his steely blue eyes.

"Steady now," King Cedric replied to one of his finest captains, though he spoke his words with good humor. "First we talk–but keep a ready hand near your hilt."

King Basil remained inside the tent with an aide as the others exited to the breezy outdoors. There they observed three men on horseback galloping northward up the field in the morning light. One of them carried a flag in muted tones of orange, brown and black symbolizing King Drogin's reign. It was a recently created emblem which Drogin valued highly, even displaying it above the official flag of Maranac. When the riders reached the encampment, they wordlessly sauntered along a pathway to the main tent with haughty expressions, their contempt for Rhiál and its allies not the least bit in doubt. While the man carrying the flag was a citizen of Maranac and a stanch supporter of King Drogin, the other two were not native to this region. One was from the Northern Isles, dressed in traditional military garb. The other, who appeared to be in charge, was a citizen of Kargoth sent by Vellan to secure these lands by any means.

Eucádus and King Cedric were both quick to note a subtle, cloudy haze within the man's brown eyes similar to that of the dying soldier from Kargoth they had talked to after the attack on the Kincarin Plains. Those who were familiar with the legend of Vellan casting a spell upon the Drusala River in Kargoth were convinced that this man had drunk from the river and had become a devoted follower of the cruel and corrupt wizard. But whether the drink was by choice, accident or deception, none could say.

"My name is Irabesh. Are you prepared to discuss the terms of your surrender?" asked the man from Kargoth with little ceremony. His nearly lifeless eyes looked down from a pale, unshaven face as his mop of jet black hair waved in the breeze.

"You presume much about our intentions," King Cedric calmly replied, not intimidated by the man's arrogant demeanor. "But if you and your associates care to join us with King Basil inside, we shall be happy to discuss many issues."

"Very well." Irabesh dismounted his steed, signaling for the others to do likewise. "But our only issue of concern is your swift and complete surrender. Otherwise these talks will be brief."

Eucádus studied the man, knowing there wasn't a shred of trustworthiness or honor in him. "And why isn't King Drogin gracing us with his presence this morning?"

"He prefers to remain across the water in Zaracosa awaiting word of our victory," he replied.

"Of course. Follow me," Eucádus said as he led the trio into the tent where King Basil waited at the head of the table. Moments later, their animated exchange was underway.

"I'll come to the crux of the matter," Irabesh said, seated opposite King Basil. His two associates stood behind him. "Your chances of victory are nonexistent as you face a larger fighting force more powerful, loyal and far more determined than your own."

King Basil grunted with contempt. "You do have a greater number of men, but I'll argue about the other points."

"Argue all you like, but you know I speak the truth, sir."

"You and your kind know nothing of loyalty!" Ranen interjected, his face flushed with disdain. "By your mindless devotion to Vellan, there is no doubt that you have consumed the poisoned waters of the Drusala. Yours is a false loyalty."

"My friend may be no diplomat," Eucádus said, "but does he not speak the truth?"

"You want the truth about loyalty?" Irabesh replied, unfazed by Ranen's remark. "I'll tell you the truth. We recently learned that traitors to King Drogin in the Hamilod Resistance passed information to you about our planned assault on your capital. But as you can see," he added with a self-satisfied smile, "we also learned that you were going to attack us before we got underway. So while you dithered, we charged at your door ahead of schedule, ready to break it down."

"What has that got to do with the subject of loyalty?" Captain Silas asked, showing mild impatience as he leaned back in his seat and ran a hand through his shortly cropped hair. "I was expecting a lesson of some sort."

"The lesson is this–don't let a young prince of Montavia and his urchin friend wander around the docks at night unprotected," he coolly replied. "Especially a prince privy to military secrets."

Eucádus, King Basil, King Cedric and many others in the tent felt a deadly chill run through them, fearing some horror had befallen Prince William and Aaron. Yet despite the emotional punch, all kept their composure.

"What are you saying?" King Cedric asked, noting that King Basil seemed unable to speak.

"I am saying that Prince William revealed the details of your attack plans to us two days ago," Irabesh replied. "For which we are utterly thankful."

"Where is he?" Eucádus demanded, pounding the tabletop. "What have you done to him and the other boy?"

"They are both fine–for now." Irabesh delighted in having the upper hand. "They are safely tucked away should we ever need them again. But my point is that it didn't take much for your young prince to supply us the information we desired. Is that loyalty?"

King Basil spoke softly, his words steaming with subdued rage. "If you harm them in any way…"

Irabesh smirked. "You'll do what exactly? Attack us?"

"We are prepared to defend Melinas to the death–ours and yours," Eucádus said.

"I think it will be more of yours if it comes to a clash of swords and a torrent of arrows," he confidently replied. "However, that can be avoided with a simple surrender. Your people will be treated justly, King Basil. Once Rhiál is reunited with Maranac, you will be astounded at the prosperity and good will that King Drogin's rule shall unleash."

"I'm only too aware of what Drogin's touch can accomplish," the King replied before placing a hand over his mouth to conceal a nagging cough. He appeared pale and tired. "My oldest son, Morton, was killed fighting Drogin's thirst for power. And Victor, my youngest, has been missing for five months after a raid in Zaracosa, though I presume he is dead as well. So do not tell me about the good will of Drogin the serpent!"

A strained hush fell over the gathering as a glint of fiery anger from King Basil of old ignited the atmosphere inside the tent. But just as quickly, the King slumped his shoulders and sighed with growing exhaustion, knowing the odds were not in his favor. Captain Silas, who sat next to him, gently laid a hand upon his shoulder in silent support.

"Let me spell out what King Drogin has in store if you still cannot grasp the logic of surrender. Maybe it will pound some sense into your royal head before subjecting your populace to more useless warfare." Irabesh's words were strident and cold. "The first wave of soldiers waiting for you upon both land and water are those from Maranac who are most loyal to King Drogin. We have purged any officers that King Hamil had installed before his untimely death in New Spring."

"Tell me, did you have a hand in planning King Hamil's assassination, too?" Ranen remarked. "Or were you only in charge of his daughter Melinda's disappearance?" He glared coldly at the man. "Just wondering."

Irabesh ignored the comment. "Standing next to King Drogin's finest fighters will be our allies from the Northern Isles and, of course, my fellow countrymen from Kargoth. We are all well trained and will show no mercy if you pursue a challenge against us."

"We had expected no less," Eucádus replied matter-of-factly. "Our troops are similarly prepared."

"That you will have to prove when our forces bear down upon you," he said. "And if that isn't enough, just a few miles south of here is a second wave of men from Maranac who stand ready to strike–not that we will need the assistance. And as for your planned attack on our ships at Zaracosa, King Basil, let me assure you that that will not happen. King Drogin has marched several companies north along the eastern shore of the lake to confront your allies from Altaga who were building rafts for your predawn invasion of our ships." Irabesh noted the trace of dismay in King Basil's eyes and upon his haggard face. "Yes, Prince William kindly told us about them as well, so expect no help floating down from the north tip of Lake LaShear. One of these days soon, King Drogin will pay a visit to Altaga in repayment for such treachery. If they think the mountains will protect them, they are sadly mistaken." He folded his arms, studying the stunned countenances surrounding him. "I think that covers everything I wanted to say."

A weighty, hopeless silence hung over the gathering. It was as if defeat had already been declared in response to Irabesh's words. As most of the men around the table cast their eyes downward, Eucádus and Captain Silas glanced at one another and simultaneously stood up. They walked partway around the table and stopped, standing opposite their enemy. Both men glared at Irabesh and his companions for a moment before a thin smile spread across Eucádus' face.

"Nice speech. Are you done now?" Eucádus looked askance at Captain Silas. "Is he done?"

"Oh, I hope so," he replied. "He does go on a bit."

A soft ripple of laughter spread among the other men like tiny waves across a pond. Even King Basil and King Cedric couldn't conceal their amusement at Eucádus and Captain Silas' antics which instantly dispelled the fatalistic gloom that had seeped into the hearts of everyone in the tent. Whatever persuasive advantage Irabesh had brought with him by his force of personality or through some residual effect of Vellan's enchantment, it was now utterly extinguished. Still, Irabesh knew he had the superior force of men behind him and that was what mattered most.

"Enjoy your little joke," he muttered. "It won't save you from what awaits if you do not surrender."

"We have no plans to surrender to you or your puppets," Captain Silas remarked, tossing a reassuring glance to King Basil. "Ride back and tell them so. Shortly you will find out what the men of Rhiál, Drumaya and the nations of the Northern Mountains are made of and to what lengths we'll fight to defend our freedom."

Irabesh stood, fuming with contempt. "These discussions are over! I'll see you on the battlefield forthwith," he said in something resembling a snarl. He signaled to his men and they followed him out through the tent flap like dark clouds in a storm. Moments later the sound of three horses were heard galloping down the field.

King Cedric looked at King Basil and offered a faint smile. "Well, my friend, I guess the moment has arrived that we've both dreaded and planned for over many fretful hours. Yet in a strange way, I'm glad it's here."

"As am I," King Basil replied, clasping his friend's hands to wish him good fortune. "It's a shame that I haven't the strength to ride with my men in battle, but I shall remain here and watch events unfold to the south and receive dispatches from the docks."

"Let's hope they are good ones." King Cedric stood and addressed the anxious gathering. "Well, it's time to yank out another loose tooth, men. Let's go!"

Captain Silas glanced questioningly at Eucádus about the puzzling comment as everyone exited the tent. *"Loose tooth?* What's that about?"

"I'll explain later," Eucádus said with a slight grin as they stepped into the cold air and observed the sun-splashed field before them. Both anticipated great and terrible events to shortly unfold, but neither foresaw how any of them would turn out at day's end.

King Basil, in the meantime, quietly called to one of his aides. "Find me two swift scouts. There is an important dispatch I need to send at once."

Voices shouted and horns blared. Orders were dispatched to the troops spread across the south and west encampments below the King's estate. Men armed with swords, knives, bows and shields, some on horseback though most on foot, began the slow march to war with colorful flags and banners waving in the cool breezes off the lake. Eucádus and King Cedric, along with Ramsey, Captain Tiber and Jeremias, led their companies down the field toward Drogin's forces under the control of Irabesh. The rippling blue waters of Lake LaShear glistened under the rising sun. Fleeting shadows played upon the field and the water as remnants of billowing white clouds sailed across the sky. Farther down the field, stretches of spruce, beech, pine and elm trees framed the field on the left and right sides. A low ridge in the center was populated with Irabesh's soldiers.

Captain Silas, along with Ranen, Uland and Torr, directed troops east to the docks. Their breaths were taken away as they drew near the large ships that had sailed across the lake during the night and now stood like mythical giants from a childhood dream. Each ship proudly flew the flag of Maranac, yet waving in the breeze above each one was the orange, brown and black banner symbolizing King Drogin himself, a drab and gaudy display that mirrored an identical line of flags that Eucádus and his men faced upon the field.

As his brave soldiers and their allies left the encampment, King Basil stepped out of the tent and looked across the battlefield and toward the lake as Garron, one of his aides, remained steadfastly at his side. A company of soldiers had also remained behind to protect the King and attend to duties in the encampment. King Basil inhaled the fresh morning air and reluctantly admitted to himself that it would be reeking with the stench of blood and death before long.

"It is too lovely a day for warfare, Garron," the King sadly commented to the young man. "I fear I shall not live long enough to see another peaceful morning or enjoy a stunning twilight along the lake again." He coughed harshly and signaled for Garron to help him back inside where he sat on a bench at the table.

"We may survive the day, sir," Garron replied, his words veiled with the thinnest veneer of hope. "Captain Silas and Eucádus ride with many of the finest men from here and abroad. Do not despair before the first sword has been drawn."

"Maybe you're right," the King said with a forced smile. "Perhaps my words are laced with despair because of reasons other than the precarious outcome of this war." He looked up and sighed. "Now that Morton and Victor are gone, there is no heir to the throne of Rhiál from my bloodline. That is one of the two things that has bothered me of late." He looked up with an air of defeat. "Perhaps that is a sign that Drogin will be victorious. Under him, Rhiál will have a king. Not the best of kings," he admitted with a sad chuckle, "but a king nonetheless."

"That will not happen because *we* will be victorious," Garron said, sitting down beside his monarch. "And should the need arise, there are plenty of good and wise men who could be chosen to lead us in your absence. It would be like years ago when a new line of rulers was established after the Maranac of old was partitioned in two. You descend from that line, King Basil."

He nodded. "Yes, though it is a short line of rulers and one of necessity after that ugly war. Yet if Maranac and Rhiál are reunited– even forcibly so–perhaps Drogin might one day be overthrown and a just ruler will take his place. The new, whole Maranac could resemble our nation of old again when it was truly a glorious place to live."

"Let's just get through today first, King Basil," Garron remarked. "Now enough of such somber thoughts. Tell me, if you will, the second thing that has bothered you of late."

The King offered a weak smile. "And you just said that you've had enough of somber thoughts." His smile disappeared and he looked at Garron with deep despair in his eyes. "I am deeply worried about Prince William and Aaron, of course. I feel responsible for whatever evil has befallen them. And if they never return..."

Garron felt a pang of sympathy for King Basil whom he looked up to in a grandfatherly sort of way. Yet before he could mouth even the simplest words of support, the distant clash of swords and the rallying cries of fighting men could be heard upon the breeze. King Basil and Garron looked at one another and their hearts sank. The fighting had begun.

CHAPTER 65

A Clash of Swords

Eucádus defiantly led the armies of Rhiál, Drumaya and the Five Clearings down the field toward Drogin's waiting troops. He rode upon Chestnut, the steed Prince William had given him. Armed with a sword and several daggers, he wore a thick leather jerkin over his clothes with a brown, weather-stained cloak draped over his shoulders. King Cedric and Captain Tiber accompanied him on his right. Jeremias and Ramsey rode on his left.

Though Drogin's forces were a half mile away, they loomed large on the horizon. The men on his front lines were mounted on horses while a vast standing army stood confidently behind them. Eucádus had often imagined this moment, glad that King Cedric decided to join him in the cause. But as he neared Drogin's army, he realized that his safe, distant musings were far different from the cold, stark reality now hitting him like a crashing wave.

"I suppose Irabesh is having similar thoughts," King Cedric commented when seeing Eucádus lost in the moment. "Your decision to come here was a wise one. I see that now even as we are about to leap into the fire."

"I still think so," he replied. "But witnessing all of this at once makes a person take pause and assess how he ended up here."

"Everyone you've guided here is thinking that," the King said. "Along with thoughts of loved ones, home and the passing years."

"And we're still behind you anyway!" Ramsey joked, eliciting nervous laughter from those within earshot. "It's been a long road, Eucádus, first from Harlow and then from the Star Clearing. But we all mean to walk the last steps with you wherever they lead us."

"This road leads to a bevy of madmen doing the bidding of an even madder wizard," Jeremias remarked. "But the men of the Fox Clearing willingly face them as well. This day is not only for the citizens of Rhiál, but for our trio of nations held captive under Kargoth's fist. I look forward to staring into Irabesh's eyes and giving him a message to send back to Drogin and Vellan."

"I hope you have a bucketful of patience, my friend," replied Ramsey, "because there is a long line of men waiting for just that chance, including me."

"I would sooner put an end to Irabesh's miserable life and let that be my message," Captain Tiber said. "But we can all dream, I suppose."

Eucádus indicated the shifting scene before them, noting that Drogin's troops had slowly begun advancing. "I'm afraid the time for dreaming is over. The blistering truth of reality presses forward." He took a deep breath, preparing his mind, heart and soul for what his eyes could plainly see. "This is it, my friends. May safety and good fortune ride with us."

With that, Eucádus and King Cedric exchanged knowing glances before a signal was given to hasten forward. The thundering sound of galloping horses reverberated across the landscape as thin, ghostly clouds of dust eddied and somersaulted across the dying field. An array of soldiers on foot followed behind with rapid steps. As the army of Rhiál advanced, Drogin's line suddenly came to a stop. In perfect unison, his riders removed the bows from their backs, preparing to fire a volley of arrows at King Basil's forces. But Eucádus and King Cedric had anticipated such a move. Before Drogin's men had drawn the first arrows from their quivers, Eucádus raised his right arm and swept it through the air in a circular motion.

In an instant, Eucádus, Jeremias and Ramsey broke to the left while King Cedric and Captain Tiber veered right, each group taking half of the equine forces with them and flanking the enemy's front line on both sides. In those few moments, Drogin's men stayed their arrows as new orders were frantically shouted at them to counter Eucádus' maneuver. But as the dust settled where the herd of horses had split, hundreds of King Cedric and King Basil's best archers were suddenly revealed to the enemy, armed and at the ready, releasing a torrent of arrows that sailed across the blue and white sky, their tips marked gold by the morning sun.

The forces of Rhiál and their allies had struck the first blow. Many of Drogin's men not quick enough with their shields were thrown from their horses when pierced by the deadly barrage. King Basil's archers fired a second volley before exchanging their bows for swords, charging forward with the rest of the army behind them. Eucádus and King Cedric, in the meantime, after guiding their forces to the east and west tree lines, drove their steeds directly at their flustered foes. Irabesh, at his front line on horseback, quickly adjusted and split his riders as well, giving the order for them to shift east and west and confront the opponent. Irabesh's foot soldiers were now shown in full, rushing forward with swords drawn and voices raised to meet their advancing counterparts in face-to-face combat.

Soon the clash of metal upon metal echoed across the battlefield, accompanied by the grunts of brutal attack and the moans and cries of the hurt and mortally wounded. The fading greens and browns of the late-autumn foliage and woodscape were tinged red with the blood of the dead, dying and injured as the rising sun crept higher in the sky over the unsettled waters of Lake LaShear.

As the battle progressed upon land, Captain Silas and Ranen led their forces to the shoreline and docks in the city. Uland, Torr and other captains in King Basil's army followed. They had swiftly passed the King's estate, now under heavy guard inside and out, and marched to Lake LaShear to face the imposing tall ships anchored offshore. But the enemy had wasted no time. Scores of large rowboats filled with warriors from Maranac, the Northern Isles and Kargoth had left the ships and made for the docks and strips of sandy beach. The women, children and elderly in town had long since barricaded themselves in their homes and shops or had taken to the road and sought safer dwellings in the woods or distant farmhouses.

As Captain Silas approached the main stone roadway running parallel to the sandy shore and the lake just beyond, he split his forces in three, sending Torr and another captain to the farthest docks and narrow stretch of beach on the left while directing Uland and two other officers deeper into the city to the right. Silas and Ranen, in the meantime, marched straight into the center of the storm with the remaining troops, tearing across the sands and among the abandoned shanties and fishing boats to the docks now teeming with enemy soldiers climbing out of their boats en masse like angry wasps issuing from their nests.

The span of time was short and breathtaking before the sounds of muted voices and pounding boots were replaced with fierce and furious cries from the collision of opposing troops. The dull clanking of silvery swords and daggers stained scarlet with blood rose above the swooshing sound of cold waves and the whistling breezes whipping off the tumultuous blue waters of the roiling lake.

King Basil observed the twin battles from outside his tent. He had recovered his strength and stepped outdoors as Garron stood close by. Several soldiers kept guard as a bonfire blazed. He watched in subdued silence, a part of him reeling with disbelief that the tragic events were actually unfolding before his eyes during that first cold and gloomy hour.

"The estate has not yet been breached," he remarked, gazing at his living quarters. The three-story, whitewashed building of clay and stone stood as a silent beacon of hope, surrounded by a rock wall and a large company of guards. "The fighting to the east is confined to the lakeside. Captain Silas will do his best to see that it remains so. Still, I wish for more detailed reports." The King turned to Garron. "Arrange a relay of riders to the estate to gage the fighting from there. Have one return to me every quarter hour with an update."

"Yes, sir," Garron replied, running off to implement the order.

King Basil, in the meantime, sat down on a small bench near the tent, refusing assistance from a passing soldier. "Thank you, but I can manage. I simply wish to be alone for a moment to think."

"Of course," the man replied, bowing his head before walking away.

Shortly after, a quartet of riders galloped off to the estate to gather information from there, the first preparing to return with his report in a quarter hour. Garron walked back to King Basil and let him know his instructions had been carried out.

"Is there anything else I can do for you?" he asked.

"How about a cold biscuit and a cup of hot tea? That should hit the spot right now," the King replied. "I'm sure you can scrounge it up among one of the camps."

"I'll be happy to fetch that for you, King Basil. No doubt you haven't had time for a proper breakfast today."

"Oh, my appetite it sated. I meant it for you. Go and find something to eat," he replied with a sweep of his hand. "Off now."

"But I'm not really..." Garron then realized that King Basil wished to be alone, noting his pale complexion and labored breaths with concern. But the King's aide kept the observation to himself. "Thank you, sir. I shall return when the first rider comes back with his report." He stepped slowly away.

"Thank you, Garron. We'll talk then."

When King Basil was finally alone, he stared down the field as the sounds of distant warfare resonated. He had no desire to talk with Garron or anybody else in these precarious moments as his gloomy perception of events attacked his courage and darkened his spirit. For brief instances, he feared that his side might not win, though the battle was still young. His doubts gathered around him like thick mist before a bleak dawn, but he did not want to give life to those nagging suspicions by uttering them to Garron and his other men. He would sit here alone and let the moment pass, hoping his frame of mind would change when the first reports reached him.

The fighting on the field continued. Soldiers, both horsed and unhorsed, battled one another in scattered groups or in one-on-one combat. The once orderly formations of armed riders and marching troops had broken down until all that remained were numerous pockets of warfare among the dying grasses and along the tree lines on the east and west.

Eucádus and Jeremias had rallied their men several times on the east side of the field to confront the forces of Irabesh. Yet despite their best efforts to keep order, the lines were continually broken as their troops were outnumbered by Drogin's first wave. King Cedric and Captain Tiber faced the same quandary across the trampled grass to the west. Ramsey, in the meantime, had fallen from his horse and fell into a skirmish on foot in the shade of the eastern woods with two dozen of King Basil's men against a similarly sized force challenging them with raised swords and unrestrained fury.

Eucádus briefly noted the broiling battle his friend had found himself in with great apprehension, but he was unable to lend a hand as he was engaged in combat with forty of his own riders against a swarm of foot soldiers along the edge of the low ridge. He swung his sword through the air with an expert hand while gripping the reins of his horse with the other, fending off soldiers that Irabesh commanded with deadly aplomb. Yet for the moment in this encounter, Eucádus and his fellow troops had the advantage as they overwhelmed their enemy with skillful blade work and finessed horsemanship.

"Let's finish this and give Ramsey and the others a hand!" Eucádus shouted to Jeremias who rode nearby.

"I was hoping they would help us!" he replied with a smirk, his sword singing lively in the air as beads of sweat streamed down his face. "But I suppose we–"

"*Jeremias!*"

At that moment, Jeremias was pulled backward off his horse by an Island soldier who had leapt up from behind and grabbed his coat, sending him tumbling to the ground as his horse bolted away. But Eucádus didn't miss a beat. He charged forward and plunged his blade into the Islander before the man brought his dagger down upon his surprised foe. Jeremias quickly recovered, jumping up and grabbing his sword that had been knocked from his hand. He struck a deadly blow at another man speeding toward him who hailed from Kargoth. Confused clouds of gray slowly dispersed from the man's eyes as death found him.

"Whether from Kargoth, the Isles or Maranac, the enemy swarms at us like a cloud of stinger gnats!" Jeremias said to the grim amusement of those around him.

"But luckily they are much bigger targets!" Eucádus shot back as he and his fellow soldiers galloped headlong at the remaining twenty or so enemy troops gathered near the edge of the grassy rise.

Jeremias hurriedly scanned the immediate area for his horse. When he saw it galloping toward the eastern trees where Ramsey was fighting, he sighed, knowing that he would be a foot soldier for a time. He took a deep breath, gripped his sword and then raced to catch up with his friends.

On the field's west side, King Cedric and his men were likewise occupied while upon their horses, hewing down a group of Islanders and men from Kargoth who had charged from behind a thicket of trees. But it was a much smaller group than their friends were facing and they dispatched the enemy with ease.

"Their sword skills do not live up to their boasting," Captain Tiber commented as he galloped past the King and turned around.

"It's not over yet," King Cedric remarked, indicating a dozen horsemen stampeding directly at them.

As the King watched his opponents draw closer, he gazed across the battlefield. His eyes absorbed the thrusts of cold swords, the dizzying flights of feathered arrows and the raising of oak and metal shields in the multitude of battles raging across the scarred grounds. He witnessed men falling, dying and bleeding on both sides. For an instant, all the cries and moans of men, the constant swish of arrows, and the heartless clanking of metal blade upon blade seemed to cancel each other out in his mind. King Cedric watched the horrors play out before him in utter silence as if he had gone deaf, allowing him to fully process what was happening here so far from home in Drumaya, so far from his wife and son and daughter. He wondered if he would ever see their faces again or if they would remember his a year from now, or five years hence should death greet him this fine autumn day upon the dying grasses among the Ridloe Mountains.

"Ready, sir?" Captain Tiber repeated his query a second time as his horse stood alongside the King's.

King Cedric flinched, pulled back into the raucous fury by the captain's strong, deep voice and the thunderous pounding of horse hoofs growing closer and closer to their position. He noted that the men with him had already lined up on either side, waiting for his command to ride out and meet the enemy. With a reassuring glance from Captain Tiber, King Cedric nodded and gave the word.

"Ride out!" he cried, lifting his sword and aiming it forward. "Let's show these scoundrels why we traveled over the Kincarin. Let's feed them the bitter taste of defeat that none will ever forget!"

The King's line bolted forward with passionate cries of victory and vengeance as his men recalled their fellow soldiers who were ambushed and killed on the plains. Soon the two forces collided in an explosion of clashing swords and choking dust, their horses relentlessly pounding the flattened grass to nothingness. A handful of men on both sides fell from their steeds during the initial impact, some losing their balance as horses collided while others dropped after the fatal thrusts of deadly blades.

Minutes into the conflict, King Cedric's horse veered off to one side of the main battle during a confrontation with a soldier from Drogin's most elite forces. The earsplitting ring of every sword strike rent the air like a sharp clap of thunder. Moments into the duel, Captain Tiber anxiously noted that the King had encountered a formidable opponent from Maranac, yet marveled that his monarch was holding his own against a younger man as he fended off each blade swing with vigor and determination. Tiber hoped to assist the King after he finished fighting an equally skillful Islander, but his eyes and ears were suddenly filled with horror when he saw King Cedric grab his upper left arm after it was struck by his opponent's sword. The King let out an anguished cry as pain coursed through his injured limb and blood trickled between his fingers.

"To the King's aid!" Captain Tiber called to any who could hurry to the monarch's side through the mayhem and dust.

Tiber, along with those who had witnessed the exchange, knew that King Cedric was now at a severe disadvantage. The King fought on as best he could though his skill with the sword was greatly diminished. The left sleeve of his shirt, partially visible beneath a protective leather vest and cloak, was soaked with blood. The King's face grew ashen. For a moment, the ruler of Drumaya appeared disoriented upon his agitated steed. His opponent smiled with contempt while seated proudly upon his horse just a few feet away. He raised his sword and pointed it at his wounded foe, pausing for a moment to bask in his assured victory.

"To think that I should take down the King of Drumaya," the man said proudly, a taunting smirk upon his whiskered face. "Irabesh will be pleased. King Drogin will be doubly pleased," he added, his smile growing wider. "But I can't even imagine what reward awaits me when Vellan hears of my triumph."

"Keep imagining," King Cedric muttered, his words strained and his face grim because of the deep gash throbbing in his arm. He raised his sword in his right hand, gritting his teeth and willing away the pain for the moment. "This fight isn't over yet!"

"I beg to differ," the man replied, glancing beyond the King's shoulder. He saw that Captain Tiber had just struck down the Islander he had been battling and was now speeding this way. "It's time to end this as I have another victim ready to take me on."

The Maranac soldier charged forward and repeatedly crashed his sword against King Cedric's blade, feeling the monarch's good arm weaken with each strike. When he saw Captain Tiber draw nearer, charging madly upon a wave of thunderous hoofs, he decided to go in for the kill. The soldier reined in his horse slightly and pulled back his sword, then charged at King Cedric who had grown tired from the fighting and the loss of blood.

Captain Tiber knew he wouldn't reach his King in time. Then as if another force had taken control of his actions, he grabbed his sword by the hilt as if it were a spear and hurled it at the Maranac soldier. It sailed though the air, reflecting sunlight off its edge before piercing the man's protective garments and burrowing into his body below the chest.

The soldier froze upon his saddle, gripping the reins with one hand as his horse slowed and trotted past the King. The man's other arm fell limply to his side and his weapon dropped to the ground. When he gazed deliriously down at the sword protruding from his abdomen, a look of disbelief registered upon his face. For a moment he was oblivious to the pain, growing lightheaded and as pale as ash. The raucous sounds of fighting echoed and faded in his mind. When he looked up, Captain Tiber had drawn near on his horse and reached for the hilt of his embedded sword, but whatever words were on Tiber's lips, the wounded soldier couldn't hear them over the heartbeats reverberating in his head.

Captain Tiber, his steely blue eyes locked onto the enemy, unceremoniously pulled the sword out of the King's attacker. The man instantly fell off his steed and died moments after hitting the ground. The captain gazed at the body sprawled upon the dried grass but was unable to evoke even a modicum of sympathy as he raced over to King Cedric to assist him.

"Let's move away and tend to your wound while the others clean up from this skirmish," he said, quickly examining the King's bloody arm and pointing northwest to a clear spot near the trees. "We must hurry before another wave engulfs us."

"Very well," King Cedric replied with a weak smile. "I'll let you bind my wound, but I'll return to the battle when I can."

"*If* you can," he said, sounding more like a son than a soldier serving under his command. "But rest assured as there are others here who will fight doubly hard to make up for your absence."

"I know they will." The King followed Captain Tiber through a narrow opening away from the several battles raging around them. "I wonder how they're faring on the other side of the field and along the lake."

"Since we're still standing, that's a good sign," Tiber replied. "So maybe things are not as grim as the sight of your wound. Now let me examine it more closely and bandage it with a strip of my cloak," he added as they neared a vacant patch near the trees. "Hurry. Time is pressing."

Though many on the battlefield had witnessed Captain Tiber's astounding maneuver, Ramsey wasn't one of them. He'd been engaged in another fight on foot with two dozen fellow warriors against a nearly equal force along the eastern tree line. Drogin's men had charged at them and soon all were engaged in one-on-one sword fights. The clatter of crossed blades ricocheted off the nearly leafless elms and beeches and the fragrant scattering of spruce trees and other evergreens. As the fighting progressed, individual conflicts took on lives of their own as the combatants moved north and south along the woods. Some took their fights into the trees or in small clearings among the towering pines and bony branches.

Ramsey was locked in a struggle with an Island soldier whose focused stare was as sharp as his sword smashing against Ramsey's weapon as the two backed into a thicket of trees. When Ramsey caught a glimpse of a soldier from Kargoth heading their way to assist his comrade, he knew he had only moments to act.

"It'll soon be two against one," the Islander muttered with satisfaction after glancing over his shoulder. "Would you rather die at my hands or face one of Vellan's spellbound slaves? Your choice."

The soldier ramped up his attack, hacking through the encroaching branches to get to his prey. Ramsey defiantly held off every swing with each backward step he took deeper into the trees. He smiled when the approaching fighter from Kargoth stumbled and landed face down upon the field, an arrow sticking out of his back.

"You'd better recalculate those odds," Ramsey said through labored breaths. "It's one against one again. No help from Vellan this time."

The Island soldier shifted his position as they fought so he could see behind him, irritated that his counterpart had been slain. In that brief distraction, Ramsey swung his sword forcefully to take down his opponent, yet the man was still too quick. He saw the blade coming chest-high and swerved sideways, avoiding a fatal blow. But Ramsey had attacked with such vigor that the top edge of his sword hit a slender tree and stuck in its bark. He couldn't dislodge his blade before the other man sprang at him. Ramsey had no choice but to leap backward to avoid a deadly swipe, desperately looking for a large stick to use as a weapon. With nothing to grab, he spun around to flee but tripped over a tree root, landing in agony upon his back. He scuttled backward on his hands and feet until a tree blocked his way. The Islander stepped forward, brandishing his weapon high with a victorious smile.

"There's nowhere to go now," he said.

Ramsey backed up against the trunk of a large beech, expecting to die beneath the tree's sprawling limbs as the remains of its golden-bronze foliage rustled in the breeze. He felt trapped like a wounded animal as the metal blade was poised over him. He looked up through the branches at the peaceful sky, waiting for the inevitable as the Islander towered above with the sword pointed downward. But Ramsey's attention was suddenly drawn away from the cobalt-blue heavens and the rich, white clouds drifting overhead. His eyes widened in surprise, not fully believing what he saw hidden among the branches. He quickly glanced down at his overconfident rival and sighed, offering a defeated smile.

"Well played, my friend."

"You fought bravely. I'll give you credit for that," he replied as he raised his sword higher, ready to bring the fight to its fatal conclusion. "May my words offer comfort upon your demise."

Ramsey grinned as he combed a hand through his mop of sweaty hair. "Perhaps," he replied, continuing to raise his hand until it was above his head, his fingers wide open. "But you know what? I don't need your empty words today."

With raindrop speed, a dagger fell from the tree, handle first, and landed in Ramsey's open palm as if conjured out of the air by magic. Before his foe comprehended what had happened, Ramsey locked his fingers around the hilt and flung the sharp blade at the soldier, lodging it squarely in his throat.

The stunned Islander floundered backward, wide-eyed and gasping for breath. The sword dropped from his hand as he frantically reached for the dagger. Light turned to darkness before his eyes as he collapsed to the ground, convulsing. Ramsey jumped up, grabbed the sword and ended his life with a swift stroke. With his heart pounding, he looked around through the security of the trees, happy to see that no one else had followed him into the woods. The harrowing sounds of warfare still reverberated outside the tree line. Assuming that all was safe for the moment, Ramsey stepped back beneath the large beech tree and gazed up through the branches again, still not believing his eyes. Sitting concealed upon a limb about a quarter of the way up the tree were two figures, both smiling down upon Ramsey after witnessing how he had escaped from certain doom.

"How in blazes did the two of you end up there?" he asked, more amused and amazed than angry.

"It's a long story, but I can give you a speedy version now," said one member of the excited duo. He climbed down the tree and hopped onto the ground as if merely playing outdoors near his home in Montavia. Prince William looked up at Ramsey, a trace of concern in his eyes. "But Aaron and I require your assistance first. We need to get to King Basil's estate."

"Why?" he asked as Aaron worked his way down.

"Because the woman in charge of the royal kitchen is a traitor!" Aaron uttered with disgust. "Nyla is a spy from Maranac."

"A spy?"

"And we know of others in her group, too," William added in desperation. "Though the war has already started, we can't let them get away after what they've done. Can you help us?"

Ramsey couldn't conceal a grin, happy to see the boys alive and well. "I'll see what I can do, considering the situation. But first I need to hear what happened. So commence with the speedy version, if you please."

Less than a quarter mile from King Basil's estate, a second battle ensued along the wooden docks and narrow, sandy shores of Lake LaShear. A row of tall ships from Maranac were anchored off the coast, each one topped with Drogin's flag snapping in the wind. Several skirmishes had also broken out in the streets of Melinas after a company of Drogin's men burst through Captain Silas' line, causing him to redirect some of his men to other locations. The clash of metal blades and the clinking of daggers were punctuated by the rhythmic waves along the beach. The sounds of warfare slowly spread out along narrow, cobblestone streets and among the trees and fallow gardens near hurriedly abandoned homes.

After waging two small battles during the initial assault, Silas and four of his men now paused briefly in a narrow alleyway to catch their breaths after their latest encounter. A half dozen of Drogin's troops lay dead around them. The captain gazed at their pallid, lifeless faces and then glanced out beyond the main street at the grim display of dead soldiers lying upon the sandy shore and slumped against the fishing shanties along the docks. He stood with his back against a stone, whitewashed building. Beads of sweat trickled down his forehead. A spattering of the enemy's blood stained his shirt beneath a tattered cloak.

Ranen stood across from him, equally exhausted yet prepared to throw himself into the next fight. "Things may look bleak, Captain Silas, but the day is still young." The piece of scarlet cloth usually fastened to Ranen's long, black hair was wrapped around his left wrist that an hour earlier had taken a stroke from an opponent's blade. But he had gotten the best of his attacker and bandaged his wound with the colorful cloth as the body of the enemy soldier lay dead at his feet.

"Do not confuse my silence for despair," Silas replied while assessing their next move. He peered out into the street with caution and then beyond to Lake LaShear where the fighting continued in spots along shore. "The way is clear for now," he whispered, addressing Ranen and the other three soldiers. He glanced at Ranen's injury. "With luck, maybe we can find a proper bandage for your hand along the way and dispose of that one." He grinned. "And perhaps a second one so you can tie up your hair again."

Ranen chuckled. "I'll accept a new bandage for my wrist, thank you, but this piece of red material was given to me by my wife before I departed the Oak Clearing to meet with King Cedric. She cut it from the hem of her favorite dress so I would remember her during my journey and in dark hours. It will stay with me always, bloodied or not. And I will wear it when I return home and see her smiling face, if that is my fate."

Captain Silas was touched by the comment. "You are a blessed man, Ranen, and I withdraw my suggestion," he replied. "May that simple memento bring us all good fortune this day." He stepped out of the shadows and looked into the street again, his attention drawn to the sounds of fresh fighting far to the left where a narrow thicket of trees bordered part of the shoreline. Silas retreated into the alleyway, his face flushed with concern.

"What'd you see?" one of his men anxiously asked.

"Another skirmish near the pines where Torr had stationed some of his men." The young captain thought for a moment. "If we make our way back down this alley and grab additional troops from the contingent we earlier passed near the common, we can circle around to the other side of the trees and surprise Drogin's men from behind. Torr will be surprised, too, but appreciative of our help."

"Let's move at once!" Ranen said with urgency, worried about his fellow leader of the Haystack Clearing. "Apparently my friend could use some of this luck, too," he added, holding up his injured wrist that sported the red bandage.

Captain Silas nodded as he and his men raced down the alley and made their way to the village green where a large group of soldiers was preparing to pursue some of Drogin's men farther into the city. He quickly explained the situation to a fellow captain and siphoned off a dozen troops to go with them to Torr's aid. Soon after, they snaked their way through a few more side streets to a point just beyond the fighting, then circled back along a thin stretch of woods and entered the trees, their blades drawn and their footsteps swift and silent. The din of sword fighting and the shouts and grunts of tired but determined men drifted through the pine boughs upon a sharp, bitter breeze. With a signal from Captain Silas, the group of seventeen soldiers burst through the tree line and scrambled toward the fighting down a short stretch of sand riddled with dead bodies, the enemy's back facing them. There were nearly fifty men already engaged in the skirmish, with Torr's group slightly outnumbered.

Suddenly Captain Silas and his dogged troops erupted in shouts of defiance, their whirling swords bearing down on Drogin's astonished men as some turned around to face the surprise assault. Torr and his men broke into smiles of triumph, and with their hope renewed, continued their attack on the enemy now from both directions. Soon their adversaries were overwhelmed in this one tiny piece of the war, though the greater conflict continued to churn away like a violent storm. Yet despite some minor injuries, for a brief moment Captain Silas, Ranen, Torr and their fellow combatants savored a small victory near the edge of the blue lake waters, their spirit and confidence bolstered.

But their jubilation was short lived.

Ranen's smile slowly disappeared when he glanced north up the lakeshore. His heart froze and his fingers tightened around the hilt of his sword. Captain Silas and a few others couldn't help but notice the swift change in his demeanor.

"What troubles you?" he asked, looking in the same direction. But he didn't need a response from Ranen, instantly seeing the problem for himself.

Slowly drifting down the lake and hugging the western shoreline were dozens of wooden rafts that presumably had been made near the north tip of the lake by their allies from the kingdom of Altaga. Captain Silas hadn't expected to see any of those rafts after Irabesh claimed that Drogin had sent troops to confront and defeat them. But now the rafts had shown up anyway, each one loaded with soldiers, some heading for the shoreline, others to the docks and several more toward the tall ships. What shocked him most, however, was that all the vessels bore the flag of Drogin. The dreary banners in shades of orange, black and brown fluttered in the breeze as the soldiers diligently paddled the rafts to their designated landing points.

NICHOLAS RAVEN AND THE WIZARDS' WEB - VOLUME 2

Ranen sighed as he glanced at the others, rubbing his neck as a wave of lethargy swept over his aching body. "Well, I guess we have another battle or two on our hands," he remarked, watching the rafts draw nearer. "Only question is—which one do we go to first?"

Ramsey, in the meantime, hiked along the edge of the eastern woods with William and Aaron trailing him like shadows. William explained how Bosh had kidnapped them with information supplied by Nyla. He sadly admitted that he had revealed King Basil's war plans because Bosh had threatened Aaron's life. Aaron excitedly detailed their clever escape from the barn early yesterday morning.

"We were lost in the woods for a time since we didn't want to stay on the road for fear of being captured," William continued. "We accidentally overslept after stopping by a stream to have a bite to eat. Just before twilight, we emerged near a large field filled with soldiers from Maranac, Kargoth and the Northern Isles and realized we had been traveling in the wrong direction."

"You saw the very troops we're battling now," Ramsey said.

"Needless to say, we crept back into the woods and turned north, heading in this direction as quickly as we could, even traveling at night until we couldn't take another step because of hunger and exhaustion." William shook his head, feeling he had made a complete shambles of the situation. "By the time we arrived here this morning, the war had already started. Had I been better armed with more than a dagger, I would have joined you on the battlefield, though what good I would have done is debatable."

"You saved my life, Will, and perhaps that is what fate had in store for you," Ramsey said. "Now it is my turn to help you get to King Basil's estate and expose Nyla and her cohorts."

"Thank you," he softly replied, still upset about what he had told Bosh. He wondered if he had made the right decision now that war swirled about them. Maybe by sacrificing his and Aaron's lives he could have prevented the current bedlam now raging around them.

"You made a choice you thought was best," Ramsey assured him in a fatherly manner. "No one will fault you for that. And even if you hadn't said anything to Bosh, chances are that this war would still be fought, only perhaps farther south and across the lake. Blood was going to be shed regardless. But we can debate that later," he said as he slowed down and made for the edge of the trees. "I think I see what we need."

"What?" Aaron whispered, fearing that they were about to step onto the field of battle and face Drogin's troops that instant.

"A horse," Ramsey replied. "Several, in fact. We must move fast while this section of the tree line is free of the enemy."

They stepped out onto a grassy spot where five stray horses had gathered away from the fighting to feed on the sparse vegetation and calm their frazzled nerves. Ramsey smiled at their good fortune and climbed on one of the steeds and held out a hand to boost Aaron up so he could ride behind him. Prince William mounted another horse and soon the trio sped off, keeping in the thinning shadows of the tree line as they galloped northward. But moments later the sound of other rumbling horse hooves reverberated through the ground behind them and to their left, growing closer by the second. Ramsey feared they had been spotted by one of Drogin's men. As he shot a backward glance, his troubled heart settled when he recognized a familiar face. He slowed down, signaling for William to do likewise.

"I had lost sight of you near the woods earlier while I was fighting elsewhere," Eucádus called out as his horse approached his friend's steed. "And by then I–" He suddenly went silent when recognizing the two figures who were riding with Ramsey. An ecstatic grin filled his face.

"I'm delighted to see you again as well," William said before he was forced to give an even speedier version of the events that had happened to him and Aaron over the last few days.

"Then onward to the King's estate–and swiftly!" Eucádus cried as their horses again took flight. "I will ride with you to the end of this tree line so I may briefly view the events along Lake LaShear. Your way to the estate will be unhindered past that point as the clash with Drogin's southern forces has remained confined to this field. We are giving them a harder fight than I guess they suspected. Now my heart will be less troubled when I return to battle knowing that you are both safe."

"But Irabesh said there is another mass of soldiers waiting behind the first line," Ramsey reminded him. "So be on the lookout."

"I will!" Eucádus promised as he reined his horse to a stop as the trees to his right thinned out and the lake appeared in view. The other two steeds galloped onward at full speed, growing smaller against the horizon. "And may we meet again soon," he whispered to himself after they disappeared like a swift breeze.

Eucádus gazed across the sparkling waters of Lake LaShear in the near distance. He viewed the frenetic movement of troops along the shore and heard the faint echoes of deadly battle, yet couldn't be sure where the balance of power had shifted from this single glance. But when he looked to the northeast, his jaw slowly dropped as he witnessed the steady flow of rafts that Ranen was also observing at that same moment. He noted with dismay the colors of Drogin's flags that appeared like a cluster of dark, ominous eyes floating upon the water. His spirits, for a moment standing upon joyous heights because of William and Aaron's safe return, now plummeted at the heartbreaking sight. Eucádus knew that this day was not even close to being over. With a deep and troubled sigh, he turned around and charged headlong back into battle.

CHAPTER 66

The Second Wave

Eucádus galloped into a whirlwind of combat shortly after he had left Ramsey, William and Aaron. Foot soldiers from Kargoth had regrouped near the western trees and charged eastward where Jeremias and his men had just finished battling a dozen Islanders. Eucádus, sensing his friends' exhaustion and seeing they would soon be outnumbered, quickly rounded up as many riders as he could to crash through the storm heading their way.

Moments later, beneath blue skies peppered with drifting white clouds, he and ten men from King Basil's ranks directed their horses south into the maelstrom. They attacked the enemy from the saddle, bringing down their blades with harsh sweeps and deadly thrusts upon their bewildered opponents who now had to combat both skilled horsemen and those on foot.

"Better late than never!" Jeremias called out when Eucádus flew by on his steed and took down a tall soldier from Kargoth. The vague, gray cloudiness in the dying man's eyes faded away as his body collapsed upon the sun-soaked ground.

"One less stinger gnat!" he quipped.

Jeremias glanced at the dead soldier before moving on, nearly convinced that he was looking at a different man than the one who tried to attack him moments ago. The native of Kargoth now seemed at peace with himself and the world. Jeremias wondered if the person had fully realized where he had been or what he had been doing these last several days in the moments before he died, all because of Vellan's handiwork.

"Look out!" Eucádus shouted to Jeremias and a captain from Rhiál who were raising swords together against a trio of enemy soldiers. A fourth man from Drogin's army bounded toward them from behind, his dagger poised to strike.

Jeremias spun around and boldly charged at the surprised attacker and killed him with a single stroke of his blade, freeing the man from Vellan's mesmerizing grip. At that moment, one of the three enemy fighters broke away and darted toward Jeremias with revenge on his mind, but Jeremias expected as much. He swooped down, grabbed the dead man's dagger and flung it at the Kargoth soldier, hitting him squarely in the chest. The wounded man froze for an instant as if he had crashed into an invisible wall. He reeled backward several steps, teetering on the verge of collapse. But a passionate devotion to Vellan sustained him for a few more fleeting moments. With crazed bravado, he gripped the knife and yanked it from his body, preparing to launch it back with his remaining strength. But Jeremias leaped up at that moment, wildly charged and plunged his sword into the enemy, killing him on the spot.

When he looked up, his face sweaty and caked with dust, he watched as a rider accompanying Eucádus slew the remaining soldier battling the captain from Rhiál. Moments earlier, the captain himself had conquered the other one with two swift strokes to his foe's shoulder and midsection. But despite the arrival of Eucádus and his men, Jeremias realized there was no time to rest after this small victory. More soldiers from Kargoth zeroed in on them. He shifted sideways to avoid a charging horse that brushed past and then ran back toward the skirmish. But as the dust settled, his pounding heart froze at the sight unfolding in the near distance.

As fighting continued on both foot and horseback amid a clamor of bloody blades and harsh cries, Irabesh suddenly appeared against the chaotic background. He slowly rode in on his black steed, a bow and arrow poised at the ready. An unsuspecting Eucádus, busily engaged in combat, was targeted in his line of sight. Jeremias, running in full stride and without a moment to spare, reached the side of his friend's horse and leaped up, grabbing Eucádus by the arm and pulling him off just as Irabesh's arrow was released.

Eucádus tumbled over the side, losing his sword but still clutching onto the reins.

He jumped to his feet at once, rattled but unscathed, surprised to see Jeremias lying on the ground on his side. He wondered what his friend had just done to him and why. The blood in Eucádus' veins grew cold and his mind reeled when his eyes locked onto the orange, brown and black feather fletching at the end of the arrow protruding from Jeremias' back. The young man slowly looked up at Eucádus, his eyes glassy, his face pale. He whispered two words with passion.

"Get him."

The request from his dying friend hit Eucádus hard. When he looked up and saw Irabesh drawing closer and reaching for a second arrow from his quiver, he understood what his friend wished of him.

"I will," he whispered back, his emotions in check until he grabbed his sword on the trampled grass. Eucádus sprang toward Irabesh, crying out like a crazed madman while still holding onto Chestnut's reins.

Irabesh saw the ferocious zeal in Eucádus' eyes as if the charging man were a wild beast that couldn't be stopped. He abandoned his bow and pulled a sword from its sheath, raising it just as Eucádus barreled down upon him, swinging his blade through the air while controlling Chestnut with the other hand. Their swords clashed with deathly force, again and again as other battles raged around them.

"You'll join your dead comrades when I topple you from that horse," Eucádus uttered with contempt. As Irabesh looked down with haughty confidence, Eucádus stepped adroitly about him. Their swords danced in the warming autumn air as the sun climbed higher in the southern sky.

"You will be joining *your* friend!" Irabesh replied, his clouded eyes looking down like death itself.

But Eucádus only grew more incensed with Irabesh's smug attitude and his slavish devotion to Vellan. As their cold blades continued to cross, Eucádus recognized the hatred each of them had for the other, yet when he looked into his enemy's dull eyes, he sensed nothing from Irabesh but an irrational loathing and an unquenchable lust for power. He knew that he couldn't let this man win, not after what he had done to Jeremias or what evil he was planning on Vellan's behalf throughout Laparia.

"Let's put an end to this now!" Irabesh bellowed. "You know your side cannot win. The second wave is on its way."

"Whether we win or not is yet to be decided," Eucádus said between deep, long-held breaths as he battled on, swinging his sword yet being blocked by Irabesh at every stroke. "But I agree on one point–it's time to end this!"

After forcefully striking Irabesh's blade one last time, causing his foe to lean back upon impact, Eucádus swiftly took a step backward. He loosened his hold on Chestnut's reins and shouted at the horse. The steed suddenly reared up on its hind legs just as Irabesh extended his arm forward and sliced his sword through the air. Chestnut's right hoof struck Irabesh's wrist and shattered it, knocking the sword from his hand. Irabesh grabbed the injured arm to his chest and cried out in pain, his head snapping back as he gazed up at the sky in blistering agony. Eucádus lunged forward and thrust his sword upward through his opponent's midsection with all his might. Irabesh felt the paralyzing sting of cold metal shoot through him and repeatedly gasped for a breath of air that wouldn't fill his lungs. His head fell heavily forward to his chest and he looked helplessly at Eucádus, his expression neither smug nor bitter nor remorseful, but simply one of utter disbelief.

Eucádus, sweating and breathing heavily, gazed at Irabesh with disgust before ripping his sword out of the man with a swift stroke, sending him sliding off his horse to the cold ground. As the life quickly drained out of his adversary, he watched Irabesh's eyes slowly begin to clear and his tight facial features soften ever slightly.

"*The second wave...*" Irabesh whispered, his voice hoarse and defiant to the very end. "*They are...on their way.*" His eyes closed for the last time as death overtook him less than a mile from King Basil's estate.

"And we'll be waiting," Eucádus replied before hurrying over to Jeremias who lay on the ground close to death.

Eucádus gripped his friend's hand and stroked his cold forehead. The two horses standing nearby partially shielded them from the sights and sounds of the fighting, but for the moment, neither man seemed aware that warfare raged around them. Jeremias looked up, his light brown eyes losing their luster as he resigned himself to death. He tried to smile as the pain slowly faded from his body. Eucádus smiled back, his heart breaking as he looked upon the dying man who had led the Fox Clearing with distinction, the youngest of the five leaders.

"Tell my dear Rebecca...that I love her," he whispered with great effort, his throat dry as he tried to swallow. "That I will *always* love her."

"I will," Eucádus replied, pillowing Jeremias' head in his hand. "That is a promise, my friend."

"I'll wait for her in the afterworld and..."

Jeremias said no more, his eyelids slowly closing as a final breath left his body. Eucádus looked upon him grief-stricken and gently let his head rest upon the ground, yet a growing anger simmered inside that would erupt as soon as he rejoined the battle. He looked up wearily at his horse and forced himself to his feet, reluctant to rejoin the fray but knowing he must as the din and clamor of war again registered in his ears. A nearby clash of swords caught his eyes and he automatically unsheathed his weapon, prepared to do his part amid such crushing sorrow. Protecting Jeremias' body from the onslaught of battle would have to wait. Something else then caught his attention. Eucádus looked south toward the low ridge less than a half mile away.

As if life were replaying itself from the moment when the heavy, white fog lifted this morning, there again upon the crest between the east and west tree lines were several long rows of soldiers upon horseback, one behind the other. The drab flags of King Drogin were scattered among them and waved tauntingly in the breeze. Behind the horse lines were countless rows of foot soldiers, mere specks against the sun-soaked backdrop, but armed and at the ready as they slowly advanced as a single unit. Eucádus sighed in despair as did all the other soldiers in King Basil's army scattered across the field. The forces of Drogin, however, stayed their swords momentarily and cheered on the new army's arrival, confident that victory was close at hand.

Eucádus couldn't help thinking so as well, knowing that the second wave of enemy fighters both on the field and floating down Lake LaShear would be impossible to counter with their remaining forces. He glanced down at Jeremias' body, suddenly doubting that he would ever get the chance to relay his friend's final heartfelt message to his wife. That, of all things occurring on this dreadful day, hurt Eucádus the most as a tear rolled down his cheek in the harsh sunlight of early afternoon.

William, in the meantime, arrived at King Basil's estate with Ramsey and Aaron. Soldiers were stationed behind the low, stone wall surrounding the building and at the front gate. The appearance of the two horses and their riders caused an immediate stir. Most were aware of William and Aaron's disappearance and many had participated in the search parties along the docks. The three visitors were allowed through the gate immediately, though the captain in charge was eager to know where the two boys had been, relieved to see them alive and well. It was a refreshing bit of news against the backdrop of fighting along the lake, though many expected the battle to sweep this way soon now that enemy reinforcements had arrived.

"We have little time to spare to tell our story," Prince William informed the captain, "but if you and a small contingent of guards would accompany us to the King's kitchen, I will explain the most relevant parts on the way."

"The kitchen?" the captain asked. "Is the Prince of Montavia hungry?"

"Nearly starving," he replied. "As is Aaron."

"But neither is here for a meal," Ramsey jumped in. He leaned down and whispered a few words into the captain's ear. The man's eyes widened when he learned of Nyla's complicity in the boys' disappearance and swiftly summoned three soldiers.

"Accompany me and our guests to the estate at once!" he ordered his men before addressing Ramsey. "We will gladly assist."

The captain and his men guided the horses to the front entrance where William, Ramsey and Aaron dismounted and followed the soldiers inside. The large flag of Rhiál suspended from an upper window was awash in intermittent sunshine and shadows as it fluttered in the breezes off the lake. They hurried to the corridor leading to the main kitchen where Nyla was usually busy at work with her cooking staff this time of day. Just before they arrived, the captain sent two of the three soldiers down another hallway, whispering brief instructions. The third soldier remained with him.

When they neared the kitchen, a pair of wooden doors at the main entrance was wide open to allow the excess heat to escape during lunch preparations. The sound of bubbling kettles, clattering dishes and workers' conversations drifted into the corridor. William requested that he and Aaron be allowed to confront Nyla on their own, so Ramsey, the captain and the additional soldier remained a few steps back.

"We'll linger close behind," Ramsey promised, uneasy about how Nyla might react if she thought she was cornered.

"We'll be fine," Aaron replied. "I want to see her face when she sees us. I'm guessing that she hasn't had contact with Bosh and her other associates since we were kidnapped, so she has no reason to suspect we know that she was involved. I look forward to our reunion."

Ramsey smirked, admitting to himself that the boys deserved at least this little moment to themselves before Nyla was arrested. "You'd better get going," he said. "We still have a war to fight."

They nodded before walking into the warm kitchen where two large fireplaces burned with crackling oak logs stacked in pyramids. A large iron kettle filled with water was near boiling as it hung above one of the blazes. Another kettle in the second fireplace simmered with the tantalizing aroma of beef stew. A multitude of stone ovens built inside the brick walls released a scent of freshly baking bread and biscuits. Oil lamps attached to the walls provided extra illumination to the large room. Barrels of warm, sudsy water were lined up against a far wall near a pantry where workers washed dishes and rinsed them off in another barrel of clear rain water. A constant chatter of voices rose above the snapping flames, clattering plates and rhythmic knives dancing upon the chopping boards. As Aaron led William to the center of the room, happy to be back in King Basil's royal kitchen, he spotted Nyla near a far counter. His heart filled with disappointment for the woman he had once given both his trust and respect.

"There she is," he pointed, whispering to William who saw her speaking to a member of her staff behind a veil of herb bundles hanging from the rafters. But before William could reply, a few of the other busy workers suddenly noticed that their long lost co-worker had finally returned.

"Aaron!" blurted out an older, teenage girl who was slicing fresh carrots. She dropped her knife on the cutting board and ran over to him, wrapping her arms around the young boy. "Where have you been? We thought you might be dead."

"And I'm happy to see you, too," he muttered, trying to catch a breath as he pried himself out of her arms.

"Nyla, look who's back!" another voice shouted as the excited staff gathered around Aaron and Prince William.

"What's all the commotion?" Nyla's voice crackled as she stepped around the drying herbs. "We have meals to prepare for some hungry–" Her dark eyes locked onto Aaron and William with ballooning astonishment, and for a moment she was speechless.

"Nyla, we found our way back!" Aaron exclaimed as if he had greatly missed her, a huge smile upon his face. William played along as if delighted to see her.

"I can't believe it," she replied, smiling nervously and exuding exaggerated relief as she fidgeted with the white, cloth cap covering her dark locks. "What a wonderful surprise. How did you get here? And more importantly, where have you been?"

"You may not believe this, ma'am," Prince William said with all seriousness, "but Aaron and I were kidnapped along the docks by some men three nights ago. By whom, we're not sure, but we barely managed to escape with our lives yesterday morning."

"What a terrible ordeal!" she uttered, somewhat relieved after the prince admitted that he didn't know who had committed the crime. "Do you know where these men are? Did you tell the guards? Did you tell King Basil?"

"Prince William and I plan to go into town with one of the captains and some of his men if the fighting subsides and show them where we were held," Aaron said before sighing despondently. "But I don't think it will do any good. Now that we've escaped, they may have fled the city."

"Well you're safe and back in my kitchen where you belong, Aaron. I'm extremely grateful for that," Nyla replied. "And you, too, Prince William. I shudder to think what a loss to Montavia it would be had you been injured–or worse."

"Thank you, ma'am."

"Now as long as you're here, how about a meal? Both of you look famished!" Nyla carried on in a motherly sort of way, leading the two boys to a wooden table in the far corner of the room. "Berta, ladle out some stew for these fine lads and round up some bread and butter. Cornelius, two cups of fresh milk from the jug over there. Hurry now!"

"You're too kind," Aaron replied as he and William took their seats. "Do you want me to return to work after I eat?"

"Nonsense!" she responded with an uneasy laugh. "You're entitled to a few days off. Now sit and enjoy your meal," she said as Berta and Cornelius darted about with their dishes, utensils and food. "In the meantime, I must scurry off on important business. I'll return shortly," she said, removing her cap and tossing it upon a counter.

"Where are you going?" Aaron asked as if saddened to see her leave.

Nyla juggled several excuses in her mind. "To meet with one of the King's advisors, of course, and discuss this terrible ordeal that has affected one of my best workers," she finally said, tapping him lightly on the shoulder as she brushed by and hastened toward the door. But when she stepped into the corridor, she was startled to see Ramsey and two of the King's men standing there. "May I help you, gentlemen?" she asked, her heart beating rapidly.

"We're waiting for Aaron and Prince William," the captain informed her. "We'll be escorting them back for more questioning to get to the root of this matter."

"That's very thorough of you," she replied. "Would you like something to eat while you wait?"

"No, ma'am," Ramsey replied. "We're fine, thank you."

"In that case, I won't bother you. It's a terrible thing what happened to those boys. I hope you apprehend the perpetrators quickly." Nyla nodded sharply as she prepared to scoot down the hallway. "I only wish I could be there when you catch them."

"Then you should join us," Ramsey added, holding out a hand and stopping Nyla from passing by him. "Aaron mentioned that you were like a mother to him, so it's only fitting that you should be there when we catch these rogues. Shall I escort you to your room so you can get a cloak? I'm sure it's chilly by the lake."

"No need," she calmly replied, taking a step back. "I just happen to have one in the kitchen. I'll get it right now."

She turned around and hurried back inside the warm kitchen, though her face was already flush and burning up. She shot past the other workers and headed toward a back doorway far from the bustle in the main section of the kitchen. She pushed the door open and muttered in frustration, knowing she had to flee the estate before her cover was blown. But as soon as she stepped though the opening, Nyla found her way blocked again. Standing there were the other two soldiers the captain had sent on ahead.

"Going somewhere?" one of them asked.

"Please step out of my way. I have much work to do," she brusquely replied.

"You'll get to your room much quicker through the front corridor," Aaron said.

Nyla spun around and saw Aaron and Prince William standing there, baffled as to why they weren't eating at the table. "Who said I'm going to..." Slowly, Ramsey and the captain stepped around the corner and stood behind Aaron and William, their arms folded and their expressions stern. "... my room?" Nyla swallowed hard, her eyes shifting, her breathing constricted.

"My guess is that you were planning to leave the estate," William replied. "Though how you'd manage to get past all the guards is beyond me."

"Why would I do that?" Nyla said with an uneasy laugh.

"Perhaps to meet up with your husband?" Aaron suggested.

Nyla flinched. "But I'm not married," she replied, scrunching up her face in feigned confusion.

Aaron smirked. "I believe his name is Bosh. And frankly, he's not a very pleasant man to hang around with. Trust me."

Nyla held up a hand to her mouth, too stunned to speak as her imagined world under Drogin's rule slowly crumbled around her.

"Nyla, it's time you had a nice, long conversation with some of King Basil's advisors," the captain said as William, Aaron and Ramsey looked on with nearly identical smirks. "I think you'll have much to talk about."

William, Aaron and Ramsey left the estate shortly after Nyla had been led away. The two boys had earlier provided directions to the building where they were kidnapped, and as best they could remember, indicated where the farmhouse was located where they had been held. Troops would be sent to both places to apprehend Bosh and his associates if they were still there.

"King Basil will have to replace Nyla," Aaron commented as they stepped into the breezy sunlight filtering through a handful of trees swaying in the breezes off the water.

"That will be the least of his problems," William said as he gazed at the lake and the field to the south. "I'd like to visit with him if possible, though I suppose he's occupied with more important matters right now."

"I'm sure word will be sent to him about your and Aaron's return," Ramsey assured him as they walked to where their steeds were tied up. But before William could reply, a soldier on horseback who had just been speaking to one of the guards near the front gate sauntered over to the trio, nodding his head in greeting.

"Prince William, I am Yurris, part of a relay running messages and updates to King Basil in his tent," he said, indicating where the King was keeping his watch. "A short while ago he was talking to me about you and a boy named Aaron who had been missing. One of the guards at the gate pointed both of you out after I heard a rumor that you had returned."

"It is no rumor. And we are fine," William replied. "When you return, please tell King Basil so and thank him for his concern."

"Better yet, you can thank him yourself if you accompany me back to his tent," he said. "I'm leaving now and am certain that your presence would do the King's spirits a world of good. His physical condition has taken a turn for the worse these last few hours. Your absence has weighed heavily on his mind." Yurris noted a flash of concern across Ramsey's countenance. "I assure you that it is quite safe there, still far enough away from the battle and well guarded."

"Aaron and I have been through our share of trouble and are not intimidated by the nearness of the conflict," William said.

Aaron looked at Ramsey, a slight smirk upon his face. "Just ask Ramsey. He can vouch for that after our recent encounter with him in the woods."

"I suppose I can," Ramsey replied, realizing that the two boys would probably be as safe there as here on the estate. "Still, watch yourself. With Drogin's troops gaining reinforcements on the water, his army might push this way at any time. You should be–"

Suddenly, Ramsey and many of the soldiers standing nearby grew quiet, their gazes cast far down the field at the low ridge between the trees. With troubled hearts, they saw that a second wave

400

of enemy soldiers had arrived. The flags of Drogin multiplied on both land and water in the last few minutes, snapping in the breeze as if announcing Rhiál's imminent destruction. William's mouth was agape at the sobering sight, wondering if their march across the plains to liberate this nation had been in vain.

"What do we do now?" Aaron asked in dismay.

"We will visit the King," William replied, remembering how he had fled from Arileez rather than confronting him in the cabin. He vowed not to run away again in the face of danger. "Now is not the time to be faint of heart. If I am to die here today, I'd just as soon do it standing beside King Basil rather than cowering in his estate."

Aaron stood tall and looked him in the eyes. "As would I, so I'll follow you to the King's tent."

"And I shall return to the battle," Ramsey said. "I've tarried here long enough and will ride back before Eucádus and King Cedric think I have deserted them." He shook hands with William and Aaron and told them that it was his greatest wish that he should see the two of them alive and well again before the day was done. "But fate and a skillfully wielded sword will decide that, so until then, I must be off. Watch them closely, Yurris."

"I guarantee it, sir," he replied.

Ramsey mounted his steed and trotted out the front gate, galloping down the field like the wind itself. William climbed on his horse shortly after, with Aaron sitting behind him. They followed Yurris to the outer road and across the field to King Basil's tent, wondering if the lands of Laparia were about to fall into an abyss of death and despair.

At that same moment, Ranen and Captain Silas looked on as the fleet of rafts moved down the lake closer to shore, contemplating their next move. Their battered forces were already spread thin, and any new effort, they feared, would at best be for show. They had had a realistic chance to defeat Drogin when dawn first broke, though the odds for victory were slim. But with these new arrivals, the arithmetic had shifted dramatically, and not in their favor.

"They move like an army of ants toward the sand, docks and tall ships," Silas remarked as he watched the rafts and fluttering flags with dread. "The day Drogin was born must have been cursed, infecting his mind and soul with a poison I cannot comprehend."

"And he has carried that scourge with him to this very hour," Ranen replied, also mesmerized in a melancholy fashion by the small armada floating upon the choppy waters.

"But we'll fight to the end no matter what he throws at us," Silas continued, his eyes still fixed upon the water as if trying to calculate any way imaginable to repel such an invincible force. He looked at his men as if they were his own brothers, offering a gentle smile wavering precariously between hope and resignation.

"What have you decided, captain?" one of the younger soldiers asked while nervously drumming his fingertips on the hilt of his sheathed sword.

"Though few in number, we will proudly meet the enemy on our shore and give them the fight of their lives," he replied. "I see some of our allies now massing near the docks for their fight. Ours will be on the sandy strip over there." He pointed to an open stretch of water well beyond the narrow, tree-lined ribbon of beach that they now occupied. "Others, I suppose, will join us when they can."

"*If* they can," someone gravely commented. "The fighting has been horrific all through the city of Melinas from what reports I heard earlier near the common."

A grin spread across Ranen's face. "Then let's do something great to generate rumors of our own!" he exclaimed, energetically jabbing his finger in the air. "If others see us charging forth, regardless of the outcome, maybe we'll strengthen their spirits and spur on our fellow soldiers during this last stand. Our labors must count for something when all is over, whether we live to see the results or not."

Ranen unsheathed his sword and raised it high in the air with an enthusiastic cry, persuading his comrades to do the same until a raucous explosion of voices rose above the trees and the gusting wind. The edges of their swords flashed in the sunlight, the metal tips clattering against one another in a deafening chorus. Soldiers engaged in skirmishes nearby on both sides of the conflict couldn't help but hear the echoes of the rousing words floating upon the breeze and witness the energetic alliance of men celebrating near the trees. Their fellow countrymen took comfort from the scene while the enemy responded with silence, their thoughts laced with scorn and mockery as they anticipated an impending victory.

"Onward!" Captain Silas ordered as his men gathered in loose formation behind him and Ranen, aiming their swords defiantly at their destination. "Let us reach the edge of the water before their first raft touches the sandy bottom. We'll give them a welcome they will not soon forget!"

They burst forward out of the thin tree shadows onto the warmer, open coastline, their voices rising to thunderous heights. They charged like angry bulls toward the water's blue edge as mini explosions of sand erupted beneath the stampede of heavy, travel-worn boots buffeting the shore. With swords waving and spirits soaring, for a moment or two the men thought that they could take on every last soldier sailing upon the rafts despite their overwhelming numbers. Yet as they drew closer to the edge of Lake LaShear, traces of doubt burrowed into the minds and hearts of a handful of the men, momentarily weakening the bond between them. But every last warrior fought through the uncertainties and plowed onward to the white-crested waves slapping against the shoreline, triumphantly arriving at the water's edge before the first raft had landed.

"Come at us if you dare!" a soldier shouted out to the men while brandishing his sword above his head, stepping into the lake as the low waves broke against his high, black boots and washed away the dirt and blood that had caked upon them since early morning.

"The forces of Drogin are not welcome here!" another man hollered across the water as he stabbed his sword into the wet sand. "We'll gladly demonstrate what we mean if you would draw but a little closer."

"Oh, they will," Silas remarked as he stared across the lake, his jaw fixed and his expression granite hard as a fine mist off the waves did little to cool his passion for a final stand against the enemy. He looked askance at Ranen as his fingers tightened around the hilt of his sword. "If there was ever a time to call forth the blessings and good fortune of your wife's keepsake, now would be that time."

Ranen grinned as his long, black locks blew in the refreshing breeze. He held up his left hand for all to see, still bandaged with the red piece of material from his wife's dress. "I have been doing so from the moment we started our run toward the water," he answered as the rafts in the fleet heading there closed in fast. "Now let us see what fruit my silent petitions will bear in the coming moments."

"We'll gladly accept any fruit, ripened or not," the captain said as another wave washed over their waterlogged boots. He was already playing out in his mind a moving picture of the first soldiers leaping off the rafts several paces from the shoreline and charging at them through the water with unbridled fury.

But before Silas could speak further, he froze, his mouth agape at a curious sight beginning to play out before him. He raked his fingers in disbelief through his shortly cropped hair drenched with sweat and lake water, unable to utter a word. The same dumbfounded expression enveloped each of his companions as they watched the perplexing event unfold upon the water. In the blink of an eye, the orange, brown and black flags of Drogin had suddenly disappeared from the flotilla approaching shore as well as from those rafts nearing the docks and the ships anchored farther away. Seconds later, a scattering of blue, silver and white banners from Arrondale unfurled above the heads of the distant soldiers who held them proudly aloft in the stirring breeze, the kingdom's emblem snapping in unison upon the cool lake winds.

"Am I alone in witnessing this display?" Captain Silas asked, still stunned in a dreamlike state. His fingers slowly loosened their grip on his sword.

"No, you are not alone!" cried a soldier from Rhiál standing next to him with a smile on his face that outshone the sun drifting among the white clouds overhead. "Those aren't Drogin's troops, sir. They're King Justin's men—but how and why I can't begin to say."

"None of us can," Ranen replied, "yet I'll happily speculate about their mysterious arrival until I learn the particulars."

Silas nodded in agreement, and for a moment, he simply smiled as a tear rolled down his face, not knowing whether to laugh or cry or shout out with joy. He turned to Ranen who caught his gaze and mirrored his boyish grin.

"Do not lose that strip of material!" he joked. "*Ever.*"

"I shall wash it in this very water and treasure it in my house when I return to Harlow," Ranen replied, now confident that he would again see the land of his birth when this battle was finally concluded, and more importantly, his wife.

Suddenly, boisterous shouts of triumph and welcome erupted from the rest of Captain Silas' men. The rafts drew nearer to shore, now close enough so that they could see the faces and smiles of those on board, knowing beyond a doubt that their allies had at last arrived. Soon armed soldiers from Arrondale jumped from the rafts while several feet from shore and stormed onto the beach amid white-capped waves and splashes of water. They had paddled down the lake on rafts built by King Basil's secret allies in Altaga to the north, the very rafts that the King's troops would have used for their predawn raid across the water in Zaracosa had things gone according to plan.

The new arrivals greeted their fellow warriors with heartfelt shouts, handshakes and hugs as a similar scene played out upon the docks, all to the horror of Drogin's troops who saw their inevitable victory turn to sudden disaster. New battles soon raged upon the shore, the docks and among the city streets, only this time the soldiers from Maranac, Kargoth and the Northern Isles were vastly outnumbered and swiftly overwhelmed by the prowess of refreshed troops from Arrondale and the renewed strength of their rivals from earlier in the day. Especially challenging were the several battles waged for the control of the tall ships where many lives were lost in grueling, close quarters combat on and below the decks. But victory was slowly and at last achieved. And as the fighting commenced in the city, with soldiers running here and there to put down the last of the skirmishes, the men of Rhiál and their allies from the west learned in bits and pieces how King Justin's men had miraculously arrived from the north tip of the lake in such grand fashion.

Days before, when King Justin and one half of his army had finally left Morrenwood for Rhiál–the other half preparing to march east to liberate Montavia–he had sent scouts ahead to consult with King Basil. When the scouts returned, King Justin was informed that forces from Rhiál were going to participate in two secret attacks, one on the fleet at Zaracosa using rafts and the other in the southern provinces. King Justin dispatched a third of his troops to the northern tip of Lake LaShear to join in the raft raiding party, knowing that such a daring attack would be dangerous and would need all the support it could muster. He realized that lessening the size of his already slim army would be a risk, but a necessary one.

But the gamble had paid off. The soldiers from Arrondale arrived at the northern tip of the lake just as Drogin's troops had begun their surprise attack on the men from Altaga who were readying their rafts for King Basil's soldiers who would never show up. And since Drogin's overconfidence caused him to send only a small force north, the troops from Arrondale had little trouble defeating them with help from the Altagans.

Fortunately, the rafts had not been destroyed. A new plan was quickly devised since everyone realized that Drogin must have learned of King Basil's forthcoming offensive. After confiscating the enemy's weapons and flags, the men of Arrondale made their way down the coast as if they were soldiers from Maranac, knowing the deception would fool Drogin's forces and buy them precious time until they could make their landing.

In the meantime, King Justin considered how to best make use of his remaining men, wondering if their trust would diminish as they watched a third of their comrades-in-arms leave before the main battle had even begun. He wondered how effective his army would be as it traversed the last weary miles on the outskirts of Melinas. It was now the same morning that Drogin's army had materialized in the cold, ghostly fog on the low ridge south of King Basil's estate.

It was after the parley with Irabesh had concluded that King Basil sent out two scouts to alert King Justin, hoping that his army was drawing near. King Justin was shocked by the news of the enemy's surprise arrival, prepared to lead his remaining men to Melinas as fast as he could though knowing they would arrive late to the fighting. But after the scouts told him that a second wave of Drogin's men was gathering deeper in the south behind the front lines, his thinking suddenly changed.

He learned that the second wave was composed primarily of men from Maranac whose loyalty to Drogin was based on fear and intimidation rather than true devotion. King Justin wondered if his reduced forces might do more good battling the fewer, hardnosed Drogin loyalists among that second wave, and at the same time, recruit those remaining soldiers who had once pledged their honor and service to King Hamil before he was assassinated. If he could turn them to his side, together they could deliver a fatal blow to Drogin once and for all. Until then, it would be up to King Basil's men and his allies to hold out for as long as possible.

After consulting with his captains, King Justin directed the troops swiftly southward, sweeping past the long stretch of woodland to their left and secretly bypassing Drogin's main force gathered upon the ridge on the opposite side of the trees. The King halted his men soon after he spotted the enemy's second wave of soldiers preparing for their assault later that morning. Their numbers were about equal. But just how many of them were truly devoted to Drogin? That was the question occupying King Justin's thoughts as he prepared to parley with the opposing forces who were surprised by his sudden arrival. The King knew that the following minutes might very well determine the outcome of this terrible war.

Eucádus watched as the army advanced down the low ridge, the flags of Drogin snapping in the breeze. The captains in King Basil's army shouted out orders from all directions, preparing to rally their remaining men for what they knew would be a final assault. Most expected not to survive the few hours left before twilight would gently touch the browning field.

Eucádus prepared to mount his horse and make for a small gathering nearby that was readying a charge south under Captain Tiber's command. Before doing so, he knelt on one knee next to Jeremias' body and covered the soldier's face and chest with a portion of the man's cloak he gently freed from underneath the cooling corpse.

"As the situation looks at present, you may not receive a proper burial when the day is done, Jeremias, so I shall give you one now," he softly said, "however simple and temporary." Eucádus found Jeremias' sword close by and plunged it into the ground near his head as a marker to complete the brief ritual, wondering where his own body would end up after the day wound to a close. "Farewell, my friend," he whispered before climbing on his horse. He snapped the reins to join his fellow soldiers, feeling empty and lost and tasting defeat in the cool autumn air.

As Eucádus neared the restless group of fighters and heard Captain Tiber shout out orders, something caught his gaze in the distance. At that same moment, Tiber and his men grew hauntingly silent as they incredulously looked southward as well, including the injured King Cedric who sat upon his horse near the captain's side. Across the field and along the tree lines, those in King Basil's army momentarily paused amid words, thoughts and actions as a fantastical sight unfolded before them.

Eucádus held his breath, his face as hard as stone as he watched the vast army of men and horses advancing up the sun-baked field amid a roar of thundering footfalls and swirling eddies of dust. But what momentarily paralyzed him and elevated his spirits was seeing all of Drogin's wildly waving flags suddenly disappear within the approaching stampede. It was as if their bearers had flung away with reckless abandon the dreary orange, brown and black emblems that marked the tyrant's forces.

"How can this be?" he whispered.

Slowly, he displayed a smile that radiated pure joy and utter relief as a spread of new banners rose up in the midst of the advancing troops. The flags of Maranac, along with the blue, silver and white colors of Arrondale, flew together as the new wave of soldiers advanced to join the fight for Rhiál. Leading the line was King Justin, his cropped silvery hair and unsheathed sword catching the golden light of afternoon. His ice blue eyes targeted the numerous battles raging around him and he directed his captains where to lead their companies to put an end to Drogin's handiwork.

Eucádus bowed his head as cheering rose from all over the field, his mind unable to comprehend this turn of events. But his heart and soul were overwhelmed with an incredible sense of euphoria at the same time. The sacrifices they had all made today, including Jeremias, had not been in vain. He swiftly unsheathed his weapon and snapped Chestnut's reins, bolting forward into the churning fury to see it through to the end as the clash of swords grew closer and louder around him.

Minutes earlier, any thoughts of victory were unimaginable to King Basil. He lay upon a cot in his tent that had been brought in from one of the encampments. He had grown increasingly weak and weary as the war and the afternoon wore on, his breathing labored and his words and thoughts scattered. Though Garron had suggested that the royal physician should attend to him, King Basil refused, allowing the war–and his life–to run the course that fate had in store.

"At least take more soup or tea," Garron insisted, sitting on a low stool next to the King's cot. "You've hardly touched either," he added as he glanced at the cooling food upon a nearby table.

King Basil started to chuckle, but only ended up coughing until his chest hurt. "You talk too much, Garron. But still, you are a good aide. Let me close my eyes and rest while you bring in someone who can tell me what is happening on the field and along the lake. That will be nourishment enough."

Garron smiled, knowing he would not convince the King otherwise. "As you wish, sir. I shall find someone at once though Yurris should be back shortly." He stood and stepped through the tent flap just as the sound of horse hooves rumbled in the near distance. A moment later Garron poked his head back into the tent, pleasantly shocked. "King Basil, Yurris has returned just as I said, but there is a visitor riding with him for you. Two, in fact, who I believe you will be most eager to see. Shall I bring them in?"

King Basil, too tired to open his eyes, wearily sighed as he waved his fingers through the air, indicating for Garron to bring the callers forward. Moments later, Prince William and Aaron emerged through the tent flap, their hearts sinking when they saw the King lying upon the cot in his helpless state. The boys glanced at one another, each silently shocked at how much the monarch had deteriorated since they last saw him.

"King Basil," William cautiously said as he stepped forward, wondering if he and Aaron should have stopped by. But Garron urged him onward. "It is Prince William. And Aaron is with me. We are both safe."

The King paused in the middle of a deep and labored breath and slowly opened his eyes, staring at the tent ceiling that dimmed the brilliant afternoon sun. "William? Aaron? Is it really you?"

King Basil slowly turned his head and tried to sit up, but was too weak and tired to do so. William and Aaron hurried to the side of his cot. Aaron sat on the stool and instinctively took the King's hand in his as he lay his head back down. Prince William stood close enough so the monarch could gaze upon him with ease.

"We're here," Aaron responded, gently squeezing his hand.

The King noted the boys with a grandfatherly smile. "Well, this is truly a pleasure to have you both back where you belong. So, my young lads, where have you been off to?"

William was about to tell him and thought otherwise, believing the truth might upset him. A wary raise of Garron's eyebrows confirmed his decision.

"Aaron and I were…lost," he finally said. "But we found our way back, sir. I hope our absence hasn't caused you any stress."

"Not anymore." The King smiled, visibly relieved. He closed his eyes again. "Now that you're both back home in Melinas, life is again as it should be. Is either of you hurt? Or hungry?"

"No, sir," William replied.

"And you, Morton?" King Basil said lethargically, squeezing Aaron's hand. "You were always fond of your mother's apple-walnut bread when she baked in the kitchen." He took a few slow breaths as if building up more needed energy to speak. "Shall I have some brought up?"

Aaron stared uncomfortably at the King as soon as he had called him by his oldest son's name. Morton had been killed last summer after the war with Maranac had begun. Aaron didn't think it was proper to let the monarch continue thinking that it was Morton sitting beside him and holding his hand.

"Sir," Aaron began. "I am not…" But when he saw William and Garron shake their heads, the boy knew what was expected of him in that delicate moment. "Sir, I am not hungry now, but thank you for thinking about me. All I really want to do is sit beside you and talk, if that is your wish. You can continue to rest and listen."

"That would be most agreeable, Morton," he replied with a joyous expression. "Perhaps your younger brother can start the conversation." He signaled to William with a weakly raised hand, though his eyes remained shut. "Victor, tell me how this war is playing out. Step outside and describe what you see."

"Very well," he replied with a heavy heart as he looked upon the King, his face pale and gaunt beneath a tangle of gray hair.

William swept aside the tent flap with one hand and held it open as he stepped partially outside and monitored the two fronts of the war–to the south on the field and east to the shores of Lake LaShear. A fresh wind blew across his face and into the tent along with a scattering of bright sunshine. He saw the chaotic movements of men and horses amid clouds of dust as a second army of men descended down the low ridge. He saw more soldiers gathering near the lakeshore beside glittering waters and foaming, white waves as a fleet of rafts zeroed in on them. The relentless clanking of metal swords and the hoarse shouts of men rose upon the air like a dull, unending echo. Suddenly Prince William shot a second glance toward the lake, looking for the flags of Drogin that had been waving ominously in the wind when he and Aaron rode away from the estate. He placed a hand above his eyes to shield the afternoon glare, wondering if he had been deceived in his first observations.

"Speak to me, Victor," the King called from his cot. "What is happening?"

"If my eyes are not mistaken, I'm seeing the flags of Arrondale flying upon the rafts floating down the lake," a surprised William spoke as he ducked his head back inside to directly address the King. "It is a most amazing sight, sir!"

"For real?" Aaron whispered, still holding the King's hand. He wondered if William was creating a tale to make King Basil feel better in his worsening state. Garron looked up with doubt as well.

"I speak the truth," William replied, stepping back outside. "It is only *too* real!"

Cheers of amazement suddenly burst forth from nearby soldiers as they witnessed the spectacle upon the water. Garron ran outside to see for himself, but as soon as he pushed aside the tent flap and stepped past William, an even louder cheer erupted as an impromptu celebration ensued. Everyone was suddenly pointing to the south, rejoicing when an array of flags from Arrondale and Maranac sprouted up like colorful flowers among the advancing second wave, replacing the dull, weed-like hues of Drogin's own banners. Garron was speechless as he looked at William, both of them beaming.

"Arrondale has arrived!" a soldier shouted, his voice piercing through the sides of the tent. "The reinforcements are ours!"

"We're annihilating the enemy!" cried another in joy. "There is victory at last!"

"Do you hear that?" Aaron said, still holding King Basil's hand. "King Justin and his men are here. We are winning the war!" He gently stroked the King's forehead as a thin smile appeared upon the monarch's face. But the King's eyes remained closed and his breathing slow and intermittent.

"That's...wonderful news, Morton," he whispered, low enough so that Aaron had to lean in to hear.

"Yes, Father, it is wonderful," he replied, his voice choking. "You saved Rhiál in the very end. You saved your people."

"And you...and your brother...shall lead them," he managed to say, his face radiating with contentment and peace.

"We shall," Aaron whispered, seeing only King Basil's pale face and recalling their many fine walks together as the shouting outside faded in his mind. He continued to stroke King Basil's forehead and watched as his eyes darted beneath his closed lids. "Rest now, Father. You have earned it."

A few moments later, William and Garron stepped back inside the tent to recount the latest happenings, their faces flush with excitement and stunned disbelief at the fortunate turn of events. But when they saw Aaron look up, his shoulders slumped and his face wet with tears, grief overtook them. They knew that King Basil had left them forever. A cold, emptiness filled the tent as the three looked upon the King's lifeless body. All were saddened that he would not be around to see Rhiál rise from its war-torn state, yet grateful that the monarch had learned that victory had triumphed in the end.

William stepped forward and rested a hand upon Aaron's shoulder, sensing the cruel anguish the boy was enduring but knowing he couldn't do anything to lessen its severity. It would have to run its natural course through him and through the kingdom in the days and weeks ahead. Rhiál was now a nation both leaderless and war weary just as winter's cold and brutal eyes were beginning to open. The young prince couldn't imagine what the long, dreary months ahead would yield.

CHAPTER 67

Lamentations for the Departed

The sun dipped in the southwest behind the jagged peaks of the Ridloe Mountains. Purple twilight gently cloaked the tree trunks on the silent battlefield and the creaky docks and fishing shanties along the sighing shores of Lake LaShear. Drogin's war to reclaim Rhiál had ended with the arrival of King Justin's troops. That final push, coupled with the conversion of many in the Maranac army who took up arms against Drogin at the very end, cast a fatal blow upon the wild ambitions of the false king. Where Drogin himself now lingered, whether in the corridors of his estate in Zaracosa or somewhere in the southern provinces of Rhiál, no one could say.

Dozens of bonfires sputtered in the cold air upon the field and along the lake as evening deepened. Men went about the task of tending to the injured and burying the dead. Tents sprouted up like mushrooms across the landscape after the fighting had concluded. Both sides suffered major losses which would affect the wellbeing of the two nations and nearly every family for years to come. But as Rhiál stood upon winter's doorstep, one of the first assignments was to reclaim the food stores that had been confiscated by Drogin's forces in the south. A frosty chill already invaded the night air after the skies had cleared. Handfuls of icy stars glittered against inky skies. The men and women on the field, tending to the sick and injured, occasionally paused near one of the fires to warm themselves. Many wandered in disbelief as they went about their trying task.

Shortly after sunset, King Justin and King Cedric paused for a meal of soup and bread that had been brought to them near one of the fires. They had met on the battlefield with their swords raised against the enemy, not having seen one another in several years. Among the soldiers and other captains now surrounding them were Eucádus and Captain Tiber, neither man having had a proper meal since the battle started that morning. All were famished though they hadn't realized how much so until the first taste of food passed their lips. But talk of such pleasantries was kept to a minimum, overshadowed by the misery and obstacles that had become part of the landscape.

"We face a long night into a cold, cruel morning," King Cedric said while sitting upon a log. His wounded arm had been properly washed and wrapped in a clean bandage.

"Though I already know your answer, Cedric," King Justin replied, "you should remove yourself to the estate where you can sleep for a while. That was quite a gash you took. There will still be plenty of work for you to oversee in the days ahead."

"Perhaps I shall allow myself a short rest in one of the tents," he said, "but I am fit to continue this evening. Others are far worse off compared to the mere scratch I received. Besides, I wouldn't know what to do with myself wandering uselessly among King Basil's corridors. It would break me right now."

"It would do so to all of us," Eucádus said in a melancholy tone. "I think it's better in the long run to immerse ourselves in the aftermath of this horror rather than avoid it. At least it will be for me." Images of Jeremias' last moments drifted through his mind. Eucádus, like many around him, had suffered terrible losses, but the grieving would have to be postponed until more immediate concerns were addressed.

Soon a small group of soldiers trudged along on foot from the southeast side of the field and neared the bonfire, hoping for a bite to eat. Among them was Ramsey whom Eucádus greeted with a hug, not having seen his friend since he had left him riding north to the estate with William and Aaron. Ramsey was delighted to see him, having feared the worst over the past few hours.

"Good news at last!" he said to Eucádus with a smile as he and his fellow soldiers were welcomed and given food and drink. As Ramsey scanned some of the faces in the fire's glow, he was relieved to see that King Cedric and Captain Tiber had both survived their ordeals. "But where is Jeremias? Were you separated in the fighting?"

Eucádus nodded, his face tightening in anguish. "Yes, my friend. Forever."

When he spoke those words, Ramsey noted the deep sorrow in the man's eyes and instantly understood. He sighed as he rubbed a hand across his weary face, his throat tightening. "How did it happen?" he whispered, listening as Eucádus described the final heroic moments of their friend.

But only a few minutes had passed when the shared grief of the group was compounded. A horseman arrived from the estate, one of many fanning out across the field and along the lakeside bearing news of King Basil's death. The monarch's body had since been borne back to the estate and only now was word of his demise being dispatched among the gatherings upon the battlefield.

"This is indeed one more black cloud over a terrible day," King Justin remarked as he stood staring into the fire, one foot resting upon a stone. "And I had so wished to talk with Basil again. It has been too long since we last met."

"He was in fragile health," King Cedric replied, "though I had hoped he would survive long enough to see his country restored to what it once was and perhaps enjoy it for a time. But I'm afraid the death of his oldest son and the disappearance of Victor, his youngest, did as much damage to his wellbeing as any illness could."

In light of the sad tidings, King Justin and King Cedric decided to make their way to the estate with a small contingent to pay their respects to the fallen King. Accompanying them were Eucádus, Ramsey and Captain Tiber, all anxious for information about their friends who had been battling along the lakeside.

The five men slowly made their way north along the battlefield on horseback, stopping occasionally to talk with other soldiers and volunteer civilians gathered among the wind-whipped tents and crackling bonfires while tending to the ravages of war. In time, the two Kings and their companions headed up the main road along the estate now lined with a series of tall torches embedded into the ground and adorned with black ribbons in honor of the fallen sovereign. The large flag of Rhiál suspended from one of the building's upper windows was also similarly decorated. A single candle blazed behind each window pane in the estate, casting the compound in a sad and subtle glow of mourning.

The soldiers guarding the main gates stood at attention when they saw the Kings of Arrondale and Drumaya trotting by on their steeds to pay homage to their departed leader. Despite King Basil's death, everyone knew that today would have turned out unimaginably worse were it not for the brave troops brought here from afar.

The five visitors were escorted inside the estate and led to a large, dimly lit library that had been cleared of all furniture except for a few wooden chairs around the perimeter. Here King Basil's body lay at one end of the room upon a polished oak bier draped with an embroidered pall of somber colors. His head, with a delicate ringlet of silver placed upon it, rested on a small, square pillow. A fireplace blazing with pine logs provided the only light save for a few flickering candles affixed to the walls.

"He looks as if the weight of the world has been removed from his shoulders," King Cedric remarked as the two monarchs stood side by side before the low platform and gazed upon the departed King. His gray hair had been combed and he was dressed in his finest garb. A hint of a peaceful smile was etched upon his face. Set upon the bier, horizontal and below his feet, was King Basil's sword, its polished blade reflecting flashes of orange and red firelight.

"Soon the weight of the world will be on another man's shoulders," King Justin said as he gently rested his hand upon the arm of the departed monarch, contemplating the solemn moment. The two Kings stepped aside, allowing Eucádus, Captain Tiber and Ramsey to offer their respects. "Well, at least the weight of Rhiál, if not the world," he quietly continued after he and King Cedric moved a few paces away. "As King Basil has no living heir, rule of this realm will be in doubt. That is an unfortunate development even with the war over. Rhiál needs stability now more than ever."

"I was thinking the same," King Cedric replied as they stood near the raging fire while the others continued viewing the deceased.

"Once Drogin gets word, he will worm his way deeper into Rhiál's power structure through methods other than the point of a sword."

King Justin nodded. "I think we need to pay Drogin a visit following the King's burial tomorrow afternoon."

"We and our combined armies?" King Cedric added with a grim smile.

"Precisely. Stern words without the hardware behind them will do little to throw fear into the enemy. Drogin needs to realize in no uncertain terms that he will pay dearly for his incursion into Rhiál." King Justin stared fixedly into the crackling flames as they danced upon the hearth. "And that same message must be delivered to Vellan as well, my friend. You of all people must realize that, living in his shadow all these years."

"The citizens of Drumaya are only too aware of Vellan's presence," King Cedric replied in a hard tone. "Though the Ebrean Forest acts as a buffer between us, we knew his forces could strike us with ease whenever he chose. I think that Eucádus and the other Clearing leaders–and their small but effective armies ready to spring to our defense–gave Vellan pause, just enough to keep him at bay while he locked his gaze upon Rhiál. But now that we defeated him here, we must press forward and not rest on this victory. We must deal another blow to Vellan's grand plans–preferably a fatal one."

"I'm glad we agree. But as winter is fast approaching, a springtime offensive would be the wisest course. Our men need to recuperate and we must restock weapons and provisions. I could call another war council in a month or so to sort out the details. But after our victory here, I suspect there will be little or no resistance to confront Vellan now that so many of our allies have seen his cruel handiwork up close."

"I suspect not," King Cedric agreed. "But the quicker we get underway, the better. As soon as winter breaks, let us unloose our armies upon that tyrant. I want to give Vellan as little time as possible to recover from his loss."

"Then I expect another visit from Ambassador Osial. I assume he will make the trip to Morrenwood a second time on your behalf."

King Cedric grinned. "He may or may not. But you can definitely count on my presence this time, Justin. I look forward to sitting in your chamber in the Blue Citadel as the snows of New Winter fall. It has been too long since we exchanged visits."

"I'm delighted to hear it. And by that time, the situation in Montavia should be settled one way or the other, too." An inscrutable smirk formed on King Justin's face which the other King curiously noted. "Matters are unfolding that may contribute to our success there–and perhaps in Kargoth as well–though I am under oath not to reveal the particulars of the mission."

King Cedric nodded knowingly, recalling his cryptic conversation with Prince William when he had first met the boy. "In a roundabout way, I was similarly apprised by the younger prince of Montavia–without specifics–that something was afoot. He visited me at Grantwick to engage my army's help in this war."

"Prince William was in Drumaya?" King Justin was both stunned and relieved by the comment, exhaling deeply as he combed a hand through his hair. "He and his brother were guests at the Citadel after the war council. They took leave for a few days while my son readied an army for the long road to Montavia, but they never returned. Scouts were sent out to search for them, but came back empty-handed. Where are they? I'm anxious to speak with them."

"William is safe at the estate. I had talked to Eucádus earlier, asking him to allow me to fill you in on William and Brendan's whereabouts."

"What a relief to have news about them. So, what have they been up to?"

King Cedric didn't know how to begin, reluctant to break the news of Prince Brendan's death. "William and his brother had left Morrenwood to seek out an audience with me, Justin, to persuade me to help you in this battle against Drogin."

King Justin smiled. "They fooled my advisor, Nedry, and me, claiming a desire to go into the countryside because of boredom."

"As I remarked earlier, William referred to the same secret mission that you had just mentioned, talking about an oath and such. I was encouraged that perhaps help from an unexpected source may come our way. It is a hopeful sign."

"A little bit of hope is justified, Cedric. But it must also be tempered with the knowledge that this secret mission may only have an outside chance of succeeding."

"Still, it is a chance."

King Justin nodded impatiently. "Yes. Tell me more of Brendan and William. Did they both ride with you here from Grantwick, or did Brendan return to Morrenwood on his own? You said that only William was at the estate."

"I did," he uncomfortably replied. "But first I should say that while in Drumaya, William told me of a rather disturbing event that happened to him and his brother. And from that, William concluded that perhaps your oath of secrecy was not so secret after all."

King Justin furrowed his brow. "Do not gingerly walk around the words you mean to speak, Cedric. Tell me exactly what is on your mind."

"Though I do not relish the task, I will do so, Justin. But it will be hard news for you to bear. It is about Prince Brendan." King Cedric momentarily averted his eyes. "He did not make the journey with us from Drumaya nor back to Morrenwood by himself. Fate led him along another road."

King Justin noted the growing tension upon King Cedric's countenance, expecting horrible news. "What are you saying? Where is Brendan? What happened to him?"

After a long pause, he finally uttered the dreaded words. "Brendan was murdered," he softly said, though feeling as if his voice had permeated every corner of the large library. "He was struck down in the Ebrean Forest by someone who–or *something* that–well, to tell you the truth, Justin, I'm not exactly sure."

King Justin paled as the blood drained from his face, unable to fully process what he was hearing. He took a few steps backward and sat down on one of the chairs. King Cedric sat beside him, briefly catching Eucádus' gaze as he stood near the bier with Captain Tiber.

"Tell me what happened." King Justin stared at the floor, his words laced with bitter anger, though not directed at his fellow monarch but solely at himself.

King Cedric patiently recounted William's story about the attack inside the cabin, hardly believing the words as he conveyed them. King Justin believed them even less, but his heart felt the tug of each sentence and the dreadful images they evoked as they wrung out the few glimmers of hope this day had provided. When King

419

Cedric finished his tale, King Justin shook his head repeatedly as he gazed at the floorboards, feeling responsible for Brendan's death.

"I still don't understand," he continued, looking up. "What kind of a creature was it that William described? I've never heard of such a thing."

"Nor have I. But William said that he–*it*–had mistaken him and Brendan for the other two men on the real mission. But being true to his oath, William offered no further details."

"I wouldn't have blamed him if he did considering the circumstances, Cedric. But I just don't know how anyone except the ten of us in my chamber could have known about our discussion. None of the others would have breathed a word. I'm sure of it."

"A spy perhaps?"

"I suppose it is possible, but how? The chamber doors were closed and guarded from the outside and are too thick for sound to readily pass through. Besides, many other delegates from the war council were congregating outside at the time, so no one could have heard anything from the corridors above the din." King Justin waved his hand in disgust. "Not that it matters now. The boy is dead and–" He wiped his misty eyes. "He was so young. His mother and grandfather will be crushed. But tell me, how has William coped?"

"Surprisingly well, especially after he arrived here and befriended one of the kitchen workers–a boy named Aaron." King Cedric chuckled. "There is a story to that, too, though one with a happy ending as Eucádus briefly informed me after your arrival."

"Tell me at once so that a little joy may find its way back into my darkened soul."

"As I only know a few particulars, I'll be quick," he replied. "We can both get the full story about William and Aaron's abduction and escape when we speak to them later."

"*Abduction? Escape?* Apparently I've missed much on the long march from Morrenwood."

After King Cedric related what little news Eucádus had imparted, King Justin felt happier knowing that William got the better of his attackers this second time around. King Cedric brought up another point that put Prince Brendan's death in a new light.

"Though he probably never realized it, Brendan's sacrifice may have aided the two men who are on that mysterious journey you mentioned."

"How so?"

"William told me that the attack in the cabin occurred twelve days after he and Brendan had left Morrenwood," he recalled. "So that would have given your two real agents at least twelve days to begin their journey without interference from the thing who assaulted the young princes. That could be key to the mission's success."

King Justin couldn't help but smile at King Cedric's word choice, but would not tell him the cause of his mirth. He folded his arms as he leaned back in his chair, contemplating where in the wild Nicholas and Leo were right now, wondering if he should dare to hope that they had already made it successfully to Wolf Lake.

At that very moment, however, as the nearby fire was easing the chill from King Justin's weary muscles, Nicholas Raven's life was being saved by a well-aimed arrow from Hannah Boland's quiver. And Leo Marsh and his guide were wending their way through the Dunn Hills back to Morrenwood with the reforged key of which the King of Arrondale dared not speak.

King Justin kept his silence and gazed enigmatically at King Cedric with guarded optimism. Eucádus, Ramsey and Captain Tiber finally strolled over toward them. But before they could engage the two Kings in conversation, muted voices drifted into the main doorway from the adjoining corridor.

Moments later, Ranen and Captain Silas stepped into the room along with a few other men, having also learned of King Basil's demise. Silas stood near his departed King for some time, visibly moved by the man's death, a leader he looked up to as a father for so many years while a trusted soldier in his army. Ranen stepped away shortly afterward when he saw Eucádus standing near the fireplace with the others and headed toward him. He greeted his fellow Clearing leader like a long lost brother. After Ranen was introduced to King Justin and spoke with him for a few moments, Eucádus took his friend aside.

"What happened to your arm?" he asked, noting a white bandage around Ranen's left wrist.

"This is but a scrape compared to what my opponent received in return," he softly replied with an amused grin. His long, black hair was again tied up in back with his wife's slip of red material.

Eucádus scanned the faces of the other men who had accompanied Ranen and Silas into the room, none who were familiar. "Uland and Torr? Where are they?"

"Fear not. I talked to them both near the docks not two hours ago. They will make an appearance later tonight," he said. "Both were helping to secure the ships that had sailed over from Zaracosa. Other than a few bumps and scrapes, they are fine."

"My heart rests easier hearing that," Eucádus said. "Still, we have lost many men from all five of the Clearings on this day."

"It was a price we were willing to pay to secure our freedom at home and abroad," Ranen replied, detecting uneasiness in Eucádus' demeanor. When he shot a glance at Ramsey nearby, he noted the same unease as a cold sense of foreboding gripped his spirit. "And Jeremias? Where is he this evening?" Eucádus looked up, his eyes filled with a palpable sorrow that conveyed more than words ever could. Ranen's face paled and he bowed his head. He needed no explanation for Jeremias' absence. "How did he die?"

"He saved my life, Ranen, taking an arrow meant for me," he answered, his eyes glassy and his voice tired. "Released from the bow of Irabesh himself." Ranen snapped his head up, his face hardened with disdain until Eucádus smiled. "But Irabesh paid the ultimate price for his deed. Jeremias' death was avenged on the spot."

"That offers me comfort, but only a little." He glanced over his shoulder at the small group gathered around King Basil's bier. "Men, both great and unsung, have fallen today. But all will leave an equal void in the hearts of those who knew them well."

Eucádus rested a hand upon Ranen's shoulder, realizing how fortunate they had been to survive this horrible day of battle and bloodshed. Yet both knew that the untimely deaths of their friends and fellow soldiers had killed a small piece of themselves inside, a living death they would carry around for as long as they survived.

CHAPTER 68

The Lines of Succession

King Basil was buried late the following morning in one of the gardens north of the estate. His grave lay next to those of his deceased wife, Imogene, and eldest son, Morton. Though the body of Victor, his youngest son, had never been found after the raid on Zaracosa five months ago, most expected that a memorial stone would be displayed one day soon for Victor near this trio of gravesites to honor the fallen hero whatever his fate. The citizens of Rhiál felt that the royal family should be together forever in death as they had enjoyed only a short time in each other's company while living at the estate. A more tranquil spot could not be found for the gravesite gently splashed in the shade of a weeping willow tree, its slender branches playfully catching breezes off Lake LaShear. The distant, snowcapped peaks of the northern Ridloe Mountains would forever stand watch, reflecting flashes of the rising and setting sun.

All through the night before the King's burial, citizens and soldiers of Rhiál had made a pilgrimage to the royal estate, asking to look upon their cherished monarch one last time. Despite the frenzied aftermath of the battle, officials allowed people to view the body, a process that concluded just before the break of dawn.

Later in the afternoon on the burial day, Kings Justin and Cedric were invited to a private luncheon after the ceremony with some of their closest captains and a few of King Basil's ministers.

Prince William and Aaron were also in attendance. The two boys had briefly met with King Justin and King Cedric during the night, but now William looked forward to spending extra time with both Kings before the task of cleaning up from the war continued.

"I can only say again how truly sorry I am for the loss of your brother, William. I was shocked when I heard the news," King Justin later said to the young prince. They walked alone outside in the cool sunshine along King Basil's private dining area. They talked of Brendan while the other guests continued to eat and converse inside behind the large windows overlooking the lake.

"I appreciate your kind words," William replied. "But do not blame yourself for his death. I detect a hint of remorse in your voice."

"You are perceptive," the King admitted, his mood shifting from somber to apprehensive. "Now I wish to learn more about the creature who attacked you and of his knowledge about the medallion. Did he say where he came from or give any clue as to his origin?"

William shook his head. "He said nothing to indicate who he was or how far he had traveled. But I suspect he had followed Brendan and me for quite some time."

"Oh?"

William recounted some strange incidents about his and Brendan's journey from Morrenwood. "On our sixth day after we had left the Blue Citadel, we were enjoying lunch on the shores of Lake Lasko. A deer wandered out of the woods, so I fed it one of my apples. Brendan, though he didn't mention it to me at the time, felt uneasy about the animal's presence, later saying something about the look of the deer's eyes. That night, we arrived in the village of Parma where we met a man on the roadside named Sorli. He claimed he had just been robbed of his horse and had beaten off his attacker before the man could steal his money."

"Claimed? You sound skeptical," he remarked as the cries of distant seagulls reverberated along the shoreline.

"I wasn't at the time. Later, Sorli bought us dinner at an inn and we agreed to journey with him the following morning since we would be traveling in the same direction for several miles," William continued. "But when Brendan and I were sitting alone after Sorli retired for the night, my brother insisted that we discreetly leave the inn at once and travel south beyond the lake along the back roads. That's when my brother told me what was bothering him, though I thought he was speaking utter nonsense at the time."

King Justin stopped walking and gazed at William as a sense of dread gripped him. "What did your bother say?"

William looked up, his eyes filled with dismay. "Brendan's instincts were correct, of course. He told me that Sorli reminded him of somebody–in an eerie sort of way–whenever he had looked into the man's eyes during dinner. Later on the road, after he had rushed me out of the inn, Brendan mentioned that he had had that same weird feeling when looking into the deer's eyes earlier in the day. I made a joke of it, asking him if he thought the deer had somehow turned into Sorli. But he was deadly serious." William sighed. "I guess *deadly* wasn't the best choice of words."

"Let's walk some more," King Justin said, pointing ahead to a lawn along the north end of the estate near one of the gardens. Here in summertime the grass was lush, and flowering trees and shrubs were abundant amid laughter and conversations in the high, bright sunshine. Now the area was awash in subtle tones of brown and gray that encouraged contemplation and whispered words more than the exuberant expressions of warmer, lighter days. "Tell me what happened at the cabin if it isn't too hurtful to revisit those moments."

Prince William offered a tentative nod. "That's when we saw the deer again, or what we thought at the time was another deer." He explained how he and Brendan had gotten lost in the Ebrean Forest and took refuge in the cabin where he later met Ramsey and his friends from the Star Clearing. He described their attack by the strange individual with a shock of white hair upon its skeletal head, and how the being's hand had magically and temporarily transformed into a bird's talon that mercilessly slew Brendan before his very eyes. "That stranger wanted the medallion, and when he was convinced we didn't have it, he demanded to know where it was. The creature knew that it was in the possession of two men who had left the Blue Citadel." William glanced at the King in bewilderment. "How could he or anyone have learned about Nicholas and Leo's mission?"

"I don't know," he replied, disturbed by William's chilling story. "But someone found out about our secret and the results were disastrous for your brother." William stopped and tugged on the King's cloak, causing him to turn around and face the young prince, noting that something was bothering him. "What's the matter? I should think that after recounting your tale, there would be nothing left of consequence to add, but you still appear troubled."

"Because there is still something left to tell, though I'm ashamed to say it." He cast his eyes to the ground and took a deep breath before facing King Justin's scrutiny. "I broke my oath, sir, that the ten of us took inside your chamber in the Citadel."

"You, William?" he replied, slightly baffled. "But you just said that even you don't know how that creature had learned about the medallion."

"That's true. I, however, broke my oath during the attack. After Brendan had been struck down, the creature came after me as I was climbing a ladder to the upper level of the cabin." William recalled the surreal moment, stirring up painful memories. "As he questioned me, I was terrified and found myself telling him about the mission. I even mentioned Nicholas and Leo by name, though I had honestly told my pursuer that I didn't know where or in which direction the two men were traveling." He turned with shame and gazed down upon the lake, finding it difficult to look directly at King Justin. "Our foe may not have been able to make use of my information as Nicholas and Leo had a twelve day head start by then, but I still broke my oath and would gladly accept any punishment that is my due." He looked up, awaiting the King's judgment.

"*Hmmm...* I suppose that must be a weighty burden off your shoulders, my dear prince." He eyed William with a stern gaze, his lips locked in a straight line and his expression unreadable. Slowly, a relaxed and forgiving smile formed on the monarch's face, his eyes filled with a mix of sympathy and gratitude. "Yet in light of the circumstances, if anyone were to be given a pass for breaking an oath under such duress, it would be you. And I can confidently say that if I asked any of the other eight members of our little cabal, they would feel the same way, too."

"Still, I feel as if I have failed you," William persisted. "Failed the entire group."

"You did not fail us, William. And if you are overwhelmed by guilt, well, you must work through that on your own time. But do not mistake my advice as cold or uncaring." King Justin walked over and sat down on a bench near a large shrub with dried leaves and tiny red berries. He signaled for William to join him. The flags of Maranac waved in the breeze upon the distant ships anchored offshore. "If you want my honest opinion–"

"I do!"

"–then you shall have it." He looked out upon the water, his mind and body relaxed for the first time in many grueling weeks. "I think, William, that you seek some sort of punishment for breaking your oath not because you feel guilty about that, but rather because you feel overwhelming guilt for not saving your brother's life. Or maybe for having survived instead of him. Probably both. But I can't offer you forgiveness for that because it is not mine to bestow upon you." The King noted a look of disappointment upon his face. "Then again, I don't think anyone could offer you such forgiveness because you truly do not need it."

"But I feel terrible," he muttered. "I just…"

"You'll just have to live with it, Prince William. And now that you're next in the line of succession for the throne of Montavia after your grandfather, you will have to get used to and live with a good many other things you'd rather not when you become king. It's all part of the job, I'm afraid."

"But I never wanted to be king or even imagined doing so," he replied. "I always expected to happily serve King Brendan some day in whatever capacity he deemed appropriate and then have authority pass to one of his future sons or daughters years and years from now. That's how it was supposed to work out."

King Justin burst out in a brief, cheerful laugh. "That's how it was supposed to work out indeed! If only, my boy. If only. You'll be part of a very exclusive circle if you ever get your life to work out the way you want it to, William. Trust me. That would be quite an achievement."

William slowly nodded and began to grin, feeling better that King Justin had been direct with him and addressed him as an adult. "So everything in life hasn't worked out for you as planned either?"

"Dear me, no! I was supposed to be enjoying these later years with my wife, after all, strolling through the fruit orchards in springtime and spoiling our great grandchildren. Instead, I just fought a war here with probably one more on the way in Kargoth." The King sighed with a slight smirk upon his lips. "Ah, well, let's not go there just yet and spoil this delightful view of the lake. There'll be other opportunities to shed tears over our regrets one day after this mess is settled–preferably while indulging in a bit of ale!"

William grunted in amusement as he leaned back on the bench and folded his arms, appreciating the sound of the King's laughter and the subtle swish of the rhythmic waves upon the lakeshore. "I look forward to it," he replied, closing his eyes for a moment as a cool breeze strummed against his cheeks and the cries of distant seagulls echoed hauntingly across the water.

For the remainder of that day and all the next, the work of tending to the sick, injured and burying the dead continued. The four remaining leaders of the forest Clearings–Eucádus, Ranen, Uland and Torr–were given permission to bury Jeremias in one of the north gardens with a stunning view of the mountains. They each spoke of their friend in a simple and private ceremony and hoped some day to travel back here with his wife, Rebecca, so she could visit his final resting place and see the lands he had helped to free.

The cleaning up along the docks and in parts of Melinas would carry on into winter as long as the heavy snow held off, though there would still be work to be done once spring made her reappearance. The ministers in King Basil's court, after some cajoling, finally convinced Captain Silas to temporarily take the reins of power in Rhiál until a new line of succession could be formed. As one of King Basil's most trusted officers and friends, he agreed.

"But only under the condition that I am not referred to as a king or monarch or any other such title," he insisted. "I will retain my rank of captain. And most important of all, I want the people of Rhiál to know that this will only be a temporary measure."

"Of course, of course!" one of the ministers replied, ecstatic upon his acceptance. "Hopefully by springtime we'll have arrived at a permanent solution and everyone can again get on with their lives."

Kings Justin and Cedric were pleased with the arrangement, having observed both the military prowess and administrative competence of the young man over the last several days. Eucádus and Ranen congratulated him as well, knowing the fragile state of the populace would be more than reassured by the choice of leader.

"But despite my new authority, I would very much appreciate your opinions about confronting Drogin in the near future," Captain Silas commented to both Kings later that afternoon as they sat with him in a small study on the west side of the estate that would serve as his office. A splash of red-orange light from the setting sun entered a multi-paned window and pleasantly tinted the room warmed by a roaring fire. Eucádus, Captain Tiber and some of the defense ministers attended the meeting as well. "You have both expressed your intentions that a trip to Zaracosa should be organized in short order. Give me a suggested timeline."

King Justin and King Cedric glanced silently at one another as if knowing what the other was thinking. King Justin turned to Captain Silas while shifting slightly in his chair. "How does tomorrow sound? Too soon?"

Eucádus grinned upon hearing the response, noting the same amusement in Captain Silas' eyes. But in order to keep a sense of decorum for the first major decision in his new station, the captain simply nodded. "Tomorrow it is. We'll sail over on several of the ships brought here during the war with a well armed contingent. I don't want to fight Drogin, but I certainly want to give him something to think about as he watches us arrive on his shoreline."

Five ships departed at midmorning the following day across the choppy waters of Lake LaShear, sailing for Zaracosa, the capital city of Maranac. With white sails inhaling a freshening breeze under milky gray skies, the vessels charted a course to the southeast for the short journey. Aboard each ship were armed soldiers who had recently fought and defeated Drogin's army, though nobody expected another battle today as the men were really there for show. Captain Silas, along with Kings Justin and Cedric, would lead a delegation to speak with Drogin and his representatives about relinquishing power and compensating the victims of Rhiál for his crimes against them. Eucádus, Ranen, Prince William and Captain Tiber would accompany them to the meeting.

"I don't expect any concessions on Drogin's part," Captain Silas remarked as the seven of them stood on deck and gazed out upon the turquoise surface of the lake as a light spray of water misted the air. "We may have to take the fight to him one of these days if we're ever to remove that scourge from this region. His alliance with Vellan must not go unpunished."

"Indeed not," King Justin replied, one hand resting upon the starboard railing as the lead ship gently rose and fell upon the low waves. "But considering the terrible defeat Drogin suffered, and in the process losing much of his manpower from the Northern Isles and Kargoth, maybe he'll be in the bargaining mood."

"Agreed," Eucádus said, wrapped in a cloak whose ragged edges fluttered in the breeze. "I'm sure the regular folk of Maranac are tired of war and may not be looking too kindly upon their leader right now."

"If *ever*," Ranen interjected, eliciting a chuckle from William.

"So perhaps Drogin will accept some sort of arrangement for his own sake," Eucádus continued. "Even some of his most loyal supporters might be abandoning him in light of his recent defeat."

"I hope you're right," King Cedric replied, his back to the breeze. "But even in defeat, I don't know if Vellan will let Drogin give up this corner of Laparia so easily. He could very well send in reinforcements once he gets word from Zaracosa. Vellan has more men in Kargoth who have drunk from the waters of the Drusala River and will mindlessly do his bidding. And additional troops from the Isles will again pole up the Lorren River to his lair come springtime."

"Let's not forget the Enári," Captain Tiber added to the somber discussion. "We already know they have helped the Islanders take Montavia as Prince William can describe in deadly detail. Why would Vellan not send some this way if he is desperate for a victory? No doubt there are plenty to spare in Kargoth."

"They are a tough and efficient fighting force," William said, recalling the predawn assault fifty days ago on Red Lodge. But after all he had been through since, it seemed like a long and dreary year had passed him by and not a mere fifty days.

After everyone had spoken, Captain Silas folded his arms and shook his head, a tiny grimace upon his face. "By our glum words, one might guess that Drogin had won the recent battle and that we are on our way to plead with him. Let us be patient and wait to see what lies across the water before we chart our course with that usurper king. I do not want to carry such pessimism with me when we disembark in Zaracosa," he said as the eastern shoreline slowly came into focus. "I suspect the atmosphere there will be miserable enough when we paddle to the docks."

The five ships lowered their sails and dropped anchor offshore early that afternoon. The low sun peeked through ragged breaks in the clouds. Many of the soldiers on board stared at the shoreline, never having expected to look upon Zaracosa while Drogin still ruled. Directly ahead and to the right was a line of wooden docks extending into the lake along the gentle curve of the water. The terrain gradually rose higher to the left where a thick support wall of gray stone had been built along the lake's edge, now buffeted by a series of low waves. At the top of the wall overlooking Lake LaShear was King Drogin's estate, a five-story building with several more levels below ground constructed of the same gray stones as the wall. Its many arched windows reflected the sullen, gray skies and the occasional spark of sunshine. A few pine trees towered nearby. Several flags of Maranac affixed above the slate rooftops snapped in the breezes rolling off the water.

Though all the observers on the ship were impressed by the sturdy elegance of Zaracosa's capitol, what attracted their attention most were two unusual sights. First, not a single one of King Drogin's emblems, the orange, brown and black flag he created to celebrate his ascension to the monarchy, could be spotted anywhere on or near the estate. Second, a large crowd of people milled about the docks and in front of the royal estate as if all the homes and shops of Zaracosa had been emptied. But whether this was a protesting mob or merely curious spectators, none could tell from this distance.

"The roads are boiling over with people," King Cedric commented as he and King Justin leaned against the ship's railing and gazed toward shore. Prince William stood next to them, thrilled to have made the trip across the lake yet wary of the sight before them.

"Surely those people haven't gathered to welcome us, have they?" he wondered aloud, glancing at the two Kings for an answer. "Or perhaps to attack us?"

King Justin shrugged. "Your guess is as good as mine, my boy. I half expected a line of armed soldiers on horseback–not this."

"Nor did I," Captain Silas remarked as he walked toward the inquisitive trio. "And before I allow any one of you gentlemen to step foot on shore, I'm sending a scouting unit ahead to determine the cause of the frenzy upon the mainland. They are heading out now as we speak," he said, pointing over the side of the ship where two large rowboats filled with men were paddling to shore. "As no one in Drogin's forces was hurrying out on boats to confront us, I'm assuming we will at least be allowed to send forth some scouts without causing any provocation."

"We'll soon see," King Justin cautiously replied as they watched the two boats draw nearer to shore.

In time the boats glided alongside one of the longer docks and tied up as a crowd of spectators hurried over to them. Slowly the men made their way out of the boats, but as he watched from the ship, King Justin couldn't tell if they were being helped onto the dock in a friendly manner or pulled up by force. Moments later, the scouting party was surrounded by a throng of locals as they were escorted off the dock and into the crowded area below the estate.

"I don't know what to make of that," he said. King Justin glanced at Captain Silas for his interpretation. But before he could reply, Prince William shouted and pointed to shore.

"Look! Two of the men have returned and are climbing into one of the boats." He leaned over the rail for a better view.

"Careful so you don't tumble over," King Cedric warned. "None of us want to fish a prince out of the water."

"I'll be fine, sir," he replied, gazing intently as the boat grew nearer with every stroke of the paddles. "Here they are!" he excitedly called when the two men were in vocal range.

"What have you to report?" Captain Silas shouted down. "What's happening over there?"

One of the men in the boat looked up with a wide grin. "Only good news, Captain Silas! But it would take too long to explain here. You must go ashore at once."

"There is about to be a public announcement," the other man added, cupping one of his hands near his mouth so that his voice carried through the breeze. "We've timed our arrival at a most opportune moment."

Silas looked at the three men of royal blood standing before him, an amused smirk upon his face. "It'll be quicker for us to learn what's going on by paddling to shore ourselves than by extracting any specifics from the scouts below. Shall we proceed?"

A short time later, five more rowboats eased up to the docks. Captain Silas had barely stepped out of his vessel when he was warmly welcomed by several of the local townspeople who had been curiously watching as the small crafts drew near. Most of the crowd though, continued to mingle around the royal estate nearby as if some national celebration were underway.

Eucádus stepped out of another boat onto the wooden dock and offered a hand to Prince William and King Cedric who both had paddled over with him. Ramsey and Ranen disembarked from the back of the vessel and looked in awe at the growing throng.

"What brings half the population of Zaracosa out of doors this afternoon?" Ramsey asked a middle-aged man in a tattered coat and mud-stained boots. His iron gray hair was tousled by the wind.

"There's to be an announcement soon from the royal balcony," he excitedly said, pointing almost midway up at King Drogin's estate. "At least that's the rumor around town. Supposed to be good news, I hear."

"About what?" Prince William asked amid the constant slap of waves against the dock pilings.

"Not sure," the man said as he curiously eyed the new arrivals. He looked out at the ships from Maranac on which they had traveled. "Are you folks anybody important?" he added, glancing at King Cedric who stood nearest to him.

William's eyes popped open as wide as windows at the perceived slight toward the King. "Don't you know whom you're addressing, sir?"

But King Cedric immediately silenced William with a stern glance and then smiled at the man. "I wish to thank you for greeting us here, my dear sir. It is a testament to the kindness of the citizens of Maranac that we hear so much about."

"Yes, of course," Prince William hastily added. "That's what I had meant to say."

The man was pleased by the King's compliment yet scratched his head, mildly perplexed. "So you folks aren't citizens of Maranac even though you've arrived upon our ships?"

"No, we're not," Eucádus jumped in as he edged over to the King's side. He sensed no trouble from the man but wanted to take no chances. "We're visitors from various nations and wish to meet with an official from the estate. Could you lead us there?"

The man burst out laughing. "Meet with an official? Good luck with that, my friends! Access to the royal estate has been prohibited since the stunning events of yesterday. If the folks of Zaracosa aren't allowed through the main doors, I don't see how you strangers washing up on our shores will be permitted inside."

"What happened here yesterday?" King Justin asked upon hearing the remark. He had just strolled up the dock, his cloak wrapped tightly about him as a steady breeze blew across the water.

But as the man was about to answer, a frantic voice drifted through the nearby crowd. Suddenly an official from the royal estate, a tall, thin man wearing an ill-fitting, brown cap, squeezed his way through the onlookers and emerged through the front line.

"A little elbow room please!" he snapped in frustration to the gawking bystanders, eliciting a few grins from some of the visitors. The man looked up at the new arrivals and smiled, unduly excited by their presence. "Welcome to Zaracosa, one and all. I was informed by your advance party that you would be visiting shortly, and your timing couldn't have been better! There's going to be an important announcement shortly."

"So we've heard," William said.

"But we haven't been informed about specifics," Eucádus added in a friendly tone. "Could you let us in on the surprise?"

"I'll do better than that. I'll take you to a prime viewing spot if you would follow me. I had a small location immediately cleared out when I learned of your visit. I'm Minister Pico, by the way." He extended a hand to Eucádus. "You must be Prince William."

Eucádus arched his brow in amusement, pointing at William. "*He* is the prince you're referring to," he said as William raised his hand and waved. Many nearby were pleasantly surprised that a royal prince from anywhere was gracing them with his presence. "Meet Prince William of Montavia, grandson of King Rowan."

Minister Pico blushed with embarrassment. "My apologies, Prince William. I had just assumed that–"

"No apology needed," William replied, doing his best to keep a straight face and make his host as comfortable as possible.

"Thank you, sir." The official turned to Eucádus once again, smiling awkwardly. "And so that I don't make a second such flub, I will kindly beseech you to provide your own introduction. You must either be King Justin of Arrondale or King Cedric of Drumaya, both of whom I was told were aboard these ships."

As the bystanders gasped that not one, but two kings were also in their midst, a buzz of excitement and fresh rumor shot among the gathering at lightning speed. Eucádus, at the same time, glanced at the minister and slowly shook his head to correct him, upon which Pico turned an even darker shade of red. Kings Justin and Cedric, however, brushed off the misunderstanding with amusement, content to observe Eucádus' gracious effort to smooth the matter over. But before the minister could speak again, Eucádus raised a hand to gently silence him.

"Sir, my name is Eucádus. I hail from the nation of Harlow in the Northern Mountains, though I serve in no governmental capacity. But please allow me to quickly introduce everyone else here so we may walk with you to the royal estate," he requested, leading the man to each member of the party individually, beginning with King Justin and King Cedric. "And currently representing the citizens of Rhiál, I am pleased to present Captain Silas."

"An honor to meet you," the minister said as he shook his hand. "And how is King Basil these days? I'm guessing that after the battles three days ago, he has much to keep him busy in Melinas and could not spare the time for this trip."

"I regret to inform you, Minister Pico, that our beloved King Basil died three days ago," Silas replied to the genuine shock of the gentleman.

"My profound condolences on the loss of such a great man," the minister said. "But a battlefield death is an honorable death, one which I'm sure will be recorded and studied for history's sake."

Captain Silas leaned in and spoke softly to the minister. "King Basil succumbed to a long illness. Still, he died an honorable death."

"To be sure," Pico replied, swallowing hard.

The minister didn't speak another word until after he shook hands with each of his remaining guests. When the introductions were over, he invited everyone to follow him to the main gates of the royal estate which were now wide open to the public. Though the distance was short, it took almost ten minutes to maneuver through the jostling spectators before they arrived at the viewing spot Pico had arranged near a line of white birch trees. He pointed to a semicircular stone balcony jutting out of the second floor of the estate where the announcement would shortly be made. Everyone in the assembly looked upward, waiting for someone to step forward.

"It's quite exciting what is planned," Minister Pico said to the dual Kings who stood on either side of him. "But as we are on the cusp of the proclamation, I will not spoil the surprise for either of you." He glanced over his shoulder and addressed Captain Silas who stood next to Eucádus. "And you, captain, will be especially interested in the recent developments which we can talk about later."

"I look forward to it."

"But in light of your news about King Basil, I think it would be better handled in the privacy of the estate."

"As you wish, sir."

"Well then, it seems we're due for a string of magnificent revelations," King Justin replied. "It's fortunate indeed that we arrived when we did."

"News has spread this way from up the coast that each of you and your armies were instrumental in defeating Drogin," Pico informed the two Kings.

"I give all the credit to my men," King Cedric replied, "as I'm sure Justin will, too." He gazed long and hard at the minister before looking askance at King Justin who was engaged in the same line of thought. "Minister, since you're aware of Drogin's defeat, and because we were not harassed nor detained upon our arrival, can I conclude that King Drogin is no longer in charge around here?"

"You may," Pico confirmed. Just then a glass paneled door on the balcony danced with the reflections of somber daylight, indicating that someone was opening it from inside. "But I see that the address is about to begin. All of your questions will be answered forthwith."

The balcony door opened wide. A tall man stepped out to a cheering crowd, though everybody in attendance had no inkling as to who he might be. He stood calmly with an inscrutable smile upon his thin countenance, patiently waiting for the crowd to settle down. Several times he raised his hands, signaling for silence. Finally, after their initial burst of mirth and pent up excitement had subsided, the people below gradually quieted, awaiting the special news.

"Thank you for being here and for your continued patience," he said. "I promise to be brief as I stand here with the distinct honor to introduce someone whom you probably didn't expect to see upon this balcony today. She will explain everything in detail, including the surprising events of yesterday." When the gentleman uttered the word *she*, there were audible gasps below and a flurry of whispers as many speculated about the woman's identity. "So without further ado, and after an absence far too long, I am honored to present to you, Princess Melinda of Maranac."

A moment of uneasy silence seized the crowd, several looking skeptically at one another. But when a young lady stepped out from behind the door and stood next to him, the citizens of Zaracosa erupted in applause, ecstatic to have the princess back in their lives. None had known of her fate since she had disappeared from Zaracosa on the third day of New Spring, the same terrible day when her parents, King Hamil and his wife, were assassinated with their driver and personal guards along a wooded dirt road.

Princess Melinda, a slender woman with long, light brown hair and hazel eyes, politely waved to the crowd as her spokesman moved aside. At the same time, a few other people stepped out onto the balcony and sat on wooden chairs that had been arranged against the wall. One of the individuals, a thin, young man with an unshaven face, walked with a cane and sat down on the chair closest to the side railing, his eyes fixed fondly upon the princess. After what seemed like several minutes of uninterrupted applause, the spectators finally quieted, eager to hear Melinda's words.

"Thank you for your generous welcome, though I have done little to earn it except walk a few steps along this balcony," she said with a gentle smile. The princess wore a dark blue velvet dress with silver trim and a white blouse, and around her neck was a string of multicolored pearls. "Though in the days ahead you will learn more about the death of my parents earlier this year, my uncle's terrible reign over Maranac and my own disappearance, I want to provide some details today so that you'll know the truth and have confidence that your kingdom and your homes are protected and no longer at war with our dear neighbors across the lake."

Another cheer arose, so many having wearied of the death and destruction waged against Rhiál by King Drogin and his allies. Despite his word that agents of Rhiál were responsible for the assassination of King Hamil and his wife, most had never believed his torturous explanation.

"First let me say—though many have suspected it—that my Uncle Drogin arranged for the assassination of my parents and the good people protecting them on that awful day last spring. Men in my uncle's inner circle have been apprehended after yesterday's events and provided proof of Drogin's complicity. My uncle was also responsible for my disappearance, though whether out of pity or others motives, he spared my life. I was secretly held prisoner in a cell below this estate so he could illegally assume the reins of power." Princess Melinda paused while the audience reacted with disgust at Drogin's crimes. "I have forgiven my uncle in my heart for his actions against me, but I know it will be difficult, if not impossible, for any of us to show that same forgiveness for what he did to my parents and to these kindred kingdoms along Lake LaShear. Only in the months and years ahead will we be able to restore our lives to what they once were. But in the meantime we must struggle along as best we can, relying on each other through the difficult times ahead."

"She is a sensible and well-spoken young woman," King Justin whispered to Minister Pico. Melinda reminded him of his granddaughter who was about the same age. "But where is Drogin? What events happened yesterday that she referred to?"

"She will address that shortly," the minister whispered back. "Patience, King Justin. Patience."

"Of course," he replied, glancing at an amused King Cedric.

"As to the fate of my uncle," the princess continued, "I will briefly recount what happened yesterday in order to dispel the rumors running rampant in Zaracosa. A more thorough public examination and discussion will be conducted in the days ahead."

Princess Melinda paused as she looked down upon the crowd, sobered by the apparent trust they placed in her. She glanced slightly to her right and caught the calming gaze of the young man with the cane which immediately put her at ease.

"Sometime yesterday, as I was informed, King Drogin was preparing to leave this estate, having received word on the previous day that his army had been defeated in Rhiál. Though he still had a considerable force in this kingdom, it was widely spread out and comprised mainly of the citizens of Maranac who were not wholly devoted to him. The vast majority of his allied troops from Kargoth and the Northern Isles had been dispatched across the lake and were either defeated or fled.

"I won't bore you with the minutia of military politics–I'll leave that to my advisors," she added with a playful smile, eliciting a round of supportive laughter. "Therefore I'll get right to the point. Yesterday it was learned that my uncle was to visit me in my prison cell before he departed, with some people around him convinced that he was going to kill me. A few thought Drogin was leaving Zaracosa for good, believing he was on the verge of being overthrown. Others, however, were convinced that he wanted to remove me from the capital city to assure that his authority couldn't be challenged after his defeat. Though we don't know his true intentions, Drogin and his closest advisors did make for my cell midmorning yesterday.

"I later learned that several guards, no longer willing to tolerate the escalating crimes of King Drogin, secretly released a few prisoners who were members of the Hamilod resistance, a small but dedicated force trying to subvert Drogin's tyrannical rule. The guards told them of Drogin's intentions, urging them to get reinforcements. So with inside assistance from the repentant guards, the Hamilod fighters gathered their local forces and stormed the estate to save my life. I wish to thank them from the bottom of my heart for their bravery and loyalty to the kingdom of Maranac and for helping to restore its lawful rule. I owe them my life."

Again, everyone burst into applause, lavishing their praises upon those who rescued their beloved princess from possibly a most horrific fate. Princess Melinda raised her hand to quiet the crowd.

"Rumors have flourished regarding my uncle's fate, so I will correct the record now. It was when Drogin and his most loyal aides were on their way to my cell that members of the Hamilod resistance stormed the royal estate. My uncle and his men were killed in a barrage of arrows after refusing to surrender and taking up arms against my rescuers. Though no one was sure what Drogin's intentions toward me were, those present at the raid, myself included, clearly heard him give the order to kill a second prisoner who had been held in a cell next to mine for nearly five months."

The people were mesmerized by this twist in Melinda's story, assuming that she had been isolated while in prison. They eagerly waited for her to continue as not a voice could be heard above the lake breezes sweeping through the bending boughs of nearby pines.

"Being separated by a stone wall, I was unable to see this man during our captivity," she continued. "But we struck up a friendship of whispered words through the small barred openings in our cell doors when the guards were not in earshot. We discussed our lives, our families and the ongoing war, as well as our likes and dislikes regarding food, art and other simple pleasures. We described ourselves to one another and created lines of poetry to while away the hours and lift our spirits. And because of his kindness and companionship, I survived my ordeal and grew stronger because of it. He told me as much regarding himself when I saw him for the first time yesterday, though we both feel as if we've known each other for a lifetime. So at this time I'd like you to get to know him, too."

Princess Melinda's words were exactly what her fellow citizens wanted to hear from their future queen. In a short time she had created a bond of trust by explaining in detail what had happened to her since her disappearance, and now that she was allowing them a glimpse into her personal life, too, their respect and affection for Melinda swelled with the volume of their rising cheers.

The princess turned to the people sitting behind her, and with a tender smile aimed at the man with the cane, she extended her hand and beckoned him to step forward. He smiled back as he stood up and walked to her, somewhat ill at ease as the crowd still cheered. They roared with delight when the young couple clasped hands and fondly gazed into each other's eyes before turning to the gathering below and politely waving.

"What a striking couple they make," King Cedric remarked. "My wife would be crying right now were she with me."

"They certainly are," King Justin replied as he distractedly stroked his chin, staring up at Princess Melinda and the vaguely familiar man standing next to her. "I must say, however, that I think I have seen him somewhere before–perhaps even met him once–though I can't remember where. It's quite disconcerting. But perhaps I'm imagining things in the heady whirl of recent events," he said as the people continued to cheer with unbridled enthusiasm.

"On the contrary," Minister Pico said. "Your instincts, sir, are most likely correct."

"They are?"

"Indeed they are," Captain Silas interjected while studying the couple with wonder as he stood behind the King. He lowered his gaze as King Justin turned to him.

"Tell me, how do I know that man, Captain Silas? And how do *you* know him?"

"Though the young man has lost some weight during his incarceration, you most likely met him years ago the last time you ventured to Rhiál and visited King Basil," Silas explained.

"It has been years since I traveled to these parts," King Justin said. "But what has that got to do with–" Then like a faded memory jarred to life by an old melody or a fragrant scent, the King suddenly realized where he had seen the man before. He spun around and again looked up at him standing next to Princess Melinda and gasped in amazement. "I can hardly believe it," he whispered, shaking his head.

"Who is he?" King Cedric asked.

"He is the next King of Rhiál," he replied, a stunned smile upon his face. "That is Prince Victor, King Basil's youngest son."

CHAPTER 69

The Many Roads Home

After Princess Melinda concluded her speech on the balcony, the crowds below reluctantly dispersed as if a grand holiday had sadly come to an end. Afterward, some of the guests from across the lake were invited to a luncheon with her and Prince Victor. But before everyone sat down for the meal, Captain Silas asked Melinda and Victor if he could speak with them alone before joining the others.

"My father's most trusted soldier will always have my ear," Prince Victor graciously told him. "What is on your mind?"

They moved to a private study overlooking Lake LaShear. A pot of steaming tea had been placed on a serving table between their chairs. With a heavy heart, Captain Silas broke the news of King Basil's death. Though the monarch had been in ill health before Victor's disappearance five months ago, the prince was still surprised that his father's condition had taken such a drastic turn for the worse. He was saddened by the news, yet his heart was warmed by the description that Silas painted of the steady stream of devoted citizens who had journeyed to the royal residence to view the King's body as it lay in state.

"Many believe that your brother's death, coupled with your own uncertain fate, took a substantial toll upon your father's health," the captain said. "But despite our loss, the people of Rhiál will rejoice when they learn that you are alive. The line of succession will continue and will count for much in this dark point in history."

"I think you would have done a fine job ruling in my stead," Victor replied, holding Melinda's hand for support. They sat on a pair of chairs near a large window overlooking the choppy, turquoise waters of the lake, Melinda still in her dark blue velvet dress while Victor wore a tan shirt beneath a brown vest and matching pants. The prince's walking cane hung upon the backrest of his seat. Captain Silas sat opposite the young couple, glad they had each other's company during this troubling time. "My father's ministers made a fine choice selecting you, Silas, even if it was only for a temporary post. The King spoke highly of your service and dedication when we last discussed the war and other affairs of state."

"You are kind, sir, yet I'm glad that you will assume the reins of power. It's what is best for Rhiál," he said, glancing around the room. A fire crackled in the hearth and shelves of polished pine lined several walls, filled with books and small treasured works of sculpted art. "This room reminds me of one of King Basil's private areas in his estate, except we now face the water to the west. How long has it been since your last visit across the lake, Princess Melinda?"

"Almost eight years," she replied, sipping from her cup of tea. "Though my father and King Basil had amicable relations, visiting each other on occasion and keeping in regular contact through their ambassadors, I was more interested in my studies than politics while growing up." She smiled as she set down her cup, glancing mischievously at Victor. "I think I saw you once or twice on my last visit. You were a tall, gangly youth who thought himself far wiser than his years, if I correctly recall."

Victor chuckled. "Perhaps you were thinking of my brother, Morton, though you are probably correct. But as I would have been seventeen at the time to your fourteen years, I shall attribute your observations then to the infatuation of a young school girl smitten by a dashing prince but not willing to admit it to herself."

Melinda smiled playfully. "I shall debate that point with you at a more appropriate time," she replied, "though I will admit to a bit of infatuation now, my dear sir."

Captain Silas cleared his throat as he reached for his tea. "I'm glad to see that imprisonment has not made either of you bitter or jaded about the important things in life."

"Our months in confinement were nothing I would wish on anybody," Victor said in a more serious tone. "And having injured a knee during my last battle only added one more difficulty to the experience. But Melinda and I decided early on in our confinements to strengthen both our minds and our spirits to keep us whole and useful for the day we might be released and called upon to lead."

"Victor and I are under no illusions, Captain Silas. We will both have moments of doubt and melancholy ahead of us," Melinda cautioned. "Yet having each other to rely upon as we weather those moments will only strengthen us and our ability to govern."

The couple looked knowingly at each other, silently debating whether to divulge a certain bit of information to the captain. A smile suddenly appeared upon their faces, indicating agreement.

"Captain, before we join the others, I think now would be a good time to let you in on a secret," Melinda said. "But you must promise not to share this news with anybody until we make a formal announcement. There is much still to be done to repair the damages of war before we take the next step."

"The next step?" Captain Silas sat back and smiled. "I assume you're talking about marriage." The couple nodded. "Well, I would hardly call that much of a surprise to me or to the public after seeing you both upon that balcony and your obvious love for one another. But if that is your wish, then I shall certainly keep it to myself."

"Oh, we intend to get married," Victor explained. "Probably sometime in Mid Summer of next year."

"Victor has already asked for my hand and I accepted," Melinda added, blushing slightly. "But that is not the secret we are referring to. There is something else, something of much greater importance we hope to accomplish with the consent of the citizens of Rhiál and Maranac."

Silas was clearly intrigued. "And I thought this day couldn't hold any more surprises. What do you intend to do?"

Victor leaned forward. "As Melinda said, we will only go forward with this proposal with the approval of the majority of our people on both sides of the water–though I don't think that that will be a problem. But what we would like to do after things settle down is to sign a treaty of reunification between our two nations, uniting them into one kingdom as they once were. Since Drogin is no longer an impediment to a peaceful reunion, maybe the time has arrived at last to bury the long forgotten disputes of the past. And though my father and King Hamil had both nurtured such a dream for the future, even they were reluctant to wade into those turbulent waters."

Captain Silas nodded approvingly. "Now that two new young rulers have arrived, you can easily sweep away the barriers of old and make this a reality. But what would you call this new entity?"

"Victor and I talked about that while in our cells," Melinda said. "And as the formerly united kingdom was called Maranac, we both thought that it should retain that name with perhaps a slight twist to help erase some of the recent unpleasantness."

"It's nothing fancy," Prince Victor explained. "Simply this– *New Maranac*."

The captain smiled. "I rather like the sound of that, preserving the old while forging a fresh path at the same time. I think King Basil and King Hamil would be proud of you both. But in which city will the royal couple reside? In Melinas? Or in Zaracosa?"

"In Bellavon, of course!" Melinda said. "Though the old capital city on the southern tip of the lake has been divided and in disrepair for some time, restoring her to shine again like new will be a goal that all citizens would strive for with passion as our individual lives are put back together as well."

"Melinas and Zaracosa would still be important administrative cities in the new kingdom," Victor added. "As King and Queen, we would install a governor in each location to assist us in overseeing the northern provinces on both sides of the lake. Melinda and I could use someone of your talents in such a position, Silas. Though an official appointment would be months away, I'd ask you to think about it while we go about repairing our respective kingdoms."

"Please do," Melinda said.

"I'm very honored by your offer and will certainly consider it," he replied. "But in the meantime, Prince Victor, I am simply happy to be a captain in your army, here to do your bidding."

"In that case, I would request that you continue overseeing affairs in Melinas until I return across the lake," he said. "I shall remain here for a couple more weeks to recuperate and to develop our proposal with some of Melinda's closest ministers. And I shall give you a list of some of my father's sagest advisors for you to put on a ship and send here to join our discussions. It will be quite a few hectic months ahead of us."

"The prospect of New Maranac coming to fruition will be a dream come true," Melinda said. "At last the people's nation will be restored to the *people* instead of serving as a plaything for the likes of my uncle and outsiders like Vellan. But thankfully, Drogin and his collaborators are no longer a threat." She sighed distractedly, enduring one of those moments of doubt and melancholy that she had referred to earlier before looking up with a smile. "Victor, we should join the others for lunch before they are finished. Captain Silas, I'm sure, is hungry after his passage across the lake."

"The captain and I will catch up with you shortly, my dear," he said as he grabbed his cane and stood up. "Silas can walk with me while I hobble along, and hopefully in that time I can convince him to take the governor's post in Melinas."

"Of course," Melinda replied, kissing him on the cheek before she left the room to join the others, her mood cheerful and light.

"She's an amazing woman," Victor said as he and Captain Silas strolled down a corridor and then up two flights of stairs, taking a brief detour along the way to the dining room. "Yet she will forever endure the pain of losing her parents by Drogin's hand. It was an evil act I don't think she can ever fully forgive, nor will many in Zaracosa or throughout Maranac." The prince led Silas to an arched window looking east and unlocked a latch, swinging the glass panel outward.

"Why are we here?" he asked.

"Drogin and his men were despised for what they did, and after they were killed, some in the ministry thought that public anger would follow them to their graves in the form of desecration," Victor explained. "Others believed that neither Drogin nor his associates were fit to be buried within the borders of Zaracosa–or in Maranac itself–for their hideous crimes. I agreed with both points of view."

"So what was done with their bodies?" Silas asked. He peered out the window to a spot Victor pointed to several miles away. The captain blinked a few times, trying to distinguish a faint flurry of tiny dark shapes fluttering against the milky gray sky.

"The corpses were loaded onto a cart at night and deposited on a strip of wasteland just beyond the tips of those distant pine trees, left to the mercy of the elements." Victor looked up, his eyes glazed with weary sadness. "A proper fate, I suppose."

"No doubt," Silas agreed, glancing at him before returning his gaze outside the window where the drifting black images slowly came into focus. Though he was too far away to hear their calls, Captain Silas could now clearly see a flock of vultures circling on the warm currents of air beyond the pine trees. Their talons were razor sharp and their wings extended in graceful flight high above the barren wasteland miles outside the city where they fed.

Captain Silas ordered the five ships back to Melinas the following morning, though this time they were bearing the flags of Rhiál which Princess Melinda had requested as a sign of the enduring friendship between the two kingdoms. And though the vessels were technically the spoils of war and now belonged to Rhiál, Prince Victor told his fiancée that Silas would only borrow the ships for their journey back and would return them to Zaracosa in short order.

"But when our kingdoms are reunited, it won't matter where the vessels are docked," Melinda replied as she and Victor watched the ships sail away across the sunny waters from an upper window of the estate. "They will be the ships of New Maranac then, each flying a brand new flag. It will be a wonderful day if that happens."

"*When* that happens," he replied, his arm wrapped lovingly around her waist as he leaned in to kiss her. "*When* that happens."

King Justin, King Cedric, Eucádus and their respective troops departed Melinas three days later on the twentieth day of Old Autumn. They said their goodbyes to Captain Silas and promised to send word in plenty of time so he or his representatives could attend the winter war council in Morrenwood.

"Both Rhiál and Maranac will want to be part of an offensive against Vellan after what he has done to our nations through

Drogin's hand," the captain said with a grim smile. "Save us a few seats at the table."

Some of the visiting troops agreed to stay behind for a short while to assist with the postwar efforts. Buildings were in need of repair, wounded soldiers required tending to, and the food stores that Drogin had hoarded in the south had to be distributed among the provinces on both sides of the water before winter arrived.

The air was brisk and the skies a brilliant shade of blue when the two Kings and Eucádus led the first line of troops west along the road back home. All were happy to be leaving without the baggage of haste and anxiety that had accompanied them on their eastward trek. But now all three men carried the indelible memories of those who had died in battle and the resultant heartache and melancholy. It was the heaviest of weights upon their hearts which they would take with them to their graves.

Ramsey and Captain Tiber led another line of men as did Ranen, Uland and Torr. Ramsey questioned Tiber extensively about Drumaya's military and his ideas for a spring offensive against Vellan as they traveled along the road like two old friends. The latter trio of Clearing leaders simply talked about Jeremias during the first few miles of their return trip, shedding tears and laughing aloud during some of their reminiscences, yet knowing how crushed his wife and the other residents of the Fox Clearing would be once they learned of his passing. None looked forward to breaking the tragic news.

When morning dawned two days later, they broke camp and continued eastward along the Kincarin Plains, having passed through the gap between the northern and southern branches of the Ridloe Mountains the previous day. When noon arrived, the several armies prepared to split and travel in different directions. King Cedric and Eucádus would continue to lead the troops of Drumaya and the mountain nations, veering southwest and making for the southern tip of the Bressan Woods. They would cross the Swift River just beyond the forest to the village of Wynhall and then march north to Grantwick.

"Though I had never expected to return to the Ebrean Forest," Eucádus said, "our forces will go back to the Five Clearings to spend the winter until our last stand against Vellan. We'll be in regular contact with King Cedric throughout the cold months to develop our strategy. After that, I suppose, we will either find victory in our attempt or perish in the effort."

"But we will aim for victory," Ranen added with an encouraging smile, the red strip of cloth in his hair blazing in the sunlight. "Then we can move our families out of the Ebrean and back to our homelands. It will be a glorious day if that happens."

"*When* that happens," Prince William replied with a melancholy grin as he bid his friends a temporary farewell. He would return to Morrenwood with King Justin, there awaiting any news from Montavia.

"My emissaries will be in contact with you, my friend, until the day of the next war council," King Cedric said to King Justin as they shook hands. "I will travel to the Blue Citadel this time where we can make plans to extract Vellan from his stronghold in Del Norác like a rotten tooth," he added with a wink to Prince William.

"I look forward to our next meeting," King Justin replied as he wished everyone safe travels. "It will be a less dreary winter when all of you–who I now consider dear friends and staunch allies–again grace the corridors of the Citadel. So until then…" He offered a cordial nod before turning around on his steed and directing his troops to the northwest for the final leg of the long road home.

The King's path would take them between the Red Mountains and Lake Lasko, covering the same terrain that William and Brendan had traveled weeks ago. They would continue north above the lake along the Pine River to the southern border of Arrondale and then onward to the capital city. King Justin longed to look upon the granite face of the Blue Citadel awash in a soft vermilion glow of the setting sun and framed by fragrant pines of deep green towering along the rushing waters of the Edelin River. But even more so, he couldn't wait to hug his granddaughter and hear any word of his son's military campaign in Montavia and of Nicholas and Leo's journey to Wolf Lake. Right now he could only wonder what news would greet him upon his return, his thoughts running the gamut from success to disappointment and back again as day slowly turned into another restless night.

The army of Arrondale moved steadily northward for the next several days as the temperatures dipped a little more each night. The skies turned iron gray and remained so for the rest of the journey, hinting of an impending snowfall. On the seventh day since the forces of Drumaya and Arrondale had separated, King Justin was nearly granted his entire wish when he looked upon the Blue Citadel from afar as it stood proudly among the snow-dusted pines in the waning light of day. Flickering beams of sunlight escaped through a tear in the clouds and softly brushed against the granite blocks on the southwest corner of the building, but only for a few moments. When the King and the forward lines finally entered Morrenwood, the clouds had mended. The lingering daylight quickly faded as a deep, purple twilight wrapped itself around the sleepy landscape.

A light flurry of snow danced in the air. Few of the citizens of Morrenwood were outdoors to greet the arrivals, but word swiftly spread that the troops had returned from war. Soon doors opened and citizens poured out of their homes. There would be much celebrating and tear-filled mourning into the late hours of night. As families reunited, houses along the city streets and throughout the countryside glowed with warm, yellow light as sweetly scented wood smoke escaped from chimneys into the frosty air. On this first day of New Winter, the long-absent army had at last arrived.

As the lines of troops, horses and supply wagons slowly made their way along the roads and into the city, many of the locals watched and cheered the returning soldiers, thanking them profusely for their service. One man, however, silently observed the commotion from the window of a nearby inn where he had been staying for the past several days. He quickly slipped on a heavy brown coat, paid his bill at the front desk and then hurried out into the cold night. He untied his horse from the side stables and galloped north out of town, crossing a bridge over the Edelin River and heading deeper into the Trent Hills. He blended into the darkness, eager to report to his superiors about King Justin's triumphant return.

CHAPTER 70

On the Eve of Vast Possibilities

Princess Megan greeted her grandfather in the large hall at the front entrance of the Blue Citadel, giving him a long hug as tears rolled down her smiling face. She wore a pale green dress with a fur-lined wrap upon her shoulders to keep off the wintry chill. When she saw Prince William standing among the men who had accompanied the King, she burst out in a smile and hugged him as if he were her younger brother, happy to see him safe and sound.

"Where have you been all this time?" she asked with a mix of joy and relief. "After Grandfather left for Rhiál, my father sent out additional scouts to search for you and Brendan after the first teams came back empty-handed, but they had no success either."

"I've been to more places than I care to remember," William replied with a weary grin. "But I promise to fill you in on the details soon, Princess Megan. It's a long story."

"I look forward to it," she replied, scanning the small crowd. "And where is that brother of yours? Where's Brendan?"

He gazed uncomfortably at Megan before looking askance at the King, searching for the appropriate words though not in the mood to address the painful subject just now. King Justin swiftly jumped in.

"That is also a long story, Megan, which we can talk about over a meal in private," he said. "Is Nedry around? There are a few matters I'd like to discuss with him, too."

Megan glanced at him knowingly, certain he was eager for any information about Nicholas and Leo. "I shall find him at once, sir, and see to it that Nedry and a hot supper are brought to one of your private rooms."

"Thank you, my dear," he kindly replied. "In the meantime, Prince William and I will speak briefly with my captains before I dismiss them for their own well deserved meals. We shall join you and Nedry upstairs in less than one hour."

"I look forward to it. And welcome back, Grandfather," she replied, kissing him on the cheek before hurrying across a stone floor and disappearing down an adjoining corridor. She had much news to tell her grandfather and couldn't wait for the next hour to pass.

A round table in a private study had been set with five place settings and laden with food–a large tureen of steaming sweet potato and carrot soup, a plate of fried sausage and mushrooms and a bowl of herb biscuits. The kitchen staff had also prepared a jug of wine, a pot of hot cinnamon tea, a plate of cheese and a small bowl of fresh butter. A crackling blaze danced in a fireplace where two people quietly conversed upon the hearth while seated on a set of wooden chairs. The room's only window, opposite the fire, looked out upon the nighttime sky subtly awash in the faint glow of the Bear Moon, just past first quarter and shyly hiding behind a mass of inky clouds.

Nedry rushed into the room moments later, fearing he had been late. He smiled when seeing the table had been set but not yet occupied. His long, gray hair was somewhat frazzled after another hectic day of tending to his official duties, his thin face sculpted with lines of worry and fatigue. He was bundled in several layers of clothing as was his habit during the colder months in Morrenwood.

"Ah, good evening, Princess Megan," he said, noticing her near the fireplace. "I received your message but apologize for not having had a chance to meet with you earlier. Meetings and such."

"No need to apologize, Nedry," she replied as she and the other individual ceased talking and stood to greet him.

"And good evening to you, Leo," he added, greeting the young man who stood protectively at Megan's side.

"Hello, Nedry," he said.

"I'm glad you'll be joining us. But who is the fifth?" he asked Princess Megan, indicating the place settings on the table. "Your messenger had only indicated that King Justin requested my presence here tonight."

"Oh, with him will be–" But Megan didn't get a chance to finish her sentence when the door opened. King Justin stepped into the study with William by his side.

"Prince William!" Nedry exclaimed when he turned around, his obvious excitement wrapped in a mantle of disbelief. "I never expected to see you here, though I'm beyond happy that you are." He hurried over to the prince and flung his arms around the boy's shoulders as if he were his long-lost grandson. "It does my heart good to see you again," he muttered on the verge of sobbing, his face buried in the crook of his arm. He released William and stood back, glancing at him with concern. "But where is Prince Brendan?"

"I'll tell you shortly," William replied, taken aback by Nedry's demonstrative greeting since he was only vaguely acquainted with the King's top advisor.

"Shall we have supper first?" Megan chimed in. "I'm sure you're all famished after your journey."

"I'm sure our journey will not compare to yours," King Justin said with an appreciative smile when he saw Leo. He stepped forward and greeted him with a firm handshake and a welcoming slap upon the shoulder. "I am beyond relieved and grateful to see you back safe in the Citadel, Leo." He glanced around the room and his smile faded. "But where is Nicholas?"

"We seem to have more questions here than answers," Megan said as she directed everyone to the table. "Let us eat while we discuss these various adventures and put our minds at ease. Grandfather, perhaps you should give an account of the war in Rhiál first, which, I assume by your very presence here, went well. Then maybe William can tell us how he returned with your army when he had left on his own many days before."

After Megan ladled out soup into their bowls and everyone began to eat, King Justin gave a brief account of Rhiál's victory over Maranac, including King Basil's death and the surprise reappearance of Princess Melinda and Prince Victor. With a hint of unease, he turned over the conversation to Prince William who quietly told how he and his brother had left the Blue Citadel, ostensibly for a few days of adventure in the countryside that turned into a harrowing journey inside the Ebrean Forest. Megan, Leo and Nedry were shocked and saddened to learn of Brendan's death and offered their condolences.

"I still find it difficult to believe what had happened," William softly said as he stared at his plate. "But I'm beginning to get used to it for what that's worth, and thank you for your kind words." He looked up with a trace of a smile though his eyes were weighed down with a perpetual and weary despondency. He and the others noticed that Nedry had lowered his eyes and cupped his chin in one hand, shaking his head continually, embroiled in emotional agony.

"Nedry, what's the matter?" King Justin asked with concern, knowing how much the man pushed himself in his job despite his advancing years. Nedry suddenly looked more tired and worn out than usual, causing the King to wonder if the governmental position was now impairing his health.

"It's all my fault," he muttered, still shaking his head and avoiding eye contact with the others. "All my fault." He slowly and shamefully looked up at William, his eyes glistening with tears. "I killed your brother."

"What?" the King replied, more confused by the comment than surprised. William was too stunned to say anything.

"It's true. It's true..." Nedry quietly wailed, his head bowed again as he took several deep and unsteady breaths. "It was that crow. And I wanted to protect the mission as well. I should have said something. I should have..."

It was several long moments before Nedry composed himself and the others could pry a complete and coherent sentence out of the man. Megan poured a cup of wine for him and encouraged the shaken man to take a few sips. When some color had returned to his face and his breathing normalized, Nedry set down the wine and straightened up in his seat, ready to speak.

"Despite my habit of worrying myself to an early grave for the safety of this kingdom," he began, "I think my first misgivings about the mission to Wolf Lake began when I saw that crow. That *crow!*" He glanced up, his eyes filled with dismay.

"First, Nedry, it is my job to worry to death about the wellbeing of Arrondale and its people," King Justin said. "So don't assume that burden on yourself. And second, what about this crow you speak of? What are you trying to tell us?"

Nedry relaxed, exhaling deeply as he sat back in his chair. "Everything I had done was for the success of Nicholas and Leo's mission. As we were preparing for it, I sensed that I was being spied upon...by a... A crow." He looked uneasily at his companions. "I assure you that I have not lost my faculties, King Justin–at least I don't think so. But when we gathered in your upper study with Tolapari that one day as he traced Nicholas and Leo's journey on the map, I happened to see a large crow on the ledge when I opened the window for some fresh air. Other crows were flying near the woods that day, but not this one. After I walked back toward the window while we were discussing the medallion, I noticed that the crow had eased its way closer to the opening as if listening to us. A strange feeling overwhelmed me as if that bird could understand us, so I hurriedly closed the window."

"You think it was spying on us?" Leo asked without the slightest bit of condescension.

"I know it sounds preposterous, but my nerves were severely rattled at that moment," he said. "I attributed my state of mind to overwork and exhaustion. But I saw the crow again while I took a walk along the orchard road, and then later outside the window of my room at night. I was convinced it was spying on me, seeking information about the medallion."

"It's not such a farfetched proposition," King Justin said. "I have heard accounts of powerful wizards casting spells upon the birds in the air and other small creatures that roam the woods, allowing them comprehension of our tongue and recruiting them as spies and such. Your suspicions, Nedry, are not unfounded."

"Thank you, sir. But sadly I am compelled to say that my suspicions were finally vindicated when I once again saw that crow for the last time on the morning when–" Nedry stopped, preparing for the consequences of what he was about to say.

"When what?" King Justin asked, his ice blue eyes locked upon his friend.

"–when I sent Prince William and Prince Brendan off on their journey across the countryside. It was on the morning after

Nicholas and Leo had left on their journey the night before," he whispered, overwhelmed with guilt.

"I'm not certain I follow you," William said. "My brother and I asked for permission to leave the Citadel for a few days. You couldn't have known that we were going to travel all the way to Drumaya, hoping to meet with King Cedric."

"No, I didn't," Nedry replied with distress. "But when you asked me to get permission for your trip from King Justin, I decided to take matters into my own hands. And the result, I'm afraid, was disastrous. You see, as a precaution, I suggested to the King that Nicholas and Leo should leave the night before their originally planned departure at dawn to conceal them from any curious eyes. And you readily agreed," he reminded the King who responded with a nod. "Immediately afterward, you gave your consent to William and Brendan's request of leave, upon which I decided to act in secret. I had the seamstresses prepare extra travel clothes for their journey which included two matching wool overcoats."

"Which we gratefully accepted," William said. "But I still don't see your fault in this matter, Nedry."

"My fault, dear sir, is that I suggested, even encouraged you and Brendan to leave at dawn on the very day that Nicholas and Leo were first supposed to have departed." Nedry paused as he took another deep breath, his voice cracking. "You see, I was convinced that that crow had overheard details of the mission, so I set up you and your brother's departure as a diversion, hoping you'd be seen leaving the Citadel by any unfriendly eyes and mistaken for Nicholas and Leo, thereby providing them cover. And when I saw that crow fly high in the air as you and Brendan left the courtyard on horseback, well, I knew I was right." He looked apologetically at Prince William with genuine remorse in his eyes. "I never suspected that any harm would befall either of you. I just assumed you and Brendan would return in a few days and that any spies following you would realize their mistake well after Nicholas and Leo were out of harm's way." Nedry shot a glance at Leo, already having heard some of the details of his adventures in the wilderness when he returned two nights ago. "But that wasn't entirely true either as you can explain to King Justin shortly. You and Nicholas were never out of harm's way."

A series of chilling thoughts raced through the King's mind when hearing those words, but Leo offered him a reassuring glance that everything had turned out well in the end. Prince William, in the meantime, contemplated all that Nedry had said and turned to him, gently laying a hand upon the old man's arm.

"I do not blame you for my brother's death. And I say that after blaming myself for so many days. It was simply a horrible result from a series of events we were barely able to hold in our grasps." William's voice was calm and sincere. "We've all made mistakes in these troubled times, Nedry, confronting obstacles most have never faced before nor should ever have to in a perfect world. And despite my young age, I've realized over the last several weeks that this is far from a perfect world. And our responses to it, unfortunately, will not be without fault either, try as we might."

Nedry dabbed at his watery eyes with the cuff of his shirt sleeve, still shaken by Brendan's death yet relieved that Prince William did not attribute the blame to him. "You are kind and wise for such a young prince and will make a fine leader some day."

William smirked, breaking the tension. "Thank you, but I'm in no hurry to test your theory." He glanced at Leo. "Now that my story is told, I'm curious to hear about your journey with Nicholas. Did you succeed? And where exactly did you go?"

"I'm curious too," King Justin said, "particularly in light of Nedry's earlier remark. What harm had befallen your mission?"

"Before I answer," Leo said, "first let me show you this." He raised his hands to his head, then suddenly froze, his eyes fixed upon Nedry. He jumped out of his seat, walked to the window and drew a thick set of drapes across it before returning to the table. "Just in case something might be out there," he joked to everyone's amusement.

"Stop teasing your audience," Megan told him with an affectionate smile. "Get on with it already."

"Yes, ma'am," he replied with mock seriousness.

Leo reached for a piece of leather cord draped around his neck and hidden underneath his shirt. He lifted it over his head, revealing Frist's iron key dangling from the end. He handed the magic item across the table to King Justin who took it with great care and wonder, smiling thankfully at Leo for his accomplishment.

"I can't imagine what you went through to find the wizard," he said while turning the key over in his hand, contemplating what a devastating blow it could deliver to Vellan's forces when the Spirit Box was finally opened. "I have so many questions, Leo. For starters, where is Nicholas? And how long did it take you to reach Wolf Lake? Before you began your journey, I had my doubts that Frist might even be alive." He gazed at the key again, almost in disbelief that he was actually holding it. He raised his eyes to Leo. "So tell me, how's the old wizard faring these days?"

Leo gazed silently at the King, upon which the monarch immediately sensed that something was wrong. "Frist, I'm sorry to say, gave his life to reforge that key. Though from what I was told, he quite willingly took the task upon himself."

"From what you were told?" Prince William asked. "Were you not there?"

"I was asleep at the time," Leo replied with a twinge of embarrassment, "but with good reason."

Leo recounted his and Nicholas' journey through the Dunn Hills with Hobin, including the attack by the two Islanders and the injury to his shoulder. "I was grateful when Frist cured me because I couldn't have endured another dose of Hobin's yoratelli brew." Everyone listened in rapt silence as he described the final meeting inside the wizard's cave. Just as touching was Nicholas' decision to leave the key with Leo and journey alone to search for Ivy.

"I can't imagine where he or Ivy could be right now," Megan worriedly said as she took Leo's hand in hers beneath the table. She looked at her grandfather, seeking reassurance that she knew he couldn't honestly give. "Do you think we'll ever see them again?"

"I hope so," he replied with a warm smile. "Nicholas is a resourceful man. He helped bring you back to me, after all."

"I suppose I can always go back after him," Leo added. "I'll take Hobin along with me. He's good to have around in a tight spot."

"So he's an accomplished mapmaker?" King Justin asked.

"Beyond accomplished from the maps he showed us."

"Hobin has been meeting with some of the administrators in the royal library," Nedry said. "From what little I've heard so far, this fellow would be worth hiring to update our maps of Arrondale and areas beyond the border. He is quite talented."

"After leaving Wolf Lake, we returned briefly to his home in Woodwater where he collected some of his best maps of the Dunn Hills to bring here to show," Leo explained. "Fortunately, the trip back to Morrenwood was much easier than the way forward. Hobin and I rode south around the Cashua Forest instead of going through it. Nicholas and I lost several valuable days by hiking through those trees without a guide."

"I look forward to meeting him," King Justin said. "But in the meantime, we have this to deal with." He held up the key. "One of my other ministers said that Gregory left Morrenwood with his army five days ago."

"That's correct," Nedry replied. "Prince Gregory had delayed his march to Montavia for as long as he thought prudent, waiting for Nicholas and Leo to return with the key. After you had left for Rhiál, your son sent out scouts to Montavia to secretly survey the capital city and beyond, including up to the shores of the sea."

The King leaned back in his chair. "And what did they find?"

"The scouts reported back that Montavia was still under siege by the Islanders, yet at peace. Apparently no fighting had broken out since Caldurian's first assault. Most of the five hundred Enári troops were stationed in Red Lodge and around the immediate area along with some Island troops for support. The majority of the Islanders were scattered throughout the other larger villages and near the borders," Nedry said. "Life was going on as usual under the circumstances, and no more incoming ships from the Isles were spotted along the coast. Prince Gregory assumed that if more reinforcements were to arrive, it would not be until spring."

"That is a bit of good news," the King replied. "Though William's countrymen are prisoners within their borders, at least they are not being starved or killed."

"That's why Father risked delaying his departure for as long as he did," Megan added. "But as Leo and Hobin arrived here two nights ago, they missed each other by three days."

"Prince Gregory planned to launch his attack on the capital city at dawn on the sixth day from his departure–which is tomorrow," Nedry pointed out. "So we can still time the use of the key to maximize his success."

"Assuming that Gregory arrives in Montavia as planned," King Justin cautioned. "But we'll have no way of knowing that and must hope that my son will make his charge tomorrow at daybreak." He gazed at the key again, anticipating the vast power it could unleash from the Spirit Box if he used it–and he was unflinchingly prepared to do so. "It seems we are gathered here on the eve of vast possibilities. Great changes in fortune await us if our combined labors pay off. Peace in our lands might be hastened through the efforts of those who have already fought and died, of those who may yet do so, and from the quiet and vital endeavors of men like Leo and Nicholas. So, just before daybreak tomorrow, we will open the Spirit Box. Though it has remained sealed by magic for twenty years, we will hope for the best. But in the meantime…" King Justin handed the key back to Leo who accepted it with a bewildered stare.

"*Sir?*"

The King grinned. "Leo, you have protected this key since it was remade and brought it safely back to Arrondale. I feel it'll remain quite secure hanging around your neck until tomorrow morning. I'll make sure you are awakened at the appointed time so we can complete this task before breakfast."

"And the Spirit Box? Where is that?" Leo asked as he placed the cord over his head and slipped the key beneath his shirt, feeling the weight of the world upon his shoulders.

"It is securely locked in an upper room," King Justin replied. "As an added precaution, I'll post a few guards outside your door tonight. Just to put Nedry's heart and mind at ease," he added with a wink to his advisor.

"Much appreciated," Nedry replied.

"And I'll certainly feel better, too," Megan said, though her solemn expression indicated otherwise to the consternation of her grandfather.

"What's troubling you, my dear?" he asked.

"I just feel bad for Carmella," she replied with a slight sigh. "I promised to let her know of our plan with the key, seeing that she was one of our group of ten who had taken the oath. But she has grown attached to that Enári creature, Jagga, these past several weeks and I think she'll be very upset. I'll take some hot food out to her and let her know what we've decided."

King Justin was slightly taken aback. "Carmella is here? And with the Enár? I just assumed they had gone to her home in Red Fern after Nicholas and Leo departed."

"Yes, Grandfather, they did. But don't look so nervous," Megan replied. "Before Carmella left, I had promised to contact her when I had new information about the key. I sent a rider to her home yesterday asking her to stop by for tea and lunch, a message we agreed upon beforehand to let her know that the key had been returned. She and Jagga arrived early last night and are camped out behind the Citadel near the river." Before King Justin could articulate his obvious apprehension, she quickly calmed him. "Do not worry, Grandfather. Jagga knows nothing, nor will he, about the key. Carmella simply wanted to be here when the deed was done. I think we owe her that much."

The King nodded, his concern diminishing. "You're right of course, Megan. None of this would have happened were it not for Carmella. But couldn't you have at least found her a spare room in the Citadel to spend the night? Winter is upon us."

Megan chuckled. "I offered, but she is set in her ways, Grandfather. Carmella is used to traveling on the road and prefers the outdoors when away from home. She also suspected that people would be wary of having an Enári creature inside these walls and so didn't want to impose."

"I suspect that Jagga wouldn't be comfortable inside either from what little I learned about him from Carmella," Leo added.

"We'll let them be," King Justin said. "Besides, it's only until tomorrow morning. Then this laborious affair will finally be over."

Shortly after supper, Megan exited the back of the Citadel. She was wrapped in a hooded cloak and carried a basket filled with a loaf of fresh bread, a wedge of cheese and a few pieces of roasted turkey. One of the guardsmen walked with her in the inky darkness, holding a torch aloft as a fine flurry of snow descended and stuck to the semi-frozen ground. Less than a mile to the east, the tiny flames of dozens of bonfires burned in an open field where most of King Justin's army had encamped for the night before the soldiers would return in the morning to their respective villages or garrisons. Another fire burned just ahead along the banks of the Edelin River where Carmella and Jagga had made their camp. When they approached close enough to hear the crackling of the flames, Megan thanked her escort and sent him back as she wanted to speak to Carmella alone.

Megan watched as his torch drifted back toward the Citadel and then glanced up at the windows, spotting a face peering out from behind one of the frosted panes. And though she couldn't distinguish the features from this distance, she knew that Leo was looking down upon her with affection and concern, just as he had said he would. He wanted to accompany Megan on her visit, but since he was appointed to keep the key safe until morning, neither Megan nor anyone else in the know thought it would be wise to allow the object anywhere near Jagga even though the Enár knew nothing of its existence.

Megan walked to the fire and soon felt its soothing heat. Suddenly a dark shape stepped away from the enclosed wagon off to the left and walked toward the fire. The glow of the blaze illuminated the subdued expression on Carmella's face as she offered a gracious smile to Megan and accepted the basket of food.

"You should have remained inside on such a cold night," Carmella said apologetically, enveloped in her multicolored cloak. She also wore a pair of beige gloves that extended to the middle of her forearms, still uncomfortably conscious of the pumpkin-colored tint imprinted upon her hands and wrists. "I'm sorry I asked you to report back to me, Megan. It could have waited until morning."

"Nonsense, Carmella. I told you I would visit and I intend to keep my word. Besides, I could use some fresh air tonight." Megan looked around for any sign of Jagga, curious about his absence.

Carmella invited her to sit on a log with her near the fire before pointing to a spot farther down the river. Megan craned her neck until she saw the faint glow of torchlight along the water's edge a short distance away.

"Jagga's down there," she said with amused melancholy. She folded her arms and gently rocked back and forth near the flames.

Megan arched her brow. "What's he doing?"

"He's searching," Carmella replied, staring into the fire. "For my medallion."

"I don't understand."

Carmella smiled, wiping the mist from her eyes. "He noticed one day that my medallion–his gift to me–was missing, so of course

I had to play along and act surprised. I told him that it must have slipped off while I was splitting wood or working my gardens or traveling on the road. Ever since then, wherever we go, he searches for hours at a time, hoping to find the medallion and return it to me." Carmella took Megan's hand and teared up. "It breaks my heart so, but what could I tell him otherwise?"

"I understand," she replied, not wanting to inform Carmella that the key would be used tomorrow before the crack of dawn to open the Spirit Box. But after stumbling around the subject, she finally uttered the words and told her friend the truth.

Carmella took a deep breath and sighed. "It was only a matter of time, I suppose, once Leo returned. And though a part of me wishes that Jagga had never given me that medallion or stolen the key in the first place, I guess this is what needs to be done despite the conflicted feelings of a silly, old woman."

"Your feelings are not silly, Carmella." Megan placed an arm around her shoulder to comfort her. "And you certainly aren't old by any stretch of the imagination. Why, you put many younger women to shame by all the work and traveling that you do."

"Perhaps, but soon I'll have to drive myself again if events play out as we expect." She looked at Megan, grateful for her companionship. "Tomorrow morning?"

"Before dawn," she whispered. "My father plans to launch his assault on Triana at that time, so we will coordinate our action with his, assuming his forces are in place. But we shall see."

"Yes," Carmella said with a weary sigh as she glanced at the wavering torchlight along the river, picturing Jagga examining every inch of ground for her treasured medallion. "We shall see."

That same evening, a man walked beside his horse among a thin spread of pine trees scattered around the base of the Trent Hills just north of Morrenwood. The steady flow of the Edelin River nearby only heightened the dense silence of the cold night. A snap of a twig caused the man to freeze in his tracks before he looked around in the oppressive gloom. He didn't have to look long before another set of eyes spotted him.

"Glad to see you made it back, Mr. Nollup." The voice drifted through the trees to his left. "You and your steed follow me and then you can make your report and get some food and sleep. No doubt you deserve both."

"I certainly crave both, Mr. Mune," the man replied with a gruff voice. "Lead on."

Several minutes later, the two men entered a small clearing where a fire burned and four other people stood close to it, conversing in low voices while they warmed their hands. One of the individuals was Madeline, dressed snugly in a fur-lined hood and cloak. With her were Commander Uta and Captain Burlu of the Northern Isles and another soldier. Madeline turned when she heard Mune and Mr. Nollup approach, glad to see them both despite her stony expression.

"I hope you have good news," Madeline said, her tone as dry as the winter air. Her eyes were fixed upon Mr. Nollup.

"Yes I do, ma'am," he replied while tying his horse to a slender tree before edging up to the fire. "King Justin and his troops returned earlier this evening. Most are camped a good distance away from the Citadel. They should pose no problem for you."

"You're sure the King himself has returned?" Commander Uta asked, massaging his unshaven face.

"Quite sure. I saw him at the head of the line."

Madeline looked up at the commander and offered a faint smile. "Then at long last, we're ready to implement our plan."

"The sooner the better," Uta replied. "One more delay and my troops would have abandoned even you, Madeline. Living in the Trent Hills these past few weeks has grown tiresome. My troops are men of action, not content to sit around and watch trees grow."

"Tomorrow morning they will get their wish," Madeline said. She directed Mr. Nollup to follow Captain Burlu to the main encampment hidden deeper in the trees where he could find food and a place to rest. When they were gone, Madeline eyed the soldier standing next to Commander Uta. "So, how are you feeling now?"

The soldier returned a steely gaze and took a step away from the bonfire before slowly raising his arms in front of him. A pained expression appeared on his face while he remained as still as a statue. Slowly, the man's body began to liquefy until the soldier from the Northern Isles transformed into the wizard Arileez. When the process was complete, the eerily familiar figure with the skeletal face and shock of white hair stood before them, clothed in garments of animal skins and other fibrous materials while wrapped in a tattered cloak. Yet Arileez appeared tired, almost disoriented for several unnerving moments until it finally passed.

"I feel fine now," Arileez brusquely replied. "But I will go and rest until you're ready to leave. I am not a plaything, after all, here to entertain you."

"Of course not," Madeline said. "But when we storm the Citadel, you will have to appear as a soldier until we can get you alone with King Justin. Then you will have to take on his appearance. So get all the rest you can. We can't afford any mistakes tomorrow."

Arileez grunted as if offended by the remark. "There will be none, I assure you." He walked off into the trees, taking much of the tense atmosphere with him.

"I thought he'd never leave," Mune whispered when Arileez was out of earshot. "I'll be glad when this is over. He could stop your heart with one look of those eyes."

"He's the key to our victory, Mune, and Vellan is counting on our success," Madeline said, though her thoughts were troubled with other matters. "Yet his difficulties of late do not bode well. His last few transformations have been a task, something Arileez claims he has never known before."

"But whether the result of an illness or some other cause, the timing is wretchedly inconvenient," Uta interjected. "No doubt I will lose some good men on this mission, Madeline, but if it is all for naught in the end because of him…"

Madeline, insulted by the remark, glared at the commander with such fierce intimidation that even Mune averted his eyes, fearing that she might lash out.

"We will not fail this time, Uta. Mark my words." Her tone was icy as she adjusted her cloak. "Just make sure your men are ready to perform as instructed."

She turned and stormed away into the trees, following in Arileez' footsteps. Mune and Commander Uta looked at one another, both relieved to be rid of the two individuals if even for a short while.

"They do tend to crowd a room by their presence, don't they?" Mune whispered, holding his hands above the flames. "Even if the room happens to be an entire forest."

Commander Uta chuckled, knowing that that would probably be the last bit of laughter either of them would hear for a very long time.

CHAPTER 71

Fire and Stone

Leo heard the steady beat of horse hooves battering the planks of a rickety bridge crossing the river. He tried to block out the noise as he lay on the cold ground among the trees, but even when he covered his ears, he couldn't muffle the annoying sound. It grew louder and louder, forcing him to open his eyes to utter darkness. But when his mind finally focused, he realized that he wasn't outdoors.

He felt the nip of cool air upon his nose as he lay on his side bundled up in several blankets. A yawning fireplace across the room contained a pile of glowing embers, the remains of last night's fire. As the monotonous pounding continued, the sound of galloping horses transformed into someone impatiently knocking upon his bedroom door in the Blue Citadel.

"*Just one more hour...*" he mumbled, his face buried in the crook of his arm and a feather pillow. His eyelids suddenly popped open when he grasped the importance of the day ahead. He anxiously felt for the metal key beneath his nightshirt. The quest to find the wizard Frist, and all the hardships that he, Nicholas and Hobin had endured in the process, would shortly be judged as either a brilliant maneuver or a complete waste of time. The hopes of many people were about to be fulfilled or crushed with the simple turn of a key.

Another knock forced Leo to climb out of bed and wrap a blanket over his shoulders to keep warm. He trudged to the door and opened it, allowing a splash of light to enter from an oil lamp affixed to the outside wall. One of the two guards standing in the corridor looked up at him apologetically.

"Sorry to disturb you, but the hour is at hand," the guard said. "When you're ready, we'll escort you to the upper room as King Justin requested."

"I'll be with you shortly," Leo replied wearily as he peered through the doorway. He smiled when Princess Megan walked down the corridor wearing a dark blue dress with a velvet stole around her shoulders.

"I thought you'd be dressed and on your way by the time I got here," she joked, fondly amused by Leo's disheveled appearance.

"I'm still getting used to sleeping in a bed again and not having rocks and tree roots sticking in my back," he replied.

Leo combed a hand through his tangled hair as he slipped back inside the room, closed the door and lit a candle in the glowing embers. He hurriedly dressed and then flung open the window drapes, revealing a dark, wintry morning through the frosted glass panes. He removed the key from around his neck and examined it in the glow of the candlelight, both excited and apprehensive about his appointed task. But with Megan at his side, he knew everything would turn out for the best. Moments later, he stepped into the corridor and joined the others as they made their way to the upper room.

"Grandfather will join us shortly," Megan said as she walked beside him. The two guards led the way down the corridor lit by oil lamps at regular intervals along the walls. Any windows they passed appeared dull and black in the predawn hour like a series of dead eyes keeping silent watch.

"I'll be glad when this is over so we can get back to a normal life," Leo whispered. "Normal at least until winter is over. Then I suppose it's an all-out assault against Vellan from what rumors I've heard."

Megan took his hand and smiled. "Let's not think too far ahead, Leo. I just want to spend some time with you, unencumbered by kidnappings, keys and miles of traveling over endless roads and wilderness. I'm looking forward to winter, hoping you can spend a good part of it next to me."

"I intend to," he replied. They turned a corner and headed up a flight of stairs into a hallway lined with decorative tapestries and pieces of sculpture set in hollow sections of the walls. "However, I do plan to go home to Minago for a spell and let my family know I'm alive," he added. "I hope Henry still remembers me."

"He'll be proud of you after he learns what you've done, as will your parents." Megan looked at him with a questioning gaze. "You *do* have it with you?"

Leo smirked as he tapped a hand to his chest, indicating that the key was underneath his shirt. "When it's over, you can keep it for a souvenir if you'd like."

"Or we can give it to Carmella," she suggested. "As there will still be magic within it, she might–" Suddenly a distant rumble echoed dully through the corridor, causing everyone to halt and look around with uncertainty. "Was that a clap of thunder?"

"It almost sounded like it," one of the guards replied, "though that would be rare at this time of year."

"We should move on," Leo said with unease. "King Justin will be–"

Another far-away sound caught their attention, only this time it clearly wasn't a rumble of thunder. The frantic shouts of men's voices and the metallic clash of swords drifted up nearby stairwells and along the walls of the corridor from distant chambers inside the Citadel. The guards glanced at each other, sharing the same thought.

"The Citadel is breached!" one said, drawing his sword. The other soldier vaulted past Megan and Leo so that one of the men guarded the couple from either side. After listening for a moment, both sensed that the fighting was still confined to another section of the Citadel, perhaps two floors below.

"Take Leo to the upper room quickly," the second guard informed the other. "I'll guide Princess Megan to a secure location." The man removed a pair of keys attached to a metal ring from his side and tossed them to his counterpart. "You'll need these."

"I don't want to leave Leo!" Megan cried, visibly shaken.

Leo placed his hands upon her shoulders and looked calmly into her eyes. "Megan, there's no time to argue. If there are intruders, you must go now," he said. "I'm sure your grandfather is being told the same thing."

"He's right, Princess Megan. I'll take you to a safe place where King Justin is most likely headed as we speak," her guard replied. "You know what is expected of you in such a situation. We have no time to discuss it."

Megan briefly fumed, but knew that her protector was correct. She placed her hands upon Leo's cheeks and kissed him quickly to his delighted surprise before stepping back.

"Go on then," she reluctantly said, hurrying down the hallway with the guard and calling over her shoulder. "But find me as soon as you can!"

"I promise," Leo replied, his eyes tenderly fixed upon her as she disappeared around a corner, her shadow and footsteps fading in the growing chaos from below.

Leo and the other guard pressed on, both wondering what forces had infiltrated the Citadel, though assuming they were after the key. Their footsteps echoed off the walls as the sounds of close quarters combat percolated in the background.

Earlier that morning in the cold, bitter darkness, Commander Uta and Captain Burlu stealthily guided one hundred of their finest fighters through the Trent Hills. They neared the outskirts of Morrenwood, preparing to storm the Citadel. Madeline and Mune accompanied the troops along with Arileez who again assumed the form of an Island soldier. An hour earlier they had passed the village of Red Fern. Madeline recalled the month-long stay at Carmella's farmhouse on its outskirts twenty years ago. She and Caldurian had taken refuge there after their failed kidnapping attempt of the King's infant granddaughter, Princess Megan.

Madeline looked wistfully back upon those days when she was young, naïve and full of hope and possibility. Caldurian first began to train her in the magic arts then, along with Carmella, and it was in Red Fern that the rivalry between the two cousins first blossomed. Madeline knew that she possessed the superior intellect and magical aptitude, feeling slighted that the wizard had shown Carmella equal attention in their training. Only when Carmella discovered five hundred Enâri creatures and the eagle Xavier hiding out in the nearby woods, and then later learned of Madeline and Caldurian's role in the attempted kidnapping, did the wizard finally turn on her. Carmella threatened to report them to the authorities, so Madeline, the wizard and their small army fled east to the Cumberland Forest, but not before a final confrontation between the two cousins.

Madeline chuckled to herself as she walked in the darkness, receiving strange glances from Mune as she silently recalled the heated argument with Carmella in her pumpkin patch twenty years ago. She doubted that her cousin had gained enough knowledge of magic over the years to reverse the orange skin-coloring spell she had cast upon her before fleeing. As the sweet scent of pine drifted through the air, she wondered if Carmella still resided in Red Fern, harboring doubts that she would ever see her again.

"You're awfully pensive this morning," Mune whispered as they shuffled across a dirt path blanketed with pine needles and small stones. "Having second thoughts about our assignment? It seems an age since we discussed it over dinner at the Plum Orchard Inn."

Madeline gazed sharply at her associate and sighed. "It's still not morning, Mune, in case you haven't noticed. And when have you known me *not* to be pensive?"

"Good point," he replied, scratching at his goatee. "I'll be glad when this mission is over so I can take some well deserved time off." He reconsidered his words and glanced at Madeline. "We are getting some time off, aren't we? What more can Caldurian and Vellan expect of us now that winter is here?"

"Replacing King Justin will be quite a coup for us all," she replied, her words absorbed in the nearly impenetrable darkness. "But since we must assume that the King returned victoriously from the war in Rhiál, I'm guessing Vellan will have other plans for us to counter that defeat." Mune sighed upon hearing those words. "But fear not. I'm sure Vellan will show some appreciation for our grueling work and allow us time to recuperate. Even I'm feeling drained. What I'd give for a few months to simply indulge myself in the study of magic. There is much more I want to learn. But first things first, Mune. We have a job to do."

"As usual," he replied with a scowl as they trudged onward. "But then I shouldn't be surprised by that answer."

"No, you should not," she said.

Half an hour later they emerged from the trees. They followed a dirt road for a short distance, briefly halting when they neared a small stone bridge spanning the Edelin River. The bridge was situated less than a mile from Morrenwood. Here is where their forces would cross, making directly for the Blue Citadel. Here is where everyone realized that there would be no turning back.

"Absolute silence from this point forward," Commander Uta instructed his men. "As soon as we're inside the Citadel, make for the sections you were assigned to and then find and detain the King. Madeline assured me that searching those particular areas will provide us our best opportunity to locate him. Send word back to me or Captain Burlu once you do and we'll send reinforcements immediately." He glanced at Arileez, now in the form of a young man in his twenties dressed in the uniform of a Northern Isles soldier. He was the key to their plan, and though Arileez had been following his orders without question, the commander felt intimidated by him nonetheless. "Remember, we want to remove King Justin from the Citadel alive and in secret after he is replaced. No one can see him leaving or our efforts will be in vain. Vellan will be anxious to speak with him while his substitute is reigning over Arrondale. But in the event that it becomes unavoidable," he sternly cautioned, "kill the King. But still remove the body in secret. Any questions?"

The commander received none and gave the order to cross the bridge, after which they veered southwest for a time along the river's southern bank before turning directly south through the trees and fields toward Morrenwood. A short while later, the dark walls of the Citadel were visible beyond the distant pines, looming like a silhouette against an equally dark sky. A few oil lamps burned inside the building's corridors, lighting up several frosted windows like watchful eyes. Commander Uta whispered last minute instructions before his men proceeded onward, veering to the right as the Citadel loomed ahead, growing closer with every step.

Soon the trees thinned out and the soldiers halted on the edge of the woods. The Citadel was less than a quarter mile away to the southwest. Here the frothy rush of the Edelin River was audible behind them to their right, its cold waters splashing over mossy rocks hidden in the darkness. A pale flicker of light blinked along the water's edge in the near distance in the same direction, most likely someone's leftover fire from the previous night. To their left almost a mile away, several bonfires burned in a large field covered with tents. Uta realized that the bulk of King Justin's troops must have made their encampment there since returning from war. He expected his mission to be swiftly executed before word could be sent to those troops. The commander gave the final signal for his men to move forward. They made a beeline toward the back entrance of the Citadel while cloaked under cover of clouds and darkness. They still had time to reach the few sentries at their post before the first hint of gray dawn pierced the eastern horizon.

"Are you ready, Madeline?" Uta whispered, his white breath rising through the frosty air. "You must work your spell fast."

Madeline adjusted the fur-lined hood covering her flaming-red hair, her words feather soft. "Am I ready? You waste your breath on such a silly question, Uta, and insult me at the same time. How resourceful of you."

"No insult was intended," he coolly replied, used to the woman's sharp tongue. "Just doing the job I'm being paid for."

Uta silently signaled to four soldiers nearby, marching two by two, each pair on either side carrying a long wooden pole across their shoulders and gripping it with one hand. Two pieces of rope were tied to each pole. Attached to the four rope ends tautly hanging from the poles was a leather sling holding a large, round granite rock. The four soldiers weaved their way toward Madeline, keeping pace with her while remaining a few steps behind as the hanging rock gently swayed with their movements.

Moments later the small army closed in on the Citadel. The soldiers silently drew their swords as they made for the main back entrance. Despite being a moving black mass that blended in with the last remnants of night, Uta expected to be spotted at any moment by the four guards whose faces he could now distinguish in the flickering light of several torches in back of them.

"Here we go," Mune nervously whispered to Madeline as he eyed the quartet of Citadel guards just ahead. Two were casually talking to one another while the other two stood at attention near a set of thick wooden doors beneath a stone archway. "Sometimes I don't think Caldurian pays me enough for my services."

Madeline ignored the comment, concentrating instead on the spell she was about to perform. Moments later, one of the guards talking near the Citadel entrance turned his head suspiciously toward the advancing troops and paused, apparently not quite sure if he saw something moving in the thick gloom. He pointed in Uta's direction as if seeking the opinion of the guard next to him. That was the only indication Commander Uta required to tell him that their veil of secrecy was about to be lifted.

"First team forward," he whispered. "Now!"

Instantly, a dozen soldiers in front of the line raised their swords and bolted toward the entrance and were soon enveloped in the faint light of the torches. The four Citadel guards heard the footfalls and a moment later detected the glint of enemy swords in the firelight. They shouted an alarm and drew their weapons. A clash of metal upon metal shattered the calm as two of the guards were quickly slain by Uta's men.

"Secure the doors!" one of the two remaining guards ordered as he battled a pair of intruders.

The guard who received the order ran with lightning fury along the left side of the Citadel while pursued by three of Uta's men. He disappeared through a small metal door, slamming it shut and locking it behind him. Unable to secure entry, the three soldiers returned to the main doors beneath the archway that were now barred from inside. They noted with indifference that the third Citadel guard had been killed, his body slumped against the stone wall.

"Step aside!" Uta yelled from a short distance away, not caring who heard him now. The rest of his army stood at the ready as the dozen soldiers near the entrance hurriedly rejoined the group.

The four men who had been carrying the large granite stone dropped it on the ground directly in line with the main doors and moved away. Madeline shed her cloak and walked toward the rock, staring at the object as if it were alive and ready to pounce. She squatted down and placed both hands upon it, her willowy body visible against the fluttering torchlight near the archway.

"What's she going to do?" one of the soldiers whispered.

"Silence!" Commander Uta said.

Madeline closed her eyes and bowed her head, muttering a string of words in a language no one there understood except Arileez. She moved her hands slowly across the stone for several moments and then froze as everyone looked on in fascination. Suddenly, a faint red-orange glow radiated from the surface of the stone like wisps of steam. Many observing the ritual thought they were imagining it at first until the stone grew as bright and hot as glowing embers. Madeline swiftly pulled her hands away and stepped back, her eyes and mind still focused upon the rock. She stretched her arms out toward the fiery orb and continued to speak the strange words, her voice slowly rising in volume, yet her tone severe and authoritative.

"*Syfálin brűl*," she commanded, her arms stiffening and her facial muscles taut.

The glowing rock moved slightly, shuddering in place as if it wanted to explode or roll away. Yet something held it back. Madeline clenched her jaw as she continued to cast a searing gaze upon the piece of granite, her expression grim and determined. She raised her hands and extended her thin fingers, repeating the command more forcefully.

"*SYFÁLIN BRŰL!*"

Like an eagle in flight, the flaming stone shot through the air, barreling directly toward the Citadel doors. At the same instant, Madeline lurched backward, off balance and slightly dizzy, yet her eyes still fixed on the fiery orb. After sailing above the surface of the ground like a blinding meteor, the glowing rock smashed into the left door of the Citadel and through the edge of the stone archway, obliterating both in a wild and fiery explosion that reverberated across the landscape like a thunder clap. The wooden door burst into flames and a gaping hole had been blown into the stone wall. The remains of the two doors were flung wide open, askew on their hinges. The back hall of the Citadel was exposed as a group of the King's soldiers scrambled within to repel the surprise invasion.

"Forward!" Uta cried, pointing the tip of his sword at the Citadel. But his men needed no further encouragement, storming the building as they cried out into the fading night. Arileez, Captain Burlu and Uta followed last of all.

Mune, however, stayed back and ran over to Madeline when he saw her waver precariously on her feet. He caught her by the arms and steadied the woman, noting a faint smile of satisfaction upon her face despite the grueling task. A few snow flurries began to fall.

"Are you all right, Madeline? I thought you were going to pass out." He retrieved her cloak and placed it over her shoulders.

"Why, Mune, I would almost think you cared about me," she replied as the clash of metal swords and frantic battle shouts echoed in the distance. "But I am fatigued, I'm not ashamed to say." She wrapped herself in the warm folds of her cloak and walked to a nearby tree, her arm linked around Mune's. She sat on the ground and rested against the trunk, closing her eyes for a moment. "Let me sit here and recover. That spell took quite a bit out of me, though I had prepared for it for days."

"Not the same as releasing flaming balls of grass into the air," Mune joked, recalling their first meeting with Uta near the grasslands.

She grinned. "No. This was more fun." Madeline opened her eyes and looked at Mune with a firm gaze, already back to business though not fully recovered. "You'd better join the others. You must help search for the King. Your team is waiting."

"I know," he said. A flicker of disappointment registered on his face as Madeline's brush with playful camaraderie disappeared. "I know my assignment and will cover my section of the Citadel. Join us when you can." He stood and ran toward the demolished entrance.

Madeline watched him disappear into the chaos, hoping he would survive. A light flurry of snow began to fall. She closed her eyes again and relaxed, exhausted after having performed her magic spell which proved to be the most difficult one she had ever attempted. Yet she prided herself on the fact that no other wizard had guided her to create that spell. She never approached Arileez for his opinion, finding him even more standoffish than Mune sometimes found *her*. And it was rare that she had a chance to consult with Caldurian these days as he was too absorbed with implementing his and Vellan's grand plans.

Madeline imagined herself apprenticing with Vellan since Caldurian seemed to have grown less close to her with each passing month despite a deep-seated affection she knew he would always have for her. Though still a powerful individual, she thought Caldurian was not the caliber of wizard he had been years ago, wondering if she should cultivate other connections when this current assignment was over. Madeline yawned and began to nod off, recalling the first time she and Caldurian had met. At that time she had claimed to want to know the world, but as her powers and associations developed and expanded, she found herself more eager to control it and bring to it a sense of order that she had convinced herself was desperately needed.

"*In time,*" she whispered wearily. "*All in good time.*"

But just as Madeline was succumbing to soothing sleep, she thought she heard a voice in the darkness, whispers drifting among the black and gray border of a new day. She opened her eyes and scanned the area along the river, for a moment wondering if some of King Justin's troops at the encampment had secretly made their way over here to help repel the attack. When she saw a tiny burst of light and a flurry of sparks near the river's edge, she snapped out of her stupor and was again fully awake. She noted a vague outline of someone leaning over the remains of the bonfire she had spotted earlier when approaching the Citadel. Madeline jumped to her feet, her body still feeling the strain from having cast such a strenuous spell. Slowly, a tiny ball of flame appeared to drift through the air, gently rising and falling as it drew nearer. She guessed that someone had lit a torch in the glowing embers and was heading her way.

"That noise surely wasn't thunder." Carmella's whispered words drifted through the air from a short distance away, the flickering torch in her hand. Madeline didn't immediately recognize her cousin's voice, not having heard it for twenty years. "And why are the back doors of the Citadel wide open at this hour? I think–"

A long, silent pause followed and the light ceased to advance. Madeline guessed that whoever was talking in the darkness had just spotted the destroyed door and stonework with shock and was now at a loss for words. Perhaps it was someone who had wandered over from the King's stables farther down the open grassy area, she speculated as the milky, gray light of morning increased ever so gently in the east.

"Something terrible has happened!" Carmella continued, now louder and with a hint of panic as the torchlight again moved closer. Madeline detected something oddly familiar about the voice. But she shoved that thought aside when noticing a shorter figure standing beside the woman in the faint glow of the light. "We have to help. We have to check on Megan and the others!"

"I will stay here," Jagga replied, his voice low and gruff. "I will probably get blamed if I step inside the Citadel."

"Don't be ridiculous," Carmella replied, hurrying forward through a veil of fine snow flurries as she held the torch aloft.

As she approached a nearby tree, Carmella suddenly stopped, startled when catching something out of the corners of her eyes. To her left she spotted a short, slender figure standing bundled in a cloak beneath the leafless branches and staring back with equal curiosity. Carmella moved cautiously toward the individual as the torchlight swept away the murky shadows, revealing Madeline's watery green eyes and strands of flaming red hair peeking beneath the hood of her cloak. Carmella was about to ask for the woman's identity, but then twenty years of separation dissolved instantly like a bubble of soap. Her mouth was agape.

Madeline, too, stood there momentarily in a state of shock. Upon seeing Carmella's colorful cloak and gazing at her unkempt head of light blond hair, she knew in an instant that this woman was her cousin. The corners of her lips rose in the tiniest of smiles when Madeline noted the long, beige gloves covering Carmella's hands, assuming them still to be the color of pumpkins. The two women gazed at each other for a long, silent moment, their faces having gently aged since their last encounter. But the fiery determination in their eyes seemed not a day older or less intense.

"Hello, cousin," Carmella said, her voice hardened with contempt. "This is the last place I expected to find you, Liney. But by the horrific looks of things, I guess I shouldn't be surprised." She indicated the smoking Citadel entrance with a tilt of her head. "But don't expect to escape responsibility for your actions this time."

Madeline shook her head without fear or intimidation. "Hello yourself, cousin. It's been too long," she replied, removing her hood, a mischievous gleam in her eyes. "And escaping is exactly what I have in mind–unless, of course, you think you can stop me this time."

Mune stepped through the broken Citadel doors, sickened by the carnage. Several dead bodies lay sprawled upon the stone floor, a mix of King Justin's troops and Commander Uta's soldiers. There was, however, no sign of Uta, Arileez or Captain Burlu. They had presumably spread out with the others to search for the King. Fresh blood stained the granite stonework in the now vacant chamber which nauseated Mune. The sound of fluttering flames in the oil lamps whispered in the background.

Mune then heard the echo of fighting from distant corridors. He knew there would be violence connected to many of Vellan and Caldurian's endeavors which is why he tried to keep as far away from them as possible. He preferred to plan such undertakings and work around the edges, but he had been unable to worm his way out of this particular affair. The sight and smell of death made him weak in the stomach. But he had a job to do, and the mercenary side of him quickly took over. If he wanted to get paid and save his life, he had to find the team he was supposed to follow and help search for the King. Mune scanned the large hallway, noting two stone staircases on either side and several archways.

"Take the left stairwell," he muttered to himself, repeating Uta's earlier instructions, "then up three flights and to the...*left again*?" He paused in uncertainty. "And then to the *right*? Or is it the other way round?"

Mune was shaken by the ghastliness of the moment, unable to recall simple instructions. But not wanting to linger in case King Justin's troops returned, he dashed up the left staircase, hoping to find any of Uta's men nearby. His footsteps echoed in the cavernous hallway as the stairwell periodically turned at right angles, but the sound was soon drowned out by a clash of swords as he approached the third floor. When he peered around the corner of the stairwell and down the main corridor, he saw a handful of soldiers battling one another at the far end in front of a large door. He wondered if King Justin might be protected behind it, or perhaps it was just one of the many spontaneous fights that had broken out. But armed with nothing but a dagger and having no intention of joining such a large fight, he stepped back in the stairwell and continued up.

Mune heard no sound as he walked along the main corridor on the fourth level. He wondered if the King and those chasing after him were fighting in a different section of the Citadel. It was a sprawling place containing several wings, with some areas utilized more than others. He quickly abandoned the floor and climbed up the final flight to the fifth level, not disappointed that the mission may have unfolded without his presence. Perhaps King Justin had already been kidnapped and replaced by Arileez while he was tending to Madeline. If he found nothing on the top floor, he would hurry back down and exit the Citadel, fearing he had little time to spare before the fortress was again secured. If captured, he guessed that he would be hauled off to a prison cell no matter which king was in charge–the real one or the impostor. Arileez would have to act like the King and keep him under lock and key to maintain his deception, at least for a short time. Mune wanted none of that and raced to the top floor.

As he walked down the corridor, voices approached around the far corner. Mune froze for a moment and then slipped behind a wooden statue in a dimly lit alcove to his right. He dropped to the ground and curled up into a ball behind the base of the sculpture that depicted a man with a short beard holding a sword. Mune guessed that he was someone of importance in the history and politics of Arrondale, glad that the obscure figure from the past provided him a hiding place just in the nick of time.

"Down the next hallway on our left," said the guard who was escorting Leo along the corridor. Mune held his breath, peeking around the base of the statue. "The last door at the end of that passage leads up to the turret where the Spirit Box resides. These two keys open the doors at the bottom and top. Then it's your turn to use *your* key."

Leo responded with a touch of humor. "There are a lot of keys in this business. I'll be glad when it's over."

Mune's ears perked up upon mention of the Spirit Box and a key. His heart beat faster. He recalled the late night meeting with Madeline and Caldurian in Kanesbury just over a month ago. Arileez and Gavin had been present along with the two locals, Zachary Farnsworth and Dooley Kramer. At that gathering, Dooley recounted how he had infiltrated King Justin's war council and the short meeting afterward regarding the medallion. He had mentioned that two people volunteered to take the medallion to the wizard Frist to have it reforged into the key to the Spirit Box.

"They must have succeeded!" Mune thought with horror. He knew that Vellan's forces would be dealt a critical blow with one turn of that key. It was his job to stop it.

He saw the boots of two men pass swiftly by the alcove, their footfalls echoing off the walls and then fading as they turned left down the corridor. Mune panicked, wondering what to do. He had come here to help kidnap and replace King Justin, hoping one day that Arileez would retrieve the Spirit Box or the key, if it was ever successfully remade. But now the key was here and on its way to open the Spirit Box. He knew he had to do something to stop the two men, but there wasn't enough time to find help as they would reach the upper room at any moment.

Mune racked his brain as he cautiously stood up, leaning on the statue for support. Slowly his eyebrows rose as a desperate plan took shape in his mind. His palms grew sweaty and his heart raced. He lowered a hand and gripped the hilt of his dagger, unable to recall the last time he had used it. Mune took a deep breath to calm down before unsheathing his weapon. It was time to jump into the game full-bore and bloody his hands.

CHAPTER 72

A Pair of Kings

Princess Megan raced down a corridor with her guardsman, the shadowy stonework and fluttering oil lamps streaming past her in a blur. She had left Leo minutes ago in another wing of the Citadel and her heart ached with each step that separated them. But she was also eager to find her grandfather, hoping he was safe. All was quiet as they weaved their way among the hallways and through various rooms, having taken a few detours to avoid areas of fighting.

"We're almost there," the guard said as he slowed down near the end of one corridor. He signaled for Megan to keep behind him while glancing left and right down an adjoining hallway. With both ways clear, he and Megan turned right as it would provide the quickest route to King Justin's presumed location.

"I shall tell my grandfather of your exemplary and courteous conduct this morning," she told the guard. They hurried down three steps near the last third of the corridor before it branched off in two directions at a slight angle to one another.

"While much appreciated, Princess Megan, I'm just doing my job," he replied. He stopped suddenly, extending an arm to halt her progress. "I hear voices," he whispered, pointing at the left turn which he had planned to take.

Megan clutched the ends of the velvet stole around her shoulders, waiting for further instructions. She heard the pounding of footfalls and a scattering of voices to the left and glanced at her protector with fear in her eyes.

"Do we go right instead?" she softly asked.

The guard shook his head, pointing back down the corridor they had just traversed. "We'll go to the other end of this hallway and circle around to the right along the connecting back corridor. Then it's through the library and out one of the side entrances." He gently took hold of Megan by the arm to lead her there.

"Yes, I understand where you're taking me," she replied. "I believe we can–"

Before she completed her thought, a chorus of thunderous voices exploded from the right corridor as well. Megan expected a mob of soldiers to rush out from both sides at any moment. But as the voices on the left grew nearer and louder, the guard smiled, recognizing some of them. His fellow soldiers were swiftly advancing.

"We've just been given some valuable time!" he said, signaling for Megan to wait against the right side of the corridor while he dashed toward the left archway just as a dozen of King Justin's soldiers hurried toward him, their swords at the ready. The men were delighted to see one of their own as Megan's guard pointed to the passageway on the right. "They're heading this way."

"We already know," the lead man replied, noting Princess Megan standing nearby. "But others may soon follow behind us, so get her out of here another way."

"I had already planned to."

The guard ran over to Megan, instinctively grabbed her hand and urged her to race back down the corridor with him as fast as she could. Just then, a handful of Commander Uta's troops burst through the right archway. A clash of swords rent the air as the shouts and cries of soldiers rose above the intensifying battle. Megan and her guard scurried back up the three steps and sprinted to the end of the hall. They turned right down another corridor alongside one of the Citadel libraries as echoes of fighting lingered in the air.

Moments later, they slipped into the library through a doorway on their left. The room was silent, vacant and dark at this early hour as a hint of gray light pressed softly against the window panes overlooking the trees and river behind the Citadel. Megan and the guard made their way to a side door and slipped out into a narrow hallway that led to a spiral staircase leading to another corridor above. They began to climb.

"Are you holding up, Princess Megan?" the guard inquired.

"I traipsed around half of Arrondale recently, so this is a breeze," Megan replied. "I'm just worried about Grandfather."

"Of course you are. We'll be there in moments."

They worked their way along several more corridors and then down another flight of steps before turning around and heading in the opposite direction. They were now beyond the area they had originally hoped to reach and began circling back, finally heading down a wide corridor awakening with the first faint traces of dawn. Megan and the guard suddenly stopped, shocked by the scene they had stumbled upon.

In the middle of the hallway, amid the hanging tapestries and fluttering oil lamps, lay the body of a dead soldier from the King's Guard, a young man not much older than Megan. A figure knelt over the body on one knee, his head bowed and his hand upon his brow as if grieving. Sprawled upon the floor behind the figure lay three more dead bodies, all streaked with fresh blood and dressed in coats and uniforms of the Northern Isles. Megan and her guard slowly approached the lone individual until he looked up, his face grim and tired. Megan, however, smiled.

"Grandfather!" she cried, running up to King Justin who stood and wrapped his arms around her.

"Megan! You're safe," he said. "But where have you been?"

"We had to take the long way to reach you, sir," the guard replied, still gripping his sword and cautiously scanning the area. "What happened here?"

"And where are your guards?" Megan asked, taking her grandfather's hands in hers, noting they were cold to the touch. She feared that he might be coming down with a sickness after all the turmoil and traveling he had endured lately.

"They moved on only minutes ago, chasing after remnants of the enemy," he said, pointing down the far end of the corridor. King Justin again looked at the body near his feet, sighing in distress. "This man saved my life, slaying that soldier over there," he said, indicating one of the Islanders.

"What happened?" Megan asked.

"Before you answer, sir, I must insist that we find a more secure location," the guard said.

"We should be fine right here," the King replied. "We have the last of them on the run. They tried to kidnap me. About ten of them. But my men were on them at once and slew three of the intruders before the others fled, surprised by the ferocity of my troops. I ordered them to pursue, refusing to hide anymore."

Megan hugged her grandfather again, delighted to be at his side. She looked up into his ice blue eyes. "Still, we should leave and find a safer place until we're certain that the Citadel is secure."

King Justin smiled. "How can I refuse my granddaughter such a request? We shall go where he thinks best," he replied, indicating the guard. "Lead on, if you please."

"At once," he replied, keeping in front of them with his sword raised.

But they hadn't taken more than ten steps when they heard voices and footfalls just around the corner ahead of them. Megan's eyes grew wide in terror, fearing that another troop of Islanders had arrived. The guard swiftly grabbed one of the fallen soldier's swords and raised both weapons high as he moved backward down the corridor, motioning for Megan and King Justin to keep behind him. A moment later, a dozen soldiers rounded the corner and headed directly for the trio before coming to a halt. Megan and her guard smiled with relief when seeing that it was King Justin's troops who had arrived. Their smiles lasted only a moment, however, when they saw the face of a man accompanying them emerge from the center of the group. Megan's jaw dropped in disbelief, unable to believe her eyes as she stared with shock at a second King Justin.

"Who are you?" she asked. Her hands trembled as she looked upon the man, and then shifted her gaze back and forth between the two identical Kings, each dressed alike and eyeing one another with burning contempt.

"Keep away from him, Megan!" the second King warned as he stepped away from his soldiers and walked toward her, pointing at his likeness. "He is an impostor!"

"Megan, don't listen to him!" the other King replied, gently placing a hand upon the arm of the young princess as if to protect her. "This is a sorcerer's trick, no doubt. He and those soldiers are not who you think."

"I don't know what to think!" she cried, stepping away until her back was against the wall. "Am I dreaming? Is this for real?"

"It is very real, but he is not!" replied the second King Justin. He glared at his mirror image standing a few feet away. "Minutes ago I was kidnapped by men from the Isles and replaced by this fraudulent being, but my guardsmen rescued me before I could be ushered out of the Citadel by the enemy. Now we're back to expose the impostor."

The other King shook his head in disgust. "What a clever tale you weave, so much so that I almost believe it myself. *Almost.*" He glanced at Megan for support. "My men repelled the Islanders' first attack when they tried to take me away by force. Now the Island soldiers have returned in disguise as soldiers of Arrondale, hoping to replace me by using this subterfuge and fooling you in the process. But it will not work."

"Megan!" the second King pleaded, attempting to convince her by the tone of his voice that he was truly her grandfather and that the men surrounding him were indeed soldiers of Arrondale.

"Granddaughter!" countered the first King with equal intensity, extending his hand to the princess.

Megan looked at her guard, silently pleading for advice. After pausing a few moments with uncertainty, he offered a tentative reply.

"I think we should detain both Kings until we get to the bottom of this royal mess," he said, glancing at the other soldiers. Though they looked like his fellow guardsmen, he began to wonder if they were also impostors. "Unless, of course, Princess Megan, you have a better idea."

"He is the real King Justin!" one of the soldiers replied, pointing to the King who had accompanied his group to this spot.

"I appreciate your conviction," Megan's guard replied, still clutching the two swords as if anticipating trouble. "But now I'm not even sure about you!"

For a long and stressful moment, a weighty silence hung over the gathering as the gray light of dawn seeped into the corridor from a row of windows. Megan regained her composure and stepped forward with growing impatience, feeling angrier and less fearful as the seconds ticked by.

"I am beyond tired of thugs from the Northern Isles and elsewhere disrupting the lives of my family and me!" she fumed, her fiery spirit reignited. "So I'm going to end this charade with one simple question." Everyone looked at Megan with wonder, awaiting her solution. "Grandfather," she continued, addressing both King Justins, "tell me what jewel you gave me for my tenth birthday. As it was a gift I treasured very much, the real King Justin will know of what I speak."

"A most wise solution," the first King replied, eliciting a smile of hope from Megan. "I wouldn't have expected anything less from my intelligent granddaughter." But before answering her question, he glanced at his counterpart, a slight smile upon his face. "Unless, of course, you would like to reveal the identity of the precious jewel that looked so beautiful upon Megan whenever she wore it. I will at least give you a sporting chance after all the trouble you've gone through to impersonate me."

"Quite gentlemanly of you, sir," replied the other King as Megan inched toward him, her confusion now dispelled. "But I don't need a sporting chance since your words have just given you up as a fraud." The first King raised his eyes in mock surprise, appearing unbothered by the accusation. "You see, the jewel I had given my granddaughter for her tenth birthday was a horse, not a gemstone." The real King Justin smiled at Megan who ran over to him and took his hand which felt warm to the touch. "She had named the horse Ruby because of a patch of red mane upon its back."

"Ruby was my favorite present ever, Grandfather," Megan said, basking in the comfort of his presence.

"As you often told me it was," he replied with a smile before looking up at his double with a wrathful glare. "And now that that is settled, my men shall arrest you and find out who you really are and who you work for, though I already have my suspicions."

"Who I really am?" Arileez laughed condescendingly, still in the guise of King Justin. "I am someone with powers you cannot even imagine, so you would do well to give me a wide berth," he replied as King Justin's soldiers raised their swords, prepared to advance upon the intruder. Arileez' voice now took on a bitter and defiant quality as he carefully scanned the corridor, determining his options for attack or escape.

"But since you failed to replace me," King Justin shot back, "the sense of invincibility you're trying to convey is a dismal attempt at best. We do not fear you, whatever you are."

"You had better!" The impostor sneered at his counterpart in the milky gray light, the depths of his eyes growing lifeless and his countenance seemingly paler the longer anyone gazed upon him.

"Go with my men now or suffer the consequences," King Justin ordered, indicating for Megan to keep behind him as he stepped forward. "I will not repeat my request."

"I would question the strength of your authority if you did," Arileez replied.

Megan's guard, who was standing closest to the impostor, moved cautiously toward him, signaling for him to walk down the corridor. But Arileez, weaponless and still in King Justin's form, raised his left arm and stared at the guardsman without a trace of intimidation, his fingers, hand and wrist suddenly liquefying and transforming into a sharp talon of a bird as the young man watched in utter horror. At that same moment, Arileez slowly raised his right arm, intending to transform and sweep it through the air and strike the guard while he and the others were mesmerized by the first spectacle. But King Justin anticipated what was about to happen, recalling his talk with Prince William about the attack in the cabin.

"Look out!" he cried, rushing toward the guard as Arileez' right arm sliced through the air, now also tipped with a sharp talon. King Justin pulled the soldier away just as the point of the talon swept by, tearing across the King's upper right arm and ripping through his clothing and skin.

King Justin and his guard tumbled to the ground as Arileez turned to strike again, but the King's soldiers were upon him in an instant, plunging their blades repeatedly into the wizard. Arileez' body snapped backward as he writhed in pain, throwing his arms into the air while emitting an ear-piercing scream that reverberated throughout the Citadel. As the swords tore through his skin again and again, Arileez' talons were unable to hold their shape. With each thrust of a blade, the wizard's natural form appeared for brief instances so that the soldiers couldn't tell if they were slaying the wizard or the look-alike King. Arileez' body then permanently reverted to its original state. The skeletal face, topped with strands of white hair, contorted in paroxysms of agony as bloodcurdling screams chilled the morning air. Arileez' royal garb dissolved back into the frayed and tattered animal skins and fibrous coverings he had worn for so many years during his island imprisonment.

When the last sword was finally pulled out, Arileez' bloody body collapsed to the floor, silent and still. Everyone looked upon it with breathlessness and racing hearts, unable to comprehend what being they had just encountered. The wizard's body and clothing turned a sickening shade of gray before bursting into flames, causing everyone to step back in surprise. The fire burned briefly before the flames died and the charred body dissolved into a pile of white ash in the pallid light of dawn.

King Justin and his guard stood up and looked upon the wizard's remains in stunned silence. The guard thanked the monarch for his bravery, but the King merely smiled as if it were nothing.

"You would have done the same for me," he replied, holding a hand against the wound on his upper right arm. King Justin was unaware that he was doing so and felt no pain amid the excitement. Megan ran to his side to examine the wound.

"Are you all right, Grandfather?" she asked, removing his hand to get a better look at the injury.

"Of course," he replied matter-of-factly, only now beginning to feel some discomfort as he looked at the bloodstain upon his fingers and shirt sleeve. "It's probably just a scratch."

"It's worse than that," Megan said. "But we'll let your physician have the final word." She hugged him, too happy to scold the man for putting his life in danger. "Who or what was that?"

"I'm guessing the very same creature that took the life of Prince Brendan," he replied, embracing Megan while staring over her shoulder at the pile of ashes. "But he'll never bother anyone again." He looked into his granddaughter's eyes and smiled, so happy to have her at his side. "Now you won't think me foolish for having tried to protect you by sending you away from here in these troubled times."

Megan smiled. "But trouble followed me anyway."

"Indeed it did," he replied with a sigh, kissing her on the forehead. His eyes widened in fear as the excitement of the moment subsided. "Leo! Where is he? What happened to the key?"

Megan's heart raced as she explained how they were separated shortly after the attack on the Citadel. "Leo should be on his way to the upper room if he's not there already, unless…"

King Justin instantly read Megan's thoughts by the frightened look upon her face. "Unless the enemy is after *him*."

CHAPTER 73

Key Developments

Leo's heart pounded. He drew a deep breath, realizing the significance of what he was about to do. He hurried down the corridor to the last door on the left with his guard who unlocked it with one of the two keys on the ring. Inside was a spiral stone staircase leading up to a small turret on the back side of the Citadel. There the Spirit Box had been stored ever since Mayor Otto Nibbs gave it to King Justin for safekeeping many years ago. The light from the oil lamps along the quiet corridor splashed upon the first few steps of the staircase within. All above was cloaked in darkness.

"There's a candle in the recess to your right," the guard told Leo while he kept a vigilant eye up and down the hallway. Leo stepped inside and found a candlestick encased in a glass globe. He lit it from one of the oil lamps. The guard handed him the key ring. "The other key opens the door at the top."

"Aren't you coming with me?" Leo asked.

"I'll keep watch down here just in case. Now hurry!"

"Wish me luck."

Leo raised the flickering candle and ascended the staircase in smothering darkness. Shadows danced wildly upon the curved walls. The bottom doorway was soon out of sight as he circled up and around, the air cold and stale. He wondered how long it had been since someone was last up here, guessing that King Justin probably sent one of his aides to check on the Spirit Box from time to time. He paused a moment, thinking he had heard a noise below, perhaps a cough or a sneeze that was amplified in the tight enclosure.

"Did you say something?" he called down to the guard. But when getting no reply Leo continued on, assuming that he was hearing things. He thought he was near the top and picked up his pace, eager to complete the task. He wished that Nicholas were here since he had played an equal part in getting the key remade. But he guessed that his friend was on another adventure somewhere, hoping that he and Ivy were both together, safe and in good health.

A dull patter of footsteps sounded below. Leo assumed that the guard was heading up either out of boredom or to warn him of approaching danger. He was about to call down into the darkness when he noted a small landing and a door just a few steps above. He hurried to the top and placed the second key into the lock and turned it, pushing the door wide open. Waves of cold shadows washed over him. Leo detected a faint hint of gray outside a trio of windows within the room, knowing that daybreak was fast approaching. The sound of footsteps caught his attention again, now much closer. Instead of stepping into the room, he turned around to wait for the guard, holding up the candlestick to light his way.

"Changed your mind?" Leo asked as the shadow of a figure appeared around the last curve in the stairwell, slowly ascending. But before he could utter another word, the face of a stranger gazed up and startled him–a short, slightly stocky man with thinning black hair and a goatee who appeared pale, tired and oddly familiar in the eerie glow of the candlelight. The stranger's sea gray eyes harbored a cold, dead quality that made Leo shudder inside. His jaw dropped when he noticed a splattering of fresh blood on the stranger's hands. "Who are you?" he demanded. "Where's the guard?"

"He won't be joining us," Mune replied, out of breath and visibly shaken. He had left his dagger lodged in the dead man's back after he had stealthily run up to the guard from behind while he was pacing the corridor. Mune was too shocked and dazed by what he had done and ran off and up the staircase, not remembering to retrieve his weapon. "Now give me the key before my associates arrive," he demanded in a low, hard voice. "They won't be as patient with you as I am."

"What key?" Leo asked, wondering how this man could possibly know of its existence. Suddenly he recognized the face as one of the two individuals he had spotted at the grasslands who had kidnapped Ivy, not letting on to the fact.

"You know what key." Mune's voice rose in exasperation. "Hand it over. Now!"

Leo reached toward the open door and pulled the key ring out of the lock, tossing it to the man. Mune caught it, glancing at the pair of keys with disgust before throwing them down the stairs in a fit of ire. "Not those keys, you fool! The one to the Spirit Box."

Leo nodded. "Oh, that one," he said, lowering the candle so that Mune's face was fully illuminated, his eyes filled with impatience and insatiable greed. "I'll show it to you," he said, his free hand rising toward the leather cord around his neck. Mune climbed up one more stair, his gaze fixed upon Leo's face, his hand reaching out.

But as Mune inched forward in anticipation of obtaining the key, Leo slammed a boot squarely into his chest and sent him flying backward. The man grunted in agonizing pain and tumbled down several steps, his cries ricocheting in the stone stairwell. Leo wasted no time and ran inside the turret and slammed the door shut, though he now had no key to lock himself in. He looked around the tiny room. It was bare expect for a small oak cabinet below the middle of three windows evenly spaced along a curved wall that faced the back grounds of the Citadel. Dull gray light seeped through the glass panes, though the room was still strewn with shadows as thick as cobwebs. He quickly lit two oil lamps on opposite sides of the wall, setting the room ablaze in yellow light. Immediately his heart sank. The top of the cabinet was empty.

"It must be inside," he whispered, keeping his nerves steady.

He placed the candle on a windowsill and then knelt in front of the cabinet, opening a set of doors below the surface with a tiny brass handle affixed to each. He flashed a smile upon seeing a small iron box with a locked lid inside, a nondescript piece of metalwork created twenty years ago by a local blacksmith in Kanesbury. He carefully removed the Spirit Box and stood up, setting the object almost reverently upon the top, wondering about the strength and destructive powers of the spirit within. He wondered if Frist's entity had survived and grown over all these years, knowing he would soon find out. Leo reached for the key hidden beneath his shirt, ready to perform his appointed task.

The door flew open behind him. Leo spun around, his heart racing. Mune stood framed against the blackened entrance, his face bruised and his clothes disheveled. A few drops of blood trickled down his forehead. He immediately eyed the Spirit Box on top of the cabinet and glanced at Leo, gritting his teeth.

"Give me the key and the box," he muttered. "I won't ask a second time."

"Good. I'm sick of hearing your voice," Leo shot back, locking gazes with Mune.

Both men remained still as the first hint of dawn pressed against the frosty windows, neither man willing to give any ground. But Leo knew he had to act soon since Prince Gregory and his troops were ready to commence their counterattack in Montavia, if they hadn't done so already. While still eyeing Mune, he slowly reached for the leather cord around his neck. Mune understood what Leo was about to do, knowing he had to stop him. He shifted his focus from Leo to the Spirit Box and back again, his face contorting in the process. He leaned back slightly, shifting his weight upon his legs, and then sprang across the room. But Leo had sensed Mune's tactic. He quickly turned and grabbed the box just as Mune jumped on his back and tried to pull him over.

"Get off me!" he shouted as Mune wrapped an arm tightly around Leo's throat, choking him while reaching for the cord around his neck with his free hand. With a surge of anger, Leo pushed off the cabinet with all his might and lunged backward as fast as he could to the opposite wall, slamming Mune against the stone while clutching the box.

Mune groaned in excruciating agony as his back smashed into solid granite. Air burst from his lungs but he hardly loosened his grip on Leo's throat. Suddenly, a deafening shriek from somewhere inside the Citadel rose up the stairwell and pierced the morning stillness, but neither man gave it a thought in the midst of their struggle. Leo, on the verge of collapse and struggling for air, trudged another few steps forward and repeated the maneuver, plowing backward into the wall as hard as he could with Mune's body in between. This time Mune released his grip, crying in pain when his head hit solid stone. He fell to the ground in a dazed heap, temporarily immobile. Leo, tired and gasping for breath, sprang toward the cabinet, his face sweaty and hot as he ripped the leather cord from around his neck and placed the Spirit Box back on top of the cabinet. With trembling hands and a racing heart, he grasped the key in his right fingers, setting his other hand on the edge of the cabinet to steady himself. He shakily placed the key inside the lock.

"It's all up to you now, Frist," he whispered, raising his eyes to the growing gray light outside the window.

Leo turned the key. The metal lid immediately flew open as an invisible force burst forth into the room like a wind gust. Leo was flung backward onto the floor and hit his head. The lights in the room flickered madly and the door slammed shut. He tried to raise his head but felt a suffocating pressure upon his chest. He could barely breath, feeling as if he were about to die. The room was silent yet his mind was a wild swirl of ferocious winds and crackling thunder that filled his entire body with searing pain. Leo tried to call out Megan's name, fearing he would never see her again, but his voice couldn't form the words. Pressure continued to build over him. He felt paralyzed, helpless and on the verge of death. Just before he closed his eyes for what he thought would be the last time, the three windows exploded outward. Showers of glass flecks spilled to the ground or were carried away on a cold winter breeze.

Leo could breathe again. His lungs filled with cold, clean air as the pressure in the room returned to normal. He slowly raised his head as the chaos in his mind dispersed. He gazed up at the Spirit Box to confirm that he had indeed opened it and wasn't dreaming. When he saw the lid still raised upon its hinges, he smiled with relief and then rested his head upon the floor, feeling exhausted as if he had hiked the entire stretch of the Dunn Hills. Leo closed his eyes as sleep overwhelmed him and a cool breeze filtered into the room through the three gaping holes in the wall.

Several moments later, Mune opened his eyes and stared up at the ceiling. His head throbbed and his back burned with pain. He rubbed his hands over his face, for a moment unaware of his location or the time of day. When he turned his head and saw Leo's unconscious body sprawled upon the floor, he sat up through his pain, wondering what had happened. He crawled to Leo, but seeing that he was no longer a threat, he stood up on his wobbly legs, his memory returning. Mune glanced at the cabinet and froze, gasping at the sight of the open Spirit Box. He gulped a lungful of icy air.

"*No...*" Mune shook his head and stepped toward the cabinet, gazing at the box in utter disbelief. "*No...!*" he repeated, swallowing hard, unable to move until his mind accepted what he was seeing. "It can't be. It just can't..." He grabbed the hair on the sides of his skull, his face contorting in spasms of shock and despair. He was nearly on the verge of tears, shaking his head and feeling as if the world had just ended.

"This wasn't supposed to happen!" he mumbled, his face as pale as snow, his eyes wide with terror. "What will Madeline say?" Mune's hands began to shake. "What will Madeline *do*?" An even more horrifying thought struck him as the pit of his stomach grew cold. "What will *Vellan* do?"

A short time earlier, a gentle fall of snow flurries sizzled and died upon the burning torch that Carmella held aloft. She gazed suspiciously at Madeline who stood beneath the barren tree and shook her head with disappointment.

"You'll never change, Liney," she sadly said. "You threw in your lot with the wrong people twenty years ago and now plow a path of destruction throughout Laparia. How could you take the side of scoundrels?"

Madeline smirked as hints of gray morning deepened in the east. "And you, dear cousin, are still as naïve as I remember from childhood. And look how far it's gotten you," she said with contempt, pointing toward the river. "You still travel around in that dilapidated cart with your mangy horses and in the company of–" She glanced at Jagga dressed in his floppy brown hat and rumpled, overly-large coat, thinking he was an acquaintance of her cousin or a stranger Carmella had picked up on the road. When she caught a glimpse of Jagga's face in the firelight as he tilted his head up, she gasped, her eyes swirling with disbelief.

"You recognize my friend," Carmella replied with satisfaction. "You aren't the only one who has connections to Vellan."

"You do *not* have connections to Vellan!" Madeline snapped. She recalled when Caldurian told her that her cousin had befriended the Enâri creature named Jagga and thus came into possession of the medallion. Madeline hated believing it then, yet here Jagga stood in the flesh, or at least in the rock and soil from which he was created. "Vellan would not want you in his presence!" she continued, her words dripping with bitterness. "But how is it possible that one of Vellan's own is in your company? Perhaps by some spell you created, though I don't see how as you apparently couldn't lift the skin-coloring charm I had placed on your gloved hands."

"I choose to be here," Jagga uttered in a gravelly voice before Carmella could answer. "*That* is how."

Madeline glared at the Enâr, not the least bit intimidated by his roughhewn features or menacing countenance. "Then you are not only a traitor, Jagga, you are a fool as well by tying your fortunes to my sorry excuse of a cousin."

"I am no traitor!" he said. "How do you know my name?"

"I know all about the traitorous Enâr who murdered a man in Kanesbury and stole the key to the Spirit Box from him," she said smugly. "And I also know that you had the key melted down and formed into a medallion which you gave to my cousin as a gift." She noted Carmella's growing discomfort. "But that is not all. I also know the fate of the medallion after she—"

"You talk too much!" Carmella said, fearing her cousin had learned that she handed the medallion over to King Justin so it could be remade into the key. The last thing she wanted was for Jagga to know, no doubt a treacherous act from his point of view. "You do not know of our business, Liney. It is impossible."

Madeline smirked. "Not impossible if one has a spy in King Justin's rafters. I know all about your secret meeting and oath."

Carmella's mouth was agape, guessing that Madeline and her associates had attacked the Citadel to steal both the key and the Spirit Box. Despite their oath and subsequent precautions, the group of ten conspirators had been foiled right from the start.

"What else do you know?" she grudgingly asked.

"Nearly everything. I know where the medallion was being taken to and what King Justin planned to do with it."

A fire of distrust ignited in Jagga's eyes. "You know where the medallion is? My friend said she lost that gift from me." He stepped toward Madeline in the growing milky light as a dusting of snow fell. "Did you steal it from her? Is that why I can't find it?"

She glared at Jagga. "Quite the contrary. You see, Carmella didn't lose your lovely medallion because she—"

"Liney, I said you do not know our business!" Carmella cried. "So I would advise you to keep quiet about matters that don't concern you."

"And just how are you going to stop me?"

"Don't think that I can't. I've trained much since we last saw each other, albeit on my own for the most part. But I am still a formidable opponent. Don't try me."

Madeline walked in a slow, lazy circle around Carmella and Jagga, keeping an eye on them all the while. Though she didn't believe her cousin could triumph in a battle of spells against her, she was still weary and weakened by the spell she had cast to blast open the entrance to the Citadel. She knew she would be at a disadvantage right now in a clash of magical skills.

"Now don't get overly dramatic on me, Carmella, or I'll turn your feet orange as well." She faced Carmella nose to nose, jabbing her in the chest with a finger. Her voice grew quiet, yet icy sharp. "But if you want me to stay out of your business, then you had better stay out of mine."

Jagga scowled and jumped between the two women, vowing to protect Carmella at any cost. "Don't touch my friend!" he ordered, nearly knocking both women off balance when he separated them. "You will deal with me if you do."

"It's all right, Jagga," Carmella said. "You need not fear her."

"Remove the pumpkin spell," Jagga demanded, "and then leave!" He glared at Madeline, his nostrils flaring, his face nearly pressed into hers.

"If Carmella can tell me where the medallion is right now, I'll consider it," she replied.

Jagga growled, raising his arms in frustration. "She does not know, woman! You are the one who stole the round piece of metal— or knows who did. Don't deny it."

Madeline bent her knees slightly to be eye level with Jagga. "Listen, Enâr, I did not steal your foolish gift to my cousin, so get that through your thick head. And Carmella didn't lose the medallion either. She gave your little trinket to King Justin who sent it off to be remade into the key to the Spirit Box by the wizard Frist himself.

That is what happened to it. Despite your sentimental attachment to her, my dear cousin had no qualms about helping to destroy you and your race. She is not to be trusted."

Jagga glared at Madeline for several moments before looking over his shoulder at Carmella. "Is this true?" he asked, his tone almost childlike.

"Tell him, Carmella. Tell Jagga that the medallion is on its way to the wizard Frist."

Carmella looked at the inquisitive faces in stony silence and then softly spoke. "I cannot tell him that, Liney, because it isn't true. The medallion is not on its way to Frist. I absolutely swear it."

Jagga smiled with relief, his faith in his friend confirmed. But a chill shot through Madeline as she studied Carmella's enigmatic expression, sensing that there was more to her cousin's words than she was letting on. Suddenly cold reality slapped her upon the face and her skin paled like snow.

"At a loss for words?" Carmella asked, guessing that her cousin had stumbled upon the truth. "That's so unlike you. If you have something to say, then say it."

Madeline fumed, her thoughts fluttering chaotically. She slowly clenched her fists. "What have you done, cousin?" she asked, her words weighed down with scorn. "What have you *done?*"

"By your horrified expression, Liney, I think you've already figured it out," she replied as the faint light of early morning increased. A frightful notion suddenly struck Carmella as well when she realized that Madeline still assumed the medallion was out in the wild. She lowered the torch and looked askance at her relative. "Tell me, Liney–just why *are* you here?"

Before Madeline could reply, a deafening and agonized shriek issued forth from the Blue Citadel, storming out of the broken doors and slicing through the air like a swift arrow. Madeline spun around and faced the back of the building, her heart racing and her breathing unsteady. Carmella and Jagga looked on, neither able to imagine the origin of such a disturbing noise.

"What has happened?" Madeline whispered, slowly raising her trembling hands to her face, clearly on edge. She suspected that that was Arileez' scream riding upon the cold air, but one filled with unendurable pain and anguish.

"Whatever nefarious deed you came here for," Carmella said, "it apparently isn't going as planned."

Madeline turned around and glared at her cousin. "Quiet and let me think!"

"You weren't trying to kidnap Princess Megan again, were you?" she asked, knowing the very mention of that failed attempt would enrage her cousin.

"Enough already, I said!"

"Or were you going to steal the Spirit Box, with or without the key?"

Madeline raised her hands and screamed out in frustration, unable to tolerate her cousin's prodding a moment longer. She lunged at Carmella with a snarl, knocking the torch out of her hand and tackling her cousin to the ground. The two women rolled and thrashed about on the frozen soil, shoving their hands in each other's faces as they shouted and sputtered as twenty years of pent-up hostilities exploded.

"You've disrupted lives around here for the last time, Liney!"

"You're a magical flop, cousin, and you always will be!"

Before they could seriously harm one another, Jagga grabbed Madeline from behind and yanked her off Carmella with a single, swift move, pulling the flailing, screaming woman off to one side. Madeline, though, twisted herself around in fiery anger and knocked off Jagga's hat when he briefly loosened his grip. She grasped his thick neck in her hands, trying to choke the bulky Enâr as she pushed back. A moment later they tumbled to the ground and continued to struggle, rolling through the dusting of snow until Jagga was on top of Madeline as she pushed against his face.

"Get off of me, you lout!" she cried.

"Remove the pumpkin spell!" he shouted back, his tangles of dark hair hanging down his face. Jagga clenched his misshapen teeth and growled at Madeline before grabbing her arms and pulling them away from his face. "I won't ask you again!"

"Jagga!" Carmella yelled as she sat up, clutching a sore elbow that had been bruised against the ground. "Don't hurt her!"

"You'll be sorry you ever met me, Enâr!" Madeline sputtered, her face red and contorted as she tried to break loose from Jagga's hold. "I'll see that you–!"

Without warning, three windows in one of the Citadel's upper turrets burst out in a simultaneous shower of glass against the milky light, the frosty shards carried away on a sudden and powerful gust of wind that blasted across the landscape with thunderous force. With her head tilted back toward the sky, Madeline saw the explosion, unable to comprehend what she was witnessing until she felt Jagga's grip loosen on her wrists. She looked up at the Enâri creature, her eyes widening in horror as she watched his face, neck, teeth, ears and hair instantly solidify into the brown and gray shades of the dirt and rock from which he was created before dehydrating mere moments later. His body suddenly collapsed upon her like a pile of sand crumbling on an exposed hillside. Madeline shrieked and flailed her arms in revulsion, frantically swishing the piles of sand and tattered clothes off her. She scrambled to her feet, continuing to sweep her hands against her body in rapid fashion, dancing about and screaming hysterically as she rid the Enâri remains from her clothing.

"*Jagga...*" Carmella breathlessly whispered, wandering in stunned amazement to where his clothes and boots lay amid a pile of sand and snowflakes while Madeline carried on in the background. Carmella gazed up at the turret on the top floor of the Citadel, a warm, yellow light visible behind the trio of shattered windows. She knew the Spirit Box had been opened but wondered about the fate of the person who had bravely performed the task. When she glanced to the east, she noticed a line of torches about a half mile away swiftly approaching, assuming that soldiers from the encampment had been alerted and were on their way.

Carmella picked up some of the sand and let it fall through her fingers, grieving Jagga's absence and feeling responsible for his demise, yet believing she had little choice in the matter. She grabbed his floppy brown hat lying nearby and held it close to her, planning to keep it as a memento of her friend, knowing she would never get over her unspoken betrayal of him.

"Madeline!" a voice called out in panic moments later.

When Carmella looked up, a short, slightly stocky man was running from the Citadel toward her. But the individual quickly veered to one side and headed to Madeline, ignoring Carmella for the moment. She didn't know who he was and really didn't care.

Mune found Madeline thrashing about in revulsion and shock, grabbing her by the shoulders to calm her down. He was about to slap his associate in the face when Madeline grabbed his wrist.

"Don't even think it, Mune!" she muttered, still breathing heavily but beginning to compose herself.

"We have to leave!" he cried, not waiting for an explanation of her crazed behavior. "Something terrible has happened!"

"I know that!" she said, pointing at Carmella.

Mune glanced at the woman kneeling on the ground and shrugged. "Who's she?"

Madeline quickly told him about the surprise meeting with her cousin after twenty years and of Jagga's friendship with her. Mune's baffled expression turned to one of shock when Madeline pointed to the Enâri creature's remains.

"So the spell Frist created inside the Spirit Box really worked," he said. "But what if it reaches–"

"–Kargoth?" Madeline asked. He nodded nervously. "I guess we'll find out when we get there."

Mune swallowed hard. "Get there? To Kargoth? To *Vellan*?"

"To the very doorstep of his stronghold in Del Norác. We have failed him, Mune. We allowed the key to be remade and used, and..." Madeline gazed sadly at the Citadel, the piercing cry from moments ago still reverberating in her head. "And I'm afraid that Arileez will not be walking out of this building again in any form."

"I saw many dead bodies on both sides of the fight," Mune said. "Caldurian underestimated the strength of King Justin's men."

"And the wisdom of his own plan." Madeline sighed. "Just another in a long line of Caldurian's schemes that have gone astray. Vellan will not be pleased."

"Perhaps we should wait for Caldurian to return from Montavia," he suggested. "No need to run off to Kargoth so soon."

"That is where I am going," Madeline said. "Accompany me if you'd like or take your chances with Caldurian. Or with those soldiers just ahead," she added, pointing to the advancing troops in the east. "Your choice."

Mune rolled his eyes, knowing he would be linked to Madeline until the end of this convoluted affair, like it or not. "We can get horses over there," he said, indicating the stables to the west. "We better go now while we still have the chance."

"Vellan will know what to do," Madeline said, tightening the cloak over her shoulders. "It's about time we took our orders directly from him. I think Caldurian has finally outlived his usefulness."

"Just don't let him ever hear you say that. He does have a temper," Mune warned.

"So do I." Madeline walked past Carmella, tossing her an icy stare as she knelt over Jagga's remains. "I'll deal with you another time, cousin."

Carmella looked up with disdain. "It's just like you to run away–again."

"If you want me, Carmella, I'll be in Kargoth." Madeline glanced over her shoulder as she and Mune hurried away. "If you have the nerve to follow."

Carmella looked away, having no desire to chase after her cousin right now. The thunder of approaching horses rumbled along the cold ground. She wondered what fate would befall the Enâri race in Kargoth now that the Spirit Box had been opened. Even after incubating for twenty years, would the spirit be powerful enough to reach Vellan's stronghold in Del Norác? She glanced east past the approaching soldiers and thought about Prince Gregory's offensive in Montavia that may have been launched only moments ago. Had the invisible hand of Frist's spirit already reached there beyond the Keppel Mountains? Or had it thinned out and exhausted itself over the many miles?

Carmella sighed and carefully picked up a handful of the cold sand in her gloved fingers. She walked to the edge of the river as it noisily rushed by and tossed Jagga's remains upon the frigid waters, watching the fine grains and falling snowflakes both silently dissolve in the growing pale light of morning.

CHAPTER 74

The Second Army

Prince Gregory and the second army of Arrondale departed Morrenwood five days before King Justin and his men had returned. It numbered a few thousand soldiers, including many from Montavia who had been training at the Citadel alongside the King's forces. Under cool, clear skies, the prince, along with his most trusted captains and the wizard Tolapari, ventured east to Montavia where Caldurian, his Enâri army and troops from the Northern Isles had laid siege to the rural kingdom beyond the Keppel Mountains. The prince rode at the head of the line upon his steed, looking much like his father would have twenty years ago. His long brown hair played upon the breeze as his sharp blue eyes focused intently upon the terrain ahead. Lines of soldiers, horses and supply wagons proceeded down King's Road in the waning days of autumn. Tolapari, riding next to the prince, couldn't help but sense his restless demeanor several miles into their journey.

"I'm guessing you're either pondering your attack strategy or worried about Princess Megan," the wizard remarked lightheartedly. "It's as if I've been riding with a statue these past few minutes, yet I can tell that the gears are turning in your fertile mind."

Prince Gregory grinned as he looked at his friend. "The latter is correct. I was thinking about my daughter and all she's been through of late. I'm deeply concerned about her safety. That is a parent's job, after all, isn't it?"

"I suppose so," Tolapari replied, his dark blue robes wrapped loosely around his large frame. His unruly mass of thick, black hair kept his head warm enough so that he needed no hood despite the morning chill. "Megan is a resourceful woman who has demonstrated that she can take care of herself. You should be proud of her."

"I am."

Tolapari detected a note of uncertainty in his voice. "But I suspect you have other worries about Megan besides her safety, in my humble opinion."

The prince chuckled. "I've never known you to have a humble opinion. Please, elaborate."

The wizard raked a hand through his hair as he lightly held the reins in the other. "I believe your daughter's affection for Leo Marsh is what's really weighing on your mind. That is especially a parent's job–keeping an eye on a daughter's suitor."

Prince Gregory smiled as he looked ahead, nodding. "You've struck the mark, my friend. But don't get me wrong," he said, glancing at the wizard. "I think Leo is a fine young man, and after all he did to help protect and save my daughter–as well as embarking on his mission with Nicholas–I have no qualms about his relationship with Megan. I'm just overwhelmed by the fact that she has grown up in the blink of an eye. It seems like only yesterday she was content to gallop around the Citadel grounds on Ruby and that was all that mattered to her. And now…"

Tolapari nodded understandingly. "Time stands still for no one."

"I know. But having to raise Megan alone for the past nine years ever since Amara died…" He sighed. "I suppose I've been holding onto my daughter for two people all this time."

"She won't be leaving you any time soon, Gregory. There is plenty of room in the Citadel for her and a prospective husband. Just think–Mr. Marsh could revitalize the apple orchards throughout Morrenwood," Tolapari said, cracking a smile.

"I suppose he could," the prince replied, his mood lighter. "Who would have thought that repelling an invasion of Montavia would give me less anguish than raising a daughter? Surely parenting is the more grueling of the two jobs."

"We haven't arrived in Triana yet to compare. First let's see what Caldurian and his Enâri horde have done to the city."

"I'm sure Red Lodge won't be the charming place that I recall from my last visit a few years ago." Prince Gregory's mood darkened again. "And I'll have to break the news to King Rowan that his two grandsons have been missing for weeks. He is quite fond of William and Brendan. Their mother will be heartbroken."

"It's back to parenting again," Tolapari said with an amused gleam in his eyes as their horses trotted across the hard dirt surface of King's Road. A gentle breeze carried the sweet scent of pine through the air. "The rigors of that occupation will have prepared you well when you inherit the throne from your father."

"Though I'm in no hurry for that to happen," he replied, "being a king will be a simple affair compared to raising Megan." He quickly glanced at Tolapari. "Only don't tell her that!"

In time they reached the end of King's Road and veered left onto River Road, traveling a few more miles until twilight settled in. They lit fires and made camp on the field south of the road along the banks of the Pine River. They continued east after a brief breakfast the following gray morning, eventually passing Graystone Garrison and then the intersection with Orchard Road that stretched north to their left. Later in the day, the long lines of soldiers and supplies passed through the villages of Foley and Mitchell. They again made camp in the southern fields when they had passed two miles beyond Mitchell's eastern border.

Before noontime the following day, the army approached the village of Kanesbury on the northern tip of the Cumberland Forest. The sun peeked out from time to time through breaks in the clouds, and the morale of the soldiers was high thanks to the cooperative weather and swift progress over the so-far accommodating terrain. As they passed through the village, spectators lined both sides of River Road to watch the men on horses at the front of the line go by, followed by companies of marching soldiers, and finally, the supply wagons pulled by sturdy steeds. Many of the locals brought their lunches and sat beneath trees to view the thrilling spectacle.

Shortly after Prince Gregory entered the village, he noticed a tall, lanky man bundled in a heavy coat with his hands shoved in his pockets, walking along the side of the road to watch the advancing lines. The prince vaguely recognized the individual, racking his brain to remember where he had seen him.

"He was at the table during the war council," the wizard said. "He is a member of the local village council."

"Of course! That's Len Harold," the prince replied, guiding his horse off to the side with the wizard and one of his captains while signaling for the others to continue on. Prince Gregory beckoned to Len Harold as he dismounted his steed.

Len hastened over and greeted the prince with a handshake to the envy and amazement of the other villagers. "I'm honored to see you again, sir," he said with a pleasant smile.

"The honor is mine," the prince replied. "I don't have much time to spare, but as I saw a familiar face, I hoped you could offer me fresh information about Otto Nibbs, your mayor. At the council, you said that he had been missing after going off alone to meet with the Enâri creatures in your vicinity."

Len appeared distressed. "He has since returned–and *how*."

He explained that their village had been attacked twenty-four days ago by a band of soldiers from the Northern Isles. "The wizard Caldurian was behind the effort, and for nine days we were prisoners inside Kanesbury, unable to send word for help." After recounting the details, including Otto Nibbs' surprise return and subsequent arrest, Len told the prince that Caldurian and his troops disappeared before dawn fifteen days ago.

"And Otto Nibbs is still incarcerated?" Tolapari asked.

Len nodded uncomfortably. "He is awaiting a public trial, being accused of betraying his village, among other charges."

"King Justin will be saddened to hear that his second cousin is in such a predicament," said the prince.

"So are most," Len replied. "Everything happened in the heat of the moment while we were under Caldurian's fist. I think everyone now secretly regrets what has happened. But still, a trial will go forth when Mayor Maynard Kurtz returns from Morrenwood."

The prince appeared perplexed by Len's statement. "Your mayor went to Morrenwood?"

"Yes. He planned to meet with King Justin and tell him about Caldurian's reappearance. He left eight days ago," Len informed him. "Zachary Farnsworth, who manages the local banking house, is currently our acting mayor."

Prince Gregory and Tolapari glanced at one another with befuddled apprehension. "It will be most difficult for Maynard Kurtz to meet with my father in Morrenwood since the King is currently fighting a war in Rhiál. And if Mayor Kurtz did go to the Blue Citadel, I think I would have known something about it. But I never met with him. I left Morrenwood only two days ago."

"That's odd," Len replied, scratching his head. "If Maynard left eight days ago, that would have given him plenty of time to arrive before you departed. Maybe he was delayed or injured on the way."

"You should inform Mayor Farnsworth that your other mayor is missing," Tolapari said.

"And your mayor previous to him now sits in a jail cell," the prince added curiously. "What an intriguing village you have here, Mr. Harold."

"Apparently so," he softly replied with growing suspicion.

"But I have more pressing business to attend to," he added, climbing back on his horse after thanking Len for his time. "Caldurian has taken his treachery and carnage to Montavia, and that is where we will stop him. Your new mayor might want to send out a search party to locate Maynard Kurtz in case he has fallen into misfortune."

"I'll talk to Zachary right away," Len replied, thanking the prince for his time and concern. He waved goodbye as the men rode off and rejoined the passing troops at the front of the line.

The army continued along River Road, and a short time later marched past the Spirit Caves less than two miles east of Kanesbury. Several tall pines towered in front of the caves, swaying gently in the steady, late autumn breezes. On the opposite side of the road stood the decaying remains of the old wooden guardhouse constructed twenty years ago as a first line of defense against the five hundred sleeping Enâri that once inhabited the caves. Now the bleak area lay abandoned and Prince Gregory urged his troops to hurry on. He felt compelled to reach Montavia as soon as possible, yet knew they would need a few more days to conclude the march.

Near sundown, they approached a road stretching north to Pigeon Lake. Prince Gregory instructed his captains to prepare their camp for the night in the field below where the roads intersected.

"Tomorrow we change course. We head north away from our path parallel to the Pine River that has reliably guided us these past few days," he later said while sitting near a bonfire beneath a handful of icy stars and the large, crescent Bear Moon dipping in the west. "After we reach Pigeon Lake, our road grows more difficult. Fields and hillocks will replace the dirt roads. We'll skirt the north tip of the Black Hills and then go through the Keppel Mountains just beyond."

"We will do so with ease," one of his captains replied. "In three more days, we'll be looking down upon the city of Triana and make our strike at dawn."

"That is the plan," the prince replied, glancing at Tolapari who looked subdued in the orange-red glow of the flames.

Prince Gregory knew that the wizard was thinking about the medallion, both wondering if Nicholas and Leo had succeeded in their mission. The prince had no choice but to depart Morrenwood when he did, having lingered as long as he could without word of the key's return. For all he knew, Nicholas and Leo could be lost in the Dunn Hills, having never found Frist at all.

"I'm sure they tried their best," Prince Gregory remarked to the wizard as the other soldiers talked among themselves. "Your instructions couldn't have been better from what my father told me, but success was never guaranteed."

"I know that," he replied. "Still, it would have been a much deserved surprise for Caldurian to see the Enâri army vanish before his eyes."

"When he sees *our* army swarming upon Red Lodge, he'll be surprised indeed."

Tolapari smiled vaguely as the flames crackled. "That's not the only surprise Caldurian can expect."

The prince arched his brow. "Meaning…?"

Tolapari looked up. "*Hmmm?* Oh, sorry. Just talking to myself, Gregory. Nothing important."

The prince stared at his friend with an uncertain glance before letting the cryptic comment pass. "Well, whatever Nicholas and Leo's fate, it was a brave and honorable attempt. I hope they return to the Citadel unscathed or I shall never hear the end of it."

"Are you afraid that Megan will send you out looking for Leo if he doesn't come back?"

"If only," he replied with a smirk, warming his hands by the fire. "I'm afraid that she'd run out and search for Leo herself!"

They departed on a cool and misty morning the next day, the line of men and supplies turning north up the road to Pigeon Lake. Without the view of the Pine River flowing lazily to their right anymore, all felt as if a dear and valued companion had left them in mid journey. But when the sun peeked out above the distant Black Hills and patches of blue colored the sky, their spirits rose and the army moved forward with renewed vigor. Before noontime, after passing through a handful of tiny villages and stretches of farmland, the choppy, gray waters of Pigeon Lake appeared ahead as a friendly beacon to guide them on the next stage of their journey.

They moved on after a brief rest and meal by the water, veering northeast over hard soil and dry grass as the northern tip of the Black Hills grew closer. Prince Gregory chose to direct his troops easily around the hills rather than through them, saving much time despite the added miles. Before nightfall, the army had followed the curve around the northernmost peaks and then turned southeast toward the open area between the Black Hills and the Keppel Mountains. Here the companies halted and made their encampment. Fires soon blossomed on the field, tents sprung up like wild mushrooms and meals were prepared. Hours of sleep passed quickly until another day dawned, cold and grim, marking the fifth day of their campaign.

The last day of autumn was upon them. Hours drifted by uneventfully as they moved southeast toward the Keppel Mountains to their left, on the other side of which lay the kingdom of Montavia. Its capital, Triana, was situated on the eastern border of the small mountain range along the Gestina River. Before midday, the prince sent out several groups of scouts, some to locate the best passageway through the mountains while others would travel all the way to Triana to spy upon the enemy before the assault was launched.

A few hours before sunset, the army arrived near the foot of the mountains as the first scouts returned, guiding the troops to a spot another mile south. Here they entered the mountain range through a narrow river valley of brown grasses, leafless trees and low mountain peaks already dusted with snow. The soldiers plodded onward until darkness settled in, again making camp for the night. Unlike previous days, the mood now was tense and subdued as the mountains seemed to encroach upon them.

"Enjoy the fire tonight, boys," one of the captains remarked as he made his rounds. "Tomorrow night we go without. We can't risk drawing the eyes of the enemy while we gather on his doorstep."

The sixth and final day of their trek commenced on winter's first day. The army weaved its way through the Keppel Mountains, crossing streams and open fields and narrow stretches of woodland when unavoidable. As they drew closer to the eastern edge of the mountain range, more scouts returned and reported their sightings. As expected, the main road running north and south along the mountains near Triana was patrolled by men from the Northern Isles.

"But they are intermittent patrols," one of the scouts informed Prince Gregory as he scratched a crude map into the dirt with a stick, "and can be easily taken out before we strike. I think they have grown lax in their guard because they've held the kingdom for two months without a challenge. They are overconfident."

"Let's not make the same mistake," the prince replied. "We will approach them as if they had only invaded Montavia yesterday and are prepared to defend their take to the death."

By twilight, they had traveled as far as they could go, having passed through the mountains to the east side. They made camp in the woods up and down the main road on the outskirts of Triana now less than a mile away. Here among the pines and leafless trees they would remain concealed until dawn, positioning themselves and refining their battle plan until the word was given to strike. Prince Gregory knew that the hours ahead would drag by, yet his thoughts and emotions galloped along as fast as wild horses.

"A few hours sleep wouldn't hurt you," Tolapari said while sitting against a towering pine, lost in thought. "Someone will wake you with plenty of time to spare."

"My body would love nothing more," Prince Gregory replied, "but I'm afraid my mind won't let me. Perhaps later. In the meantime, I shall walk among the trees to clear my head. Maybe the fresh air will tire me out."

He nodded to the wizard before wandering off through the leafy undergrowth, thinking not about tomorrow's attack but about his daughter instead. He hoped that Megan wasn't feeling lonely wandering the Citadel corridors in the middle of the night these last few days, sleepless and full of worry like her father. How he wished he was back home with her and his father, enjoying a warm meal and a pleasant laugh in front of a roaring fire. One day soon, he hoped.

CHAPTER 75

Âvin Éska

Caldurian stood at a window in his shadowy bedroom at Red Lodge, gazing out east across the inky waters of the Gestina River. The dawn of winter's second day approached, yet the eastern skyline still lay charcoal black as night reluctantly loosened its grip. A fire burned in the nearby hearth. The wizard, his black cloak wrapped over layered garments, folded his arms and sighed while caressing his short, pointed beard. Though content with his recent revenge upon Otto Nibbs, he still felt bored and unfulfilled. Despite pushing Kanesbury to the brink of destruction before deserting it hours before dawn nineteen days ago, he still craved greater power. He yearned for the public adulation of a wider audience. More importantly, he thought he deserved it.

Achieving that goal wouldn't have been a problem if Vellan's long choreographed plans hadn't gone awry. Over the past several days, informants from the south had made their way to Montavia, apprising the wizard about Drogin's defeat in Maranac. The terrible news had been surprising, but what bothered Caldurian the most was being stuck in a pitiful little kingdom awaiting word of Vellan's next move. Yet apparently Vellan was in no hurry relaying those orders, secure in his stronghold in Kargoth.

"Perhaps he doesn't know what to do," Caldurian whispered to himself in the chilly gloom. He pressed his forehead to the window pane, searching for answers in the darkness. "Perhaps someone else should be in charge. Someone like me."

Though Vellan had begun training Caldurian in the magic arts twenty-seven years ago, Caldurian now felt less allegiance to the wizard with each passing day. He deemed himself a significant power in his own right, determined to stamp his mark upon Laparia. He stepped back from the window as snippets of a plan swirled in his head, a plan he had never spoken about to anyone. He had forced himself to grow accustomed to it as if stepping closer and closer to a raging fire until comfortable with the increasing heat.

Caldurian reached inside one of his deep, cloak pockets, feeling for a glass vial. It contained the last of the potion that Arileez had drunk to free himself from his island captivity. Vellan had prepared the mixture which allowed Arileez to break through the confinement spell that once held him. But he secretly added another potent bit of magic to the liquid to slowly reverse Arileez' powers after he consumed it, including his unique transformational abilities. Caldurian calculated that sometime after Arileez would assume the form of King Justin and act as Vellan's puppet in the Blue Citadel, the potion would run its course and reduce Arileez to a mere mortal. He would then be forever trapped in the identical King's body, not knowing why his powers had failed, but learning to accept his role as monarch while doing Vellan's bidding.

The wizard removed the vial from his pocket and held it up to the light of the fireplace, gazing through the amber glass at the liquid contents. He always wondered if he could use this same potion against Vellan, though doubting he could easily get him to consume it in some ordinary fashion. Caldurian would have to be most clever if he were to introduce it into Vellan's system. Even then, he didn't know if it would have any effect on such a powerful wizard. Still, he thought about it off and on for nearly three years ever since he first learned about Arileez' existence and was recruited by Vellan to sail to Torriga with the magic potion. Though Caldurian hadn't admitted it to himself back then when he kept some of the potion, he now realized that he had been subconsciously plotting Vellan's demise since that time.

Caldurian slipped the vial back into his pocket, wondering if he would be bold enough to implement his plan. The thought of replacing Vellan both unnerved and excited him. A knock at the door scattered his thoughts. He spun around and called out.

"Who disturbs me at this early hour?"

The door opened and Gwyn walked into the room. The Enâr was attired in a leather jerkin beneath his weathered, gray cloak. A small sword hung from his side. Light from the corridor splashed onto the floorboards until an Island soldier standing guard outside closed the door to give them privacy. Caldurian kept most of his Enâri troops at Red Lodge and in the vicinity to do his bidding after the invasion, though he had sent a handful out to each of the major villages with their Island counterparts to report back at regular intervals. Though he worked with Commander Jarrin and his men from the Isles as Vellan wished, Caldurian never fully placed his trust in them. He did, however, keep a company of the Islanders at Red Lodge to use as guards in a show of cooperation.

"What is it, Gwyn?" he asked, sitting down in a chair near the fireplace as the Enâr stood rigidly at the door. Though the room was immersed in thick gloom, the wizard could see that Gwyn was upset.

"Red Lodge is under attack. Men have stormed the main gates but are not yet inside."

"*What?*" he cried. Caldurian jumped up from his seat, appearing bewildered as if such a possibility had never before entered his mind. His mood quickly shifted to anger. "Jarrin's men have been lax in their patrol of the border!"

The wizard flew to the window and flung it open as Gwyn rushed to his side. A sharp, winter breeze cut through the warm air inside, disturbing the flames in the hearth. Caldurian stuck his head through the opening, detecting the frenetic movement of shadows in the darkness below near one of the minor east gates as the unmistakable metallic clash of swords and gruff shouts of men rent the predawn stillness. Though he couldn't see any of the fighting near the main southern gate from this angle, Caldurian heard an even more fierce battle rage in that direction.

"What are your orders?" Gwyn asked.

Caldurian swung the window closed and locked it, staring at the glass panes. His facial muscles tightened as he juggled a dozen thoughts. He turned his head, throwing a sharp glance at Gwyn.

"Kill them, of course," he replied. "But capture whoever is leading this offensive. I want information. And send warnings to our Island friends in the nearby villages. They may be under siege soon, if not already."

"As you wish."

"No doubt King Justin has his finger in this episode despite his latest effort down south." The wizard sighed with disgust, annoyed with himself, annoyed with Vellan, and most of all angered that another one of his schemes was beginning to unravel. "But the King will get what's coming to him soon enough." Caldurian imagined Commander Uta and his troops storming the Citadel any day now to replace Arrondale's monarch with Arileez. He trusted that Madeline and Mune would not let him down. As Gwyn hurried to the door, the wizard called him back. "Wait. One more thing."

The Enâr spun around. "Yes?"

"Take King Rowan and his daughter-in-law to the main level near the north entrance. Get a dozen of your best troops, those who can ride. I will meet you there momentarily."

"What are you going to do?"

"Provide myself some added security in case events take an ill turn," he replied. "And, Gwyn, bring two of the Island guards with you." The Enâr furrowed his brow. "I'll explain later. Hurry now!"

A short time earlier, Prince Gregory's army had emerged from the woodland spread on the eastern slopes of the Keppel Mountains and made its way to Red Lodge in the inky darkness. Before moving out of the trees, they waited for a band of patrolling Island soldiers to pass south along the main road. Afterward, the army of Arrondale encountered no resistance until they arrived at Red Lodge. Before the assault, Prince Gregory directed some of his soldiers to the east, west and north sides of the wall surrounding King Rowan's compound. The bulk of his men would attack the main entrance at the south. A mix of Enâri and Island troops stood guard at all gates. A handful of the Enâri walked as lookouts along the top of the stone wall, illuminated now and then in the glow of oil lamps placed around the stone enclosure.

A short time later in the predawn darkness, the signal was given and Prince Gregory's men attacked. Some soldiers scaled the walls with ropes and hooks while others used small battering rams to break down the smaller gates and burst inside. As fighting commenced within the cobblestone compound, a fierce group of Enâri creatures stormed out of the main gate with several Island soldiers behind them, their cries rising in the air above swinging swords as they charged at the enemy. Despite the intense opposition, Prince Gregory knew he had outnumbered Caldurian's troops and urged his men onward.

"Break through to Red Lodge!" he cried, directing his men from atop his horse amid the swirling mob. Tolapari was near his side. "We must find King Rowan!"

"If he is alive," the wizard grimly commented before thrusting his sword into an Island soldier who had slipped through the onslaught of men and rushed at him with a crazed look in his eyes. The wizard removed his bloody weapon from the dead soldier who collapsed to the ground, and then shot a warning glance at Prince Gregory. "We must also find Caldurian before he causes any more mischief. He can't get away."

"He won't," the prince replied, pushing his steed onward as his men finally flooded through the main gate into the sprawling courtyard. The fighting soon spread out among the trees, shrubbery and buildings in the frosty gloom. "To Red Lodge!" he shouted, directing a large contingent of men to the main building where a throng of Enâri gathered near the wide front steps, waiting with swords drawn. The windows in all the buildings were now fully aglow as the centerpiece of Triana came to life.

"Let's not keep them waiting," Tolapari said as he and Prince Gregory jumped off their horses and joined the rush to Red Lodge as the Enâri guards sprang at them.

But after a brief battle near the front doors where a few of Prince Gregory's soldiers and several Enâri had been wounded or slain, the main entrance to the building was breached. Even the addition of several Island troops who had rushed over from the nearby garrison had done little to stop Prince Gregory's progress. He, Tolapari and many of his soldiers burst through the thick wooden doors and fanned out through the building as the fighting continued outside. Enemy troops stationed within continued to resist as scattered fights erupted among the various rooms and corridors.

"Find King Rowan and his daughter-in-law," the prince instructed his troops. They spread out down several hallways and up a stairwell leading to the two upper floors.

"We'll find them, sir!" one of his captains replied, rushing past with some of his men and disappearing down a side passageway.

Prince Gregory hurried along the main corridor with Tolapari and several soldiers at his side, searching a number of rooms as the sound of sword fighting echoed within the royal residence. The prince grew more moody and silent as they moved onto another section of Red Lodge.

"Patience, Gregory," Tolapari said, noting his friend's growing unease. "We will find them."

"Will we? I'm beginning to wonder," he replied as he glanced out a window at the fighting across the compound. A hint of daylight painted the eastern horizon. "Princes Brendan and William have been missing for weeks since they left the Citadel. If anything happens to their mother or grandfather in the meantime…"

"It would be most unfortunate," the wizard replied. "But don't let your imagination determine their fates. It'll drive you mad. Continue the search."

Prince Gregory nodded as they left the room and moved on to the adjacent one. "You're right, of course, which is why my father and I keep you around for your calm advice as often as we can."

"As you should," he quipped. "And if your father were here right now, he'd say–"

"*We found him!*" a soldier cried out. He bolted around the corner and ran toward Prince Gregory. "By the north entrance."

Prince Gregory's eyes lit up. "King Rowan?"

"No, sir," the man replied, out of breath. "It's the wizard. Caldurian and a dozen of the Enâri have just fled Red Lodge. A few Island troops are with them. Five of us found them and tried to prevent their escape. I was sent to get reinforcements."

"Take us there," ordered the prince. "Quickly!"

The soldier led Prince Gregory and the others around the corner to the left where they hurried past a line of fluttering torch lights attached to the walls. After rounding the next corner to their right, they headed directly toward the adjoining outer corridor along the west side of the King's residence. The window panes passing alongside them were still tinted charcoal black from the fading night's last gasp. When they turned right again into the north corridor, a cold gust of air pinched their faces as it poured in through a wide open door. An Enâri creature lay dead near one of Prince Gregory's wounded soldiers who stood against the wall to prop himself up. His left shoulder was stained with blood.

"Caldurian and his followers fled outdoors while we fought off several others," the soldier told Prince Gregory, appearing pale yet eager to assist. "Three of my fellow soldiers went after them."

"Let me see your wound," Tolapari said, gently taking hold of his arm.

"I'll be all right once it's bandaged," the soldier said, wincing in pain. "You'd better go after Caldurian. He seemed in an awful hurry to get his troops out of here."

"He won't get far," the prince replied, signaling to one of his men to stay behind and assist the wounded soldier. He led the others out the door into the cold dawn.

"I'd cast a spell to ease the pain," Tolapari explained to the soldier as he hastened through the doorway. "But right now I can't spare the time. Or the magic."

The area outside the north entrance contained several gardens, many trees and a large pond blanketed with a thin layer of ice. The din of battle raged mainly to the east, west and south sections of the compound as dozens of skirmishes erupted and diminished in strength as the minutes drifted by. Vague morning light continued to intensify behind clouds along the eastern horizon. It slowly illuminated the gray outline of Arrondale soldiers battling the Enâri and Island troops upon the cobblestones, among the trees and by the stone wall.

To their left in the near distance were the King's stables. Prince Gregory had just glanced that way when over a dozen horses shot forth through the doors of the main stable house and charged toward the western gate. Atop the galloping steeds were a group of Enâri creatures holding tightly to the reins as they leaned forward. Two soldiers from the Northern Isles accompanied them, bundled in their long, brown coats against the morning chill with hoods draped over their heads. Prince Gregory and his companions were taken aback by the brash escape, but only for a moment as they charged toward the stables. When they reached the main stable house, their lingering astonishment turned into bewilderment. There, standing outside the doorway with a thin smile upon his face, was the wizard Caldurian. Gwyn stood loyally at his side, scowling and silent. Prince Gregory's men unsheathed their swords and circled about.

"So glad you stopped by to pay us a visit," Caldurian said to the prince when recognizing him in the receding gloom. "To what do I owe this pleasure?"

"Well, I'll give you credit for standing your ground," Prince Gregory grudgingly replied. "I had expected you to be fleeing on one of those horses."

"Why, when I'm having so much fun here?"

"That is about to end," Tolapari said, stepping out from behind the men into the pale light. "Where are those riders going?"

For a split second, Caldurian showed genuine surprise and a hint of trepidation when he recognized his fellow wizard. "You were the last person I had expected to see here, Tolapari. It's been far too many years."

"Not enough. Now answer my question," he gruffly replied. "Where are those riders going?"

Caldurian glanced at the western gate where the last of the riders were disappearing through the stone archway in the wall, the same gate that William and Brendan had escaped through just over sixty days ago. "They have their orders," the wizard coolly replied, "and they will dutifully follow them."

"Where is King Rowan?" Tolapari persisted, gazing intently at his foe as if trying to read his thoughts and facial features.

"In a safe place," Caldurian said. "And if you ever want to see him alive, you will extend to me the utmost courtesy and respect." Gwyn softly chuckled at the comment.

"We don't have time for this!" Prince Gregory said with growing disgust.

"No, we definitely don't," Tolapari muttered, an exasperated sigh escaping his lips. He focused a stern eye upon his fellow wizard, and then as quick as a heartbeat, he extended both arms at Caldurian, palms upward, and shouted. "*Âvin éska!*"

A brief gust suddenly washed over Caldurian, tousling his hair and garments as he involuntarily inhaled a deep breath of the cold morning air. He stood there as if paralyzed, his face contorted with shock and surprise. He teetered drunkenly on his feet for a brief moment and then collapsed to the ground in unconsciousness.

"Caldurian!" Gwyn cried out, rushing over to him. He knelt at the wizard's side, frantically trying to awaken him.

Prince Gregory spun around, gazing at Tolapari in dismay. "What have you done?"

"If I performed that spell correctly," he replied woodenly, "Caldurian should recover shortly. His powers, however, will be diminished for some time," he softly added, his face turning pale, his eyelids unblinking. "As will mine."

Tolapari's knees buckled and he crumpled to the ground. The world darkened around him as echoes of warfare faded to silence in his head.

CHAPTER 76

The Chase

The two wizards regained consciousness minutes later as the initial impact of the âvin éska spell subsided. Prince Gregory knelt over Tolapari as his eyes slowly opened and darted about. He sighed in exhaustion, though a faint smile crossed his face.

"Are you all right?" the prince asked, his voice unsettled.

"I'll recover soon," Tolapari replied, sitting up with difficulty as Prince Gregory and another soldier assisted him. "I just hope my magic abilities will, too." He noted the questioning look upon the prince's face. "There's no time to explain now," he said, standing up with help from the others. He glanced at Caldurian who was only beginning to stir. He appeared ashen and dazed, having endured the brunt of the spell. Gwyn stood dutifully beside him. "You had better send soldiers after the Enâri who just bolted through the western gate. I have an uneasy feeling about them."

"As do I," he replied, signaling to one of his captains. "At the very least they are off to find reinforcements. They must be stopped."

A young soldier hurried over. "Your orders, sir?"

"Captain Grayling, gather some of your fastest riders and pursue the Enâri who just fled west," the prince ordered. "Stop them at all costs."

"My pleasure, sir!" Grayling picked three soldiers with him and they sped off around Red Lodge to recruit more riders and retrieve their horses near the main gate.

As the morning light and the sounds of fighting grew around them, Prince Gregory called for his men to move out. "We'll be exposed here soon. Make for the garrison," he said, pointing west. "It appears we have reclaimed that building. Bring the wizard and his Enâr with us, under a vigilant eye, of course. Despite Tolapari's claim that his powers have diminished, I still don't trust the man."

"The feeling is mutual," Caldurian muttered, appearing as if he had just awakened from an all-day sleep. He shuffled forward with Gwyn at his side under the watch of several armed soldiers, strands of gray hair dangling in front of his eyes. His back was bent as if he had been transformed into an old man.

Soon they arrived at the garrison which was heavily guarded by Prince Gregory's troops and several of King Rowan's soldiers just released from captivity inside. The harsh clash of swords echoed throughout the air from nearby skirmishes. The men at the garrison were excited to see their leader and equally astounded that Caldurian was his prisoner. As the prince ushered everyone inside, Captain Grayling and nearly two dozen armed soldiers sped by upon their horses, making for the western gate in pursuit of the Enâri creatures and the two Islanders who had fled a short time ago. The soldiers standing outside the garrison cheered on their fellow warriors as they disappeared through the archway in the growing milky light.

Captain Grayling led his men northward when they reached the main road outside of Red Lodge. He noted fresh tracks upon the hard dirt surface and could easily follow the Enâri creatures. The captain, never having heard a single story about the riding prowess of Vellan's willing slaves, was confident that he and his men would catch up to them shortly.

"What of the terrain ahead?" Grayling asked, speaking to a man named Grezza who was riding next to him. Grezza, a soldier of Montavia, had been training alongside King Justin's men in Morrenwood when his native land was attacked.

"This road stretches on for many miles north," he replied, "following the natural curve of the Keppel Mountains and the woodland tract near its foothills."

"Then we shouldn't have trouble following them," Grayling remarked as the rhythmic pounding of horse hooves disturbed the somber silence of a brand new morning. The tips of the towering pines to their left and the awakening peaks of the nearby mountains reached for the iron gray clouds sailing overhead.

They had ridden only a few minutes when the tracks of their foe veered to the right along another tree-lined road, this one much narrower and weathered with wheel ruts and dry puddle holes from previous pounding rains. The soldiers now rode in pairs, slowing their gait out of concern for the horses' footing.

"We can't lose them!" Grayling shouted.

But just when his hopes had begun to dim, the trees suddenly thinned out and the open meadows and hilly terrain beyond filled his vista in the growing light.

"*There*, captain!" Grezza shouted out, pointing left. "They're making for those grassy mounds across the field. They've turned off the rode just up ahead."

"And so will we," he replied. Moments later, he signaled for everyone to veer to the left into the frosty meadow. They now pursued their quarry to the northeast, swiftly gaining on them to the soldiers' delight.

"They have badly miscalculated," Grezza told the captain moments later. "We can slow down and allow our horses to rest."

"Why would we do that?" Grayling skeptically replied.

Grezza pointed out two grassy hills just ahead and the narrow valley between them that the Enâri troops had entered. "Those two hills converge into one very shortly. The Enâri are trapped! They must turn around and confront us or abandon their horses and climb over the steep hill beyond. I'm guessing they'll do the former."

Grayling motioned for his men to slow down as they approached the valley entrance. When they arrived, he halted the line, allowing the horses to briefly rest. The thin, brittle grass lay brown and speckled with hints of frost in the growing light. The captain rubbed his whiskered face, momentarily lost in thought as a light breeze swept across the meadow.

"You look troubled," Grezza said, looking askance at him.

"More curious than troubled," he replied. "It's apparent that the Enâri did not know the layout of this terrain, so I'm guessing they were not rushing to get reinforcements or they would not have gone this way."

Grezza nodded. "They would have stayed on the road and gone to the next village where more Islanders are stationed."

"Exactly. So what are they planning?" Captain Grayling said. "Why have they traveled out here in the middle of nowhere on Caldurian's order?"

"Perhaps they will soon tell us," another soldier commented as he pointed ahead into the valley. "Look."

Slowly emerging around a curve in the narrow passageway between the hills were the Enâri creatures, still atop their horses with the two Island soldiers tucked in among them. When they saw Captain Grayling and his defiant line of soldiers blocking the entrance, the Enâri halted and talked among themselves. The two sides studied one another in silent curiosity, analyzing their options. Grayling's men, however, were better armed and outnumbered their opponent. Though barely able to distinguish the faces of the enemy from this distance, Captain Grayling sensed that the Enâri were apprehensive about their next move.

"They don't know what to do," Grezza said.

"Or they're eliminating their options," Grayling replied.

In a unified display, the Enâri forces drew their swords and raised them high above their heads, the metal blades dully reflecting the tame morning light. The two Island soldiers with them sat silently upon their horses, hooded and impassive, as if unintimidated by the events that were about to unfold.

"They've made their decision," one of the men whispered.

The captain grinned. "Apparently so." He sat up proudly upon his steed and called out to the Enâri. "Soldiers of Vellan, lay down your weapons and dismount your steeds and no harm will come to you! That I will promise–but only this once. Choose any other course of action and the consequences will be severe."

An icy silence blanketed the landscape as Grayling's soldiers waited impatiently upon their horses. In one motion, the Enâri creatures thrust their swords forward and cried out defiantly, their exclamations guttural and garbled, but not unexpected.

"They have chosen," Grayling said matter-of-factly. "Men, ready your bows. We'll make the first strike in this affair. And let's be sure it's the only one we'll require."

"You can count on it, sir," Grezza replied as he retrieved his bow and a small quiver of feathered arrows attached to the side of his horse. He slipped an arm through a strap on the quiver, affixing it to his back as did his fellow soldiers. He patted the hilt of his sword still secured in its sheath, eager to take on the enemy.

"Look sharp now," Grayling told his men. "Here they come."

With swords held high, the Enâri forces snapped the reins on their steeds and charged forth down the valley in two wide lines, the pair of Island soldiers riding in the center of the back row. The pounding hooves reverberated between the grassy hills and along the surface of the cold ground like a steady roll of thunder.

"Arrows ready!" Grayling shouted. "Wait for my order."

The soldiers of Arrondale and Montavia steadied themselves upon their horses, the animals anxious and jittery as the opposing forces barreled at them. Grayling's men were spread out in a single, curving line with the captain directing the maneuvers from the middle of the formation. He gripped his sword, preparing to thrust it forward when he uttered the command to fire.

"The tall Enâr is mine," one of the soldiers joked, eliciting chuckles from his fellow soldiers.

"Steady now," Grayling calmly replied as the harsh voices of the approaching Enâri grew louder, their chiseled faces and wild eyes growing clearer in the brightening dawn. Soon their hideous shouts and cold, hard grunts overwhelmed the sounds of the galloping horses. "Aim to kill. They are fierce fighters if it comes down to hand-to-hand combat. Let's finish this now." The captain took a deep breath as the Enâri were nearly upon them like a fast moving wave. "Release on my command."

With bows raised, the line of soldiers sat poised like statues, their fingers itching to let loose a barrage of arrows as the moving target grew larger in their sight. Captain Grayling observed his adversaries as if they moved in silent slow-motion, his mind briefly shutting out all other distractions as he focused on the unabashed grit reflected upon their crazed expressions. He noted an unquenchable fire in the Enâri eyes and the stony grip of their thickset fingers upon the hilts of sharp swords. Yet when he glanced at the two Islanders in back through an opening in the line, he couldn't help but notice their less than equal fervor for the mission, wondering why they were partaking in such a suicidal run. Surely they were not as devoted to Vellan as were the Enâri, unless, of course, they had accidentally drunk from the Drusala River in Kargoth and were under his magical influence. Grayling decided that that must be the case just as he was about to drive his sword into the air and shout out his order to launch the arrows.

Suddenly his eyes caught a glimpse of bright clothing peaking out from beneath one of the Islander's long, weather-stained brown coats—a vivid, colorful fabric of autumn hues with fine embroidery, entirely out of place for an Islander. A harrowing chill seized the captain just as his lips began to form the command to fire, the truth revealed to him in a heartbeat. Then several things happened at once.

The tips of the trees in the west began to sway as the men drew back their arms and bowstrings to the breaking point, awaiting Grayling's order to fire. The Enâri thrust their swords forward and cried out, determined to break through the opposing line. A violent gust of wind tore through the hills and across the meadow from the west just as Captain Grayling shouted as loudly as he could, his words nearly consumed in the gale.

"*Stay your arrows!*" he cried out. "*Stay your arrows*! *Spare the Islanders!*"

Grayling's men had but an instant to digest his impassioned words, wondering if they had heard their captain properly. But Grezza, sitting next to Grayling and glancing at him askance, caught the movement of the captain's lips and the horrified expression upon his face and instantly knew that something was wrong. Grezza fought every impulse in his strained muscles to launch his arrow, finally loosening the tension on his bowstring in the last instant and tossing down the weapon before drawing his sword to defend himself. His fellow soldiers reluctantly yet obediently did the same as the wild wind rushed over them and the Enâri forces prepared to crash through the line.

But the disturbance in the air vanished as quickly as it had materialized along with the raucous cries of the Enâri, who for a split second rode upon their horses as if frozen, their swords raised and unmoving, their faces hardened with expressions of vengeance and contempt. To the shock of Captain Grayling and his men, the limbs of the Enâri riders suddenly fell from their bodies like melting clumps of snow and crumbled in the air, hitting the ground as piles of swiftly drying soil. Swords clattered as they hit the cold surface, the fingers that once held them having eroded into nothingness. Pairs of boots dropped like weights, filled with dry dirt that spilled out of the tops. The heads and torsos of the Enâri suffered similar fates, disintegrating upon the horses and pouring to the ground in streams of sand and soil as their ragged uniforms and cloaks collapsed into lifeless piles upon riderless saddles and frosty meadow grass.

Grayling and his men looked on with mouths agape, their eyes wide in disbelief as the once charging horses quickly slowed down and trotted past them, as if happy to be relieved of their unnatural burdens. The two horses carrying the Island soldiers took their cue from the other steeds and reduced their speed, eventually halting before Grayling and his men as the line closed up and stopped them from advancing.

"What just happened?" one of the soldiers uttered, excited yet stunned. Still, he kept his sword raised, wary of the two Islanders before him. But when they made no sudden move, he let his guard down slightly, though his befuddlement rose to the clouds.

"I can't explain the fate of our Enâri foes," Captain Grayling said as he sheathed his sword and quickly dismounted. "But I think I can now explain some of the mystery of this strange morning."

He signaled for Grezza to join him as he hurried to the pair of horses patiently standing there with the Island soldiers still atop them. Grayling rushed over to one of the steeds as the hooded soldier on top slowly bowed his head toward the captain. Grayling flung back the soldier's hood. But instead of the defiant face of a Northern Isles' native, there to greet them was King Rowan of Montavia, his mouth bound with a piece of cloth and his hands tied to the horn of his saddle.

"*King Rowan!*" Grayling said, quickly removing the gag from around the monarch's face.

Grezza hurriedly removed the hood from the other rider. His heart jumped into his throat when he saw a woman's gentle face framed with long, blond hair, thickly braided.

"*Lady Vilna!*" he cried, hurriedly yet gently untying her gag with shaking hands. "My utmost apology!"

"You have nothing to apologize for," said the mother of Princes Brendan and William. "You helped save my life, but more importantly, helped to save the life of our King."

"For which we are both eternally grateful," King Rowan replied with a tired smile as Captain Grayling untied his bonds.

When King Rowan and Vilna were helped down from the horses shortly afterward, Grayling introduced himself and told him what had just occurred at Red Lodge. "But I cannot explain what happened here to the Enâri creatures, sir. Perhaps Prince Gregory and the wizard Tolapari can provide us some answers."

"Let's pay them a visit at once," the King said, happy to see some of his soldiers among Grayling's group. "I'm eager for answers about this unusual turn of events–and for some news about my two grandsons."

The soldiers who had been battling Vellan's troops at Red Lodge experienced the same gamut of emotions after a sudden gust of wind brushed across the compound. For a brief moment, the Enâri forces turned into the rock and soil from which they came before collapsing into piles of dry sand, scuffed boots and tattered uniforms. A clanking of swords echoed across the compound as their weapons fell to the cobblestone in eerie unison.

The men of Arrondale and Montavia, whether holding their weapons in mid stroke or running to assist a fellow soldier, suddenly stopped and gazed upon the silent battlefield as the peculiar breeze quickly died away. Soldiers from the Isles, whose numbers were far fewer as the bulk of their forces were scattered among the other villages, stood in stunned silence. Many, now vastly outnumbered, laid down their arms and surrendered. Some of the Islanders fighting on the periphery fled the compound, either running to a nearby village to warn their comrades or escaping from the kingdom to start a new life, having grown weary of the war.

But those occupying other villages in Montavia needed no informants to learn of the events at Red Lodge. Caldurian had placed a small number of Enâri troops in each location to serve as his messengers and spies, and when they disintegrated in front of their Island counterparts, no explanation was required. Many panicked at the sudden misfortune, fearing that a huge army of wizards from the west had invaded to avenge the deeds of both Caldurian and Vellan. Even Commander Jarrin was unnerved when the Enâr he had been speaking with near a campfire disappeared right before his eyes during a sudden and chilly breeze.

To King Rowan's delight, he later learned that many Island troops deserted their units as rumors spread of their impending defeat. The few Islanders who stayed their ground were soon killed or imprisoned when Prince Gregory's troops, alongside the freed soldiers from King Rowan's guard, spread out across the countryside village by village over the next few days, decimating the Island scourge all the way to the Trillium Sea. There, the last of the ships that had once carried the Island invaders to shore, now retreated to their archipelago homeland with skeleton crews in shameful defeat.

Inside the garrison near Red Lodge, shortly after the fall of the Enâri, Caldurian stared incredulously at the opposite side of his prison cell, his head throbbing mercilessly. He and Gwyn had been locked in a small room until Prince Gregory determined their fates. Moments earlier, the wizard had been sitting on a bench against one wall, still reeling from the effects of Tolapari's spell. Gwyn paced along the opposite side, feeling as if he were again trapped inside the Spirit Caves.

"We're not getting out of here any time soon," Caldurian had said, trying to calm the Enâr. "I've lost my powers and I believe we're outnumbered."

Gwyn snarled as he trudged back and forth along the wall. "My fellow Enâri do not fear these invaders. They will fight to the death!" he sputtered, spinning around to face Caldurian. "They will not be—"

Those were the last words Gwyn had uttered before his body momentarily froze into the likes of a stone statue before collapsing onto itself. Caldurian watched in helpless amazement as Gwyn disappeared before his eyes in such a stark yet unceremonious fashion as a cool stream of air flowed into the chamber from somewhere, gently brushing across his face.

Now, Caldurian gazed at the pile of dry sand and clothing, imagining the ghastly sight outside the garrison as the pain in his head throbbed. Soon the rattle of keys caught his attention and the door opened. Tolapari stepped inside carrying a cup of steaming liquid. He indicated for the guard who had let him in to leave.

"I'll be safe," he assured him. "Caldurian is no threat for now." After the guard left and closed the door, Tolapari walked over to his fellow wizard and handed him the cup.

Caldurian looked up with a tired sneer. "First you take away my powers and now you want to poison me. Why didn't you just kill me from the start?"

Tolapari smiled. "At least I didn't take away your sense of humor, such as it is. Drink this herb elixir. It will greatly ease the ache in your head you are most likely enduring. I consumed some earlier, having prepared the dry ingredients beforehand. My spell affected me as it did you."

Caldurian relented and took the cup, swallowing the hot liquid a few sips at a time. Soon the tension in his face faded. "What did you do to me?"

Tolapari sat down on the other end of the bench. "It is a spell called the âvin éska, and since you are questioning me about it, I must conclude that you were never taught it or knew of its existence."

Caldurian took another sip and glanced contemptuously at his fellow wizard. "No. Apparently Vellan skipped that lesson."

"Not surprising. Perhaps he feared that you might use it on him someday despite its deleterious effect on the user."

"So now we are both without our powers?"

"Temporarily–if I performed the spell correctly," he said. "It took me many days to prepare for it, and if properly cast, our powers should come back in the weeks to come. Yours may take much longer since you absorbed the brunt of the spell."

"*Should* come back?"

"We'll see. But it was worth losing mine to keep you in line, Caldurian. You are nearly as bad a menace as Vellan."

"I try," he muttered, taking another sip. He indicated Gwyn's sandy remains. "Apparently the medallion had been successfully remade into the key and used. Well done."

Tolapari was taken aback. "You knew of that? How?"

"I can't reveal my secrets–and spies–but it's irrelevant now. The Enâri have been defeated," he said. Caldurian set the cup down and rubbed his forehead. "I can't even imagine the look on Vellan's face when all his soldiers, workers and guards in Del Norác disappeared before his eyes."

"That was most likely their fate," Tolapari said. "His realm will be at a standstill for some time, though he will still have his Island supporters who traveled to his lands as well as any locals who are devoted to him, willingly or otherwise. But many might have second thoughts when they see that the bulk of his forces have been destroyed."

Caldurian laughed grimly. "Now I suppose King Justin and his allies will sweep into Kargoth and put an end to Vellan once and for all. Is that his plan?"

"King Justin's plans are his own. But I suppose you will get a chance to talk with him before it is all over."

"He had better hang me or shoot an arrow through my heart while my powers are gone, because if they come back, I shall return with a vengeance."

Tolapari snickered. "As if we didn't already know that." He looked up at Caldurian with genuine sadness in his eyes. "That is why Vellan never passed on the âvin éska spell to you nor probably to any other students he had trained over the years. You, he and others like you are vengeful sorts, absorbed with yourselves first and foremost. You just wouldn't trust each other with such knowledge because you would ultimately use it for your own advantage."

"And you wouldn't?"

"Nor haven't. Frist taught me that spell years ago when I was his apprentice. It is a defensive tool that he hoped I would never have to use," Tolapari explained. "He had no fear that I would ever use it against him or others to advance myself. That is how we are different, Caldurian. You and those like you sit at the center of your worlds, and chaos and destruction is usually the result. Nothing else matters."

"I do what I do to bring order to a chaotic region," he replied with a sharp edge to his voice. "Things get messy along the way, but some day the end result will be worth it."

"Some day." Tolapari shook his head, glancing at the wizard with a skeptical eye. "I'm sure that's what you tell yourself to sleep well at night, but I'm convinced that even you don't really believe that, Caldurian. You're no different than a common thief or a charlatan. You just have better resources at your disposal."

"Spare me the lecture. You have no idea what motivates me to behave as I do, to make the sacrifices I do."

Tolapari sighed. "That's precisely your problem, Caldurian. In the end, it is *only* about you–or Vellan, or whomever. Your kind is on a perpetual quest for power and control. You live well at others' expense," he said. "A simple matter really–just small men with twisted views seeking their warped vision of greatness regardless of the consequences." He stood and knocked on the cell door for the guard. "You could have done so many good things with your talents, Caldurian, if only you didn't get in the way of yourself."

"Think as you like," the wizard muttered, his eyes fixed on Gwyn's remains as the door opened. "You'll never understand."

"Probably not." Tolapari sadly shook his head. "Enjoy the drink," he replied as he left the chamber, leaving Caldurian alone with his muddled thoughts. The door swung shut and the key turned, locking them both inside.

CHAPTER 77

The Long Road to Spring

Three days later, on a cold, sunlit morning, a messenger from the Citadel arrived at Red Lodge. Though some of the physical ravages of recent warfare had been cleaned up by then, the deaths of those who had sacrificed their lives to retake Montavia would never be erased. Black ribbons of mourning had been strung about the courtyard and in the villages throughout the kingdom. Many somber memorials had already been held to honor the valiant deceased and would continue throughout winter.

But there was still much work to be done against Vellan and his allies before the nations of Laparia could live in peace. This weighed heavily on King Rowan's mind as the messenger handed him two sealed notes he had carried from Morrenwood. One was from King Justin and the other from King Rowan's grandson, Prince William. After delivering the correspondences, the courier left to find Prince Gregory and present him with other messages from his father.

"What news from the west?" Vilna asked her father-in-law. They sat in a small study near an eastern window as a blazing fire crackled in the hearth. Sharp rays of sunshine sliced through thick panes of glass.

"Good news," King Rowan said with a smile after opening the first letter. "Rhiál has been victorious in her battle against the forces of Maranac. Drogin has been defeated." He glanced up with subdued surprise after reading a few more lines, peering over the top edge of the parchment. "*Permanently* defeated. He will never again bother his fellow countrymen or their neighbors across the lake."

"I will not shed a tear for him," Vilna replied as she worked on a piece of embroidery during one of the few moments of relaxation she and the King had enjoyed since Caldurian's invasion.

"And Prince Victor has been found alive! Princess Melinda, too," he excitedly added as he read further. "They will rule their respective kingdoms on either side of Lake LaShear. Finally, there will be peace for our southern neighbors."

"I suppose Caldurian knew of this during our captivity and kept it from us to stomp out any glimmer of hope," Vilna said with a contemptible smirk.

"He's paying the price now," he replied, his expression growing sterner. "All is not good news though. There was an attack on the Blue Citadel by men from the Northern Isles. It happened on the same morning Prince Gregory and his forces arrived here."

"The Citadel was breached?" Vilna asked, setting down her embroidery in stunned disbelief, her eyes filled with dread. "Was anyone hurt?"

"Yes. Several of the King's men," he sadly responded as he continued to scan the letter. "But the other side fared far worse. King Justin promises to provide more details at another war council he is calling near the end of this month." The King looked up. "I shall definitely be attending," he added with a determined glint in his eyes.

Vilna shook her head in dismay. "Vellan has grown strong indeed to boldly attack the Citadel with his Island puppets. But now that the Enâri have been defeated, he might think twice about disrupting the lives of so many throughout the region."

"We can only hope, but I wouldn't wager any coin on it," he said as he set aside the first letter and broke the blue wax seal on the second one from Prince William. "Now I'm most eager to read the words of my grandson. It seems like years since he and Brendan escaped from here on that horrible night."

"Tell me of my sons," Vilna eagerly asked, again picking up her embroidery though she was too excited to concentrate on her stitches. "When will they return? And why didn't Brendan pen a missive to us as well?"

"Perhaps he's engaged in meetings with King Justin and his ministers," King Rowan proudly replied as he glanced at the first few lines of William's letter. "After all, Brendan is the highest ranking representative of Montavia at the Citadel. He probably appointed William as his corresponding secretary to keep his brother out of mischief," he added with a chuckle as he continued reading. "And I've no doubt that they–"

The color suddenly faded from King Rowan's face as he absorbed the words on the parchment. The note quivered in his unsteady hands as he slowly learned about the strange death of his grandson among the trees of the Ebrean. Vilna couldn't help but notice the swift change in his demeanor and felt her chest tightening, expecting the worse.

"What's troubling you, Father-in-law?" she hesitantly asked. "What ill news has William sent? Judging by your expression, the news could be nothing *but* ill."

King Rowan looked up, slowly setting the letter down upon his lap, his eyes glassy with tears. "It is the most grievous news, my dear," he said, his voice choked and his thoughts reeling. "It is about Brendan, I'm sorry to say." He put a hand to his eyes as tears flowed down his face. "So sorry to say…"

The following day, four days after the Enâri troops had been destroyed, Prince Gregory and the bulk of his army departed Triana. He left a contingent of soldiers behind to help secure the kingdom and track down any stragglers from the Isles who were hiding out in the hills and about the countryside. King Rowan promised to attend the next war council especially in light of his grandson's death.

"All the tragedy and misfortune of these dark days lead back to Vellan," the King said, his face careworn and ashen as Prince Gregory prepared to depart. "I will help defeat that tyrant if I have to break into the fortress of Del Norác myself."

"Pray that it doesn't come to that," he replied. He wished the King goodbye and good fortune. "And again, my condolences to you and Lady Vilna. It is both grievous and unfair that such tragedy has again struck your family. My heart goes out to you."

King Rowan nodded, unable to speak for a moment as he wiped away a tear. "When my son was killed four years ago on that mountain survey, I blamed myself for giving him that assignment, vowing thereafter to protect his sons with my very life if required." He sighed with an air of defeat. "But it seems that fate strikes when and where it pleases whatever our plans to the contrary, showing us who is truly in charge." He took a deep breath to compose himself, nodding to the prince with a stern expression. "And it *is* most unfair."

Tolapari accompanied Prince Gregory on the long road back under gray skies and intermittent snowfall. Caldurian rode with them under heavy guard to face his judgment at the Citadel, remaining silent and stony faced. Three soldiers rode in front of the wizard, three more behind him and one on either side. Despite the loss of his powers, Prince Gregory wanted to take no chances with Caldurian and considered him just as dangerous as he had always been.

The road was slow and uneventful with only a minor adjustment to their course. When they arrived north of Pigeon Lake, instead of taking the road south back to River Road, the army continued eastward, gradually veering south between the Wetwood and Cumberland Forests. The prince decided it would be wise to bypass the village of Kanesbury on the return trip, fearing reprisals from its citizens should they get word of Caldurian's presence.

"I expect my father will pronounce the first judgment upon the wizard," Prince Gregory guessed. "Or at least I hope so. He has had to deal with that scoundrel and his trail of chaos for far too many years. Others can stand in line to exact justice in due time."

"It will be a very long line," Tolapari said. "Though I suspect your decision has been influenced by the fact that Caldurian arranged for the kidnapping of your infant daughter twenty years ago."

The prince looked askance at Tolapari as their horses trotted along a dirt road. "I will not deny it. Caldurian deserves whatever punishment comes his way and will get no sympathy from me. And may Vellan's fate be thrice as bad."

"And soon," he added as the eaves of the Wetwood stretched out in the near distance to their right, dusted with freshly fallen snow. A mournful wind whistled across the dry, grassy fields of central Arrondale as the army trudged onward.

After six days of traveling, they arrived in Morrenwood under a veil of early afternoon snow flurries. All were exhausted yet in high spirits. Prince Gregory greeted his daughter with a hug inside the Citadel, happy to see her again as Leo stood protectively at her side. The prince proudly shook his hand after speaking to his daughter.

"Well done, Leo!" he said, referring to the key. "You and Nicholas accomplished an amazing feat for the citizens of Laparia. I want to hear all the details."

"I'm sorry I didn't get back before you had left," he replied. "We could have better coordinated your strike against Caldurian with the opening of the Spirit Box."

"Regardless, he and his Island accomplices were given the surprise of their lives when the Enâri literally crumbled before their eyes." Prince Gregory glanced about as many of his captains and other soldiers talked and wandered around the main hall. "Where is Nicholas? I want to offer him my congratulations as well."

"That's a story best told over a bowl of hot soup, Father." Megan took his hand and smiled. "If you can break away from here, I'll arrange a quick supper for the three of us. No doubt you'll be going over the details of your military campaign with Grandfather, Tolapari and others long into the night. We will not have a chance to speak today otherwise."

Prince Gregory smiled and kissed his daughter. "You know me too well, Megan. I will set aside my duties for an hour or so and dine with both of you and learn the latest." He signaled to Tolapari who was engaged in conversation nearby. "Tell the King I shall be detained for a short while by his lovely granddaughter. He will have no choice but to excuse my tardiness." The wizard smiled and nodded as the trio disappeared through an archway.

Megan, Leo and Prince Gregory were soon enjoying bread and pumpkin soup in a small room by a roaring fire. Leo spoke of his and Nicholas' adventures and of the key's return. Prince Gregory was both heartbroken and fascinated by details of the Citadel invasion and of Leo's ordeal after he had unlocked the Spirit Box.

"One of the physicians confined Leo to bed for three days," Megan explained. "He was deathly pale when we found him on the floor in the upper turret."

"I was beyond tired for several days," Leo said. "Whatever emerged from the Spirit Box nearly killed me, or so I felt at the time. I thought I was going to suffocate. I'm better now. Healthy enough to go on a mapping mission with Hobin one of these days."

"You'll stay here until warmer weather arrives so you can fully recover," Megan insisted with a smile. "I'm tired of seeing all the men in my life leave my side for weeks at a time. You can send a messenger to your parents to let them know that you're well. I'd much prefer you spending your free hours in the Citadel library poring over maps of Arrondale rather than rushing off to climb more mountains with Hobin. At least for a few more months."

"I promise not to leave your side until spring," Leo replied, gently taking her hand in his before glancing at Megan's father.

Though Leo planned to say nothing to Megan in the near future to keep her from worrying, he hoped to travel south with King Justin's army on their expected march to Kargoth when winter passed. After his and Nicholas' success in the Dunn Hills, Leo knew he could contribute more to the fight against Vellan even though he wasn't a professional soldier. He had learned so much recently and felt both proud and obligated to help defend the kingdom in any way possible. But he also wanted to prove to Prince Gregory and King Justin that he was indeed worthy of Megan's love. He hoped his motives were slanted more toward the honorable than the self-serving, yet he couldn't deny either feeling as he squeezed Megan's hand and smiled. He didn't know how or when he would break the news to her, having plenty of time to think long and hard about it before the melting of the snow.

Later that day, Prince Gregory learned more about the Citadel invasion from his father. Commander Uta, Captain Burlu and most of the Island troops had been killed during the attack.

"Though damage had been extensive, the repairs were done quickly," King Justin told him as they wandered through the back hallway and surveyed the new masonry near the breached entrance. "Several fine men of Arrondale were lost that terrible morning," he sorrowfully added. "Yet we overwhelmed the enemy in the end. The few survivors are imprisoned in Graystone Garrison."

"How did they get inside? Your letter was vague on details."

"Carmella was camped outside when the attack commenced," King Justin said. An oil lamp fluttered and cast uneasy shadows upon the wall. "She later told me how her cousin, Madeline, and the woman's associate, Mune, assisted in the assault. Carmella said they have since fled to Kargoth."

"*Madeline?*" Gregory sighed as he rubbed a hand over his unshaven face. "Megan's old nursemaid. It was she and that Mune fellow who tried to have her kidnapped in Plum Orchard before mistakenly nabbing Ivy."

"Caldurian and his accomplices have been a plague on this household for two decades," he replied as they wandered across the hallway and down an adjacent corridor.

"The wizard has been a plague upon Kanesbury for that long as well," said his son, telling the King about Caldurian's recent nine-day invasion of the village. "Len Harold gave me a description upon our recent chance meeting."

King Justin sighed with disgust. "Caldurian is a walking storm cloud. But now that he is our guest, temporarily declawed, as it were, I'll have a long talk with him if it will do any good."

"He could still be dangerous, Father. Use extreme caution."

"I'll be careful, my son. After all, I survived an encounter with that horrific creature who assumed my form," he said with a hint of bravado. "Caldurian doesn't loom so large to me at the moment."

"You could have been killed, Father."

King Justin chuckled. "Oh, I hardly received a scratch."

"Not according to Megan's description."

"Nonsense. Look." King Justin stopped and rolled up the garment covering his upper right arm and showed his son. A fine, pale line ran across his skin, the only reminder of the once bloody wound. "That creature struck me nine days ago and this is all that's left of his handiwork."

"Exactly one week and it's almost completely healed?" Prince Gregory furrowed his brow as he examined the marking. "How is that possible?"

"I'll attribute it to honest living and the fresh pine air," he replied before growing silent. Again, the sound of fluttering oil lamps filled the empty corridor. "Unfortunately, Prince Brendan was not so lucky. His was a grave wound from that same mercurial hand. His mother must have been devastated by the news of his death."

"I saw the anguish in Vilna's eyes when I spoke to her before I departed Red Lodge," he replied. "But I cannot truly imagine her pain. I wonder how I would have felt if Megan had been—"

The King held up a hand to silence his son. "Times are bad enough. Let's count ourselves lucky and not speculate on what ills might have been. I do not have the heart to do so."

Prince Gregory smiled and wrapped an arm around the King's shoulder as they continued down the corridor. "Wise words from a wise man, Father. As usual."

King Justin met with Caldurian the following day, offering him lunch in one of his private chambers. As a precaution, two guards were stationed both inside and outside the room. Caldurian suspected that the King was simply trying to extract information by allowing him time outside his locked room in one of the upper levels. King Justin admitted as much with a sly grin, yet the two men enjoyed their lunch with cool civility.

"Vellan will expect you to launch an attack now that you're overflowing with smugness from two victories," Caldurian said, dipping a crust of bread into his stew. "I also expect that that is what you'll do once the weather turns cooperative in the spring."

"A pity you can't be with him," the King replied.

The wizard looked up, his gaze sharp. "What makes you think I'd want to?" The remark caught King Justin off guard. "Vellan has made many mistakes trying to achieve his goals. I'm no longer afraid to say that I grow weary of implementing his misguided plans. Even with his vast resources, he has taken on more than he can achieve."

King Justin sat back in his chair, contemplating the wizard's stunning words and wondering why he revealed such a thought. "I don't know whether to believe you or not. Are you serious? Or is this some sort of deception?" Caldurian offered a faint smile in reply. "In either case, I shall keep a close watch on you. As to your previous point, I think you are correct that Vellan knows we will come after him. He may actually be worried for a change now that he doesn't have the Enâri to protect him."

"But he still has a substantial army," the wizard reminded him. "Many of the locals are loyal to Vellan."

"Most are under his spell."

Caldurian raised an eyebrow. "Loyal nonetheless. Whether they were forced to drink from the Drusala River or consumed the water willingly or by accident matters not. Also, troops from the Northern Isles have been streaming in for some time. Don't be convinced of victory yet. There is still a formidable force in Kargoth."

"But one we can now beat," the King replied. "All those years of weaving deadly plans like a pair of poisonous spiders are finally catching up to you and Vellan. You're both tangled in your webs." King Justin sipped from a mug of hot tea, glancing over the rim at his adversary. "I'll bet you never expected us to remake the key to the Spirit Box or find the wizard Frist." Caldurian appeared bewildered. "Oh, save your feigned puzzlement. I know you were aware that we possessed the medallion. I know all about your spy in the rafters."

Caldurian's eyes widened with surprise. But after a moment of contemplation, he decided that none of it mattered anymore. "My compliments to you, King Justin. How and when did you find out?"

"I can't reveal all my secrets," he said. "Unless you're willing to reciprocate."

"In what way?"

"I want to know about that strange entity who was going to take my place. Surely, you must know something about him."

"I know that he failed his mission." The wizard sat back and pushed his empty bowl away. "I am talking to the *real* you, after all."

"But he came so close," King Justin commented with a hint of grudging admiration. "It was an ingenious plan. Vellan could have controlled the fate of Arrondale without releasing an arrow or raising a sword against my people. Diabolically ingenious."

"But a failure nonetheless." Caldurian gazed at the crackling fire across the room. He was genuinely saddened at Arileez' demise, believing that his fellow wizard could have rivaled Vellan in power and influence if left to his own devices. "Arileez–that was his name–was a unique specimen. A rare mutation among the true wizards with special powers that set him apart from the others. Not surprisingly, he was both feared and shunned, isolated for most of his life."

Caldurian recounted stories about Arileez' banishment as a young boy from the Valley of the Wizards and of his imprisonment on the island of Torriga. King Justin listened with fascination, yet felt pity for the extraordinary being who had wounded him and nearly usurped his monarchy.

"You and Vellan used and manipulated him," the King said in a reproachful tone.

"We did," he shamefully admitted. "After I gave him the potion to break his confinement spell, the Umarikaya was happy to do our bidding, never having a chance to live life on his own terms."

King Justin felt a heightened sense of distrust for Caldurian despite the fact that he was speaking freely. He provided details of Arileez' death in the Citadel corridor, shocking Caldurian with images of the wizard's violent demise at the points of several swords.

"I almost wish we had never used Arileez in this manner," Caldurian admitted.

"So do I. He nearly killed me with a vicious swipe of a talon," the King said, telling Caldurian about the stunning transformation. He rolled up his sleeve and showed Caldurian the faded remains of his injury. "An odd thing that such a wound would heal so fast. This Arileez was a unique fellow indeed."

"*Indeed.*"

Caldurian stared at the wound with growing interest, thinking immediately of the potion Vellan had created to release Arileez from his island imprisonment. The remaining drops of that liquid were in a small glass vial deep inside one of his cloak pockets. Vellan had added a second spell to the potion that would have slowly diminished Arileez' powers, rendering him a mere mortal. But death had saved Arileez from that confining fate. Caldurian assumed that that second spell had somehow reversed the damage Arileez had inflicted upon King Justin. But he said nothing about that second spell or his theory, thinking it best to keep them secret for now, or at least until revealing the information could work to his advantage.

As they drank their tea, Caldurian smiled inside with grim amusement, knowing how lucky King Justin was to have been wounded by Arileez himself rather than by the sharp edge of a knife or the point of a sword wielded by the wizard's hand. The King would never have recovered as swiftly, if at all, had he received a blow from either of those inanimate metal objects rather than from Arileez' own bone, skin and blood in the guise of a sharp talon. A most fortunate injury, he lightly mused as he poured himself more tea from the steaming kettle between them.

After their meal and conversation, King Justin and two of his guards escorted Caldurian to his room on an upper level. Two other guards kept watch outside the door while another pair was stationed at the entrance to the corridor. The King had even placed two additional sentries outdoors below the window to Caldurian's room as an added precaution. As one of the guards unlocked the wizard's door and opened it, Caldurian turned to the King.

"Thank you for lunch. I had feared it might be my last meal," he said with grim humor.

"Your fate is still to be decided," King Justin replied. "Your offenses are numerous and against many throughout Laparia. Others will be consulted before your sentence is pronounced."

Caldurian nodded. "I suppose I should be grateful, but I suspect there will be a noose around my neck or an arrow through my heart when all is said and done."

"It will be a collective judgment," the King replied. "Nothing will be settled until after the turn of the year."

"Then I still have plenty of time to sit and think through the winter months."

"It is a long road to spring, Caldurian, so use your time well."

"And it is a long road to Kargoth," he said with a hint of defiance in his voice. "You do the same as you plan your next move."

King Justin gazed warningly at the wizard. "Do not think that we won't be monitoring you closely. Tolapari's powers will return before yours, so we will have a gauge to measure you by."

"I had no doubts that you'd do just that," he replied.

The King sighed. "Good day, Caldurian."

As he turned to leave, Caldurian called to him. "One more thing, sir. You never told me how you found out about my spy in your council chambers. I've at least earned that bit of knowledge after all I revealed to you over lunch, have I not? I'll suffer a fitful sleep without the answer."

The King turned around, silent for a moment. "I see no reason to keep the information from you any longer. After all, I will have my guards thoroughly examine every room from now on before any such meeting is ever convened again."

"Wise move," he quipped. "So how did you find out?"

"Quite simple. Madeline told me."

Caldurian's jaw dropped. "You have her imprisoned in the Citadel, too?" Surprise, and a hint of anger, was evident in his darting eyes. "Where is she? Can I speak to her?"

King Justin raised a hand. "I slightly misspoke. Madeline didn't tell me directly, but had told her cousin who spoke to me afterward. You trained Carmella for a short time, so I've learned."

"That was twenty years ago," he replied, recalling the tumultuous time at Carmella's house. "She didn't have the aptitude that her cousin does in the magic arts. I haven't seen Carmella since I fled from her abode in Red Fern." Caldurian grinned. "Pity. Had I trained her longer and coaxed her to my side, she wouldn't have brought that medallion to you but to *me* instead. Then again, Carmella had a nasty streak of honesty and good nature running through her, so my efforts would probably have been in vain."

"Probably. From what I learned about Madeline, Carmella and her cousin are opposites in so many ways."

"Where is Madeline now?" Caldurian pleaded to the monarch with saddened eyes. "I truly would like to speak to her, even under the watchful eyes of your guards if you so order. I'm pleased that she wasn't killed during the assault."

"She is not here," the King admitted, carefully studying the wizard's expression. "Madeline is on her way to Kargoth."

"*What?*" Caldurian stood with his back to a corner of the doorframe, his mind reeling with images of Madeline meeting with Vellan and serving as his new apprentice. "Kargoth? Are you sure?"

The King nodded, noting how upset Caldurian seemed upon hearing the news. "Madeline and Mune left for Kargoth after they spoke to Carmella outside the Citadel. Their meeting with her wasn't on the friendliest of terms. Madeline and Mune fled after Commander Uta's assault failed." Caldurian slowly fumed, taking it all in. "Uta and most of his men didn't survive. The remainder of his troops were taken prisoner and provided me what information they could."

Caldurian stared at the floor for some time before speaking. "So Madeline chose to seek out Vellan rather than return to me in Montavia." He looked up, visibly hurt. "She abandoned me."

"Carmella told me that her cousin was rather disillusioned with the current state of affairs," King Justin said.

"*Disillusioned*? Really?" Caldurian's words oozed bitterness and betrayal. "So she crawled to Vellan–and that little traitor Mune went with her. I–" He disgustedly waved a hand through the air. "I wish to be left alone please. I need to think."

"Very well." King Justin indicated to his guards to close the door and lock the wizard inside. "We'll talk again, Caldurian. As I said earlier, it is a long road to spring. I'm sure you'll have much to decide in the interim."

"Undoubtedly," he muttered, stepping into his room as the door was closed and locked behind him.

King Justin sighed, tired from his long conversation and battle of wits with the wizard. He dismissed the two guards who had accompanied him to lunch, telling them that he wanted to wander the corridors alone to clear his head. He made his way to a quieter, less frequented wing of the Citadel, enjoying the hint of cool air wafting through the passageway as the oil lamps fluttered hypnotically and cast restless shadows upon the walls. The light behind the windows was gray and dimming as twilight softly encroached upon the frozen hills and snow-covered pines of Morrenwood.

"There you are, Justin," a voice echoed between the narrow walls moments later. "You're late for our meeting."

The King looked up as Tolapari made his way down the corridor, his footsteps ricocheting off the stonework. The wizard greeted him with a smile.

"Dear me, it completely slipped my mind," the King replied.

"Not to worry. You're not that late," he said, studying the King's faraway expression. "You look out of sorts, Justin. Did your meal with Caldurian not go well?"

"On the contrary. I learned much." The two walked along the passageway. "It was taxing at times as I wasn't always sure whether he was speaking the truth or deceiving me. But it was worth the effort. Next time I'll invite you along."

"I look forward to it, I think." Tolapari cracked a smile. "After casting the âvin éska spell, I don't think Caldurian is anxious to see me yet. Perhaps in a week or so."

"Perhaps."

"In the meantime, we must discuss preparations for the upcoming war council. It is only fourteen days away."

"I don't expect this gathering to be as large or as boisterous as the first one. After all, the convening parties are all in agreement that we must confront Vellan this spring. All that's really left to do is plan the particulars. It should go rather smoothly."

"But there are quite a few particulars," Tolapari said. "The biggest of which is the very individual you've just lunched with." He halted beneath a shadowy archway framed by the glow of light from the adjoining corridor. "What do you plan to do with him?"

King Justin looked about, making sure that no one else was in earshot, but the connecting passageways were both empty save for the two of them. He lowered his voice anyhow, his ice blue eyes roiling with concern. "What do I plan to do with him? I do not trust Caldurian anymore than I can manipulate fire in my palms or cast a sleeping charm upon another. Even at his most sincere, I question the very words uttered by his lips. I think that wizard is nearly as dangerous without his powers as with them. He could probably cause just as much mischief whether wandering the roads and woodlands of Laparia or sitting behind a locked door in the Citadel."

Tolapari appeared nonplussed. "So you're going to...?"

The King smiled as if the answer was obvious. "I'm going to take Caldurian with us when we march to Kargoth. I'll always distrust the man, so I might as well keep him at arm's reach under my careful watch. Besides, maybe he'll be useful to our cause."

Tolapari appeared doubtful. "How so?"

"Caldurian feels that his friends have betrayed him. Maybe we can use that division in his ranks to our advantage."

"I don't know," the wizard replied. "If it comes to choosing sides, in the end I think Caldurian would run back to his friends in spite of their differences. Tread carefully in those waters, Justin."

"That's why I have you to advise me," he replied. "You can always cast the âvin éska spell again should Caldurian regain his powers and come after us," he lightly added.

"That's a dangerous proposition," he warned. "When Frist trained me in the finer points of the spell, he said it should never be used twice on the same person as its debilitating effects would grow more potent for both the purveyor and the recipient. And the spell shouldn't be cast by the same person without several intervening seasons to ensure a proper recovery. It's a spell of last resort."

"I jest, my friend, because of the seriousness of our plight. So I will utilize your eyes and vast wisdom instead to closely monitor Caldurian over the next few months. I need to know just how tight a rope to keep around him when we depart for Kargoth." King Justin signaled for him to continue down the corridor. "Now we can discuss an even more pressing issue."

"And what is that?" the wizard asked ominously.

"Why, what to feed and where to house all the ancillary guests when the principals meet for the second war council," he replied, chuckling. "They certainly kept the Citadel kitchens and staff in a whirlwind during their last visit!" King Justin ran a hand through his hair and sighed. "I can't wait until spring, Tolapari. The campaign against Kargoth will seem so much easier than the planning for it."

"Aren't they all?"

The King nodded wearily as their footsteps gently echoed down the darkening corridor. "Regardless of the weather, I think it's going to be a long winter, my friend. A very long winter."

END OF PART SEVEN

PART EIGHT
LOOSE THREADS

CHAPTER 78

An Invitation to Dinner

Katherine Durant stood behind a tall pine in the frosty autumn darkness, her eyes fixed upon Dooley Kramer's house just up the road. She was hidden in a stretch of woods on the same side of the dead-end lane as his small, dilapidated dwelling, having watched the place since long past dinnertime. Most residents had retired inside for the night. The streets lay quiet and vacant. The Fox Moon, two days past full, peeked over the eastern horizon behind a veil of inky clouds. Midnight, still hours away, approached with catlike stealth.

Katherine shifted her position, careful not to rustle any dry leaves or snap a twig. Dooley still remained inside his single-story house, a few of its windows glowing dully behind cracked wooden shutters. Zachary Farnsworth, who lived at the far end of the narrow street on the opposite side, had wandered down to his neighbor's house half an hour ago. The leaf-littered road was terribly dark with thick patches of trees on either side. Katherine, her breath rising in small white puffs, took comfort in the murky surroundings. She couldn't see much through the hedges growing wild around Dooley's house and longed to hear what the two men were discussing inside.

After Caldurian's mysterious departure eleven days ago, Maynard Kurtz resumed his duties as acting mayor in light of Otto's arrest. Maynard's first duty was to appoint Zachary Farnsworth to the village council after Ned Adams had resigned to rebuild his gristmill. Two days later, Maynard abruptly left for Morrenwood, planning to consult with King Justin about Caldurian's reappearance. Before departing, he recommended that Farnsworth assume the duties of acting mayor until his return, expressing his utmost confidence in the local bank manager. Since the other four council members had no objections–none of them being interested in the position after having lived through Caldurian's iron rule–Zachary Farnsworth was unanimously appointed. Little fanfare accompanied the announcement as people were too busy repairing their disrupted lives and damaged property.

Katherine had privately shuddered upon hearing the news, assuming that Farnsworth must have made a deal with Caldurian and had somehow hoodwinked Maynard to worm his way into power. She was eager to expose Farnsworth before he could do further damage to the village, but knew it would take time and patience to gather proof. Now, she waited silently in the woods on a cold and cheerless night, having repeated this vigil on successive evenings.

Katherine shivered, wrapped in a heavy cloak with the hood draped over her head. It was another monotonous night, one of many she had endured ever since Paraquin had alerted her to the periodic, late night excursions of Dooley Kramer and Zachary Farnsworth. She furrowed her brow as the smell of pine sap invaded her nostrils, wondering where they had traveled to on those previous occasions in a horse-drawn cart laden with cut wood and other supplies.

She had twice spied the two men leaving in their cart from Dooley's house in the dead of night. And counting the one other time eighteen days ago that Paraquin saw them leaving Kanesbury with a letter signed by Caldurian, she calculated that their departure was always at six-day intervals. She had never seen them leave in the nights in between when she kept watch until Dooley's lights were extinguished. So if they stuck to that schedule, she expected them to leave again tonight.

As the cold tormented her, she wished the two men would hurry up and confirm her suspicions. If they left again tonight, then she would implement her plan in six more days. Perhaps they would lead her to Adelaide–if she was still alive. She hung on to that hope, recalling Paraquin saying that he had heard Adelaide's name spoken between Dooley and Farnsworth eighteen nights ago. Katherine wildly imagined the depths of their connection to Caldurian and the strange happenings in Kanesbury.

A noise startled her. The impatient grunting of a horse near Dooley's house drifted through the air. Then all was quiet again, the two men apparently not any closer to leaving. Katherine sighed with only mild disappointment, happy that the occupation of Kanesbury had ended which allowed her to hide here without fear of arrest. Caldurian and his Island forces had mysteriously disappeared in the middle of the night eleven days ago. The citizens of Kanesbury awoke deliriously happy the following morning to their newfound freedom. After nine days of captivity, a celebration and the rebuilding of lives had begun at once. Except for her Uncle Otto.

The former mayor of Kanesbury still remained a prisoner in the village lockup, awaiting trial on abetting the enemy and other charges. Katherine knew in her heart that her uncle was innocent, somehow having been framed for his alleged crimes just as Nicholas had been. She wondered where Nicholas might be right now, hoping he was warm and out of harm's way. Her thoughts were close to the mark as Nicholas and Ivy were recovering in Illingboc two days after the inferno on the *Bretic* and their ordeal on Karg Island. Katherine also thought about Paraquin's whereabouts, hoping the kind soldier had escaped from Caldurian and his fellow Islanders and was perhaps making an honest life for himself somewhere in Laparia. But their fates were out of her hands. She waited impatiently for Dooley and Farnsworth to make their next move because *her* next move depended upon them keeping to their six-day schedule.

Katherine sighed again. She thought of Lewis, thankful to have him as a loving and steadying force in her life during the past few weeks. She was confident that their relationship would evolve into a solid and enduring one. She grinned, not sure how Lewis would react if he ever found out about her recent sleuthing in the woods. Suddenly voices emanated beyond the trees near Dooley's house. A door slammed shut. When Katherine glanced up, she noticed that the interior lights had been extinguished.

Soon the sound of wagon wheels rattled along the lane. A horse-drawn cart with two figures in front drew ever closer and slowly passed by as Katherine looked out from her hiding place.

Square copper oil lamps, one attached to each side of the cart, burned with a demonic glow. She guessed that Dooley and Farnsworth were on their way to River Road where they would travel east out of the village as on the night when Paraquin and his fellow soldiers had stopped them for questioning. She couldn't imagine where they were going or how many times they had made this trip, but vowed to find out the answer six nights from now. In the meantime, there would be much work to do.

When the wagon rolled out of sight, Katherine stepped out of the woods and trudged home, longing for sleep. Now that she was convinced of the six-day pattern, she wouldn't have to waste time spying over the next few days. That would leave plenty of time to set her plan in motion and put to rest any suspicious questions from her mother and Lewis about her evasive behavior of late. She didn't enjoy being deceptive with her loved ones.

She soon turned onto the street where she lived, passing by the Water Barrel Inn. The establishment was quiet tonight. A few lights burned inside and the sweet smell of wood smoke issued from a chimney. Katherine hurried past until she neared the next corner on the left where her house stood among a cluster of pine and maple trees. She assumed her mother was fast asleep until she noticed an oil lamp burning on the front porch railing. Had her mother left it out for her, Katherine wondered, sleeplessly awaiting her return? A moment later, she heard a familiar voice in the shadows. A figure wearing a hooded coat stood up near the front steps.

"I was beginning to think you had left Kanesbury," Lewis said as he walked over to Katherine, gently taking her hands. "I walked around the village looking for you before returning here to wait."

"We didn't have plans tonight, did we?" she asked, delighted to see him yet fearing she may have mixed up her days because of the recent spying.

"I just wanted to see you," he replied. "Lately it seems I have to make an appointment to spend any time with you after sunset."

Katherine blushed. "*Sorry...*"

"Your mother said you had been out walking again." Lewis looked into her eyes as he held the tips of her fingers. "If you wanted company..."

Katherine looked up with understanding and kissed him on the cheek. "I know I've been difficult to find lately, but I promise I'm free for the next several nights. We can spend as much time together as you'd like."

"That'd be wonderful. And maybe you could tell me why you've been wandering around the village all alone so late at night–if that's what you've been doing."

Katherine's expression hardened and she stepped back, feeling that Lewis didn't trust her. But amid the glow of the lamp light she noticed only genuine concern in his eyes, not a hint of distrust, and her mood lightened. She took his hand and led him back to the porch steps where they sat down.

"Lewis, have you been worrying about me that much lately?"

"You could say so." He gently wrapped an arm around her shoulder. "But if you have some reason not to tell me your business, I'll try to understand. After all, out of safety for others, I didn't give you details about the resistance movement I was in when Caldurian had control of the village."

"And it caused me many sleepless nights, thank you," she said, resting her head upon his shoulder. "But I trust you completely, so there's no reason for me not to involve you in my little escapade. But I must warn you, it could be dangerous."

Lewis chuckled. "That crazy wizard was hours away from letting his soldiers march me out of the village hall to be killed. How much more dangerous could it get?"

"You have a point. But still, I'm not sure of all the obstacles I might–we might–be facing. We can't take this lightly."

"We won't," he promised, giving her his undivided attention. "So you'll finally tell me what this mystery is all about?"

Katherine sat up and thought for a long moment before speaking. "Better than that–I'll show you." Lewis wrinkled his brow. "But first I must arrange a few matters before I can reveal anything. Absolute secrecy is required if this is to work."

"All right," he replied, filled with intrigue. "I'll let you decide how to proceed. Just know that I'll be there beside you every step of the way."

"I'd like nothing better, Lewis. It's been so lonely these past few days keeping this secret from you and my mother–and even from Constable Brindle."

"Constable Brindle?" Lewis' eyes popped wide open. "What's he got to do with this? What exactly are you involved in, Katherine?"

She smiled inscrutably and gently pressed a finger to his lips. "Remember, Lewis–absolute secrecy. I'll tell you as soon as I can, but I promise you won't have to wait any longer than six days."

"Six days?" he mumbled as Katherine's finger still rested upon his lips. "What happens in six days?"

"With luck, answers to several mysteries will be revealed. In the meantime, you'll just have to trust me." She removed her finger. "Can you do that?"

"I'd be a fool not to," he replied, kissing her in the soft glow of the lamp light.

Katherine visited her uncle in the village lockup the next day. Otto Nibbs, dressed in a white shirt, brown vest and matching trousers, his long, thinning hair tied up in back with a black band, sat despondently in a chair in a tiny stone room which had served as his home for the past fourteen days. He appeared thinner, his appetite having waned. A feather filled mattress and pillow lay on the floor along one wall. An oil lamp burned on a small table. Otto stood when Katherine walked in. They hugged, delighted to see one another.

"I can't stay long," she said after they exchanged pleasantries. "I'm going to speak to Zachary Farnsworth about hurrying up your trial instead of waiting for Maynard to return from Morrenwood."

"I could have made that request through Constable Brindle," Otto replied, offering Katherine his seat. "I'm innocent, after all, and will let it be known from every corner of Kanesbury. I would never betray our village or anyone it in."

"I know that, Uncle Otto, as do most, I'm sure."

"That wizard framed me, Katherine." Otto silently fumed as he paced about. "He must have put a spell upon me, forcing me to go from house to house in the middle of the night and warn people about his impending attack. I can't remember doing that, so it must be the only explanation." He flung his arms in the air and sighed before settling down and smiling. "Sorry for getting so worked up."

"You have a right to, Uncle Otto. But I'm here to help."

"Katherine, you had told me to keep quiet about demanding a swift trial until you snooped about for a bit." He looked at her expectantly. "Did you find what you were looking for?"

"I'm close, Uncle Otto." But before he could ask another question, Katherine held up a hand. "As I told you earlier, I can't divulge what I'm doing for all our sakes, but I'm on the verge of a breakthrough. That's why I'm going to approach Mr. Farnsworth–with a little help from a good friend."

"Who?" Otto noted the cautious expression upon her face and nodded understandingly. "I know. I know. All in good time."

"Please be patient. It's for your own good–and for others' safety, too. In the meantime, not a word to anyone. Not even to my mother when she visits."

"Very well," he quietly replied, his tone gracious.

"I'm sure she'll bring you a warm meal. There was a kettle of soup simmering over the fire earlier."

"Hot soup would be lovely," he remarked. "Constable Brindle and his men have been nothing but kind to me, but their culinary skills do not match their investigative prowess, though even that is wanting in my particular case."

Katherine grinned, happy to see his sense of humor still intact, but her heart was heavy, knowing she would have to leave here without him. She said goodbye shortly afterward, and when she had left, Otto resumed sitting in his chair, quietly contemplating the fate of his fellow villagers in the wake of Caldurian's raucous arrival and stealthy departure. He had already forgiven his neighbors in his heart for turning against him, knowing that the wizard had deceived the good people of Kanesbury amid his string of threats and punishments. Most, if not all of his neighbors, probably regretted the outcome of events. But since the gears were already in motion for a public trial, however slowly they moved, Otto accepted the fact that that is how everything would be resolved in the end, for good or for ill.

Under a whisper of snowflakes, Katherine walked along the busy streets of Kanesbury later that morning, her mind racing with a myriad of tasks to complete, the most important one being a visit to Amanda Stewart. She moved along the side of the road, oblivious to all else as she hurried to her destination, the hem of her hooded cloak sweeping against the cold ground. When she reached the Stewarts' home, Katherine knocked on the front door, surprised to see Amanda answering the door.

"Good morning, Katherine. I didn't expect you on your day off," she said with delight, beckoning her guest inside the hallway and closing the door behind them. "What brings you here today?"

"You, Amanda, if you can spare a few moments."

"For you, Katherine, always. You and Sophia are like family." She took Katherine's cloak and hung it on a wall peg. "Most of the staff is off today as people are still getting their own homes and lives in order after what that horrible wizard had put us through. We can talk in the side parlor."

"I appreciate this more than you know," Katherine replied as they walked through the hallway. "And I promise not to take up too much of your time."

"Let me worry about that, dear." Amanda sensed a trace of anxiety underlying Katherine's demeanor. She stopped and looked at the young woman in a motherly fashion, raising a questioning eyebrow beneath her silvery hair. "You seem troubled, Katherine. What's bothering you?"

"I need to ask a favor of you, Amanda. A *big* favor."

Amanda nonchalantly swished a hand through the air. "After all the last minute dinner party jams you've helped me out of, a favor is the least I can do in return."

Katherine smiled as a wave of relief washed over her. "Speaking of dinner parties, I was hoping that you could host a very small one here at your house."

"Sounds lovely," she replied with no reservation but with much intrigue. "For what reason? And who will be attending?"

"The guest list will be small. Only five. You and Oscar, of course, and my mother and me, and..." Katherine's heart beat wildly as her nerves started to get the best of her. She did her best to remain composed and casual. "Oh, and Zachary Farnsworth, too."

"Our new acting mayor. Seems we've had a lot of those lately," she said with a soft chuckle as they continued to the side parlor. "Oscar has wanted to invite Mr. Farnsworth over and pick his brain. Business and the like. But I suspect that you desire to talk to him about your Uncle Otto's situation."

"Something like that."

"Why not then? I'd be more than happy to oblige. Perhaps sometime next week or the one after?"

Katherine tried to conceal a budding frown as she looked up at her friend. "I hope you won't think this forward of me, Amanda, but would it be at all possible to hold it in five day's time?"

Amanda performed a quick mental calculation. "That would be on the twenty-eighth of the month, the last day of Old Autumn."

"Winter's Eve is a special day, after all," she replied with a forced grin.

Amanda sensed that there was more to the young woman's request than met the eye, but would allow her to explain in her own time and manner. When they reached the side parlor, they sat by the fireplace that gently crackled with a low blaze.

"Tell me more about this dinner party," Amanda said.

Katherine fidgeted nervously, knowing she couldn't tell her friend the full truth. She couldn't risk letting her knowledge of Farnsworth and Dooley's collusion with Caldurian reach back to their ears until she was ready to strike. Amanda would have to be kept in the dark as much as possible for the time being.

"It shall be a simple but elegant affair," Katherine said, promising to help with the meal preparations beforehand. "However, there is one task I would request of you if you're agreeable."

"And what is that?" Amanda curiously asked.

"Would you be so kind as to invite Mr. Farnsworth yourself?"

Dooley Kramer was splitting wood on the side of his house later that day when Farnsworth stopped by on his way home from the banking house. Twilight deepened among the trees as an orange and purple glow lingered above the southwest horizon. Dooley glared at his neighbor when Farnsworth informed him that he would have to make the next delivery to the swamp alone.

"Why?" he asked, grunting with contempt.

"Because I shall be dining with Oscar Stewart and his wife that evening," he replied, trying not to sound boastful. "Amanda stopped by my office this afternoon and invited me. And now that I am a public official, it would raise suspicions for someone to see me sneaking out of the village in the middle of the night. Am I right?"

Dooley scowled, insulted that Farnsworth addressed him as if he were a child. "Once again, you reap the rewards with dinner parties and appointments to public office while I get stuck doing all the dirty work," he muttered, his ax striking a piece of wood he had set upon a large, flat rock and splitting it in two. "I served as a spy in the Citadel, and what did that get me? When do I get a seat on the village council? When do I get invited to swanky parties and fancy dinners?" He wiped the sweat off his brow with a brush of his shirt sleeve. "And now I have to go to the swamp by myself? Hardly seems fair. I really don't like that place."

Farnsworth sighed, shaking his head. "I told you that these things would take time, Dooley, but now that I'm mayor, the rewards are soon to flow your way, too. I'm in a position to make that happen. But the good news is that this will be the last time you have to go to the swamp."

Dooley looked up. "Oh?"

Though not another soul was in the vicinity, Farnsworth stepped closer and lowered his voice. "When you leave in five days, I'll have finished hiring someone to take care of our persistent problem. So you see, things are looking up for you already."

"*Take care of?*" Dooley set the tip of the long ax handle on a piece of wood and rested one hand upon it as if it were a cane, wondering if Farnsworth was serious about ridding their lives of Maynard and Adelaide. "You've talked about this before, Zachary."

"I know, but with Caldurian around, it was difficult to make arrangements with my outside contacts. Now things are nearly set."

"Are you sure you've found someone reliable? Someone who can–" Dooley swallowed uncomfortably. "Someone who can do the job right?"

Farnsworth nodded. "I've talked to some of the people who helped me contact Caldurian in the first place. They are very loyal and responsible–for a price, of course."

Dooley scratched his head as a bead of sweat trickled down his brow. "Why do I even have to go to the swamp next time if the person you hired is only going to–well, you know."

"My employee is coming up from the south where the war against Rhiál hadn't gone as planned, so I've heard. This individual had hoped to make his fortune there, but left when opportunities dried up," he explained. "He's more than happy to get any work he can for now in these parts."

Dooley shrugged. "Still, why do I have to go to the swamp?"

"Because you will be driving our employee there."

Dooley's eyes widened. "Why me?"

"I certainly can't do it! I'll be having dinner with the Stewarts. But don't worry. All you have to do is pick him up by the bridge past the Spirit Caves and then drive him into the woods along the swamp. He'd never find the entrance on his own."

"But he's a killer!" Dooley frantically whispered. "I don't want to sit next to him."

"A killer for hire," he corrected. "And you've hung around worse people lately, so get over it. Anyway, after he completes his job, you'll give him his pay that I'll provide and then drive him back to the bridge. After that, he'll go on his merry way into the wild and you'll return to Kanesbury." Farnsworth smiled reassuringly. "Then neither of us will ever again have to worry about Maynard Kurtz or Adelaide Cooper burdening our lives. My employee will be well worth the investment."

Dooley thought about it for a moment, taking comfort in Farnsworth's steady words. "I suppose you're right. Still, I feel uneasy about this. What's the guy's name?"

"I don't know his real name, Dooley. People like him don't pass out that kind of information." A breeze swept by, rustling the remaining autumn leaves littered about the house. "Only his closest associates would know, I'd imagine."

Dooley looked up. "How much are you paying him?"

Farnsworth smirked. "Plenty. I'll drop it off to you on my way to dinner with the Stewarts, not a moment before." He raised a hand before Dooley could protest. "And it's not that I don't trust you with the money, but there's no sense in having it misplaced or stolen before then. After all, you did lose that key. And poor Arthur Weeks ended up paying for it with his life."

"No need to bring up the past," Dooley sputtered, his face feeling warm in the cool air. "I'll drive him to the swamp if that's what it'll take to put this sorry matter behind us."

"That's the spirit, Dooley. And when Maynard and Adelaide are gone, life is going to be completely changed for both of us," he replied. "Mark my words."

"It had better be a big change in my case," Dooley demanded, picking up the ax and setting another chunk of wood on the stone to split. "I want my fair share–and soon. No more excuses!"

Farnsworth stroked his chin, knowing that Dooley's impatience, immaturity or inadvertent slip of the tongue could cause him trouble down the road. Worse yet, Dooley might one day show some fortitude and hold their past deeds over him, demanding a greater share of the social and monetary profits to buy his silence. Farnsworth always knew he would probably have to do something about his neighbor, too, and in the back of his mind he had long anticipated such a corrective action.

Whoever he hired to purge Maynard and Adelaide from his life could easily do away with Dooley as well for a higher price. He imagined Dooley driving the assassin to the swamp to presumably do away with Maynard and Adelaide and then paying him afterward for his services. Dooley would never suspect that he would be the third and final assignment for which the man had been hired. Dooley's corpse would join Maynard and Adelaide's at the bottom of the swamp where the trio would slowly fade from the village's memory. Farnsworth savored the image before offering a quick wave goodbye.

"I promise that you'll get your due," he said as he wandered up the road to his house as the sound of splitting wood reverberated through the crisp air. "No more delays. No more excuses."

"And soon!" Dooley refrained, raising his ax in the deepening twilight.

"Sooner than you think," Farnsworth whispered to himself as he shuffled along the shadowy road, a thin smirk forming upon his face. "Sooner than you think."

CHAPTER 79

Setting the Table

The next five days swiftly passed. On the twenty-eighth day of Old Autumn, the table was grandly set for Amanda Stewart's dinner party. As evening approached, sweet wood smoke lingered above the village like ghostly tendrils. The crisp air delicately frosted window panes and squeezed the last bits of life out of the browning grass and fallen leaves pasted to the frozen ground. The first quarter Bear Moon drifted overhead through a veil of feathery clouds.

Zachary Farnsworth arrived at the Stewart residence on time, dressed in one of his finest shirts and silver-buttoned vests, topped with a dark gray evening coat. He graciously thanked his hosts for the invitation as they sipped a hearty red wine by a blazing fire in the side parlor. Later, Katherine and her mother knocked at the front door. Upon hearing their voices in the front hallway, Amanda politely excused herself and soon returned to the parlor with the two women as Farnsworth and Oscar continued talking near the fireplace.

"I hope you don't mind, Zachary, but I also invited two dear friends of mine to help us celebrate autumn's last night and add some sparkle to the conversation."

"I'm delighted," he replied as he greeted the new arrivals with a smile, displaying the friendliness and charm he thought would be expected from one in his position. But deep inside, Farnsworth seethed, wondering why Amanda had invited Otto Nibbs' sister and niece. Surely this dinner was not all about *him* anymore. He believed that Amanda had an ulterior motive and suspected that he wasn't looked upon with the respect he had earned in his new position. He decided, however, to behave with civility and grace to see where the evening would lead.

When Morris announced that dinner was ready, Amanda escorted everyone into the main dining room. They sat at one end of a long rectangular table of dark cherry wood covered with a cream-colored runner with decorative stitching laid lengthwise down the center. Several candles flickered on the table while a roaring fire crackled in the hearth. Katherine sat directly across from Farnsworth and gave him a brief but cordial smile, her heart beating rapidly. She felt as if he could read her thoughts and knew what she planned to do. She was determined to keep calm, knowing that much depended upon her evenness of mind and meticulous planning. She took a deep breath and a sip of wine and relaxed, looking forward to enjoying a delicious dinner. Dessert, however, would be another matter.

"The table looks lovely," Sophia remarked, admiring the gold-edged plates and polished silverware as two young women from the kitchen staff served their meal. A platter with a freshly baked loaf of bread, a crock of butter and a wedge of cheese had been placed upon the table along with a pot of steaming tea.

"I decided to use my best tableware this evening to celebrate our gathering and our renewed freedom," Amanda replied. "From the look of the place, you wouldn't suspect that two weeks ago this room was filled with soldiers from the Northern Isles whose crass table manners, I'm guessing, were akin to those of the Enâri!"

"I can vouch for that," Katherine said over the light laughter. "Many of the soldiers I served had appalling etiquette and boundless appetites." She glanced at Farnsworth, her nerves more steady and her confidence growing. She knew that if she had been able to deal successfully with dozens of uncouth soldiers, she could certainly handle anything Zachary Farnsworth might throw at her. "Mr. Farnsworth, you would have been shocked and saddened to have seen the inside of this beautiful home during Caldurian's occupation."

"I'm sure I would have," he said with feigned disgust before drinking more wine. "Fortunately, I was allowed to continue working in the banking house. Apparently that troublesome wizard had enough sense to know that some day-to-day operations of the village had to continue to keep up any semblance of order. Still, I heard enough stories about the terrible things that went on here."

"Horrible things!" Sophia remarked as she removed a cloth napkin from a silver ring and placed it on her lap. "It's unfathomable the harm that some people in this world will do to others. The disruption of lives and livelihoods that that awful wizard and his soldiers brought down upon our village is unconscionable. What would possess a man to do such things?" Amanda sadly shook her head in response as Farnsworth looked uncomfortably at his plate.

"Well, we shall never let that happen again!" Oscar assured his guests as they began to eat. "The other council members and I will soon meet to discuss steps to better protect our village in these uncertain times. We hope you'll attend some of those meetings, Zachary, when time allows."

"Of course," he said. "I look forward to it."

"Excellent!" Oscar replied, popping a piece of beef into his mouth and washing it down with some wine. "Now not wishing to pass judgment, I do believe that Maynard Kurtz was unwise not to seek help from King Justin right after Otto's disappearance when rumors of an attack were floating about the village. Then when Otto reappeared a month later to spread his dire warnings which were punctuated by the fire at the gristmill, Maynard again should have sent word to Morrenwood for military assistance. Caldurian still would have launched an attack, but King Justin's troops might have arrived in time to free us and crush the wizard and his men."

"That makes perfect sense in hindsight," Katherine said. "But I suppose Maynard was just doing what he thought was right, don't you agree, Mr. Farnsworth?"

The guest of honor looked up. "Far be it from me to criticize my predecessor, but if he had acted immediately, things may have turned out differently. Still, credit where credit is due. As Maynard recently left for Morrenwood to speak with the King, perhaps he has finally overcome his past hesitancy. That's something in his favor."

"Better late than never, I suppose," Amanda said.

"Let's not be too harsh," Oscar jumped in. "Maynard has been a wise and upstanding citizen all his life–and a good friend, too. Only since he was appointed acting mayor did I silently question some of his actions, or lack thereof," he added with a bewildered frown. "Oh, and on a related topic, Len Harold stopped by to see me two days ago after Prince Gregory and his troops passed through the village. Len had spoken to him."

"Really? What did he have to say?" Sophia asked curiously.

"According to him, Maynard never arrived in Morrenwood even though he left here fifteen days ago. I wonder why the delay?"

"I wondered the very same thing myself," Farnsworth jumped in, knowing full well that the *Maynard* who went to Morrenwood was Arileez himself, on his way to the Citadel to supplant King Justin and serve as Vellan's puppet. "Len Harold had informed me as well. I waited a couple of days before taking action to see if Maynard might send word that he had safely arrived. But as I haven't yet heard anything, tomorrow I will seek volunteers to trace Maynard's path and determine if he was delayed or, perish the thought, injured along the way." Farnsworth sighed, hoping he appeared concerned enough about Maynard's well-being. "But since everyone is preoccupied with getting their lives back in order, if I have to go myself, I will."

"That's commendable of you," Amanda said. "Putting the welfare of others ahead of your own is the mark of a good leader."

"I agree," Katherine said. She poured herself some tea and looked askance at her hostess who discreetly nodded in response. She now wanted Amanda to ask a prearranged question to Farnsworth about her uncle to establish a legitimate reason for her and her mother being here tonight.

"And speaking of the welfare of others, Zachary," Amanda continued, trying to sound as casual as possible. "Have you given any thought to Otto Nibbs' trial? As Maynard is not here–and who knows when he'll be back–is it possible that you might consider taking charge of the proceedings?"

Farnsworth set his fork down and gently patted his lips with the cloth napkin draped over his lap. "It has crossed my mind," he said, "seeing that it would be unfair to let Otto languish in the village lockup as Maynard gave me no specific date as to his return. Yet I don't want to step on Maynard's toes and usurp this responsibility from him. He was the acting mayor when Otto was incarcerated, so Maynard should be the one to oversee the public proceedings."

He noted the disappointment on Sophia and Katherine's faces, realizing that this dinner party was nothing but a ruse so that Amanda could help her two friends curry his favor on behalf of Otto. Farnsworth didn't particularly care when Otto's trial took place or whether he presided over it or not. All he worried about was whether Otto would be declared guilty by at least fifteen of his twenty-one fellow citizens who would be randomly chosen to sit as jurors. If Otto were declared innocent of the charges, he would reclaim his seat as mayor. All of Farnsworth's work to climb to his current position would have been in vain. He needed Otto to be guilty.

Farnsworth once guessed that the sooner the trial was held, the better his chances for a guilty verdict since most people would still be upset with Otto for trying to save himself. But nineteen days had gone by since Caldurian had pronounced Otto's sentence, and some of the simmering resentment and ill feelings against Otto were cooling. A few people were even quietly suspecting that Otto's various crimes may not have been all they seemed now that they had had time to think. The wizard Caldurian was involved, after all, and that left a very large question mark in the minds of many, though none had any proof to exonerate Otto. Perhaps it was already too late to achieve the verdict he desired. Farnsworth needed Otto to be guilty, realizing it might come down to him rigging the selection system or handing out some well-placed favors to achieve his goal.

He gazed at his fellow dinner guests, wondering if there were even fifteen people in Kanesbury dishonest enough to turn against Otto Nibbs, an amiable and respected man to nearly everyone before Arileez briefly assumed his identity and marred his character. Perhaps he might have to employ more drastic measures to hold onto power. Farnsworth seriously considered the possibility, wondering what would happen if Otto tried to escape. Perhaps he might *accidentally* be killed during the escape, conveniently solving his problem. He considered the anonymous individual he had hired who would go to the swamp later this evening to permanently eliminate his three other problems, namely, Maynard Kurtz, Adelaide Cooper and Dooley Kramer. If he could somehow rehire that person to secretly pay Otto a visit in the lockup in the middle of the night sometime soon... Farnsworth smiled inside, imagining how the village would grieve when they learned that Otto Nibbs had taken his own life out of an unrelenting sense of guilt and shame because of his questionable deeds. Indeed, it was another avenue to consider so he could secure his place in Kanesbury society.

Amanda lightly cleared her throat, drawing Farnsworth's gaze. "Well, Zachary? Have you made up your mind?"

"*Hmmm*? Oh, I guess I have," he replied with a thin smile. "Weighing both sides of the matter, I've come to the conclusion that more people would be properly served if we proceeded with a trial as soon as possible. I'll talk to Otto tomorrow to see if this is acceptable and to make sure he's had enough time to prepare to defend himself." Farnsworth reached for the loaf of warm bread and ripped off a small piece. "I'll also let Constable Brindle know so he can put his case together on behalf of the village." He looked up at Katherine and Sophia. "Is this satisfactory to you both?"

"Very much so," replied Sophia with a relieved smile. "I'm quite appreciative of your efforts, Mr. Farnsworth."

"As am I," Katherine said as she raised her teacup and took a sip. "It was fortunate that we met tonight and were able to discuss this matter without rancor or distrust."

"Fortunate indeed," he said, catching Amanda's gaze.

Amanda smiled with a tinge of guilt. "I suppose it's no use pretending, Zachary, that this dinner was planned solely for my husband and me to get more acquainted with you. You're too perceptive to believe that. My dear friends, Sophia and Katherine, had planned to speak to you about Otto's trial, but Katherine asked if I might intervene to help move things along. So, as Oscar and I were planning to invite you over one of these days anyway, I saw no reason why we couldn't boil two chickens in one kettle." Amanda gently patted his arm. "I hope you're not offended by my slight deception, Zachary."

Farnsworth sat back in his chair and grinned. "Not in the least, Amanda. In fact, I'm embarrassingly flattered that others at this table think so highly of me. I am merely a citizen of the village just like the rest of you," he said, briefly eyeing Katherine. "So please, think nothing more of it. It has been a wonderful evening so far, both the company and this fine meal."

Oscar raised his wine glass as a show of appreciation for the man's kind words. "But rest assured, Zachary, that later you and I shall go off to one of the parlors and sample a fine vintage I've been saving. There we can have a long talk about politics and business and whatever else strikes our fancy."

Amanda laughed lovingly. "And we three women completely understand that you men don't want us around bothering you. So after we all have dessert, Sophia, Katherine and I will take tea in another room for our own private chat."

"As you wish, my dear," Oscar said, leaning over and kissing her on the cheek.

"Speaking of dessert," Katherine said, "Lana, one of the kitchen girls, asked me to check on her sugar glaze for the cinnamon bread. She was trying a recipe I had concocted for the party here during the Harvest Festival. I promised to peek in after dinner."

"My Katherine is always looking out for others," Sophia proudly said.

When the meal concluded, Katherine excused herself to step into the kitchen. But when she stood up from the dinner table, her facial muscles tightened and she immediately placed a hand upon the edge of her chair to steady herself, appearing lightheaded.

"Are you all right?" her mother asked worriedly.

"What's the matter, dear?" Amanda said.

"I'm fine," Katherine softly replied, standing still for a second or two before her countenance relaxed. "I guess I rose from my seat too quickly. I'm quite all right now," she added, walking slowly toward the doorway with a pleasant smile. "Now don't let me put a damper on this evening. Continue your conversation. I'll be back momentarily." She exited the room.

"My, but I do hope she's not putting on a brave face," Amanda said, fidgeting with a turquoise bead necklace she wore. "It'd be a shame if she missed the rest of the evening, especially when she was so adamant that I hold the dinner on this particular night."

"Oh, is something special about tonight?" Farnsworth casually inquired as he reached for his wine.

"It is the last day of autumn," she replied. "Katherine had mentioned that fact when she asked me to play hostess. Whether or not that's the reason, I'm not sure. But she was rather set on this date." She shrugged before picking up her glass, only to find with disappointment that it was empty. "Oh well, you can ask her about it when she comes back, Zachary, if you'd like. In the meantime, more wine, anyone?"

After leaving the dining room, Katherine went to the kitchen now toasty warm from the heat of the fireplace. Lana was busy at one of the island counters glazing a loaf of cinnamon bread with sugar icing. Katherine walked up and complimented her on her artistry.

"It looks so delicious," she said amid the bustle of the other workers.

"Thank you for suggesting this recipe the other day," Lana replied. "I sampled some earlier and you're right–it is delicious. You and Amanda's guests are in for a treat."

"They are, but unfortunately, I'm not," Katherine replied, appearing suddenly tired when Lana glanced up. "I wish I could stay, but I'm not feeling well at the moment."

"I hope it's nothing you ate!"

"No. The meal was excellent. I'm just out of sorts. Maybe I'm coming down with a spot of something or other," she said with a weary sigh. "Could you be a dear and inform Amanda that I went home for the night? With my deepest regrets, of course. I'll stop by tomorrow if I'm feeling better and apologize in person."

"Of course. Do you want somebody to escort you home?"

"No, I'll be fine. But if you would go out to the front hallway and grab my cloak without anyone in the dining room seeing you, that would be lovely," Katherine added with an appreciative smile. "I'll wait here and leave through the kitchen. I don't want to make a fuss and spoil everyone's evening."

Lana understood and retrieved Katherine's cloak. Moments later she bid her goodnight as Katherine stepped into the shadowy backyard and closed the door behind her. A faint glow of moonlight filtered softly through the thin layer of clouds, bony tree branches and fragrant pine boughs.

Katherine veered left and hurried across the brittle grass to the nearby street. When she briefly caught sight of the door to the ice cellar, she couldn't help but recall when Nicholas had escaped from Constable Brindle amid the excitement and chaos of the Harvest Festival, wondering where his path had led him. Was he still in

Arrondale, she wondered? Or even in Laparia? Wherever life had taken him, she hoped that Nicholas was safe and happy.

As she neared the clump of maple and pine trees on the edge of the property, Katherine smiled in the darkness as a shadowy figure emerged from within them and walked over to her. She immediately recognized the lean silhouette vaguely illuminated in the moonlight and moved toward it.

"Right on time," she whispered, taking Lewis' hand in hers. He had become an unexpected and pleasant breath of fresh air in her life, and someone dear to her heart. "Are you ready?"

"I've been waiting six days for you to explain this mystery of yours," he replied. "Where are we going?"

"Not far. Just a few blocks away. But we'll keep to the trees and the shadows," she added with an air of intrigue. "I'll explain everything along the way."

"Lead on," Lewis replied, affectionately squeezing her hand.

Katherine smiled at him as they crossed the road and hurried north up the nearest street, heading for Dooley Kramer's house. She was glad to have company this night, excited by the pursuit yet fearful of what she might find. Her emotions settled down and she began to whisper to Lewis about all she had been doing over the last several nights. As he listened in stunned amazement, Katherine noted the look of disbelief in his eyes. The gravity of what she had been doing and what she was about to do suddenly hit her. She now realized just how fortunate she was to have Lewis at her side and in her life. Katherine held his hand tightly as they entered a thin stretch of woods, their steps in sync as they drew nearer to their destination.

CHAPTER 80

Beside Murky Waters

Katherine and Lewis hid in the shadows alongside Dooley's house. A single light burned inside. A line of dry, straggly hedges leaned toward them in the frosty night, the spindly branches catching traces of moonlight from the west. Their eyes were fixed upon the horse and cart near the front of the property facing the leaf strewn road. Shortly after they had stealthily made their way to Dooley's home, they peeked into the cart, disappointed to discover that it hadn't yet been loaded with supplies. A pile of old blankets and some firewood scraps were the only items within.

"On previous nights when Dooley and Farnsworth made their journey, the cart was already filled with wood and sacks of food and other supplies," Katherine whispered as she and Lewis kept watch. "Everything had been covered with blankets. I was daring enough to take a look one night while they were still inside."

Lewis was about to comment but held back when the light in Dooley's house went out and the front door opened. He pointed as Dooley's dark figure emerged and trudged toward the horse cart, a lit candle in his hand. Soon the two copper oil lamps affixed near the front of the cart were illuminated, casting an eerie glow. Dooley blew out the candle and tossed it in back with the wood and blankets.

"Let's get this over with, Barley," he muttered, affectionately slapping the horse. His words sounded lazy and tired as if he had recently indulged in a few mugs of ale. "We'll do the work as usual while he lives it up." Dooley spat on the ground and climbed up on the seat with a bit of a struggle.

Lewis glanced at Katherine and noted the growing panic in her eyes, realizing that she had expected Dooley to first load the cart before leaving. Now they had lost their chance to climb into the back, conceal themselves and follow Dooley to his destination. Before Katherine could speak, Lewis brushed his fingers along the ground for a small rock. When he found one about the size of a plum, he tossed it over the single story house in a high, graceful arc, sending it plummeting noisily through brittle tree branches on the other side and landing with a thud in a pile of dried leaves. Dooley craned his head to the left as he clutched the reins.

"Who's there?" he called out, his unsteady voice flushed with fear and suspicion. "Zachary, is that you?" Upon receiving no reply, he sighed and climbed down off the cart. He removed one of the oil lamps and wandered toward the opposite side of the house, wondering if he was hearing things. "What now?" he muttered, spitting again in the road. "I want to get this over with and..."

As Dooley's voice faded away, Lewis signaled for Katherine to follow him. They dashed along the hedges and hurried to the cart, careful to avoid stepping on any twigs or dried leaves. Though the darkness concealed them for the most part, both felt vulnerable as if they were out strolling beneath the morning sun. When they reached the cart, Lewis helped Katherine climb onto the back and then scrambled up himself, grabbing a blanket for each of them. They lay down upon the dirty floorboards littered with pieces of leftover firewood and covered themselves with the damp, dirty blankets just as Dooley reappeared around the corner of the house. He walked back to the cart, reattached the oil lamp and climbed upon his seat with a tired grunt.

"*Now* we'll go, Barley," he muttered, grabbing the reins and giving them a gentle snap.

Slowly the horse moved forward and Dooley guided it onto the road and to his right. The steady clip clopping of Barley's hooves along with the grinding of the wagon wheels allowed Katherine and Lewis to shift their positions and get comfortable without being detected. A short time later, Dooley had driven a few blocks through the village and soon arrived on River Road. There he turned east and rolled out of Kanesbury, passing between Maynard Kurtz's farm to his left and Adelaide Cooper's small house on his right just moments before he crossed over the village borderline. It was a couple of miles to the Spirit Caves and to the wooden bridge just beyond. There Dooley would pick up the man Farnsworth had hired to eliminate their problems in the swamp. He shuddered, contemplating what was about to happen, taking little comfort that it would not be directly by his hand. He breathed the chilly air, his body feeling as cold inside as it was without. How he wished the night was already over, dreading the anxious hours ahead.

Katherine and Lewis traveled along River Road for several minutes, hidden beneath their blankets, breathing slowly and steadily, not daring to move. The cold rising up from the floorboards, the constant jarring of the cart as it rattled over the bumpy dirt road, and the stale, hideous odor of the blankets made for a long, dreary and uncomfortable ride. Katherine, lying on her left side, wondered how Lewis was enduring the trip. He, though, was happy to be tagging along, imagining with dread what might have happened to Katherine had she undertaken this risky adventure on her own.

When the cart hit a particularly deep rut about a quarter mile from the Spirit Caves, Katherine had to bite her tongue to keep from shouting furiously at the driver. Finally, when she could tolerate the stench of the blanket no longer, she risked taking a peek out from underneath to inhale the cool, sweet air and revive her spirits.

She held her breath and slowly lifted the edge of the blanket near her head and peered through the opening. It was nearly pitch-black outside and she wondered if Dooley would even notice her if she removed the covering entirely. Feeling courageous, she raised the blanket a little higher and detected the faint glow of the two oil lamps through thin spaces between the front and side wooden planks of the cart. She looked up at the cloudy sky. The first quarter Bear Moon had dipped farther in the west and was completely obscured as the clouds had thickened in the last half hour. When she craned her neck farther, she noted the outline of the back of Dooley's head and shoulders as he dutifully drove the cart, apparently oblivious to all around him except the road ahead. Katherine suddenly felt a warm breeze upon her face and looked straight ahead, noting Lewis' smiling face looking back at her from beneath his raised blanket.

"Are you all right?" he silently said, mouthing each word.

Katherine nodded and smiled back. Lewis extended his left arm, entwining it lovingly around hers until their fingers interlocked. They smiled at one another again, for a few moments unaware of the rickety cart traversing the bumpy road as it passed by the Spirit Caves and continued to the wooden bridge farther up the road. The young couple, caught for a moment in the soft, timeless contentment of a waking dream, moved their lips closer to one another as a cool breeze shot across the top of the cart. Suddenly they were pulled back into the harsh present when the dull, steady rumbling of horse hoofs turned into a clattering echo upon the wooden planks of the bridge. Katherine realized they had approached the western edge of the swamp, wondering how much longer their journey would take. But when Dooley reined in his horse as they crossed the bridge, Katherine and Lewis both assumed they had reached their destination. They simultaneously flipped the blankets back over their heads to await what would happen next.

Dooley, in the meantime, brought the cart to a halt after it passed over the bridge which spanned an eastern portion of the Pine River, its icy waters mirroring the deathly gloom of the sky. He guided Barley to the right side of the road near a handful of spindly trees growing along the western tip of the swamp. Here the swamp was narrow and more open to view, but as it stretched farther eastward, it gradually grew wider, bordered by the Pine River to its south and River Road to the north. The woods around the water's edge grew thicker and wilder as one headed east, hiding the vast majority of the swamp from the view of passersby.

Dooley looked about, the glow of the oil lamps shrouding the area with a pall of melancholy and hopelessness. He felt sick to his stomach, thinking too much about what he was preparing to do, about what Farnsworth had ordered him to do. His squeamishness turned into cold fright when he saw something shift in the shadows just ahead, swiftly moving toward the horse and cart. He sat up straight, now wishing he had brought along a knife with him for protection, chiding himself for being unprepared. But he had been so nervous and out of sorts these last few days, especially tonight, that he left home without thinking things through.

"Dooley Kramer?" A man's tired and scratchy voice called out from the shadows near a tiny point of glowing light.

"*Yes...*" Dooley whispered before clearing his throat. "Yes," he repeated, this time much louder.

"Good," the man said, stepping into the glow of the oil lamps and briefly studying his driver. "Take me where you need me to be. The sooner this is done, the better."

Dooley nodded, his heart racing and his hands sweating despite the cold air seeping through his thin gloves. "Climb on board, Mister...?"

The tall man, just under forty years old and smoking a pipe, locked eyes with Dooley. His whiskered, wind-burned face beneath a tattered hat made him look older. When he climbed up onto the cart, Dooley winced and held his breath for a moment before he could adjust to the smell of smoke emanating from the stranger's clothing. The man took another draw on his pipe as he leaned against the wooden backrest just as Dooley was about to snap the reins.

"Not so fast," the man said, exhaling a stream of smoke scented with cloves. "First I want to knew how long until we get to where we're going. Then there's a little matter of my fee that your employer promised."

Dooley squirmed in his seat, bristling at the comment that Zachary Farnsworth was his employer. "It's not far. Less than a mile up the road. And as to your fee," he added, trying to keep his voice steady as if he were in control of the situation, "I'll pay you half now and half after you finish." He reached into one of his coat pockets and pulled out a small leather pouch filled with coins and handed it to the man. "Is that acceptable?"

The man untied the leather strings and poured some silver and copper half pieces into his hand and quickly counted them. "Fine," he sharply muttered, carefully placing the coins back into the pouch and shoving it in his pocket. "Let's go."

"At once," Dooley said, his shoulders slumped as he looked askance at the man. "Do you have a name?"

Dell Hawks offered a thin smile. "Yes, but you don't need to know it. I prefer to keep anonymous when I can in my line of work."

"Of course," he replied.

"Can we get moving?" Dell said in an almost friendly tone. "I want to get this over with and get paid so I can move on to other

576

jobs. And you, I'm sure, want to return home to a good night's sleep. So the sooner we leave…"

"Say no more," Dooley said, snapping the reins and guiding the horse back onto the road, all the while wondering how he had ended up in such a bleak situation as his surroundings passed by like ghostly visions.

The next several minutes dragged by like a tiresome dream. Dooley felt as if he were moving but making no progress, condemned to an eternal journey as payment for the horrible things he had done and for the evil that he was about to unleash. He spotted the turnoff just ahead on the right near a large rock half buried in dirt. He slowed the horse to a trot and pulled off onto a thin strip of brittle grass and weeds bordering the tree line, continuing until they found a narrow path disappearing into the thickening trees. Dooley followed it for a short distance before it veered right deeper into the woods and closer to the swamp. There were no soothing calls of frogs or crickets tonight as the cold air and deathly darkness encroached upon them.

Dooley nervously tugged at his collar, feeling as if he were suffocating. He glanced at his mysterious passenger, barely discerning the man's outline in the sickly light. As his hands quivered and his body grew colder, he wondered how the stranger would complete his task, yet didn't truly want to know the ghastly details. He resigned himself to years of sleepless nights, questioning if he should ever have thrown in his lot with Zachary Farnsworth. He wished he had never stolen the key to the Spirit Box from the talons of the wizard's eagle twenty years ago.

At last they reached the end of the path near the water's edge. The pungent swamp smells Dooley recalled from previous excursions had lessened with the onset of colder nights. But the place still gave him the chills with its misshapen trees and snakelike vines standing guard while a murderer for hire sat next to him. He shuddered, wondering if he could go through with this as he brought the cart to a standstill.

"Here we are," Dooley said, swallowing hard. "Now what?"

"Now you tell me where they are," Dell Hawks replied. "Then I'll do the job I was hired for."

"Okay then." Dooley's heart pounded as he deeply inhaled the crisp night air to calm his frayed nerves, but his chest ached and his throat felt constricted. Dell Hawks noticed his unease and chuckled.

"Relax. I'm doing this, Dooley, not you. Calm down and tell me where the two individuals are. In the meantime, you can wait here while I take care of business. Afterward, you can drive me back to the main road."

Dooley nodded, staring uncomfortably at his feet. "All right. They're... They're over..." He pointed through the gloom to the island across the water where a faint yellow light burned behind the nailed shutters in the tiny house on stilts. "One of them, the older woman, is locked up in that house. I'll give you the key to open the padlock on her door. The other one is in a small shack to the right. He's asleep, so you won't have any trouble with him."

"Asleep?" Dell asked skeptically. "How do you know that?"

Dooley's faint laughter fluttered nervously in the darkness. He removed his hat and anxiously combed a hand through his tangled blond locks. "Trust me. He's fast asleep and isn't going to wake up any time soon."

"Odd," he replied. "But if you say so. Now tell me how to get over there."

"There are two boats hidden nearby. Follow me." Dooley climbed down off the cart as if in a trance. His legs felt like they might buckle and his footsteps were those of a drunken man, though the ale he had consumed a while ago had since worn off.

Dell Hawks joined him on the ground, standing beside Dooley as he removed one of the oil lamps from the cart. Dooley's shaky hands caused the pale circle of light to waver back and forth among the legion of tree trunks and decaying undergrowth.

"Want me to hold the lamp?" Dell offered good-naturedly.

"I'll do it. You can take it with you when you cross the swamp. I'll still have the other one."

"All right," Dell replied as Dooley held the lamp at arm's length in front of him. "So, where are the boats?" he added with a hint of growing impatience.

"This way," Dooley said with an air of finality, signaling for him to follow. "We hid them deep in the woods, though I don't know why since nobody else knows about this place that I'm aware of."

"That's good," Dell casually replied as he trailed close behind. He slowly removed a freshly sharpened dagger from a leather sheath attached to his side. "That makes this a perfect spot for committing unsavory deeds." He gripped the dagger tightly in his right hand, inching closer to Dooley as he prepared to pounce swiftly and silently upon him, ending his life with a swift stroke from behind. Now that Dell knew all the necessary particulars about his assignment, Dooley Kramer was of no use to him and would be the first to go. "Your employer wisely chose this location."

Dell Hawks believed that Dooley's next sentence would be his last as he slowly raised his dagger in the thick shadows, ready to grab him with his free hand and end his life with a swift stroke of the blade. Dooley fumed in that same instant, annoyed that everyone looked upon him as Farnsworth's subordinate and not as an equal. A split second before Dell Hawks leaned in to grab Dooley and claim his first victim, Dooley spun around while holding the oil lamp high, nearly pushing it into Dell's face, his mounting anxiety momentarily replaced by a wave of vexed frustration.

"With all due respect, sir, I am not in the employ of Zach–!"

With icy clarity, Dooley saw the raised blade gleaming in the light and flinched, stepping wildly backward and crying out. Dell Hawks had instinctively turned his head at the same time to avoid the glare of the light, sparing Dooley's life in that moment.

"What are you doing?" Dooley screamed, almost stumbling over his feet. He scrambled to get away from Dell Hawks before backing himself against a tree.

"I was going to make it quick and painless," Dell replied with annoyance, his eyes fixed on his target quivering beneath a canopy of bony branches. "But you made that impossible by turning around," he added with feigned disappointment, waving his sharpened blade back and forth in the air.

"What are you saying?" Dooley whispered, though he already knew the answer as he felt his insides freeze up. But before he could utter another word, Dell Hawks stepped forward, his expression vacant and cold. Dooley's jaw dropped. His limbs shook. But not knowing what else to do, he threw the oil lamp, nearly hitting Dell in the face before running back toward the cart in a full-blown panic. Dell swept to one side just in time to avoid the flying object that landed behind him. It crashed to the ground and went out. But he didn't miss a beat and pursued Dooley around the cart, his steps slow, easy and confident compared to Dooley's frantic maneuverings.

"There's no avoiding this, Dooley," he said matter-of-factly, staring at his intended victim who stood on the opposite side of the cart in the dull light of the remaining oil lamp. "I'm going to reach you sooner or later. You know that, don't you?"

"Keep away from me!" Dooley feebly ordered, taking a series of cautious steps alongside the cart and moving closer to the horse every time Dell Hawks took a step in the opposite direction toward the back of the cart. "Why are you even doing this?"

Dell chuckled at the naïve comment. "You mean you still haven't figured it out?" He paused near the back corner of the cart. "You're a liability to your boss. An unpredictable risk he can no longer tolerate." Dooley, his face tinted in the glow of the remaining oil lamp, stared at his pursuer in confusion. Dell shook his head in grim amusement. "I'll say this as simply as possible, Dooley. Zachary Farnsworth hired me to kill *three* people, not two. You're the third victim on my list."

Dooley absorbed the words like a slap to the face, looking at Dell Hawks in disbelief. Yet a part of him at last began to absorb the reality, needing only a moment to allow the revelation to fully sink in.

"Zachary wants to have me killed? Wants to have *me* killed?" Dooley turned his head at a slight angle, his eyes still fixed on Dell Hawks. "*Me?*"

Dell shrugged. "Can you blame him? I don't know all the particulars about what's going on around here, but apparently you do, and I'm guessing it's not a pleasant story. And judging by your fretful manner on the way over here, I'm also guessing that you're not one to be trusted for long with a secret. Apparently Farnsworth believes that, too." He took another step around the corner of the cart and now stood directly in back, resting the tip of his dagger on one of the wooden floor planks. Dell, his eyes locked upon Dooley standing near the horse at the opposite end, didn't take notice of the pile of tattered blankets strewn about the cart amid the murky shadows. "That's why he included you in the job when he hired me. Understand?"

Dooley stammered in the darkness, trying to come up with a response to buy himself more time while simultaneously attempting to make sense of Farnsworth's treachery. At last he blurted out the only words that came suddenly to his frazzled mind. "I'll pay you more money to kill *him* instead! Deal?"

Dell Hawks bit the side of his cheek to keep from laughing. "*Hmmm...* Interesting proposition," he said, caressing his whiskers as if giving the suggestion some serious thought. He casually moved to the other back corner of the cart and now saw Dooley directly ahead in his line of vision. Dooley still stood by the horse in the pale light as if frozen in place, breathing heavily like a tired rabbit taking a much needed break in mid chase, knowing his next mad dash from his dogged pursuer might be his last. "Why don't we sit down and talk about it?" Dell continued, making an obvious display of placing his knife back in its sheath. "I'm not averse to making a bigger profit out of this deal."

"*Really?*" he asked with childlike hopefulness.

"Really," Dell replied, taking another slow step alongside the cart in Dooley's direction, oblivious to the subtle movement of the blanket pile among the shadows. "So, what are my services worth to you?" he said, drawing closer to the light, a faint smile upon his lips. "What can you offer me to murder Farnsworth instead of you?"

Dooley adjusted his hat and scratched the back of his head, hemming and hawing before speaking. "Well, I was thinking that maybe..." As he hypnotically observed Dell inching one step closer, his heart beat faster. He noted the same vacant expression in Dell's eyes as from their first encounter. The fog lifted from his mind. This man was not interested in a deal and intended to kill him no matter what. Dooley turned, finding his footing again and extricating himself from his deer-like trance. He scrambled around to the other side of the horse, keeping Dell Hawks opposite him. "You don't want to deal with me! You have no intention to!"

Dell scoffed as he stopped and leaned against the horse, gazing at his prey across the saddle. "You couldn't afford me." He pulled out his dagger, eyeing Dooley as he slowly inhaled the cold swamp air. "But that doesn't matter. And do you know why?"

Dooley swallowed nervously, feeling a burning sensation in the pit of his stomach. "Why?"

"Because I'm ending this now!" Dell dropped down and dove beneath the horse's underside, grabbing one of Dooley's legs and nearly throwing him off balance.

"No!" Dooley yelped, kicking and pulling away as hard as he could so he wouldn't fall down, flailing like a swimmer drowning in a lake. He kicked Dell square in the face with the boot of his free leg. "Get off me!"

Dell grunted as a searing pain shot through his skull, releasing Dooley's leg as he boiled over with white-hot rage. "You're dead now!" he shouted, springing to his feet and slicing his knife through the shadows. Dell Hawks bolted after Dooley who had ran to the back of the horse cart. "You'll wish I had killed you earlier after I get through with you now!"

"Get away from me or I'll throw the rest of your money in the swamp!" Dooley cried, his hand slapping the back of the cart and catching a splinter as he raced around it to the other side, trying to keep his pursuer at bay. But the hired assassin was quickly gaining ground. Dooley thought he might have to make a run for it through the dark woods if he was ever going to survive the night.

"I don't care about the money now!" Dell sputtered as he circled around the rear of the cart a second time, slowing down just enough to veer past the first corner. "I just want you dead! Do you hear me–*dead*–you little–!"

In the next instant, Dell Hawks cried out in agony and lurched backward as a searing pain shot up through his abdomen, his nerve endings on fire and nearly paralyzing him as he struggled to take a breath. At that same moment, Lewis leaped off the back of the cart and planted his feet on the ground, a blanket dropping from his shoulders. He gripped a piece of maple wood that he had rammed into Dell Hawk's body, stopping him cold. Lewis raised his arms, wielding the stick of firewood like a deadly weapon in front of Dell's hunched figure. Katherine remained standing upon the cart, similarly armed and watching Lewis' every move with wondrous pride.

"Drop the knife!" he ordered, standing a few steps away from Dell who stood hunched over, moaning in pain and gasping for breath as he tried to speak.

"Who–? Who–?" Those were the only words Dell could utter as he attempted to stand up straight and catch a full breath. But before Lewis could respond or take another step closer, a harrowing scream ripped through the gloomy night. Dooley Kramer barreled toward Dell Hawks from behind in a full sprint, crying out furiously, his eyes bulging and his face contorted. Seeing his enemy momentarily incapacitated, he plowed his body straight into Dell Hawks, shoving him in the back with the full force of his weight just as Dell was beginning to recover from Lewis' strike.

"Try to kill me, will you?" Dooley shouted, nearly pushing Dell off his feet and sending him sailing past Lewis and staggering headfirst into a thicket of trees by the edge of the water. Dell Hawks bellowed out in pain as he tumbled to the ground among piles of decaying undergrowth. He grunted hard when he hit the dirt and tree roots, lying there, silent and unmoving, as Lewis and Katherine looked on in stunned disbelief. Dooley bent over with his hands on his knees, the last ounce of strength having left him, gasping for breath as droplets of cold sweat dripped from his forehead.

"Lewis, are you all right?" Katherine anxiously asked from atop the cart.

"I'm fine," he replied, offering her a helping hand down. Katherine hugged him briefly, but then Lewis stepped protectively in front of her in case Dell Hawks should make a run for them again. But as there was no movement from the trees in the next few moments, he began to think that the man was too tired to move or perhaps badly injured. "Stay here, Katherine, while I take a look."

"Wait! Let me get the lamp from the cart," she replied, hurrying around to unhook the remaining fixture.

Dooley looked up in the gloom as she did so, still out of breath. "Katherine Durant? How did you...?" He bent down again and breathed deeply, not sure if he was imagining other voices or was perhaps caught in an unending nightmare.

"Yes, you heard right, Dooley," Lewis replied. "Katherine is here–and lucky for your sorry self that she is!"

Katherine hurried back with the oil lamp, shedding light upon their surroundings. Dooley slowly stood up, appearing haggard, frightened and hatless as he gazed upon his unlooked-for rescuers in disbelief. Katherine and Lewis stared back with pity and shame.

"How'd you get here?" he whispered, his breath rising to the treetops. "*Why* are you here?"

"It's a long story, Dooley, part of which you'll have to tell us," Katherine said.

"If you know what's good for you," Lewis added, raising the piece of maple wood with a threatening gleam in his eyes.

"Fine! I'll tell you everything," Dooley replied, still panting. "After what happened here tonight, I don't care anymore."

"You mean after you found out that Zachary Farnsworth is neither your friend nor protector," Katherine coldly remarked.

Dooley nodded. "That, too."

"First let's check on him," Lewis said, indicating the spot where Dell Hawks had disappeared into the trees.

Dooley agreed, not fully convinced that that particular threat had been eliminated. "There's another lamp over here. If it's not damaged, we could use the extra light."

Dooley walked toward the front of the horse cart with Lewis and Katherine closely following, neither of them trusting him out of their sight. When Dooley found the other oil lamp, banged up but still usable, he relit it using a small twig and the flame from Katherine's lamp. With the added illumination, he found his hat lying on the ground and popped it on his head. They returned to the spot where Dell Hawks had fallen amid the undergrowth and found him lying facedown and motionless, his hands planted beneath him as if he had been trying to soften his fall.

"Get up!" Dooley shouted, kicking the bottom of Dell's boot. He glanced at Lewis. "I don't know his name, but Farnsworth hired him through some of his questionable connections."

With growing impatience, Lewis bent down and rolled the body over, drawing gasps of disgusted surprise from the others. Dell Hawks stared blankly at the sky with open eyes, his cold, right fingers still gripping the handle of his dagger, the blade of which lay plunged through his blood-soaked coat and lodged firmly in his chest. Katherine looked away as Dooley breathed a silent sigh of relief.

"I guess you won't have to worry about him anymore," Lewis said coolly, casting an eye upon Dooley.

"Apparently not."

"But you still have a lot to answer for." Lewis scowled with disdain before prying Dell's fingers from the dagger and removing it as Dooley looked on with horror. He cleaned the blood from the knife by running the blade over the weeds a few times and then wiping it off using the edge of Dell's coat. When Lewis stood up, the knife gleamed in the lamp light. "And you'll provide those answers to Katherine and me right now if you know what's good for you."

Dooley nodded nervously, taking a step back. "Can we at least get away from that?" he asked, pointing to the dead body.

"I agree," Katherine said, leading them to the cart where she and Dooley set the lamps on the back floorboards. "Now, Dooley, it's time for us to ask the questions and for you to answer them. Keep in mind that we just saved your life. And from what Lewis and I heard of your conversation with that dead man, you can't go home again and show your face to your friend, Zachary Farnsworth, if you know what's good for you."

Dooley turned his head and spit. "He's no friend of mine!"

"Agreed," Lewis said. "Now tell us why you're here."

Dooley gazed at the young couple, awed by their bravery and intrigued by their presence. "I might ask you the same question."

"We followed you!" Katherine snapped. "We know you and Farnsworth are connected to Adelaide Cooper's disappearance, so don't look surprised. I was given information about that from one of Caldurian's Island soldiers who had learned about your late-night journeys outside of Kanesbury during the occupation." Dooley tried to conceal his stunned amazement, but was unable to do so. "We know more than you think, Dooley. So you can give us the rest of the facts here, or we'll take you to Constable Brindle right now and you can explain yourself in front of the whole village."

"Don't make us prove how serious we are," Lewis said, displaying the knife. "Katherine, I and a lot of others are fed up with people like you worming yourselves into our lives for your own profit. Now it's time to pay up."

Dooley gazed upon them, realizing he owed them his life and recognizing that he was backed into a corner. With a helpless sigh, he slumped his shoulders, knowing he was at the end of his rope.

"Well, Dooley?" Katherine asked impatiently.

"All right! All right! I'll tell you everything," he sputtered, releasing a stream of air through his lips. "But keep in mind that this scheme wasn't all fine wine and roasted pheasant for me either!"

CHAPTER 81

The Confession

Dooley ripped off his hat and flung it to the ground. He paced inside the circle of pale light like a caged animal, frantically combing both hands through his mop of dirty blond hair. When he stopped and faced Katherine and Lewis, his dark eyes were fixed hard upon them, his thin, triangular face taut with bitter frustration.

"I should never have stolen the key from that stupid bird!" he groused, his words punctuated by a long sigh and more stubborn silence as he began to pace again.

"What key?" Katherine inquired with a touch of compassion, sensing that Dooley would tell her everything if she could only pry the first few words out of him. "And what about this bird you speak of? I don't understand."

"Neither do I," Lewis said, holding Dell Hawks' knife at his side. "We're running out of patience, so talk to us."

Dooley turned to his rescuers, taking an angry step forward as he slapped his arms to his side. "The key to the Spirit Box. *That's* what I'm talking about! I stole it from that eagle–the wizard's eagle– twenty years ago." He took a deep breath, his face flushed and sweaty. "I was ten years old and didn't know any better. I hit– I hit the bird with two stones. The key dropped out of its beak and the eagle flew away. I could tell it was badly injured." Dooley cast his eyes to the ground in shame. "I held onto the key ever since, well, up until a few months ago."

Katherine and Lewis looked on in amazement. Though neither had yet been born during that tumultuous time in Kanesbury, both were well versed in the particulars of the Enâri invasion twenty years ago and Caldurian's arrest and expulsion from Arrondale. Katherine had been regaled with stories by her Uncle Otto who had witnessed the events firsthand, having stood eye to eye with Caldurian after the wizard had been apprehended by King Justin's troops.

"My uncle told me about Caldurian's eagle, Xavier. The bird had swooped down and stolen the key from his hand after King Justin turned it over to him with the Spirit Box," she recalled. "Though my uncle sent the box to the Blue Citadel for safekeeping years later, no one ever knew what became of the key."

"That's because I had it," Dooley confessed. "I kept it secret for over fifteen years until…"

Lewis looked on with suspicion. "Until what?"

Dooley frowned. "Until Zachary Farnsworth discovered what I possessed–or at least suspected what I possessed–and concocted a plan to use it for his advantage." He told them how Farnsworth had befriended him about five years ago after first seeing him with the key. Up until that time, the two men had been neighbors who were merely cordial to one another in passing, keeping their business and personal lives to themselves. Only after a night of drinking together at the Iron Kettle Tavern did Dooley fully reveal to Farnsworth the existence of the key and how it had come into his possession. "Once Zachary knew the truth, he held it over me. He let it be known in so many words that it would be terrible if the authorities found out that I stole the key. Or worse yet, if Caldurian somehow discovered that I had wounded his eagle in the process."

"He blackmailed you," Katherine said, noting the anguish in his eyes yet unable to feel sorry for him.

"He did, though not saying so directly," Dooley admitted. "Zachary convinced me that if he could contact Caldurian, we could return the key to him for a price, pretending that I had won it in a game of dice from some locals. I had my doubts, but Zachary insisted on trying and so I let him, though I had little choice."

Katherine scowled. "What did the wizard pay you in exchange for the key? Money? Power?" She shook her head with disgust.

"It was more complicated than you think," Dooley said. "Not everything went according to plan."

"Meaning?" Lewis asked.

Dooley sighed, prepared to reveal the worst of his crimes. "Meaning that Zachary and I made our deal with the wizard, but a few things went awry."

"Such as?" Katherine asked, her gaze fixed upon him with an intensity that both intimidated and flustered him.

"Mind you, it took Zachary four years to track down the wizard through a long line of intermediaries before finally meeting him," he replied, as if that was somehow an excuse for his behavior. "Then it was another year before Caldurian arrived in Kanesbury to meet Zachary and retrieve the key."

"When was that second meeting?" Lewis asked.

"On the first night of the Harvest Festival. Caldurian went to Zachary's house to pick up the key. Only thing is, by the time their meeting took place, the key had been stolen a few hours earlier."

"Stolen?" Katherine cast a disbelieving eye upon him. "You had the key for twenty years, only to have it stolen just before the wizard was about to take possession of it?"

"It's true. Zachary had convinced me to give him the key so he could make his deal with the wizard, but I had my reservations all along. I wanted a guarantee that we would climb the ladder of power in Kanesbury before Caldurian got his prize, or at least receive some advance payment for our trouble."

"So it was all about power," she said with a frown. "And it seems to have worked seeing that Zachary is now the acting mayor."

"It worked all right–for him!" Dooley shook his head with resentment. "But the deal almost went sour because the key had been stolen. You see, while Zachary attended the party at the Stewarts' house that evening, I broke into his home and took the key back before his meeting with Caldurian. Unfortunately…" Dooley went silent, his face ashen as painful memories returned. Katherine and Lewis waited for a response, seeing that he was on the verge of speaking while gathering his troubled thoughts. "Unfortunately, the key was stolen again that very night, only this time from my house, though I wasn't there at the time." Dooley looked up guiltily. "But Arthur Weeks was. The individual who stole the key killed Arthur during the robbery."

Katherine gasped. "You lied from the start, Dooley, accusing Nicholas Raven of Arthur's murder. But I could never understand why. I thought you might have killed him and were pointing a finger at Nicholas to save yourself. But it was all about the key, wasn't it? You didn't tell the truth to Constable Brindle because that would have revealed how you and Zachary were plotting with Caldurian."

Dooley nodded as he wiped away a few tears streaming down his face in the darkness. "I know! I know! And poor Arthur, he knew nothing about the key at all. Zachary hired him simply to lie about Nicholas, to tell Constable Brindle that Nicholas had returned to the gristmill later that evening on the night of the robbery."

"You and Farnsworth had your dirty hands in a lot of affairs that night," Lewis said. "Dealings with a mad wizard and framing a man for robbery and murder. Did you do the latter to get Nicholas' job, or was their some connection between the two?"

"Very perceptive," Dooley replied. "Getting rid of Nicholas was part of our deal with Caldurian, but it was all about your Uncle Otto in the end, Katherine. He was at the center of everything."

"What are you talking about?" she fearfully asked.

Dooley stared at her as if the reason was obvious. "Caldurian hated your uncle with a passion after what Otto did to him twenty years ago. He had sent for King Justin's soldiers who then arrested Caldurian and his apprentice, Madeline," he explained, "driving them from the village like common criminals."

"Because that's what they were!" Katherine said.

"But powerful criminals," he cautioned. "And a bit crazed, if you understand me. From what Zachary and I had gathered from our few meetings with Caldurian, and by studying his subsequent actions, that wizard was obsessed with having his revenge upon Otto, and believe me, nothing was going to get in his way."

"And he hired you to help?"

Dooley squirmed with guilt. "At first we only planned to negotiate with the wizard to get a fair price for the key, allowing him to save Vellan's prized Enâri creatures. That's all! I swear! But Zachary handled the particulars, so as part of the deal, Caldurian also hired us to help him get his vengeance upon your uncle." Dooley appeared mentally exhausted. "I just wanted some money, that's all."

Katherine stared at him, a white-hot hatred burning inside her. "You must be so proud of yourself, Dooley."

"No, not at the moment," he flatly replied. "Not for that or a good many other things."

Lewis gently rubbed a hand upon Katherine's back, sensing how upset she was yet knowing that they both needed to hear everything no matter how painful it might be. He glared at Dooley in the pale light. "What did you and Farnsworth agree to do?"

"Our main task was to get rid of Nicholas Raven."

Katherine shuddered. "Get rid of him? You mean kill him?"

"No! Caldurian just wanted him removed from his home, leaving the manner of doing so to us. The wizard knew that Nicholas lived on Maynard Kurtz' property. He needed him out of the way in order to enact his plan."

"So you framed Nicholas for the robbery," Lewis said, "whereupon Constable Brindle had him arrested."

"Until he escaped."

"You're lucky Nicholas didn't go after you before he fled the village," Katherine remarked, "though part of me wishes he had."

Lewis smirked understandingly in the shadows. "Explain something, Dooley. It was common knowledge that Nicholas planned to travel to Morrenwood and join up with King Justin's guard. So why did you and Farnsworth create such an elaborate ruse to frame him in the first place? It seems he was already doing the job that you two were hired for *for* you."

Dooley nodded. "I agree, but Farnsworth thought we could sweeten the deal to curry favor with the wizard. Getting rid of Nicholas would be the easy part, but Zachary hoped if we removed him in such a way that allowed me to take over Nicholas' job at the gristmill, then we would be able to offer Caldurian a–" He suddenly caught himself, reluctant to reveal that his list of crimes included treason against Arrondale.

"Offer Caldurian a *what?*" Katherine echoed apprehensively, wondering just how deep Dooley's treachery ran.

Dooley looked down as he ground the tip of his boot into the dirt, not wanting to answer. Though aware of all the wrongs he had committed, only now was the severity of his crimes fully registering with his conscience. His shame and embarrassment were fully on display when he looked up with trembling lips.

"Zachary informed the wizard that maybe I could act as, well, sort of a spy for him if Ned Adams hired me to take Nicholas' place." Dooley exhaled as some of the mental and moral burden slipped from his shoulders. "Since Nicholas made occasional deliveries to the Blue Citadel throughout the year, maybe it was possible that..."

"That you could weasel your way in there somehow and serve as Caldurian's eyes and ears?" Lewis coolly remarked.

"I never thought it would come to that!" Dooley exclaimed. "Or that it would even be possible, but by dumb luck..."

"*Oh, Dooley...*" Merely by studying his furrowed brow and faraway look, Katherine guessed that he had infiltrated the chambers of the Citadel, wondering with horror what damage he had inflicted upon the kingdom. "Though I'm afraid to ask, I must know what you did after Ned Adams sent you to the capital with his trust."

After a fair amount of hemming and hawing, Dooley broke down. He told them how he had rather easily made his way into King Justin's chamber and hid among the rafters before a meeting of the war council convened–all with the unwitting help of Len Harold.

"But in my defense, I didn't hear anything that went on during that first meeting–the war council itself–as I accidentally, well–" Dooley swallowed, his embarrassment obvious. "I sort of fell asleep. It was rather warm up there as the fires were blazing and I was exhausted from days of traveling."

Katherine and Lewis glanced at each other, unable to conceal faint grins. Both were happy that Dooley's first attempt at spying had been a disaster.

"You said you didn't hear anything at the first meeting. What did you mean by that?" Lewis asked. "Was there a second council?"

"No," he replied. "After I woke up and most of the delegates had drifted off into the hallway, four new arrivals showed up in the King's chamber. Hearing the voice of one of those visitors was a shock, to say the least, as he was the last person in Laparia I would have expected to see there."

"Who?" Katherine asked, wondering how Dooley Kramer could possibly know anyone paying a visit to the Blue Citadel.

Dooley shrugged. "Believe me or not, it was Nicholas Raven in the flesh. Our Nicholas, meeting with King Justin and a handful of others left in the room. Soon they closed the doors and had another private meeting."

"Nicholas?" Katherine, though pleasantly surprised to hear his name and to learn that he was safe, was not totally convinced that Dooley was telling the truth.

Lewis, noting how Katherine's eyes lit up upon hearing the news, decided to attribute her reaction as being relived that Nicholas was safe rather than as a sign of any lingering affection for him. Still, he was astounded by the news, eager to hear more.

"Nicholas had always said he wanted to join the King's Guard, but are you sure it was him?" Lewis asked. "And who were the three people with him?"

"From what I could gather on my perch, Nicholas was accompanied by another man about his age named Leo Marsh, an older, somewhat eccentric lady named Carmella, and, believe me again or not, the King's granddaughter herself, Princess Megan."

Katherine, her arms akimbo, cast a skeptical gaze upon him. "Are you simply making up stories to buy yourself time? Because if you are, Lewis and I will drag you to Clay Brindle's doorstep right now–and don't think we won't!"

"I swear I'm telling the truth!" Dooley extended his hands with childlike innocence, pleading for them to believe him. "Zachary Farnsworth just tried to have me killed, and frankly, you two people are my only allies right now. So what reason do I have to lie?"

Lewis smirked. "He does have a legitimate point– amazingly."

"I suppose he does," Katherine agreed. "Continue."

Dooley nodded appreciatively as he gathered his thoughts, wondering how much about the meeting he should reveal. While most of it wouldn't get him into any deeper trouble than he already was, there was a nugget of information he didn't want to divulge. Thinking about it only reminded him how easily he was becoming a person the likes of Caldurian and Vellan–cold, heartless entities who viewed others as things to be used or as inconsequential as the fallen leaves of autumn that they treaded upon without thought or notice.

Dooley briefly talked about some of the high points discussed at that second meeting as best he could remember, recounting how Nicholas had met Princess Megan, and then later, Leo, on his travels to Morrenwood and the seaside village of Boros.

"It was on their way to Boros that the princess was nearly kidnapped," he continued. Dooley said that Nicholas spoke fondly about a young woman named Ivy who was kidnapped in Boros after being mistaken for the princess. "She was nearly rescued later along the shores of the Trillium Sea. But whoever Ivy was, Nicholas was heartbroken by her absence and vowed to find her again."

"I hope he does," Katherine said with a heavy heart, worried for both of them. "Nicholas seems to have had quite an adventure. But why did he go back to the capital city?" she asked, eager for more information. "And who is Carmella?"

"That's the most interesting tidbit of the story," Dooley said, "as it helps explain some of the mysterious events in Kanesbury during the Harvest Festival."

"What are you talking about?" Lewis asked. "How are they possibly connected?"

"Carmella, in her travels, had befriended one of the Enâri creatures awakened from the Spirit Caves," he said. "The creature, named Jagga, presented her with a small medallion as a gift. Nicholas and his new friends happened to meet up with Carmella and Jagga somewhere on the road and then traveled to Morrenwood together."

"Why is that so interesting?" he asked.

"That medallion, as I overheard, was actually the key to the Spirit Box. Can you believe it? Jagga had stolen the key and subsequently melted it down to secure his freedom." Dooley noted the disbelief on Lewis and Katherine's faces. "Carmella told King Justin and the others that Jagga admitted to stealing the key from a man named Arthur Weeks. He admitted only to stealing it, though logic tells me that it was Jagga who killed Arthur in my house after I had stepped out to talk to Zachary. Had I been there, I might have been lying in a pool of blood on my floor as well." Dooley exhaled exhaustedly, considering how fortunate he had been. "How Jagga found out that I had the key, I'll never know, but this story proves my innocence. I didn't kill Arthur Weeks!"

"Fine," Katherine said. "We believe you on that point, but it doesn't excuse all the other horrible deeds you've done."

"No, I suppose not," he replied, his brief moment of triumph deflating. "I have committed some awful crimes and am willing to face the consequences if I can bring down Zachary Farnsworth with me. But most of this is his fault," he muttered. "If I hadn't listened to him in the first place, a lot of people wouldn't have been hurt."

"Nicholas for starters," Lewis said, though Dooley barely heard his words.

His mind drifted to the meeting that he and Farnsworth had attended in the gristmill with Caldurian and his associates. It was then that Dooley learned how Arileez had tracked down two young men from Morrenwood to a cabin in the Ebrean Forest, killing one of the unwitting decoys in a fruitless search for the medallion. He guessed that the two travelers must have been the sibling princes of Montavia who were in King Justin's chamber during the second meeting. Dooley felt responsible for the one boy's death, having given instructions to Gavin to follow the pair and alert Caldurian as to their destination. It was only a matter of time until Arileez pursued and confronted them, shattering their lives forever. Dooley's spirit had slowly withered with this stark realization in the back of his mind, but he didn't have the heart to tell Katherine and Lewis. He had confessed to enough transgressions already. One more probably wouldn't lower their already low opinion of him.

"Like Nicholas for starters?" Lewis repeated a little louder, noting that Dooley had drifted off. "Are you listening?"

"*Hmmm?*" Dooley looked up, realizing he was still standing among the shadowy trees near the swamp as the horrible memories faded from his mind. "Yes. Like Nicholas. What I helped do to him is unforgivable."

"That would be up to Nicholas to decide," Katherine said, "if you ever see him again. I don't know if he would dare step foot in Kanesbury after what so many people put him through."

"I expect he has more important matters on his mind now," Dooley said, piquing their interest. "While meeting with King Justin, Nicholas and that other fellow, Leo, volunteered to seek out a wizard named Frist, the one who cast a sleeping spell upon the Enâri twenty years ago. He created that thing growing inside the Spirit Box."

"I recall Frist's name," Katherine replied. "But why would Nicholas and Leo need to find him?"

"To remake the key, of course, and the magic within it," he said, briefly explaining what he had learned from the wizard Tolapari. "But I don't know where Nicholas and Leo were going since the meeting ended before that was discussed."

"You still never told us why Caldurian wanted you to get rid of him in the first place," Lewis said. "What threat could Nicholas Raven pose to such a powerful wizard?"

"Nicholas wasn't a threat," Dooley clarified. "More of an inconvenience."

"How so?"

"Everything revolved around Caldurian's desire for revenge upon your Uncle Otto," Dooley explained, eyeing Katherine uneasily. "But in order to implement his plan, he needed more help."

"Besides you and Farnsworth?" she asked.

He nodded. "Caldurian needed help from someone who didn't actually know he was providing the help, namely, Maynard Kurtz."

"Maynard!" Katherine was flabbergasted. "I cannot believe that someone as honorable and decent as Maynard Kurtz would be tangled up with a vile wizard like Caldurian."

"He wasn't," Dooley replied, resting an elbow on the side of the cart. "Like I said, Maynard didn't know he was helping the wizard. In fact, Maynard hasn't been aware of anything for about the past two months or so."

Katherine felt a cold stab to her heart, fearing the worst. "What have you done to him? If you've hurt him in any way…"

"I didn't do anything to Maynard," he assured her. "Another wizard named Arileez did–a strange yet clever wizard who is in the employ of both Caldurian and Vellan." Dooley noted the strain and impatience upon Katherine's face, sensing that she wasn't in the mood to interrupt and ask questions. "At Caldurian's command, Arileez cast a sleeping spell upon Maynard and then, well, he simply took his place."

Lewis shrugged. "Took his place? What do you mean?"

"Just what I said. Arileez took Maynard's place in Kanesbury society. On one occasion, he even assumed Otto's identity, too. You see, Arileez has a unique ability among wizards to take on the appearance of any person–or even an animal–and retain that shape for as long as he wants."

"That's preposterous!" Katherine said. And though her words sounded sincere, her heart wasn't fully convinced that Dooley was telling an extravagant lie. Could such a thing actually be true? On a few occasions she felt that Maynard had been distant to her, not in a smug or mean sort of way, but in his overall physical and emotional presence. She could never explain Maynard's behavior and simply attributed his cool demeanor of late to constant worrying, overwork and the painful disappearances of Nicholas and Adelaide, the two people in Kanesbury most dear to him.

"It's true," Dooley insisted, his expression showing no signs of deceit. "I saw it for myself right in Ned Adams' gristmill. One moment the phony Maynard Kurtz was standing before my eyes just as you are now. Then to emphasize some point or other in a dramatic way as wizards have a tendency to do, he transformed into his original self." Dooley shuddered, recalling Arileez' skeletal face and shockingly white hair. "Believe me when I say that that effective demonstration seared itself into my memory. Arileez isn't the most pleasant specimen of wizards to observe, but he made a most convincing Maynard Kurtz."

"A Maynard Kurtz who was a respected, upstanding citizen, yet one who could now manipulate people and events according to Caldurian's wishes," Katherine said with growing bitterness.

"It was part of Caldurian's plan to frame Otto," Lewis concluded with equal disdain. "That's why they needed Nicholas out of the way, fearing he would uncover their deception."

Dooley nodded. "With Nicholas around, Caldurian wouldn't have been able to secretly meet with the impostor Maynard as needed. As I said, Nicholas' presence on Maynard's farm was merely an inconvenience." But despite his explanation, Dooley still noted a trace of skepticism on Katherine's face. "However, if you still don't accept my word, I can prove it to you."

Katherine sighed wearily. "How?"

"By showing you the real Maynard, of course. He's over there on the island," he said, pointing across the murky waters. "Along with–"

Katherine and Lewis noted a flicker of shame upon Dooley's face, emphasized by his downcast eyes and fidgety body. They looked at one another, their astonishment at Dooley's string of reprehensible deeds giving way to a deadening numbness the longer he talked.

"Now what?" Lewis asked. "No sense holding back, Dooley. You've come this far with the truth, so spit out the rest."

"I know," he glumly replied, fending off his last impulses to conceal the truth. He finally looked up, too exhausted to wage the battle anymore. "She's over there, too. Adelaide, I mean, if you haven't already guessed."

"Adelaide?" Katherine's heart ached for the sweet woman, imagining what distress he and Farnsworth had put her through. "Under a sleeping spell?"

"No, nothing like that. But don't fret. She's perfectly safe!" he hastily replied. "She's locked up in a cozy little place–"

"As your prisoner, Doooley!" Katherine stepped forward, making him flinch and dart away from the cart like a startled deer.

"I said she's fine! That's why Zachary and I made periodic trips out here to bring her supplies and such." Dooley scratched his head. "Had she been under a sleeping spell like Maynard, that would have made our lives so much easier."

"Dooley!"

"Bad thing to say! I know," he cried out, holding up a hand to keep Katherine at bay as she inched closer to him with Lewis at her side. "Anyway, Adelaide made the unfortunate mistake of catching Zachary and me placing the stolen items from the gristmill in Nicholas' shed that night. She fled, but we had no choice."

"So you kidnapped her?" Lewis snapped.

Dooley nodded guiltily. "Zachary held her on his property for a short time before we took her to this swamp. We never let Caldurian know as he would have questioned our competence regarding his other assignments. Then, after Arileez placed Maynard under a sleeping spell, we were ordered to get rid of his body–permanently. So Zachary and I hauled him out here, neither of us having the nerve to kill either him or Adelaide. As awful as we've behaved recently, we're not murderers."

"But Zachary took one step closer by hiring one to get rid of you," Katherine reminded him.

"You've got a point there. Still," he continued, raising his index finger to emphasize his next argument, "if Zachary and I hadn't concealed Adelaide and Maynard here at the swamp,

Caldurian or Arileez probably would have killed the poor things themselves–and perhaps Zachary and me in the process. So in a weird way, we saved their lives, don't you think?"

Katherine clenched her fists, wanting to pummel Dooley. "I think you're reprehensible!" she said, doing everything to hold her temper in check. "And nothing you say will excuse your foul deeds, Dooley Kramer." She took a deep breath to calm herself, glancing at Lewis' unruffled exterior for moral support. "Still, you shed some light on the strange goings-on in Kanesbury of late–though at the point of a dead murderer's knife–so that will count for something. But now your next step is to release Adelaide. After that, you'll have much to explain once Constable Brindle hears about all of this."

Dooley hunched over the side of the cart in defeat. "*I know… I know…*"

"Enough talk," Lewis said, sliding Dell Hawks' knife under his belt. "Take us to the island."

Dooley looked up, pale and trembling as he considered what was to become of him in the days ahead. "Must I?" He swallowed hard. "Must I face her again?"

"Take us to Adelaide," Katherine ordered. "Now!"

"All right, all right," he replied, feeling as if he were slogging his way through a horrible dream. "The boats are hidden over here," he said, pointing to a small thicket of trees as a defeated sigh escaped his lips. "Follow me."

CHAPTER 82

The Last Step

They glided over to the island on two boats, Katherine and Lewis in one and Dooley in the other as they silently dipped their paddles into the cold water. The oil lamps resting upon the bow of each boat cast feeble arcs of light upon the inky surface. Soon they landed and disembarked, pulling the boats onto shore and taking the lamps with them. Nearby to their left stood a small shack-like structure on wooden stilts where Adelaide had been kept prisoner. Faint yellow light seeped through cracks in the wooden shutters nailed to the windows. To their right among shadows and dried weeds was a stone and wood shed. A thicket of trees grew between the two structures.

"You'll find Maynard Kurtz in there," Dooley said uneasily, pointing to the shed. "He's sound asleep under Arileez' spell. That will prove I was telling the truth." He removed a key from his coat pocket. "I'll release Adelaide in the meantime, though I don't think she'll forgive me."

"I wouldn't expect so," Lewis replied.

Dooley walked away and sighed, knowing one person who could never forgive him as he had died in a cabin deep in the woods. Prince Brendan's death would forever weigh upon him. "Wait!" he called out, hurrying back. He reached into another pocket and withdrew a small leather pouch containing half the payment for Dell

Hawks. He handed it to Katherine. "Zachary gave me this to pay our dead friend. Use it to compensate Adelaide and others in Kanesbury as you see fit. I know it won't nearly cover the misery they suffered, but..." He cleared his throat, visibly upset. "The rest of the money is on the man's corpse. You can take it when we leave."

"All right," Katherine replied, moved by Dooley's gesture as she dropped the pouch in her cloak pocket. "Now release Adelaide at once while Lewis and I check on Maynard. Hurry please."

He dashed off toward the little house with the oil lamp to guide his way. Katherine, in the meantime, took hold of Lewis' hand with a sense of trepidation, anxious about what they might find. She looked into his eyes for reassurance as he held up the other lamp, the pale light offering them little comfort.

"Are you ready?" he asked, gently squeezing her fingers.

She nodded and the two of them walked slowly to the shed, their hearts beating rapidly as a sense of foreboding overwhelmed them. When they reached the entrance, Lewis handed the lamp to Katherine before pushing hard against the warped door to open it. A flood of stale air escaped through the widening gap as the bottom scraped against the dirt floor. Lewis took the lamp and stepped into the shed first, looking around as the light filled the dark crevices and illuminated a tapestry of gray cobwebs. His eyes immediately locked onto a large figure sprawled upon the floor and wrapped in several tattered blankets. Katherine inched up beside Lewis and gasped when she saw the body, stiff and lifeless at first glance. She and Lewis looked at one another with growing unease before stepping closer to the body and kneeling down next to it. Lewis held the light near the head as Katherine carefully removed the folds of the blanket covering Maynard's face.

"Do you think he's...?" Lewis didn't complete the sentence, noting Katherine's fearful state. But when she pulled back enough of the blanket for them to recognize Maynard's face and the long strands of silvery-black hair framing it, Katherine smiled, beaming with relief.

"He's breathing!" she whispered.

"He looks to be in good health," Lewis replied, moving the light closer. "How long did Dooley say he's been out here?"

"Long enough." Katherine gently shook Maynard on the shoulders, hoping that the real acting mayor of Kanesbury would rise from his deep slumber. "Maynard, wake up," she softly pleaded. "It's Katherine Durant." But Maynard didn't stir even after she shook him harder and called out his name a little bit louder, all to no avail.

"Dooley spoke the truth," Lewis said, "both about the shape-shifting wizard and the sleeping spell. But how are we to wake him?"

"I don't know if we can," she replied, her eyes fixed upon Maynard's peaceful expression as her mind grasped for a solution. "Still, we found him, and that's one obstacle we've overcome."

"But what do we do with him? We can't leave him here."

"We'll have to find a temporary safe place." She stood up and smoothed the wrinkles out of her cloak. "But, Lewis, we must keep this a secret for now. If word ever gets back to Zachary Farnsworth before Maynard recovers, there's no telling what he might do or who else he might send to track him down. Remember, Farnsworth will now think that the real Maynard is dead, along with Dooley and Adelaide. We shouldn't do anything to change that perception until we decide how to act."

Lewis agreed. "We'll think of a place to hide him. For now, let's find Adelaide and Dooley and get away from this swamp. I can't stand it anymore."

"Me either," she replied. "If ever there was an appropriate spot for Farnsworth to conduct his nefarious deeds, this is definitely the place."

Dooley, meanwhile, walked across a dirt path toward the house, carrying the oil lamp in one hand and clutching the key to the padlocked door in the clammy palm of the other. Strings of awkwardly constructed sentences drifted through his mind as he tried to compose an apology to Adelaide for all he and Farnsworth had done to her. He didn't expect to receive the woman's forgiveness and understanding, though he hoped she would let him have a few uninterrupted moments to make his speech. She would surely have her say afterward, but in the end, the laws of Kanesbury would have the final say before rendering its judgment.

Dooley froze as he neared the bottom of the ten steps leading up to the house, suddenly realizing that the citizens of Kanesbury might not be the only ones who could cast sentence upon him. He had already admitted to Katherine and Lewis his crimes against Arrondale which they would most certainly mention to Constable Brindle. Now he suspected that King Justin might sit in judgment before him after this sorry affair was over, wondering with rising fear what royal punishment might fit his crimes. Years of imprisonment? Dooley glumly imagined himself growing older and wasting away inside a cell in one of the King's garrisons.

Banishment was another possibility Dooley considered as a dull ache settled in his heart. Though he would still retain his freedom, he wondered where he would go if the King sent him to the border of Arrondale with the directive never to return. He imagined himself wandering friendless and lonely along empty roads and across barren fields for a lifetime. As an added consequence, King Justin could ask his allies not to offer sanctuary within their borders to the traitorous Dooley Kramer, thus making his life miserable to his dying days as he explored the cold, desolate regions of Laparia and beyond.

Dooley pictured himself aging gracelessly and in misery until his dying days. Yet that final day of his life might come sooner than he'd prefer if King Justin decided upon death as the appropriate punishment. Had he really committed such terrible deeds to deserve that hideous fate? He halfheartedly tried to convince himself that he hadn't been such a horrible individual, but as a chill drove the last bits of hope from his heart, he knew deep inside that a sentence of death was a distinct possibility and rightly so. He wondered how many people had been killed, injured or had their lives disrupted as a result of his assistance to Caldurian, and indirectly, to Vellan. He couldn't imagine the number, nor did he want to know.

Dooley stared at his feet inside the wavering circle of sickly light cast from the oil lamp. He had wasted enough time thinking. Now he had to act. He looked up at the house looming above and uneasily inhaled a lungful of the cold swamp air.

"First things first," he whispered, nervously combing a hand through his hair. "Adelaide gets to scold me before anyone else can have a go at it. It's the only fair way."

After taking another deep breath, he trudged up the ten creaky steps one at a time, ready to face his first of many judgments. As he slowly ascended with his head bowed, Dooley didn't notice the pair of wide eyes watching him through a crack in one of the front shutters. They swiftly disappeared when he reached the door and held out the key. He knew the time had arrived for him to begin paying for his misdeeds.

With a shaky hand, Dooley inserted the key into the rust-coated padlock and turned it. A metallic click rose and died in the damp air. He set the oil lamp on the last step below the small upper platform and then removed the padlock and left it hanging from the latch. He had always dreaded coming to the swamp with Farnsworth to see Adelaide every six days, feeling terribly sorry for her but making an effort not to show it. The journey always left a dull, gnawing pain in the pit of his stomach and usually ruined his appetite the following day. Dooley sadly noted that Farnsworth never seemed to have been bothered by such symptoms. Maybe tonight would go a small way toward redeeming himself.

He clenched his jaw and hesitated before grabbing the handle and pushing the door open. A flood of soft light and warm air spilled through the widening crack.

"Adelaide?" he gently called out when not seeing her standing in the middle of the room where she usually waited upon their arrival. "*Adelaide*? It's Dooley," he said, stepping into the room. "I'm alone tonight since–"

His blood ran cold when he saw Adelaide lying on the floor upon her right side near the fireplace, unmoving, a shawl falling off her shoulders. Dooley raced over to her, leaving the door wide open which allowed cool air to waft inside. When he noticed her eyes were closed but that she was still breathing, he felt only a little better, though still feared the worst. A straw broom lay alongside her. Dooley guessed that she had collapsed while sweeping the floor to while away the dreary hours in confinement. He feared he may have her death upon his hands if he didn't get some help soon.

"Adelaide! Please wake up!" he cried, kneeling beside her and touching the back of his fingers to her cheek. Her skin felt warm and he took that as a positive sign. He gently shook her shoulder, hoping that she might have only fainted. "Adelaide, can you hear me? It's Dooley Kramer. I've come to–"

She stirred. "*Dooley?*" The single word was faintly uttered by the woman, though her eyes remained closed and her lips barely moved. "Is that really–*you?*"

"Yes!" He nearly shouted as his heart beat faster. He studied Adelaide's careworn face beneath her disheveled gray hair, her frail body bent at the knees. "Can you understand me, Adelaide?" He leaned in closer and pushed aside the straw head of the broom which rested near her face. His spirit rose when he saw movement beneath her eyelids. "Open your eyes, Adelaide. Open your eyes. Wake up and talk to me."

Slowly, Adelaide raised her eyelids as if responding to his plea. She appeared tired and disoriented yet kept a confused stare locked upon Dooley's countenance. He smiled, and after a few moments, Adelaide seemed to recognize the familiar face.

"*Dooley?*" she whispered.

"Yes," he replied, almost giddily. "It's me. Are you hurt?"

She paused, her thoughts seemingly adrift. "I don't remember falling, but I think I'm okay. A few sore limbs maybe. A bit dizzy perhaps."

"I'll help you slowly sit up," he said. "We'll take it one step at a time, all right?"

Adelaide nodded, raising her left arm and resting it upon Dooley's shoulder as he leaned in closer to support her. "Thank you," she kindly replied.

Dooley beamed with gratitude that he was able to assist her for once in his life. He helped her to sit up on the floor, not noticing as she wrapped her right fingers tightly around the broomstick. He leaned back and glanced at her face and head for any signs of injury, still on his knees and showing much concern.

"Adelaide, I wanted to sat that—"

Suddenly Dooley lurched forward, clutching both hands to his stomach, his breath knocked out of him as a pain shot through his body. Adelaide pulled her right hand back as if withdrawing a thrust sword, having rammed the tip of the broom handle squarely into his abdomen. Before Dooley realized what had happened, she scrambled to her feet while still holding onto the broom, accidentally hitting Dooley in the chin with the handle.

"*Ow!* What are you doing?" he muttered with barely enough breath as he looked up at Adelaide looming over him, his eyes watering from the stinging pain.

"Did you think you could keep me locked up forever, Dooley Kramer?" she sputtered, fully awake and recovered from her feigned injuries. "Well, mister, I don't think so!" She waved the broom like an ill-trained swordsman. "I saw you coming up the stairs without Zachary this time, so now it's an even match–you against me!"

"But, Adelaide, I'm here to–!" Dooley felt the straw end of the broom hit him square in the face when he tried to stand up, sending him tumbling backward, his eyes and mouth filled with dust grains and dirt. "Stop that!" he shouted, rubbing his eyes as he spit out the cold, soily taste in his mouth. As he got to his feet, his head bent down while furiously wiping at his face, Adelaide hit him several times over the back with the broom.

"I don't know what you and your friend are up to, but I'm not letting you get away with it anymore!" she hollered, poking the straw bristles repeatedly into the side of Dooley's head as he rapidly spun around to keep his face away from the crazed woman's broom. "And why did Zachary go over to the shed tonight? I saw the other light heading that way." Adelaide demanded an answer between her labored breaths as she continued hitting Dooley with the broom.

"That wasn't Za–!" The forest of frayed broom bristles again slapped Dooley in the face when he turned to Adelaide to offer an explanation. He whirled around in a blinding, dizzying circle, coughing and sputtering, unable to get his bearings. He felt the cool draft pouring in from the open door and knew he had to get outside and away from Adelaide so he could regroup and calmly explain to her what was happening.

"I don't want to hear your falsehoods!" she shouted. "And I refuse to spend another day in this wretched place!" The woman's face tightened with the pent up rage that had been festering inside her for weeks. "You'll have to kill me if you want to keep me here any longer!" she shouted, accompanying the remark with another crack of the broomstick across Dooley's hunched back.

"Stop it!" he yelled as a stream of stinging tears poured from his eyes as he blindly tried to find his way to the door. "Stop it, you crazy woman!" He again felt the coolness of the swamp air wash over him and hurried to the open doorway through a haze of tears and black spots, barely able to discern the knotty floorboards beneath his boots as he scrambled to get away from Adelaide's incessant beating.

"Get out of here, Dooley, and don't come back!" Adelaide hollered, raising the broom but holding back her next strike as he bounded sideways out the door as if drunk, nearly tripping over his own feet and rubbing at his eyes with one hand while blindly reaching for the door frame or the staircase railing with his other. "And when Zachary shows his face around here, I'm going to–!"

Her words were cut short by a deafening crack of wood and a petrified scream in the darkness. But both sounds were instantly swallowed up in the night. She gasped as she helplessly watched Dooley trip and stumble backward against the rotted wooden railing on the left side of the staircase, snapping it in half and falling into the shadows below. Cold, heavy stillness flowed into the room. Adelaide stood frozen in place, her eyes wide in horror and her mouth agape. She let the broom drop to the floor, wondering if what she had just witnessed had really happened. She then heard a flurry of distant voices swiftly approaching and snapped back to her senses. She grabbed the broomstick as a weapon and rushed to the doorway, gazing with shock at the broken railing, her heart beating wildly. She picked up the burning oil lamp on the topmost step and carefully walked down the staircase, her first taste of freedom after a long string of lonely, gray days.

Adelaide held the lamp higher after she planted her feet on the ground, glancing around frantically in the darkness. The voices drew nearer amid the faint glow of another light. She now expected trouble from Zachary Farnsworth, but her resolve had been fortified after her encounter with Dooley. She gripped the broom handle tighter, ready to make what she thought might be her last stand. Still, she planned to make it a good one as two shadowy figures emerged through the darkness, one carrying a lamp similar to hers that gently rose and fell with every footstep.

"Stop right there, Zachary Farnsworth!" Adelaide stepped forward, raising the broom and holding the light in her outstretched hand. "I fought off Dooley Kramer and I'll do the same to you and your friend. I'm not scared anymore, so consider yourself warned!" Her heart pounded and her arm quivered, but she clenched her jaw, ready to face the last battle.

"Adelaide, it's me, Katherine Durant." The voice sounded light and sweet in the oppressive gloom as if a breath of springtime had invaded autumn's final hours. "I'm with Lewis Ames. We're here to rescue you."

Adelaide couldn't believe her ears. The friendly, familiar voice blanketed her trembling body and drove the fear and darkness from her mind. She lowered the oil lamp and dropped the broomstick as an astonished smile slowly enveloped her face. "*Katherine*? But how could you possibly..." She was speechless as Katherine and Lewis hurried over, their faces visible in the combined light of the lamps.

"Are you all right?" Katherine asked, filled with worry as she wondered what had transpired since Dooley left her side.

"*Oh, Katherine!*" Adelaide replied with unbounded relief as she reached out and flung her arms around the young woman while tears of joy streamed down her face. Lewis, holding the lamp, quickly grabbed the second one from Adelaide as the two women held each other. Adelaide buried her head in Katherine's shoulder and sobbed for some time. Katherine quietly assured her that everything would be all right and that Zachary Farnsworth was nowhere in the vicinity.

"You have nothing to worry about anymore," she promised as Adelaide stepped back and wiped the remaining tears from her eyes.

"But how did you find me?" Adelaide inquired, stunned that Katherine and Lewis were standing there.

"It's a long story," she replied in a motherly fashion, looking upon the woman who appeared older and frailer since she last saw her. Yet a rugged determination swirled deep within Adelaide's steel blue eyes and Katherine knew that she would survive this harrowing ordeal after some much needed rest and friendly company. "We'll answer all your questions in due time."

"But where is Dooley?" Lewis asked. "We heard a scream and rushed over. What happened here?"

"Something terrible," she said, her voice choking up. Adelaide pointed along the side of the staircase. "He's over there, but in what condition..."

Katherine and Lewis glanced at each other, dreading the worst. When they looked up and noticed the broken railing on the staircase, they regretted not accompanying Dooley to the house. Katherine took one of the oil lamps from Lewis.

"Wait here, Adelaide, and we'll take a look," she gently said.

"No. I'm coming with you," she firmly responded. "I have to see what I did, accident though it was."

"All right." Katherine took her hand as Lewis led the way to the side of the staircase, all dreading to see what they feared in their hearts had occurred.

As the pale light of the two lamps dispersed the thicket of shadows, the outline of Dooley's shape grew visible against one of the round wooden stilts holding up the structure. As they drew closer, the light gently fell upon Dooley Kramer's dead body couched in a thick bed of dried weeds. All were shaken by the sight of him lying sprawled out upon his back, his head and one arm bent at awkward angles. Both of Dooley's eyes were wide open. He blindly gazed up through a canopy of tree branches at a mass of gray clouds drifting silently overhead like a lone eagle in mournful flight.

CHAPTER 83

Some Much Needed Rest

Adelaide was stunned when Katherine and Lewis led her to the shed where Maynard lay sleeping under Arileez' spell. She stared in horror at his peaceful face for several disbelieving moments.

"I thought Zachary and Dooley had carried in a dead body that night," she whispered, gently touching Maynard's warm, pale cheek. "So I guess this is good news." Adelaide dabbed her watery eyes with the corner of her shawl. "Still, to think that Maynard has been here all this time under my very nose."

"There's nothing you could have done," Katherine assured her. "Lewis and I tried to wake him to no avail, so you wouldn't have had any better luck. We'll need to consult someone who knows a thing or two about magic to help Maynard."

"We could contact the wizard at the Blue Citadel who Dooley mentioned," Lewis suggested. "I believe his name was Tolapari."

"If he's still there," Katherine replied, reminding him that the war council was held about five weeks ago. "In the meantime, we should take Maynard somewhere safe, but not in Kanesbury. No telling what would happen if Zachary Farnsworth catches wind of this before we talk to Constable Brindle."

"I agree," Lewis said. "Who knows what a cornered man might resort to in order to hold onto power? Maybe I can find someplace where–"

"No need to," Adelaide gently interrupted. "I know exactly where we can take Maynard."

"You do?" Katherine asked.

"The son of a dear departed friend of mine lives on a farm a mile or so east of Kanesbury. Emmett Trout and his wife, Lorna, run the place with their three children. I'm sure they'll be happy to take Maynard in for a time until we can cure him."

"And will they take you in, too?" Lewis asked. "You can't suddenly reappear in Kanesbury without sending the village into an uproar. Let us quietly inform Constable Brindle about what's happened before we make a move. Katherine and I will bring Clay to your friends' farmhouse and then to the swamp so he can decide how to proceed against Farnsworth. It's most important that you and Maynard are restored to good health first."

Adelaide grimaced. "As to Maynard, of course. But me? I feel fine," she insisted. "I survived here all this time, didn't I?"

"Yes, you did," Katherine said with a caring smile. "But all the difficult days you endured will catch up with you soon enough. Use this extra time to recover and to keep an eye on Maynard. Lewis and I must return to Kanesbury to keep up a normal appearance, but we'll try to visit if time allows.

Adelaide nodded, knowing the young couple had her best interests at heart. And deep down, she admitted that she could use several days, perhaps even longer, to get some proper rest and nourishment. She thought she had definitely earned it.

"But before we leave for Emmett and Lorna's farm," she said, "I need to know why Maynard and I were brought to this horrid place. I know Caldurian was involved because he visited Farnsworth when I was imprisoned in his cellar. But other than a few overheard scraps of information, I don't know the entire story." She emitted a weary sigh. "What exactly is going on in this crazy world of ours?"

After they explained to Adelaide all they had learned from Dooley and told her how they had secretly followed him to the swamp, she returned to the house with Katherine to retrieve a few of her things. Lewis, in the meantime, carefully wrapped Dooley's body in a blanket, lifted him over his shoulder and carried him just inside the trees. With a mix of unease and sadness, he buried him in a shallow grave using a shovel he found in the shed. He and Katherine planned to return with the constable to exhume the body as part of his investigation, believing the corpse would remain better preserved underground than lying in the shed. They also feared that if Farnsworth or his associates should return in the meantime, the body might disappear to cover their tracks.

When Katherine stepped outdoors with Adelaide a short time later, Lewis had completed his grim task. Their next job was to carry Maynard's body to one of the boats and cross the swamp. Lewis wiped his brow with a coat sleeve as they trudged once more to the shed. Though the first pale light of dawn still lay many hours away, everyone felt as if they had lingered here the entire night.

"I'll lift him under his shoulders and you take him by the feet," Lewis instructed Katherine as they stood over Maynard's body. "He's much larger than Dooley, so I'll need some help. Let me know if you have to stop and rest."

"I'll do my best," she replied, gazing at Maynard's face. His eyes and thoughts were still closed to the world. She wondered what dreams, if any, occupied the man's unending hours of sleep. "And to think all this time we believed that Maynard was journeying to Morrenwood to consult with the King. What other lies has Zachary Farnsworth fed to the citizens of Kanesbury?"

"I hate to imagine," Adelaide whispered, "though I fear we'll find out in due course. Then we'll know the real extent of the damage he and Dooley have caused. I'm sure it won't be pretty."

They drifted across the swamp in somber silence. Lewis sat in one boat with Maynard, taking the shovel he had removed from the shed. Katherine and Adelaide paddled the other. When they reached shore, they carried Maynard to the cart and laid him in back, covering him with the additional blankets. Lewis saved one tattered covering to wrap around Dell Hawks' body. He buried it in a second hastily dug grave among the low shrubs and weeds just inside the tree line, but not before retrieving the other half of the money that Dooley had given to the hired assassin. He handed the leather pouch with the silver and copper half pieces to Katherine to keep with the first one.

NICHOLAS RAVEN AND THE WIZARDS' WEB - VOLUME 2

"Maybe we can do something good with that money," he said. "Something to reverse the damage that Farnsworth and the wizard have caused."

"It will take a lot to accomplish that," Katherine sadly remarked as she and Adelaide watched Lewis dig a hole among the trees not far from where they had left the horse and cart. The two women held up the oil lamps to provide light. "Unfortunately, even a bucketful of coins won't be able to undo the misery inflicted upon our friends and neighbors. Time can only accomplish that task."

After the body was buried and Lewis enjoyed a short rest, the trio boarded the cart, anxious to leave. Lewis took the reins and soon they were heading back up the narrow wooded path, eager to break free of the suffocating grip of the swamp. Adelaide sat between Lewis and Katherine, enjoying with childlike innocence the play of cool air upon her face and the scent of fragrant pine boughs standing guard at intervals on either side of the trail. The branches of other trees, now bony and bare on winter's eve, created an archway of sorts above them as they traveled with quiet urgency. Soon the swamp lay behind them and they exited the woods, arriving back onto River Road still awash in night shadows and blanketed with a mass of thick clouds sailing sluggishly above.

In time they crossed the wooden bridge where Dooley had first encountered Dell Hawks, and then continued westward past the Spirit Caves at a steady pace until they were about a mile from the eastern border of Kanesbury. Adelaide soon pointed out a right turn up the road and Lewis reined in the horse to a gentle trot.

"There's Willow Road," she said. "Just a few minutes north and we'll reach Emmett's farmhouse. No doubt he and his family will be fast asleep, but I suppose waking them can't be helped under the circumstances." Adelaide's face was creased with worry as she glanced over her shoulder at Maynard who was still in a deep slumber. "We have to help him," she whispered, fearful that she might never talk with her old friend and neighbor again. "We have to save him no matter the cost."

As they pulled into the farmstead, a large brown dog popped out from behind the doors of a barn and dashed toward the strangers like a swiftly moving shadow. Its loud barks pierced the inky night. Moments later, a light appeared inside an upper window of the small house adjacent to the barn. A large oak tree towered above it on the left side. Soon the front door opened and a tall man stepped out into the gloom holding an oil lamp enclosed with a glass globe, the soft yellow light casting away the darkness around him.

"Horace! Quiet!" His deep voice immediately silenced the dog who raced over to the man and walked protectively at his side as he approached the cart. He held the oil lamp in one hand and raised a stick of firewood in his other. "Who's there?" he asked, standing a safe distance from the cart and holding up the lamp though unable to distinguish the faces of the visitors.

"Emmett, it's me, Adelaide Cooper from Kanesbury," she said, recognizing the man's voice.

"*Adelaide*?" Emmett immediately tossed aside the piece of wood and hurried to the cart, trying to recall the last time he had seen the woman who had visited his home on a few occasions. "What brings you here at this ghostly hour?"

"I apologize for the inconvenience, but I'm with three friends of mine," she said, her voice nearly at a whisper. "And we desperately need your help."

Emmett saw only two people sitting next to her and caressed his whiskered face. "Where's the third one?" he asked, his brow wrinkled with curiosity.

Adelaide sighed. "That, I'm afraid, will take some explaining. May we come in?"

Half an hour later, Katherine, Lewis and Adelaide were seated around a table in front of a large fireplace in a sparsely furnished kitchen with Emmett Trout and his wife, Lorna, who had since waken up and put on a kettle of tea. Lewis and Emmett had earlier carried in Maynard's sleeping body and laid him on a spare feather mattress in an adjoining room. As hot tea was poured into clay mugs and passed around, Katherine began recounting a condensed version of the harrowing events of that night and of the previous weeks in Kanesbury. Emmett and his wife listened in stunned fascination, knowing some of the local history regarding Caldurian and the Enâri creatures, yet finding the exploits of Zachary Farnsworth and Dooley Kramer equally intriguing.

"I heard news of a murder in the village early this autumn," Emmett said, "but never learned if the case was solved. Later, the borders of Kanesbury were closed for a while due to redlin fever." Katherine smirked. "We've had quite a time of it lately." She asked her hosts if they wouldn't mind housing Maynard and Adelaide for an unspecified number of days, or perhaps even weeks depending on Maynard's condition, until they could bring Constable Brindle to their home. Emmett and Lorna were more than willing to offer what space and food they could spare since Adelaide had been such a close friend of Emmett's mother.

"Gilbert, my oldest, will be delighted to give up his room to Maynard and sleep downstairs," Lorna said. "He's eager to build a cabin with his father in back of the property and live on his own."

"Except for meals," Emmett added with a laugh.

"He'll probably insist that this is the first step." Lorna got up to put on a second pot of tea and rounded up a plate of herb biscuits to serve to her guests.

"We're very grateful," Katherine said, "and will compensate you for the additional cost."

Emmett shook his head and held up a hand to signal his polite refusal. "Adelaide was a dear friend to my mother and to my family. We're more than happy to help. We won't accept even a copper quarter piece from either of you."

"But Katherine and I won't be compensating you," Lewis said, explaining about Farnsworth's payment that was supposed to have gone to Dell Hawks. "We insist that you take a few silver half pieces for all your trouble compliments of our fraudulent acting mayor. It's the least he can do after all the havoc he's caused."

Emmett grunted with laughter, flashing a smile beneath a full head of long, stringy hair. "Well, that puts an entirely different spin on the story. After what you've told me about this appalling man, I'll be more than happy to deprive him of a little bit of his wealth to help care for Adelaide and her friend."

"And though Lewis and I will ride the horse back to the village," Katherine added, "you can have the cart for the farm. I don't want to risk Farnsworth spotting that on the streets of Kanesbury. He will most likely assume that it was either left at the swamp or taken as a bonus payment by his hired assassin."

"Excellent point," Emmett said, impressed with the young woman's foresight as he turned to his wife. "It seems we'll have an extra piece of equipment on the farm and some spare change to boot thanks to that conniving man. Are you okay with that?"

Lorna nodded, wanting to voice her comments regarding Zachary Farnsworth's disgraceful character. Instead, she pointed to Adelaide sitting in the chair closest to the blazing fire. Sometime during the conversation, Adelaide bowed her head to her chest and had fallen fast asleep, her breathing steady and deep as the heat of the crackling flames washed over her. Katherine smiled.

"That's probably the first decent night's sleep she's had in quite a while," she said, imagining the mental torment that Adelaide had endured while all alone at the swamp. "I think she deserves a good many hours more."

"She shall have it right here," Emmett assured her. "And no one in Kanesbury, especially Zachary Farnsworth, will be the wiser."

Katherine and Lewis departed an hour later after Adelaide had awakened from her nap. She was sad to see them leave, yet knew they had to return to Kanesbury so as not to arouse Farnsworth's suspicions. As they left through the front door, she promised to keep a constant eye upon Maynard, hoping for a miracle recovery.

"We'll return when we can to visit and keep you updated," Katherine said as she hugged Adelaide goodbye.

"Lorna or I can always ride into Kanesbury if we ever need to see you," Emmett promised. "We'll figure things out."

In the meantime, Lewis unhitched the horse from the cart and then he and Katherine thanked Emmett and Lorna once again for their help and wished them good night. Lewis climbed onto the steed and extended a hand to help Katherine up. She sat behind him, her arms gently wrapped around him as they quietly rode off in the gloomy night and returned home to the deserted village streets. Kanesbury lay silent and dark when Lewis finally said goodbye to Katherine in front of her house. The windows were dark, though her mother had left an oil lamp burning on the front porch railing to welcome her back.

"Your mother is getting used to your late nights out," Lewis said as they stood below the front steps holding one another close.

"One day I hope to explain to her why," Katherine replied, her affectionate gaze fixed upon Lewis' eyes. "I'm just glad that you were with me to share in all the fun."

Lewis grinned. "More fun like this and we might not get to enjoy spending more time with each other." His expression turned serious. "Things could have gone badly tonight, Katherine. And the danger still isn't over. We have to be careful even after you talk to Clay Brindle. Until Zachary Farnsworth is in the village lockup–or better yet, in King Justin's custody–he's still a threat to both you and the village."

"And to think I shared a meal with him at the Stewarts' house this evening," she said. "Well, the sooner I talk to the constable and let him know what's going on, the better. I'll arrange a day when we can return to the swamp and Emmett's farm with Clay and show him our proof."

"I look forward to it," he said, kissing her softly on the lips. "In the meantime, stay out of trouble, Miss Durant. I'm beginning to think that you enjoy these daring adventures."

"As long as you're by my side," she said, returning an affectionate kiss and wishing that the night was still young. "But now you must go home. If I don't get any sleep, I'll be useless tomorrow when I talk to the constable."

"You'll do a wonderful job," Lewis assured her as he climbed on the horse.

He smiled and waved goodbye to Katherine and sauntered down the street, his heart both light and melancholy. He watched as she slowly climbed the porch stairs and disappeared into the house with the flickering oil lamp, closing the door behind her and adding another layer of dreary darkness to the night.

CHAPTER 84

Growing Suspicions

Zachary Farnsworth lifted his coat collar as he stepped out of the house early the next morning. The first day of winter had arrived, bringing with it leaden skies and feathery light snow. He trudged to the banking house, eager to face another day of ink-stained ledgers and manipulating numbers if only to keep his mind off the events of yesterday. Dinner with Oscar and Amanda Stewart and their guests proved to be a lovely evening despite Katherine Durant's abrupt exit. But when he imagined Dooley Kramer's final excursion to the swamp, he grew pale and took a deep breath. He couldn't bear to glance at Dooley's ramshackle home as he hurriedly walked by, knowing he had sent his neighbor to his death.

Farnsworth repeatedly told himself that his actions had been necessary if he were to move up in Kanesbury society. He had grand plans to acquire wealth and position and needed to clear his life of all extraneous distractions. Dooley had been a distraction, one of several loose threads that needed to be snipped. He silently congratulated himself for having the courage to make the tough decision.

In a day or two, someone in the village would make an inquiry into Dooley's absence and the questions would begin, followed with an investigation by Constable Brindle and the usual search party. Farnsworth planned to play along and participate in a search since Dooley was his neighbor, but in time the investigation would come to a dead end. As there would be no signs of a struggle or a robbery in Dooley's house, some might think that he had gotten lost and injured in the woods or had fallen into the river after a night of drinking. Despite taking on more responsibility by helping Ned Adams plan the rebuilding of the gristmill, Dooley would still be seen as remaining true to his self, and that meant indulging in too much ale after working hours, often times late into the night.

Farnsworth sighed, mentally preparing himself for that next bump in the road. But given a little time, he hoped to pass over it and enjoy the fruits of his labor. And with his newly acquired power, he convinced himself that maybe he actually could do some genuinely good works for the village in addition to those benefits he envisioned for himself. If such were the case, he believed his fellow villagers, even if they ever discovered the truth, would probably thank him for seizing power and making their lives better. He convinced himself more and more of this with each step he took.

As the snow danced in the air, Farnsworth straightened his shoulders and picked up his pace, feeling better about himself again. He turned off his road and continued into the center of the village, convinced that his questionable actions were really just what the village of Kanesbury needed–a necessary remedy to cure a stagnant community that didn't even know it needed his help. He smiled, realizing how lucky his fellow villagers were to have him selflessly guiding their way through the rigors of life. He hoped in the end that they would appreciate all of his hard work and sacrifice.

After unlocking the banking house a short time later and offering his employees a hearty good morning when they arrived, Farnsworth slipped on his coat again and excused himself for a few minutes as he headed back out into the cold streets.

"Village business," he pleasantly remarked to a young woman seated at a worktable near the front door. She was carefully preparing a duplicate of a contract to be signed later in the week. "I'll be back shortly," he added as the woman neatly copied each word with a quill pen dipped in black ink.

"We'll keep an eye on business, Mr. Farnsworth," she replied, returning to her task as he stepped outside and closed the door.

Farnsworth smiled as he walked down the street to the village lockup, certain his workers were delighted that their manager was also the mayor of Kanesbury. He sensed their overwhelming pride and thrived on their unspoken recognition every time he walked by. Just another benefit of the job he told himself as he passed the village hall and approached the lockup next door. A large, bare maple tree stood between the buildings, a tall and silent sentinel watching over the handful of passersby going about their morning errands among the gentle swirl of snowflakes.

Since Amanda Stewart had graciously invited him to dinner last night, albeit at Katherine Durant's request to secure an early trial for her uncle, Farnsworth wanted to officially let Otto know as soon as possible that he was granting the favor. Such an action on his part, he believed, would curry favor with the Stewarts and prove to them that he could be a reliable public servant as well as an influential friend. He wanted to make sure his first impression as mayor with Oscar and Amanda was a memorable one. A quick trip to the lockup to speak with Otto was well worth the tiny effort.

As he neared the building, the door opened. Sophia Durant stepped outside, dressed warmly in a maroon cloak and fur-lined gloves. She was draping a hood over her head when Farnsworth called out to her. Sophia looked up with a smile as the acting mayor of Kanesbury walked over.

"Good morning, Zachary," she said as he hurried up the few steps and met Katherine's mother underneath a narrow overhang extending the length of the small building. "Or would you prefer *Mayor Farnsworth?*" she added with a friendly laugh.

"Don't build me up too much," he replied with equal humor. "After all, I'm only the acting mayor until Maynard returns, or, as I sincerely hope, your brother Otto is found innocent of his charges. In the meantime, *Zachary* is just fine, Mrs. Durant."

"Very well, Zachary." Sophia stepped back to allow him some room on the floorboards beneath the overhang to keep out of the snow. Though his large body towered over her small frame, she was not intimidated by the imposing figure. "And speaking of my brother, I just talked with Otto and told him the good news about his trial. I thank you again for helping to hurry matters along."

"I'll do my best, Mrs. Durant," he replied, though inside he was eager to put Otto's situation behind him one way or another so he could go about his business. "I just left the banking house so I could officially tell Otto the wonderful news. Shall I assume he was happy to hear it from you first?"

"And how!" she answered, beaming with a grateful smile. "He looks forward to speaking with you about the particulars."

"Good." Farnsworth wrapped his arms around his chest as the bitter cold cut through him. "I'm glad to help out in any way I can," he said. "By the way, Mrs. Durant, how is your daughter feeling this morning? I was sorry to see Katherine leave dinner so early last night. We were having such a delightful time."

"Katherine is fine, so no need to worry. She accompanied me here to visit Otto this morning and is still speaking with him," she said. "I have some chores to finish, so I slipped out early."

"Wonderful. I'm glad to hear she's feeling better."

Sophia laughed. "Katherine recovered quickly as she was already out of the house when I arrived home last night. No doubt out on one of her long evening strolls of late, probably with Lewis Ames, her latest gentleman admirer. I'd tell Katherine you inquired and said hello, but you're sure to see her inside."

"I look forward to it," he replied, offering Sophia his arm and assisting her down the stairs to the snow-dusted dirt road. There he smiled and wished her a good day before they parted. Farnsworth hurried back up the steps into the lockup. He was eager to get Otto's visit over with so he could return to the banking house and lose himself in his ledgers and in the joyful musings of warmer and more prosperous days to come.

After he entered the building and hung up his coat on a wall peg in the entryway, he noted Katherine's cloak hanging nearby. He stepped into the main room where several logs crackled in a fireplace across the room from where Constable Brindle kept a desk to oversee his duties. A narrow hallway led out from an opening in back of the sparsely furnished office to an area where two small holding cells were located, each comprised of stone walls and a thick wooden door with a small barred opening. A single individual occupied one of the cells today. Farnsworth immediately noted

Katherine Durant standing near a far window and quietly talking to Tyler Harkin, one of Constable Brindle's deputies, the only other person in the room. Tyler nodded from across the room to acknowledge the mayor's presence while listening to Katherine.

"Thank you so much for your time," she said a moment later to the young deputy constable as he escorted her toward the door where Farnsworth waited. "And good morning to *you*," Katherine added, smiling at the mayor. "I had stopped by to see my uncle."

"Of course you have, telling him the good news from last night, no doubt." He discreetly eyed the deputy and silently shooed him away before giving his full attention to Katherine.

"I wish to thank you again, Mr. Farnsworth, for agreeing to hurry along his trial," she said as they walked into the entryway.

"My pleasure," he replied as Katherine was about to reach for her cloak. "Allow me." Farnsworth removed the cloak from its peg and placed it upon her shoulders from behind whereupon she securely fastened it with a metal clasp, her face tightening with dismay as she reluctantly accepted his kind gesture. "Oh, wait," he added, bending down and removing a few dried, prickly burrs that were stuck to the hem of her garment. "You must have brushed past a burdock bush. Pesky little things, aren't they?" He stood up. "Done."

"Thank you," Katherine said as she turned around to face him, now pleasantly smiling again. "By the way, I'm guessing that you're here to see Uncle Otto, too."

"For a brief visit. He and I will surely talk extensively about the trial later," he said. "In the meantime, how are you feeling? You missed a wonderful time last night. Your mother was particularly charming company."

"I'm glad to hear it," Katherine said with a genial air while images of the terrible events at the swamp swept through her mind. But she managed to keep up a pose of charm and grace as she looked into Farnsworth's dark, piercing eyes, wondering what other ill deeds he had committed. "My mother said she enjoyed herself immensely. I'm sorry to have missed it due to my sudden illness."

"Another time perhaps." Farnsworth smiled as he prepared to open the door for her. "Still, I'm glad you made a swift recovery. That's the most important thing."

"I went directly home and slept the whole night through," Katherine replied as she gathered up the folds of her cloak, ready to depart. "Now I feel like my old self again."

Farnsworth glanced at her with a confused smile, wondering if he had heard her correctly. "Your mother said that–" But he quickly held back the words he had intended to say, keeping his smile intact. "–that she really regretted you were unable to stay. Oscar and Amanda said as much at the dinner table, too."

"How kind of them," Katherine said as he opened the door for her, allowing a cold draft to slip into the room.

"Good day now and please watch your step," he added, gazing at Katherine as she stepped out the door and into the veil of light snow.

"Good day to you, Mr. Farnsworth," she replied before fading into the grayness of the wintry street.

Zachary Farnsworth paused before closing the door, bothered by the contradiction in Katherine and Sophia's stories but not quite sure why. Nor was he even sure why he had caught himself before mentioning it to Katherine, yet was glad he did. He shook his head and brushed off the incident as he walked back into the main room where Deputy Harkin sat on a high stool at a table that served as his desk, eager to speak with him.

"Did Miss Durant visit with her uncle for as long as she needed?" he asked, eyeing Tyler Harkin as if he might have done something wrong.

"Of course, Mayor Farnsworth," he replied. "I allowed her into his cell to speak with Otto uninterrupted."

"Good. Very good, sir," he replied more kindly. "You did exactly as you were supposed to. But did the young lady have any other matters she was displeased with? When I saw her talking to you as I entered the room, it seemed as if she was–"

"No, sir!" the deputy interjected. "Miss Durant voiced no complaints. She was simply asking to speak with Constable Brindle as soon as possible. I told her he was out at Bud Chasen's farm again and probably wouldn't be back until later this morning. It seems that Bud lodged another complaint about his neighbor's goat," he said with a smirk. "They still haven't fixed the hole in their pen."

"I see," Farnsworth replied with an amused nod. "Was there anything you or I could have helped Miss Durant with? I hate to see any citizen of Kanesbury unserved by their public officials."

"As do I," the deputy agreed. "I offered to help but she was reluctant to tell me what she needed. She insisted on talking to Clay in person. Miss Durant will return tomorrow when she has time."

Farnsworth casually shrugged his shoulders which put the deputy at ease. "Oh well, then I guess it's no business of ours. Don't give it another thought."

"Very well."

Farnsworth smiled as he headed toward the back hallway, tossing the dried burrs he had pulled from Katherine's cloak into the fireplace. He removed a set of keys to the prison cells that hung on a hook near the hall entrance. "I won't keep you from your duties any further. I'm going to talk to Otto briefly and then return to the banking house. Carry on," he added cheerfully before drifting down the shadowy hallway where his smile quickly melted from his face.

When he reached Otto's door, he paused before knocking, wondering why Katherine was so eager to meet with Constable Brindle. Surely it must be about Otto's upcoming trial and nothing more, he concluded. Yet the knowledge that Katherine had lied to him about sleeping through the entire night only moments after Sophia offered a contradictory story bothered him like a nagging mosquito. But he let it pass for the moment and knocked on the door to officially inform Otto about the latest news regarding his trial.

As noontime approached, Farnsworth had gotten little work done in his office. His thoughts constantly turned to Katherine Durant and what he believed was a feigned sickness on her part the previous night. He wondered why she had gone to all the trouble of asking Amanda to host a dinner party with him as guest of honor and then slip out shortly after it had gotten underway. And why did she need to speak with Constable Brindle about a matter she refused to reveal to one of Clay's deputies? He leaned back in his chair, a sense of unease and suspicion slowly wrapping itself around him like gray shadows at twilight.

His thoughts shifted to Dooley Kramer and his journey to the swamp last night. Farnsworth speculated that that unsettling situation was what really had him upset right now. He wondered if he should have gone with Dooley on that fateful trip to make sure everything went according to plan. He nervously drummed his fingers on the desktop, debating whether to take a quick trip to the swamp to reassure himself that the situation stood as he imagined it, as he had paid for it to be. No one should be occupying the small house or the shed on that little island now, and the horse and cart that Dooley drove to the swamp should have been removed by the nameless assassin he had hired. That's how things *should* stand and probably did. Farnsworth tried to convince himself of this before diving into his work again. But when he slipped on his coat a while later to leave the banking house at lunchtime, his suspicions got the better of him. He stopped at the station of one of his employees on his way out.

"Mr. Keswick, there's a small matter I must attend to this afternoon. I'd like you to manage the house in my absence," he said, his demeanor calm and casual. "I doubt I shall be back by closing. Lock up at the normal time."

"Happy to, Mr. Farnsworth," he replied, enjoying the idea of being in charge in his superior's absence.

"Very good then." Farnsworth offered a hint of a smile as he walked away and exited the building, buttoning up his coat as he stepped into the cold, cheerless street.

He was less than eager to return to the swamp, but nagging doubts urged him on. Deep down, he guessed that he had been destined to see this through to the end. But after today, he hoped never to visit that dreadful, watery site again, though he resigned himself to it invading his dreams from time to time. An adequate price for the triumphs that life would soon bestow upon him he reasoned while walking home to get a horse and cart for his impromptu excursion. Soon he climbed upon his steed, snapped the reins and rode down to River Road, dreading the weary journey ahead.

A gray, oppressive silence weighed heavily upon Farnsworth as his horse trotted along the desolate road, a fine, intermittent snow falling. He passed only one individual during the trip, a man driving a cartload of hay presumably to one of the nearby dairy farms. He and Farnsworth silently acknowledged each other as they passed until an eerie stillness again reigned over the barren landscape. Soon he passed the Spirit Caves and crossed the wooden bridge just beyond. Shortly after, he veered off the road to his right and disappeared into a stretch of sparse woods that quickly thickened around him. He guided his horse down the narrow path deeper into the trees toward the swamp, stopping as he neared the water's edge. He dismounted, scanning the area in the dim light of early afternoon.

The murky water lay still and sleepy. Farnsworth noted the fresh impressions of wheel and horse tracks etched in the hard ground along with a slew of boot prints among the patches of dirt and dried grass. He was confident that Dooley and his hired assassin had arrived here last night. He scanned the pattern of prints across the ground, some in a detectable oval shape while others veered off here and there. He wondered if there had been a commotion during the night. Perhaps Dooley had put up a struggle or tried to flee when realizing his fate. Farnsworth wandered over to where the two boats were hidden in the underbrush. He knew his curiosity wouldn't be satisfied until he paddled over to the island to check things out.

After stepping in one of the boats, he pushed off using a paddle and swiftly made his way across to the island where he disembarked and pulled the boat ashore. He wandered over to the shed, noting the door was slightly ajar. As he stepped inside, a wave of relief washed over him when he saw that Maynard Kurtz' sleeping body was gone, guessing that the man was now lying beneath the swamp. Farnsworth smiled, relaxing a bit now that one obstacle had been permanently removed. But something else about the shed's interior looked different, something minor and out of place, though he couldn't put a finger on it.

He hurried to the house next, noting that the scent of burning wood was absent. Also missing was a thin trail of bluish-gray smoke snaking out of the small chimney on the side. Another good sign he mused with almost giddy delight, believing his problems were finally behind him. But when he saw the broken railing on the upper right side of the staircase, his heart fluttered. A straw broom lay upon the ground nearby. He slowly climbed the ten steps to the front door which was closed but not fastened with the padlock. He paused to study the broken railing and then glanced down to the ground at a handful of large splinters sprinkled among the dried weeds. Had

Adelaide taken a spill, accidental or otherwise? Farnsworth scratched his head and went inside.

The yawning fireplace greeted him, filled with a pile of cold ashes and half burnt logs. Everything else seemed undisturbed, looking like it always had whenever he and Dooley ventured inside. He peeked into the other rooms, and finding the place empty, stepped outside and stood on the top platform and pondered the situation. Pale daylight filtered through the treetops. The frosty, sharp scents from the swamp calmed the acting mayor of Kanesbury, allowing him to clear his mind and visualize what might have happened.

Since Adelaide was nowhere in sight, his first guess was to assume that she was also lying beneath the swamp with Maynard Kurtz, and most likely, Dooley Kramer. Farnsworth inhaled the bittersweet air, feeling more convinced than ever that he had gotten his money's worth. His worries about Katherine Durant and her sudden and mysterious illness began to fade. He chuckled, realizing that she was merely a young girl who simply might have been bored eating dinner with a bunch of older folks and found a clever way to skip out early and spend an evening with her latest love instead. He admired her ingenuity and his mind was set at ease.

Then he spotted something peculiar from his perch and his curiosity was stirred once again.

Farnsworth gazed at the wooded area between the house and shed, noticing footprints embedded in the soil in one spot leading into the trees. The weeds and undergrowth in that area were noticeably disturbed, as if someone had recently walked into the woods at that point. He turned up his collar, his thoughts now somersaulting again. Who had gone into the woods, and why? He wondered if his paid assassin had buried the bodies instead of sinking them to the bottom of the swamp as instructed. He fumed for a moment before realizing that it would have been more work for the man to bury the bodies, not less. He scrambled down the stairs to investigate. Only moments ago he thought his life was in order. Now an element of disorder and uncertainty had returned. Katherine Durant's clever escape from dinner again entered his mind, though he did not know why.

He noted that the footprints were pressed deeper into the soil in this spot than those across the water. And since the ground was just as hard over here, he speculated that the individual must have been carrying something heavy, no doubt the body of one of his victims. Farnsworth didn't have far to go before he saw a low, elongated pile of freshly dug dirt in the drowsy afternoon light, immediately recognizing the signs of a shallow grave which sent a sickening chill through him. What disturbed him more was that he could find only one grave in the vicinity after frantically searching the wooded area. Had his hired man buried only one body and sent the others to a watery grave? It didn't make sense. But needing to know the truth, he rushed back to the shed to grab a shovel. When he looked inside, he noticed it was missing, realizing that that was the minor detail which had bothered him earlier.

Farnsworth returned to the gravesite and searched for the shovel, thinking the assassin may have tossed it aside in the underbrush. When he couldn't find it, he wondered if the man had taken it with him across the water, though unable to fathom why. Finally, he decided to do what he didn't want to do–kneel down and dig away the dirt at one end of the grave with his bare hands. When his fingers touched what felt like the tip of a boot through a piece of soft material, he shuddered, yanking his arms out of the dirt. He repeated the process at the other end, scooping up soil and tossing it aside until the blanketed face of a dead individual stared up at him.

Farnsworth paused, wiping his brow. He wondered what his employees at the banking house would say if they could see him upon his knees, his fingernails encrusted with soil from a murdered victim's grave. He was reluctant to reveal the identity of the corpse, feeling sick to his stomach, but since he had come this far he knew there was no turning back. He reached for the edges of the material and slowly pulled them down over the victim's head and face. But before he completed the task, his hands began to shake when his fingers were suddenly entwined with long locks of dirty blond hair. He leaned back in horror when Dooley Kramer's pale, lifeless face was fully exposed. He remained frozen for several moments while hunched over his neighbor's dead body, his gaze locked upon Dooley's closed eyelids and ashen face as he silently tried to absolve himself of any responsibility for the man's death. He wondered how and why he had come to be in this particular place in life. A satisfying answer eluded him as the sickly scent of death permeated the air.

After reburying Dooley's corpse, Farnsworth paddled over to the other side of the swamp, eager to leave the island behind. Light would be fading soon and he wanted to depart before the darkness swallowed him up in the ghostly aura now taking hold among the creaking trees and along the water's weedy edges. But before he left, he again examined the scattered footprints near where he had tied up his horse. He assumed that the prints, messily laid down in an ovular shape, were those of Dooley as he possibly evaded the assassin he had unwittingly brought to the swamp. If so, he wondered why Dooley was buried on the island if he had been killed over here. Or had Dooley fled to the island and then met his demise over *there*? The prickly questions gave Farnsworth a headache.

He continued to study the prints, some more distinct than others. A few veered off into the narrow stretch of woods along the water. Farnsworth followed them into the tree line, wading through dried undergrowth and some low hanging branches. As on the island, it didn't take long for him to find another freshly dug gravesite, and lying nearby, the metal shovel that had disappeared from the shed. He wondered why the man would bother to bury either Adelaide or Maynard's corpse over here. Perhaps both of the bodies were in this one gravesite as he couldn't find another one.

He carefully removed some of the soil at one end of the grave with the shovel until he uncovered the face of the deceased, once again wrapped in an old blanket. Since the body was large in size, he assumed that it must be Maynard Kurtz sprawled out before him, asleep for the ages. He knelt down and pulled away the layers of material covering the face, expecting to reveal the familiar long strands of silvery-black hair that were the hallmark of Maynard's appearance. But when the whiskered face of a total stranger stared blankly back from the grave, Farnsworth flinched and jumped to his feet, wondering whose corpse he had dug up. It took only a few moments, however, for the pieces of that puzzle to logically fall into place. He realized that he must be standing over the man he had anonymously hired to do his killing. He scratched his head, his mind overwhelmed until a bolt of lightning-like clarity struck him, making him realize the danger of his situation.

If both Dooley and his hired assassin were dead, then who had killed them? It only made sense that either Adelaide or Maynard had rendered the fatal blows, hard as that was to believe. Had Maynard finally awaken from his sleep and saved them both? Or had Adelaide escaped and somehow heroically carried Maynard's body away to safety after defeating her foes? Regardless of the answer, Farnsworth knew that the circumstances spelled out his doom. Both individuals he had imprisoned were now free and had the ability to bring him down. His rise to power had come to an unexpected end, and he wondered if he could ever again show his face in Kanesbury.

Farnsworth reburied the body, miffed that he had not gotten his money's worth. He silently cursed in the growing gloom for not checking Dooley's body for the pouch of silver half pieces. Or maybe the man he just reburied had the money in his possession instead, but Farnsworth didn't have the heart to search for it now. He could always come back another day. Now it was time to go home—if that was even an option anymore.

Farnsworth tossed the shovel into a clump of dried ferns with a weary sigh, wondering if his twisted plans had been worth the effort. He contemplated where in life he would be right now if he had never walked past Dooley's house five years ago and saw him on the doorstep fingering that key hanging around his neck. Would he still be managing the banking house for Horace Ulm? Perhaps, though he thought he'd probably be dying of boredom behind his desk without having achieved his current station as acting mayor of Kanesbury, a role now in jeopardy.

And it was all Dooley Kramer's fault. It was Dooley's fault for stealing the key and inadvertently enticing him into this life of crime. It was Dooley's fault for being both incompetent and a liability, thus forcing Farnsworth to have him killed. It was *all* his fault, he thought with a scowl as he turned around and headed back through the trees to his horse. But he hadn't taken a handful of steps away from the gravesite when he felt a slight tug on his pant leg.

Farnsworth looked down at his boots, his thoughts still in a muddle. He noticed that his left leg had brushed against a burdock bush and pulled off some of the prickly spurs. He grunted with mild disgust as he reached down to pick them off one by one, still more upset with Dooley and his own shifting fortunes than with this minor inconvenience. But when he pulled off the last burr and tossed it aside, a paralyzing chill suddenly gripped him. Farnsworth stood up straight, his eyes open wide and unblinking.

"She was *here!*" he whispered in horror. Now it all made sense–the dinner party on that particular night and Katherine's abrupt departure. Those events could not be explained away as mere coincidence. Katherine Durant, and perhaps others, must know about his involvement with Maynard and Adelaide's kidnappings, his partnership with Dooley Kramer and his alliance with Caldurian. It was the only logical conclusion. But how did she find out? And more importantly, what was she going to do about it?

Farnsworth returned to his horse, wondering what to do as he ran his hand across the animal's soft mane. He now understood Katherine's desire to speak with Constable Brindle–she wanted to expose him to the authorities and have him arrested. He was disgusted that she had acted so civilly to him in the village lockup when all the while she was plotting his demise. He wondered if the Stewarts were involved, or perhaps Katherine's friend, Lewis. And where were Maynard and Adelaide now? No doubt somewhere under Katherine's protection, secret and safe. They above anyone else could point the finger of blame at him and destroy his life forever. And once Katherine talked to Constable Brindle tomorrow, it would all be over. If he was going to flee, he knew he would have to leave before sunrise. Yet if he chose to stay and fight, he would have to lay the groundwork in a similarly constricted timeframe.

But what could he do? With the possibility that so many people knew of his transgressions, how could he stop them without killing them all? He considered other options as the dusky light dimmed and the restless grunts of his horse disturbed the oppressive silence. After much tortuous thinking, he arrived at a possible conclusion that might buy him some time if Katherine was the only person who knew of his involvement. If many others were already aware of his guilt, he guessed that they would come after him whether Constable Brindle had been informed or not. But if Katherine held this knowledge in secret, he convinced himself that maybe he could persuade her to keep it that way until he made some long-term plans. He realized it would require swift and intricate maneuverings, yet nothing more complicated than what it took to get him where he was right now.

Farnsworth decided to give it a try. He had risked too much to give up his gains so easily. He could run away from Kanesbury if needed, yet he was prepared to take one more calculated risk first. But he would need the assistance of one of his local contacts, the one who had initiated the chain of communications enabling him to hire the assassin who was buried in the trees. Farnsworth didn't require another kill though, having something else in mind. His contact, who lived in the countryside outside the western border of Kanesbury, would work on short notice for the right amount of money. But first, Farnsworth had to get rid of the two dead bodies as a precaution, a task he reviled yet knew was necessary should an investigation ever be launched despite his latest plan.

He sighed, lamenting the unfairness of it all while bracing himself for the task ahead. He turned around and trudged back into the trees, looking for the shovel he had tossed into the ferns.

The deepening dusk had wrapped itself around the trees and settled upon the water's moody surface by the time Farnsworth dug up Dell Hawks' body. He lugged it upon his back and deposited it into one of the boats and then removed the two oars and tossed them in the second vessel. He went back and refilled the grave with soil, certain that after a long winter's snowfall and the wild growth of spring, no one would ever know a body had been buried there. He paddled across the swamp in the second boat after tying the first one behind him and towing it across the water. Upon reaching shore, he went inside the house as the precious rays of daylight slowly faded. There he found an oil lamp and lit it before returning outdoors to dig up Dooley's corpse. When he finished, Farnsworth searched the body for the pouch of silver and copper half pieces as he had done on the first, muttering when he found nothing. He guessed that Katherine had taken the money, knowing he couldn't do anything about it as he carried Dooley's body to shore and placed it in the same boat with the first one.

After catching his breath and wiping the dirt off his coat and pants, he grabbed a bundle of rope and a small ax from the shed. In mechanical fashion, Farnsworth cut the rope into several long pieces and tied the two bodies to the boat itself, glad that the darkness concealed the horrid details from the judging gaze of daylight. After double checking his knots and convinced that the bodies were securely attached, he towed the boat across the swamp amid the sickly light of the oil lamp and stopped when he neared the center. After positioning his boat alongside the other, he grabbed the ax.

Farnsworth took a deep breath as beads of sweat dotted his forehead. He reached over into the other boat and repeatedly hammered the ax blade into the bottom of the vessel until he punctured the surface. A gush of cold swamp water poured through the opening and slowly filled the boat. He briefly smiled at his success before untethering his boat from the damaged one. He paddled a short distance away to watch and wait. Slowly, lethargically, the damaged boat and its two corpses were pulled down into the murky water in ceremonial silence, swallowed whole by the swamp and leaving no trace of their existence. Farnsworth imagined the ghastly hulk steadily descending in the frigid, grimy water until it reached a final resting place. Time and nature would erase all traces of this misfortune from his life, and hopefully someday, from his conscience.

He paddled back to shore with one more job to complete. After pulling the boat ashore, he tossed the four oars on the ground, planning to burn them at home. He again took the ax to the boat and created a gash in the bottom, sending up an explosion of wooden splinters with each stroke. When a large enough hole was created, he pushed the boat out onto the water, aiming the bow toward the center of the swamp as the vessel began to fill. He watched with fascination, silently encouraging it to move as far away from shore as possible. Soon the boat stopped as it took on more water. Farnsworth was satisfied that it had floated to a deep enough spot. He vigilantly observed the vessel sinking at a slight angle as if it were being consumed in one bite by a giant watery creature lurking beneath the surface. When the second boat had vanished, he flung the ax and the oil lamp as far as he could across the swamp, hearing them both plop into the water, a final punctuation to the loathsome deeds he had undertaken that night.

Now, having sufficiently covered his tracks, Farnsworth was ready to return home and move on to the next phase of his plan. A strange feeling of satisfaction overwhelmed him. After placing the four oars in the cart, he climbed on his horse and slowly made his way through the darkness to River Road. He felt less afraid of what might face him back in Kanesbury now that he deemed himself in control of the situation again.

With the deepening night and the Bear Moon hidden behind thickening clouds, he wasn't worried that anyone would spot him entering Kanesbury. He would cross the eastern border, pass through the village, and immediately exit in the west. Before he could go home and sleep, he needed to hire a man for a spur-of-the-moment job tonight, someone reliable who would disappear into the shadows when it was all over. Come morning, Farnsworth was confident that he would have his life back in order, just as he had always planned and bargained for, and knew that he deserved.

CHAPTER 85

An Uneasy Truce

Several hours later, before the first hint of light touched the eastern horizon, Kanesbury lay still and silent, wrapped in winter's deepening chill. A veil of thick clouds sailed sluggishly overhead like a massive ship upon a nearly windless sea. The tips of distant pine trees wavered against the inky skies as if anticipating an impending change in the atmosphere.

Suddenly, a violent gust of wind from the west ripped across the village and nearby locales, creaking barns, tree branches and homes while scattering the leftover dried leaves of autumn. The vigorous breeze, originating in an upper chamber of the Blue Citadel, had burst outward from Morrenwood in an ever widening circle and soon overwhelmed the village of Kanesbury. But mere moments later, it faded away to nothingness while continuing on its eastward trek, leaving no damage in its path nor waking a single soul. In time, faint traces of dawn appeared like a painter's soft brush stroke across the horizon as morning arrived, without fanfare, on winter's second day.

Then everything changed in a heartbeat.

The usual calm of the village was shattered as residents drifted out of their homes amidst their daily routines, hearing the first rumors that swirled about like snow. Whether splitting firewood, going to market or brewing a kettle of tea at a bakeshop, individuals soon caught word of a terrible and shocking ordeal that had befallen their community. People were again reminded of the fear and distrust that gripped them when Ned Adams' gristmill had burned and Caldurian's Island troops had conquered the village. The unpleasant memories lingered like ghostly curls of wood smoke above rooftops on a misty morning.

Katherine Durant was putting on a kettle of water over the kitchen fireplace when she heard a frantic rap at the window. She glanced up, surprised to see her neighbor from down the street tapping upon the glass pane in back of the house. Katherine unlatched a hook and pushed open the window.

"Matilda?" she asked with mild surprise to a woman about her mother's age as cold air flowed into the room. "What's the matter?"

"Sorry to bother, Katherine, but I saw you through the glass as I was walking up the road," she said with a trace of urgency. "I'm on my way to the lockup."

"What for?"

"Hank Pillet just delivered a load of firewood to my house and told me a crowd was gathering there in the street," she replied. "Something terrible happened, though he didn't know all the details. He thinks someone died, or was killed maybe. He wasn't sure as he only heard snippets of conversation as he passed by. With your uncle being there, I thought you'd like to know."

Minutes later, Katherine and her mother hurriedly trudged up the road to the village lockup, wrapped in their warmest cloaks as they speculated about the latest trouble. Both were worried about Otto's safety, especially Katherine, now that she knew of Zachary Farnsworth's intentions toward Kanesbury and its citizens. But she didn't mention those disturbing matters to her mother, not wanting to cause her any more heartache.

When they arrived, about thirty people were milling about on the dirt road near the front steps. Tyler Harkin had just walked out the front door with Zachary Farnsworth, Len Harold and another deputy constable, all looking anxious as they talked to one another before turning to address the crowd.

"Deputy Constable Harkin will now speak," Farnsworth said, pointing to the pale young man with a head of thick brown hair who appeared uneasy at having to explain the situation. "He'd like to dispel the rumors swarming around our village."

The deputy constable stepped forward, unconsciously tugging at the hem of his coat. "Mayor Farnsworth suggested that I say a few words and explain what happened earlier today. As many of you already heard, Constable Clay Brindle was attacked this morning in the dark on his way to work."

"Is he dead?" someone shouted.

"No, he is not dead!" Tyler snapped, some color returning to his face. "No one is dead. As best we can figure out, Clay was robbed along the woody road near his house. He was hit in back of the head and pushed down, badly twisting an ankle." A gasp of revulsion rippled through the crowd. "He received a few cuts and scrapes, but his assailant fled before Clay even knew what happened to him. Unfortunately, he never saw the man's face."

"Where is Clay now?" a woman cried out.

"He's home resting comfortably," Tyler said, explaining how one of the local physicians had tended to him. "Clay's wife is looking after him now. But that said, it will be a couple of weeks before Clay is back on his feet. The physician told me that the ankle injury was severe but that the constable was fortunate to be alert and lucid considering everything he endured. Things could have been much worse. In the meantime, the other deputies and I will do our best to keep matters running smoothly in Clay's absence."

A barrage of questions was suddenly launched at Tyler Harkin as the villagers inched up closer. Farnsworth locked gazes with Sophia Durant who stood near the edge of the crowd with her daughter. He acknowledged her with a polite nod and made his way over as the others continued to bombard the deputy constable with their queries.

"Rest assured, Sophia, that your brother was never in any danger," Farnsworth kindly told her as he stepped away from the crowd with the two women so they could talk in private. "I spoke with Otto this morning and told him what had transpired."

"Thank you so much, Zachary," she replied, taking his hands in hers. "After what Katherine told me this morning on our way over here, I had feared the worst."

"It appears to be a random act," he said, gently squeezing Sophia's hands as Katherine watched with concealed dismay.

"May we see him now?" Sophia anxiously asked.

"Of course," he said, turning to the second deputy who remained standing near the door of the lockup. He raised a hand to get his attention. "Deputy Nasby will be happy to take you inside as I have to return to the banking house."

"Thank you," Sophia said, indicating for Katherine to follow.

"I'll meet up with you in a moment, Mother," she said. "I need to speak with Mr. Farnsworth about a few matters first."

"All right, dear," she replied, making her way to the deputy who escorted her inside.

"How may I help you?" Farnsworth politely asked.

"In light of these awful developments, I was wondering if this will affect my uncle's trial." Katherine looked up with a pleasant demeanor, forcing herself to behave civilly while trying not to think about the crimes he had committed.

"I thought that might be on your mind. Unfortunately, Miss Durant, I must postpone Otto's trial since Constable Brindle will be incapacitated for a time. Clay, after all, is in charge of presenting the case against your uncle, as distasteful as he may find that duty. I informed Otto of the change this morning. He took the news well."

Katherine nodded, gazing dejectedly at the ground. "I understand, Mr. Farnsworth, and I suspected as much. It seems that matters are out of our hands."

"It is a shame," he replied, catching her eye and noting a hint of unease. "Perhaps by spring, or even late winter, circumstances might be more amenable to holding a trial. I think by then that Maynard should be back from Morrenwood, assuming he has reached the capital city. I still haven't had a chance to recruit any volunteers to search for him since we've not received word from Maynard since he left. *Hmmm*, but I do wonder where he could be," he said, thoughtfully stroking his chin. He studied Katherine's face for any sudden change in her expression at the mention of Maynard's name. He detected none. "But if he should return soon, then this trial will be out of my hands as I will no longer be mayor."

"Time will tell," she softly replied.

"Indeed. But now I'm forced to deal with this situation, much to my displeasure," he remarked with a sigh as he stared at the crowd that fluttered about Tyler Harkin and Len Harold like bees around a hive. "It's quite a shame, Miss Durant, that such a horrible act was carried out against someone like Clay Brindle."

"I quite agree, Mr. Farnsworth."

"I mean, could you ever imagine–" Farnsworth shifted his gaze from the crowd back to Katherine, lowering his voice, though his words were hard as stone. "Could you ever imagine something that horrible befalling one of *your* loved ones? Your mother, Sophia, for instance? Or your dear friend, Lewis Ames? Just a vicious attack out of nowhere, sudden, with no warning. I suspect it would send shivers through you just contemplating such a terrible fate for either of those individuals." He looked silently upon Katherine, her eyes widening in mild horror and her complexion turning as pale as ash. "I know it would upset me to no end if something like that happened to any of my close friends, such as Oscar and Amanda Stewart, who have shown me such kindness recently. I couldn't bear to think how I'd feel if either of them were assaulted in the dead of night. It'd be horrible. Just horrible." He shook his head as he glanced past the crowd, speaking to the cold, gray morning. "A sad, sad thing when ghastly deeds are inflicted upon the people we most love."

An uneasy lull hung over the conversation before Katherine could finally speak. "Yes, Mr. Farnsworth. I see your point." But her words were slow and unsettled as she cast an uncertain glance upon him, wondering who this man really was, feeling the chill of his unspoken threat coursing through her body.

"So be vigilant when you're out, Miss Durant. This incident may have been an isolated event, but one can't ever be too careful."

Katherine stiffened her resolve, her voice growing stronger. "I would advise you with similar words, Mr. Farnsworth. You may be equally threatened if some unknown assailant is still lurking about."

"True," he replied. "That is why I will employ extra eyes to keep me apprised of anything unusual happening in the village. Clay's deputies can only do so much with the day-to-day problems we have around here, right? But so as not to wound their pride or drain the village coffers, I will discreetly hire a few trusted men with my personal funds to act as my eyes and ears, reporting to me any possible signs of trouble around here, signs of anything–suspicious."

"*Suspicious?*"

Farnsworth nodded. "People meeting with others in secret perhaps. People going to places they ordinarily would not. Things like that. As I said, just as a precaution." He sharply raised his eyebrows before leaning in and whispering close to Katherine's ear. "But let's keep this development a secret between the two of us, shall we? No need to concern the others."

Katherine pulled back, her heart racing. Though she couldn't explain how, she realized that Zachary Farnsworth was on to her. Somehow he had figured out that she was aware of his illicit activities and was now subtly threatening her and her loved ones should she ever go public. Would he really bring harm to her mother or to Lewis? To the Stewarts? The thought of Clay Brindle recovering from his injuries provided the only answer she needed.

Katherine didn't know what to say as her thoughts whirled and doubt crept into her previous resolve. Did Farnsworth really suspect her, she wondered, or had she only imagined it? And how could he have known? But since she had planned to meet with Constable Brindle today and tell him everything–on the very day that the constable was severely injured and perhaps nearly killed–she didn't find it difficult to believe that Farnsworth might have arranged for the appalling incident. She felt sickened to think what else he might do to fend off his enemies and the truth, fearing for the safety of her loved ones and close friends.

As Katherine composed her thoughts and calmed down, she realized that defeating Farnsworth would not be as easy or as uncomplicated a task as she once thought. The lives of others could be in danger depending on what she did next. She had to think through her steps thoroughly and with caution. And though her uncle would have to endure a longer incarceration since his trial was delayed, she now thought that that might be a positive thing as it would allow Adelaide and Maynard more time to recuperate before revealing themselves to the public. At least it would help Adelaide, she reconsidered, wondering if Maynard would ever wake up from his unnatural sleep.

"You do what you have to do to protect the village," she said, her words tired and defeated. "And I'll watch out for myself, just as you suggested. In the meantime, your secret is safe with me."

"I'm glad we have an understanding," he replied, flashing a brief smile. "So glad indeed. Now do enjoy your day, Miss Durant."

With that, Farnsworth turned and walked down the street in the gray light of morning, heading for the banking house as if it were just another day. Katherine, though, felt dead inside, contemplating if his hired eyes and ears were already watching her. She sighed, wondering if she could trust *any* acquaintance or stranger who might pass her by in the cold and dreary days in the long winter ahead. Her life, and now her plans to expose Farnsworth, felt frozen in place.

END OF PART EIGHT

NICHOLAS RAVEN

AND THE

WIZARDS' WEB

is concluded in

VOLUME 3

~ CHAPTERS 86 - 120 ~

~ Books by Thomas J. Prestopnik ~

Nicholas Raven and the Wizards' Web
an epic fantasy in three volumes

A Christmas Castle
a novella

The Endora Trilogy
a fantasy-adventure series for pre-teens & adults

The Timedoor - Book I
The Sword and the Crown - Book II
The Saving Light - Book III

Gabriel's Journey
an adventure novel for pre-teens & adults

Visit Thomas J. Prestopnik's official website
www.TomPresto.com

Little Falls Public Library
10 Waverly Place
Little Falls, NY 13365
(315) 823-1542

Made in the USA
Charleston, SC
03 August 2015